GARD

Clarissa McNair w̶̶̶̶̶̶
Mississippi but went to c̶o̶l̶l̶e̶g̶e̶ ̶i̶n̶ ̶N̶e̶w̶ ̶Y̶o̶r̶k̶ ̶w̶i̶t̶h̶ ̶a̶
degree in American history. She then went on to
qualify as an interior designer and has since had a
variety of jobs and travelled widely, living in Canada,
America, Italy, England and Cyprus. In Rome, where
she lives now, she was a news broadcaster on Vatican
Radio and also wrote and produced political
documentaries. While writing *Garden of Tigers*, her first
novel, she was in charge of international publicity for a
film company based in Rome and Los Angeles.

# CLARISSA McNAIR

# Garden of Tigers

Futura

A Futura Book

First published in Great Britain in 1988 by
Century Hutchinson Ltd

This edition published in 1989 by Futura Publications
Copyright © Clarissa McNair 1988

ISBN 0 7088 4320 4

Printed and bound in Great Britain by
Cox & Wyman Ltd, Reading

Futura Publications
A Division of
Macdonald & Co (Publishers) Ltd
66–73 Shoe Lane
London EC4P 4AB
A member of Maxwell Pergamon Publishing Corporation plc

*This book is dedicated
to all my friends who told me I could write it.*

## Acknowledgements

I wish to thank Larry Addington, Stephen Altschul, David M. Anderson, Johnine Avery, Chap Barnes, Jane Cavanagh, Victor Ciardello, MME, Heather Hanley and Stanley Rosenfeld, Chantal Laurent, Suzanne and Lee Liebolt, Judith Oas Natalucci, John Siemens, Frank Spelar, Dorry Swope, and particularly Tom Walton III.

Special thanks to Ron Edens who word-processed the manuscript from its original 942 pages to the last draft, and to my ever-optimistic editor, Rosie Cheetham.

# Prologue

Twelve for dinner was typical at the Palazzo de Leone. Nina gazed up, beyond her husband Claudio animatedly discussing Le Mans with the family lawyer who had propositioned her for the hours between two and four on Wednesday and Friday afternoons when he had access to an apartment on the Gianicolo overlooking St Peter's. She stared at his very fat cousin with the platinum choker set with cabochon rubies. Elena had been not quite all right since the kidnapping, and suffered from a fear of starvation after ninety-seven days of bread and water chained to a bed. She looked past Claudio's mother with the permanently etched frown, except when regarding her only son with an expression bordering on veneration. Nina looked past Claudio's twin aunts from Milano who came to Rome twice a year to eat ice cream at a place near the Pantheon and to be entertained by lovers in a hotel on the via Veneto. Nina's glance flew to the ornately decorated ceiling twenty-four feet above them; she silently counted each rosette like a golden cabbage as though the exercise were a mantra to keep her sane. *Uno, due, tre, quattro, cinque, sei, sette, otto, nove, dieci* times one, two, three, four, five, six, seven, eight, nine, in the other direction. Sometimes she counted in pig Latin just to tease herself.

A diamond as big as a fifty-lire piece sparkled on her left hand as she reached for the goblet of garnet-coloured wine. The rosy-cheeked bishop from Florence was explaining why the Church had allied itself with the Christian Democrats on the divorce referendum. The Duke and his most recent Duchess nodded appreciatively at his remarks. They had four annulments between them: the Church had always been understanding. Nina smoothed the raspberry silk of

1

her newest Valentino and crossed her legs and tried to pay attention. Her husband's grandfather gnawed on his bread-stick and stated decisively, 'The only mistake Mussolini ever made was getting us into the war. He thought the war was over.' Everyone ignored the old man. He was positive that the war raged on, outside the palazzo, in a Rome of the 1940s. Nina's father-in-law smiled absently. He was thinking of his mistress, Simona, and of their child that would soon be born. He wondered when he dared excuse himself to go to her.

Nina thought: I keep trying to belong here. She looked at the faces around her, at the long table. Animated, smiling, flirting, attractive faces lit by the radiance of the venetian glass chandeliers. Yes, decided Nina, remembering the Countess's words so long ago at the party on Park Avenue. It is a garden of tigers.

Seven polished black Cadillacs were double parked in front of the funeral home. The longest one, the hearse, sat in the parking lot with its back door already open, a black flap trimmed in chrome, open at an angle like a cellar door. The hearse's driver, a skinny man in a black suit and a black chauffeur's cap, leaned against its long gleaming expanse and mopped his red face with a white handkerchief.

Across town the red line of the thermometer on the back porch by the kitchen door was easing up to ninety-two degrees, and it wasn't yet ten o'clock in the morning. The coloured maid was upstairs in Nina's pink bedroom, tying the sash of her charge's best dress as the little girl fidgeted with a yo-yo her brother had given her.

'Come on, now,' pleaded Ellen. Her white uniform was damp with perspiration. 'You don' wanna be the one to mek your momma late. Lemme fix your hair. Nina! Sit down.'

'But why are we gettin' dressed up if we're not goin' to church?' Nina asked for the third time.

Ellen sighed as the response came from the doorway where Virginia stood. She was wearing a black linen dress with a choker of pearls around her long neck. Her black hair was shoulder-length, held back from her face by tortoiseshell combs.

'We are going to church.'

'But Ellen says it's Saturday and we don't go on Saturday. Not till tomor . . .'

'Nina, this is different. You know that Daddy told us all last night that his mother died.' Virginia had always found it difficult to call her mother-in-law by the family name and sometimes it showed.

'This is a ceremony for Big Momma. We're going to the funeral home first. Daddy and Bart are already there greeting people. After that we'll sit in the chapel and Dr

Mills will read from the Bible. That will be exactly like church.'

'When can we come home?' asked the little girl, swinging her legs back and forth from the height of the pink dressing table bench. It was covered in a glazed chintz of pink roses identical to the roses on the wallpapered ceiling.

'Then, after the chapel service,' continued Virginia, 'we'll get into cars and go to the cemetery.' She said this slowly and as she spoke it suddenly occurred to her that she might get someone to take Nina home before that long drive to Lakewood. Why should she go to the graveside, too? It is going to be a long day for all of us, she thought to herself as she pulled on white kid gloves, finger by finger.

Nina watched her beautiful mother in the mirror and wondered if she would grow up to be pretty. She stared at herself as Ellen brushed recalcitrant curls from one brown hand to another and then captured them at last in the mother-of-pearl barrette. People say I look just like Mother, but I think they are only trying to make me feel better, Nina decided.

Virginia was silent as she drove downtown. She really died. Virginia let out a deep breath. After all those years of martyrdom in that big four-poster telling everyone she was about to go any minute and wouldn't they be sorry they hadn't come to visit her more often. She stopped the car at a red light and changed the gear into neutral. She remembered how disappointed she'd been when her new mother-in-law-to-be hadn't arrived in Natchez for the wedding. Duncan had told her a story about a sudden illness but she'd later heard the truth from her sister-in-law Leticia.

Big Momma and Leticia had boarded the train in Jackson carrying big round hat boxes and little square cosmetic cases, and a porter had followed them with a trunk of clothes on a trolley. Just a short while after they were settled in their seats and the train was gaining speed Big Momma began to shriek in fear.

Virginia had to smile at the thought of those two women left in a field beside the railway tracks with all their bags around them in the tall grass. Big Momma had sat herself down on the trunk and bawled out her daughter for not having investigated the presence of tunnels between Jackson and Natchez. Leticia had known that her mother refused to ride the escalator at Sears but as Big Momma hadn't taken a trip since her husband had died, which was at least a decade before, her daughter had been just as surprised as the other passengers by her outburst.

Virginia could almost feel sorry for Leticia when she thought of her in the midday heat with that virago, waiting for hours for the taxi to be sent from Raymond to return them to Jackson. Almost feel sorry for her, thought Virginia, for she and her sister-in-law felt a great tension in each other's presence. Leticia had spent the next day calming her mother, had unpacked and supervised the maid as she pressed all of her clothes and returned them to the two big wardrobes, then packed herself off down to the station again, to get on the train alone.

Weddings and funerals, thought Virginia disjointedly.

The car passed big houses with green lawns, then a new shopping centre with an impressive parking lot, and then Bailey Junior High School, a football stadium under construction, the Millsaps College entrance gates, and then the older section of town with its narrow shady streets. They drove by the street where Big Momma had lived and she hoped that Nina wouldn't say anything. She didn't. At last they were on Capitol Street and passing the Governor's Mansion with very dressed-up people getting out of cars and crowding towards a receiving line that must have begun at the front door. Capitol Street was wide and clean and lined with shops. There were two banks, Primos Restaurant was there and a sign proclaiming John Juniker, Jeweller. Mississippi's two biggest department stores, amiable rivals, sat like giants catty-cornered across the street from each other. There was the square white Krystal which Nina loved for its tiny square hamburgers between pocketbook rolls. Her brother Bart called them 'mouse meat', which made her laugh. Jackson's best stationery store was on Capitol and the only place in town to buy a musical instrument was next door. The bottom of the street became tattier with every block away from the Governor's Mansion and every block towards Farish Street, which was the main artery through the Negro section. This was dotted with pawnbrokers' and luncheonettes with screen doors that squeaked and slammed every time a man in a T-shirt, his black muscles wet with sweat, walked in for his lunch away from the construction site. Hard hats of bright yellow like upside-down turtles lined the kerb as men sat eating sandwiches and drinking beer on the sidewalk. Farish Street had pool halls and clubs with music late at night and pocketed here and there every block was a sign that said in hand-crayoned letters, EASY LOANS, WE CASH CHECKS, or WE BUY ANYTHING. This was a part of Jackson as foreign to Virginia and Nina as China. They knew that Ellen lived there and that was all.

Rice and Parkinson's is just like a house, decided the little girl as she caught her first glimpse of the red-brick building with the panelled white front door and the paned windows centred between pairs of white shutters. Like a perfect little doll's house, thought Virginia as she glanced at the precisely trimmed box hedge.

The funeral home stood on the corner of a busy downtown street but at this hour, approaching noon on a Saturday, and in this heat, no one was about. Virginia parked easily and farther away than she had to, purposely giving herself that extra glimpse into her compact mirror, that extra adjustment to Nina's white socks that never stayed up, and a last extra moment of composing herself as she walked.

Once in the front door, the mother and daughter experienced a new kind of heat, the humidity of too many people in too small a space. There was the scent of face powder and hair spray but above all, there was the heavy fragrance of flowers: of orchids, of camellias, of lilies, of magnolias, of roses, and of gardenias. I've never seen so many roses in all my born days, thought Virginia. Nina clutched her mother's hand and thought: It's just like a party. Strangers bent to kiss her, to exclaim over how old she was, how tall she was, how pretty she was. Often they patted her face with a warm, moist palm. Nina could see that there seemed to be hills of flowers all the way up to the ceiling.

6

They lined every wall. The carpet was thick and felt soft under her black patent shoes and she gave a little springing jump which made Virginia squeeze her hand and give her one of those 'don't do that' looks. The next room was the same. Flowers and people and that oppressive airless atmosphere. Suddenly a woman embraced her mother and began to cry.

'Virginia! Dahlin, Ah'm so glad you're heah! Ah . . . Ah . . . Ah cain't believe she's gone!' the woman in lilac sobbed. 'Ah hope Ah'm in good taste,' she murmured.

Virginia felt confused and then, recovering, said soothingly, 'Oh, Leticia, you look wonderful. Considering everything . . .'

Virginia was sure that had they greeted each other alone Leticia would never have felt the need for such a display of grief. All for effect, like her dear brother.

Without warning Leticia fairly fell to a kneeling position in front of Nina. 'Ah'm your Aunt Leticia. You remember me from Christmases ago, don't you? Wal, I shore remember you!' and with that she planted a big wet kiss on the child's cheek with full scarlet lips. They left their bright imprint on her white skin.

Nina was silent and staring at yellow hair which turned under in a perfect roll. A black straw hat sat upon it, held firmly in place by an evil-looking hatpin at the little girl's eye level. Aunt Leticia's maroon-painted fingernails flashed by Nina's face as she toyed with her black curls.

'You shore have gotten mighty pretty, little lady.'

Suddenly she took Nina's hand from Virginia's and said, 'Honey, let me take Nina for a while and you kin jus' relax and talk to people.'

Nina felt herself pulled along in her aunt's wake. A man or a woman would call her name and she would look up and hear them say the same silly things about her and then her aunt would begin moving again through the knots of full skirts and the spectator pumps and the men's seersucker suits of light blue and tan. Nina's aunt corralled her in a corner and knelt again.

'Ah want you to be a good girl and come with me. We're

7

goin' down this hall to a special room.' She carefully wiped a glistening tear from her brown eye with a white lace-trimmed handkerchief that was already spotted with mascara stains. Nina thought: She has eyes just like Daddy's.

A man in a black suit, a doleful expression on his tired face, nodded respectfully to the woman and the little girl in the pale yellow pinafore as they made their way down the long wide hall.

'If he gits paid to look like that,' murmured Leticia, 'there would never be enough money in it for me.'

Nina was relieved to be away from all those strangers but then she worried that she was so far away from her mother. And Bart? Where was Bart? Leticia had her hand in a firm grip and was walking purposefully towards the first doorway. The hushed voices of the mourners had receded but suddenly there was that heavy cloying sweetness again and flowers, flowers, flowers – on stands, in pots, in wreaths, masses of them. There was something shiny in the middle of the room, big, like a car or a boat. Nina was curious about what it was, but held back with a fear she had never experienced before. With a quick motion Leticia lifted her into the air towards the centre of all the flowers and over the boat and said, 'Kiss Big Momma goodbye.'

Nina had her hands out to keep from falling on the sleeping woman with the white face and the blood-red lips. There was grey hair combed over a white satin pillow and hands – old, crepey, veined with blue, heavily powdered hands.

Virginia entered the room as Nina began to scream. In a tangle of bare arms and small kicking feet and Leticia's gold bracelets the little girl was soon sobbing in her mother's arms as Virginia patted her sweat-soaked dress. Several things kept her from slapping her sister-in-law across the face. The first was her sense of decorum. Then, of course, she had her crying child to consider. How do these things happen in families, she wondered as Leticia explained, 'All Ah wanted was to give her the chance to say goodbye for the las' time.' Virginia could not decide if it were sincerity and ignorance, or the malicious nature Leticia and Duncan seemed to share, that had prompted her behaviour.

Like a cheap version of Death the man in the shiny black suit materialized and stood with folded hands at the foot of the coffin. He was used to these scenes but one had to be vigilant, he reminded himself, echoing the words of his boss. There had been several times when relatives had actually jumped in with their loved ones. This meant emergency calls to the hair stylist and the make-up artist and a lot of repair work. He frowned as the child whimpered and then decided to intervene in his capacity as a grief therapist.

'Perhaps I may be of assistance,' he whispered to Leticia, who turned to him with a flash of her brown eyes and said curtly, 'Shut up.'

He took a step backwards in that obsequious little ballet step he practised in front of the mirror at home and tightened the muscle in his jaw. These people! Rude though they are, I must assume they are overcome with emotion and forgive them. He sighed the sigh known to all martyrs and actually quoted to himself: They know not what they do.

Virginia glanced quickly over Nina's head at the still body of Big Momma. She'd seen her looking worse in her nightgown in that closed and gloomy Carlisle Street house, and half expected her to flutter her eyelids and whine in that self-pitying way that she was thirsty and 'Dudn't anybody 'round here care if Ah haf to ask fer a drink of water? Do Ah haf to beg to git a drink from mah own fam'ly?'

Virginia looked away as though by thinking it, it might be persuaded to happen, and the wax-like hands might move aside the coverlet and then the entire woman might rise to a sitting position and ask her, 'Why are ya jes' standin' there, Va'ginya? What on earth are ya'll staring at me for?'

Her daughter-in-law straightened her shoulders to keep from shivering and strode from the room. The place smells like ether. I guess when you read about death, she thought, as she wiped Nina's face in the crying room across the hall, it smells like this. This is what writers mean, she decided as she mechanically held a Kleenex in front of Nina and commanded, 'Now, blow.' The attendant hovered behind her solicitously, a spot of black in a womb-pink velvet room.

9

Yes, thought Virginia, this is what death smells like in Mississippi in August.

Virginia had been the only child of a couple who died in an automobile accident when she was two years old. Their funeral in a driving rainstorm would always be with her, the way Big Momma's would never be forgotten by Nina. Little Virginia's Sunday school shoes had sunk in the earth at the graveside and, crying with shame and confusion, she had had to be lifted out of them. She remembered looking back over the shoulder of a big man and under the dripping eaves of a black umbrella and seeing just the red straps sticking out of the thick brown mud and, beyond that, a few feet away the yawning chasm of the freshly dug grave.

The next day the orphan was sent from Arkansas to live with her maiden aunt in Natchez. Virginia Avery grew up to be stunningly beautiful, so beautiful that people on the street of the little town would turn their heads to gaze at her, would stop their sidewalk gossiping to give her their full attention as she passed, and would mention to their neighbours that they had caught a glimpse of her at the social hour after church. Virginia was pursued by every boy in the Delta, invited to every dance, where she danced every dance, and was proposed to no less than thirty-one times before her twentieth birthday. Aunt Lillian wanted to know what she was waiting for. Virginia didn't know.

That spring she was introduced to Duncan McLean by the Baptist minister. Duncan was six years older than she; he came from Jackson and was resplendent in his Navy uniform. His handsome face with clear-cut finely chiselled features, his big brown eyes that made her feel she was almost blushing when he stared at her, his deep laugh, and his easy confidence with her, were enough. 'Oh, he is so good-looking,' her aunt exclaimed every single time she saw him.

When Duncan asked Virginia to marry him that summer she accepted with the strongest rush of happiness she had ever known.

10

Her aunt sold the dining room furniture to pay for the wedding reception and Duncan never let her forget it.

Duncan liked to say that he came from a family of doctors. His own grandfather had been a surgeon at the Battle of Vicksburg in the Civil War and later had had a small Mississippi town named after him for his heroism in quelling a yellow fever epidemic. Now the town was a filling station and a cinder-block general store that advertised RC Cola just above the sign that said McLean, Mississippi.

Behind his charm, and beyond the camaraderie that had made him so popular at medical school, Duncan McLean possessed a cold ruthlessness that was destined to make him unhappy every day of his life. Virginia's aunt didn't see it, nor did the sweet Virginia herself, until after the wedding. Their honeymoon on the Gulf Coast was marred by Duncan's anger that the bride's second cousins from Memphis had not attended the wedding ceremony. He had counted on their coming and had counted on his making a good impression, for they had money and practically ran the largest bank in the city. He blamed Virginia and he blamed her Aunt Lillian. Virginia had nothing, absolutely nothing to bring into the marriage except those family connections, thought Duncan. He had discovered at the reception that the family ties were not at all close, not even close enough to send a wedding gift! He fumed, and he blamed Virginia, and he told himself he'd made a mistake.

Virginia sat in a white wicker chair on the broad porch of the Hotel Bellevue and stared out at the tranquil water; it was still, not a whisper of breeze ruffled its surface. She pushed a strand of dark hair into place with a fine-boned hand and then absentmindedly smoothed her pink and white flowered skirt. The flowers blurred suddenly, and she bit her lip, refusing to give in to the tears. Aunt Lilly had been hemming the dress only two nights ago as the women had sat for the last time at the kitchen table in Natchez and excitedly talked of the wedding plans.

Sunday afternoon, thought Virginia. Yesterday seems like years ago. She pressed her palms together and took a deep breath. Yesterday Duncan said he was the happiest man in

11

the world and told me how beautiful I was and kissed me again and again in front of everyone. All his KA fraternity brothers called him lucky and made toasts . . . She closed her eyes and could see the scene. And now he says I am stupid and naïve and he's made a mistake. She gasped to suppress a sob. All because the Lanahans didn't come. Something about Cousin Jack being on the board of a hospital . . . and when I said I didn't understand he said, 'And you never will!' and slammed the door of our room and now he's gone.

Duncan was going to be somebody. Though there were several doctors in his family his own father had held a job with the Illinois Central Railroad. Duncan, from the age of twelve, had hated telling anyone what his father did for a living. He was a kind, slow-moving, amiable gentleman. Duncan's mother was a harridan, a nagging possessive dissatisfied shrew. Nothing her husband did was good enough, and her sharp tongue made his hours at the ticket window, out of her reach, very happy. When he was home he was often behind the house whistling as he tended his little garden. He loved his roses and he loved his children.

Leticia, Duncan and Angus were showered with his unreserved affection but it was their mother they each took after. Their father was pointed out as an example of what happened to those without ambition. 'Ambition' was one of their mother's favourite words. Her philosophy of life could be illustrated by two short phrases: 'getting there first' and 'survival of the fittest'. Nothing more and nothing less. At least two generations of McLean children sitting at dining room tables steeped in misery, hiding uneaten okra or turnip greens in soggy bundles in their laps, blinking back tears, could trace the source of their woe back to this woman her family called Big Momma.

Duncan was smoking a Camel on the dock. He leaned gracefully against a piling, wearing a light blue polo shirt open at the neck and white slacks. His handsome sunburned face looked untroubled. A woman stared at him and remarked to her daughter, 'Doesn't he look just like the Arrow collar ad?'

12

Too soon to do anything, he was thinking. I'll be getting my orders in a week, so I won't do anything now. Too many people would ask questions. They might think something happened on the honeymoon and . . .

Duncan could not bear for anyone to think of him as anything less than strong, masculine and charming, and he was, in fact, all these things.

It's imperative to behave as a gentleman, went through his mind as he watched a sailboat round a buoy with a great fluttering of clean white sails. Funny, but when I first met Virginia I was sorry I'd enlisted but now it'll work out just fine. Probably be stationed in Pensacola and then off after that. She'll be all right there in an apartment near the other officers' wives. When I come back we'll get a quick divorce and people can say it was the strain of separation. That decided, he neatly flipped his cigarette end-over-end into the blue water.

The hotel dining room was crowded with at least a hundred pinkly sunburned couples who sat at small round tables and chattered noisily. The waiters were high-spirited boys with their first summer jobs, and the diners' conversation was punctuated by their shouts of distress to busboys or to each other and the clank of falling silverware.

Duncan was silent, only becoming animated when their waiter approached to pour more ice water. Virginia waited; she sat very still in her strapless aqua dress and waited for him to notice her, for him to say something to her. When he did not, she began to cut her roast beef into smaller and smaller pieces, wondering if she would be able to swallow them. The room was filled with laughing people but Virginia and Duncan seemed to be clinging to an ice floe which bobbed in an ocean of everyone else's happiness. Virginia ventured, 'It's a lovely hotel, isn't it?' Duncan did not answer. 'Why don't we get up very early tomorrow and go swimming before . . .' Duncan looked sharply at her and she stopped in mid sentence. She swallowed and cleared her throat in embarrassment.

'Should I go back to Natchez?' she asked as casually, as lightly as she could, as her heart pounded in her ears.

Duncan shook his head while buttering a biscuit and she felt a wave of relief. It's going to be all right. I'll make it be, she thought as she looked at his strong face.

Virginia had turned a corner in her life. She went from a girl who did as she was told by a loving aunt to a woman who did as she was told by a domineering husband. She would rarely question, even silently, his motives or whether his orders, for they did amount to that, were right or wrong. No man had ever told her what to do. She had coyly laughed and flirted if one had so much as insisted she give him a second goodnight kiss. But they were boys and Duncan was a man. Duncan was her husband. Virginia decided she would do as Duncan decided. She wanted to be a good wife. What else was there for her to be?

Life is what happens when you've made your plans. Duncan was posted to a ship shortly after the honeymoon. Virginia had become pregnant within two minutes of losing her virginity, so when Duncan returned on his first home leave, he had a son. He never brought up the subject of divorce.

Pearl Harbor and World War Two intervened. Bart was five years old, a quiet boy with dark hair and his mother's big grey eyes, when his father returned from the Pacific, covered in ribbons. The boy was so frightened of the tall stranger with the deep voice that he wet his pants as he sat on Duncan's dress whites. The naval officer and war hero threw his son across the room where the little boy's head made a sickening crack against a corner of the coffee table. It signalled the beginning of a childhood filled with bullying and cruelty.

Virginia suffered, too but she suffered as a fellow victim and was not strong enough to lessen her husband's severity. Her pleas on Bart's behalf seemed to anger Duncan even more. She wrung her hands in the next room; she shut off the kitchen tap and anxiously listened to Duncan's rages directed at the child.

Duncan perceived his wife's gentleness as weakness, as an invitation for anyone to take advantage of her. He saw her good humour and her attempts to please or placate as just

14

another sign of her subservience. But worst of all, he saw these characteristics in his small son and resolved that the boy should grow up to be strong, aggressive, with a mind of his own and, of course, imbued with the fiery ambition that Big Momma had kindled in himself.

The family lived about thirty miles from Jackson on a small farm with half a dozen coloured sharecropper families. They worked it with a few acres each of corn, cotton and soybeans; there were also a hundred head of cattle, some chickens, and some pigs. Both Virginia and Duncan liked to ride, so Duncan kept three very handsome horses in the barn nearest the house. The house itself was white clapboard, a one-storey rather sprawling structure set well back from the dirt road in a grove of pine trees. Virginia had planted red roses which bloomed several months of the year in great profusion along the split-rail fence that lined the long driveway and behind the house blue morning glories curled around the kitchen door and white petunias grew in window boxes. Each room had fresh chintz curtains and many of the prints that Aunt Lillian had given to Virginia hung on the walls.

Jackson was growing, fast becoming a city, and the young Doctor McLean was gaining a reputation as a fine eye, ear, nose and throat man. He was thinking of specializing in ophthalmology and had bought a plot of choice real estate on Fortification Street where a new office could be built.

Duncan would drive to the hospital in the capital to make rounds and then on to the office he shared. He would pass little Bart with his school books trying to hitch-hike to school, for there was no bus service so far out. It didn't matter if it were a February morning of bone-chilling rain or a warm pale yellow day in April, Duncan would not stop, and Bart, after the first few times, would not turn to watch his father's car disappear down the road. He kept his thumb out, his arm straight, never stepping back, hoping some farmer would materialize in a pick-up truck on his way to Jackson to buy supplies.

When questioned by Virginia, Duncan snapped, 'Do him good,' never raising his head from the newspaper.

One March evening when Bart was ten, he arrived at the supper table flushed and excited. He was nervous about asking his father for anything but maybe this time it would be all right. He had paced in the back of the house, rehearsing his words, for nearly fifteen minutes.

'Dad, I want to ask you a favour.' Bart clenched his fists under the table, thinking this might slow his heartbeat.

His father stared at him, his fork in mid air.

'The Four-H Club is having a contest to see who can grow the best crop of corn and well, I . . . do you think that . . .' he stammered as his father continued staring.

'What is it?' Duncan asked, irritated by what he saw as his son's spineless nature.

'He wants to . . .' began Virginia but Duncan cut her off with a look.

'I want to know if I can have forty square feet to plant the corn on. I need forty square feet. Somewhere . . .' He paused. 'Just until the contest is over in June,' he blurted.

Duncan took a sip of water and swallowed. 'Seems fine to me. Maybe back behind the brooderhouse would be a good place. Go talk to Isaac tomorrow and tell him I said it's all right.'

The little boy grinned and Virginia smiled at both of them. They finished their meal in a different kind of silence that night.

It was a dry and sunny April which all too quickly became May, then June. Bart devoted himself to his little stand of corn, weeding, setting up a complicated sprinkler system, and constantly worrying that something might go wrong.

'Guess what!' he shouted as he hugged his mother in the kitchen. 'I went over to Jimmy's house and then he came over here and said my corn was much higher than his. And it is!'

Virginia smiled. 'You spend every single minute out there after school and even before breakfast checking on it. It doesn't dare not grow!'

'I think it's that fertilizer from the hen house that I mixed up with the stuff Isaac gave me . . .'

'It's you, Bart! It's you! You have a green thumb!'

16

The boy beamed at the praise. Virginia tweaked his freckle-covered nose. 'Did you say the judges are coming next week?'

'First, the preliminary judges are going to see everyone's corn,' Bart corrected her. 'Then' – he drew out the word with elation in his voice – 'the real judges will only go to see the corn that the preliminary judges have picked.'

The first judges arrived on the following Wednesday. The corn was magnificent; each of the rows was perfectly tended. Virginia watched the three men and her little Bart, so proud in his new overalls, leading them to the plot behind the brooderhouse. As they were leaving to get into their trucks she couldn't resist calling from the kitchen steps, 'Would ya'll like a glass of iced tea?'

The judges exchanged looks and accepted her offer gratefully, for it was one of the first truly hot days of June. They sat around the kitchen table as Bart leaned against the refrigerator.

'Bart, I wouldn't tell you that if I didn't think it was true. I wouldn't want to get your hopes up,' said Mr Flanders. Mr Clark wiped his forehead with a checked handkerchief and nodded.

'Tell him what?' asked Virginia.

'Well, Miz McLean, your Bart is sure to win first prize tomorrow when the judges drop by. His corn is far and away the finest we have in the contest.'

'Oh! That's wonderful news!' She poured herself iced tea and lifted her glass towards the three men and her son. 'To Bart's corn!' she toasted.

Mr Clark, Mr Flanders and Mr Bailey shouted, 'Hear, hear! To Bart's corn! To First Prize!'

Bart stood with skinny folded arms across his chest and beamed with pride.

They told his father at dinner and he had seemed pleased, too, though not nearly so pleased as his mother. Bart couldn't sleep. He kept thinking of tomorrow. He just had to go and look at the corn one more time to make sure everything was perfect, that not a leaf had fallen to mar the perfection of each row. Then he had to go to school and get

17

through the entire long day and then get home again in time to watch the judges look at his corn.

Every hour at school the next day seemed like two hours to the fourth-grader. He didn't dare tell any of his friends what the preliminary judges had said, even when they asked him why he was smiling so much. That afternoon, as he ran up the driveway under the oak trees hanging with Spanish moss, he saw three men getting into a green pick-up truck. He reached the driver just as he turned the ignition key. The motor came to life as the man said, 'Sorry, son. We don't know what to say. There must have been some mistake . . .'

Bart was clutching his school books under one arm. 'A mistake?' he cried.

The truck pulled out of the driveway. Bart watched it go, leaving a long horizontal cloud of dust, like the ghost of a giant caterpillar, all the way down Pear Orchard Road. Suddenly, his mother was beside him with her arm around his shoulders.

'Come on, Bart, let's have some lemonade. Let's sit in the kitchen and . . .'

'What happened?' he demanded, wrenching away from her. He ran to the brooderhouse and then right around to the back and stopped in horror. There was nothing but brown earth and a few of the broken green stalks that had not been entirely ploughed under.

Isaac was standing there, arms limply at his sides, his dark face full of pain.

'Mistuh Bart, I din' know I din' know I din' know what ta do. Your daddy came out here las' night and tole me ta plough it undah. I din' know what ta do . . .'

The old black man put his hands over his face. 'He tole me I hadda do it this mawnin' for sure.'

Bart knew he was too old to cry but he did anyway, and then Isaac walked quickly across the expanse of dirt and crushed corn that separated them and took the boy in his arms. He fell to his knees on the ground and held Bart's head against his ragged overalls and rocked him back and forth for a long time.

*

18

Nina was born that same year in the Baptist Hospital. Bart, a skinny ten-year-old wearing blue jeans, a blue sweater and a khaki windbreaker, saw her for the first time through a wall of glass when she was a day old. He adored her from that moment on.

The next year the McLeans moved into the new house on the Old Canton Road just outside Jackson.

This is very grand, thought Virginia as she watched the movers carry crate after crate of new furniture through the garage and up the back steps. I don't know what we're doing with six bedrooms!

The two-storey house with gardens and a fish pond and a fountain behind was antebellum in style. Nina learned quickly that the six fat white columns in front were to lean against for daydreaming and to hide behind in times of trouble. Before she could talk she was instinctively staying out of her father's way.

When Nina was four she took her first aeroplane trip, spent the night in her first hotel and had her first taxi ride. Then she was led by her mother to a long room with a shiny floor like the kitchen at home. Boys and girls stood or lay in their cribs and cried. The very room pulsated with wailing, sobbing children. Nina put her face against the softness of Virginia's tan coat and clutched her hand with all her strength.

A woman in a white dress was talking at her in that voice that adults use with children. 'Why don't you come with me and see the toys we have?'

Nina felt her mother's hand pull away and in one swift movement was lifted over the rails of the nearest crib. The little girl was insulted; I'm not a baby, she thought. Panic swept her like a fever as she saw her mother's back, the tan coat, getting smaller and smaller in the distance down the long aisle between the cribs. Double doors swung open and closed behind the figure. Nina saw her mother turn to look at her through the round window in the left-hand door, and then she was gone. The woman undressed Nina and took her clothes away; a scratchy nightgown was pulled over her head and tied behind.

The night was one of tears and of remembering her mother's backward glance framed in the circle. Nina buried her face in the pillow and sobbed silently, wondering why her mother had left her in this terrible place. The next day a doctor came. He was wearing a white coat like the one she'd seen her father wear, and he was very gentle with her. She was later taken on a moving bed to a room full of shining metal and that same kitchen floor, and the doctor with the kind smile bent over her with something that reminded Nina of a net for scooping goldfish out of the pond in the back yard. He told her that it smelled like roses. But it didn't and she vomited all over the strange kitchen and they had to begin again.

Later she tried to tug the blindfold away and they, someone, tied her arms to the bars of the crib and told her she could not cry, she was not allowed to cry. 'It will only be worse,' a woman's voice said.

It was five days and nights. All that time Nina choked back tears in the darkness with tied hands and thought of her mother's face in the round glass and wondered why she had left her.

Her father came one day with his booming loud voice. 'Nina! How's mah girl? How's mah girl?' But she wouldn't grasp his big hand when he reached down for hers. She had only one eye bandaged now and was taken home on the plane to her pink room with the roses on the wallpaper, where a doll bigger than herself was the surprise. Her mother showed her how to put her feet in the elastic stirrups and walk with the doll as if they were dancing. Little Nina with the eyepatch, silent, pensive, stared vacantly at the enormous doll with the yellow wool hair and the red and white striped pinafore. The brightly painted smiling face stared back at her as her parents made enthusiastic noises.

'There was a problem for a while,' Virginia told her later. Nina became short of breath and could hear her heart beating in her ears when she didn't know where her mother was. The child would rush from room to room of the house with a fist in her mouth to stifle sobs as tears poured down her face. In the grocery store she panicked when Virginia

20

moved out of sight behind a display of vegetables. And if her mother left the house without her, Nina would press her face against the screen of the dining room window and watch the station wagon pull out of the driveway, stop at the corner partially obscured by the pine trees and then accelerate and disappear. The little girl was always positive that she would never see her mother again.

In time the house became safe and then the woods behind and then the Robinsons' house and then the Grenfells' farther up the street. One hundred yards farther was not, however. When she was five, her very plump, usually giggling coloured nurse would waddle with her to the nearby kindergarten. They would say goodbye and Nina would find her small wooden chair at the table with the modelling clay or would lie down on the floor with the other children among scattered wax crayons and colouring books. But within a quarter of an hour she would be home again, standing on the back steps in the garage, straining on tiptoe to reach the doorknob to let herself in, to make sure her mother was there. This happened every day for four weeks until at last it was decided that it was of no use to take her.

'We thought Nina'd have to go to a special school but before the first grade she snapped out of it. My friends felt so sorry for me,' Virginia remembered. 'Why, I was so embarrassed!'

Nina was a tomboy who loved her dolls. She marked with a pocket knife how far up the butterbean tree she'd climbed so that the neighbourhood boys would believe her. On other days she studied the Jackson telephone book in order to change every doll's last name. Ellen taught her how to thread a needle and how to cut out little clothes for them and she'd sit in the breakfast room for hours at a time labouring over her giant stitches. Her three favourite dolls would sit propped between the sugar bowl and the salt and pepper shakers watching her. Ellen would be ironing or mixing up batter for a cake and Nina would think: This is what I want when I grow up. I want to have six children and bake things for them and sew their clothes and make them happy.

21

Silky was always at the back door on the other side of the screen, a black shining curly-haired cocker spaniel with large brown eyes and a rather melancholy set to his head. Nina would sometimes talk to him as she sewed just a few feet away and the dog would wag his tail with delight at the sound of her voice. Silky waited for his mistress to return to his world – the world of being barefoot, of catching crawfish down by the creek, of looking for four-leaf clovers, of lying in the tall grass of a field talking lazily of cloud pictures.

At night, in the summer, they would go out with the Robinson boys and the Grenfell brothers to catch lightning bugs as the tiny green and yellow lanterns floated among the pine trees. The children vied for who'd caught the most in their jelly jars and when they heard their mothers' voices calling them for baths and bed would, with a great sense of benevolence, unscrew the lids and let the little bugs fly away into the warm night.

McCallie, the military school in Chattanooga, Tennessee, was decided upon for Bart and he was packed off when he was fifteen and Nina was five. It was a source of great amusement to Duncan that the only other boy from Jackson in Bart's class was the son of a very prosperous bootlegger.

Duncan's practice was flourishing and he had money to join the Country Club for Wednesday and Sunday afternoon golf games, money for an even more expensive Packard car, money to build a lodge for his poker-playing cronies with a refrigerator and a pool table and special racks for his hunting gear, which included boots and jackets and hats and, of course, a dozen rifles which stood upright in a glass case.

Virginia joined the Women's Auxiliary, which consisted of a few dozen doctors' wives and, within three years, she was its vice-president and then its president. She was lovely, with a sweetness to her that women liked. It was a sincere gentleness that never made her women friends feel that, even with her considerable beauty, she might be a threatening figure. Besides, wasn't she married to the most handsome man in town?

Duncan McLean was popular with everyone, from little

22

children whom he examined for glasses before the start of the school term, to their mothers who anxiously powdered their noses in his big modern waiting room before being called in to speak with him. He was pioneering the fitting of contact lenses with several of his patients, who were delighted with the change from spectacles, and his elderly patients revered him for his expert surgery in removing cataracts. There was no one in Jackson who hadn't heard of Dr Duncan McLean. If they had not personally met him, they knew someone who had been treated by him and who would sing his praises. The only exceptions to this were the nurses who had served him in the operating room. Several had been reduced to tears by his tongue-lashing when they had been a fraction of a second too slow in handing him an instrument, and there were many hospital orderlies who stayed out of his way.

A great part of Duncan McLean's popularity was his almost political control of any social situation. A social situation could be assessed by the number and the status of the people involved. Duncan was a smiler, a joker, a laugher, a back-slapper, and knew just how long, to the second, to hold a woman's hand to make her feel attractive, but not long enough to annoy her husband. Nothing was afoot, of course, for Duncan's energy, all his energies, were funnelled into his practice, into his golf game, and into having more money than last year. Money was the god he worshipped. Money and status. But, of course, status was determined by how much money you had. What else was important?

He'd bought an ashtray at a little country store and put it by his chair in the den. Virginia dared to say it didn't 'go' in the room and moved it. Duncan secretly agreed but kept it out on the table for another week in defiance, and then took it to his lodge where, if it belonged anywhere, it was more appropriate. It was white ceramic with hand-painted red letters spelling out the question: If you're so damn smart why ain't ya rich?

Duncan was undeniably wealthy by Mississippi standards. He bought land in the northern part of the state, he bought more land in Calhoun County, he bought oil leases and cattle. He hung on to the farm, wisely predicting that some day it would be sold to developers for a hefty price to be parcelled into little one-acre plots for one-family dwellings.

Duncan went away every few months for medical meetings. The first ones were local affairs on the Gulf Coast. Virginia hated to go; she hated to leave Nina, even with Ellen, for the usual four days or long weekend. But most of all, she hated to be at Duncan's side, all dressed up and adoring, and then later alone in the hotel room to be stingingly criticized for some imagined but unforgivable transgression. Virginia worried: If I thought something were terrible I just wouldn't do it, but I never know what he will be angry about next. It's as though he is watching me, longing for something to happen so that he can have an excuse to vent his rage.

Virginia was not an introspective person. She was practical, not given to tears, and had learned from her aunt that to expose your emotions, other than sincere thank-yous or profuse apologies for being late, was bad manners. Jea'.ousy was bad manners. An argument at the dinner table was bad manners. To confess, when asked by a friend, unless your very closest friend, that you didn't think her dress suited her, was bad manners. Virginia was well brought up and the perimeter of what a lady did or did not do was defined enough to give her a sense of security, a sense of balance, throughout her entire life.

Virginia always knew 'the right thing' and, of course, one did the right thing without thinking.

It was second nature for Virginia to choose an appropriate wedding present, just as it was second nature for her to have all her Christmas cards stamped and in the mail by 10 December. Parties at the big house were smoothly organized and executed, with the right food, the right linen napkins, and the right flowers. Enough drink would be delivered the night before by Mars, the bootlegger, for Prohibition would not be repealed in Mississippi until the mid 1960s. Ellen and her Aunt Marie would rush silently in and out of the kitchen, wearing spotless white uniforms, serving and clearing, just as Mrs McLean had taught them. Parties in

24

the back garden were illuminated by Japanese lanterns that hung from the trees or candles protected from the wind by graceful hurricane glasses.

Duncan's 'eye meetings' were held at the Greenbriars in West Virginia one May. A more important one was held at Hilton Head Island in South Carolina that autumn. The next year Duncan decided to go to one in London. He loved to talk about these trips before he took them and to mention them upon his return. His patients, especially, were suitably impressed. Dr McLean began to order his shirts hand made from Hong Kong, with his initials carefully embroidered in tiny capitals on the left-hand pocket. He'd gone to a medical meeting there and someone had introduced him to an excellent shirtmaker. Virginia and Ellen were hysterical with laughter one afternoon upon opening one of the newly arrived boxes of shirts. A confused Chinese had sewn every monogram backwards.

Duncan went to an eye meeting in Rio de Janeiro and came back to Mississippi with a vicuna sport coat. In the spring of 1958 very few Americans could have told you a vicuna was a small mammal with hooves that lives in the Andes and is much hunted for its soft undercoat, which can be woven into exceptionally fine cloth. It was that summer that the Sherman Adams scandal erupted, its revelations rocking the Eisenhower administration with its solid Republican abhorrence of luxuries. Adams had to resign as the President's Chief of Staff over his acceptance of a gift in the form of a vicuna coat. For months everyone loved the story, particularly Mississippi Democrats, so one can imagine Duncan McLean with his friends at the Nineteenth Hole, sipping bourbon after a good game of golf and hot showers.

'What the devil is a vicuna coat, anyway?' laughed Harvey Waters.

Duncan smiled, as his pals echoed Harvey. 'Yeah, what's it look like?' 'I wouldn't know a vicuna coat if I found it in my closet.' They went on and on.

Duncan, his timing perfect, as always, said to the crowd around the table, 'You're all in luck, gentlemen. I just happen to be wearing a vicuna coat.'

Duncan went to New Delhi and returned bearing a tiger skin, complete with the head, its jaws open exposing terrible long white teeth. Nina made a face as she put her fingers timidly inside. Her father laughed and told her that he'd shot it with a silver bullet.

Virginia didn't go on these longer trips and it was with relief when she drove him to the airport to catch his plane to Atlanta, then on to New York and points beyond. The house became a happy place without him. Nina and her mother would have hamburgers and chocolate milkshakes for supper. Nina would play records and invite friends over to spend the night.

'It's like Christmas,' the girl would say. 'Only better, since he's not here!'

Dinners with the three of them, for Bart was away at school, were either half an hour of great unpleasantness or half an hour of silence except for the sound of chewing. Virginia was a loud swallower and would sometimes catch Nina glancing at her. The swinging kitchen door made a swish-swish noise as Ellen came in and out of the room to serve and then to clear.

'Mother! We're like animals at a trough! How I hate it! Please send me away like Bart!'

Her mother told her she was too young to go away and that she would go away to college.

'Years from now!' Nina clenched her fists.

It did seem an eternity of sitting in the pale blue dining room. The wallpaper was printed with scenes of tranquil Chinese in wide-sleeved robes, strolling for ever from pointy-roofed pagoda to serene pond. The chandelier glittered brightly over the highly polished Sheraton table. Nina sometimes thought: I'm going to scream, for often the only words spoken during the entire meal were by Ellen. 'Is it all right to serve the dessert now, Miz McLean?'

Occasionally after dinner Nina would try to watch television in the den. Her father would sit in his red leather chair, referred to as 'his throne' behind his back. As he glanced at *Life* magazine or read an AMA journal his left hand would explore his nasal passages and every once in a while he would drop dried brown items into the red leather wastebasket beside him. Nina would be repulsed and quietly leave the room. Virginia complained once that he was disgusting but Duncan said it was his house and he could do as he pleased.

Sometimes he would remove his finger from his nose and point it at Nina and say, 'I hate you. I'm going to get rid of you.' Nina was so young when this started that she was bare-chested and barefooted and wearing shorts with elastic so that she could dress herself. That first time, she had silently gone out to the backyard to be with Silky. She sat like a little cross-legged Indian, snaggle-toothed and pony-tailed, with long arms and legs, skinny and confused, with tears falling on her dog's black head.

Year after year as a little girl Nina conscientiously tried to find something good about her father. She gave him every chance, made every effort, even composed little notes, telling him that she loved him but that she would love him more if he weren't so angry at Mother all the time. She was young enough to be naïvely positive, as she stood on tiptoe, placing them in between his smoothly ironed white hand-kerchiefs in the top bureau drawer, that he would never trace the letters back to her.

Duncan would read one as he stood in his expensive suit, in his monogrammed shirt, in his hand-made shoes, in front of the mirror. Then he would simply drop the little folded note, much like the notes second-graders pass back and forth secretly in school, into the hall wastebasket as he strode towards the winding staircase and down for breakfast. Virginia found five of them there in the course of a year.

Nina waited patiently for signs of change. She watched her father when he wasn't looking and tried to detect a difference in his face, in his voice, anything. She was sure that, once he understood he was not behaving in a kind way, that he would be different. In stories at school things happened like this. No one was bad or unkind once they were given a chance to be good. Nina waited but nothing changed.

Duncan suffered from asthma, which he blamed on his

wife and child. 'You upset me!' he would shout from his end of the dining room table.

'Why, Duncan,' Virginia would murmur, 'we don't mean to upset you.' She would appear genuinely sorry for him but the truth was, the three women of the house had banded together in an alliance whose strength lay in making fun of this tyrant.

Virginia, Nina and Ellen shared many hours of hilarity in the breakfast room in the afternoon. They could laugh, as Ellen ironed and Virginia wrote out a grocery list and Nina had her after-school cookies, over the previous evening's performance.

'Miz McLean, what you goin' to do 'bout the chandelier?'

'Do about it? What can I do about it?' shrugged Virginia.

Nina was studying the contents of the refrigerator, waiting for inspiration.

'Nina, shut the door,' said her mother.

'I am really hungry,' moaned the girl, 'but I don't know what I want to eat.' She sighed dramatically. 'Maybe I feel like a sandwich.'

'Well, you don't look like one,' responded her mother, as she always did which, without fail, made Nina giggle.

'But is something wrong with the chandelier?' insisted Ellen. 'I was skeered to go in and look.'

'Let's look now.' Virginia walked towards the swinging door. She turned on the light switch and the three of them gathered in the dining room and looked up expectantly. Ellen held a wooden spoon, Virginia held clothes for the cleaners, and Nina held a piece of bread and a jar of pickles.

'Mother, I was staring and staring last night, and I couldn't see the dim one he was talking about . . .'

'That's because there aren't any dim ones to see.'

'He's supposed to be an eye doctor and he can't even see,' said the little girl disgustedly.

'Miz McLean, there ain't nothing wrong with that chandelier,' giggled Ellen.

Virginia turned the switch off and on and then off and then on again and they laughed as they stared up at its twinkling pendants.

Nina snarled in her perfect mimic, 'Cain't even run the house properly. Cain't even tek care of a chandelier. Cain't even unnerstand what Ah'm talking about. You're stupid, stupid, stupid. Gonna haf to shell out money for a housekeeper.'

'Stop it,' begged Ellen as she wiped her eyes on her apron hem. 'You sound jes' lak him and you're givin' me the creeps.'

Nina growled, 'That's cause you're stupid,' and the three of them laughed uproariously.

They all did their part to protect each other as best they could. Ellen would listen from the kitchen and steel herself, during the heat of a tirade, to push open the swinging door and announce that there were three kinds of ice cream for dessert and who wanted what flavour? Virginia became a master of diversionary tactics and, during particularly awful bouts of taunting and ridicule, would, with a sweep of a pretty hand, knock over her water goblet. In the ensuing confusion of mopping up the little river and pulling up the damp placemat and moving a plate of biscuits, sometimes Duncan would stop and sometimes she would upset a second goblet.

If Ellen stayed too late to catch the last bus, sometimes Dr McLean would offer to drive her. This was not a show of generosity on his part. He was thinking of himself, considering his reputation, for no Mississippian would allow his wife to drive in that section of town after dark. If anything had happened to Virginia all eyes would turn to Duncan and the blame for any incident would be placed squarely on his shoulders. But now Virginia insisted upon taking Ellen home and, without discussion, her husband allowed it, for Ellen was terrified of Dr McLean after a nightmarish ride down Farish Street at eleven o'clock one night. She had screamed at him to stop; she had pleaded and begged as she clutched the back of the front seat just inches behind him. He never said a word, but bore down on the accelerator with more and more force as the speedometer edged up past eighty miles per hour and then past the one-hundred mark. Trucks and cars were pulling aside, bicycles and pushcarts were pushed on to sidewalks; the headlights swept over black faces with white teeth as figures leaped, hand in hand, to safety, and Ellen heard shouts behind them. They reached her house and the maid almost crawled out of the back seat, trembling, with knees buckling, grasping her paper bag of leftovers from the McLean dinner table. She made her way up the porch steps and stood next to the glider as her three youngest children danced around her, demanding, 'Momma! Momma, what happened?' Through tears of fright, Ellen watched the fancy black car slowly disappear as it turned left at the weed-choked vacant lot. She was to remember a hundred times as she bent to remove a dinner plate at Dr McLean's side, how he had called after her, 'Goodnight, Ellen,' in a perfectly normal voice.

Even little Nina tried to defuse the snipings of her father, the slings and arrows of sarcasm that led to the more serious scenes. If there was trouble after dinner, Nina, usually at her desk upstairs labouring over math homework, would come to her mother's aid.

'If you cain't run the house, jes' say so, and Ah'll fork out money for a housekeeper. Jes' put an ad in the *Clarion Ledger* and pay somebody to . . .'

'What do you mean, Duncan? All because I've decided not to have the garage painted this year?' Virginia would say in her controlled voice.

'A chile kin see it needs to be painted! Why, everyone who goes by on the Old Canton Road . . . Don't you have eyes?' he would sneer.

'Well, all right,' Nina might hear her mother say.

Nina would move silently from the top step down the eleven stairs to perch on the landing. Bart had taught her to walk on the edge of the steps nearest the banister or right next to the wall. 'Since the wood is nailed down at the ends, there's not a lot of play there,' he had explained to a mesmerized little girl, who dreamed of becoming a famous detective.

Virginia would sometimes be able to leave the den after an exchange, but if she weren't quick enough then Duncan

30

would begin again or even call her back to stand in front of him as he sat like a despot in his enormous chair.

'You're stupid!' he would taunt his wife. He would be flushed, his handsome face quite red, his mouth set in an ugly snarl. 'Stupid, stupid, stupid!' Then he would shake out his newspaper, muttering to himself.

'Why am I stupid?' Virginia might ask him calmly.

He would crumple the paper on his lap, newly enraged. 'Why? Why?' he would shout. 'Well, if you haf to ask . . .'

Virginia sometimes pursued it one step further. 'I don't understand.'

'If ya don' understand by now, ya never will!'

At this point, Nina would walk downstairs, pass the open doorway without glancing at her parents, and go into the kitchen, where she would noisily find the right pan and sort through several lids and pull herself up on the counter to reach the top cupboards for a box of popcorn and the bottle of cooking oil. Virginia could always escape Duncan by saying 'Going to see that Nina's all right.'

It was a typical evening in the big house, with the porch lights aglow and the giant magnolia trees casting long shadows towards the road. The camellias and the gardenias were likely to be in bloom, making the air sweet; the violets lining the brick path to the wrought-iron gate in the garden were perfectly manicured, the dolphin fountainhead, almost buried in garlands of fig ivy and honeysuckle, made a soft gurgling noise and the Mercedes was in the garage for the night. Any one of many people might drive past and remark to a companion, 'That's Dr Duncan McLean's house. He's a fine man.'

Nina was about seven when she decided that this 'fine man' might not be her father at all. There was a mistake and some day it would be straightened out. Marilyn's father became her first choice, for he teased the two girls and called them his 'little birds'. Once he had driven them to Leo's skating rink and had read an entire *Clarion Ledger* while they, beribboned and brightly leotarded, had giggled and clung to each other with ankles like spaghetti amidst the groaning noises of the organ music. Patsy's father was funny and knew more riddles than Patsy. Nina had liked it when LuAnn's father had patted her on the shoulder after she'd fallen off the swing. 'Are you all right?' he kept asking as Nina nodded, 'I'm okay'; though her knee would be purply-green by school the next day.

But Marilyn's father was Nina's favourite. If he was her father Nina never went so far as to think that that made Marilyn a relative. Not did she imagine that anything had to have occurred between him and her mother. That would have been an affair and whatever that constituted, other than a grown man and woman kissing in a parked car, it was deemed absolutely impossible in Jackson. Nina was positive that no one in Jackson had ever had an affair; certainly none of her parents' friends or her friends' parents. And Mother? Out of the question. Neither the practicality nor the logistics of it all erased the longing to be someone else's daughter.

Nina sought to please Marilyn's father and found the rewards immediate and satisfying: a laugh at something she'd said, a little compliment about how well she tossed the basketball into the hoop on the garage door once when he drove in from work. And one time he had joked to her mother as they all stood in the McLean driveway with her sleeping bag for Marilyn's spend-the-night party. 'We love having her. Matter of fact, we might just keep her.'

Marilyn's father, as a focus of affection and of daydreams, lasted for what was a long time for a little girl. However, when Marilyn moved to Biloxi and Sheila Walker became Nina's best friend, his possible paternity was usurped by the genial Mr Walker.

When Bart came home Nina's world changed. She would race down the stairs and through the hall, through the kitchen and out through the garage, to where a car filled with his friends or, even more exotic, a checker cab, would be parked. Bart might be grabbed from behind as he said goodbye to his companions, or leapt upon as he tried to pay the taxi driver. He would then drop everything, whether it was the duffel bag from McCallie or the small suitcase from New York, to embrace her and throw her, laughing, into the air and then catch her as she shrieked, only to spin her around full circle as her long legs flailed about. Then he'd deposit her on the driveway with a wide grin and, as he mussed her hair, he'd introduce her. 'This is my little sister.'

Nina would look up and, mirroring his smile, would think, giddy with delight: Bart's back.

The two of them never had very much time together. That realization made every moment special. They had grown up as members of nearly different generations, for when Nina was given her first bicycle, Bart was getting a driver's licence. From the age of fourteen Bart had had a summer job, at his father's insistence, which was fine with the boy, for it meant pocket money and a measure of independence, including reasons not to spend time at home. It upset his mother, for she thought he was far too young to do construction work for the State Highway Commission with grown men. He was too young; he never told her he'd had to lie about his age for several of those first summers. At eighteen he went down to the Coast and signed up to be a roughneck on an offshore oil rig. The work was dirty, noisy and dangerous, but it paid very well and Bart was putting his money aside.

Bart took the little black-haired girl with him everywhere those few days that he was home. If he were going out in the car he'd always call her and they'd buy ice cream cones on the way back. If he were walking to a friend's house he'd yell up the stairs that she and Silky could come, too. Putting gas in the station wagon, picking up something at the drugstore or at the cleaner's, Nina and Bart were together. It was amazing, thought Ellen, how they looked more alike every year. Both son and daughter had their mother's face, particularly her big grey eyes, but Bart was now as tall and as well built as Dr McLean.

Ellen was ironing and listening to them chatter in the kitchen, Nina was sitting on the counter by the sink, and Bart was arranging sheets of washable tattoos beside her. The girl was meticulously cutting out a picture of an anchor with her mother's brass desk scissors and Bart was putting a damp piece of paper on her kneecap.

'What's that one, Bart?' asked Ellen.

'It's a rose. I hope this is . . . hmmm . . . no, no, Nina, don't bend your leg yet . . . ahhh . . .'

Nina was giggling. 'I wanted this anchor there, you dummy! Not some flower. Can you get it off me?'

'No, Nina, I have hesitated telling you,' began Bart solemnly. His grey eyes were serious. He looked up and winked at Ellen almost imperceptibly.

'Tell me what?' asked the little girl as she stared down at the red rose with curiously blue leaves. Her legs were slender, like a little colt's.

'Weeeeeelll,' sighed her brother, 'these don't ever come off.' He spread his hands in a hopeless gesture. 'You now have a rose on your left knee and you are going to have to learn to live with it. I, personally, think it's really beautiful, really very, very nice . . .'

Nina stared at him open-mouthed. Her grey eyes were wide. One green ribbon of a pony tail was undone and hung below the shoulder of her sunsuit, giving her the appearance of someone who had already had several adventures in the day.

'It is there, my girl. Maybe you could keep it covered for a few years until we can think of a way to tell Mother. She is . . .'

'Baaaaaaart!' Nina yelled. 'For ever! You mean, this stoo-pud rose is on me for my whole life!'

Ellen started to laugh quietly and then Bart did, and then, at last, after she had studied first one face and then the other, Nina joined in.

Bart taught his sister to throw a softball as straight as an arrow. He taught her all the knots in his old Boy Scout handbook. He told her stories about military school and later stories about Columbia and New York City. She loved his tales about 'the place that never sleeps', which to her sounded like an Indian name, with more movie theatres than you could count and hundreds of people on every street corner all day long waiting to cross. It sounded as unreal to her as the Land of Oz. Bart took her sailing in a bluejay one summer almost every afternoon for two weeks and, at the end of that time, she could handle the boat without a second thought. She was nine that year.

Nina kept her head down as she undid the jib sheet. She was fumbling and slow.

'Hey, up there in the bow! You asleep or what?'

'No, I . . .' Nina began to cry.

Bart was confused as he took two or three quick steps and swung himself over the centreboard housing to the little girl. She was sitting cross-legged, veritably buried in yards of sail.

'Did you hurt yourself?' He grabbed both her hands in his. There was no sign of blood, no mark at all. This wasn't like his brave little Nina, who never cried with him. She didn't cry over big bruises on banged knees or cuts that he winced to examine; she hadn't cried when they were out in that storm and the water had turned the colour of ink.

'What's the matter, Nina? Tell me.' He cupped her chin in one hand and forced her to face him.

She looked heartbroken, big dark eyes filled and re-filled with tears. She had a runny nose, her lower lip trembled with the promise of many more tears. Bart sat on the bow next to the mast and scooped her and the jib on to his lap, but she still wouldn't tell him what was wrong. She muttered between sniffles, 'I'm afraid. I'm afraid to be away from the house today.'

'Nina, tell me why. Did something happen at home? Did Dad say something to scare you?'

At these words, she pulled the jib over her head and sobbed uncontrollably. 'He wants to get rid of Silky,' she wailed. 'He said . . . he said . . . I heard him tell Mother . . . I was on the stairs last night when they were fighting and . . . he said I was too attached.'

Bart clenched his fists. He'd go home and take care of this with his mother and then with his father, if necessary. Goddamnit! Nina adored the little cocker spaniel, and why shouldn't she?

The sun was hot and bright in the sky. A motorboat raced by, breaking the stillness with a loud buzzing noise and rocking the bluejay with its wake. Bart patted the only exposed part of his crying sister, which happened to be a small red sneaker, and at last she came out from under the canvas and wiped her eyes on her shirt tail.

'He's not going to do anything. I'll make sure of it,' Bart promised. 'You know how he says things and then nothing happens . . .'

'Yeah.' She sniffled and then began to cry again. 'When I was in first grade I heard him tell Mother I was too old to play with dolls and to "git rid of 'em".' She mimicked him exactly. 'But Silky,' she cried. 'Oh, Bart, don't let him hurt Silky! I love Silky so much.'

'Nina.' He handed her a paper towel. 'Here, blow your nose. There, that's better. Now, look. I'm nineteen years old which means I'm an adult, a grown man. I can drive a car and I can almost vote. I can do anything I want to do.'

Nina looked at him intently. She had always known that Bart could do anything he wanted to do, but it was different to be told this by him.

'I want you to come to me whenever something is wrong. Just tell me and I can take care of it. I'll make it right. Nothing bad is going to happen to Silky. I promise.'

'But how can I come to you when you're in New York?' She suddenly felt nine years old and very little and very helpless again.

'I'll give you my phone number and teach you how to make a collect call, and all you do is get a dime – I'll give you a dime to hide somewhere – and you walk to the phone booth outside Brent's drugstore, and in a few minutes you can hear my voice.'

'What if you're not home? What if you're not in the dormitory?' she corrected herself. Her voice quavered.

'Then you can tell whoever answers the phone that you are Nina calling from Mississippi and that it's very, very important that Bart McLean call you back as soon as he can.'

'Okay,' she said, toying with the jib sheet.

'Listen,' he finished. 'I'm always with you.'

She looked up at him adoringly, the tears still wet on her face. 'Yep, I know.'

'Always thinking of you, kid.' He smiled and winked, and then leaped gracefully to the stern, pushing them off from the dock. 'Let's just float around today and not use the sails. Let's just pretend we're on our way far away . . . just floating.'

Nina giggled. 'Let's pretend we're floating all the way to New York!'

Duncan's anger altered course with a grown son at the dinner table. He didn't pick on Nina or his wife to the same extent, for perhaps he feared his son would challenge him and he might have to back down. But Duncan went after Bart with renewed enthusiasm for confrontation. He criticized his grades, his friends, his clothes, his haircut. Duncan would feign fatherly interest in Bart's plans and then make fun of his hopes. Bart never raised his voice, would often say 'Yessir', and, after the main course was served and the dishes were cleared, would politely ask to be excused.

Duncan refused to pay for Bart's tuition if he majored in business instead of pre-med at Columbia. Bart said sadly to Nina, 'I don't want to be with sick people all the time. Dad just doesn't understand. I try to talk to him, but I can't.'

Bart took a job in a Manhattan hotel's dining room as a busboy and struggled to keep his grade average up with this great bite taken from his study time.

Duncan cut his son out of his will every month or so, reinstating him in between appointments with his golfing buddy lawyer in handwritten notes on prescription pads, which he would read over the phone. Duncan was careful to convey the impression that Bart was useless and that he, as a father, was giving him every chance to make good.

Bart seems like a nice boy, Joey Chasen thought. He stands very well and has good manners, but he's been away for years, and who knows what problems there are? Duncan must have a hard time with him. A shame when a man's only son doesn't turn out. Poor Dunc.

Nina knew her father didn't like her brother and thought that he hated her because she looked like her mother. But that didn't make sense because, when she was with her father at a wedding reception or having Sunday lunch at the

Club, her father would put his arm around her when he introduced her to people and call her 'my beautiful daughter'. She recoiled at his touch. It's like that time the Carson boys put their pet snake around my neck, she shivered. Nina remembered her mother telling her she had to kiss him goodbye before his trip to South America. There was all his luggage in the hall and it was early in the morning before she had to get up for school, so she was in her nightgown and very groggy. She'd kissed him all right and then scampered up the stairs to her pink bathroom to make faces in the mirror and to brush her teeth five totally separate times, spitting into the basin with a vengeance.

Nina was aware from an early age of his two sides – the public Dr McLean, who was mentioned when she bought school notebooks at the drugstore, was the person she knew nothing about.

'Oh, you must be Dr McLean's daughter,' beamed the grey-haired woman with thick glasses behind the cash register. 'What a daddy you have!' Yes, thought Nina, smiling politely. 'He is just a wonderful, wonderful man! I got these here eyeglasses from him last fall, and he saved my Aunt Bessie from goin' near blind with cataracts! She loves him. She came all the way down here from Clarksdale to have the operation. She jes' can't say enough about that daddy of yours! And I, well, I'm the same way!'

Nina was a little statue with a frozen smile as she listened. At last, someone wanted to pay for cigarettes and she could leave the store. I hate him, I hate him, she thought as she kicked at the gravel beside the road. Why are people so dumb?

Virginia came into Nina's room that night as she was turning out the light. She sat on the edge of the high spool bed and took Nina's hand in hers, giving it a little pat. 'Go to sleep, now.'

'Wait, Mother. I want to ask you something.' Nina lowered her voice to a whisper. 'Why don't you get a divorce?'

Her mother sighed in exasperation. 'Oh, Nina! Don't start this again. You ask me every week!'

'Why won't you tell me why not?' insisted the girl. 'You hate each other. It's miserable in this house. I hate him and so do you, and he hates us.'

'Stop it!' said Virginia, standing up with her arms akimbo.

But Nina didn't stop. 'He tells us he hates us. Tell me why you don't get away from him,' she persisted.

Silence. Virginia stared, with head turned away from Nina, out of the open window. Insects were thumping against the screen and there was the soft sound of fluttering moth wings. There was the faint noise of the television coming up the staircase.

'I want him to pay for your college,' Virginia replied.

Nina was elated, but only responded with, 'That's eight or nine whole years away, Mother! The judge will make him give the money for . . .'

'Maybe, maybe not. Everyone loves your father in this town and no one would want to believe anything bad about him.'

'People are so stupid!' Nina banged her fist on her mattress. 'That phoney smile, that phoney laugh, that phoney . . .'

'Go to sleep. Stop all this. It won't do any good.' Virginia bent down quickly and kissed her daughter on the forehead, and then pulled the sheet up and turned back the edge.

Nina watched her mother's silhouette open and close the door. For a second she was surrounded in light and then she was gone.

'Won't do any good,' whispered Nina. 'Won't do any good to say "no" to him. To say this is what I want. To say don't do this to us!' Tears burned her eyes. She visualized her beautiful mother in the kitchen only the afternoon before. The kitchen, that place for conspiracies and confrontation between the women of the house. Ellen had been ironing a light blue skirt as they talked about the eye operation Terry Wharton's little boy was going to have.

'Exactly the same as yours, Nina. The lazy eye thing. Tightening a muscle at the side.' Virginia wrote 'flour' on the grocery list and then opened a cupboard door and checked for vanilla extract. Nina knew that her father hadn't wanted to operate on his own daughter; she knew that the operation had taken place in New York, that the surgeon was one of the country's best, but now she asked, 'Why didn't you tell me, Mother, that I was going to a hospital? Why didn't you tell me it was an operation on my eye?'

Virginia's back was to her. She answered casually, 'Your father thought it was better not to.'

Nina began to remember things. It was as if it had only happened yesterday. Her feet in the brown penny loafers pressed down on the bottom rung of the kitchen stool. Her hands smoothed the pile of just ironed pillowcases on the table before her. 'Why didn't you tell me it was a hospital? I was old enough to talk, old enough to understand. Why didn't you tell me anything?'

Virginia wrote down 'confectioner's sugar' and said in an even voice, 'Your father didn't want me to.'

Nina felt her face flame. 'Why didn't you tell me you were coming back? Why didn't you ever come to visit me?' She looked down at her hands on the wooden table and thought of them tied. Remembered the darkness.

Virginia closed the cupboard door with an air of finality and then put the list in her large brown leather pocketbook. Nina stared at her profile. 'Your father told me it was the best thing. Not to. He . . .'

'Not to visit me?' Nina's voice was tinged with tears.

'He thought . . .'

Nina fairly ground her teeth to keep from screaming in rage. 'What did you think? What did *you* think, Mother? Did you think it was the best thing?' She stood up suddenly and the stool rocked back and forth until she grabbed it. Ellen put the iron down and Virginia, still holding the yellow pencil, stared at her daughter. 'What did *you* think, Mother?' shouted Nina as she pushed open the swinging door and ran up the stairs three at a time to her room, to Kleenex, to geography homework, to forgetting before dinner.

Now she lay in bed and bit her lip. I won't be like Mother. I won't be like that. I won't ever be like that, she vowed. She wiped her angry tears on the hem of the sheet and lay there for a long time listening to the insect noises of the spring night.

Nina was later to claim that she didn't sleep until she was at least twelve. Her relatively few experiences with lying down and drifting into the 'land of Nod', as her mother told her she should, were so lurid with nightmares that she decided to sit up all night. Every night. For ever. Nina must have dozed off occasionally in those years, but usually the little girl sat with her pillow propped behind her, cocking and re-cocking a cap pistol. She knew it wasn't real, she just thought that a glimpse of it in her shadowy room might act as a psychological deterrent to any would-be trespasser. She spent hours playing mind games in the dark, waiting for dawn. Nina allowed herself to sleep when she could see that the clothes draped on the rocking chair were really clothes draped on the rocking chair. That was the deal. She was filled with superstitions like some primitive who'd been pulled screaming into the twentieth century, into a world of arithmetic and shoes. She couldn't sleep with bare ears, they had to have locks of hair covering them ever since she'd watched Van Gogh and the razor in *Lust for Life*. Some ghoulish girl in school told her about a gang in Memphis who went around killing people by poking hatpins up their noses, so she couldn't sleep with her nose uncovered. She'd heard that the Japanese liked to pull out fingernails, so she had to sleep with clenched fists. No chance of closing her eyes with the closet door open or without a thorough check under the bed with the kind of flashlight adults keep in the garage. These checks were conducted roughly every twenty minutes. She slept under a quilt one entire summer to give herself better odds against a stabbing attack. Virginia was mystified. Werewolves were a big problem. Escapees from Parchman State Penitentiary were a major worry. Her father was out to kill her. Maybe it would be something quiet at night, like a lethal injection, for he is a doctor, after all, or a simple strangle job, or the old pillow suffocation routine. He's threatened at least a dozen times to get rid of me, hasn't he, Nina worried.

Nina wasn't the only one in the Old Canton Road house who was afraid of being murdered. Sometimes, inexplicably in a pleasant mood, Duncan would call Virginia into the den

41

as he watched the news before supper. Virginia would try to smile as he offered her a glass of sherry: already poured and beside his own bourbon on the table to his right. She would sit perched on the edge of the couch across from him in the pine-panelled room, pretending to be so overcome with interest in the latest newscast that she would forget to bring the glass to her lips. After a moment, she would rise quickly and say, 'Oh, I have to tell Ellen not to put salt on that fish tonight,' or 'I forgot to tell Ellen about dessert,' and stride from the room. Ellen would usually be spooning steaming vegetables into serving dishes or bending over the oven, heating the dinner plates. Mrs McLean would hurry past her to the sink, then, as the maid watched, she would carefully pour the dark crimson liquid from the delicate stemmed glass directly down the drain.

Neither woman ever spoke of it to the other.

Nina plotted murder the entire year she was twelve. Unlike her mother, she found no satisfaction in soothing troubled waters, in getting through a tension-filled breakfast, one more supper, one more Christmas day.

Nina hatched at least two hundred nefarious schemes and discarded them all. There were plots from Bart's paperbacks, of course, and she'd watched *The Alfred Hitchcock Show* at Sheila's house a couple of times but had ruled out even his so-called perfect crimes.

How, she wondered, was she supposed to plug in an electric heater and then casually throw it at her father in the bathtub, when he always took showers? It had to look like an accident, she was positive of that. Nina had seen the black and white striped pyjama-ed prisoners from Parchman working in one-hundred-degree heat beside the road. They cleared the tall grass with scythes as they hobbled along in leg irons under the eye of a khaki-clad guard bearing a rifle. Would it be worth it, she wondered, lying in bed at night staring out at her pine tree? Would it be worth it to save Mother and Bart and Ellen? She had no idea what a judge would do with a twelve-year-old murderess. Maybe they'd send me to the gas chamber. Maybe I'd get to pick my last meal, the way I've read in the *Clarion Ledger*. Nina was suspicious because everybody always asked for the same thing: fried chicken, corn on the cob, biscuits, lima beans and chocolate cake. Amazing, thought Nina, but that's just what I would ask for. I wonder if it's a sign from God that I should kill him.

If only I had thought of this when I was nine, I could have gotten away with it. I know he has a gun in the Mercedes glove compartment, and one on the top shelf of his closet, and one in his desk drawer. If only I were not so old!

Nina discounted using a gun as quickly as she discounted the prospect of Hell. She and her mother were sent as Dr McLean's representatives every single Sunday to the First Presbyterian Church, while he stayed home reading the paper. According to Dr Mills everyone, no matter what they did, was destined for that eternal barbecue. She'd asked her mother about it and Virginia had sighed and told her not to worry and then murmured something Nina did not understand about Hell on earth.

Nina decided to let God take care of the murder. She was positive that he understood how much better the world would be without her father; she even thought she could persuade him through prayer, to arrange the 'accident' without implicating her. She began to pray every night and during every gym class, every time she sharpened a pencil, every time someone commented on the weather. She prayed for lightning to strike her father on the golf course. There were three afternoons a week for this to happen. It is so simple, she thought. Hitchcock would be delighted.

Nina prayed and she waited and she prayed. An entire summer went by and then the autumn. Lightning never struck Duncan McLean.

The very first Mercedes Benz in the Magnolia State was bought by the popular eye surgeon, Dunc McLean. Nothing gave him as much pleasure as manoeuvring the resplendent black car into a parking space at the Country Club; he gloried in the curious looks at a traffic light, and he positively gloated when asked a question concerning his new and very expensive acquisition. He thought a great deal about how he must look in the driver's seat, for he knew he was a good-looking man, and shouldn't he have a good-looking car, as well?

When Nina heard its purr as it entered the garage she ran up the stairs (three at a time) like a rabbit to her room. She usually did homework until the call for supper, but this year she was reading all Bart's books. *From Here to Eternity*, *The Caine Mutiny*, *Kon Tiki*, all the Mafia paperbacks, all the Erle Stanley Gardners, and several Dashiel Hammetts. She imagined Bart reading the same page and read and re-read anything underlined as though she had come across something of amazing significance. Bart, in his sophistication, would only have marked very important passages. His tattered *National Geographic*s resided in stacks, ten issues high, under Nina's bed. The little girl studied the photographs of deserts, oceans, mountains and wide plains as though she were memorizing the shapes and colours. She stared at veiled women in crowded marketplaces and vowed to see it all for herself some day.

From her bedroom Nina could hear her father's footsteps in the downstairs hall and then the clink of his car keys in the silver dish on the hall table. She knew that he would sit in the den until 6:28, when Chet Huntley and David Brinkley would bid each other goodnight. Then he would rise from his chair, switch off the television, and stride through the hall to the dining room, where everything was ready: flowers, silver, linen napkins. A frosty glass pitcher of water with ice cubes sat on a straw mat at his wife's end of the long oval table. If everything were not ready, if Duncan sat down and had to wait even thirty seconds before Ellen hurried into the room bearing the first of many platters, or if Virginia were not in place, there was trouble. If Duncan noticed a window open even a quarter of an inch, he would have something to shout about during the entire meal, for hadn't he put in air conditioning at great expense and did they want him to throw money down the drain, paying to cool off the entire state of Mississippi? Was he the only one who understood the value of money?

Nina and Virginia had heard this rhetorical demand thousands of times. Virginia was a wizard with the tiny

44

household allowance her husband gave her and bought clothes and shoes for herself and Nina at one of Jackson's cheapest department stores. Even then, she hid the bills, and Ellen helped her to get any big boxes out of sight before he got home. Oh, the value of money! thought Virginia, as she remembered Bart's last visit. He'd had just four days here for Christmas and, unfortunately, arrived the day after his father had sold an office building. Duncan ordered him to find a twelve-foot ladder and several grocery boxes and plenty of newspaper. Poor Bart spent two days in the old building, removing all the light bulbs from the high ceiling sockets and then half an afternoon packing them carefully for later use.

Nina studied the *Life* article. She sat on the front steps, against a white column, and hungrily stared at the black and white photographs. The object of this fascination was a girl just a few years older than Nina, but light years away from her life. The grinning cheerleader celebrating her seventeenth birthday, the smiling girl being picked up by a handsome boy with a crew cut for a movie date, the teenager with triumph on her face being pulled on water skis behind a speedboat filled with attractive friends, all sporting perfect Colgate teeth. The title of the article was 'Discovering the Fun of Being Pretty'.

Nina's feelings about seventh grade were comparable to the way many young men regard the draft – with a sense of inevitability and with the trepidation that wakes you early in the morning, convinced you will not measure up. Nina was a member of the post-war baby boom. All the twelve- and thirteen-year-olds all over Jackson, from school to school, were funnelled after their sixth-grade graduation into a September hot auditorium in one of two junior high schools to hear what was expected of them for the next three years. The speech at Bailey was delivered haltingly and with copious notes by a round little man sweating profusely, who wore the mantle of principal as one would some new and rather ill-fitting trousers, for he had been a football coach until the last losing game of the previous season.

An hour after his speech Nina was leeringly asked by the boy across the aisle in seventh-grade English class what 'fuck' meant. She turned and asked the girl behind her. There was always and would always be that artlessness to Nina. No matter what she said or how she said it, there would remain the innocence of the girl who asked the little red-haired teacher's pet, 'What is "fuck"?'

Her mother did not volunteer very much. Nina was given a booklet, published by Kimberly-Clark, best known for manufacturing the plump little mattresses that most girls Nina's age kept stacked neatly in a corner of their bureau for that day when their bodies would signal that these strange items would be worn between their legs, hooked on a bizarre G-string of elastic that never stayed where it was supposed to. The book was pale blue, titled, *What Every Girl Should Know* and, after a very motherly sort of letter to the reader, contained page after page of diagrams of pear-shaped organs and the good news that, yes, you could ride a bicycle on 'those days'. Nina was appalled and asked her mother how long this was going to go on. Every month! And every month for thirty years! That's twelve times thirty! That's three hundred and sixty times a minimum of four days. That's one thousand four hundred and forty days. Gee whiz, she thought. All day and all night of all those one thousand four hundred and forty days that's times twenty-four. Nina put down her pencil in horror and disgust. She was going to *bleed* for thirty-four thousand five hundred and sixty hours. She wished she could use the ridiculous things, with the blue line 'away from the body', as pillows in her old doll's carriage.

Nina was almost fourteen when her mother called her into her bedroom and sat on the edge of the bed, looking faintly confused. 'Nina, it's time we talked.'

'We're always talking, Mother. What's going on?'

'I want to tell you a story.'

Nina grinned. Her mother never told her stories. Her mother was too pragmatic to ever make up things. What was this all about? She was most interested in the way her mother seemed to find this difficult.

'Let's just pretend that you are out in the car and you are way out of town . . .'

'By myself? I don't have a licence yet.'

Her mother cleared her throat. 'Well, let's pretend it's next year and you do have your licence, and you are way out of town and it is late in the afternoon, and there is a thunderstorm . . .'

Nina immediately wondered if her father might perhaps be out on the golf course on this imaginary afternoon and then directed her attention to her mother again. Nina was intrigued, for this was so unlike her.

'There is lightning and thunder, and it's pouring down cats and dogs and getting dark, and you have a flat tyre. Now what would you do?'

'I'd stay in the car and play the radio until someone drove past me on the road, or . . .'

'Oh, no. I forgot the part about . . .' Virginia sighed. 'Let me add something,' she said in confusion, plucking at the hem of her wool sweater nervously. 'You see that there is a hotel in the distance with the lights on, and you get out of the car and walk to the hotel. The man behind the desk tells you that he has no vacant rooms. You ask if you can sit up all night in the lobby until you can get help for the car in the morning. There is a man right there who says that he has two beds in his room and that you would be welcome to stay with him.' Virginia looked down at her lap, nervously. 'Now, Nina, what would you do?'

Nina thinks this is all nonsense. Why is Mother behaving so strangely? 'Well, of course, I'd tell the man that it's great that I can share the room . . .'

'Oh, no! Oh, no!' cried Virginia. 'You can never, ever spend the night with a man in the same room! Never! Not until your honeymoon!'

'But, Mother, it . . .'

'Nina! I don't want you to ever forget this story!' and with that Virginia McLean rose and left the room, walked down the hall and descended the stairs with a sense of great relief

47

over the accomplishment of a motherly duty well executed.

For the next year Nina was to be positive, and to express the opinion vociferously to many girlfriends, that to 'do it' and to become pregnant, all a girl had to do was not be wearing a Kotex in the same room with a man, and the minute it was night, a light sort of like Tinker Bell would shine forth from the male, somewhere in the region of his trousers, and like a magic ray, would enter the female, somehow, perhaps through her navel. It was a very scary thought.

Nina was what would be diplomatically termed 'a late bloomer'. Seventh grade and the advent of dating and brassieres and lipstick and stockings were difficult for a tomboy with a flat chest who didn't secretly smoke, and would rather have arm-wrestled with a boy than hold hands in some soppy movie.

She was amazed during a rag-tag neighbourhood game of football, when she began to score touchdown after touchdown. Robby took her aside and told her that the boys she'd always played with had been instructed by their mothers not to tackle her any more. Nina walked home by herself and never went to the vacant lot again.

Most of Nina's friends carried fat wallets, filled with photographs of Bailey football players, their best friends, and their true love of the moment. Nina's wallet snapped closed easily, for every transparent plastic pocket was empty save three. There was a picture of Elliot Ness in one and two slices of baloney carefully folded in the others. Her wallet tended to become rather oily, but she thought this was certainly better than running the risk of starving to death when one had the option of being prepared and, anyway, she explained to a friend, 'I change my baloney every week.'

Nina's first date was to attend a football game, which was cancelled because it was the day that President Kennedy was assassinated in Dallas. Nina was horrified when cheering erupted from one classroom to another after the news of the shooting came over someone's radio at lunch time. When the principle announced John Kennedy's death over the public address system, the entire school shook with jubilation. Students did tap dances of joy, standing on their desks, and others shouted, 'Now we'll have a Southerner for President!' Rebel yells echoed up and down the corridors. Mr Hanes, Nina's history teacher, tried to bring his class to order. He shouted for silence in the room and when he got it he said, 'You all know that I have about as much use for Kennedy as I do for a garbage can, but he is the president. Now pipe down and read chapter nine before Monday.'

When the principal returned to his microphone to say that he was considering cancelling the big game 'as a sign of respect', Nina felt sickened at the boos of her friends, and also a strange personal guilt, for hadn't she just that morning wished that anything, tuberculosis, a broken leg, anything, would happen to save her from sitting next to Herbert Decker in the bleachers, and then in the back seat of the Lincoln with Mrs Decker at the wheel for the drive home?

Nina lived in a place that thought of itself as the centre of the universe. Thirty years before, H. L. Mencken and Charles Angoff had run a two-part series in the *American Mercury*, which ranked the states from good to bad, 'from civilized to barbaric'. Their criteria included wealth, literacy, education, entries in *Who's Who in America*, symphony orchestras, crime, voter registration, infant mortality, transport, and the availability of medical attention. In the final standing Mississippi was last. Behind every state in the Union. Its situation hadn't changed in 1963.

There were occasional calls for secession, as there had been one hundred years before. Washington was full of idiots who wanted to take away our states' rights and New York was full of damn Yankee liberals. Nina grew up thinking that 'damn Yankee' was one word. No one outside of the South had an inkling of what Mississippi stood for, and what's more, they, those damn Yankee liberals, all wanted to enforce laws that would endanger and eventually destroy our Southern way of life. At the root of all this fear, and indeed it could be called paranoia, had been the idea that President Kennedy would enforce laws putting an end to segregation. Mississippians refused to use the word 'integration' and compromised, with a bad taste in their mouths as they said it, with the word 'desegregation'. This meant the coloured people, or Negros, would be in schools sitting next to white children. This meant mixing of the races, which was forbidden somewhere in the Bible and, at last, the most heinous of all situations – miscegenation. What would become of white supremacy?

It was Governor Ross Barnett and his Lieutenant Governor Paul Johnson who 'stood tall in the fall' and barred the doorway of Ole Miss when James Meredith tried to register as the University of Mississippi's first Negro student. Mississippians bore Meredith no personal malice, for he was just a pawn in the Northern liberals' hands. He happened to be the right colour and they used him to invoke their will against the Great and Sovereign State of Mississippi. These last words could be depended upon to induce Rebel yells and shouts of approval whenever they were invoked by a politician. Usually a crowd would then begin to sing 'Dixie' and, if there were a band, it would play in earnest. The thump, thump, thump of the drums and the horns' blaring notes would stir every listener to patriotic fervour. Someone was sure to shout, 'Long live the Confederacy!'

So as Nina heard the applause of her best friends all over the wealthiest school in the state, she knew the hatred of Kennedy had nothing to do with him or his wife's clothes or his being a Catholic. It had everything to do with his brother Bobby who, as Attorney General, had locked horns with Governor Barnett on the green Oxford, Mississippi, campus.

How ironic that it would be the new Southern president from Texas who would enforce the Civil Rights Act and put an end to segregation in the state of Mississippi and, in fact, all over the United States. The life of a Mississippian, whether he be black or white, would never be the same.

For years, Ellen had arrived at the McLean house at half past six in the morning, six days a week, and cooked breakfast. Then she cleaned the house and did laundry, she prepared and served lunch, and then ironed. She began to prepare supper in the middle of the afternoon and, at last, after serving it and washing all the dishes, she would catch a

50

bus for the trip home to her side of town, home to her six children and to her husband, who couldn't seem to hang on to a job. She was paid the going rate of twenty-seven dollars a week. No Jackson housewife would have dared to rock the boat by paying her maid more than that.

She was Nina's second mother; the girl's first thought after school every day was: What will Ellen say when I tell her! Ellen was usually in the breakfast room ironing. She was ready to listen to how exciting it was to have Steve, the most popular quarterback, say something at the pencil sharpener, or to hear that Peggy Sue had been caught smoking in the bathroom. She gave advice as she rolled out biscuit dough and punched circles with an upside-down water glass; she gave encouragement as she iced a chocolate cake with quick flicks of the knife glittering in the light. It would never be enough to say that Nina loved her. But Nina knew from her mother that Ellen could take her children to the zoo and buy them hotdogs, but that they could not sit on a bench to eat them. Nina knew that Ellen had her own bathroom in the garage and her own drinking cup off to one side of the pantry. Nina realized that if she rode the bus home from school and there were only a few whites and plenty of empty seats, that the coloureds would have to stand huddled together in a crowd behind an invisible line in the back of the bus. Nina thought, it's as if they aren't clean. Public places like the airport and filling stations had four public restrooms and two drinking fountains, one labelled 'white' and the other 'coloured'. But Ellen cooked all the food, and Ellen did all the washing, and Ellen had taken care of Nina when she was too little to take a bath alone.

The teenager never made her bed, dropped clothes where she pleased, and saw nothing wrong with wearing a blouse for a few hours and tossing it in the laundry hamper to be washed and ironed. Yet, Nina felt the system was wrong.

Dr McLean treated Ellen and her family for any medical problems and never charged them, and his colleagues did the same. 'Luke may have an ulcer?' Dr McLean's friend, Dr Blackburn, would take care of it. Ellen's children wore Bart's and Nina's old clothes; Nina's mother usually gave them Whitman's Samplers of assorted chocolates for Christmas, along with a hamper of fruit and a very expensive wool blanket. The elderly laundress who washed and ironed all Dr McLean's shirts and had been doing his clothes since he was a little boy on Carlisle Street was given a flannel nightgown one year, a pair of shoes the next and, of course, the fruit and chocolates. Dr McLean might be woken in the middle of the night with a call from Sheriff Butler and within half an hour a deputy would ring the front doorbell, asking for bail money for Travis, who was drunk again. Duncan McLean always gave it to him, and the next morning Travis would be on the phone, full of apologies and gratitude. He ran the farm and did a good job most of the time. In ways, it was all an extension of the old plantation system – a dependency and a benevolence.

One evening after supper Aunt Leticia drove in from her house in Canton, which was now twenty minutes closer on the new highway. The family settled themselves in the living room with its high ceiling, dove grey walls, white moulding and silk brocaded curtains. Leticia never failed to feel a stab of envy as she looked at this house and compared it to her own small frame one. She was well off for a widow, but she resented how generous her brother was with 'that Virginia'. Leticia had to admit her sister-in-law's taste was unerring. Even the rather strange wall hangings from China were beautifully framed and placed where they could be admired. Goodness! Duncan did bring a lot of peculiar things back from his trips, she thought, as her eye caught the amber glass eye of the tiger's head. I wouldn't know where to put that!

The windows, which ran almost from floor to ceiling, were open and the dusk outside was full of cricket songs. Ellen had gone home so Virginia brought in a silver tray, bearing tall glasses of iced tea laced liberally with mint leaves.

Aunt Leticia had radically changed in appearance in the ten years between her fortieth and fiftieth birthdays and had become a scrawny bird of a woman with few feminine characteristics. The features that made her younger brother Duncan so handsome were not pretty on her. They had the same eyes, but the identical nose and mouth seemed thick and graceless on Leticia. Above her mouth was a noticeable moustache which made Virginia never fail to think upon greeting her: Why doesn't she do something about that moustache?

Leticia was flat-chested, with a hacking smoker's cough which came from deep inside her small frame and frightened people when they heard it. She sometimes had to actually put down her Camel cigarette in order to place both spidery-fingered hands over her mouth. Her hair was entirely grey now, still worn in the tightly rolled pageboy of her youth. Winter or summer Aunt Leticia always dressed in a cotton shirtwaist with her monogram in contrasting thread over her small left breast; for the winter months in Mississippi she added a wool cardigan in any one of two dozen colours. The dresses, in thirty or forty colours, were identical, with self belts and sleeves that rolled up just once above the elbow. They were full-skirted and Leticia thought they were the perfect attire for a bookkeeper.

Nina told herself not to stare. Do all the McLeans have these other sides? she wondered. Nina rarely saw her aunt, but whenever her parents were out of town, which was sometimes two or three Saturday nights a month during the Ole Miss football season, Leticia would telephone. The prim bookkeeper, the respectable widow of the accountant, perfectly groomed right down to her toes, would have locked herself in her house for the weekend with several bottles of bourbon, then she would reach for the telephone. Usually Nina would answer as she sprawled on the den couch watching television with Ellen. The unintelligible growling on the line never failed to drain the colour from her face. Then Ellen would answer the next call and the next.

'It does sound like Aunt Leticia,' Nina would say and Ellen would nod.

'The next time she calls, Ah'm gonna tell her that Ah'm gonna haf to tell Dr McLean on her. She's skeered of him.'

'Dr McLean doesn't trust her,' Virginia remarked once to Ellen in the kitchen, 'and she doesn't trust him either!'

How the two women laughed over that!

'She mus' smoke sixty Camel cigarettes a day, Miz McLean, and you know they is strong.' Ellen was emptying an ashtray after one of Leticia's afternoon visits. 'That nicotine-stained moustache!' She shuddered.

'She told me she never drinks less than fifteen Cokes a day!' said Virginia as she wrote 'get more Cokes' on a grocery list.

'Lord have mercy!' exclaimed the maid, her hands up in horror. 'That woman gwan die for sure from all dem Camels and Coke Colas!'

Tonight Leticia wore a mint green dress with an emerald monogram; her feet were encased in white patent leather with a green bow flat across the vamp of each tiny size five shoe. She spread out yellowed documents on the marble coffee table which, at first glance, looked like property deeds. 'Now, these, Duncan,' said Leticia, clearly relishing her moment of conveying information to her brother, 'are great Uncle John's slave papers.'

'What?' gasped Virginia, in surprise. She moved her iced tea glass, wiping the damp ring on the table with a white handkerchief, then she leaned closer for a better look.

'Didn't Duncan evah tell ya?' Leticia dragged deeply on her cigarette and blew smoke out of her nose, tilting her head way back. 'Great Uncle John had three plantations, and Lord knows how many niggrahs.'

Nina, kneeling on the floor, didn't have to look at her mother to feel her wince at the word. In the past two years everyone who was the least bit educated had made an effort to enunciate the o of the last syllable.

Just goes to show, thought Virginia, being brought up in Jackson doesn't necessarily mean you aren't country.

'Look on the bright side,' Nina had once remarked. 'She's stopped saying "nigger", and that was a major step.'

Hating her fingers to touch the paper's stained edges, Nina began to read aloud. 'I hereby acknowledge the receipt of one buck Negro, aged about twenty, with good teeth and in good general condition.' She whispered, 'Two hundred dollars,' as she put the page down. They were people, she thought. People like Ellen.

54

'Two hundred dollars was a lot of money in those days,' nodded Duncan.

At ten o'clock Nina and Virginia walked Leticia down the brick path to her car parked on the street. She always had a blue Impala. Nassau Blue, Capri Blue, a romantic island colour of blue for this car named after a fleet animal of the African plains. Nina had read in the *World Book Encyclopedia* about herds of impalas, and all she could visualize at first were hundreds of Aunt Leticia's blue Chevrolets, all humming along at ten miles per hour in clouds of dust, their little blue chrome-trimmed tail fins glinting in the hot African sunlight.

Nina lay in the dark staring at nothing for a long time and then turned on her side and looked out the window at her pine tree. Its needles touched the roof below her window and in a year or two would reach the screen. A year or two, she thought. Years of school loomed ahead of her, years of silent dinners, years of hearing her parents argue. Years until she would be old enough to go away to New York, to places in the *National Geographic*. An eternity before she would be old enough to leave Mississippi behind and to find a place where she belonged.

# 2

Nina stared out of the train window at the fields of green and felt very far from home. Summer was over according to the calendar but the landscape of Westchester County looked well tended and lush with the promise of June all over again. Nina's new watch with the white leather strap showed that it was twenty past three. This day may last for ever, she thought. At six o'clock her mother had driven her to the Jackson airport for the flight to Atlanta. There was a saying in Mississippi that if anyone died they had to go through Atlanta to get to Heaven, and Nina believed it. She'd barely made the connecting flight with five minutes to buy pralines and magazines, and then there had been a long taxi ride to Grand Central Station and now this train.

Nina brushed her hair from her face with the same gesture her mother used. The tall slender girl in the pink flowered shirtwaist and white high-heeled sandals was determined to look as though she'd made this trip dozens of times before, but she was thinking with panic, I'm going to spend four years in a place I picked out of a book. What if I hate it?

At least she knew what Briarcliff looked like, but that was small comfort. She could visualize the main building like an ivy-covered house with a classroom wing and offices on the ground floor and dormitory rooms on the first and second. She could see the front door and the fountain in front of that in the centre of the circular gravel-covered driveway. She knew that if you stood with your back to the front door you would see two modern classroom buildings directly in front of you and the new glass-walled high-ceilinged dining room to the left. It was filled with round tables and black wrought-iron chairs with flowered aqua cushions. Four dormitories like small frame houses were sprinkled on the campus but

56

Nina was glad to be assigned to the main one. She felt this was a good sign.

The catalogue told her that each room contained two single beds, two bedside tables, a dressing table and stool, a mirror, two desk chairs for the two desks, and two chests of drawers. One for me and one for Adele Forrest Wickham. Nina bit her lip at the idea of a roommate from Park Avenue, but there was no time to worry about her now, for the train was coming into the station of Briarcliff Manor and there was high-pitched chaos as girls grabbed suitcases and dragged bags down the aisle. Most of them, including Nina, had shipped their trunks in the middle of August and would find them, like old friends, in their respective rooms.

Taxis that weren't really taxis but wood-panelled station wagons waited at the bottom of the platform with drivers surveying the new crop of students. Nina shared a car with two girls from Texas who introduced themselves and then talked only to each other. She hadn't thought that anyone in the South dressed the way they did and tried not to stare at their simple linen suits and low-heeled shoes. She was reminded of the glossy photographs in the *Glamour* magazine college issue. The seven amateur models gazed from the pages with all the self-assurance that being perfectly groomed, well dressed, young and beautiful would give anyone. Beneath their feet had been printed their names and 'Briarcliff College, Class of 1972'.

Nina had raced to the kitchen wailing, 'Ellen! I can't go! I can't possibly go there and be with those people!' Nina looked down at the white shoes that she and her mother had thought were perfect. That afternoon at McRae's everything had seemed perfect, and now, thought Nina miserably, everything looks wrong. Her mother had bought and bought, overruling Nina's protests, for the girl was terrified of what her father would say when the bills arrived. She shuddered at the thought of that dinner table scene.

The two girls knew each other from some place called Rosemary Hall and were talking about someone named Pippa who'd been married over the summer.

The taxi glided noiselessly through a landscape of trees

whose leaves were dappled with soft September sunlight and whose branches sometimes parted to show large two-storey houses set well back from the road. They were grey shingled or of old brick and every single one of them was as large or larger than the McLean house back in Jackson. They passed an expanse of grass that could have been a golf course, and fenced rolling hills that looked like part of a riding school.

At last the car pulled through gates and down the winding driveway Nina recognized from photographs. Dow Hall had cars in front of it overflowing with girls and luggage. Parents were kissing their daughters goodbye and in the centre of all this activity a beagle was racing around the fountain chased by a small boy in red shorts calling, 'Harry! Harry! Come back!' Nina thought: Everything is where it should be. Except me.

She found room 210 at the top of the stairs and discovered her roommate bending over an open suitcase on the floor. Adele stood up and smiled. Her long, straight, cornsilk platinum pageboy swung forward. Nina stared at the oval face, the rather wide-set blue eyes and thought she was the most beautiful girl she'd ever seen. Small gold hoop earrings adorned her ears; her shining hair was held back by a wide black velvet band.

The jeans, the square-necked black T-shirt, the black espadrilles, were all cause for panic. Nina thought: She's too perfect for words. I feel like a sweaty overdressed hick. They tried to talk.

The train. Classes they'd requested. Where exactly was Jackson? Within minutes the room was crowded with freshmen who knew Adele, who introduced themselves to Nina then lounged on the two beds in blue-jeaned insouciance. It's like Purgatory, thought the girl from Mississippi as she rummaged through her trunk. She desperately wanted to be free of the insipid flowered shirtwaist and the high-heeled shoes. The girls chattered and laughed around her.

'Hey, you guys! Dinner!' shouted someone from the hall and they all stood and began to clump in their loafers down the wide wooden staircase. Nina thought: I won't make it here. I don't look the way they do. I don't talk the way they do. I can't go to dinner all dressed up. I can't go at all. I'll say I'm sick.

'Hey!' It was Adele's voice. Nina looked up from the pile of sweaters on the floor. 'We're the same size, I bet. Wear these.' Adele tossed the perfectly faded jeans to her new roommate.

Someone else leaned in the doorway. 'Adele, are you coming or not?'

Nina was yanking the white nylon slip over her head. 'Nina and I will be down in a few minutes. Save two places.'

From that moment on Adele Forrest Wickham was to be Nina's best friend. There were one hundred and sixty-four girls in her freshman class and by Thanksgiving she knew every single one by name. The girls she knew best were the ones she lived with. These were the ones who cavorted in the hall in their underwear, who sprawled in nightgowns and curlers watching old films in the TV room, the ones whose doors were open with the radio playing and a bridge game in progress, the ones who gave her her phone messages, and the ones who borrowed her history notes. Nina saw them when they needed to wash their hair, when they announced imminent suicide over an impending zit, when they looked like Hell after cramming all night for a French quiz.

She had been dropped into a strange and exciting world and she vowed to learn everything all the others took for granted. She learned that Emma Willard was a school and not a person and all about Farmington and Choate and Exeter and Deerfield. She learned about Yale and Ivy Club and the Whiffenpoofs. Wednesday was a half day of lectures and the girls were encouraged to go to the city in the afternoon and see plays and visit museums and art galleries. Nina did it all. It was like inhaling pure oxygen.

That first time she'd taken the train alone was the time she would always consider her first taste of New York. She longed for Bart to be with her. All his stories, all his descriptions were coming to life. She went to the Metropolitan Museum and then wandered down Fifth Avenue in the bright sunlight staring hungrily into shop windows. She

59

crossed 58th Street in front of the Plaza to hear the wild beat of a rag-tag army of musicians beneath a fountain. It wasn't working because, of course, there was a water crisis and also because, as she overheard in the crowd, 'This is Manhattan!' There were five trumpet players and two bass drummers and a lovely girl with long straight shining brown hair wearing a man's lavender shirt playing a trombone. A large girl was playing a tuba and there was a boy with a saxophone and a man with a clarinet and two more girls shaking tambourines and gourds. Fourteen, Nina counted, fashionably ratty, chicly shaggy, unanimously unkempt, in love with what they were creating, in front of two hundred people. Refugees from offices with ugly chairs on rollers and sealed windows were in love with it, too. Money poured into the trumpet case, open on the sidewalk, lined with shiny purple velvet. Nina threw a quarter in and backed away as others behind her made their offerings. She felt happy to be a part of that crowd. There were foot-tapping business-suited men, and children on the shoulders of blatantly intrigued out-of-towners. And just as that rhythm and that yellow white autumn day became too good to bear with the trumpets all together in one soul-searing moment, the fountain towering behind the musicians showered forth glittering cascades of water, and silently, and not meant to be noticed, Nina saw a jet soar slowly past a top corner of the Plaza and disappear from view.

Briarcliff, thirty-seven miles away, with its campus of tall oak trees, was full of a different kind of excitement. Nina thought simply being there was an adventure. She rather naïvely admired all her professors, save one. She liked the small classes and felt comfortable in blue jeans after the tension of planning never to wear the same thing twice in one week of high school. Why, one girl at home had never worn the same dress twice in a year!

Life was full of blind dates for she was always ready to answer the desperate cries of a friend who had a cousin who had a fraternity brother who . . . The boys were short, tall, aggressive to the point of savage, and shy to the point of silent. Nina made her own fun. There were the dull ones

60

and the decent ones and the ones so bad they were memorable. On Sunday night girls who wanted a laugh would follow her up the stairs with her suitcase, pleading, 'Nina, tell us! Was he just awful?' But if he was loathsome he always had a nice roommate and if the roommate was eccentric and kept lizards in a flowerpot then there was always someone funny and cute who lived across the hall or sat with them at dinner. Nina had good times.

She learned to drink milk before parties and she learned what to drink at parties and how to leave the third glass of it in the ladies' room. She learned how to apply eyeliner on a moving train and how to pierce ears with an ice cube and a circle pin. This, too, could be done on a moving train. She learned how to say 'no' on the first weekend with no hurt feelings and how to leave her date standing in the hall outside her hotel room. She learned how to say 'no' on the second weekend with a hint of promise in her half smile. She learned how to finesse the third weekend altogether and to be gentle about never seeing him again. The boys were from Amherst, and Williams, and Trinity in Massachusetts and Connecticut. They were all from all the Ivy League schools: Princeton, Yale, Columbia, Cornell, Penn, Harvard and Brown. Dartmouth was a bit far away and really, said a senior, 'They're like animals up there. The woods of New Hampshire do something to them.'

Nina did something to them, too. The Mississippi girl was a beauty. No one would dispute that. But there was more to her allure than the even features, the high cheekbones, the sparkling eyes, the full mouth. Nina froze in photographs and looked merely attractive; nothing more came across on a flat piece of paper. It was as if she hated the idea of permanence and couldn't decide what expression to convey, what thought to think as the cold eye of a camera focused upon her ever-moving spirit. So the spirit refused to show itself and the image was of a pretty girl, nothing more. But telling a story, wailing over a C minus in French, or answering a telephone, her face took on the radiance of an actress with all spotlights upon her and an audience in the palm of her hand ten minutes into opening night.

'She performs,' said an angry Susannah to Adele on a Sunday afternoon. 'You should have seen Larry staring at her right after I'd introduced her. I mean we'd had this incredible weekend together and we were packing up the car to drive back here and she bounded out of the quadrangle with three of his fraternity brothers tagging along behind her like beagles and she was laughing. About to die laughing over purple socks!'

'Purple socks?' questioned Adele looking up from painting her toenails bright red.

Susannah, full of irritation, banged her fist on the bureau. 'I don't know the story about the purple socks! I refused to listen! But, Adele, you're her best friend and if you don't tell her to stop taking people's boyfriends away then she's not going to have any female friends!'

'Listen to me.' Adele's voice was tight, authoritative. 'You know Nina. There may be seventeen things you can't stand about her but what you're going on about is *not* one of them.' Adele twisted the little bottle closed with two sharp jerks of her wrist. 'Nina is the most loyal friend I've ever known.'

Susannah was silent. She'd never seen Adele so coldly logical. Logical, yes, sure, that was Adele. But this was rock-bottom, icy, don't-you-dare-dispute-this rationale.

'Nina can be careless and unthinking but she doesn't cross her friends and you are her friend. And I'll bet' – Adele stopped and then breathed out – 'that if Nina were alone with Larry all she'd talk about would be what a great person you were.'

Susannah continued to lean with one elbow on the bureau but began to play with one long strand of blonde hair as Adele went on.

'And if she performs, she performs. It's part of Nina. She performs at the lunch table. You've seen her. You were there when she acted out the garter snake story.'

Susannah remembered. Why, Myra had laughed so hard she'd started to cry.

When Susannah still didn't say anything, Adele asked gently, 'Did Nina really do something terrible?'

Susannah shook her head. 'I guess not. She just . . .'

Nina was on the landing then and they heard her laugh as she heaved her suitcase in the doorway. With a flash of her grey eyes and a big grin, she fairly exploded, 'You won't believe my weekend!'

'We probably won't,' smiled Adele. 'I bet, for once, nothing happened at all. Liz says her brother is afraid of his shadow.'

'Ha!' snorted Nina, pulling off her plaid jacket. 'But not afraid of mine! He put his hand on my breast . . . on Friday night!'

Susannah stared without speaking.

Nina made a face. 'I told him I couldn't make love to him because I . . . well, I said the first thing that came into my head after drinking that scotch . . .'

'What did you tell him?' the other girls insisted.

Nina sighed. 'I told him I was anthropomorphic.' They howled with laughter. 'He let me alone after that.'

'Goddamn!' hooted Myra from the doorway. 'Sounds contagious to me.'

That night Nina lay awake in the dark. She could hear Susannah's voice all over again. 'She performs. Tell her to stop taking people's boyfriends away.'

But what if Susannah's right? Do I perform? Do other people see me and think that, too? Nina was hurt. Surprised. Off balance from the criticism. At least Adele stuck up for me. She brushed away sudden tears then silently pledged to stop flirting. At least, she amended, I won't flirt so much. Feeling sad and unfairly maligned, she suffered for a long time and at last fell asleep.


Nina finally lost her virginity after a year and a half of flirtatious foreplay. She hadn't expected to. It happened in the Taft Hotel in New Haven, on the night of, no, the morning after, Fence Club's Christmas Dance.

'Frankie, Frankie, Frankie,' she sighed, feeling his lips on her shoulders. His dark hair was rumpled and his brown eyes were glazed with desire. The pale coral dress was deftly unzipped in one quick gesture which, thought Nina, is pretty impressive. She was leaning against the wall of the cheerless little hotel room. The mirror above the bureau reflected a bed with a white chenille spread and one straight-backed chair. The only light came from the street.

Sometimes in this funny half glow, this hazy world of kissing and being kissed and feeling weak Nina would think of Temple Drake and a voice in her head would murmur the Falkner heroine's words, 'Something is happening to me,' and Nina would have to fight herself not to give in to that pressure of strong muscles and soft mouth and the face usually pressed against her small perfect breasts.

Nina was sure they had proceeded far enough for her to push Frankie away when he suddenly lifted her like a doll and placed her squarely on the double bed, whose springs squawked in protest. He jerked off the black bow tie and tore open his tux shirt with all the tiny pleats she'd toyed with all evening. They'd danced to Lester Lanin and drunk great quantities of scotch and laughed over silly in jokes of his fraternity. Later, much later, she'd been the only girl playing pool with Frankie and his two best friends at the club. She was younger sister as good sport – the kind of younger sister who never complained and tried hard to keep up. She was sometimes coy, sometimes cynical with her 'Oh, give me a break' moan and a slitting of her big grey eyes. She was innocent and sexy and playful. They adored her. Each one would have liked Frankie to tire of her, each one longed for the day when she was no longer invited up as his date and they'd be free to dial her Briarcliff number.

'Frankie?' she whispered tremulously.

His handsome face had changed and he looked intent and determined in the half light. Nina felt the bumps of the chenille under her fingers. Frankie's tiny ruby studs were falling on the floor and he was wrenching his hands free from the french cuffs and letting those little gold circles of cufflinks fall, too. Nina rose on her elbows and pulled the bodice of her dress over her bare breasts just as she saw his jaw harden and his face assume an expression very new to her.

64

She could only say, 'No, no, no! Frankie, please! No!' Then his mouth and tongue literally stopped her cries. The three a.m. stubble of his beard was rough against her and his knee was like a stone between her legs . . . immovable, hard and pressing. Nina realized for the first time in her life that she was not as strong as a man, not as strong as a boy. Had they all been letting her win all these years at Indian wrestling just the way she'd discovered their mothers had told them to stop tackling her at football that autumn afternoon so many years ago? Nina tried to scream and when he refused to release her she bit his tongue hard and his head snapped back in pain and surprise. In a voice tinged with tears she commanded him, 'Let go! Stop it!'

But all Frankie could think of was his own need and how in a few moments she would stop protesting. Nina. Scarlett O'Hara come to life. He'd wanted her for weeks, he'd wanted her ever since he'd seen her at that mixer shaking her bare shoulders above the white tube dress, smiling, at that Ray Charles song. The shining mass of jet black hair surrounded a perfect oval face. Then she'd been somebody's guest for dinner at Pierson the next weekend and she'd had every Yalie within earshot on both sides of the long narrow table hanging on her every Southern-accented syllable. Frankie loved that mouth and that long-legged walk. The boys had laughed at her and she had innocently laughed at herself with such playfulness, such a teasing joy in her face that no one could take their eyes from her. She was bright and played dumb, and when she really didn't understand she was quiet and watched people as though she had paid for front row centre seats at a play. And she could say the lines afterwards. She knew all the lines by heart. Frankie held both her slender white arms over her head easily in one of his large hands that were used to plucking footballs out of the air.

He ripped off her flimsy panties in a quick motion and stared at her flat white belly and the black triangle of hair and the long expanse of her slim legs. Nina heard the zip of his trousers and writhed with new strength. No, she kept thinking. Not like this. Please not like this. His black satin cummerbund flipped towards her face and she felt the softness against her cheek.

'Frankie! Frank-ee!' she cried out and he, in shock, realized too late that she was the virgin his fraternity brother had bet she was.

Afterwards Nina pushed him away and wiped her tears on the cummerbund. This Frankie was weak, with eyes closed and helpless and still, and no longer the animal she'd fought against. He slept there on top of the spread, naked and muscular and strange to Nina. She curled up in a foetal position and watched the off-on-off flash of the neon light that advertised Coca-Cola reflecting on the flowered wallpaper.

Well, it's happened, she thought, and at last fell into a deep and dreamless sleep.

She wakened before dawn and stared at him. Frankie had not moved since he had rolled his body off hers; he lay there still face down, arms and legs spreadeagled, with the light in one-second intervals illuminating the perfect smooth planes of his strong back and buttocks. Nina slid carefully from the bed, wincing at the squeak the springs made, and in four minutes she had washed all traces of the captain of the Yale football team from her. In seven minutes she was in the lobby of the hotel with a suitcase, walking past the dozing night porter sprawled in a lumpy red armchair. His Sunday newspaper had been opened to the sports page when it had fallen to the floor and Nina saw the headline: 'Yale Trounces Harvard 21–0, Wellington Scores for Bulldogs.'

'How come you're back so soon?' Adele looked up from her cross-legged position on her bed and tossed several sections of the New York *Times* on to the floor.

Nina didn't answer at first. She dragged the suitcase over to its place under the window, laid it on its side and yanked at the zipper. 'I didn't wreck your dress, anyway,' she said. 'Don't panic. I . . .'

'Nina! What's with you? You know I don't care about the silly dress!' Adele sighed in exasperation. 'You went off on Friday afternoon for a weekend with *the* Frank Wellington and *the* best dance of the year at Fence Club which I've taught you is *the* club at Yale and it's . . . it's . . .' She squinted at the little silver Tiffany clock. 'It's twenty-three minutes past nine on Sunday morning and you should be having bloody marys with him and complaining about how much you had to drink last night.'

Nina was unpacking listlessly on her knees, tossing things on to her bed. She suddenly stood and walked to the little stool in front of the dressing table.

'Seeing my parents was okay but not the greatest. Do you know that Mother . . .'

Nina brushed her hair away from her face and stared into the mirror. Adele continued to chatter then stopped abruptly.

'What happened? Don't keep me in suspense! Are you sick? Did you come back because you don't feel well? I know he didn't get hurt in the game,' she insisted. 'Everyone in five states knows exactly what happened at the game.'

Nina stared at Adele's reflection and then at her own. She whirled suddenly. 'Do I look different?' she demanded.

'Well,' stammered Adele, at an uncharacteristic loss for words. Adele was known as the Cool Blonde at several fraternities up and down the eastern seaboard. She was pointed out to the Briarcliff freshmen as 'Adele Forrest Wickham. She looks just like Grace Kelly, doesn't she?' and 'As if that isn't bad enough, her father is one of the ten wealthiest men in the United States.' Adele said slowly, 'You look tired, if you really want to know.'

'But different?' insisted Nina, who had turned back to the mirror and was seeking something new in her grey eyes, something changed in the way she held her head. 'I've been de-virginized,' she said softly, almost to herself.

Adele screamed. 'My God, my God, ohmygod!' she shrieked, leaping to a standing position on the bed. 'Oh my God!' She was blue-jeaned and barefooted.

Nina laughed. 'Adele, cool it! You'll wake people up!'

Adele sank to her knees and then sat again with her hands over her mouth and her blue eyes wide with astonishment.

'Frank?' she whispered. '*Frank?*'

'Course! I went there to see Frank. Honestly! Do you

67

think I'd accept a date with Frank and then lose my virginity to the conductor on the train?'

Adele rocked with laughter. 'Nina! We've talked about it for two years and now it's happened! Ohmygod!' she cried again. Suddenly she was in control. 'Tell me everything that happened. How do you feel? What did he say? Was it in his room? Was it after the game – God, I hope so, his coach would kill him if . . . but then again he played so well they could throw that theory out the . . .'

Nina seemed to be seeing herself for the first time. She crossed her legs and winced. 'I hate to tell you, Adele, but it hurts.'

'It does? It really does?' hissed her roommate in her Long Island lockjaw. 'Did you discuss it? Did he say he loved you? Did he undress you? Did you throw all your clothes on the floor and then just simply *melt* together? Or were you really businesslike, like Mrs Robinson with Dustin Hoffman?' she breathed. 'No, of course not! My God! Frank Wellington doesn't remind me of Dustin Hoffman. He's more like Rhett Butler.'

'He calls me Miss Scarlett, rather, Mis Scahlet, when he's teasing me,' interjected Nina as she pulled on blue jeans. She flounced on her bed and kicked off brown alligator flats. 'Okay, if you want to know what happened.' She leaned against the wall, pulling up her pillow behind her. Adele was hypnotized and staring. 'The dance was great. He is a terrific dancer. During the waltzes I guess we were sort of melting together. He kissed my shoulders a lot but then anyone would have . . . I mean, that dress and all . . .' She smiled. 'Everyone loved the dress, Adele. I was in the ladies' room with two Smithies and they wanted to know if it was an original.'

'It is,' said Adele quickly. 'Now get to the real story.' She wrinkled her forehead with concentration.

'Don't wrinkle!' warned Nina.

'Okay, okay!'

Nina began. 'I don't know how to figure it out. One minute we were dancing and I could feel him against me . . . you know . . . there . . . but that's normal.'

68

'I think it's abnormal if it isn't there,' sighed Adele. 'I don't think I've slow danced with anyone for three years without . . .'

'Without the third leg!' giggled Myra in the doorway. 'Can I come in, you guys?'

Myra Bernstein was Brooklyn through and through. Her dark pixie haircut made her look fifteen but her street smarts gave her a few years up on Adele and Nina. They liked her raunchy sense of humour in small doses and appreciated her tough brand of common sense. Myra envied them their well-bred waspiness. It was something for ever out of her reach.

'Absolutely!' said Nina, feeling less serious about what had happened with each passing moment in the company of friends. 'You are about to hear about someone near and dear to you losing her virginity.'

Myra whooped. 'With Frank Wellington! Goddamn, tell us everything!'

'I am so surprised,' murmured Nina. 'I didn't expect it to be that way.'

'Is he any good?' whispered Myra from her position on the floor leaning against Adele's bed.

'How should I know?' shrugged Nina. 'It happened so fast. One minute we were walking to the Taft and he had his arms around me and we were having a hard time getting to the Taft . . .'

'A *hard* time!' hooted Myra. 'Bet ol' Frank was having a hard time!'

Adele gave her a withering look and Nina continued.

'He was kissing me every few steps and I love the way he kisses . . . so I wasn't exactly resisting and it was cold and clear and there was a half moon. It was like daylight with all the snow. I guess we'd had a lot to drink . . .'

'Oooooooh!' moaned Myra as she pulled a loose thread from her Snoopy sweatshirt. 'They *all* say that . . .'

'Well, it's true! On Saturday there was the game and then there was a victory party in somebody's room and then Frank came in and we drank a zillion toasts and he doesn't have to play till after Christmas so everyone was giving him

69

drink after drink and then there was a sort of pre-dinner cocktail party at Fence . . .'

'What'd you wear?' interjected Myra.

'That.' Adele pointed to the yards and yards of coral satin hanging from the back of the closet door.

'Ooooooooh!' was the reaction.

'Your favourite cousin from Wellesley was at Fence with Henry again,' Nina said to Adele, and they both made a face.

'So what was the dance like?' asked Myra.

'Glorious!' Nina's face shone. 'There were flowers everywhere and crystal chandeliers and Lester Lanin played all these songs I liked . . .'

Adele thought: How innocent she sounds.

'And Frank . . .' She stopped. It was difficult to describe him now for he wasn't the same person any more. Am I either? she wondered. 'Frank was very nice to me until . . .'

She hesitated and Adele said, 'Don't wrinkle your forehead.'

'He's good-looking and big and he loves to be the centre of things. He carried me up the winding staircase over his shoulder like a sack of meal and everyone applauded and yelled! I pretended to be furious, of course . . .' Nina smiled. 'And he pretended to have to calm me down.'

'This was at the dance?'

'Yes, that was the beginning . . .' She moistened her lips. 'It was all fun, it was all such great fun. He said . . . the only thing he said' – Nina tried to remember exactly – 'was, "tonight's the night", but I didn't really understand that he meant *that*.'

'How many weekends have you been to New Haven to see him?' Myra insisted.

'This is the third one but he calls Nina all the time and last week he wrote twice . . .' Adele answered.

'He's a senior. I heard that seniors can't go without it for more than a week or the sperm has no place to go and it has to go somewhere . . . it has to escape . . .' Nina felt panicked.

'Oh, Nina!' groaned Myra, seeing her face. 'They jack off constantly. Those Yalies aren't exactly monks. Somebody

70

told me they have circle jerks after every meeting of Skull and Bones.'

'I don't want to think about it.' Adele sniffed delicately.

Nina was silent. The hall phone began to ring loudly. It was right outside their door and usually Adele or Nina was the first to reach it. Myra was on her feet immediately.

'I'm not here. You haven't seen me,' shouted Nina as Myra said smoothly; 'I don't think she's back yet. Hold on and I'll check her room. May I tell her who's calling?'

Nina and Adele stared at each other like matching bookends from their single beds separated by the night tables, legs crossed Indian style in blue jeans. Both wore black turtlenecks and both had hair that fell below their shoulders, but Nina's was black and thick and waved slightly whereas Adele's fell like silk in a straight shining pale sheaf.

Myra stuck her head in the door and asked, 'Oh, Adele, is Nina around? Ooooh, she's not back yet? Ooooh, can I take the number? Ooooh, will you tell her Frank Wellington is trying to get in touch with her?' Adele laughed as Myra mimicked Lily Tomlin and returned to the hall.

'I don't want to see him again,' said Nina quietly.

And she didn't. He was furious. He was enraged. He felt rejected and his friends knew about it, which made it worse. He'd either raped her which was why she wouldn't have anything more to do with him, or she had gone to bed with him willingly and hadn't liked it.

Frank dialled her number several times a day, every day for a week, and was told by Myra or Adele or Susie or Libby or Kim or Sandy or Mitzie that Nina McLean was not in her room. He began to call at seven in the morning and at ten forty-three just before the switchboard closed for the night.

'Talk to him!' insisted Adele. 'I can't stand to be waked up any more. I can't stand to hear his voice. I can't stand to lie to him any more.'

Frank would walk through the quad after lunch, after his 3:30 class, and after dinner, spring lightly up the stairs to his third-floor room and, without speaking to either Rob or Lew, would tear off his sheepskin jacket and dial the Briarcliff number he knew by heart.

71

At last Nina went to the phone and when Frank heard her soft 'hello' he felt rage and rejection all over again, and instead of saying he was sorry, he missed her, he wanted to make it up to her, he said entirely different things. 'You, Scarlett O'Hara, went too far with me and you know it!' Nina was astounded. He continued, 'You led me on. You teased me. You wanted it and now you want to play little miss wronged virgin. You're a flirt and a cock-tease who got what was coming to her!'

'Go to Hell!' said Nina, putting down the phone. Her face was flushed and her hands shook. She'd never told anyone to go to Hell before. She repeated his words to herself again and again. A cock-tease? Did I lead him on? She trembled. A cock-tease. Could it have been my fault?

'I just don't want to do it again!' she insisted to Adele. 'If I see him, he'll expect it, and I didn't like it. He was rough and I might even be pregnant and it hurt and I want to forget that it ever happened.'

The absence of Frank Wellington in her life bothered her not a whit even though some of her friends said Nina McLean was a fool to let him go.


Adele put down her fountain pen and closed the textbook. She ran her fingers over the title – *Abnormal Psychology* – and sighed. Wish I were in here. Maybe I am. 'Adele FW, Caucasian Female, 20 years old. Lied to her best friend about her virginity.' About losing it. No. About who took it from her. No, that isn't right, either.

Adele looked out the library window. Am I jealous, she wondered? No. I guess I just wish I could go through my share of Geralds the way she does. He won't last another two weekends and then there will be someone else for her to be in love with. And she really loves them! Adele smiled. Love? She put her hands on either side of her face and leaned heavily on her elbows. She abruptly thought of her mother and moved them away. 'Stretches the skin, darling.' Mother! Well, Mother would never know. Not unless my sneaky cousin, that beast at Wellesley, had actually seen something. Had she? The thought plagued Adele almost as much as what had happened on the dock. Behind the boathouse, on the boat, in that field. God! How many times with Jack! How many times had she let him do those things?

Jack. Rosy-cheeked, fine-featured, with that smile that dared her not to return it. As a six-year-old Adele had stared at his hands on the tiller of a boat, she had watched his hands knot a bowline, tie a shoelace and endlessly wipe back that almost white cowlick he laughingly called his pompadour. And Jack, as an eight-year-old, had known she was watching him and had watched her back. After all those summers together in Watch Hill, all those days measured by how many times you could get into that cold Atlantic water and swim against the undertow or dive through the breakers and all those weeks of July and August measured by dinners in Sunday clothes and 'no bare feet please' at Grandmother Forrest's big grey-shingled house on the hill overlooking Narragansett Bay. The gin games afterwards on the front porch until it was too dark to see. The 'got you last' tag that drove their parents crazy and evolved into teasing tennis matches at the Misquamicut Club. A dozen summers of this and then just one afternoon changed everything.

On the dock in her white shorts and a pale pink pullover Adele had sat staring at the horizon. The dock was nestled on one side of a spit of land that stretched far out into the bay. It had been built by her grandfather and was known as the Forrest Dock but no one ever used it except her and Jack. The big house was far above them on a bluff that commanded a view of the bay and then of the ocean beyond. A fluttering of sails and then the soft bump against the end of the pier announced his arrival. She usually ran down to help but this time she simply watched him spring from the bow of the Snipe and felt the boards shake under the weight of his landing jump. He looped the bowline around a cleat and came striding towards her in shorts and a crimson T-shirt that said Harvard CREW. Jack, the only sophomore to make crew, she thought. He was proud of that.

'What's so funny?' he grinned, seeming enormous above her.

'Nothing.' She smiled more broadly. He sprawled beside her and lay down full length, resting his head on one elbow.

'How tall are you now?' she asked.

'Exactly six feet and one inch. If you ate Wheaties you could beat me up, probably.'

'I don't like Wheaties,' she smirked, 'and it wouldn't take Wheaties to put you in your place.'

Adele didn't move. She later thought of the way she'd been sitting, knees up and feet straight towards the end of the dock. She thought of his face close to the hand supporting her weight. She hadn't stirred. She hadn't done anything. She was sure he had made the first move.

Jack stared at her. Her pale blue eyes were the colour of his. Sky blue he called them, the colour of that aquamarine ring his mother wore. Adele's hair was blowing in the wind. Long strands of the palest gold.

'I'd like to put you in your place,' he mocked. They were silent. The breeze cooled their skin and smelled of the sea. He stared at her feet in the white thong sandals. Her toenails were the same pink as her sweater and each toe was perfect, he thought. He put his big hand on one of her ankles as though to encircle it and found that he couldn't move it away. Electric shivers had gone through him. Adele felt the same current and parted her lips to take a deep breath or perhaps to stifle a gasp.

Damn! He could feel the erection through his cotton shorts. Could she see it? He didn't dare look down but he didn't move his hand away either. Later he thought: If only I'd behaved like a little kid and rolled off the dock into the water. We could have laughed and forgotten it. But no, I had to squeeze her slender elegant foot until she cried out and that cry was something wild and sexual and then I couldn't remember who she was or who I was and I knew only that I wanted her against me. I wanted to be inside her and I wanted that mouth on mine and I wanted that cry to come again and again with me controlling it.

Adele stared at him as he helped her to her feet, and with one hand around her small wrist he had pulled her behind him down the long expanse of dock. She remembered all the 'crack the whip' games and the thousands of times he'd reached out to help her from the dinghy to the Snipe, from the Snipe to the point. And in the ocean. All the times he'd groped for her hand when she'd been pulled under by a wave and they'd both been pounded in the surf mercilessly. But he'd never let go and when the water had receded they'd be standing waist-deep in the swirling mass and the millions of grains of sand would make it look more like dishwater than the Atlantic. Hair slicked back like a seal, eyes blinded from salt, coughing, she'd have only his hand as the undertow sucked the sand from beneath her feet and the water boiled around her. But Jack would have a firm grip, their wet fingers would be locked together, and he would drag her away from the force of the next wave growing in a wall of blue behind her.

With one swipe of his arm he'd knocked the paddles that leaned against the boathouse flying. They clattered into a pile like pick-up sticks and into the tall grass that bordered the clearing. He pushed her against the grey shingled building and held her head firmly as he kissed her. He drew it out, suddenly confident that she would not resist. Adele felt his mouth on her forehead and then he kissed the side of her face and when she felt his mouth move towards hers she realized her lips were slightly parted and waiting for him. Wanting him, wanting him, have I spent years wanting him? flashed through her mind as she felt the hard maleness of him against her bare thighs. Adele's fingers dug into his shoulders and she thought: Harvard Crew shoulders, and he thought: Her hands are like fire burning through the thinness of my shirt. Her knees were wobbly and she kept thinking: I feel so small. In seconds her shorts were around her feet and she found herself beneath him on the ground, beneath that face with eyes closed, beneath that bare chest, that amazingly soft mouth, beneath something else that caused her to scream when it rammed into that place that was her most secret place of all. Her voice was muffled by his hand. She stared at him watching her and his face seemed detached from the body that moved slowly up and down above hers. She gasped and he said, 'It's okay now.'

75

He whispered, 'It's okay,' again and again and watched the fear leave her eyes.

'No, no, no,' cried Adele but she didn't mean it and he knew she didn't mean it and they stared at each other and he felt as though he could fall into her soul and be lost for ever. Adele would later remember the slow rocking motion and the way his eyes had looked and that moment he had stopped and asked if he were hurting her and she had felt herself filled with him, with this part of him, this maleness she'd tried not to see a thousand times in the last three summers, under bathing trunks, under tennis shorts. Inside of me, she thought. Deep inside of me.

'All right?' he asked again in a whisper. She nodded and he had begun again to rock back and forth and the pain was suddenly less and she'd opened her eyes to see his face contort and his jaw clench and then he had torn his body away from hers and she had drawn her knees up to hold them together and to make the wrench of his leaving her less. She watched the spasm of his orgasm and reached for him and he'd gripped her forearm from where he lay on his back in the grass.

'Jack! Jaaaaaaack! I know you're there! Jaaaack!' came the shrill voice of his sister Melanie from the bluff.

'Damn! Don't move!' he hissed. 'She won't come down. I told her there are snakes down here. I told her I saw three last week.' Jack saw Adele's face and laughed silently.

'Come up and get changed for dinner. Grandmother wants to have it early tonight.' Silence. 'I know you're there. I know you can hear me!' Melanie waited a moment and then she walked back towards the house as Jack knew she would.

Adele lay on her side and watched Jack's face as he pulled blades of grass from her hair. He looks different. Her eyes widened when she saw the blood on his shoulders and he turned his head and saw it and smiled. Then he took one of her small hands in his and examined her fingernails caked with blood. 'We're both bleeding.' And with a quick gesture he grabbed his shirt and handed it to her. Adele was confused, and seeing this he bent down and kissed the pale

76

skin above her blonde public hair. She wondered if she should protest but didn't. Then she felt his lips on her thighs carefully licking her. His soft tongue went back and forth over the smeared blood and when she felt the warm throbbing inside her begin again the piercing shriek of Melanie began again.

'Damn! She never gives up!' he muttered and gently mopped the wetness from Adele's legs with the already crimson shirt.

God, we were crazy, thought Adele, staring out the library window. Melanie, the little snoop, the tattletale since she was born, the stool pigeon, the . . . I can understand why people in the Mafia kill tattletales. Or whatever they call them. Stoolies. Nina told me they call them stoolies.

Somehow they'd gone up the hill separately and somehow Adele had reached her own room up the stairs off the kitchen without anyone really noticing her. After a bath and in a white dress and a necklace of seashells she'd sat across from him in the grand dining room overlooking the bay and had eaten lobster and murmured thank you and no thank you to the maid who served. She'd heard her mother talk about a letter she'd had from her father, who was in Europe on business till the twenty-third of July. She remembered every detail of that dinner, especially Melanie's sharp glances at her. She told herself that Melanie knew nothing. Adele had stood on the bluff a hundred times and could never see the paddles leaning against the boathouse. The roof of the boathouse and the dock and the boat tied at the end of it but nothing else. It wasn't possible that she had seen anything.

Adele didn't dare glance at Jack but he watched her with admiration, thinking: Cool, cool Adele. He began to dig at a lobster claw with a tiny silver fork. When he had pulled out the white juicy meat and dipped it into the little bowl of melted butter he wiped his mouth on the linen napkin and thought of licking Adele's blood from her thighs and the urgency began beneath his trousers and he felt his whole body come alive with wanting her.

'Why, Jack! You're bleeding!' Melanie's voice cut across

77

the quiet conversation of his grandmother and the two women. Adele looked at his white-shirted broad shoulders and saw blood seeping through in small dark spots.

'Shaving,' he laughed but no one else joined him and his grandmother said, 'What happened?' and his mother said quizzically, 'Jack?'

'Angry seagull?' quipped Adele, trying to give him time to think.

'No,' he sighed. 'I didn't think anything of it before but it must have happened when I was diving. When I was under the Snipe trying to straighten the rudder. I must have scraped myself.'

Tory, Adele's mother, offered, 'There's iodine in my bathroom cabinet. Go up and help yourself after dinner.'

'Thanks.' He'd smiled easily and dinner had continued with Melanie watching both of them out of her narrow-slitted brown eyes. Melanie resembled no one in the family – dark straight brown hair, a small, usually tightly pursed mouth and a rather thick waist above thick legs.

That had been the summer before Briarcliff. How many times had she almost told Nina and then pulled herself away from such a dangerous confidence? So, at last, after Nina had had the night with Frank Wellington she had allowed Paul, dear Paul, hanging-on-to-her-every-word Paul, to think that she had relinquished her virginity to him. It meant nothing to her. His kisses would start to feel good after a while and then when she thought she liked them he would stop and begin to carefully remove her clothes. Sometimes, Adele thought he was going to hang up everything. He is so finicky, she despaired! If I ever dug my fingernails into him he'd probably excuse himself and be off in a flash for a tetanus shot. But he had solved the problem with Nina because now she could talk about sex and pretend that her only experience was with him. Adele sighed and thought of Jack. A senior at Harvard and then he'd go to Harvard Law School. Ha! He was one of those she had mocked to Nina just before lunch, but he wasn't really. He was Jack. Jack Forrest. Her first cousin.

*

Sprees in the city were sudden and usually initiated at five in the afternoon when Leslie or Mary Ann or Kim raced up and down the hall begging for somebody to take the train in to meet friends at Malkan's. 'I need two girls!' they would cry. 'I have dirty hair!' someone would shout. 'I have a quiz tomorrow at eight thirty!' someone else would call. 'But Eric always has adorable friends!' Kim was likely to croon.

Hundreds of preppies called Mike Malkan's East Side watering hole home. The red-walled bar with a few booths and fewer tables overflowed every night of the week with tweed-jacketed Princetonians and Yalies in crew-necked sweaters and even boys from UVa in bright red or yellow trousers who had driven all the way up from Richmond. These were the drinkers not yet involved in too much marijuana. These were the social animals who loved leaning on a bar with an arm around a girl from Briarcliff or Bennett and not the hippies who inhaled a hand-rolled cigarette in solitary. These were the football players and the track stars and the prettiest girls from everywhere who loved the music and the feeling of a crowd all listening to the same song and the clink of beer mugs or ice cubes and loud toasts made to entire fraternities.

Nina met Doug Steiner there.

He asked her to marry him before they were introduced, as she looked up from her glass and saw that wide, wide grin and the brown eyes that girls talked about in moaning voices. Nina laughed and it wasn't until he'd gone down on bended knee in the crowd that she spoke to him and he detected her Southern accent. 'Oh, all right, I'll marry you! But first, tell me how you feel about divorce. I don't want to be stuck with you for ever!'

It was time to catch the last train back but he insisted she have dinner with him the following night and said he'd come to Briarcliff to pick her up at seven. She smiled but tempered it with a shrug and then allowed him to help her into her black velvet blazer. She could feel his hands resting on her shoulders after he rather protectively turned up the collar. He put his face against the cloud of her shining black hair and she arched her back and drew away to walk towards

79

her date for the evening who stood holding the door open. She kissed George goodnight under the clock at Grand Central Station and ran with the other girls towards track eleven.

'Nina, my God! How did you meet him? What did he say to you? Did you walk over to him or what? Where was George? In the men's room! You're so lucky I can't stand it!' they cried, once on the train. It had begun to move before they had even fallen giggling into the facing seats.

'Who are you talking about?' asked Nina.

'Doug Steiner, you fool! You know, the six-foot tall black-haired brown-eyed one . . . the one you can't miss in a small crowd of a thousand people. That one!' crowed Kim.

'That's Doug Steiner!' Mary Ann and Kim shouted at her. 'He goes to Penn!'

Nina said, 'I know. He told me,' and proceeded to take off her jacket in the overheated car.

Kim was writhing in her seat, saying, 'Oh, he's beautiful!' when the avuncular conductor suddenly stood over them.

'Is there anything wrong, young ladies?'

They collapsed in giggles and paid him for their tickets.

'Nina, Nina, my child,' gushed Kim. 'Doug Steiner's father *is* Marine Midland Bank along with a few other things. He stands to inherit a cool twenty million dollars on his twenty-first birthday.'

'Golly ned,' said Nina. 'Too bad they couldn't dig up an extra and make it a million for each year.' Her friends shrieked at her show of boredom. Funny, Nina hadn't thought that Kim, with her father, or Leslie or Mary Ann would be impressed with that. They seemed to have twenty million each, anyway.

'He's asked me out for tomorrow night,' she told them with a trace of pride in her voice and they gasped in delight mixed with envy. Wouldn't it be fun to marry someone loaded, she thought, as the train clattered towards Westchester County. To go back to Mississippi only to give presents to Mother and Ellen and Bart. To go back with a handsome husband who adored her and who was a millionaire. Wouldn't that be something?

The next evening was a nightmare. The great Doug Steiner arrived an hour late after four girls had spent practically two hours fussing over what Nina was to wear. They thought he'd take her into the city, and she hadn't asked – to their mutual horror – so there was the problem of being too casual and underdressed or overdone and looking as though you were trying too hard. Adele alone was not excited.

'Be careful, Nina. This is somebody who has a bad reputation at deb parties. Watch out.'

'I vote for understatement,' declared Kim, who was on her knees in front of Nina with a palette of eye shadow. Nina sat on the stool trying not to blink as Mary Ann sprayed her bare arms with Chanel.

At last the hall phone rang announcing a guest for Nina McLean and she made her way down the hall with a veritable retinue of voyeurs.

'I'm so nervous,' worried Nina. 'I won't be able to talk.'

'Let me know when you can't talk and you can be my roommate!' insisted Leslie, only a little facetiously, for she was known to be driven crazy by the hyperactive Susannah.

'Do the belt one notch looser so it sort of slides down on your hip bones and pull the sweater down once in the back.'

'Good luck, little Miss Corn Pone,' hissed Tracy Sanders as she walked past the little gathering.

'Have you got the curse or what?' demanded Myra to the retreating levis in the high-heeled red leather boots.

'Class of 1972 Bitch. Every class has one,' said Leslie.

'Jealous as a cat.'

Nina smiled wanly. Everyone had leapt to her defence. Nothing could diminish the excitement she felt. Not even Tracy. Her dressers had defended her because in some way they felt she was their creation.

'Oh, God!' Nina whispered at the top of the stairs. 'I look awful, don't I?'

She didn't and they told her she didn't. She was wearing a white mohair sweater of Kim's and a straight black skirt of Adele's that just grazed her knees and a pair of black suede pumps from McRae's, of all places, that all her dressers had

81

proclaimed were perfect. She wore Adele's silver earrings, a wide silver band of Mary Ann's on each wrist, and carried her black blazer. They had all decided she was perfectly dressed for any place Doug Steiner could take her. Nina descended the front stairs slowly after Kim made the thumbs-up sign and Adele had given her one last warning look. Just out of sight of the hall below they leaned over the banister watching her in their blue jeans and turtlenecks.

As Nina reached the last step masculine admiration was expressed by the long, low wolf whistle. 'Doug, hi,' she breathed a bit shyly as he approached her and it was then that she smelled the alcohol. The grey Rolls-Royce was parked squarely at the front door so no one could miss it. Nina excitedly repressed the urge to confess she'd never ridden in one, never even touched one, she giddily thought. There were rustling noises behind her as she signed out in the large leather book on the lectern and she wondered if all her friends were tiptoeing down the stairs to watch her getaway. Once in the car Nina again smelled the liquor on his breath and wondered what to do.

Thirty-five minutes later, after Doug's telling her she was in his father's Silver Cloud, they were passing signs to Cold Spring Harbor which Nina thought was on Long Island. Dinner was in a very romantic candlelit place with windows facing the sound; attentive waiters stood in dark corners prepared to leap forward and satisfy the slightest whim of their wealthy customer. Douglas Jacob Steiner Jr put away four double scotches and an entire bottle of red wine in silence and ate almost nothing. The maitre d' stood over their table and inquired solicitously if anything had been wrong with the steak.

'No, no, 'slutely fabulus . . .' he slurred.

'Doug, I have to go back now. It's late.'

''Kay, we're off.' He stood up and grasped the table edge for balance.

'Doug.' Nina put her hand on his sleeve. The cashmere jacket was soft against her fingers. 'Doug, you have to pay.' When he turned to her his face was vacant, his eyes unfocusing. 'Pay. You know. Money. For dinner.' Twenty million dollars or not, she scowled, he's drunk as a skunk.

'Oh, oh, oh,' muttered Doug. 'Sure. Here.' He thrust a one-hundred-dollar bill in the maitre d's hand and lurched towards the door. Nina followed him to the parking lot. He navigated the narrow shrub-lined path very well, she noted. Cold air is probably all he needs. After all, she said to herself, he's huge. His body is madly neutralizing all that alcohol. Doug fumbled with the door of the Rolls then managed to swing it open and get in. Nina wondered if she should go back for help, go back to call a taxi, do something. But I don't even know what town I'm in. I can't just call a taxi and have them drive me fifty miles back to school.

Doug belched loudly as the windscreen wipers whirred back and forth. The car had not moved. Laughing at himself, he turned on the ignition and slowly proceeded along the Long Island Expressway.

Nina grimaced. I'll never get back on time at this rate.

Suddenly the car stopped and with a moan Doug threw himself at her.

Like a wounded bear, she thought as she pushed his face away from her. 'Oh, God!' she cried out when she saw the drool on his chin. 'Doug! Get away from me! Stop it!' she shouted and with all her strength shoved him towards the steering wheel where the noise of the horn caused him to jerk upright, blinking.

His moment of passion entirely forgotten, he suddenly floored the accelerator and then began to cackle to himself. 'Let's pretend we're in England! I like England! Nina, ya like England?' The Silver Cloud crossed the median with a lurch that snapped Nina's head back. She shouted his name a dozen times but he didn't seem to hear her; he giggled moronically as the lights sped by.

'One hundred miles an hour! Le's see what this ole baby can do!'

Nina begged him to stop the car. Thank God there's no traffic going back to the city at this hour. What hour, she wondered. How fast, she wondered. Don't think of numbers she told herself. How fast, she wondered again.

'One hundred and five!' Doug crowed.

Nina turned her face into the soft upholstery of the Rolls-Royce and then pulled herself into the back seat. She crouched on the floor in a foetal position, wondering if she should take off her high heels the way women were advised to do in plane crashes. My shoes from McRae's. Probably be found hundreds of yards from the crash. I'm furious. Just when life was getting to be fun. And if I don't die this is going to hurt a lot.

Sirens screamed behind the Rolls and at last Doug heard them. The car slowed then purred to a stop. Nina popped her head up and with great joy saw the two policemen at Doug's window. One opened the door and helped her out.

'You all right, miss?' he asked politely. Nina felt like falling into his arms.

Doug swayed as he stood in the headlights of the squad car parked behind them on the shoulder. Its rooftop red light still turned.

'You sure you're okay?' insisted the young officer, and Nina nodded.

There was the sound of running water and a strange splashing noise. Douglas Jacob Steiner Junior was carefully peeing on the highway patrolman's shining black boots.


Nina was dead set on making International Relations her major field of study but Dean Harkins refused to waive the language requirements.

'I don't think you could count that year of French in high school back home,' she confessed to the Dean. '"Bonn jewer!" she'd say every day.' Madame Thompson had never been out of the Delta until she had arrived in Jackson to teach French.

Nina decided to major in American History which she loved, but her weekends got in the way and suddenly she was on academic probation. The next semester her name was read out at the school assembly as being on the Dean's List and the audience broke into surprised titters. 'Nina McLean doesn't study!' said a worldly freshman afterwards. 'There must have been a mistake!'

Nina had never been so proud of anything in her life. She'd made Dean's List after a school career of Ds and Cs and hating her Mississippi teachers who said things like 'Ain't that real good?' She wrote her mother about it, of course, addressing the envelope to both of her parents and pretending she was writing only to Virginia.

Her mother wrote back, 'There is going to be a divorce.'

'Oh, God, how so like Mother to treat it as if it were something out of her power. As though it were something she could not take credit for or take charge of. There is going to be a hurricane. There is going to be a flood,' she complained to Adele.

'You're glad, aren't you?'

'Course I'm glad. I think this means I may never have to see him again. Ummmmm . . . well, maybe one last dinner. It says here he is moving out of the house around the first week of June. I'll be back by then. Rats.'

Rats is right, thought Nina as her mother parked the station wagon in the driveway that evening in June.

'Dinner's on the table but we thought we'd wait for you. It is the last time, you know.'

Nina kissed her mother's cheek and then made a face. 'I know it. Don't worry. I won't throw anything.' Like confetti, went through her head as she pulled open the back and began to reach for one of her three large suitcases.

'Lawsy! Look at chew! Jes' look at chew!' screamed Ellen in her white uniform, running through the garage. They embraced and laughed.

'Ellen, are you drinking those milkshakes?'

'I done gained three pounds since we last saw you. And your dress!' cried Ellen. 'Oooooooo-eeeee! Is this New York?'

'Nina has the same roommate who keeps giving her clothes,' put in Virginia. 'I've never heard of such good luck in all my born days!'

'Adele's gained exactly three pounds like you and thinks she is popping out of all these incredible dresses, so I'm wearing 'em until she is wildly thin again!'

The three women each carried a suitcase into the front hall.

Her father, who was sitting in his red leather chair, stood up as she entered the den and she awkwardly kissed his cheek.

'Did you have a good trip?' he asked as they walked into the dining room.

Ellen retreated quickly to the kitchen. She was thinking: The last time, the last time, the last time, as she counted the biscuits and covered them with the linen napkin to keep their heat in.

Nina sat in her old place with her back to the Old Canton Road window. She pretended that her father was any other guest at any other dinner table and she was as vivacious – 'as New York vivacious,' she told Adele on the phone, 'as I could be.' She told stories about her friends and made sure she emphasized how attractive and how wealthy they all were. There was Karen, the daughter of the head of General Motors, and there was Mimi, the heiress to half the oil in Texas, and the twins from Capetown whose last name was De Beers. There was the daughter of a maharajah and a princess from Austria was in the senior class. Myra's father was chairman of the board of Associated Enterprises, which ran half the department stores in New York and California. There was Libby, whose father started what had become the Holiday Inns and there was Kim, whose grandfather started Woolworth's.

'Daddy ate it up. I knew he would,' Nina reported to Ellen the next day in the breakfast room.

Ellen laughed. 'Dat's de firs' time I see any a' ya'll smile at dat table!' She arranged the freshly ironed pillowcases in a pile and reached for the Coke bottle which she filled with water to use as a sprinkler. She splashed Mrs McLean's pink linen blouse and then the iron, which sputtered and angrily hissed. Ellen looked at Nina, lounging in shorts, a halter top and barefooted, and asked, 'What are those girls really lak? What's it lak to have a mill-yun dollars?'

Nina told her all about Adele. The way she looked, the way she talked, and the way a Rolls-Royce had picked her up to take her to New York only the day before yesterday. 'You'd like her. And she'd like you. She already does! I've told her all about you!'

Ellen giggled, 'Lawsy!' as she put the iron carefully down on the embroidered collar.

'Adele is my best friend. She worries about things just the way I do.'

'Like what?' asked Ellen sceptically as she replaced the iron on its metal stand.

'She worries about her father, for instance, because he is really and truly old.'

'Laws! How kin that be?'

'Her mother was this famous model, her picture was everywhere. You've seen her. I know you have. You'd recognize her face. Anyway, Charles Wickham saw her face and found her and married her and he was twenty years older.'

'Oooooh!' Ellen shook her head. 'A May–December match.'

Virginia came into the kitchen. 'What am I missing?' So Nina had to tell it all over again.

'But still, after all this time Givenchy, Chanel and Christian Dior, the French designers particularly, like to give her discounts for her clothes.'

'As if she'd ever need a discount in her life,' remarked Virginia as she poured herself a glass of iced tea from a frosty white pitcher.

'I don't know. Maybe she doesn't take the discount but she does have closets of clothes. Adele showed me when we were alone in the apartment. There are closets there you can walk into and she has one closet for evening stuff and one for daytime things and one for summer and, because her favourite colour is this ice blue, she has a whole section of a closet just for her jackets and sweaters and coats in ice blue.'

'Oh, I just cannot imagine living that way!' exclaimed Virginia.

But Nina, sipping Coke from a red Dixie cup, bare feet on the kitchen chair across from her, could.

*

The next day Dr McLean moved all his things out, or rather, Ellen and Virginia and Nina did. They filled suitcases and put his shoes in big brown grocery bags from the Jitney Jungle and drove them in the station wagon down the Old Canton Road about half a mile to his newly purchased house, which was large, but 'nondescript' said Virginia and 'needs paint' put in Ellen. The three of them unpacked his suits and hung them in his closet and arranged his bureau drawers with freshly laundered shirts and then they turned around and went home for another trip.

They finished at lunch time as Dr McLean examained a would-be cataract patient. Nina lit candles at the dining room table and she and her mother toasted each other with glasses of ice water.

'Imagine! This is the first time we've ever had candles!' exclaimed Nina as they passed bacon, lettuce and tomato sandwiches back and forth on a silver tray. Her father had never allowed it. 'Cain't see whut Ah'm eatin'!' he'd bark. It was high noon and ninety-seven degrees but Nina felt exhilarated as though she were gulping champagne. Why was Mother so quiet?

Virginia chewed the white bread and decided it tasted like cotton. Should I tell Nina the truth? No, she'll never find out otherwise and what possible good would it do for her to know? She put pepper on the red slices of tomato before her. I guess I would like her and Bart to think I was strong enough to stand up to him after all these years of bowing under. Nina was chattering happily, something about Adele's last final exam. Virginia could only think of Duncan after dinner that night, sitting as usual in the red leather chair, and his voice, calm, deep, simply informing her that he was going to marry another woman. She winced at the memory of his commanding her to file for divorce. And I did what he told me to do, right down to the twelfth hour. Just like always. Nina was laughing as she passed her mother the sandwiches. My daughter won't be like me, thought Virginia.

It was to be a different kind of summer for all of them. Dr McLean rented an apartment so that he could live there

88

comfortably while his house was being renovated. Virginia kept thinking of him going past on the Old Canton Road in his Mercedes to an apartment furnished with a few of the living room things and the tiger skin rug. She was invited to spend July with her friends the Edwards family on the coast, and decided to go. Bart was taken into a real estate firm in San Francisco and after a weekend in Jackson said goodbye. Nina accepted Adele's invitation to come to Watch Hill and discovered she loved the ocean, and she had not forgotten how to sail.

On 1 September Virginia moved into a small house about thirty miles from Jackson. Tall pine trees lined the road to it and woods surrounded it on three sides. The house on the Old Canton Road, the setting for years of acrimony, was put up for sale.

Briarcliff began again, minus several friends who'd married, who'd flunked out, or transferred to state universities, or simply decided that the two-year Associate of Art degree was what they wanted and not the four-year Bachelor of Arts degree.

Paul looked at his watch, abruptly closed his notebook and then the thick sociology text. He knew that it took exactly eleven minutes to cross the quad from the library and to make his way up two flights of stairs to his room.

'There he is! I told you so! Set your watch by him!' laughed Dorsey and Hal.

'Hey, knock it off,' grinned Paul. 'You're just jealous.' He pulled off the tweed jacket and the long wool maroon scarf. His blue eyes were clear and his cheeks glowed from the brisk walk.

'And there he goes!' hooted Hal. 'Area code! Nine! One! Four!' shouted Dorsey as Paul's fingers moved.

'Cut it out, you guys!' He threw a green corduroy pillow from the couch at them as they slammed the door. It bounced on the door frame and fell to the floor. 'Hi, how are you?' he smiled into the phone.

'I'm . . . wait a second . . . Nina's got the stereo going full blast and the door is . . .'

'What's going on there? Sounds like a party.'

'Nina is learning to do this strange kind of dance and there are about seven girls in our room. Oh, Paul, it's not a strange dance! I sound like Nina! It's just a normal two-step and she can't get the hang of it!'

'So are you coming down on Friday? There's a party at Ivy that night and we've got a band coming from New York. Should be pretty good, and then on Saturday we're playing Brown and then there's the usual stuff.'

Adele was wondering what to wear. 'How does the weather look?'

'I promise it'll be clear blue skies if you come. I'll be on the horn with our Maker the minute we hang up.'

She laughed. 'You want me on Friday?' she teased and then regretted it.

'You bet!' he answered as always.

'Okay, I can leave right after economics and take the bus, but maybe someone's going down and I can catch a ride.'

'Great. See you day after tomorrow,' he ended.

'Bye.'

Adele faced the closed door of her room and heard the giggling and the music. She walked down the back stairs to the lounge and sank into one of the big brown leather chairs, sweeping a candy bar wrapper out of the way and propping her feet on the chair across from her. Alison, as usual, was staring at the television, oblivious to everything but the black and white shadows on the screen. The candy machines and the coffee maker and the Coke machine stood in a line behind her. She felt in her jeans pocket for a quarter and then realized she didn't want anything.

Paul. Another weekend at Princeton. And all I can think of is whether I should take my winter coat or not. Nina would be so excited and I am like Alison sitting there in a coma. I can't blame Paul! What is it? Adele asked herself for the twentieth time in that many weeks. She smiled. Nina has this idea that once you do it they will become ravenous beasts and will never let you out of bed. Adele sighed. She thought of Paul last weekend after the dance. They'd gone back to the Princeton Inn and she'd walked slightly ahead of him down the hall with its little framed prints to her room. He'd come in and closed the door and smiled. I like his blond hair, Adele had thought. I like the way it looks all feathery in the wind. He'd reached for the top button of her dress as though he were undressing a child. She had turned around obediently and waited for him to finish. Eight buttons, she thought. Eight pale blue self-covered buttons. Then he'd gravely helped her pull the sleeves down and then, whoosh, it had been expertly lifted over her head and arranged on the chintz armchair beside the bed. She had turned to face him as he yanked at his tie. 'Let me,' Adele had said. That was a little different, she thought now as she stared at her red leather flats across from her. What is it? I like his body. I love his smile. I like him. Mother adores him. Dad only met him once. What had Nina said to Leslie? 'It's probably a danger signal if your parents think he's so great. May mean he's low on the sex appeal scale.' Nina's little theories! She'd never met Paul. Wonder what she'd really think of him? And he of her? Nina, who never threw a crushed wad of paper in the direction of a wastebasket without murmuring 'I'm gonna live for ever,' and if it bounced on the rim and fell on the floor she dashed over and retrieved it with a 'Damn!' If it went in she smiled as though it did in fact guarantee immortality. Immortality . . . live for ever . . . living for ever with Paul. He was about to bring up marriage again. She could feel it. He was a senior this year and would be at Chase Manhattan next summer. It was all set. He'd signed a lease for an apartment already and within a year planned to buy into a cooperative. All set.

'Hey, what are you doing down here?' called Nina. 'I thought you'd pulled a Judge Carter!'

'Crater!' laughed Adele.

Nina flounced into a chair and then out of it again to put a quarter in the candy machine.

'Hey, do you want to be the man or shall I do it alone? Look at this!'

Adele stared as her roommate began to two-step around the room, unwrapping the Hershey bar.

'Pretty good,' nodded Adele, watching the figure in tight blue jeans and yellow sweater.

'Pretty good? I'm gonna sweep Carl right off his size eleven feet next weekend!' Nina took another bite and called over her shoulder, still two-stepping, 'Just call me Ginger!'

It was after Christmas vacation when Nina was summoned to the Dean's office. Dean Louise Harkins looked very motherly with her short grey permanented hair and her eyeglasses on a silver chain that rested on her broad bosom. Her plump frame was encased in a grey and black tweed suit and little no-nonsense pearl earrings were affixed to her ears.

'Nina,' she began and then rose and handed the confused girl a box of Kleenex. Nina accepted it and continued to stand in the doorway.

'Close the door, please,' said Dean Harkins as she lowered herself into the large wing chair in front of the window.

Nina obeyed. She held the Kleenex and with her other hand reached up to absentmindedly finger a strand of long hair that had escaped from the ribbon of her pony tail. She wondered if she should have changed from jeans for this appointment but there had been no time. This was her nonstop classes day. One right after the other from eight o'clock to four-fifteen.

'I have some sad news for you, dear. Your' – the pause went on for ever. The beat of a heart, the intake of breath and then the words – 'father has died.'

Relief suffused Nina's arms and legs in a warm rush. She placed the Kleenex on a corner of the Dean's desk and said, 'Thank you.'

Dean Harkins half rose to throw her arms around the tall slim girl in the plaid jacket. She waited for the sobs, for the pain to strike the composed figure. Why, she must be in

92

shock. 'You'd better sit down, my dear,' she commanded gently.

Bells were ringing for the third period and Nina said, 'Is that all? I have a class.'

Dean Harkins put on her glasses and leaned forward, squinting as though she were not seeing clearly.

'Ummmm, do you want me to have my secretary make arrangements for you to go home?'

'I don't think so. I really don't think so,' answered Nina and she turned and walked to the door and opened it and was lost in the crowd of girls with books, hurrying to class, clutching notebooks and gym clothes and hockey sticks.

Adele persuaded Nina to go to Mississippi. It was Adele who paced back and forth in their room, telling her to go if only for her mother.

'Go for her sake. Go to be with Bart. Go because you should.'

Nina sat on her desk, still wearing the red and black lumberjack jacket and her long knee-high black boots. They were dripping melted snow everywhere but for once neither of them saw fit to mention it. 'God, Adele. I don't want to go. I've only been back from Christmas for four days. I had my chance to see him Christmas day and I didn't.'

'You didn't see him?' asked Adele in surprise.

'No!'

Silence. The imminence of Charles Wickham's death was always with them and now it had been Nina's father who'd died. Dead in his mid fifties. 'I couldn't go to see him, Adele. I know you won't understand.'

'Try me.'

'He got married to that woman last fall. The woman from Georgia. I told you, didn't I?'

Adele nodded.

'Wow!' Something occurred to Nina. 'That was a pretty short marriage. October, November, December. Poof!'

'What happened over Christmas?'

'He called Mother and had her relay the message to me and to Bart that if we went to see him in his new house up the Old Canton Road that he'd give us each fifty dollars.'

93

'You're kidding!'

'No, Adele. This is the way my family is.'

'I wouldn't've gone either.'

'Bart went and he got his money, but he came back to the house and he said he felt ill. Then he tried to give me the envelope and I wouldn't take it. He was almost crying. You see, he hadn't gone to get the money, which is what, twisted though it seems, Daddy *wanted* . . .'

'You've lost me . . .'

'Daddy thinks money can do anything, can buy anything and if you have it, you have power over people, over everything they do or don't do. So when he offered money and Bart went to see him, he proved his point just one more time . . .'

'But Bart didn't go for the money.'

'I know that. You know that. Bart knows that.' Nina bit her lip. 'But Daddy just used the money to tell himself he was right about money and people and greed.'

'Goddamn! He's a real vulture!'

'Was! *Was, was, was, was*! And now he is *nothing* and I don't see why I have to show up at his funeral.'

Adele helped her to pack and stood outside the phone booth by the snack bar while she telephoned her mother. It was Adele who called the taxi for the train station. And it was Adele who pressed a Hershey bar in her hand as they hugged goodbye in the front hallway by the book that listed comings and goings and overnights. 'I've taken care of it! Just go!' she insisted.

Nina slept soundly until the wheels of the Delta jet bumped down on the runway of the Atlanta airport. When you go to Heaven, she thought wryly, you have to make a connection in Atlanta. Guess he won't be going to Heaven, she decided with finality as she put on her coat. Now walking down the long carpeted tunnel, like being inside a giant vacuum cleaner hose, she sensed the all-too-familiar distance again. Nina listened to the soft Southern accents swirl around her, but felt apart, alone. She wondered if she looked like someone whose father had died.

The short flight from Georgia to Mississippi was in darkness. The farmland below, even five minutes from either capital, was without light of any kind. When she made her way running in the drizzle from plane to open glass door of the Jackson airport she expected her mother to come surging through the crowd but instead it was Bart who wrapped her in his big strong raincoated arms. Nina felt the tears then. For Bart, she said to herself. For the pleasure of feeling safe and loved.

'Come on, kiddo! Let's get your suitcase and get out of this place! You know you're forty minutes late and I'm bored stiff! High winds, the radio said, coming up from the gulf!'

Nina couldn't stop grinning at him as he grabbed her red and white candy-cane-striped canvas tote bag and put one arm around her shoulders. She heard a woman in the crowd behind them say, 'Dr McLean you know just . . .' and was happy when the words were lost in the confusion of greetings.

Bart has rosy cheeks and looks taller and more handsome than ever, thought Nina. 'So, how's Mother?' she asked as he swung her suitcase into the back of the station wagon. The parking lot was half empty and great expanses of shining asphalt shone with pools of rain water under the arc lights. The new airport had been named after one of their father's golf-playing cronies.

'Okay, I think.' Bart slammed the back gate closed and then walked around to open the passenger door for Nina. 'Let's hurry. There're tornado warnings out.' He looked up at the dark sky and Nina felt the cold wind on her stockinged legs as she pulled her coat around her on the front seat. 'You know. Typical Mother. She's just not talking.' He turned the ignition key and went into reverse in a wide curve. 'How are you?' He smiled lightly and reached over to muss her hair.

'I could be even . . .' Nina almost said 'happy' and then saw his face sag strangely and didn't. '. . . even perfectly all right.' Bart nodded as he turned on to the highway. His profile, the perfect stamped-on-a-Greek-coin profile, was illuminated by the headlights of oncoming cars. A minute later the rain began in earnest with a swoop noise as though a giant bird's wing had swept across the roof. Bart reached for the radio and twirled the dial and then, as if he'd just thought of something, turned and grinned at her. 'Hear that?'

'What?' She stared through the windscreen, which ran with rivers of water, making her feel as though she were in a diving bell plunging to the bottom of the sea.

Bart floored the accelerator, turned off the highway and sped along the narrow country road. 'Bart!' cried Nina, suddenly frightened. 'What are you doing?'

'Don't you hear it?' he shouted excitedly. The radio was loud now and the Everly Brothers twanged their guitars and sang, 'Wake up, little Susie! Wake up!' as the car bucked along the back road between Jackson and Brandon. Then she heard it. The wail of the Illinois Central. The whistle was not a wail the next time but a sharp sudden cry very near them in the darkness. 'Watch this! Hold on!' The car raced towards the signal crossing as the red lights flashed. Like cherry cough drops they seemed to melt and run down the windscreen as the roar of the train became a deafening wild noise that made Nina think of horses stampeding, of being trampled by thundering hooves. The Everly Brothers were with them too in that moment: 'What are we gonna tell our friends when they say "ooh la la!"' The clang clang clang of the warning bells was punctuated by the crack of the flimsy white pole blocking them from the tracks and in suspended seconds, with Bart's face a mask of manic euphoria and Nina's eyes closed against the light from the locomotive as bright as the sun, the station wagon sailed over the rails as the whistle shrieked like a woman being murdered with a butcher knife. Behind them clattering tons of metal roared down the track towards New Orleans. They heard their breath in ragged gasps as the noise of steel on steel was pulled away from them and disappeared into the rain-soaked night.

The radio had been silenced, and the rustle of Nina

96

pulling her heavy winter coat away from her perspiration-soaked sweater seemed loud in the interior of the car. She felt feverish. The brother and sister drove on without saying a word.

A few miles from home Bart suddenly pulled the car off the road and began to cry. He put his hands over his face and slumped towards the steering wheel. The headlight beams shone straight ahead through the rain and dissolved on the periphery of the woods beyond.

'Bart,' she soothed. 'It's okay. It's over now.'

He looked up at her flushed face lit only by the phosphorescent dials on the dashboard. 'Strong little Nina.' Tears shone on his cheeks. 'Only you could sing that and get away with it. Could mean it. Could be so perfectly "all right", as you put it.'

Nina was confused. 'I don't know what I was humming. Some tune keeps running through my head.'

Bart smiled and wiped one cheek with the heel of his hand. 'From *The Wizard of Oz*? You really don't know?'

Nina shook her head.

'Ding dong the witch is dead, ding dong the wicked witch is dead . . .' his voice sang tremulously and then the sobs began again. Nina took her brother's head on her shoulder and smoothed back his soft black hair. Tears stung her eyes as she wondered: How many times has he been the one to comfort me? 'Always thinking of you, kid,' she remembered. Poor Bart. His face was hot with tears, his raincoat wet with rain; the windscreen wipers slapped slapped slapped against the pounding storm and the drops on the roof drummed like bullets. She held Bart for a long time, feeling very old and very cold inside. Well, he is dead, she decided. And we're alive. He didn't kill us after all.

'Red!' hissed Nina. 'I don't believe it!'

'Shhh! Here they come!' shushed her brother.

'Not maroon, not wine, but Merry Christmas red!' she continued, uncowed by Bart's dirty look as the two women made their way across the crowded room.

'Nina! Bart! Dahlin'! Ah'm so glad to see ya!' Aunt Leticia fairly wailed, putting out her arms in the red wool suit. Still got the moustache, noted Nina. The brother and sister allowed themselves to be embraced and then stood back to be introduced to the second figure in red.

'This is your daddy's new wife.' Old wife, new widow, flashed through Nina's mind. Thank God Mother hadn't come.

She extended a small hand towards Nina who took it and then Bart, always perfectly mannered, murmured, 'It is very nice to meet you,' and the petite middle-aged woman with the Florida tan and the blonded hair nodded wordlessly.

'Well, she's not a floozette actually,' Nina said quietly as they were approached by the Presbyterian minister and his demure round wife who had the air of someone about to pass sandwiches at a tea. Always looked that way, even if you met her buying stockings at Kennington's, thought Nina. 'Yes, yes, thank you,' she nodded and when the couple had turned away continued to Bart, 'I thought she'd be about twenty-seven wearing a pound of swimming-pool-blue eyeshadow so I . . .'

'Oh, Mrs Gordon! We certainly do appreciate your coming,' Bart was saying smoothly. But it was Nina she turned to.

'When are you gonna give up that Yankee school and come back down here where you belong?'

'Why, I . . .'

'Bart, I don' know how you kin as the man of the fam'ly allow this to . . .'

'Mrs Gordon, there is someone over here from Clarksdale who was asking about you . . .'

It happened again and again, she was to tell her mother later. 'You know, Nina, we want you back home . . .' 'You could have a job with Bubba's bank by jes' snappin' your fingers . . .' 'Ah'm afraid to ask what kind of ideas those Yankee perfessors have been puttin' in yer pritty head . . .' Nina shuddered. Come back? she thought. Never. She imagined that she had become another person south of Atlanta, that the confident popular Nina of Briarcliff, who knew her way around Manhattan, who could get a taxi with an outstretched arm, who could order from a menu in French without hesitation now that Adele had taught her how, simply evaporated below a certain latitude. All these people knew me as an unhappy little girl with an important father, and now, I am . . . someone who can order from a menu in French? My important father is dead, I am older and I've gone a long way from here. But not far enough away and not long enough for these people to see I'm different when I come back. Couldn't anyone see I never belonged? Can't they see I don't belong here now?

Bart put his arm around her shoulders and gave her a squeeze, then he took the arm of a woman convulsed in tears and led her over to Dr Jasper's wife for words of comfort. 'Ah wanna tell y'all both that your daddy . . .' Nina's thoughts turned back to Aunt Leticia and the new widow. That red is pretty strange. Wonder if they planned it. 'Your father was one of the fannest men that evah walked this earth,' said a large woman dogmatically as her ample bosom heaved with emotion under a black crepe dress. Nina concentrated on the string of pearls that floated on the expanse like little white buoys on a dark sea.

'No, no, no thank you,' said Nina firmly as her aunt took her hand to pull her towards the open casket. You can't get away with that again. I'm older now. She had known where he was all morning and she and Bart had marked off their territory as far away as possible. They stood to the left of the archway that led into the viewing room beside a lectern that Nina kept putting her elbow on and then removing. It held a large white leather guest book, its pages edged with gold. Nina shuddered and tried not to even look in the direction of the enormous polished wooden coffin.

Bart had said in his only moment of showing his wicked old self, 'Should go over and put a few dollar bills in. He'd like that. I'm sure those lawyers had to talk him out of being buried with it all.' Nina broke into a delighted grin and then found herself being embraced by her father's secretary.

'This place hasn't changed much since Big Momma's funeral, has it?' she said to no one in particular as still another elderly woman came forth to praise the illustrious surgeon, the humanitarian, the good citizen, the pillar of the community, the great man.

Nina's black leather pumps were not made for standing, her grey tweed suit not made for the too-warm central heating. Nina felt cranky, tired, but curiously unmoved by the displays of grief around her. She tapped Bart on the arm but he didn't turn towards her immediately. 'We're downtown. Want to go to the movies when this is over?'

He looked at her then and she was astonished to see his face contorted with the effort to hold back tears. She was sorry then. He seemed weak, somehow diminished by it all, whereas I, she thought in confusion, feel . . . feel free. I feel as if someone has untied me. This is the last time I'll ever be in the same room with him. She took a step forward, putting herself one pace farther away from the archway.

Sobbing came from the centre of the room behind her and Nina realized it was her aunt and the new widow. Aunt Leticia's voice carried over the hushed murmurs of the mourners. 'Oh, mah dahlin' brother! How ah loved you so!' and then a new voice, words muffled by sobs. 'Jes' when ah'd found you! You weren't with me long enough!'

'Excuse me,' said a man to Nina who turned as a flashbulb went off in her face.

'Hey! What is this?' exclaimed Bart with annoyance. 'What are you doing here?'

'Mrs Garrison hired me for the day. I'm afraid I'm a little late. The rain, you know, has . . .'

Nina rolled her eyes as Bart moved aside and let the photographer through the archway. White flashes caught the tableau at the coffin and saved the scene for the enjoyment of someone in another generation, another year, or perhaps just Aunt Leticia next week when she would sit down, pour herself a Coca-Cola, light a Camel cigarette, and pick out her favourite proofs.


Five days later after economics class Adele opened the door of their room and saw Nina still in her winter coat curled up asleep on her bed. Adele tiptoed to the desk and began to read the next day's sociology assignment. She glanced up from the page and stared at her roommate, willing her to waken. She'd missed her. Best friend, confidante. Her mother had said maybe she should change roommates after freshman year, that maybe the two of them would get on each other's nerves. 'That's a small room, after all, darling,' had been her comment. But the two girls hadn't been anything but close since that first funny awkward dinner of the first day. Adele later told her, 'I couldn't believe what you looked like! Thought Briarcliff being full of beautiful girls was just a myth and then I draw a roommate who looks as though she could take on the world with one smile!' Nina had evidently never been told she was even pretty, had never had a real date, had never been kissed, and had grown up in this strange big house in Mississippi with a tyrannical father. Nina thought of Briarcliff as freedom and so did Adele, at last freed from the confines of Farmington with its rules, rules, rules. Both of them steered clear of those who thought of Briarcliff as a ritzy finishing school for girls whose grades had kept them out of Wellesley, Radcliff or Barnard or Smith. They were the sulkers as far as Adele was concerned. Nina had told her how she'd sat on the steps at home and marked the listings in the big college handbook with pencilled check marks. There were all the schools around New York City marked, then all the girls' schools and then all the ones with under eight hundred students. Briarcliff and two others had been given three marks and she'd applied to all three colleges, praying that her father would not insist upon her going to Ole Miss. All three had accepted her. When Adele heard this part of Nina's story she was very impressed but Nina explained immediately. 'Ever heard of geographical distribution? I'm a token hick from the Magnolia State, that's all!' How the two of them had laughed over it.

Six o'clock, going on six-thirty. 'Nina,' Adele whispered. 'Nina!' more loudly. 'We're going to miss dinner if we don't go now. Do you want to come?'

Nina opened her big grey eyes and smiled. Stifling a yawn

she stood up and shook herself. 'What am I doing sleeping in my coat? Like some old Bowery bum!'

Adele pulled on a parka while Nina brushed her hair and the two of them clattered down the stairs and out the side door. It was a short walk to the dining room which sat like a giant aquarium in a field of snow.

'Sorry about your father,' said Leslie and touched her arm in the cafeteria line.

Nina nodded. 'Thanks.'

'Too bad about your dad,' whispered Kim as she unloaded her tray beside Nina's at the round table.

Nina nodded, 'Yes, thanks.'

Adele glanced at her.

'I was sorry to hear about your father,' said Alison in that twangy Wisconsin accent.

'Okay, okay,' snapped Nina.

They all ate in silence after that. When the others were gone Adele said, 'Look, everyone's just trying to be nice to you! No one knows what to say when somebody dies. Don't be a bitch. It's not becoming.' She grimaced. 'You're not a bitch. You don't know how to be one, so don't try.'

Nina took a gulp of milk and said, 'Adele, I know everyone assumes I'm sorry because that would be the normal thing, but he wasn't a normal person and I'm not sorry and I hate all this pretending. It's been a strange four days . . .'

Adele saw Myra approaching in that silly Snoopy sweatshirt that amounted to her uniform, she wore it so much. Uh-oh, not now, she thought. Myra was always up on the gossip. Always knew it all.

Myra bent down with her hand on Nina's shoulder and said, 'Hey, I'm sure glad your father died!'

Nina looked amazed and then burst out laughing.


'Telephone! Adele! It's person-to-person for you!' shouted Leslie over the banister from the second floor as Adele and Kim plodded up the stairs with their arms full of new textbooks for the spring semester.

102

'Coming! Thanks!' Paul never called person-to-person and he was the only man in her life now, and Mother wouldn't, so who could it be? Adele's heart pounded when she heard Jack's voice. She saw his face, she felt his face, when he said, 'Hi, kid.'

'Oh, it's you,' she tried to be nonchalant.

'Yeah, just me. Your sailing pal, remember?'

She didn't answer. They'd decided that last summer, that last time behind the boathouse, to avoid each other for the rest of their lives if necessary until the feelings went away. And he was breaking his promise. 'What's up?' she asked casually as Kim walked by wearing blue jeans and pink curlers. Adele wanted to demand, 'Why are you calling me! How dare you!'

'How would you like my roommate and me to sweep you and a friend away for the evening? Dinner in New York. I have to be there tomorrow afternoon and Charlie's in town. Remember my roommate? We're staying with your parents.'

She didn't answer. She had calculated only the day before yesterday that they hadn't seen each other since Labor Day weekend of her freshman year and now it was January of her junior year. More than two whole years had passed.

'You still there? Just take the train in and meet us at the Plaza. Half past six, the Palm Court?'

Silence from Adele.

'I can hear you breathing and if you don't have sense enough to say yes to a big deal at Harvard Law School then I'll say it for you. "Yes, Jack, see you tomorrow."'

'Okay,' she said in barely a whisper and hung up.


'What's the matter? Don't you want to go?' Nina stood in the middle of the room holding three dresses on hangers. Their hems trailed the floor.

'Sure I do. I just . . .' Adele put her hand up to her forehead. 'I wonder if I'm getting the flu.'

Nina sprang into action and within seconds had a bottle of alcohol and a thermometer out.

103

'No, Florence, it's probably nothing serious,' smiled Adele, sinking dramatically back on her pillow.

'You look thinner. You are probably feverish from malnutrition. I've been watching you, you know. You're thinner since Monday.'

'Sure I am. Seven chocolate chip cookies for lunch every day will do that to you.'

'Of course you were ridiculously thin when I met you and you are still the second skinniest person in 'he dorm.'

'Who's first? You?'

'Did I tell you they called me Beanpole in the sixth grade?'

Adele allowed Nina to take her temperature and watched her hold up one dress and then the other. 'I think black since it's the Plaza. Wow! The Plaza! Isn't that exciting, Adele!'

Her New Yorker roommate nodded and tried to keep her lips closed. It was only exciting when you thought it was and for her it was just a convenient place to meet. She'd been there a hundred times.

'Are you going to wear your black dress, too? The one with the low back?'

Adele shrugged. She felt a pain starting in her stomach. What if Jack is breaking his promise because his feelings have gone away? What if it no longer bothers him to see me? What if he thinks it is all over? What if I have no effect on him? What if he falls in love with Nina? Oh, God, that would be easy. What if he can look at me and feel nothing and remember nothing and I am still suffering this way? All I have to do is tell Nina the truth and she'll find a way to brush him off, to be aloof. Nina would never go after somebody else's property. Well, not on purpose. She's just so vivacious and beautiful the property comes to her. But isn't Jack for Nina and Charlie for me? How can Jack and I be a couple when Nina knows we are cousins? Why did I act absolutely star-struck on the phone? Should I call him back and make him tell me what is going on?

'I cannot wait to meet this cousin of yours. I was a little disappointed when he didn't show up at Watch Hill last summer. Lucky me! I used to get to see his sister at Fence Club!' Nina clutched her throat and gagged.

Adele took the thermometer out and read, 'A hundred and one. We can't go.'

'Let me see that,' cried Nina, and grabbed it away. 'You're absolutely normal, Adele! What is wrong? For heaven's sake, it's the Plaza!'

Adele shrugged. I have to tell her or I have to go and pretend nothing's wrong.

'Just teasing.' She leaped from the bed. 'Let's knock 'em dead! Tomorrow afternoon after art history I'm going to soak myself in Diorissimo, and you will look fabulous in that dress with my silver sequinned evening bag if you wear these earrings . . .'

And they did the nearest thing to knocking 'em dead.

'Goddamn, Forrest! Why didn't you warn me!' sighed Charlie Brewster as the two tall girls came swinging through the revolving doors as if they owned the place and made their way to the centre of the lobby. Charlie straightened his tie. He was broad-shouldered, brown-haired, brown-eyed, with a contagious smile.

Jack had taken this table on purpose. He wanted to see Adele before she saw him; he wanted one good look with no one watching.

Nina whispered, as they walked heads high, shoulders back, 'Oh, Adele, I love this place. I love the doormen, I love the flowers, I love this green and pink-flowered carpet, I love the chandeliers, I love these shops right out in the middle of the lobby, I love the limousines outside the front door, I love everybody being in a hurry . . .'

'Nina! You are driving me nuts!' hissed Adele.

They now stood in front of a maitre d' who smiled and said, 'Ladies?' Nina eyed the tiered platform of marble crowded with silver plates of fancy pastries. The waiter behind Louis thought: Lord in heaven, it's Snow White and Rose Red. Each more stunning than the other. He stood riveted to the spot until Louis, in what was planned as a smooth reverse, almost tripped over him. 'This way, please. Mr Forrest's table is in the corner.' Louis gave Eddie a piercing glare. Nina and Adele followed him into the square enclosure of palms, past clusters of green velvet chairs. It was an island of subdued voices and tinkling ice cubes and the muted chink of china cups against their saucers. The violinist was playing a waltz.

'Waltzes make me weak,' whispered Nina.

'I don't have to ask who is the cousin!' grinned Charlie. 'You look like twins!' He looked from Jack to Adele. 'I'm Charlie Brewster.' He smiled at both girls.

'What'll you have to drink?' Jack nodded to Nina.

'Scotch and water, please.'

'Adele?'

The way he said her name was different from the way anyone else said it. Her heart pounded in her throat. 'Vodka, please, with tonic. Thanks,' she said coolly.

'Adele and I missed you at Watch Hill last summer,' began Nina.

Jack tried to smile just enough to be polite. He wondered if Adele were reacting to anything. She seemed brittle and far away.

'I missed being at Watch Hill,' he said smoothly. 'I hear you sail. Where'd you learn?'

Nina began to talk about Bart and turning the boat over and the stories about water moccasins. Jack was teasing her about the Magnolia Blossom nickname he'd heard his Aunt Tory refer to, but he was keenly aware of the pianist playing a song from *Gigi*. Not that one, he thought. He remembered the scene with Gaston at Maxim's and recognized the strains of 'She is not Thinking of Me'.

Charlie ordered another round of drinks and surveyed the stunning blonde beside him. She looked uncomfortable. As though she could have been photographed for the cover of *Vogue* but as though her lunch hadn't agreed with her.

'Adele?'

She smiled and stared at him. Better stop it. Better shape up, she thought. 'Sorry. I am off in another world these days. Tell me what Harvard Law School's like. Is it all it's cracked up to be, or simply more?'

'More!' he declared. 'And the longer I'm there the less I feel like being a lawyer.'

'Why? What are they doing to you?' Adele laughed that

tinkling laugh of her mother's and the evening finally got off the ground.

An hour later they were walking down Fifth Avenue towards '21'.

'Only a few blocks. Don't mind, do you?' asked Jack.

'Never!' swore Nina. 'You are with somebody so hungry that she could crawl to a restaurant on her knees if necessary.'

Adele was horrified but the men laughed. 'Nina, you wouldn't! This is Fifth Avenue! You wouldn't!'

Nina grinned. 'Just making sure you were awake, Adele!'

'See what I put up with!'

'And what I put up with!' said Nina, putting her arm around her friend.

Damn, they are exquisite, thought Jack. Nina with those big grey eyes and that white skin like porcelain and that devastating smile that says, I'll never be unhappy. And Adele! With skin like moonlight and the blonde hair that falls like silk on to the stand-up sleeves of the black satin dress. She still hasn't looked at me. Was this a good idea?

In minutes they had descended the steps surrounded by little painted iron statues of jockeys and were inside the restaurant. Jack felt a spasm of desire when Charlie drew Adele's coat from her shoulders and the long smooth expanse of her back was exposed. Cut to the waist, he thought. Hmmmm, and if you sat facing her you'd only see the tailored coolness of her.

The maitre d' nodded, 'Good evening, gentlemen, ladies,' and they followed him into the downstairs dining room.

There was a long dark wood bar and tables covered with red and white checked tablecloths. Nina looked up, for the ceiling was hung with toys of all kinds, little trains and cars, and model aeroplanes; the occasional helmet and baseball glove dangled between fire engines and toy rocket ships. It looks like a boy's room, she thought.

Brewster's son rated a good table as did anyone named Forrest or Wickham, so they were seated by the door. Lee Radziwell walked in behind them on the arm of someone decidedly gay. Charlie nodded at the head of CBS and his glamorous wife, Babe. People pointed them out, too. 'Looks just like her mother, doesn't she?' said one woman clearly as she exited and they all laughed. 'She was talking about me, of course,' chirped Nina. 'I *do* look like my mother!' she insisted when they booed her.

'Yeah, and we're Jack and Charlie!' teased Jack, and when Nina didn't laugh Adele explained that Jack and Charlie had been the bootleggers who founded '21' during Prohibition. It had originally been a speakeasy.

Adele decided Charlie was very nice and actually much more fun than Paul was these days. She didn't move away when he took her hand in his under the table after dinner and absentmindedly stroked her thumb with his. It's fine, just fine – she held her breath – as long as I pretend Jack isn't here. I can't look at him. I can't let him see what I feel. Will he ask Nina out again? Will he kiss her goodnight? Oh, God – she took a swallow of Grand Marnier – why did I come here?

Jack watched Nina plunge her spoon into a dish of chocolate mousse with all the happiness of a child. 'Where do you live when you're not at Cambridge or Watch Hill?' she asked suddenly.

'Oh, my family lives outside Philadelphia. Have you ever heard of a place called Chestnut Hill?'

She shook her head.

'Well, it's not so different from Westchester County, really. Same kinds of houses, same kinds of people, I guess. You'll have to come down some time.' He stopped, sensing Adele had heard. 'Get Adele to bring you.'

Nina was blissfully unaware of the glances exchanged between cousins. Hate flashed in sparks from Adele's blue eyes. Charlie missed it, too, for he was lighting a cigar, wondering if it would bother anyone and having a devil of a time with the match.

They all said goodbye in the middle of the cavernous Grand Central Station. Nina was given a peck on the cheek by Jack, which rather surprised her and Adele was kissed on the lips by Charlie. She thanked him profusely for all the fun and then pretended to be involved with something in her evening bag when Jack moved next to her. Nina and Charlie were laughing over a joke as Jack whispered to his cousin, 'Call you tomorrow. Will you take the train in for lunch?'

Adele turned abruptly, never raising her head or acknowledging his words, and stalked towards platform eleven.

'I'm being abandoned!' called Nina, running to catch up with her. 'Bye!' She turned and waved. The two pairs of black peau de soie heels clattered noisily over the marble floor and then the roommates disappeared from sight through the arch to the left of the giant Kodak ad.

Charlie and Jack ascended in silence, two tall figures in dark suits, on the only escalator still running this late and went out through a side door of the Pan Am building to hail a cab for the Wickham apartment.

Well, I survived, thought Adele on the train. Nina was asleep across from her. Thank goodness I didn't tell her anything. What a mess. No, it's not a mess. It's just nothing. Why couldn't he leave me alone? Why did he have to do this? Tears stung her eyes and she felt angry and sad and afraid. What if I never get over him? Why does he want to see me again? Why did he do this tonight? I hate him. I hate him. He'd caught her staring at his hand as it rested on the checked tablecloth. She'd seen the fine golden hairs that sprang above his knuckles. She'd thought of his fingers and crossed her legs with such force that she'd kicked Charlie and he'd knocked his scotch flying straight up into the air. Damn him. He is playing with me. He's stronger than I am and can have sex and forget it, or maybe he simply wants it again. A return match just for fun. I hate him, she thought. I hate him. Why did we ever touch each other? Why did we ever meet? Why is my mother his father's sister? Why can't I stop wanting him?

'Briarcliff! Briarcliff Manor! Next stop!' Nina stirred and they were helped off the train by the round little conductor who asked if they were being met. 'It's okay,' said Adele. 'I see a taxi. Thanks.'

Twenty minutes later they were in their separate beds three yards apart. Nina was sound asleep and Adele was lying in the dark in misery. *

109

Most of the girls at Briarcliff College ignored Vietnam – after all, any male they knew had a deferment and was safely tucked away in college or graduate school; ignored Students for Democratic Society; and were rather playful about the women's liberation movement, for they felt totally optimistic about the life the potential husbands they dated promised to provide for them.

Jacqueline Kennedy married Aristotle Onassis the weekend of Nina's first mixer at Columbia. The girls oohed over her Valentino dress in *Time* magazine but Kim declared, 'I could never do it with a man that short.'

'What about all that cash?' demanded Leslie, and Adele quipped, 'Mother says, "Marry for money and you pay for it every day of your life."'

Nina leapt to the conclusion that the Wickham marriage was one-sided as far as wealth went and it wasn't until some time later that she learned that Tory Forrest had come from a gilt-edged background, too.

Richard Nixon was swept into office by his silent majority in a landslide. It was the dawning of the *Age of Aquarius* and the music from *Hair* was playing up and down the halls of Briarcliff dormitories. Neil Armstrong landed on the moon and took that 'one small step for man, one giant leap for mankind'. Americans were beginning to parrot 'Have a nice day' and were making jokes about the porno movie, *I Am Curious Yellow*. Woodstock, the rock music festival in upstate New York, drew 400,000 people. Jefferson Airplane, Jimi Hendrix, Joan Baez, Janis Joplin, The Family Stone, and the Creedence Clearwater Revival were the pop stars Adele and Nina listened to.

Charles Manson represented the black side of the hippie movement and the gruesome murder of Sharon Tate made headlines around the world. The drowning death of Mary Jo Kopechne in an automobile driven by Senator Edward Kennedy, the only surviving Kennedy brother, seemed to have finished his political career. Skyjacking became a word and bomb threats in New York City reached one thousand a month. Angela Davis in California was the most famous black advocating revolutionary action, and the Chicago

110

Seven were on trial in Chicago. The Vietnam War continued.

Simon and Garfunkel crooned about 'the sound of silence'. A freshman in a pony tail picked out the notes by ear one rainy afternoon at the piano in Dow Hall.

*Portnoy's Complaint* was a best seller and people waited in lines to see *Butch Cassidy and the Sundance Kid*, starring Paul Newman and Robert Redford.

The Pentagon Papers, tracing three decades of growing American involvement in Vietnam, were leaked to the New York *Times* and created a panic within the Nixon administration. Watergate was still only the name of an apartment complex in Washington. Ping-pong diplomacy made a splash in the press and the publishing firm of McGraw-Hill released the memoirs of Howard Hughes, which would be proved a colossal hoax perpetrated by Clifford Irving.

Myra strolled down the hall in her underwear, reading *Everything You Always Wanted to Know About Sex* to anyone who wanted to listen. Leslie's copy of *Love Story* had been tear-stained enough to strain legibility.

Nina's class of one hundred and sixty-four had shrunk to eighty girls by Graduation Day in May of 1972. Nina's mother at last met Adele's and the women embraced by the fountain as though they, too, were best friends.

Almost everyone wore Bermuda shorts under the royal blue robes on the hot spring day for the ceremony; afterwards they sprinted to their rooms to change into dresses and run down again to pose for photographs, to kiss classmates goodbye, to meet the long-talked-about older brothers and the fiancés, to swear that they would write, and to supervise the loading of trunks into station wagons.

Adele was off to San Francisco, much to Nina's disappointment, who had opted to find an apartment in New York City. Adele's mind had been made up since junior year, since the day after the dinner with Jack and Charlie at '21'. Bart's address had been scrawled on a sheet of notebook paper with the message: 'If you change your mind about Paul, marry Bart and we'll be related.'

Nina embraced her and began to cry and then Adele

111

began to cry and Myra came leaping at both of them, telling them to 'grow up!' which made them laugh and turn and ask where her Snoopy sweatshirt was.

'I've given it to Dean Harkins to bronze.' Myra had plans to work as an assistant buyer for Marshall Field in Chicago. Leslie was going to Paris, where her father was the American ambassador, and Kim was doing nothing at one of her parents' houses in Hawaii until 'the spirit moves me'. They made promises to keep in touch and waved until limousines and station wagons were out of sight.

An hour later the campus was deserted and nearly silent. Dean Harkins locked her office door for the last time of the school year and nodded to Lucy, the elderly maid, in the lobby of Dow Hall. She was busily picking up discarded programmes headed 'Briarcliff College, Class of 1972', under the school coat of arms. The heavy white paper was printed with an alphabetical list of all the girls' names. It was the last time they would share the same page.

# 3

Nina turned the key in the lock and realized that Mississippi was part of her past. She would never go back and there was no one, nothing, that could make her. Mississippi and her childhood could be something squinted at from a great distance, something she could trade on as exotic background. She could mention it when it suited her purposes, to add allure, to spice a conversation with a funny story. She could roll her eyes as she sipped cognac late at night and make herself as romantic a heroine as she pleased.

Mississippi was no longer real, she decided as the door swung open.

New York, thought Nina! She resisted the urge to shout out the window of the tiny apartment on the fifteenth floor. 'I have arrived!' She wanted to scream at the dozens, no, the hundreds of little windows that faced her as she looked southwards across 54th Street. There was the Citicorp Building with its white sliced-off silhouette of a roof, and the Chrysler Building with its art deco curlicued design, and the Pan Am building half a mile away, and all the minor buildings between them filled with exciting people and elegant shops. Nina had learned that every twenty blocks from north to south equalled a mile and that every ten avenues crosstown from east to west was a mile. She memorized the avenues from Fifth to where she lived by saying Mississippi Power and Light, which made perfect sense to her but caused several people at a cocktail party to shake their heads and look perplexed. 'Madison, Park and Lexington!' she'd beamed triumphantly. 'And then, of course, it's easy, you pick up the numbers again with Third, Second and First.'

How lucky I am, she thought. An apartment shared with two girls who'd graduated from Briarcliff the year she had been a freshman. Vague friends of a vague friend; one working for *Glamour* and one for *Newsweek*. Nina was sure it was the perfect situation for her. The apartment was a studio in a nice doorman building which went for the bargain rate of $300 a month and, with three of them, they each tossed in $100 plus any extra for their telephone calls. Seemed sensible. But it is small, they'd warned her, with only a living room, a kitchen and a bathroom. Nina's bed was a cot that rolled out of a closet into the living room every night and Lydia slept a foot away on the couch that unfolded into a double bed and Carol slept on a single bed in the kitchen with her doberman named Rommel. Lydia had no dates and was on a nonstop diet of cottage cheese which she drowned in ketchup and called 'a la Nixon'. Carol picked up men in Central Park with the help of Rommel, who excelled in major attention-getting tricks like biting a man's *Wall Street Journal* right out of his signet-ringed hand.

The premise was they shared everything but, in fact, the inverse was true. Why, even the refrigerator shelves were labelled 'Carol', 'Lydia', 'Nina'. Carol's shelf was always empty, which stirred in Lydia the darkest suspicions whenever she saw Carol so much as chewing gum. Their parsimonious attitude was annoying to Nina and she often left the apartment to keep from making a sharp comment. Twice, as she was taking a shower, Lydia entered the bathroom, calling 'Knock-knock! I took eleven cents out of your purse since I bought toilet paper today!'

Fights between Lydia and Carol were full of bitter accusations and recriminations. The last one Nina witnessed was particularly memorable. Lydia claimed in screams of anguish that Carol had rubbed all her Gucci shoes with sirloin and fed them to Rommel, who'd torn each $85 pair to shreds. 'This,' shrieked Lydia, 'is revenge for my forgetting to tell you that your latest pick-up called!' Lydia sat on the living room couch, eternally eleven pounds overweight, with dank hair hanging in her face, and stared mournfully at the six Gucci shoes riddled with teeth marks. Carol stood, slim, bleached blonde, kewpie-doll pretty, in the kitchen in a red cotton skirt that barely covered her pantyhose crotch seam and unconcernedly ate baked beans out of an open can. Her

114

long platinum hair was brushed back into a loose pony tail. As the sleek doberman growled and leapt for the red ribbon she said calmly, 'Stop it, Rommel!' and fed him beans from her spoon. Clutching a brown leather shoe to her breast Lydia began to weep in the living room two yards away. 'Covered in drool!' she cried. 'My Guccis!'

Carol left the apartment to meet someone for a drink at Trader Vic's and Nina left for a phone booth. The younger brother of someone she'd dated at Columbia knew of an apartment. She arranged with relief and trepidation, after seven dimes and seven phone calls, to move to 90th Street and Second Avenue. The place was falling apart, she was warned, often had no heat and was in a rough neighbour- hood; but it was empty and there was no problem about taking over the lease. The next evening Nina settled the phone bill and Lydia, who had a good heart, helped her into a taxi with her suitcases. 'I just can't believe you're leaving,' she said for the tenth time.


Nina woke on her cot in what she called the Master Bedroom – or should it be the Mistress Bedroom, she wondered – and stared at the ceiling with its new coat of white paint. It made her back hurt to think of all those days last week on the borrowed stepladder. In the end she'd called a telephone number listed in the *Village Voice* and five black painters had arrived with everything but paint. Three of them stood around in white coveralls and sneakers and New York Yankee caps and waited for the other two to return with buckets of off-white Sherman Williams number thirty. Nina had shaken hands and offered them beers and in a half hour they were in full swing. They told her they had all been born on January thirtieth and that's why they had formed the company and that's why they were so compatible and she believed every word. The painting corps scraped and played the radio at a deafening volume, trailing canvas drop cloths from room to room, working at a very fast clip and singing loudly. They were awfully good with a medley of Ray Charles hits. In two days the place sparkled. Nina paid them one hundred dollars and five six-packs of Budweiser.

The next morning the linoleum had arrived and been laid in twenty minutes over the kitchen floor, which was simply eighteen by twenty-two feet of splinters. Such an expanse of the bold black and white zebra-skin pattern had made Nina jump, but she thought of Africa, of the Serengeti, and nodded to herself: it stays. The rest of the apartment's floor was covered with shining black deck paint.

Every room was hung with pictures that her mother had brought up in May on the graduation trip. There were seascape prints, and her favourite etchings that went all the way back to Aunt Lillian's house in Natchez. Nina filled the fireplace that would never work with geraniums of pink and coral, and a tall palm tree, orphaned by the previous tenant, stood in one corner of the living room facing 90th Street. Since the apartment stretched the length of the building, the kitchen and the living room were the brightest rooms with the largest windows. The kitchen overlooked a rather scruffy back garden. A tiny bathroom with a giant bathtub was two steps from the kitchen sink. Nina's first act had been to paint a wide green racing stripe around the tub and then paint all the toenails of its clawed feet the same bright emerald. The three middle rooms had windows that opened on to a not very scenic air shaft so Nina simply added colour. One wall of her bedroom was emerald green and one wall of the room off the kitchen was the brightest yellow. The closet room in the centre was pristinely white.

Nina was good with flowers and had made a deal with the old character who sold them in the Yorkville section on 86th Street. She always bought what he had left over on Mondays and Thursdays for almost nothing and took them home where she cut their stems at a sharp angle and soaked them for several hours in water with aspirin tablets. The apartment was usually filled with daffodils, daisies and zinnias.

'So I have the apartment,' she said aloud without meaning to. Now I need a job. She sighed and wondered if it really

116

were ten minutes of nine. Grimacing at the little Tiffany clock Adele had given her one Christmas she got out of bed and walked into the kitchen. I probably need a psychiatrist, she decided. Why am I making such a big deal of this? She flicked on the last nine minutes of the *Today* show and talked at the figures on the screen. 'You have a job and you have a job and you have a job and all the people who wrote your clever little lines have a job and the cameramen filming you as you say them have jobs and . . .' She made a face and switched off the television. I can't bear the idea of having to be somewhere every single day. Well, five days out of seven is really every day and to sit there and be told what to do and to be painfully aware that my lunch hour is sixty minutes long. She reached for a Tab and yesterday's paper. Flipping open to the entertainment section she chose the afternoon movie.

Nina's life revolved around a thorough reading of the New York *Times*, her movie, and a trip to pick up this silk blouse or that velvet jacket at the cleaner's. Then she would wash her hair and dry it carefully, give herself some sort of herbal facial, do her nails, and be ready for that evening's dinner date. She enjoyed getting dressed up, enjoyed being admired, and experienced a keen delight in teasing, in flirting.

No one could be more of a coy romantic than Nina. A dinner companion would bask in her affectionate gaze across a candlelit table; she would summon reservoirs of energy in telling a story on herself, making it funny and slightly self-deprecating to incite feelings of protectiveness within the lawyer or banker holding one of her soft, perfumed-at-the-wrist hands. By the time it came to tasting a bit of his dessert and allowing him a spoonful of her chocolate mousse, intimacy had bloomed. 'I love it! I could live on it! I could swim in it naked!' she might exclaim and across from her, his face would assume what she called 'the trout look'. Whoever it was they all shared certain qualifications: good-looking, Ivy League, moneyed and, sooner or later, 'the trout look'. This expression was a mixture of stunned adoration, pulsing desire and please let me take

117

care of you, you are so fey and need someone solid to lean on. This last emotion, Nina imagined, she could see right around the eye area.

Nina kissed them soundly and knew how to gently stroke a sideburn for maximum sensitivity; she knew whether or not to allow her coat to fall open as they pressed themselves against her in a descending elevator. She liked taking a man's arm and innocently angling his elbow into her breast as they walked up Third Avenue for Sunday brunch. But perhaps, most important of all, Nina knew which ones would be enchanted by her capricious play and which ones wouldn't put up with it. It was games.

'A flirt! A tease! A bitch!' said Craig Standish as he slammed a squash ball against the front wall. Joe Hamilton, son of the old Senator, echoed his sentiments as he volleyed. But both thought she was lots of fun and resolved to call her for another date. Nina would have laughed and laughed had she been able to overhear them two hours later at the bar in the Knickerbocker Club. There, over scotch, freshly showered, they both professed to have made love to Nina McLean. It was there, too, that eyeing each other over their drinks, they each decided the other was lying.

Nina had never considered herself beautiful nor did she ever believe in the sincerity of a man who told her she was. She did think she was attractive. The attractiveness, she was positive, had little to do with her looks but hinged on her vitality, the way she talked, the way she told a story. The energy for this had to be summoned.

Perfumed and smiling she took a deep breath to open the door of her apartment, perfumed and smiling she strode into the lobby of the Yale Club, perfumed and smiling she sailed through a restaurant in the wake of a maitre d'. Ascending in elevators she flicked open a compact for a last check, convinced she would see smeared lipstick, and saw, in fact, never anything other than a very pretty, rather anxious, perfectly made-up face. She was still the Nina of Briarcliff days who, with pounding heart, stood at the top of the stairs

118

preparing herself to meet Doug Steiner. She was the same Nina who had whispered, 'I look awful, don't I?' Often, arrived inside the front door of an apartment, she bolted to the nearest bathroom to yank a brush through shining hair and to accustom herself to the murmuring voices and bursts of laughter emitted from the living room. 'Not so bad,' she consoled herself time after time in a stranger's medicine-cabinet mirror. Then she would make her way down the hall to the periphery of the crowd; she would scan it for a familiar face, for the best-looking male, notice what people were drinking, assess what the other women were wearing and when greeted was prepared to summon her most radiant smile.

It wasn't false; it was necessary. I want to be gobbled up on my own terms, when I'm ready, she thought. Nina had to watch, to gauge the tempo before navigating a sea of faces, before responding to an introduction. She was a high diver summoning a moment of concentration before springing off the board into a mid-air dance of twists and turns.

And so, when her hostess took both her hands and gushed, 'Nina, I'd like you to meet Sidney Fischer. He's an engineer,' she could turn bright eyes to the humpty-dumpty figure in bottle-bottom glasses and joyfully inquire, 'Oh, what do you engineer?' Sidney Fischer would go pink with pleasure and swear that the best thing he'd ever done in his life was to go to MIT.

'Adele! You sound as though you're next door!' Nina tore open the box of Oreos on the kitchen table and stared at them hungrily, not daring to take a bite. 'What do you mean, you're back! You just left!' Nina reached for a chocolate cookie. 'Right. It's number three oh seven East 90th. Top floor. Listen, the paint fumes are better, but be warned. If we feel dizzy we can just leave.' Laughs. 'Oh, I'm so excited. I want to hear everything! Bye!'

Nina pulled off the cut-off jeans and yanked a T-shirt dress over her head. It came exactly to her knees when she

119

tied the straw belt around her waist. She snapped a big yellow plastic heart on each ear.

'Can't believe my little eyeballs!' shrieked Nina as she watched Adele slowly make the third landing and then begin the fourth flight of stairs.

'What a place you've got!' panted Adele. 'Laughed my head off over your letter. You mean you didn't bring Rommel with you?'

They embraced in the doorway. Adele is too thin, thought Nina. She was wearing white trousers, a blue and white striped jersey, and seashell earrings.

'Tab?' called Nina as Adele walked through the apartment.

'Fine. Love it.'

'Go all the way to the living room.'

Adele settled herself on the bright yellow couch. 'I like this, Nina,' she said, feeling the soft leather. She surveyed the fireplace with its carved mantel and the large mirror above it. Nina had placed brass candlesticks there and dozens of yellow daisies in a big copper vase.

'Just the colour of a New York taxi. On sale at Bloomie's. Had to have it when I heard my rent was only $134.74.'

'How ludicrous! Five rooms! What's the seventy-four cents all about?'

They laughed. Nina handed her a glass and sat in one of the round wicker chairs.

'It's one of those shotgun apartments, someone told me. You know, bang-bang-bang, one room after another and no hallway.'

They used to call them railway flats. Same idea,' said Adele, looking up at the high ceiling. 'The kitchen and this living room are enormous! What are you going to do with the three rooms in between?'

'The white one will be for wardrobes and clothes. The German who owns it apologized for there being no real closets so he lent me those old-fashioned wooden wardrobes. Then, I can have *two* bedrooms!' Adele smiled. 'What about you? You've only been gone a month! What's happening? Hey, are you getting married to Paul? Is that it?'

Adele took a sip from the tall green glass and the ice

cubes moved and made a loud noise. A taxi honked on Second Avenue and Nina waited. 'Paul has been really putting the pressure on me.' Adele looked tired. 'I came back to have a talk with him face to face.'

Nina grimaced. 'You don't really want to marry him, do you?'

'Good ol' Nina. Can always depend on you to cut through all the bullshit.'

'Is that it?' Nina insisted.

Adele wiped fine beads of perspiration from her upper lip. 'Don't know any more.'

'Why doesn't he give you a little space? Why did you have to come back here? Why couldn't he have flown to you?'

'Because his work is very important. He couldn't just take off and fly to San Francisco for a few days. He's in a really competitive position right now.'

Nina didn't answer, but she noticed Adele's hand was trembling. 'Have you found an apartment yet?'

'I'm sharing with Kim, who got tired of sitting under a palm tree and now thinks San Francisco is the centre of the universe.'

'Fantastic.'

'I don't have a job yet but I really am not sure what I want to do. With a degree in art history . . .'

'Well, join the club!' Nina put the Tab on her old trunk which served as a coffee table and leaned back in the wicker chair.

'Nina, aren't you worried about money?'

The brunette shook her head, smiling. 'My first week in New York I got a cheque from Mother for ten thousand dollars.'

'Wow,' breathed her friend. 'Just out of the blue?'

'Out of a clear blue sky. Mother said in her letter that she wanted to make up a little bit for what Daddy had done with the will. Said she'd gotten plenty of money for the divorce and wanted me and Bart to have what she called "a cushion".' Adele was mystified. 'Oh, Daddy cut us out of his will. Actually he left us each a thousand dollars just so we couldn't contest it.' Nina shrugged. 'Very cagey.'

'I cannot believe it,' Adele said slowly and distinctly. 'What a monster.'

Nina continued, unfazed. 'But I'm going for job interviews next week. I don't want to live on that money from Mother and suddenly realize it's evaporated. That thought terrifies me.'

'What about men?'

'Whaaaat?' asked Nina innocently. 'What men?'

The phone rang as if on cue and Adele raised her eyebrows.

'Ricky, hi! No, I'm just talking to a friend. No! Come on! Don't be so silly!'

Nina smiled at Adele, who lifted her glass and mouthed the toast, 'To men.'

'Tomorrow, I can't. Sorry. Monday night? Ummmm . . . let me check my book. Stop making fun of me! I think *you* talk funny. Matter of fact, I can hardly understand you half the time . . .' Laughter.

Nina glanced at her Metropolitan Museum diary. 'Monday is perfect. Eight o'clock here? Do you want to come up and see my palatial digs or should I come down?' Silence. 'I might be too tired later.' Laughter. 'It depends on how well you treat me at dinner.' Silence. Making a face at Adele. 'No promises.' Laughter. 'Bye.'

Adele shook her head. 'Well, *you* haven't changed! Why can't I get away with that stuff! How do you do it?'

'What stuff?' Nina shrugged. 'It's called charm, Adele.'

Her old roommate groaned. Nina sat down again and crossed her long suntanned legs. 'How long are you going to be here?'

'Don't know.'

'Adele, are you all right? You look exhausted.'

'I am tired of thinking.'

'Look! Why don't I call Ricky back and get him to bring a friend on Monday night . . .' Adele was shaking her head but Nina continued. 'He is attractive and fun. He's with Salomon Brothers and he graduated from Yale about four years ago . . .'

'I can't. I am practically about to marry Paul!'

122

'Practically! About!'

'Well, it's almost definite. He's after me to get married now. He's gung-ho to get married this summer.'

'Why now?' Nina took a swallow and absentmindedly shook the ice cubes in the glass. 'Why can't he let you have a year on your own? You've just escaped the confines of Briarcliff . . . of being cooped up in a room with me for four years. Tell him you want some time.'

Adele was staring into space. Nina saw that she had tears in her eyes and was silent. They seemed to stay in her blue eyes for a moment, a very long moment, and then silently rolled down her pale face. Nina stood and handed her the paper napkin from under her glass. Then she left the room and went to the kitchen to stare out the window for a count of thirty elephants. When she returned Adele was her composed self, smiling bravely.

'Blow your nose,' Nina ordered gruffly, 'and don't smile if you don't want to.'

Adele laughed and burst into tears again.

'Let's take it from the top, as those Broadway directors are supposed to say . . .' Nina grabbed her long yellow legal pad from beside the phone and her fountain pen. She scrawled in big letters across the top of the page, P.A.U.L. 'Do you want to do this now?'

'Won't do any good. I've done it in my head a hundred times,' sniffed Adele, hating herself for crying like this.

'In your head alone isn't doing it with me on paper! So . . .' she finished, dividing the page with one long vertical line from top to bottom. 'Now you have to answer everything, since I've never met him.' It was sheer chance that she had not but now Nina didn't want to meet him and be forced into giving an opinion, for she felt the marriage was wrong if Adele was suffering this way. She refused to be a factor in any decision that Adele made, so by not meeting him, she could stay relatively out of it.

'Let's do the good things.' Princeton graduate, she wrote.

'Magna cum,' said Adele, wiping her nose with the little green cocktail napkin.

123

'Okay. Socially he's tops. Ivy Club, Princeton Club. What else?'

'The Racquet Club. Piping Rock . . .'

Nina wrote everything in capital letters in the left-hand column. 'Describe him.'

'Well, what do you mean?' asked Adele.

'Good-looking? Appealing? Cute? Best features? What is his best physical point?' Nina smiled. 'You lost your virginity to him, after all. There must be *something*,' she smirked.

Adele ignored the obvious innuendo. 'He's blond, he's six feet tall, he has a good face, a nice smile, blue eyes . . .'

'Body?'

'Good. He plays squash and tennis. He's in good shape.'

'Sex appeal?'

Adele blushed.

Nina thought she'd hit a nerve. Quickly she said, 'Okay. Good background. You wouldn't be afraid to have his parents as grandparents of your children, right?'

Adele frowned. 'You're crazy, Nina.'

'Well, it's something to think about. By marrying someone you automatically give your children a whole bunch of relatives. What if you were killed in a plane crash and his parents or his sister had to raise your children? Would you mind?'

'He's an only child.'

'Well, would you mind his parents?'

'No, come to think of it, I wouldn't. They're all right.'

'Okay, that's settled.' Nina was still printing. 'Good sense of humour?' Adele nodded, wondering when she'd last laughed with him. 'Kind to animals? Do dogs like him?' Adele smiled and nodded. Of course, Nina would be listing all her priorities. 'Generous?'

Adele thought. 'He doesn't tip that well, I've noticed that.'

'Generous with you?'

'What do you mean? Restaurants? We go to very expensive restaurants.'

'Does he ever give you presents?'

'This gold bracelet for Christmas.' Adele toyed with the gold links on her slender wrist and remembered the pale blue Tiffany box it had come in.

'Okay. You would say on the whole he is generous enough?'

'I guess.'

Nina put 'generous' in the middle and then a question mark. She stood and stretched. 'You want another Tab?'

'Let's split it.'

When Nina returned she grabbed the pad again.

'Last thing. Profession. Income. Future. What do you think?'

Adele poured the brown liquid into their glasses and watched the fizz rise to the top. 'That's fine. He'll be president of Chase Manhattan at the rate he's going. We'll have an apartment, then a house in Westchester or New Jersey when I get pregnant, and . . .'

'Oh, another thing. Do you think he'll make a good father?'

Adele nodded.

'A good husband?'

Adele sighed. 'Yes, I do. But I wonder . . .'

'You wonder if he would be a good husband for you?'

Adele thought: I am going to tell her. I am going to tell her about Jack. It's eating me alive.

'Okay,' said Nina. 'One thing you haven't hit upon. What don't you like? Right now he's an angel, he's everybody's dream, but what's wrong with him?'

Adele stiffened and started to say, 'He isn't Jack,' but as she opened her mouth to speak the phone rang.

'Sorry!' Nina leapt for it. 'Myra! Let me call you back in an hour. Oh, you're on the WATS line. Well, then call me back. No, I'm just with Adele and we're in the middle of something. Yes, she's fine. I'll tell her you said hello. Bye.'

Adele rose to leave, grabbing her Mexican basket-bag and swinging the leather strap over her shoulder.

'Adele! Wait! Do you love him? That's the most important thing!'

'Sure. I met him freshman year. We've been together ever since. Of course I love him.'

Nina stared at her. 'Let me walk you down. I want to pick up some things at the deli.'

They descended the stairs in silence and kissed goodbye as Adele stood beside the open door of a taxi. 'You seeing him tonight?' Adele nodded and tried to smile. 'Don't be pushed.' Nina put her hand on Adele's arm. 'Remember when you told me I could do anything I wanted? Well, so can you.' She leaned in the window. 'So can you, Adele.'

Nina watched the taxi hit all the green lights going down Second Avenue and disappear in the space of five seconds.

'Mrs Wickham? Hi, it's Nina.' She looked at her bare feet and thought she really liked that shade of pink polish. 'Oh, I'm settled. The apartment is painted and all I need is a job, of course, and maybe a decent bed. Then my life will be in order. Is Adele around?'

'She's sleeping. I was going to call you later today because I was sure that you would want to know.'

'Is she sick?'

'She came in yesterday from seeing you and fainted so I called Dr Peel and he came over and the next thing we knew she was having blood tests and now, just this morning, the test results confirm that she has mononucleosis.'

'Oh no!'

'Yes, I'm afraid she is going to spend the entire summer in bed.'

The Wickhams occupied one floor of a building on Park Avenue and 75th Street. Room after room was filled with paintings and a mixture of modern and antique furniture. The front hall was lacquered a dark Atlantic ocean blue with pristine white woodwork; these walls were covered with black and white Beardsleys in wide silver frames. A venetian mirror with its frame of twinkling glass was the first thing you saw when the private elevator doors opened, reminding Nina of a mass of stars on a dark blue sky every time she faced it. I actually used to feel sorry for people who lived in apartments, thought Nina, the first time she stared out the living room window. They were high enough to see the skyline of Central Park.

Nina visited Adele several times in the next two weeks but after about ten minutes Adele's eyes would start to close and Tory Wickham would materialize in the doorway of the large blue bedroom with her finger to her lips and motion that it was time for Nina to leave. Nina would take one last look at Adele, her blonde hair splayed over the white eyelet pillowcase, her thin figure under the pale blue sheet, and follow Tory down the long blue-lacquered hallway.

Once she stayed and had tea with her in the white living room. Did Mrs Wickham always look about to be photographed, she wondered. Today she wore a white caftan and gold sandals. Gold love-knot earrings adorned her ears and a narrow gold band held the thick mane of straight hair away from her absolutely expressionless oval face.

The former cover girl had been dubbed The American Classic and had even made the cover of *Life*. She hated the label, complaining that it sounded like an automobile, but it had stuck. She had given up the idea of Hollywood to be the wife of Charles Wickham, whose spectacular deal-making was the stuff of legend from Wall Street to Zurich. At forty-one she was simply an older version of Adele, thought Nina. They shared the same shining pale hair and the straight patrician features that had taken Grace Kelly from Philadelphia to Monaco.

'You mean to say you haven't met him yet? How extraordinary!'

'I didn't go down to Princeton very often. Most of my weekends were at Yale or Trinity or Penn now that I look back on it.'

'Paul is wonderful. Just wonderful. Charles and I have known his parents for years.'

Nina was surprised. Adele had never mentioned this.

Mrs Wickham returned the teacup to its saucer on the marble coffee table and shook her head. 'I thought we could all plan on a wedding in August but this . . . this' – she shrugged – 'postpones that.'

127

'Maybe Adele could go back to San Francisco for the winter and get a job and then, next summer . . .'

Mrs Wickham looked at her sharply. 'Why should she do this San Francisco thing? She doesn't have a job. She doesn't know what kind of job she wants.' She pushed a gold bracelet higher up on her tanned forearm. 'I don't understand it. It's not as if she's giving up anything to marry him, the way I did.' She stared at Nina. 'He is so perfect. They are so right together. Why risk tossing it all away for some little job earning $150 a week and some dumpy little one-bedroom apartment on Nob Hill?'

Nina realized it was useless to discuss it and wondered with sorrow if Adele had decided the same thing. Later in the elevator, after kissing Mrs Wickham goodbye, she repeated the words: 'This San Francisco thing . . . risk tossing it all away . . .' How awful! Adele's mother really thinks that Paul is the best she can do!


Nina was painting her long nails with clear polish. The receiver was on her shoulder, with her neck bent to hold it; she was wearing pink bikini underwear and nothing else at the big round kitchen table. It had become what she called her 'office' and was where she wrote her mother, paid bills, kept her diary and, of course, dropped her dry cleaning and groceries after the climb up the stairs. 'So how do you feel?'

'Exhausted. It is rather depressing to think that I haven't had one swim and I've been staring at the ocean for weeks!'

'Has Paul been coming up on the weekends?'

Silence.

'He's coming next weekend. He sends roses every week.'

'Great.'

'Remember how we put a question mark by the side of "generous"?'

'I've got the page in my wall safe. You want me to change it?'

Adele laughed. 'Oh, Nina, I am so tired. I'm sorry. I have to sleep again before dinner.'

'What do you do all day?'

'I sit on the porch like someone in a sanitarium. With a little blanket over my legs, being waited on hand and foot.'

Nina sighed. 'Don't complain too much or I'll arrive and strangle you! It's ninety degrees here!'

'Nina, I'll call tomorrow. I just' – yawn – 'can't talk any more.'

'Get better!' commanded Nina, and put down the phone.


God, if it weren't for Nina, thought Adele as she stretched in the wicker chair and closed *The French Lieutenant's Woman*. She pulled the lime green sweater around her shoulders and rolled down the cuffs of the pale green trousers. I can hardly wait for the next instalment of where Doug Taylor took her last night or John Haskell or whoever and what happened with Donald at dinner.

Nina and her men! Adele remembered that conversation freshman year with Susannah and wondered if she hadn't slightly missed the truth. The truth was that Nina did perform, her eyes did become brighter, greener, bluer, depending on the colour she was wearing, when she met someone new, when she told a story. Her stories were the same stories whether she related them to Adele or to her date but her mouth seemed to look fuller, her hair seemed to need to be flicked back over her shoulder suddenly and she would widen her eyes and tilt her head ever so slightly up at the male. Yes, she did perform.

Adele knew, too, that Nina had thought of her college beaux as sparring partners. Someone to dance with, kiss, maybe grapple with in the back seat of a car, or on a sofa in the fraternity house, and maybe, but not always by any means, to make love to. But it was sparring all the same. The male of the species was a challenge and usually a conquest. And the funny thing was, they never knew what hit them. Adele was not surprised that the Frank Wellingtons of the world were after Nina. The star quarterback, the class president, the stroke of the Harvard crew, no one had ever been immune, no one unattainable once Nina had entered a room.

Adele sighed. Nina was a natural. She stared down at the dock and at the blue, blue bay extending all the way across to the houses of Stonington. Tomorrow Jack will be here. And Paul. And someone named Sandra! If I told Nina, the old pro, how I felt, she would help . . . she would advise a relapse, at least. No, she wouldn't. She'd help me find a way to tell him. Adele shook her head. I've seen him once since the last time we made love and that was the time in New York, with Nina. She felt sadness like a weight press against her. Guess there's nothing to tell. Paul will be here so I won't ever be alone with Jack and the idea that he'd call and ask to bring someone says a lot, too. There's nothing to say, is there? She wrinkled her forehead and picked up the book, but didn't open it.

She thought of the first time for the one hundred thousandth time and then of the second time, which may have been more important than the first, for we were accomplices then. We both knew what was going to happen and we let it – no, we made it happen. Jack. Adele felt prickles of tears in her eyes. I cry, or almost cry, a lot, she thought. It must be mono. The feeling that I can't do anything. The feeling that Mother is taking care of everything from when I take a nap to what I eat. Oh, Jack, she wept, fumbling for the Kleenex in her trousers pocket. His face was before her as though it were yesterday.

The second time. He'd been behind her the next morning as she'd walked to the garage to get her bicycle. She'd had postcards to mail at the village post office and clutched them in one hand, along with a pair of sunglasses. His voice had made her jump. 'Can I come?' He'd smiled as she turned. 'Sure, if you want,' she'd answered with racing pulse as she dropped the postcards in her wire basket. They'd coasted halfway down the big hill, side by side, then he'd waited in the grass by the flagpole with his bike resting against the stone wall and watched her go into the little building. A flash of her long tanned legs, the shine of her blonde hair in the early morning sun, and he felt desire all over again. She came out, rolling up the sleeves of her turquoise jersey, and looked at him and at the way he was staring. As she gave her

130

kickstand an upward push he said, 'Let's ride to the point and see if the Heflin place has been sold yet.'

She agreed and they coasted down the hill to the village, past the docks on one side and past the shops on the other. There was the store that sold seashells, and the pharmacy, and the shop that sold Lilly Pulitzer and Pappagallo. They rode by the postcard stand and the second-hand-book place and Fiore's, which was where their grandmother ordered all her groceries. They came to the merry-go-round, which was supposed to be the oldest in the United States, with its hand-painted horses that bore real horsehair manes and tails. Jack and Adele had ridden those horses as children and had squealed with excitement when they'd leaned out far enough to catch the gold ring.

It was three minutes peddling uphill, then suddenly they were alone in front of the four-storey mansion that had gone on the market after the death of its eccentric owner the previous September.

'Come on,' called Jack, who dropped his bike in the tall marsh grass and began walking up the long driveway. Adele followed without question. Hadn't they been doing this kind of thing for as long as she could remember? 'No one's bought it, yet.' Jack looked up at the sign and the phone number of the real-estate agent in Westerly.

'Maybe a foundation or a school,' remarked Adele, walking on to the porch that faced away from the road and out at the ocean. She shaded her eyes from the sun and looked down at the surf as it poured in white froth over the sea wall at the base of the cliff. The noise was deafening, for the water was rough, and boiled and hissed below them. She could feel Jack beside her. They were very much alone up there with the wind and the house with its thirty-five empty rooms, every one of them facing nothing but Ireland.

The night before, Jack had lain in bed after painting his shoulders with iodine and thought: It was a mistake. Anyone can make a mistake. We don't do it again. Now it's happened and we know what it's like and we must forget it. 'No, I can't forget it,' he whispered aloud. The curtains

131

made a sudden flapping noise as a breeze from the bay disturbed them.

'Adele,' he said softly and she turned. He was two feet away, tall, tan, wearing a dark blue polo shirt and khaki shorts. His eyes looked troubled. 'Adele,' he said again when she didn't answer. 'I want you.' Then he had taken her in his arms and they had stood there for a long time.

'I can hear your heart beating,' she whispered into his shoulder.

'I think it's yours,' he teased, and knowing her so well he tightened his arms around her, predicting rightly that she would playfully try to move from his embrace. They lay down in the grass beside the porch and he laughed and said, 'Just our luck to have somebody get interested in the house today,' and she suddenly felt very afraid of what they were about to do.

Jack was lying on his side with one arm over her. She kept her eyes open, watching his mouth dip towards her again and again as he kissed her eyelids and her nose and at last her mouth.

'We can't do this! We can't do it,' she insisted, knowing that they would, knowing that she didn't have the strength to push him away.

He drew up on his arms above her as though doing a push-up and stared down at her. 'Tell me. Tell me,' he demanded. 'Tell me you don't want to.' Adele looked into his blue blue eyes. There was a great expanse of matching sky behind his face. 'Tell me!' he commanded. 'And I won't ever touch you again!'

When Adele did not answer him he lowered his long hard body against the length of hers. She obediently raised her arms as he pulled her jersey away and then she watched his blond head move above her breasts as he licked her nipples, which stood hard and defiant in the cool wind. She watched him rise to a kneeling position, yanking their few clothes aside; her espadrilles made two soft thud noises as they landed in the grass. Naked, he began to kiss her and when his mouth left hers she squirmed with outstretched arms to reach him, to touch him, this new discovery.

132

Jack took her hands in his and said, 'No. Not yet. Let me do things to you. Let me make you like it.'

I already do, thought Adele. She stroked his sun-streaked hair as he kissed her flat stomach and moved downward, then she tried to wrench away but his big hands held either thigh firmly.

Adele stared at the white clouds scudding across the sky and listened to the surf below the cliff as Jack tenderly, methodically, made her helpless, and carried her ever so gently past the point of comprehension. He did not stop until she begged him, then he became a part of her. Jack looked down at this face, this face with eyes closed and lips parted, this face he had known for ever. Adele called his name a dozen times in their fevered dream-like lovemaking. Sky and earth were blotted out, ceased to exist, as did the sound of the sea. They only knew of pounding hearts and Adele's cries of 'Jack!'


'These came for you about ten minutes ago, darling.'

Adele turned quickly, guiltily, at the sound of the footsteps on the porch, as though she had been caught doing something very wrong. 'Oh, Mother, thanks.' She took the red roses and pulled at the little white square envelope. She knew what it said. It always said the same thing: 'Love, Paul.' She smiled more for the benefit of her mother than for any other reason, as Tory sat on the opposite wicker chair.

'I can hardly believe the summer's half over.'

'I can,' answered Adele rather petulantly. 'It's been the longest summer of my life.'

'Well, in two weeks you can have another blood test. I must say you look wonderful, dear. Faintly suntanned, good colour. No one would dream you'd been so ill.'

Adele sensed her mother had something on her mind to say about Paul, about weddings. She didn't want to hear. Not now. Particularly, not now.

'Mother, I'm going to have a sleep before dinner. I can hardly keep my eyes open.'

'Fine. Good idea. Walk slowly.' Her mother took the roses and the book and put them on the wicker table. Then she folded the white cashmere lap robe. 'Remind me at dinner. There's something I want to talk to you about. Why don't we plan on a wedding at Christmas?'


Adele towel-dried her hair in front of the mirror framed with seashells. Her bedroom at Watch Hill was very much like the others: big, high-ceilinged, with a comfortable double bed, two fat armchairs and a bureau beside the door to the adjoining bath. Tory had redone the house after her mother had died and Adele's room was painted a lemon yellow with white woodwork and fresh yellow and white flowered curtains and slipcovers. Adele stared at herself in bewilderment. If I didn't know myself I'd say I actually appeared happy! She saw the red roses Missy had put in a big white vase beside her bed. They reflected over her shoulder along with the red roses which had come yesterday. 'I don't even like red roses!' She slammed the silver-backed hairbrush down. When am I going to tell Paul that red roses make me think of funerals! Damn! She slammed the hairbrush down again in a rare burst of temper.

'Del?' Her mother stood in the doorway. 'They'll be arriving soon. Paul is picking up Jack and Sandra in New York so they'll all be here before dinner.' She noted her daughter's expression.

'What is it? Don't you feel well?'

'I'm fine, Mother. Really I am.' Adele was thinking: If anyone asks how I feel one more time I think I'll scream.

'This thing with Sandra sound serious.' The older woman smiled knowingly. 'So maybe you and Paul should plan to give them time alone.'

Adele thought: I'm going to be sick I'm going to be sick I'm going to be sick all over this glass-topped dressing table all over this blue rug. She nodded and began to rub her hair again with a vengeance. The large white towel covered her face and only when she had heard her mother softly close the door did she drop the towel, pick up the brush and slam it down yet again.


'Bart! How nice to hear your voice!'

Virginia Avery McLean stood by the kitchen phone, smiling. 'Where are you?'

'I'm in San Francisco, of course! I just wanted to call and see how you are.'

'I'm making a sandwich. It's terribly hot here.' Virginia rattled on rather disjointedly.

'Are you going to do anything special for the weekend, Mother? Any Yacht Club things?' he asked, with a voice full of hope that his mother would not be alone.

'I'm going out tomorrow night with the Evans,' she lied.

'That's great. I'm off in about two hours to drive up north to Novato. Linda's parents have a big place up there. It should be fun.'

'That's nice, Bart.' Virginia dipped her index finger in the tall iced-tea glass carefully so as not to allow the ice cubes to make a noise, then she silently licked the bourbon from her finger. 'Drive carefully, dear.'

Bart stood in his office with the view of the city spread beneath him and stared at the receiver. Strange. She seemed to have simply hung up, forgetting to say goodbye. He shrugged and began to toss papers into the pigskin briefcase. The Hollison deal. The shopping complex. All of this could wait until Tuesday. Suddenly, he decided to leave the briefcase behind. His desk was clear. He glanced around the white room with plants lining one wall; the modern paintings hanging above them in pale blues and greens looked very well there. That fussy decorator had been right after all. The other wall opposite his chrome and glass desk showed the California sky, clear and blue for once, way past the little island of Alcatraz.

'Have a good time,' Bart called to Susie as she looked up through thick spectacles and smiled at his retreating figure. The light tan summer suit, the light blue shirt, the blue and cream tie, the long-legged stride, the black hair, the grey eyes, the face of someone who could have been in a movie. Susie Williamson never failed to sigh when he passed her desk.

Overdressed, thought Adele rather smugly at dinner. She tried not to stare at the streaky-blonde-haired, blue-eyed Sandra across from her. Dark roots. Probably had to put off an appointment till the first week of September. Rather large hands.

'So what is the difference between Newport and Watch Hill?' she was chirping.

Paul laughed, Tory Wickham smiled at Jack's mother, Ann, and Jack started to answer. 'Let's put it this way, Sandra . . . ummmm . . . how should I put it?' He turned to the others as his date waited expectantly.

God! thought Adele. How gauche she is! Nina would never utter something like that and Nina used to drop bombs like a pyromaniac in her innocent way. Adele decided to bail her out. I'm not a total bitch, she reminded herself. 'I guess Watch Hill is a lot more casual than Newport.'

'That's true,' agreed Ann Forrest, thinking: If the girl has any smarts at all she'll drop the line of questioning. Ann was a straightforward woman, quiet, dark-haired with fine features and a rather shy smile.

'What do you mean by that?' Sandra asked brightly. 'The clothes, the lifestyle?'

Oh, Lord deliver us, thought Ann. Anyone who ever said something like 'lifestyle' was finished in her book. The delicate brunette deftly lifted the backbone from her sea bass and put it on the plate beside her water goblet. She is rather good-looking, she admitted. I can understand my son's physical attraction to her, but she is graceless.

Tory began to respond, hoping that her discomfort was not evident. 'Newport is more oriented towards black-tie dinners and dances. Dinners for forty are typical, dinners for a hundred are usual . . . but here . . .'

Paul interrupted. 'Watch Hill is perhaps more family-oriented. Summer people have been coming here for

136

generations and . . .' He stopped, realizing families had been going to Newport for generations, too.

Christ, thought Adele. No one was going to tell her that most people with a house at Watch Hill thought the way everyone carried on at Newport was not even worth thinking about! People in Watch Hill wore sneakers and rode bikes in old pullovers and didn't wear Lilly Pulitzer underwear and didn't fight over having a visiting European prince to dinner under a marquee on their ten acres of backyard with black-tied men and women in long dresses dancing to an orchestra. Why, Watch Hill was for clambakes on the point by the lighthouse, for a yacht club where it was all right to walk through sopping wet. Newport, thought the Forrests and the Wickhams, was simply *overdone*.

Nobody here, thought Paul, who'd only visited Watch Hill eight or nine times, ever seemed to want to be *there*.

Overdressed, thought Tory. The silk dress for dinner was definitely not right. She and Ann and Adele were all wearing flowered cotton dresses, were bare-legged, with only a slash of lipstick, whereas this girl was stockinged and high-heeled and made up as though she were about to have dinner in a New York restaurant.

Jack smiled. 'I think we've done a lousy job of explaining Watch Hill to you! Newport has Bailey's Beach Club and big formal parties and the America's Cup, and we've got the Misquamicut Club for occasional parties and the Yacht Club and our big front porches for grand gatherings of six good friends for drinks to watch the sun set.'

The subject had been changed and Missy had come in to take their plates away. Adele thought that Jack was staring at her as she spooned cream over the strawberries but she couldn't be sure. Marry her! Her mother was totally wrong. Sandra Billis, young lawyer from St Louis, presently of Washington, DC. Ridiculous. Adele felt much better than she had before meeting her and actually smiled when Paul winked at her for no reason at all as they left the table.

'Please leave your name, number and any short message after the tone. Thank you.' Nina's Southern accent recorded

137

well. Someone had said it was the friendliest machine they'd ever spoken to. 'User friendly' someone had laughed, and then she'd had several calls after that dinner party from people who had teased her about the drawl. Nina stood in the middle of the zebra-skin-printed linoleum and listened.

'Beeep.' 'Nina, this is Tad. Call me if you want to go out to the Hamptons this weekend. I think I'll drive out for Saturday lunch, we can stay with the Lyles again and then come back after Sunday lunch. I have work to do on Sunday afternoon so . . .'

Nina nodded. Of course. He would have work to do on a Sunday afternoon. She clutched the towel around her and marched back to the bathroom where she turned off the hot water and stepped into the frothy clouds of bubbles.

'You're kidding! Tell me you're kidding!' insisted Adele.

'Nope. I'm almost packed, with the ticket in my hand. Wow, how I wish you were well and could sprint away with – '

'Nina! Why can't you do something normal? Like coming up here for a long weekend or for a week. I'd love to see you. You don't have to – '

'I'll see you when I get back. And I do have to. I feel exploding with adrenaline and suddenly thought it's always one thing or the other: people have the time for a trip and not the money or else they have a job which means money but they don't have the time. I have both. When I come back I will get a job in two seconds flat.'

Adele agreed. 'If you want to, you probably will.'

'I'm just taking my vacation first, that's all.'

Adele wanted to offer advice. She'd been to Europe three times with her mother, once with a group from Farmington and once to London to stay with her grandmother for a week of theatre and the ballet. 'Nina,' she began, trying to think of something important to convey.

'Yes?' Nina wrote 'shampoo' on a piece of paper and put a question mark beside 'white sweater'.

'Ummmm . . .' There was just so much to say! 'Don't

138

drink the water, not even when you brush your teeth . . . and don't . . .'

'Oh, Adele! I'll be fine! You know me!' She lapsed into the strongest possible Southern accent: 'I always depended on the kindness of strangers!

'I'll mail you a thousand postcards,' she promised. 'Don't worry!'

Adele hung up the phone and shook her head. If if if Nina were ever drugged in a Parisian movie theatre and if if if the white slavers managed to get her on a plane to some remote Arab kingdom, Nina would give them all such a hard time they'd be happy to fly her back to civilization or, more likely, she'd bat her big grey eyes at the king and he'd marry her in a ceremony covered by all the major world newspapers. Adele picked up *The French Lieutenant's Woman* and tried to concentrate.

Nina clattered down the stairs and out the door to find Schneiderman and give him a post-dated rent cheque. He was a portly figure leaning over a frothy beer in the darkness of the bar on 89th Street. She watched him tuck the envelope into a grimy shirt pocket and with dirty fingernails fumble at the button flap. Then to the drugstore for razor blades and Tampax though certainly European women used them, didn't they? Can never tell, she decided, putting an economy-size box in the wire basket along with Crest and hand lotion and tiny plastic packets of shampoo.

The suitcase was open on the zebra floor, overflowing with several piraeas, enormous cotton scarves Nina used a bikini cover-ups and as shawls in the evening, espadrilles, high-heeled sandals, a white mini, white slacks, black silk trousers, and jerseys in five bright crayon colours. A Panama hat was on a chair and a tangled mass of jewellery was plopped unceremoniously into a clear sandwich bag. 'There!' she crowed triumphantly to the TV broadcaster who reigned over the big round kitchen table littered with the packing's rejects. 'New Yorkers suffered as a hear wave pushed Manhattan's temperatures into the nineties . . .' Nina flicked off the little set. Who cares? she asked herself. Today New York, tomorrow Paris!

*

Dear Bart, Arrived aboard this flying tunafish can with bizarre types. Sat with woman going to Nepal to start a crafts clinic teaching macramé. Does Nepal need this? A man with hair below his shoulders sang folk songs off-key for about one thousand miles. Someone who looked like a prizefighter wearing a beret finally took his guitar away over Ireland. Paris is bright and sparkling. Don't know what to see first! much love, Nina

Dear Adele! Why didn't you tell me it would be like this! I've wasted my entire life on the wrong side of the ocean! Now I am sitting on the banks of the Seine with a real Parisian who is adorable and speaks about twelve words of English. He is a terrific dancer and we've been together since yesterday afternoon. No! Dancing! Are now drinking wine and sharing a baguette from this little bakery we found open at six a.m. I am in love, love, love. No, not with Michel . . . with Paris! love, Nina

Dear Mother, Paris is a dream! It's like every movie I've ever seen about it! There are so many things I should see but all I really want to do is sit at sidewalk cafés and stare at people! Will go back to the Louvre tomorrow and Versailles the day after. much love, Nina

Dear Bart, Why don't you play hooky and come over here? Find me in care of Paris American Express until the 10th then same address Madrid, then Lisbon, then Rome. Eurailpass is stroke of genius. I just take a taxi to the station and stand under the schedule board and get on whatever train is leaving. I have one tiny suitcase weighing more than I do. Am getting stronger but arms are getting longer. Think of you so often. love, Nina

Mother — Wonderful little village yesterday an hour from Paris and darling hotel with flowers everywhere and such a nice family. The daughter spoke English and I wrote down phrases to be memorized at a later date. Much later since in a few days I will be in Spain. I miss you! love, Nina. And love to Ellen, too!

Dear Adele, I am not berserk about Madrid. Bolted out of bullfight. The sidewalks are so hot that my shoe heels sink into them. Like walking around in chewing gum. The Prado is overwhelming. Will go back again to really look at certain El Grecos. How's your white blood count? Paul? love, Nina

Dear Mother, The Algarve is the most beautiful place I've ever seen! A Portuguese count feeds me fried squid for lunch and we sunbathe all afternoon, then listen to this mournful fado music all night. The water is a pale blue-green and so clear you think you can see the bottom of the world. I am as brown as I can be! love, Nina. love to Ellen, too.

Dear Adele, Oh, my god, a Portuguese count has asked me to marry him and he is divine and wouldn't I be a great countess? His parents are divorced for ever and his father is away for the summer and his mother lives in St Tropez and has blonde hair and green eyes and sounds formidable. I won't get to meet them. Even though he is a count he is fighting in Angola and has to go back on Wednesday. It's all wildly romantic and what should I do? love, Nina

Dear Mother, Venice is like fairyland. Castles on islands across blue expanses of lagoons. Everyone goes on about the smell but I must be too excited to notice anything that isn't glorious. Maybe I will buy a canoe and get 'Nina' stencilled in gold across the bow and just stay. love, Nina

Dear Adele, Rome is spectacular. Every corner, every little street has something lovely to look at. The people seem happy about life, I adore the language, and the shoes are to die for. I've bought six pairs and consider myself rigidly disciplined. Home soon. My flight is in three days so I will rush back to Paris on a night train with plenty of bread and cheese. Will call you when I land at Kennedy! Nina

*

141

Adele sprawled gracefully, for all that she did had grace, on the chaise longue and gazed out at the royal blue bay, wondering idly if one could get bedsores from wicker over the span of an endless summer. 'Nina!' she laughed into the receiver. 'You have been going on about Italy for fifteen minutes! So it was your absolute favourite place?'

'Adele,' began Nina earnestly from her kitchen. She wore white bikini underwear, gold hoop earrings and a very deep tan. 'I felt different there. Not quite me. There was something in the air that made me think I would be happy to stay. Sure I know I'd miss New York and you, etcetera, etcetera, but I thought Rome had a different kind of excitement.' Nina could never keep her own secrets. But this didn't qualify as a secret. It was in the category of 'I'll just think of this once in awhile and know that it exists and be happy about it'. Nina felt like a child at summer camp who hides a chocolate bar above her bunk on a wide rafter. But she was in the habit of telling everything to someone, gauging reactions, asking advice. It started with Mother and with Ellen after school each day and then of course there had been Adele. Nina's confidantes were female and, from the beginning, her confidences were usually about males. 'Adele, I have to tell you something, but promise me you won't breathe a word of it. I mean – '

'Of course I won't!' Adele sat up almost imperceptibly straighter and looked at her tank watch. God. Don't let Mother pop out on the porch now and insist I hang up. It's been thirty-five minutes.

'When I was in Rome . . .' Adele was thinking: Of course, she fell in love with an Italian. I mean it's de rigeur. 'I talked every morning with this nice man at the hotel. He owns the hotel and always sat across the street at the little coffee bar with his cronies. All of them in their suits reading their newspapers until the sun hit their table at about eight-thirty. He'd tell me to go to the Villa Borghese to see the horses parade through early in the morning or to get myself to the Sistine Chapel and take the shortest tour possible. This and that. The best place for ice cream is such and such . . .'
Adele thought: Well, at least he owns a hotel and isn't a

waiter at the coffee bar across the street. That's to be thankful for. 'He knew how much I loved Rome and asked me why I was going back to New York. We talked. He speaks English very well. I asked how difficult it was to find an apartment and he told me it wasn't very for a foreigner. The rent laws are hilarious, Adele! That afternoon we met with his uncle on a tiny street between Piazza di Spagna and Piazza del Popolo . . .'

'Wow! That's the ritziest area!' breathed Adele from Watch Hill.

'I know. Anyway, I now have an apartment in Rome!'

Adele gasped. 'Nina! But do you want an apartment in Rome?'

'Yes! Why shouldn't I live there for six months? Maybe even a year. The idea of . . .'

'Are you two girls still twittering away?' Tory stood in her pink-flowered Bermuda Shop one-piece bathing suit and shook her head. A bell of white-blonde hair moved slightly. Every perfectly pedicured toenail on a slender tanned foot had been lacquered white mother-of-pearl. Not one grain of sand clung to her. It wouldn't dare.

'Neens, we've got to hang up. Mother's just back from a swim and . . .' Tory readjusted the striped beach towel around her shoulders, gave a shake to the pink bathing cap and opened the screen door. 'Tell her I said to come up any weekend at all. We'd love to *see* her.'

Adele didn't relay the message. She had felt, though never had it spelled out, that her mother would have been happier had Nina been from some old Savannah family or maybe from Charleston. Mississippi was a place that no one ever mentioned in *Town & Country*. And no one who ever got married in the New York *Times* ever came from a place like that. She waited to hear her mother's bare feet on the polished wooden floors and then the creak of the stairs as she mounted them. 'You can't just move to Rome! I think you're nuts! It's an exciting thing to fantasize about, but you should get yourself a job you like and then next summer go back and spend your entire vacation in Rome. That's enough to – '

143

'Adele!' the sharp voice came from the bedroom window above the porch.

'I have to hang up! Talk to you tomorrow!'

Nina put the phone down and with legs still on the kitchen table, barefooted, barelegged, ankles crossed, she reached for the newly developed photographs in their bright yellow envelope. She smiled. Roma.


Tad took Nina by the hand and led her through the milling guests. They tipped arms balancing champagne tulips and people laughed and said, 'Hi, Tad!' and he was kissed and she was introduced to one black-tied man after another and appreciated, she would think, as their eyes met hers. The fuchsia silk was okay after all, for the women all wore the same sort of short dress with various types of shoes from white sandals to silver sling-back pumps. Nina's were dyed to match her dress which had been re-cut with no back at all after her being a bridesmaid for Susie last summer. Aunt Lilly's amethyst earrings sparkled at each ear and above them clustered two clips of pink silk flowers holding back her waves of black hair which cascaded loosely below her shoulders.

'Nina!' screamed Mimi of Briarcliff days, of running up and down the halls in underwear, of all those rides to Boston. 'You look terrific! Are you in the city now?'

'You look terrific too!' Nina laughed as they hugged, awkwardly clutching drinks and paper napkins and purses. Mimi's hair had grown out quite brown and suited her far more than the blonde pixie cap. It was chin-length and shining.

'Tell me everything, Nina!'

'I just got back from Europe yesterday and – '

'Did you have a good time?'

'The best!'

'Do you have a job lined up?'

'Well, no . . .' This was the worst thing about not having a job, suffered Nina. You get embarrassed at parties.

'Oh, I'm sorry for being so rude! Mimi, this is Tad

144

Overton. Tad, this is Mimi Arden. We practically lived together for four years – '

'Lived together and died together!' burst in her friend. 'Some of the things we went through! Remember the time I fell asleep under the hair dryer and ended up with third-degree burns on my neck?'

Before Nina could respond Mimi was clasped by one braceleted wrist and dragged away by a tall man who merely nodded to them. Mimi, wide-eyed and spilling champagne, was speechlessly swallowed up by the crowd.

'My God!' sighed Tad, wiping his brow with a handker-chief.

'She's nice,' smiled Nina. 'Just a little . . .' A waiter took her empty glass and handed her a full one. 'Let's go outside. Bound to be cooler.' When they reached the flagstone patio and could look down the slope towards the ocean, Nina sighed. 'Ninety-nine acres on the sea! Nothing like having a little weekend cottage!'

Tad laughed. 'I love the way you're not impressed, but you are.'

Round tables and chairs were filling quickly as guests carrying their dinner plates sought out friends to sit with. White candles in white paper bags lined the walkway from the swimming pool to the dance floor which had been set up to the left of the thirty-foot buffet table. Where the peripheral lights shone on this island of colour and music, the grass stretching down the hill was as green and smooth as a billiard table. Nina looked back at the four-storey Tudor house. Every window was ablaze with light; laughter and voices floated out in the soft air. Nina turned her attention to Tad who was telling her that it was someone's birthday. He had a good strong profile, she was thinking, and if she didn't really listen, not with total concentration, she wouldn't feel so . . . what was it she felt with him exactly?

'Taaaaad! Dahling!' This whoop like an Indian's came out of the semi-darkness. 'Where have you been keeping yourself?' Not waiting for an answer a large woman simply threw herself into his arms.

'Ummm uh, Countess . . . how nice to see you!' he recovered.

'Nice to see me? Your mother did teach you manners but really my dear, you could show a bit more . . . who is this creature?' She faced Nina, who was trying not to giggle at Tad's confusion. He was blushing; she could practically feel the heat from him in the dark.

'I'm Nina McLean.'

The woman with the very white powdered face below nearly orange hair wrinkled her brow in concentration. 'Oh! How very Scandinavian to introduce oneself . . . hmmmmmm.'

'Nina is – '

'Tad, darling, would you mind terribly getting me some champagne?' the Countess chirped at him. He turned away and she said in a low voice, 'Known him since he was a litle boy with skinned knees and a runny nose.'

Nina did her best not to laugh. Tad had explained to her in the car on the way out of the city how important it was that he had been made a vice-president of Morgan Guaranty before September first. 'In terms of my career,' he had said solemnly as he carefully put on the indicator to change lanes.

'Now, darling, from *whence* do you come?'

'From Mississippi,' responded Nina, feeling like a little girl. Heavens! Did this woman in the lavender and blue-flowered caftan with that amazing hair treat everyone as though they were scruffy children who had wandered into her living room?

'Mississippi! My dear, how frightfully exotic!'

Nina thought the English accent at odds with her superlatives, with her exclamations. The only English accents she'd heard had been voiced in subdued tones, in a calm manner. Tad reappeared at the Countess's elbow but she ignored him except to take the glass he extended. 'But what an orchid you are! And what do you dooooooo?'

'I . . . I . . . Lots of things . . .' she stammered, and then laughed. 'But no one is paying me for doing any of them!'

'Oh?' cried the Countess, considering this. Then she exclaimed, 'I must run away! I have people waiting . . . however . . . hmmmm.' The Countess seemed to be making a decision. 'Tad, would you be an angel and hold this?' She thrust the champagne glass at him and then the ostrich-feather fan and began to rummage through a gold metallic evening bag. Tad held the fan upside down with distaste as though it were a dead chicken then he looked to the right and to the left as though consoling himself that no one was looking. 'Oh, never mind,' fussed the Countess. 'Nina! Let me look at you! she commanded, snapping the bag closed. The older woman peered at Nina's face in the darkness and Nina peered right back thinking that the face was neither attractive nor unattractive. She had to be in her sixties.

Her blue eyes were bright and rather far apart; her nose had been broken long ago before they'd known how to set things properly, which had put a stop to her aspirations to the stage. Her mouth was painted in a full scarlet bow, the only spot of colour in the ivory-complexioned face which had 'never seen the sun', she was wont to declare. Big-boned, a handsome woman, were the phrases that came to mind. Her hips seemed to undulate under the yards of flowered fabric but perhaps, Nina would think later, it was simply that the heels of her shoes kept sinking into the soft grass.

'If you ever decide to change your position in life, telephone me. I cannot find my card and shall have to contact Tiffany's on Monday and order new ones. Tad can find me.' She turned to him and gave him a little peck on the cheek. 'I know I treat you badly, darling, but I just . . .' she sighed dramatically.

'It's the martoonis on the train. I'm a witch with men after martoonis.'

And with that declaration, full of apology and self-knowledge, she seemed to drift away, vanishing between the knots of people chatting under the trees in the candlelit darkness of the September night.


Adele could feel her eyes closing. She could hear the murmur of voices around her on the porch but the cool darkness, the tiny sip of brandy she'd been allowed, the long day, had lulled her into a state of pleasant exhaustion. She

147

heard the scraping noises of the porch chairs and felt Paul's hand on her arm.

'Come on, Adele, let me walk you upstairs.'

The others said goodnight and she nodded drowsily. Paul gave her his 'this is just a goodnight kiss' kiss that she knew so well. He always gave her another kind of kiss when he wanted to make it a preliminary to lovemaking. After the bedroom door closed, she stripped off her dress and, naked, pulled back the sheet and slipped into bed. Adele was so tired she didn't notice that she had left the bedside lamp on.

The others talked for a long time, past midnight. Jack kissed Sandra on the landing, wondering if it had been a good idea to invite her for this second weekend. Then he went downstairs again to stand on the porch and remember. He remembered what it was like to have Adele, the little kid Adele, sitting next to him in one of her Sunday dresses after dinner. Fighting and bickering over who was winning at Spit or who had won at gin. Jack thought of the Adele who had stood with him on these steps hundreds of, no, maybe thousands of evenings, looking up at a star-spattered sky and across the black expanse of water lit by its own little stars of boats with their running lights. He thought of the Adele who knew as many constellations as he did.

Realizing he could see his shadow on the lawn, he turned to Adele's bedroom window above the porch. A light was on. She was still up. He locked the front door behind him, a reminder that things had changed over the years, and tiptoed up the stairs and down the hall to her room. He held his breath as he turned the knob. They'd laughed over Adele's squeaky door as children. Jack tightened his muscles in anticipation but the door opened silently.

Adele lay on her back like a splendid statue. The sheet had been pushed away and was crumpled around her waist, her small, perfect white breasts shone like alabaster in the lamplight. Blonde hair was splayed like gold on the pillow; her eyes were closed and she was breathing deeply. Deeply asleep, thought Jack standing over her. He turned out the light after a moment of staring and then bent down in the darkness to tenderly kiss her lips.

*

148

Adele sat on a canvas chair in the shade beside the tennis court. 'Nooooo!' shouted Sandra as she missed a shot.

'Yeeees!' called Jack as he slammed it back.

Paul was standing them both and doing a great deal of running. 'You take over with Sandra.' Jack bounded away, tossing his racket on the grass. Adele watched him lope towards her. White tennis shorts, white Lacoste shirt, brown legs. She felt her pulse quicken.

'Don't ask me how I feel today,' she remarked.

'That bad, huh?'

She nodded. The brandy had sent her reeling after months of no alcohol and she had spent a long night with strange dreams. Jack sat on the grass at her feet so that he could watch the game, such as it was; Sandra was so uncoordinated. He leaned towards her and said, 'You're not still mad about that night at "21", are you? I haven't seen you since then. Not one Christmas. Not one Thanksgiving. Nothing.' He held a leaf in one hand and stroked the tiny veins with one finger.

'No, of course not,' she said crisply.

'I just wanted to see you, that's all. Thought that . . . I don't know what I thought . . .' His voice trailed off as he watched Paul's lean figure thwonk a really beautiful serve. Of course, it was not returned by a groaning Sandra, who was wearing espadrilles instead of sneakers and a mint green tennis outfit.

'You going to marry him? Aunt Tory says it'll be soon. She wants a Christmas wedding.'

Adele saw no reason to answer. 'Mother says you're about to marry Sandra, too.'

Jack laughed. 'So are you going to or not?' he insisted. 'I don't see a ring.' He hoped he sounded light, with banter in his voice.

Adele frowned. How can he ask me that! He's so detached. It's a big joke to him. I still dream about him and he just acts as though there were nothing ever between us. How I hate his insolence! 'Don't worry, you'll get an invitation.'

Jack felt as though he'd been slapped across the face. She

has no feelings for me at all. My Adele. Funny, I always think of her as mine but . . .

Paul was grinning and running towards them with a white towel around his neck. 'How's my favourite invalid?' He bent down and kissed Adele's upturned face. Jack stood and slowly walked towards Sandra, who suddenly seemed clumsy and loud and the wrong colour blonde.

At dinner that night Adele thought, maybe this weekend had to happen. Maybe I had to have the truth thrown at me and now I can get on with my life. Stop daydreaming about something that happened a long time ago, that never should have happened, that was wrong, probably illegal. Thank God we never told anyone.

'Adele! Are you with us?' called her mother, breaking in on her thoughts.

'Oh, yes, Mother, what is it?'

Everyone laughed. Missy stood at Adele's elbow like a round short statue in her white uniform. Her white hair was caught in a knot on her neck and her pink cheeks glowed from the heat of the kitchen.

'Missy is taking dessert orders. Lemon sherbet or strawberries?'

Missy removed the untouched food from Adele's place and wondered what was going on in this house. 'Sherbet, please, Missy.' Adele was in a state over something since yesterday when they'd all arrived. Not eating anything and sleeping through breakfast! And Jack! Missy'd come across Jack before dinner behind the garage with an axe chopping firewood. His face was red and his tennis clothes were soaked in sweat. He was furious at something that had happened. She'd known those cousins since they were first coming here as kids when their grandmother was alive and something was going on. She knew Jack had always been the one to slam doors and storm out to the garage for the punching bag but it'd been taken down years ago and he evidently had grabbed the axe instead of his gloves.

Paul and Jack were laughing over something and Adele tried to pay attention. 'Ahh, bankers! All alike!' joked Jack.

'And lawyers! What do they know? They can exacerbate a

problem until the poor client can't remember why he first asked advice . . . !' Laughter.

'Remind me when I'm fat off people's problems not to put my money in Chase Manhattan . . .'

Adele smiled. Forget it, she said to herself. Forget it. He will always be my cousin and the things we did were just games to him. He's probably had a hundred girls since me, and that's fine. Doesn't matter. Her eyes flickered to his face, sunburned, grinning, laughing, making a joke, blond hair almost white from the sun. Then she looked at Paul. Blond, blue-eyed, kind, solid, soon to be her husband. Don't throw him away. After dinner she took his hand and led him down to the dock and when they were right on the spot where Jack had grabbed her ankle that July afternoon so many daydreams, so many summers ago, she pulled Paul to her and kissed him hard and long and deeply with her tongue, hoping she wasn't still contagious. He was pleased and surprised and responded ardently. Exorcism, thought Adele. I will exorcize my cousin from my body and my soul and my heart. Starting with my body . . .


'Oh, Chas,' cooed Tory, extending her cheek for a kiss. 'I just couldn't hold dinner a minute longer.' Those aquamarine eyes flashed from the tanned face, her perfect smile was outlined in pale peach lipstick.

'How are you, Tory?' he asked, almost absentmindedly. 'Looking well, as usual. Oh, Jess, put that stuff in the back hall. Thank you.'

Charles Leslie Wickham was a very good-looking man at sixty-two. His hair was silver but he had a full head of it. He still played a good game of tennis when the opportunity presented itself and he was deeply satisfied when his Savile Row tailor reminded him he had the same measurements as thirty years ago. Charles took off the Cartier watch, reset it six hours back and then fastened the dark brown alligator strap.

Late as always, tired as always, Tory thought. Why does my husband bother coming up at all? He'd be much happier spending the weekend in an office somewhere, New York, London, anywhere, going over some dry as sawdust financial report. Charles had begun to seem vague to Tory. Vaguely polite, vaguely good-humoured.

'Daddy, hi!' Adele came down the stairs wearing a short flowered pastel dress. Too thin, he thought. Her gold bracelets clinked as she embraced her father. 'How's the world traveller?'

'Jack, good to see you!' Charles extended his hand to his handsome nephew, the only member of the family for whom he felt genuine affection. Jack and his mother, thought Charles. They're all right. 'Ann! How are you, my dear?' He patted her arm and she leaned forward to brush his cheek.

'Daddy, this is . . . you remember Paul?'

'Nice to see you again, sir.'

Not a very firm handshake, thought Charles as he nodded and said, 'Been a long time, hasn't it?' Rice's boy, but not as aggressive.

'And this is Sandra.' A short young woman with a tousled mane of streaked blonde hair stepped forward. 'It's a pleasure,' she simpered.

Ann winced. Where did my son find this one? she wanted to say aloud.

Tory began to take charge. 'Everyone, why don't we have a drink on the porch? Chas, are you hungry? Missy's kept something warm for you.'

'No, thanks. I had dinner, such as it was, on the plane. I'd love a drink, though.'

'Coming right up!' grinned Jack at his elbow. 'The usual, Uncle Charlie?'

The older man felt keen pleasure. Jack was the only person in the world who'd ever got away with calling him Charlie. The two of them entered the large living room. Its four front windows overlooked the wide porch and beyond that the shimmering royal blue expanse of Narragansett Bay. The other quartet of windows viewed a rock garden perfectly tended, a scene of green and white, for Tory had specifically instructed the gardener to plant only white flowers this year. The pale blue walls were hung with sailing prints banded in silver frames above low white bookshelves which were filled to capacity with the latest novels and old copies of *The New Yorker*. Beside the large grey stone fireplace was a chaise littered with plump down pillows covered in light blue sailcloth. At its head stood a brass lamp and at its foot was folded a pale blue afghan. Above the mantel hung a painting by Winslow Homer. Charles had bought it from the estate of an old friend and he treasured it. This room is at its most inviting, thought Charles, in the evening hours or on a foggy afternoon. There was a chill in the air and with a small prickle of disappointment he saw that Tory had neglected to have a fire laid.

'Bring me up to date on everything that's happened around here,' he requested as he took the straight scotch from his nephew and settled himself at one end of the dark blue and white chintz sofa. 'You having one? Fix yourself a drink and sit down, unless you're needed on the front porch.'

'I'm not needed anywhere!' said Jack rather cynically as he dropped the ice cubes into a tall glass. He added a lot of vodka and very little tonic. It was good to see his uncle again. He tossed in a slice of lime after giving it a quick squeeze.

'So what's this I hear about Adele getting married?' asked Charles when Jack had seated himself in an armchair across from him.

'You'll have to ask her about it, sir. She hasn't said all that much.'

'So I haven't missed a lot of toasts at the dinner table?'

'No, you haven't.' Jack lowered his voice. 'You'd think Aunt Tory was the one about to marry Paul.'

Charles laughed. 'Now I know what's going on! It's all crystal clear. And how's Washington? Old Judge Potter still walking around creating havoc with those decisions he insists upon handing down?'

'He's a helluva guy to work with! The best hour of this entire summer was drinking with him at the Hotel Madison bar. He had me convulsed with his stories.'

'He's a character all right. I remember crossing swords with him in the early fifties . . .'

Ann rocked on the porch, listening to Tory and Sandra talk about New York as opposed to Washington. Paul had an opinion once in a while and Tory kept insisting that Boston was the most civilized of all American cities. Ann could see the two men in the living room through the window when she rocked the chair backwards. And the sight of them together in deep conversation made her happy. Charles Wickham was a hard man to know, an absent man from all their lives, but whenever Jack had needed advice he had been there. Long distance to London, long distance to Paris, it didn't matter. 'Mom, should I go to law school and worry about getting drafted every minute or should I just enlist and get it over with and them come back and start at Harvard?' All the questions a son wanted to ask a father had been answered by Charles. She heard loud masculine laughter coming from the living room and smiled. Sometimes she thought she should have married again. Barry's death from cancer had been when she was so happily married, though. It had been several years before she could imagine even looking at anyone else and Jack and Melanie had certainly been enough to keep her occupied. The Forrest money had made her life very easy and summers here with her mother-in-law, sister-in-law, and Adele, her children's only first cousin, were lovely interludes. The Wickhams were Ann's only family. She heard Charles laugh again at something Jack was telling him. Tory seemed on edge. Probably is unused to hearing him laugh, thought her sister-in-law. I don't think the two of them do much laughing together.

'I'm going up to bed, my boy.' Charles patted Jack's elbow. 'Tomorrow I intend to swim several miles and then trounce you on the tennis court.'

'Hah!' whooped Jack. 'And if you lose, you can blame it on jet lag, right?'

'Don't believe in it. It was cooked up by Madison Avenue to excuse people who drink too much on planes . . .'

'Goodnight, Uncle Charlie,' called Jack to the retreating figure already halfway up the stairs.

This house always smells the same. Like the sea mixed with that lemon polish I wish Tory would change for

154

something that doesn't smell like anything, thought Charles as he made his way down the hall. He opened the last door on the left and walked in. His bags had been unpacked and his dressing gown lay on the bed. Charles had worn no pyjamas for years, for all the years he had slept alone. He stepped under a warm shower for a few minutes and then dried himself quickly and brushed his teeth and slipped into bed. The soft green walls are nice. Restful. Not a hotel tonight, he thought gratefully, and turned off the bedside lamp.

Charles couldn't sleep. Jack. Good boy. Ann has done a good job with him. Sometimes I wish Adele were different. Oh, doesn't bear thinking about . . . He tossed and turned, listening to the sound of the breakers outside the window.

Tory looks the same. Always the same. That beautiful face. He remembered seeing it everywhere he went that one winter, on magazine covers perched on newsstands from New York to Chicago to the Los Angeles airport. He'd read the *Life* story on her and learned about her rather genteel upbringing and it had appealed to him. She was capable and orderly and her cool good manners when they finally did meet were the closest approximation an American had ever come to the gentility of a well-brought-up Englishwoman.

Charles had grown up in London's East End. There he had felt the heavy hand of England's class system and at the tender age of sixteen, with no public school background and no Oxford or Cambridge before him, had decided to try New York. He had arrived like thousands of other immigrants and been processed in the cattle market of Ellis Island. His first job had been obtained literally upon landing – sweeping the docks. His next job was as a messenger boy for a shipping company, then he became a clerk for Atlantic Overseas, and then someone's assistant. He went to night school after working ten hours a day, and then it had been only a matter of three years before he was noticed by someone who could make a difference. My mentor, smiled Charles in the dark. Harry Flanagan, who teased the Cockney right out of me and taught me how to dress and advised me to bathe more often and gave me my own desk.

155

Harry had decided that Charles Wickham could make it. Charles knew this and would have given his life rather than disappoint Harry. At the unreasonably young age of twenty-eight, Charles Wickham was veritably running, without a title of course, Atlantic Overseas. It was only a few years later that he had money enough to invest, and the know-how gleaned from listening to know where to invest it. He passed from his thirties to his forties with no love affairs and no family save an elderly mother to whom he sent cheques in London. It's all timing, isn't it, thought Charles. Everything is. From the affairs of a corporation to the love affairs of men. I was ripe for Tory Forrest and she for me. She is a beautiful woman, considered Charles, but you get used to beauty. Rather quickly. Charles sighed and turned over restlessly. It was four o'clock in the morning in Zurich. At last he closed his eyes and sleep came.

Adele lay on her bed in the yellow bedroom at Watch Hill, barefooted, thankful that it was the Tuesday after Labor Day, thankful that the house was empty again. Her mother and Ann had gone to a cocktail party at the Beach Club and she had privacy at last. 'How was Southampton?' she said into the white phone.

Nina kicked off her green sandals and put her feet up on the facing kitchen chair. 'I met such an interesting person.'

'Oh! Ooooh!' Adele cooed. 'What's he like?'

'This is a woman, Adele! I've never met anybody like her before. She was sort of flowing in folds of flowered chiffon that reminded me of Monet's *Water Lilies* and she kept materializing like some spirit, a sprite among the trees. She's a countess.'

'The Countess of Avondale?'

'Yes, that's who she is. Do you know her?'

'She did our front hall and was supposed to do the entire apartment but something happened – '

'What do you mean? She's a decorator?'

'Exactly. She's got terrific style but something happened. I think she ran away to hunt wild boar in Java, or was it

156

elephants in Kenya? Anyway, Mother was livid because she never finished the apartment. The blue lacquer hall was her idea and framing all the Beardsleys in silver . . .'

'She told me to call her and maybe . . .'

'She's always inviting people for drinks. She knows everybody.' Adele was thinking: Please go, Nina, and get involved with someone – or something – that will keep you in New York. A man, a job, anything. Adele couldn't seem to convince Nina that it was a bad mistake to sweep off to Rome to live when she hadn't tackled her first job, hadn't even survived a first year in a city where she spoke the language. Nina seemed to have a block about the job hunting. Adele knew she spent hours taking walks and going to museums and movies as if postponing the inevitable commitment.

'Now tell me about Paul. You haven't said a word about him or your weekend.'

'Fine. Red roses. Two bunches last week. It pleases Mother.'

'Damn! Forget your mother! Does it please you?'

Adele frowned. 'Nina, I know that he is the person I will marry. He is right for me.'

'Your mother tells you that!'

'No! That's not really fair, Nina!' Adele bent her knees and drew them under her on the yellow quilted bedspread. 'He is everything a husband is supposed to be.' She stopped. 'And that's not his fault!'

'Are you going to marry him soon?'

'I still want time. Time for myself. I want time to see if I can earn my living. Does that make sense?'

'Yes.'

Adele was thinking. 'I want to go back to San Francisco, live with Kim, and get a job. You've been on your own a lot longer than I have. Not just this summer, but the four years at Briarcliff.'

'Why don't you try to get a job with an art gallery out there?'

'That's just what I intend to do. The minute my white blood cells get themselves in order! Oh! I hear the doorbell

157

and the maid is off today. It must be the groceries from Fiore's. Call you tomorrow.'

'Bye, sickie! Get better! I miss you!' Nina put down the phone and smiled suddenly. She stared at the vase of daisies before her on the kitchen table and imagined the Countess in a yellow caftan and matching pith helmet being borne regally through the jungle on a litter. 'Well, I *like* her!' she said emphatically.

# 4

Nina sprawled on the yellow couch, doing thigh exercises casually as Adele sipped iced tea in a wicker chair across the room. 'So who do you want to invite for your homecoming? The "Adele Has Been Sprung Party"? The "Nina Is About to Go Job-Hunting Celebration"?'

Adele laughed. She felt so much stronger now. 'How many can you have here, Nina? Say, thirty?'

'Oh, no! Lots more than that!' Nina swung into a sitting position. 'Let's really simplify this. Let's just invite every single person we know!'

'The sun of Portugal has baked your brain,' Adele stated flatly. 'You've finally lost your mind.'

'Really, why not?' Nina was excited by the idea. 'At least a third won't be able to come, but they'll be pleased that we invited them and then they'll owe us an invitation, and then there are those men who've asked me to dinner and I should technically once in a while have tickets for a concert and invite them, but I never have and probably never will. I can pay everyone back in one fell swoop and so can you. I think it's a terrific idea.' She padded barefooted to the desk and returned with her big yellow pad and a fountain pen. 'Okay, you start.'

The page was full of names inside of twenty minutes.

Nina lavished flowers on the apartment and put a smoked ham, eighteen-pound turkey and sandwich makings from the deli on the kitchen table; a bar was set up in front of a living room window. By nine o'clock the railway flat was filled with people holding glasses and leaning against walls and in doorways, talking, talking, talking.

It was not an unmitigated success for Susannah's escort was drunk on arrival and fell down an entire flight of stairs. His crumpled form seemed lifeless as Paul bent over him but suddenly he smiled crookedly and introduced himself.

'Hi, I'm smashed.' Around midnight a candle on the coffee table set Lisa's long hair on fire as she dipped forward to kiss her date. Someone from Goldman Sachs splashed out the flames with a full glass of white wine and was astonished that instead of being thanked he was met with outrage. Lisa stalked away to pull herself together in Nina's bathroom. They'd opened all the windows for a while and someone had grabbed Nina's Diorissimo off her bureau to spray away the awful smell.

At six the next morning in the kitchen cluttered with ashtrays and dirty glasses, Nina and a bleary-eyed trio were discussing Vietnam and the Johnson administration policies towards the war.

Adele telephoned at noon and said, 'I don't want to go to San Francisco now. I had such a good time. I don't want to leave. And wasn't Linda incredible with that feather boa that kept shedding in everybody's drink? And Paul was off with that veterinarian for hours . . . I never thought Paul would have anything to say to a veterinarian!'

'And did you see Louise with Rick! Remember him? He asked me out to dinner and I was on the phone with him when you were here in June about to find out you had mono? Louise was crawling all over him! And he wasn't exactly pushing her away. Now you've seen *the* Louise!'

'Was the dress sprayed on or did she manage to sew herself into it using mirrors?'

'Don't ask me. What a body!' exclaimed Nina. 'And Paul is not exactly ugly! You look wonderful together and are going to produce all these blue-eyed tow-headed children.'

'What did you think of him, Nina?'

'I like him. I really did. But I only said hello and goodbye. I watched him during a lull around midnight, and he seems outgoing enough and people like to talk to him . . .'

'Hmmmm. That's true.' Adele was silent. 'Do you want me to take a cab over and help you clean up? It'll go so much faster with the two of us.'

'Absolutely not! How can you imagine doing something like that! Should I remind you you're moving across the

160

country tomorrow morning! I am sure you have a few things to take care of.'

'I want to get out of here for a while. I really do. I'll be there in fifteen minutes.'

So the two of them in jeans and sneakers and T-shirts had gone at the damage together. Adele was ambivalent about returning to San Francisco, especially since she was getting along with Paul so well. Nina told her to take deep breaths and to know it was the right thing.

'Mother has been harping for the past three days on my talking to my father. She wants him to call three gallery owners in San Francisco to set up interviews for me! I don't want this, Nina!'

'Of course you don't! You're going there to do things on your own.'

'Mother just won't let up on me!'

'Look,' said Nina, waving a soapy dishcloth from her position at the sink. 'Where is your father now?'

'He's in New York. Probably at his Pine Street office downtown.'

'On a Saturday?'

Adele nodded.

'Why don't you call him?'

'But, Nina! I don't want him to help me!'

'I know you don't That's just the point. Make sure he knows you don't!'

Adele thought this would surprise her mother. 'Funny. But Daddy and I never talk. Absolutely never. Mother runs everything and I assume just fills him in when he arrives from the airport.'

'So there is the good chance that your mother will intercede and your father will do this without your even knowing it, thinking that you want it done, right?'

'I hadn't thought of it that way.' She reached for the phone and dialled.


Nina reached for the phone, picked up the receiver and didn't dial several times on Monday and four times on

Tuesday. On Wednesday afternoon she didn't touch it, only stared at it, and on Thursday she dialled and hung up on the first ring. Nina traced her index finger down the tissue-paper-thin page of the Manhattan directory. For the seventeenth time. 'Avondale, the Countess of, 799 Park Ave.' read the entry. 'Wow!' breathed Nina between bites of an Oreo. A Butterfield 8 number. She swallowed. 'It's just too much.' I want a job, she thought. I cannot bear the idea of an employment agency and being sent to a grimy little grey office with a typewriter in the centre of the desk like a shrine. I don't even know how many words a minute I type. 'And with a little luck,' she said aloud, 'no one else will ever know either.' I do want this job. If, in fact, there is a job. An offer to change my position in life? That could be a job. Nina wondered if mere proximity to someone like the Countess could change her, Nina, into someone more dramatic, half as romantic a figure as the older women who had seemed to float in diaphanous robes through that otherwise predictable weekend with Tad.


'Darling! Of course I remember you! So you did call after all!'

'I . . .' Nina made her voice strong and clear. 'I want to change my position in life,' she declared.

'Well, of course you do!' came a musical laugh in response. 'We *all* do! And if we have any sense, all the time! Just get into a taxicab and tell the nice man to deliver you to 799 Park. I'm waiting.'

'But now?' Nina thought: My God, I have to pull myself together.

'What better time?' came the cry.

'Well, I'll be – '

'I have the moooost charming man who's just flown in from the Lebanon who's simply dying to meet you! Hurry!' And with that the receiver was put down.


The apartment itself had fairly embraced her as she stood uncertainly in the doorway. 'I do confess it's a bit over the

162

top for the afternoon,' gestured the Countess with one arm out bidding her to enter. The walls were covered in light pink watered silk and the tall narrow paired windows were curtained in geranium coral velvet to the floor trimmed with silver-coloured gimp and held back to expose Park Avenue traffic by heavy silver cords. The furniture, Nina would decide, was delicate and French, and anything that normally would have been gessoed gold was silver. Every piece of fabric, upholstery, every pillow or cushion in the room was of coral or geranium or the palest pink possible like the walls. 'It glows,' Nina murmured as she stood on the Aubusson carpet.

The Countess was laughing. One hand held a glass of red wine and the other, very theatrically, a white lace-trimmed handkerchief. She wore a caftan of white which fell to the floor and actually trailed behind her a few inches like the train of a wedding gown. Her hair glowed brightest copper; her blue eyes were mischievous as she directed Nina to a pink sofa.

Nina would think later that she felt him rather than saw him that first time. Suddenly he was before her taking her hand and bringing it almost to his lips. The pencil-thin moustache tickled her knuckle as she stared at the shining black hair, the olive skin, the eyes black as jet. 'I've heard very much about you,' he said in accented English.

'Oh no, you haven't!' teased Nina. 'No one in this room knows very much about me! I could be a double agent for Bulgaria . . . Why, I might even be a triple!'

He straightened up, amused, as the Countess trilled, 'I told you she had a great deal of spirit!'

'May I get you a glass of wine?' he asked. 'Red or white?'

'I think red would be very nice.' Nina put the hand he'd held in her lap and wondered why such a simple gesture would make her feel so light-headed.

'This is all rather new,' the Countess was saying. 'Diana Vreeland has her deep ruby red living room she calls a garden in Hell and I suppose I have my garden in Purgatory!'

'Paradise, Contessa! Paradise!' was the smooth response.

'Well, Paradise or Purgatory it's vibrant, isn't it? Now, Nina, you have wine, don't you? Good. Tell me all about yourself.'

Nina took a sip of the Burgundy. 'I was born in Mississippi in a thunderstorm and I suppose for about eighteen years after that all I could think of was getting away from there as fast as I could . . .'

The Countess tittered. She noted Nina's cream-coloured tweed suit and the gold love-knot earrings and the simple gold bracelet. She sits well and hardly anyone sits well on that down-cushioned sofa. She moves well, stands well. The faint Southern accent is an asset. An air of vulnerability. Well-bred. Her mother must have been someone with manners, with a sense of the genteel. Certainly not the offspring of a sharecropper.

'And now' – Nina raised one black eyebrow – 'now, I am here sipping wine with you, wondering how you will change my position in life!' She smiled one of her most radiant smiles and the Lebanese smiled back. I love that suit, thought Nina, forcing herself to look at the collection of tiny brightly-coloured enamel boxes on the coffee table. And his shirt is so white it must be almost blue. Dazzling against the bronze skin. Strong face. God. An Arab chieftain would have a face like that. Never been in a pink living room drinking wine with an Arab chieftain in the middle of a Friday afternoon before. With a Countess besides.

'I am so glad you remember that phrase,' the Countess was saying, 'because it is something I cling to. Whether colouring one's hair or discarding one's husband, one can always change one's position in life.' She paused and like a bird, tilted her head to one side. Her question startled Nina. 'You're not thinking of marrying Tad Overton are you?' Nina's big grey eyes widened as the Countess continued from her little French Regency armchair. The folds of the white caftan had fallen to the side exposing gold flats and slim ankles. Her face, decided Nina, had nothing pretty about it, poor woman, but the eyes were very kind and alert and the teeth were like little pearls. Old-fashioned teeth, she thought, the kind that women in old photographs had. Not

164

Cheryl Tiegs teeth or Julie Christie or Lauren Hutton teeth. 'And don't marry anyone like him either!' the older woman was reiterating as the Lebanese laughed. 'I can look at you and know you play the part and they see this, too. These men!' She made a dismissive gesture with one slender hand. Her wrists and ankles match, noted Nina. Her fingers were long and lovely and delicate; manicured, with nails the colour of the wine in her glass. 'Why, someone like Tad will swallow you whole before you know it!'

Nina laughed then. 'He hardly looks dangerous to me! That's why I am probably not fascinated enough to consider marrying him!' She paused. 'To be quite honest and fair to Tad – he hasn't asked me either!' The Lebanese stood to pour her more of the wine as Nina extended her glass. This was the best thing for me, she decided, as she felt herself sink another inch deeper in the pink velvet cushions. If I were home I'd be pacing from one room to another feeling sorry for myself.

'Oh!' chirped the Countess. 'He will! Nina, you see, you look exactly the sort of wife anyone like Tad would want and there may or may not be different things inside you but a man will be so entranced by the . . . by the . . . oh,' she tut-tutted herself, 'I'll be very Madison Avenue and say "packaging"! They'll be so taken with the packaging that Nina will be lost, or not lost, simply never discovered.' Nina stared at her. An older woman had never talked to her this way, had never shown this much interest. 'And that, I think, would be rather a shame.' She turned to the dark man beside her in the pink brocade wing chair. 'Mar-Mar, darling! You are so silent!'

His voice was deep, smooth. 'I'm just looking,' he replied.

Nina felt the beginning of a blush suffuse her neck and throat. 'The last time anyone looked at me like that,' twittered the Countess, 'was in the late forties, just after India had her independence and all was upside down. I was several hours' flying time – Christ, the planes those days were unbelievable! – north of Calcutta visiting the Janpur family. The daughter's wedding was to be in twelve days and the elephants were being prepared and the kitchens were simply rife with servants and the gardens were filled with gardeners and there were dozens of little turbaned men with peacock feather dusters whose sole purpose in life was to climb ladders and dust pendants of chandeliers . . .'

Nina was lost in the monologue but Mar-Mar interrupted. 'Contessa! Tell us about this "look"!'

'Oh, yes!' She put down her wine glass and with palms together leaned forward. 'It was the bride's half-brother by another marriage. He was only twenty-one and I was . . .' She waved one palm outward and shrugged, 'I was older. A little bit older, let us say.' She sighed and her eyes were cast upward at the cream-coloured ceiling with its bands of carved moulding as though she were reading from it. 'Oh, this maharajah was divine! Absolutely nut-coloured! With big dark eyes to drown in! He'd shot his first tiger at eleven and walked into a room like a young god!' She sighed and put one graceful hand to her breast. Her audience waited. 'So that look, that look across the banquet table twelve days before the wedding . . . well, that was the beginning of . . .' She became coy. 'Well, something that was very, shall we say, sweet? That lasted for nearly two years . . .' Mar-Mar was amused and she chided him. 'I know exactly how long it lasted because the young bride had borne twins and was in confinement again and we were all rejoicing . . .'

'Did you live in India for all that time?' asked Nina.

'Oh, I came and I went. India can be oppressive so one must get away. My husband was British and we would have leave to go to England every so often and that was a respite.'

'Oh.' Nina suddenly felt as unsophisticated as a wild daisy in the rose-coloured parlour. Mar-Mar winked at her as though reading her mind and she smiled faintly. 'Was he the Count?' she asked shyly and was met again with laughter from the Countess.

'No, the Count came later. Let's see. There were two husbands in between this one in India and the Count of Avondale.' She gestured towards a round glass-topped table with a cloth of strawberry-coloured linen hanging to the carpet as if to include lovers in between her various matrimonial forays. At least two dozen sepia photographs of

166

handsome young men gazed from their silver frames. They looked melancholy, sensitive, and even a bit lovesick but above all, sleek as greyhounds. Well-bred noses, decided Nina. And skin as smooth as a dance floor.

'It's late,' she said as the Countess reached for a lamp. It was dark outside the windows and two glasses of wine on an empty stomach were not the best idea. 'I must go now.' She stood, putting her empty wine goblet on the table with the little boxes. 'Thank you for the wine. I've had a lovely time.' Please, prayed Nina, offer me a job.

With a little whoop the Countess exclaimed, 'It is past seven! I had no idea! I have people waiting for me!' A swish of the caftan later she was holding the door and Nina was thinking – using desperate brainwaves, she'd tell Adele – Please offer to change my position in life, please. 'Mar-Mar, be a darling and take Nina to dinner?' she pleaded to Nina's horror.

But Mar-Mar seemed pleased and said, 'I'd be delighted if she has no plans. "21" will be crowded but they'll find us a table.'

'And while you're having dinner, please persuade her that I am not a promiscuous madwoman just because I live in an eighteenth-century bordello.' Nina smiled a brave smile as she wrapped the printed silk scarf around her neck. No job, just talk, she thought sadly. 'You will come on Monday at nine, won't you, darling?' The older woman reached for her hand. It was as soft as the petals of a flower. 'I work very very hard when I work, but by Friday at four I've often wound down and need red wine and company . . .'

'Do you mean – are you offering me a job?' Nina wanted it spelled out and even later that same evening she would panic that the Countess would forget and be surprised to see her three days hence.

'Of course! Be my assistant! The last one, silly girl, ran away to marry a Peruvian diplomat. Didn't she ever read Helen Lawrenson's *Latins Are Lousy Lovers*? A dreadful mistake. She shall rue the day.' She tittered, 'Every night.'

Mar-Mar kissed the Countess and guided Nina into the hall in a series of practised motions. The Countess closed her apartment door just as the elevator arrived. 'A quick getaway or we'd be standing there for hours,' he smiled as they descended.

'You don't have to take me to dinner, you know,' Nina said with dignity.

Mar-Mar gave her a long look of interest. 'I know I don't. I rarely bother doing what doesn't appeal to me. Life is too short.'

Mar-Mar was right. There was a table for them – by the door of the front room, connoting his status. Nina remembered Adele and her cousin Jack and that nice Harvard Law School roommate. Funny that I never heard from Jack again. Those blonde good looks and now I am here with someone just as dark as he was fair and just as handsome. Flip side of the coin. Foreign.

'Pimm's Cup, Mr Sarkis?' the maitre d' leaned over them.

'Love it,' nodded Nina, wondering what on earth would be placed before her. 'Is Mar-Mar your real name?' she asked as he spread a red and white checked napkin over his lap beside her on the banquette.

'No. It's diminutive for Omar. I've known the Contessa so long that she feels it's affectionate and' – he shrugged – 'I permit it.'

Suddenly Nina realized he was stuffy. Just as stuffy as Tad in his own way. Just as full of self-importance. Just as tight. But – she stared at his white French cuffs peeking from beneath the exquisitely tailored grey flannel suit and thought: There is something very animal-like and lithe about him. He seems muscular, coiled, controlled, whereas Tad is a known quantity, all in the open. Nina wondered suddenly what Omar would be like if he lost his temper, lost control, drank too much. Took off his clothes.

'And you?'

Nina realized he was asking what she wanted. 'Order for me, please. I'd love to feel taken care of, suddenly.'

He looked up at the waiter. 'Two orders of Senegalese soup, two sirloin steaks on the rare side, and green salads.'

'Tell me all about the Countess.' Nina waited for him to begin but he stared at her mutely as though thinking of

168

something else. She began again, determined to remain unflustered by his intensity. Arrogance in spades. 'Does she often do things like hire assistants without asking if they graduated from the first grade?'

He nodded. 'The spirit within her is all. She is like a wild thing at times.' It was then that Nina wondered if he had been to bed with her. 'She judges with her heart, with her first glance. Snap decisions. A look at the colour of the wine and she imagines she can tell if the bottle is good or not. She is like this in all the endeavours of her life.'

'How did you meet her?' I wonder if they are lovers went through her mind again.

'In Paris, years ago. I was a student and she knew my father. He told me to call her. I was at the Sorbonne for a while and knew no one. I had only a book of telephone numbers. I think . . .' He hesitated. 'She was like a mother to me or rather, like an aunt. Kind and loving and protective, and her house – do you know Paris?' Nina shook her head. 'Well, in the very best part, very elegant and always filled with people. La Contessa!' he laughed. White teeth as white as the shirt gleamed as he thought back to those days. 'She was between husbands and several men were in love with her. When I rang the bell late in the afternoon I would often see a shadow at an upstairs window – usually her bedroom window – and I would wager with myself if the maid would be dispatched to answer the door and let me enter or not.' He smiled at Nina. 'Often not.'

The soup arrived and they turned their attention to it. Nina reached for her glass of wine. 'What do you do exactly? Why are you in New York? Are you a Muslim?'

He laughed at her. 'Is any of that important to you? Really important?'

Nina laughed then. It wasn't. The wine suddenly hit her and she thought, he is terribly handsome, he is paying for my dinner and he won't rape me and cut my throat or cut my throat and then rape me because I met him on Park Avenue. 'But tell me about your life,' she insisted.

'I play when I'm not working and when I work I like it so much that I think I'm playing.'

169

'So what is *it*? This work, this play? You are talking around me in riddles.' Nina smiled slowly. I feel so good. After all, I have a new job!

'I'm a banker and a broker and I deal in real estate, in investments.' He raised his eyebrows. 'I get on and off planes, catch the Concorde when I can, and talk on the phone to Europe when I'm here and to New York when I am there.' He shrugged as he wiped his mouth on the napkin. 'Boring.'

'Oh, it can't be. You said life was too short to do things you didn't want to do. So don't tell me now that you'd let time go by being bored.'

He reached out and with one finger touched her nose teasingly. 'You're like a little fox. Do you know that?' Seeing her reaction he responded, 'And that's the second time I've made you blush.'

Nina felt the electricity between them. Unmistakable volts of it. Zillions of watts, she'd confide to Adele. He was older, cooler, more in control than any of her college beaux. She sensed his unpredictability and it excited her. Nina pushed her hair off her shoulders and retorted, 'You're probably too jaded ever to blush. Too cynical about the ways of the world, the wiles of men.' Is this me, she wondered giddily, or is it all this wine after nothing but popcorn for breakfast?

'I don't blush because I usually have the upper hand in dealing with someone across the table . . .'

'Well, I'm not one of your silly bankers with a contract before me. I'm Nina and this is a steak!' He laughed as she mocked him. 'Don't compare me to one of your business protagonists. I'm not in their league.' She hesitated and then grinned. 'I mean, they are not in my league.'

That seemed to delight him. 'A terror, aren't you? Tell me, do men run away from you in fear?'

Nina lowered her eyes as she put down her wine glass. 'Some do.'

'And some don't.' Omar put his warm smooth hand on hers and she looked at it and thought what a lovely colour it was against her own. The current flashed between them again but instead of giving in to yet another blush she said

170

firmly, 'Omar, I must eat if I'm to keep up my strength.' She arched her wrist and reached for her fork as he laughed at her.

Later in the taxi he put his arm around her shoulders and pulled her to him. Oh no, thought Nina. Just when I think I know how to handle him at dinner, it's suddenly after dinner and he has all the advantages. The street signs, yellow with black numerals, flipped by, fifty-seven, fifty-eight, fifty-nine, as the driver took advantage of a run on green lights and sped up Park Avenue. When we hit a red light he'll kiss me, she decided, and then all will be lost. I feel very, very weak. Nina could sense the strength in his arm and in his large hand holding hers in her lap. She turned her back to his chest as he pulled her closer and was aware of his strong flat stomach. Playfully elbowing him she asked, 'Squash or tennis or skiing?'

'All of the above and polo when I can.'

Sixty-two, sixty-three. There was silence except for the traffic noises outside the speeding capsule. A pothole bounced them closer and she realized he had put his face in her hair and still she watched the numbers flip by. Seventy, seventy-one. 'I'd invite you up for a drink,' she began and he finished, 'But you're frightened to.' Nina turned to face him. 'I'm the terror, remember?' It was then that he pulled her to him and held her there tightly. Her hands went up to his chest as though to keep their faces apart. Omar looked faintly amused at the futility of the gesture as he pressed his mouth hard against hers. Nina's fingers on the starched shirt front were spread wide and her right palm could feel the hammering of his heart as the taxi at last slowed for the red light on Eighty-seventh Street.

'Oh my God!' cried the Countess when she opened the door on Monday morning. 'Am I too late?'

Nina was confused. 'It's only five of nine and you are already here. How could you be – '

'Let me get a good look at you.' The Countess peered into Nina's eyes.

171

'Too late? What's happened?'

'Mar-Mar!' whispered the Countess with coral-painted lips.

'Omar! What's happened to him?'

'No! Not to him! Never to him! It's what's happened to *you*, darling!'

Nina began to laugh. 'Countess, I didn't! I didn't! I swear that we didn't!'

'You didn't?' The Countess clapped her hands in joy. 'Thank God! It's far too soon! Now come in and let's get to work!'

'The office,' she explained as Nina followed her down a taupe lacquered hallway covered with prints framed in a dark gold, 'was a second bedroom but it works quite well.' The Countess began clearing off a tiny loveseat covered in pale blue velvet. Samples of fabric were everywhere imaginable as if someone had been holding them to the light and in the midst of making a decision had suddenly been called away. Wallpaper books were heaped in piles on the floor with little rectangles cut out of this or that open page. The oriental rug was dark blue and rust where Nina could see it and the room itself was a surprising deep blue. A French Regency desk bore a blue telephone and a metre of chintz in blue and green with the cardboard tag proclaiming it to be from Schumacher. An appointment book bound in brown calf was open to October and several pens cluttered a silver tankard with a coat of arms engraved on the side.

'Now, you' – the Countess turned to Nina – 'may work on this side table if that's all right.' She sighed as though resenting an intrusion and continued, 'I'll have to let Dorothy come in and dust. She arrives at ten and putters a bit. Putters, makes lunch.' The Countess waved one hand with a jangle of gold bracelets. 'There's a telephone under that mess somewhere. No, the left-hand side. That's right. We've two extensions, thank the Lord. Sabrina did do some very good things and here's the list of suppliers we use and all the phone numbers and the clerks who are the favourites.' The Countess leaned over Nina who was seated at her new desk. 'Jennie at Clarence House is good and so

172

on . . .' She pushed at her mane of red hair which looked a little wild this morning. 'Why don't you just listen to me as you pick up a bit, darling, and at lunch I'll fill you in on who everyone is.'

The Countess was on the telephone non-stop for three hours, placing orders for a penthouse on the East River, discussing fees with an upholsterer, and comparing estimates to clean a painting with several restorers recommended by several art gallery dealers on Madison Avenue. As an unseen clock across the hall ping-ping-pinged the hour of noon she put down the phone. 'I think I have cauliflower ear,' she said, giving her left one a couple of taps with her palm as though to get the circulation going. 'My heavens!' She turned to face her assistant. 'I scarcely know the place! It's a miracle!'

'I thought if I stacked all the wallpaper books on that bureau in alphabetical order we'd be able to get at them better and I've started new files for the billing. If we have files for each house instead of for each – '

'Don't tell me!' cried the Countess with hands over both ears this time. 'This is wonderful! As long as you understand the system I shan't have to!' She stood up. The orange caftan nearly matched her amazing hair.

Nina waited. She had no idea if the puttering Dorothy had set the table for lunch in the dining room or if they would eat off trays and continue working or if she should go home for a sandwich on her own. What would a Countess have for lunch? A baked potato dolloped with caviar and sour cream and a glass of champagne?

'Lunch!' trilled the Countess. 'Do you have strong feelings about peanut butter?'


Nina loved wearing the pale violet satin dress with the low scalloped neckline, and she loved sitting next to Omar in the dark as the first chords of music filled the symphony hall of Lincoln Center. Last week had been the opening of the Metropolitan Opera. She and Omar had sat seventh row centre and smiled just before the curtain went up so that the *Daily News* photographer could put the first night's audience on the middle page of the next morning's edition. Last night had been one gallery opening after another. The first had been black tie at the Museum of Modern Art. It was still warm enough for the crowds to spill out into the garden and walk and talk and have drinks between the sculptures. Salvador Dali had been there, wearing a tuxedo with trousers a little too short, so that all could see his silver socks. After an hour of circulating, they had excused themselves and made their way through the people for the drive up Madison, with Amos at the wheel of the limousine, to several of the smaller galleries.

Nina felt Omar's arm next to hers and thought, how handsome he is in a dinner jacket! And this dress! Adele said it was wrong with her colouring and had casually thrown it at Nina as she was packing for San Francisco. Nina had taken a taxi home with all the things Adele had insisted she have. 'Otherwise, Mother will deliver them straight to the Reject Shop and someone awful will buy them for five dollars each. So whatever you want is yours! Wear everything in good health, or at least have a good time if you refuse to be healthy!' This last was a running joke between them, for it was Nina who drank Diet Pepsis for breakfast and cooked popcorn every day, and it was Adele who had succumbed to mono.

Adele. Wonder how she's getting along? At least she has that apartment and a good friend and roommate in Kim. And a whole country between her and her mother! When is she going to wise up that her mother manipulates her? Her mother pushes and pulls and, while she doesn't use the sledgehammer technique of a screamer, she slowly pulverizes Adele's objections like a mortar and pestle into the finest dust. Nina remembered with a shudder the Tory Forrest Wickham opinions on San Francisco and Paul. Then she thought of her own mother, of her calm voice on the telephone every Sunday or Monday night. She was always excited about Nina's new job, excited about Omar, and on the whole, sympathetic and enthusiastic about everything in

174

her daughter's life. How lucky I am, mused Nina. And how I miss her. And Bart, too.

Applause ruffled through the audience and then, in unison, became loud. Omar turned to her and asked, 'Did you like it?' and she nodded. Beethoven's *Pastorale* began.

Adele looked at her watch and at the phone, then at Kim's typewriter. I should write her, I should write her! Otherwise I am asking for a million-dollar phone bill. She reached for the phone and then hesitated.

'When you call Nina,' came Kim's voice from the other room, 'tell her I said hello and never trust anyone in pinstripes.'

Inevitable, Adele sighed. 'Okay. Here goes.'

The phone rang and rang in Nina's empty apartment. The kitchen light was on; there was a shiny green metal box that looked like a fishing tackle kit on the kitchen table filled with various cosmetics. A silk scarf was draped over a chair and three brass bangle bracelets were beside the big white pitcher of daisies.

'No answer,' called Adele to Kim, who was on the green living room rug doing leg exercises.

'Means she's having a good time! Means she's still out with her sheik father figure!'

'Do you really think that?'

'He is fifteen years older and she did *hate* her father. Draw your own conclusions.'

'But she dated so many men her own age at Briarcliff and she liked them.'

'Men? Is that what they were?' panted Kim. She lifted her leg off the floor. 'Thirty-eight, thirty-nine, forty. New York is full of men and look who she's picked for the last couple of months. Someone almost double her age who takes good care of her.'

Adele frowned. 'He sounds too dangerous to take care of anyone. Nina'd better be taking care of herself.'

It took three evenings of dialling before Nina answered her phone. 'Nina! Where've you been?'

'Cannot believe it! Let me pull this coat off. There.' Nina struggled with her black military reefer with the gold buttons down its double-breasted front and kicked off gold sandals. Her black jersey trousers were covered by a black jersey tunic, which was artfully draped from the left shoulder to the mid-thigh. Nina yanked off two wide gold cuff bracelets and fairly shouted into the phone. 'Now! How are you? I've missed you!'

'I don't think you've missed anybody because you haven't been home for days. I happen to know. How is the Leb?'

'Don't call him that, Adele! He's fine! But I want to hear about you first. Have you found a job?'

Nina had never heard Adele sound so happy. She was working in the European paintings department of a small auction house called Grafton and she loved it, and she adored her woman boss and thought San Francisco was just right for her.

'Do you hear from Paul?'

'Sure. Letters all the time. He calls on Wednesday nights and we talk.'

'What about other men?'

'Weeeeeell, Kim wants to fix me up . . .' There was something shouted in the background but Nina found it unintelligible.

'Then let her. You can't live like a nun in San Francisco!'

'Oh, yes, you can. That'd be easy because ninety per cent of the men seem to be gay or are about to become gay. I swear, entire days go by when I don't see one red-blooded heterosexual male.' They laughed. 'Now tell me everything,' insisted Adele.

'I'm having an adventure.'

'I'll say you are! You've got an incredible life if you spend all day with the Countess and all night with the Leb.'

'I *do not* spend all night with the Leb as you insist upon calling him. His name is Omar, Adele.'

'I just think he's awfully foreign.'

'Well, he is awfully exotic and awfully good-looking and awfully sexy.'

'Watch out, Nina!'

'I have not succumbed to his charms, in case you are about to ask.'

'But you're about to.'

Nina laughed. 'How do you know that?'

'I can tell. You're on the line about it. A tap in the right direction and you'd be in bed with him.'

Nina thought of his mouth. How could anyone's mouth be that soft? She remembered one Sunday afternoon when she was a little girl out in the country feeding a horse sugar cubes. That's it exactly, she realized. Omar has velvet lips. 'Mmmmm, maybe.'

'Nina! Is he married, for heaven's sake? He may have three or four wives stashed somewhere.'

'I don't know. And the Countess doesn't even know. She says he has never mentioned a wife or marriage even in theory . . .'

'Don't you think you'd better find out before you take off your clothes?'

'Oh, Adele, of course I will! I'm just playing a little.' Am I? she wondered suddenly. Or is Omar the one playing? 'I'm very unavailable and pushing him away. We get along pretty well. I love going to "21" and I love his black driver.'

'What?' cried Adele thinking the connection was strange.

'His driver. His name is Amos and he's from Alabama. He's a riot.'

'Oh God, Nina!'

Nina continued. 'Omar is actually fun once he decides not to be so tight. He needs to play. He's the product of too many boys' boarding schools. This place called Victoria in Egypt and Gordonstoun and then there was somewhere in Switzerland . . .'

'That's an awful lot of boarding schools for one person . . .' Adele's voice oozed with cynicism.

'He wasn't happy.'

'Oh.' Adele made a face in San Francisco.

'When are you coming back east? Christmas?'

'No. Big break with family. With Mother, actually. Daughter finally decides to untwist umbilical cord from neck. I'm spending the holidays with Kim in Hawaii.'

177

'Terrific idea. How is Kim?'

'She has an assistant buyer's job with I. Magnin and loves it, and she is dating a lot.'

'Let her fix you up with dates, Adele. Have some fun. Paul isn't there to take you out. Don't think for a minute that he doesn't have drinks with people after a long day at the bank. Have fun. Don't do it to look for a replacement for Paul, just do it for yourself. In maybe a year or two you will be married and you might, just might, look back and wish you'd had one or two great evenings on the town with someone other than the man who's going to be your husband for eternity.'

'Oh, God. Are you ever down on marriage!'

'No, I'm not! I'm just having fun. The dinner parties Omar takes me to! Oh, Adele!' She stopped. 'One night I sat between John Lindsey and Beverly Sills. Barbara Walters was across from me. You know how in New York everyone automatically says, within ten seconds of hearing your name, "And what do you do?" I go to all these parties and half the people there are world famous for what they do! It is a tiny bit intimidating.'

Intimidating! Maybe someday I'll be able to tell Adele about the dinner at '21' when I ordered an artichoke just because Omar did and because it sounded exciting and how I tried to eat it with a knife and fork. Omar softly touched my elbow and I saw that he was pulling the leaves away with his fingers. That awful Jackie Sandler was sitting there, Nina remembered with a shudder. She saw it all and said brightly to the dinner party of eight, 'You're a long way from home, aren't you, dear?' Nina had blushed crimson and reached for her wine. Omar responded with no love lost for one of the bitchest women in the western hemisphere, 'Not as far away as I hear you are.' Jackie, who'd married into society, the daughter of a bankrupt Colorado saloonkeeper, swallowed, and it was her turn to go red. There was silence broken by Nina, who felt awash with sympathy for the older woman trying to disguise a crepey neck with ropes of pearls above the yellow silk designer suit. With a big smile, Nina announced, 'I've probably come farther than anyone. At

178

home we eat with our feet.' Everybody had enjoyed it enormously and even Jackie had managed to smile, at once both grateful and ashamed.

'Does he hover or toss you to the sharks?' Adele was insisting.

'Neither. He gives me briefings in the car. Who is who and what they do. He introduces me as though I were the most important person there, and he winks at me once in a while. I know I can always go over in a crowd and slip my arm in his and he will turn and be pleased, and then I am folded into the group he's with . . .' She sighed. 'It's hard for me. I make mistakes. I used to get too dressed up. I got Parkins that novelist confused with his fiercest critic, the *New York Review of Books* columnist, Parker! That was last week at a cocktail party and I wanted to die on the spot. Just wanted to ask for hemlock with a splash of white wine.' Nina frowned. 'Sometimes I really feel like I'm from Mississippi . . .'

'You're great, Nina! Don't feel that way! Everybody makes little "fox passes" as you used to say!' Nina laughed then. 'Listen, I have to hang up. It must be three in the morning there!'

'Used to it! I'm so glad you called. I'll do it the next time! Remember, let Kim introduce you to people! That's an order! And call Bart!'

'Maybe.'

'I want to tell you that I have worn the violet dress five times and I love it, and Omar loves it, and the black and white Chanel suit is terrific with my red silk shirt, and you won't believe this, but I wear it with a chocolate brown silk blouse, too, and I thank you a zillion times. I am only afraid you're going to fly back and repossess!'

Adele was thinking how much she wished she were in Nina's kitchen right now. Feet up on chairs, Tabs in tall glasses, and the whole evening to talk.

It took them another three minutes to say goodbye, with each having urgent last-minute thoughts to convey.

Adele walked from her bedroom into the green and white, plant-filled living room, where Kim was watching Nina Van

179

Pallandt, blonde and leggy, smile at Johnny Carson's teasing questions.

'Clifford Irving made her and made her what she is!' hooted Kim. 'Imagine sleeping with someone and then telling all on coast-to-coast television!'

'Nina, *our* Nina, says "hello!" She hasn't given herself to the Leb yet. I'm going to take a shower and fall into bed. G'night.'

'G'night.' Kim's attention was riveted to the television.

As Adele soaped herself slowly in the shower Jack flashed into her mind. Jack. She thought of what he had done to her. The release. The way she had felt afterwards. During. God. Afterwards, at dinner, sitting across from him. Jack. Damn him. She turned off the water with angry little jerks on the taps and reached for the fluffy green towel.

'We'll have to plan on Roman shades for that long expanse of windows at the Walkers',' the Countess was saying.

Nina visualized the view from the penthouse and sighed aloud. 'Oh, it's going to be heaven.' The river in the sun, the lights on the water in the evening, the changing colours of the sky.

'I think it should be something like that, yes,' came the preoccupied voice. The Countess was examining samples of sailcloth, chintz and cotton duck.

'What about that linen?' called Nina.

'Wrinkles too much. But I think you're on the right track. We could use a pale blue and mix the indoors and the outdoors . . . just extend everything past the glass, so to speak.' The Countess found what she wanted and tossed it to Nina. 'What do you think of that? That soft blue will pick up the blue in the paisley cushions very nicely.'

Nina nodded. She continued to be amazed at the Countess's memory for colour, for the design of a chair. Why, she could tell you where a rug had been worn or the position of a standing lamp in a bedroom she'd seen only once ten years before! She remembered clothes, she remembered jewellery. It was a highly-developed visual memory. 'So order . . . what did we say?'

Nina flipped the pages of her red notebook. 'Fifty-two yards if they are to be Roman.' She picked up the phone and dialled Schumacher.

'If delivery time is more than four weeks don't order it. It's near enough to this Jack Lenore Larsen,' called the Countess with another pale blue sample in her hand.

Nina felt she was absorbing knowledge like a sponge. When they visited a client, the Countess moved quickly over a room and Nina followed two paces behind her, scratching down notes frantically. 'Two wing chairs, to be re-covered. One three-seater sofa, two two-seaters, look for a more modern rug. Consider ethnic. Now, for the dining room . . .'

Dining rooms in New York City apartments were seldom that. They became guest rooms, playrooms, studies, everything but dining rooms. Walls were constantly being knocked down and put up as co-op owners changed their minds, had children or sent those children away to school.

'People decorate when their lives are changing,' she learned from the Countess. 'So don't let it ruffle you when they can't decide things. Usually' – she raised one brightly painted maroon fingernail – 'there is something else more important transpiring under the surface.' Yes, or had just transpired. The new marriage. The birth of a baby. The divorce. The death of a husband. The remarriage. The arrival of stepchildren. 'And there simply are people who have to be nudged in the right direction. Makes you wonder how they get dressed in the morning. Never show them more than three samples. Couldn't make a decision about wallpaper if their lives depended on it!'

Besides the psychology involved there was general knowledge that was all new to Nina. Her mother, Virginia, had what almost anyone would agree was 'good taste' so Nina had grown up knowing how to set a table beautifully, how high to hang a picture. She had an innate sense of colour which the Countess had immediately seen in the way she dressed. The older woman, however, was well aware that she was taking on a novice. She realized that she'd have to explain why the pleats were turned forward instead of back on some upholstered chairs, how many inches of hem were appropriate for a quilted bedspread, why chintzes with borders took so many extra yards. 'But,' she had trilled merrily as Nina took notes that first week, 'I don't have to unteach you anything!'

'What do you mean?'

'Well, if you'd come to me with a degree from the New York School of Design I simply would not have had a thing to do with you. I would have given you a glass of wine and said farewell.'

'Why?' Nina was mystified.

'Because they'd give you lectures in an enormous auditorium and fill your head with facts that aren't facts at all. For instance, yellow for all rooms with northern exposure. Sounds all right but have you ever painted a room blue with northern exposure? It's lovely. Ever so much better than yellow! You'd be filled with "facts" that I disagree with and I'd have to . . .' The Countess groped for a word. 'I'd have to deprogramme you!' She threw up her hands with a jingle of silver bracelets.

Nina laughed. 'So my head is empty, my mind's a blank and you're happy!'

'Yes, darling! Exactly!'

Nina despaired of knowing French antiques from Italian, one century from another, one cabinetmaker from another. 'Go into my bedroom and pick out books. Start with eighteenth century and go forward. Since you're wild for Italy maybe Italian is best for a beginning. Take them home and don't just stare at them until you're blind but trace the drawings. It's the only way to remember the curve of a leg, the way a cornice looks, the carving on a bureau or the drawer pulls. Get paper and fine-leaded pencils from the top drawer in my desk. Use the airmail paper in the tablet. Take as many books as you can carry.'

So it began. Nina's crash course in antiques; how to tell the finest silk from second best and why a painter must come to an apartment three times in one day to check the colour of the wall in the changing light. She was a quick study and the

Countess was delighted with her energy and her practicality.

'Your imagination is for later,' she told her new assistant. 'First, learn the rules; then you can break them.'

Nina gazed mournfully into her glass of milk as though she were watching a fly do the breaststroke across its white expanse. Nina and the Countess drank Perrier all day long and milk with lunch.

'Darling! Do anything you please!' the Countess was saying. 'Just don't fall in love with him! Make love hanging from the chandelier in the lobby of the Plaza but don't fall in love with him!' She swallowed a bite of the peanut butter and chutney sandwich and couldn't resist adding, 'And don't fall from the chandelier either.'

'I'm not! I'm really not in love with him.' Nina's voice was firm, the tone was direct. If only she could convince herself. 'He is good-looking but so are lots of men. Robert Redford is good-looking but . . .' She shrugged. Redford paled, quite literally, beside Omar. 'He is sexy but so are lots of men. Paul Newman for instance. Take Paul Newman.' Yes, thought Nina, take him. I don't want him. I want Omar. 'And he's clever. But so is . . . oh, what am I going to do?' she wailed.

'Oh! God! You *are* in love with him.' The Countess appeared vaguely irritated.

'I don't even know if he's married or not! And there is something in me . . .'

'All right. First, have another sandwich. Dorothy has made some with honey from the Vanderbilt hives on Long Island.' The Countess expressed maternalism with her assistant and Nina secretly loved it. 'What if – let's just imagine he is married – what does that mean?'

'Well, he doesn't bring her to New York, that's for sure. I know all his flight schedules and he calls me from Kennedy and says, "Can you meet me at such and such for dinner in two hours?"'

'All right. She's not here. But he is . . .' The Countess raised one slender finger. The nail was lacquered rosy pink.

'Now there are usually thirty-one days in a month and he is here more days than not and you think, and by the way, so do I, that all the days on this side of the Atlantic -- or at least the non-Chicago, non-Los Angeles days -- he is with you and only you.'

Nina nodded. 'It's non-stop. It's only when he goes away to Paris for a week or to London that I get sleep and lay off the wine, and recover.'

'So even if he is married he prefers to be with you. Am I right?' Nina looked more forlorn than ever. 'Oh, dear,' chirped the Countess. 'I keep forgetting you haven't been out of Mississippi that long.'

Nine floors above the islands of Park Avenue, the Countess of Avondale's living room was filled with guests. Champagne sparkled in the fragile tulips held by manicured fingers, tilted towards brightly painted lips; quaffed with more gusto by clean-shaven men in dinner jackets. The Countess always described the watered silk covering the walls as 'that colour pink of the geraniums one sees in window boxes in the south of France'. The gessoed sconces bathed the several dozen faces in a soft glow and the perfumes of the women scented the air. The tinkling piano notes of a Cole Porter melody could be heard amid the buzz of voices, the occasional peal of laughter, and the excited greeting of a new arrival.

Nina stood tall and slender in the doorway, on the threshold, between the empty dining room and the crowded living room, and watched. Briarcliff was just a rehearsal, she thought. But this is New York. This is the real thing. Some people she recognized from *Town & Country*, some from photographs on the Countess's desk or the bureau in the dressing room. The publishing heiress Millie Bancroft floated by on a cloud of Diorissimo, her silver-coloured sheath shimmering with several thousand bugle beads. Warren Hubbel, the playwright, was in the far corner with his new wife, the Broadway dancer. Sidney Fitz, the economist from Harvard, was laughing over something. His

184

bow tie was crooked. Feminine hands reached for it as Nina stared. Wendy Townsend cooed at him and he stopped his conversation with her husband and both men turned their attention to her. Anna Buccini, the opera diva, made her way through the crowd swishing grandly in a fire-engine-red chiffon dress. She kissed her manager, John Heiden, loudly on each cheek as he playfully ogled her barely concealed breasts. Ross Maynard stood beside the bartender as he measured out scotch into a tall glass.

'Darling.' A soft hand was on her bare arm. 'Come with me and I'll introduce you. Who would you most like to meet?'

'I think . . .'

'Warren would adore you. His play before last was all about a family in New Orleans who were losing their minds in unison.' The Countess, looking much less than her sixty-plus years, radiant in the gold brocade caftan, raised her eyebrows one inch closer to her deep orange hair. Canary diamonds sparkled at each ear. 'In unison,' she repeated, 'and on stage.'

'I want to stand here just one minute more. And look at everyone . . .' Nina sighed. 'Their clothes, the way they hold their heads . . .'

The Countess gazed at her protégée fondly. It was nearly a perfect profile if there were such a thing: a straight nose, just long enough to show breeding, rather full lips, now parted in anticipation, ready to smile at something amusing or good that she, in her youthful optimism, was sure would happen, and a well-defined chin and high clear forehead. The raven-black hair fell loosely on to the ropes of pearls the Countess had lent her. A present from that adorable French baron, oh, so long ago! The Countess had shown Nina how to powder her bare shoulders and they were pale and satiny next to the ivory silk dress. She saw the girl's wide-set shining eyes drink in the scene; she saw her inhale music and colour as though it were the rarest scent.

Omar, darkly handsome, was standing in the front hallway giving a white silk scarf to the maid who already held his chesterfield. Lila Hutchins nodded to her hostess with a tight smile as she put her hand possessively on the arm of her husband. He looks much younger, noted the Countess. There was Deirdre Whitman barely speaking to Howie Hastings even though everyone in the room knew she would be named as the other woman in his bloodbath of a divorce settlement. And Paul Carter, laughing so easily, with the martini, may go to prison soon on that insider dealing case if his Wall Street partners don't see fit to bail him out. Aloud, without meaning to, the Countess said, 'A garden of tigers.'

Nina turned. 'What did you say?'

'A garden of tigers. This room. And if the room is in the Seizième Arrondissement or in Cadogan Square or over-looking Piazza Venezia, it's all the same. A garden of tigers.'

Nina wondered if the Countess were serious. Her face looked older and her eyes were clouded with . . . regret? 'Countess, let me get you a glass of wine,' she said to the older woman. 'I was just thinking that I can't stand in doorways all my life. Once I'm in the room I'm in great form. I have to always force myself to walk in – whether with a chair in front of me or only a glass of something to drink.'

The Countess nodded. 'Right, darling. No more standing on thresholds. Someone should embroider that somewhere or crewel it or whatever. You know what they say,' she tittered, once more her old self, leaning towards Nina conspiratorially.

'No, what?'

'They say,' the Countess said wickedly, 'that needlework is a substitution for masturbation!' They giggled together. 'And I think of all these women who I know who are madly involved with silly pillows night after night!'

Nina moved away smiling and nodding over her shoulder that she'd be back. That was the moment she felt his eyes upon her. Someone was watching her and Nina thought: It's as if I'm wading into the ocean and someone on the beach, a safe distance away, is scrutinizing me, my bikini, everything it doesn't cover. She reached the bartender and when the two glasses were in her hands turned to find the Countess. Nowhere to be seen. Swallowed up by the tigers who laughed and flirted and played in the pink garden.

'Thank you.' A tall man smiled down at her, taking the glass from her left hand.

'But!'

'I know that it was meant for the Countess but she's been taken care of so you can give it to me.'

Nina's bright eyes slitted as she looked up at him. I never look up at anyone, went through her mind. He must be over six feet one. 'Have you been watching me?' she asked teasingly, not without a note of suspicion. 'Has it been intriguing? Are you mesmerized?'

'Riveted.' He grinned and introduced himself. 'I'm Mickey Keeling.'

'Nin – '

'I know who you are. The Countess's new assistant. How is she treating you?'

'I adore her!' Nina blurted quickly as if to ward off a condescending remark about her too-red hair or her too-loud voice. 'I really adore her.'

'So do I. Did you expect . . .' He stopped and looked into her clear grey eyes. 'Never mind. You did, of course.'

Nina continued to look up at him. Dark brown hair, a little mussed, light brown eyes with flecks of gold in them as though the wine he was drinking was somehow lighting them. She actually took a step backward, for his even-featured face with its quick smile seemed too close. His broad shoulders beneath the dinner jacket seemed almost too broad, too strong. Mickey Keeling took up space in a room. A vitality to his movement even if merely lifting a glass to his lips gave him a sphere of sorts, a field of action, and Nina was inside it and felt vaguely uncomfortable. 'You played football, didn't you?' was the first thing that came into her mind.

'Junior year in college. One game.' He looked rueful. 'It was the end of the world for me when a knee injury put me out. All over. Funny.' He smiled slightly and looked very intently at her. 'The twists and turns of fate.' Mickey stared at Nina until she lowered her glance to the pleats of his white dress shirt. His dinner jacket was open, exposing a wide band of maroon silk around a narrow

187

waist. Still staring, he spoke. 'What do you think about?'

Nina was caught off guard by the question but raised her eyes to his. 'I only talk about what I really think about when I'm eating peanut butter and chutney sandwiches with the Countess.' She smiled only slightly when he laughed. He puts me off balance, she decided, but she continued, 'I'm not due to talk about thinking for another seventeen hours.' Flipping her black shining hair over one bare shoulder, she moved away, into the crowd, towards Omar who beckoned her with one crooked finger.

He kissed her chastely on each cheek and whispered, 'Beautiful. Ravishing,' and she whispered back, 'You smell delicious.'

Curt Bellamy embraced her awkwardly from behind. 'Nina! Haven't seen you since the Whitney show! How are you?' he bellowed.

She liked him. Silver-haired, old enough to be my father and so sincere I could trust him to behave as one. 'I'm wonderful,' she beamed and the men laughed. 'Have you heard that we're doing your neighbours' penthouse?'

'The Walkers'?' he asked in astonishment. Nina nodded. Omar's eyes were on her pale shoulders. 'I thought they were getting a divorce.'

Nina twinkled knowingly. 'I don't think they are. But' – she hesitated for effect – 'the Countess says lots of marriages can't stand the strain of decorating.' They laughed as she continued, 'So give them another six months together.'

'Excuse us, Curt.' Omar took Nina's arm and steered her over to the piano where the tuxedoed player crooned, 'I've Got You under my Skin'.

'Omar! What is it?'

He looked at her long and hard. 'Are you coming home with me tonight?' She put her glass on the piano and swallowed. Omar's voice had an undercurrent of urgency. 'You know that I want you. That I have wanted you ever since we kissed in the taxi weeks ago. How long can we go on this way?'

Nina looked down at her fingers curved around the stem

188

of the wine glass and felt his voice and the notes of the song wrap around her as softly as the Rubelli velvet she'd ordered for Mrs Hanson's dining room curtains.

'Are you married?' she asked without warning.

Omar almost stepped backwards. 'Not at this moment.'

Nina didn't allow herself the luxury of relief, but plodded on. She'd rehearsed this so many times and would not be deterred. Only the setting was wrong. She hadn't counted on fighting with 'You're the Top' in a crowded room. 'What exactly does that mean?'

'Am I married emotionally or on paper? What are you asking?' He brought the vodka in the heavy cut-glass tumbler to his lips.

'Are you married? I want to know before I make love to you.' She realized that she was being stared at again. It was Mickey Keeling across the room. Not smiling. Not toasting her. Just watching. Almost as though he could hear her. But that was ridiculous.

'. . . You're the tower of Pisa . . .' sang the young man four feet away. 'You're the smile . . . on the Mona Lisa . . .'

'I've been married since I was fourteen.' Omar's voice was matter of fact. 'And betrothed since conception.' He sipped the vodka and again his dark eyes sought hers. 'Does that answer your question?'

'Where is she?'

'Geneva. In a house there. Outside Geneva.'

'Do you have children?'

'No. Is the inquisition over?' His voice was cold.

Nina's heart was pounding under the ivory silk. Omar who held her hand in taxis, who made her knees buckle when he kissed her goodnight but had refused to enter her apartment. Omar who took her arm at party after party and introduced her as though she were a princess. Omar who tweaked her nose in restaurants and called her his 'little fox'. This Omar was married to someone who lived in Switzerland. 'Do you ever see her?'

'Sometimes.' He stared at his ice cubes as though reading tea leaves. 'Nina' – he turned his dark-eyed gaze upon her again and, not for the first time, she noticed how long his

189

black lashes were – 'I want to make love to you. Do you want that?'

Nina did want it, but she resisted letting him know she did. I can't push him away any longer, she thought. Nina was pleased that she'd been both coy and cool till now and she knew the Countess was surprised that she could suffer so over Omar and never let him suspect. She'd slept with men after many fewer dinners, after many fewer fantasies. But Omar possessed a faintly menacing quality and he was older and she wasn't sure she always fascinated him and now, she knew that he was married. Yes or no? she asked herself. I must decide this minute. And with either answer, Nina knew she would be sorry. Yes or no, she would regret it.

'. . . You've got that thing, that special thing, that thing that makes birds want to sing . . .' crooned the pianist.

Oh, damnit. 'Let's go,' was all she said.

From the doorway just inside the hall she turned to seek the face of the Countess in the crowd but all she saw was Mickey Keeling standing beside the Chinese screen, glass of bourbon at chest level, watching.


It was a private elevator like the Wickhams', was her first thought, or rather, a private stop, with the doors opening into the hallway of the apartment itself. A maid in a black dress and white apron came to take their coats and then Omar said, 'Bea, we won't be needing you until breakfast,' and Nina thought: Breakfast seems a century away. He saw her face and put his arm around her then and pressed her hard against him and she felt safe and at once, very unsafe, but he seemed to sense it and held her face in his hands and kissed her forehead as though she were a little girl. 'Let's have something to drink,' he smiled, 'or dinner? We haven't really had dinner, have we? Shall I have the cook prepare something?'

'I'm famished! Where's the kitchen?'

'Follow me.' Omar led the way through the dining room and the pantry, flipping light switches beside each doorway. Picassos hung on every wall. The rooms were beige as

190

though their non-colour were in deference to the primary colours of the paintings. The kitchen was white, pristine, spacious enough to roller skate in. Nina began to feel better. She twirled the Countess's long pearls backwards and bent over to inspect the refrigerator's contents. Laughing, they made brie sandwiches and dabbed caviar on croissants. They sat at the white Formica table on white wooden kitchen stools and drank champagne out of amber-coloured goblets from Egypt. Omar teased her and she reached up and yanked at his bow tie. 'Oh, look what you've done?' he complained. 'It took me twenty minutes to get that right.'

'Well, are you going to sleep in it?' mocked Nina and then she realized yes, they were going to take off their clothes and they were going to go to bed together. Brie sandwiches in the interim or not. She blushed and he teased, 'The little terror.' Nina's high heel slipped off the rung of the stool and made a 'clump' noise on the linoleum floor. He lifted his glass towards her and she did the same. They both sipped; she in cream silk and he in his dinner jacket with the black tie dangling over the white pleated shirt, in the white kitchen. There was silence except for the hum of the refrigerator. Omar took her hand and led her stocking-footed through the pantry and through the dining room with eight chairs arranged along each side of the long table and into the front hall and down a long corridor. 'Oh,' she began but he turned to her and stopped her protests with his kiss and she felt without strength as she did in taxis, as she did on her front steps, as she did whenever he pressed his mouth to hers. Omar picked her up as though she were a doll and carried her into his bedroom.

The mink spread had been turned back as always, the bedside lamp was softly glowing, the heavy dark green velvet curtains were drawn against the noises of Fifth Avenue twelve storeys below. He put her on the big bed and, bending down, began to undo the pearl buttons of the dress's bodice. She watched his face and raised her arms obediently when he pulled the silk from her and then she let him pull the stockings off and at last when she was clad only in the cream-coloured panties and the Countess's pearls,

191

she crossed her arms over her bare breasts. His lips sought the nipples she tried to hide and when his mouth touched them Nina cried out almost in pain at the intensity of the sensation. He jerked away his shirt, his studs dropping on the thick carpet; his trousers and cummerbund fell in a dark heap that he stepped away from disdainfully.

He knelt with one knee on the mattress, his chest and shoulders, his stomach, well-muscled and tanned. 'Nina. Come to me.' She didn't move. 'You have to make up your mind.' Omar's voice was gentle as though coaxing a wild animal to eat from his hand. 'You're afraid, aren't you?' Then he lay on the bed beside her and they both stared at the white-panelled ceiling, breathing heavily, but not touching. 'We won't if you don't want to. It's up to you.'

Nina thought: No, it isn't up to me. It's Omar, always Omar, who knows how to do things, what to do. He does everything so well, without hesitancy. He is pretending it's up to me. His hand touched her face, then he turned and was against her. His skin was warm and Nina found herself saying, 'I want. I want.' She did want. I've thought about it long enough. Considered it from an intellectual viewpoint for hours and now I simply want. She wanted, she felt, she ached with wanting and still his lips, his tongue, his fingers played with her. He pulled away from her arms and then she felt his face between her thighs. Gasping, she tried to push him aside but his tongue softly explored her, his fingers brushed her like feathers. 'Oh, what?' she cried out. 'What are you doing?' Nina suffered with wanting him. 'Oh, please, Omar, please,' she whispered. 'Why is it like this?' She tried to catch her breath.

His laugh was silent. 'Like what?' He was on top of her then, one elbow on either side of her head. She gazed into his face, at the thin moustache above his mouth. The black eyes sparkled like polished jet. 'I want to play. All night.'

'No, no, no!' Nina shook her head. 'I can't stand it.' She dug her nails into his shoulders. 'I can't go on.'

'Oh, Nina.' He smiled at her then began to lightly touch that place, that place that pulsed with wanting, until she cried out. But he seemed to pay no attention to her voice and entered her carefully, almost methodically, as she called his name in desperation. Omar's eyes were closed and he bit his lower lip as though deep in thought. Nina wrapped her arms around his neck and gasped again and again as he slowly rocked back and forth, edging the two of them towards the crevasse of orgasm and then at last, as Nina cried his name once more, he allowed himself to come.

# 5

White roses filled the living room. '"To my little fox!"' sang the Countess, tucking the card back into the tiny envelope.

'You are as happy as if they were for you!'

'Well, I am partially to thank or to blame, whichever way you'd like to look at it!' The Countess surveyed the latest arrangement of a dozen. 'I do hope he doesn't keep sending them on the hour like this! I'll be out of vases by noon!' She raised a nearly orange eyebrow. 'You must be handling that man very well, Nina. I've known him a long long time and this isn't normal Mar-Mar behaviour.'

Nina stared at the figure in the voluminous royal blue robe. Morocco. From a prince. Moroccan, of course. 'He's married,' she said softly.

The Countess turned, her hands outspread with bright coral nails flashing. 'Darling!' she clucked and then, recovering, added brightly, 'But it isn't a total loss. Look at all these roses, for instance!'

Nina sighed. 'He's asked me to go to Europe with him after Christmas.'

'Well, go! Absolutely! You shall go! I'll help you pack! Where? Paris? London? St Moritz? Skiing?'

'I didn't ask.' Nina sighed again. 'It was all sort of hazy last night.' She stared at the sunlight filtering through the sheer undercurtains of the long windows. 'It was like nothing . . . nothing I've ever known.'

The Countess laughed. 'Of course it was! You've been giving yourself to little boys, to college boys of all things! They have no finesse. The word "tender" only comes into their tiny minds when ordering a steak.'

Nina thought of Frank Wellington. 'You're probably right about that.'

'Well, let's make plans!' The Countess held a notebook. 'Before the phone starts ringing again.' She glanced a bit anxiously down the hall towards the office. Usually the two of them never left it before noon for lunch. The living room was solely for entertaining. 'First, you leave for Mississippi for Christmas in two weeks. The twenty-third. Then back here and off with Omar on what date?'

'Should I go?'

'Why ever not?'

'Should I get more and more involved with him?'

'Are you having a good time?' Nina smiled and nodded. Her eyes were bright when she thought of Omar and of the way he looked at her. 'Do you have fun with him?' Nina nodded again. 'Then play it out. He obviously likes the way you've held him at arm's length so continue, but now it will be a bit trickier . . .'

'I've been to bed with him, for pete's sake! How can – '

'I admit it's more difficult now. Just never let him think he has you. Don't talk about love. Let him come round to that. Wait for him. Make love for all you're worth but don't talk about it with him.'

Nina stared. She'd bitten her tongue so many times in the dark last night when he was on top of her, when he was kissing her, and afterwards when he was stroking her hair away from her face early in the morning before dawn. She'd nearly burst with wanting to declare 'I love you'. She was confused. She'd never wanted to say it before. Oh, sure, she'd told Adele a hundred times that she was in love. Could I have been in love with so many boys, in love so many times under so many full moons, for so short a time? But love is not tangible, she thought. It's in your mind, your imagination. So if you think you're in love, you are. But never before had Nina wanted to stare into someone's face and say 'I love you'. She had always been the recipient.

'Don't make him feel trapped or he'll run away. You'll lose him.' The Countess moved two roses a little to the left in the alabaster urn. 'There.' She turned. 'Now what about the fabric for the Frazier dining room chairs?'

And so the day began.

*

Nina resisted the impulse to close her eyes as the lights of the chandeliers blurred above her and behind Omar's face. 'Floating,' she purred and he gently pulled her a little closer. The waltz seemed to have been written for them.

'We dance the way we make love,' he said.

The strapless black silk dress swirling around her legs felt sensuous on her skin between panties and black lace suspender belt. Omar liked suspender belts and bare thighs. Omar liked the dress; and so had Millie Bancroft; and so had the Countess when she'd dumped it out of the yellow bag the day before. 'Who's the designer?' Millie had inquired an hour before in the powder room of the Pierre. 'Oh, I . . . I don't know,' Nina had stammered. 'It's not an original . . . it's . . .' No, she'd never tell anyone but the Countess what it really was. A sixty-dollar nightgown from Bloomingdale's. 'Can I get away with it for the Black and White Ball?' she'd pleaded and the Countess had pronounced it, 'Elegant. Especially with your bare shoulders like that. Yes, pull down the straps and be careful when you laugh. Your breasts are small enough, lucky you, to not have to worry about a thing underneath. Oh' – she'd clapped her hands – 'I can't believe how soigné you look in it!' With the Countess's large square pavé diamond pin right at the lowest point of the V-shaped neckline and simple diamond clip earrings 'from that Spanish pretender to the Bourbon throne', the effect was of simple elegance.

'You're wonderful at this,' complimented Omar as she followed his quick steps and then pirouetted back into his arms.

'I learned at Briarcliff in my room,' she grinned. 'Kim and I used to fight over who'd be the man. She said she couldn't teach me if she didn't know how to be a man and I said how was I supposed to learn it backwards and then become a woman! Myra got involved and said she could do it either way. We called her the "bisexual waltzer". She gets all the credit for me.'

'Nobody in their right mind would take all the credit for you!' Nina made a face at him and he dug his fingers into her slim waist which made her cry out softly. The sound was

196

familiar to both of them. 'Stop making me think of making love to you all the time,' he hissed at her as their thighs brushed.

'Stop making me make love to you all the time,' she retorted.

'Ahh!' he laughed delightedly. 'You're lucky to be dancing in this ballroom and not in a suite upstairs.'

'Beast! Animal!' she retorted. The music seemed to stroke Nina's bare shoulders; her shining black hair flipped across her face as Omar pulled her even closer. Their legs brushed together. 'Watch out!' He winked at her. 'You and I can't be horizontal for at least another two hours.'

Amos stood like a sentinel beside the long black limousine, only coming to life when he picked out Nina's dress. 'She is lak a young Liz Taylor, I swear to God!' he often insisted to his wife. 'Only more delicate, somehow. She really probably doesn't look 'zakly lak Liz Taylor but lak . . .' Amos wished Lavinia could see Nina. Lavinia thought everybody looked exactly like somebody in the movies and she would know who Nina looked like. 'Why, Mr Sarkis, he looked a lot lak another Omar. Omar Sharif, 'cept his face is not so wide and his eyes seem brighter, more lak . . .' Amos opened the door and settled his charges. In a few moments he had expertly manoeuvred them out of the quagmire of too few taxis and too many people desperately seeking them. Only a few blocks away and five minutes later Nina and Omar were being shepherded to a booth in the front room of '21'.

'Mr Sarkis,' murmured the maitre d' attentively, as he saw to their order of Pimm's Cups.

'Omar! How've you been?' A short man wearing glasses stopped by the table and pumped his hand.

'Omar!' gushed a woman with white hair, breaking away from the group she was with. She kissed him on both cheeks as he rose, holding his napkin. He introduced Nina and the woman nodded at her and then turned her attention back to Omar. 'Lovely to see you!' and she was gone.

It was past midnight when they'd finished dinner and were again in the car. 'Come back with me?' He squeezed

197

her hand. Nina was bone-tired but she felt a need to be in his arms. All night. She could have him all night. She nodded and he squeezed her hand again and leaned forward. 'Amos, we won't be taking Miss McLean home tonight.'

Nina liked it best when they were alone. Usually that was in his big bed. Sometimes they woke before dawn and talked quietly with the soft grey light slowly turning to day, allowing her to gradually make out the planes of his strong face beside hers on the pillow. Nina loved hearing about his being a child, about growing up in a big country house in the mountains outside Beirut. It was cooler there in the summer; it was an escape from the summer heat, a place for him and his five brothers, for his uncles, aunts, cousins. 'I used to sit beside the wall outside the mosque with Saladin – he was two years older – and we'd count lizards, keeping score in the dust.' Omar had laughed as he described himself in heavy leather sandals, with a nose he had to grow into, late for supper. 'Our competition would always be close.' He turned and looked up at the ceiling, smiling at the memory of the white-hot days, of that beloved brother. 'Sometimes Saladin would get the last lizard, sometimes I. Then we'd say "just one more" as the call for supper would come again.'

Nina noted that his accent would lose its easy American quality and would take on a foreign cadence, sometimes English-accented, but at other times, a formality with the words as though he became again a young man, uneasy with the phrasing. He had been that way the first night at dinner and sometimes it returned when he was remembering his past, long before New York, long before Nina. His life had changed when he was eight and had been sent away to school in Scotland, 'I was too small, too dark; an Arab in a world of tow-headed, blue-eyed Anglo-Saxon boys,' he explained quietly, leaning on one elbow over Nina's face. One of his fingers stroked that wave at her temple over and over again in the long silences between his sentences. 'Unhappy was not the word for what I was. I used to ache inside, I missed my family so. And the system of fagging for

198

the older boys terrified me. There was one boy called Rupert Evans. When I heard him call my name across the hall my legs would turn to water. It was like a telephone ringing in your belly and you can't answer it. You just . . .' His finger began its gentle methodical stroking again as Nina lay still and listening. 'You just get through it. Somehow.'

Nina thought of the little boy Omar and of the man she knew. 'How do you ever know when you belong?'

'Who says anyone belongs?'

'You do. You do now. You do in New York.' Her mind flitted to Geneva, to the wife he never ever spoke of, the wife he never answered her questions about, to the places he went when he was not with her.

'Nobody belongs. Sometimes I think that.' He sighed; his voice was heavy with pessimism. 'We all pretend. It's all a game, Nina.'

'But why do some people appear so comfortable, so . . .'

'Because they are good at the game, that's all.'

'But why do I . . .'

He dipped down and kissed her mouth quickly. 'Because you haven't decided who you are yet. When you decide then you can play the game.'

'But then who are you?'

Brrrrrrrrriiiiiiiiiing went the alarm and then the voice on the radio began, 'This is WNIS with the seven o'clock news. In Beirut last night . . .' Omar frowned as he leaned over and punched the radio into silence. 'I am a Lebanese banker worried about my country,' he said ruefully as he got out of bed. Naked, muscled like Michelangelo's David, he turned to look at her and added, 'Playing a game.'


Christmas edged closer with each cocktail party, with each invitation to stop over for egg nog, with each dinner party. Omar was perpetually beside Nina with his arm often around her waist loosely all evening as they stood in a living room clutching glasses, chattering. At the Michaelsons' under the mistletoe which hung from an archway he kissed her so long and so ardently that several of the men broke into applause. The women separated and wondered what it would be like to kiss such an intense, handsome man and studied Nina's face afterwards as though it might tell them.

Nina arrived in Jackson feeling elated by life and happy to confide everything to her mother. Except that she slept with Omar, except that he was married. Virginia listened, excited, pleased and a bit overcome at Nina's descriptions of the parties, of the rooms she was decorating. She heard about the penthouses overlooking the East River and a two-bedroom on the fiftieth floor of a building and a co-op with a garden behind that the Countess wanted to do entirely in yellow flowers.

Bart called on Christmas Eve morning from San Francisco and told them that he was fogged in and couldn't come unless he could manage to rent a car and get to the Los Angeles airport in four hours and that unfortunately everyone else had the same idea and the flights were booked solid. Both women were very sad not to see him and hung up determined not to show too much disappointment to the other. They went to the candlelight midnight service at church and on Christmas Day to an open house in Woodland Hills and later on to a concert of carols given at the Old Capitol.

'You look simply beautiful!' Virginia breathed as she kissed her daughter goodbye at the airport. 'You're all grown up with a career and your own apartment and a man who is in love with you.'

'Oh, Mother!' laughed Nina as she rearranged her winter coat over her arm.

'It's thrilling for you! It's all just happening!' continued Virginia.

Nina didn't say what flashed through her mind. No, Mother, I'm *making* it happen.


The Countess invited forty to celebrate New Year's Eve and she and Nina simply 'cancelled', as the Countess put it, the day before. Caterers, the drink deliveries, the extra help were supervised by the little skinny Dorothy, who could do anything, it seemed. The black woman ordered everyone around save the Countess. 'Them plates go over there,' she commanded the temps from the agency. 'And them wine glasses go over there. And we better polish them silver trays before we set out the . . .'

Nina brought her dress over to the apartment and bathed and dressed at six. She and the Countess wandered up and down the hall from bathroom to bathroom like two girls at Briarcliff. Nina was surprised to see how attractive a figure the older woman had in her light blue slip and her eyes must have shown it as she stood behind the Countess who sprayed herself up and down with perfume from an old-fashioned atomizer.

'I had this made up for me in Egypt and I get someone to bring me back a supply once in a while. Can't keep it very long, unfortunately.' She smiled. 'Oh, I know what you're thinking. And yes, it's true. Oh, how many men have told me I look more beautiful without my clothes! And not one has ever complimented me in a suit or a real dress, even if the bloody thing cost three thousand dollars!'

Nina thought the delicate feet and ankles that gave her the baked-potato-on-toothpicks look were just right on the nearly-naked woman. But clothes with waists and shoulders were all wrong; she was made for lingerie, for caftans, to loll on pillows wrapped in scarves.

The Countess's robin's-egg-blue silk caftan made Nina wish that Adele could be there. Diamond clips were on her ears and her bright hair, newly rinsed with a shade called Pale Persimmon, was full and brushed upward like flames. Anything but pale. Nina wore forest green velvet. The Countess, like a greedy child fishing sweets out of a box, had dug her hands into her jewel case and then looped several silver chains set with emeralds around her neck.

'That maharajah,' said the Countess as she stood behind Nina at the dressing table mirror and fastened the clasps.

'Oh, the one with "the look"?'

'No, this is another one. There.' She stepped away as Nina turned to face her. Nina's eyes had taken on a green

201

cast. The Countess had shown her how, with a few whisks of a sable brush, to make her cheekbones even more prominent. Her face above the square-cut neckline of the dress and the delicate necklaces was radiant with anticipation. Omar would be ringing the doorbell soon.

The living room was crowded when the Countess and Nina made their entrances. There were little gushes of greeting from the perfumed glittering women and embraces and compliments from dinner-jacketed men. Dorothy had lit all the candles for some reason and they raised the temperature of the large, high-ceilinged room by at least five degrees. 'But the effect is charming!' everyone insisted. 'Looks like some religious ceremony is about to take place,' murmured the Countess to Nina.

'Shall I go around and blow them out?' the girl asked, thinking there must be three dozen.

'No. Leave them. People will remember this but they are going to drink more to stay cool . . .' She turned towards a friend who kissed her on both cheeks.

'You must be Nina!' said a heavily made up woman with a diamond necklace. Her face had been too tanned over too many Hobe Sound winters and she was probably a bit younger than the fifty years she looked. 'I'm Lila Hutchins and I want to talk to you!' Nina tried to smile but the woman's tone was hard, not really friendly. 'I want to get my cottage done on Fisher's Island and want you to persuade the Countess to . . .'

Nina apologetically explained, 'I'm afraid she's adamant about not doing things outside the City.'

Lila gave a sigh of exasperation as Mickey Keeling approached. When she saw him she looped her arm through his and, noting the look that flashed between him and Nina, said, 'I see you've met the great American poet.'

'Yes, we've met,' Nina nodded. What was going on?

'Well, see what you can do with her!' Lila's tone was sharp, unmistakably annoyed. Did she mean what Nina could do with the Countess or what Mickey could do with Nina? 'I'm going to get more gin. Are you coming?' Her question, as imperious as any command, was directed at

202

Mickey. He shook his head as she pushed her way through the crowd. She was tall and slim and held her head very high; her posture, her stride belonged to someone not used to being thwarted.

'Wow!' sighed Nina.

'She's in one of her "the world just isn't behaving as I want it to" moods.'

'Charming.'

'Yes. You are.'

Nina stopped smiling. 'Why do you stare at me?' She thought of that particular time when Omar and she had been discussing making love as they stood beside the piano but there had been parties in between then and now; parties where he remained at one end of the room; times when she'd been aware of him just watching her.

'You enchant me. You are a chameleon.'

Nina sipped from her glass and when she lowered it she raised her grey-green eyes to his brown ones. The irises did seem to be flecked with gold. She hadn't imagined it before; and here in the candlelight the effect was heightened. 'A lizard?' she began to laugh. 'But . . .'

An arm went around her waist and Omar kissed her cheek. 'Not allowed.' She tried to sound tough.

'Not allowed!' Omar fairly growled, smiling, as she pulled away. 'Hi, Mickey! How goes it?' He extended his hand.

'So-so. I'm ready for next year,' Mickey responded. 'Only two hours thirty-seven minutes to make up a list of resolutions I will have broken by the seventh of January.'

With Omar by her side, Nina found bantering came easily. 'Don't make such hard ones to keep.'

He noted the arm around her waist, the bright eyes, the teasing tone of her before him in dark green velvet. 'Maybe I should resolve to make other resolutions.' His voice was serious. Mickey excused himself and turned into the crowd.

'Did I hurt his feelings?' Nina asked Omar in a low voice.

'Don't know. Perhaps you did hit a sore spot. He doesn't seem happy with his life right now.'

'Is he a poet?'

'I wouldn't say full-fledged but then what do I know of poets? I always think of him as a banker. A financier.'

'But I heard . . .'

'He's had several books published, but that was years ago. I don't know what they're like. Never picked one up.' He put his arm around her more tightly and as his fingers stroked her bare arm below the cap sleeves she felt the current between them. 'Are you coming to London with me?'

Nina shrugged. Games. Games. Oh, how I want to go! I'll go to Cleveland with you! she almost cried out. 'When?' Her voice was nonchalant. As if she went to London only when she had nothing better to do. A last resort.

'January. Will you or won't you?'

'I will. I can't wait!'

Omar winked at her. 'Claridge's keeps a suite for me and you'll love London.'


Manhattan sunlight in January has a weak and watery quality, as though seen through the frosted glass of a dentist's office door, thought Nina. She pulled her bright cardinal-red quilted coat around her more closely in the wind. Omar teased her about not buttoning things, about being in a hurry to get out the door, about not wearing gloves. She sighed as she waited for the 'Don't Walk' light to change on the corner. It seemed that the city was ever so slowly recovering from the effects of the hectic holiday and the days fairly crawled. Fabric houses were short staffed as one person after another jubilantly announced that they'd taken advantage of a special fare to the Caribbean. Even Luther, the upholsterer, had closed his shop. Omar had been away since the second of the month and Nina felt suspended in aspic, waiting for him to call, waiting to know when to pack for London. Maybe that's why I accepted Tad's invitation for dinner tonight, she mused as she moved with the crowd across 79th Street. She stepped gingerly over the ridge of slush and dirty snow that lined the kerb and then began to walk quickly downtown over the wet and shining sidewalk. Nina cradled the heavy wallpaper book at a different angle in her arms and smiled. Omar. I do miss you. And so far, you seem to love me. Nina thought of the Countess's countless warnings over peanut butter sandwiches. Only the Countess is making January bearable, Nina decided. She was always her bright self, full of anecdotes about liaisons and flirtations with a prince or a baron or even a king 'of that tiny tiny country that got swallowed up by the Russians'.

'Miss McLean,' nodded the grey-haired doorman as she wiped her black leather boots before traversing the gleaming marble-floored lobby. 'Will you take the mail up to the Countess?' He handed her a sheaf of envelopes and she thanked him and stepped into the waiting elevator.

Not good, she thought after pushing the button for nine. I must talk to her about all these invoices. Maybe today I will simply write cheques and get her to sign them. Whenever I reach for the chequebook the Countess wants me to confirm an order's arrival date or get someone on the phone who can expedite a delivery.

The Countess swung open the door before she could ring the buzzer. 'Oh, darling!' she cooed delightedly. 'Guess who just called because he missed you at home!' Today the caftan was a shocking pink which fought with the orange hair but, thought Nina, remembering the Countess's words: If you're going to break a rule, break it to smithereens. She was waved in on a slight breeze of Egyptian perfume.

'Omar called me?'

'None other than Mar-Mar himself and he misses you desperately and is bored silly and cannot wait to ravish you in the fog the minute your plane lands at Heathrow.'

Nina pulled off the coat. She knew better than to ask what Omar had really said. The Countess was a paraphraser and preferred the 'gist of things' to direct quotes. 'Is he calling back?'

'But of course he is!'

'Did he say he would?' Nina sought the Countess's white-powdered face for clues. Rice powder. Doesn't destroy the pores.

'Well, he will!' exclaimed the Countess brightly. 'Now,

205

what I think . . .' There was the sound of a key in the lock behind them. The door opened and Dorothy entered in the old beaver coat the Countess had given her two winters before. With her dark little wrinkled face surrounded by fur she looked like some wild fabled forest creature caught between human and animal form.

'Why, mawnin' Contessa and Nina! Thought I'd git here early today and catch up with my caftan ironin' and do a lil' bit of . . .'

The phone began to ring then and the Countess fluttered at Nina to take it in the bedroom. Ten minutes later she floated out into the hallway where the two women stood discussing a grocery list. They turned to her as Nina fairly sang the news. 'I leave day after tomorrow for London!'

I'm mean, decided Nina as she cut into her swordfish. I'm rotten and mean and thoroughly vicious. Why does he bore me so? Why can't I be nicer? Tad was talking about the commodities market. 'If you're daring enough to venture into futures . . .'

Futures, thought Nina. Futures as toasted on New Year's Eve with Omar's smiling face before her. Futures as what shall I pack? Futures as a suite at Claridge's with just about the most attractive man on earth. And futures as in how could he stay married for ever and not be enough in love with me to do something about this marriage, this engagement or entanglement, whatever you wanted to see it as, since conception. And here I go, off to commit adultery across the Atlantic and I'm so excited about it I could burst. Fucking on Fifth Avenue wasn't enough.

'Would you like another glass of wine?'

'Ummm . . .' Nina was flustered, remembering where she was. Macmillan's, Third Avenue, surrounded by preppies, well groomed and well dressed and well brought up. Well schooled and if not all of the former, undeniably well heeled. 'Love it!' she declared and then continued, determined to be nice, to be good to dear Tad who was nice, who was good. 'And would love to hear all about what's happening at the bank.' She leaned forward feigning great interest and teased, 'I want the scoop on who's got their hands in the till, and who's sleeping with whose secretary and who is embezzling like mad about to buy a ticket to Brazil!'

Tad laughed. 'I knew it was wrong to let you get involved with the Countess. You're starting to think like her.'

He is good-looking, decided Nina. If you didn't know him. And he is decent. Maybe this dull decency he radiates is what negates any sex appeal. Maybe I will always be drawn to married Lebanese who disappear for weeks at a time while I stall with someone like Tad, waiting to be summoned to a faraway foreign hotel. It occurred to her then that perhaps she should tell him she was going to London, but then she thought: Why must he know? He knows I'm sleeping with Omar. But then she worried: What if he thinks, since he hasn't seen us together, that it's over and I mean to begin something with him, that I am suddenly receptive to him after all these months . . .

'I'm very glad you're with her on a day-to-day basis. Certainly my mother knows her as well as anyone but I think they have a sense of competition about parties and people they know and so I wonder if . . .'

Nina realized Tad was trying to understand. He seemed suddenly more human and less banker when he talked about the Countess. 'You really are fond of her, aren't you?' She looked up at him over the edge of her wine glass.

He nodded. 'Really am.' He reached for his fork. 'She's one of a kind.' He hesitated and then added, 'Like you.'

'Thanks.' There it was. The 'trout look' in spades. She smiled though she didn't feel much like it. 'I hardly think we're in the same category.'

'What do you mean?'

'Well, it's just that . . .' Nina searched for a way to grasp the idea. 'She is a countess and she . . .'

Tad seemed unimpressed. His mother had explained to him that the Countess could never have been married to the Count of Avondale. If he were English, then he'd have to have been an Earl. Tad wondered how many Americans would catch that. Obviously, very few. The poor Countess,

207

he thought. Well, I won't be the one to blow the whistle.

'But you could be a countess if you wanted to be. If you went to Europe with the right introductions anyone you wanted would marry you.'

'Oh, Tad!' She didn't believe him for a minute. But then, there had been the Portuguese count. She had forgotten him entirely. 'What I want to say is that the Countess – what is her name? Do you know, she must have a name and I've never heard anyone call her Mary, or Liz or . . .'

'Neither have I. She's been the Countess ever since I met her a few years ago.'

'She told me . . .' Nina began and then a sense of loyalty stopped her. Why had the Countess said she'd known Tad since he was a little boy? 'What I was thinking is, she knows how to do things and I feel I'm just learning.'

'Things like what?' Tad poo-poohed her. 'Your table manners are fine.'

Nina laughed. 'Okay, now that you ask, I will tell you. I had this stunning blonde roommate at Briarcliff and I watched her. For four whole years. She took it for granted that she never experienced a pang of hesitation over what to pack for the weekend or what to wear to a dinner party. She grew up knowing how and what . . .'

Tad stared at her. 'All I know is that you're from Mississippi but you gleam of Briarcliff and you seem to instinctively know how to do things.'

Nina looked at her plate. 'I've had to learn. This roommate helped a lot. The Countess helps a lot.' She turned her big grey eyes towards him. 'I grew up where everyone thinks squash is a vegetable.'

She was serious so Tad, to his credit, did not give into waves of laughter. He concentrated on snipping the end off his cigar. Nina knew it and she appreciated it.

Two hours later as he helped her out of the taxi she said, 'Sorry I can't ask you in for a drink but I'm . . . I have to pack.'

'Where are you going?' His voice was interested. He was not the same Tad she'd seen last summer, not the same Tad she'd accepted the dinner date with.

208

'I've had a wonderful time, Tad. Thank you so much for the – '

He kissed her then, very hard, too hard. It was the kiss of someone who hasn't quite mastered the technique yet. She broke away, one eye on the waiting yellow taxi beside the snow-banked kerb. 'Tad, I like you so much, but . . .'

He nodded. 'I know. Don't say it. Just tell me where you're going and maybe we can have dinner when you get back.'

'London.'

'With Omar,' he stated flatly.

Nina wished she could erase the look that clouded his eyes. She nodded. Her black hair moved on the shoulders of the black wool coat. 'I had a good time with you,' she said softly.

Suddenly his arms were at his sides and they were separate people shivering on a brownstone porch surrounded by slush and the noise of night-time Second Avenue traffic. 'Call me if you ever . . . change your mind about anything.' His voice was businesslike. Nina fumbled in her purse for the key. He was down the seven steps and had his hand on the door of the taxi when she looked at him again. Tad called her name and she thought, oh, please don't make me feel worse than I do. 'If you ever need anything . . .' The sentence hung unfinished in its own little cartoon cloud of vapour from his warm breath in the cold air as he slammed the door and the taxi rolled away.

Omar looked down at her and smiled. Her dark hair was tangled on the white pillowcase around a face he always thought of as impishly angelic. Was that good English? He wondered what his favourite teacher at Gordonstoun would say. Nina stirred in her sleep as Omar removed his watch. He put his coat over the chair then sat down and removed shoes, socks, still staring at her. The note he'd left was on the little desk. Across Claridge's notepaper he'd scrawled in black ink:

Dear Fox — So sorry not to meet you at Heathrow. Know if you're reading this that my driver has delivered you to the right place. Money in drawer. Room service for just about anything. My last meeting is at half past three. Can't wait to see you! O.

'Mmmmm,' she cooed in her sleep as she felt his warmth beside her. Omar kissed her shoulders, white as cream, then gently lifted her arm and kissed the silkiness inside one elbow. As his tongue flickered over the curve of one perfect breast she opened her eyes. 'Omar!'

He smiled, white teeth showing, eyes twinkling. 'Did you think it was room service?'

She pulled him to her then and covered his neck with little playful kisses until he firmly held her face in his hands and put his mouth upon hers. They both felt the familiar wave then: that heat, that shortness of breath, that weakness along with the surge of energy. Nina grasped his shoulders as the excitement took hold, as it always did. She loved the thick black hair on his chest, the way it grew in the pattern of a T, the coarseness of it against her own soft breasts. Omar's fingers stroked her flat stomach for a moment as she sharply inhaled with the tension he was creating beneath his wide strong hands. They never spoke once they'd kissed, once it began, but both separately drifted away. They were conscious of pleasing the other and only conscious of their own pleasure as clouds or when their own fingers became too weak to continue the methodical stroking. Omar would wait until Nina cried out and then he would kiss her hard and hold her in his arms, for she had told him she felt she was falling. Not only falling away from him as her back arched but falling into a void; with eyes closed and mouth open, sometimes with deep silent gasps, she held his shoulders until she had no strength. Then he would raise himself on elbows and gently enter her and Nina would begin to come again. Afterwards, this afternoon in London, they lay in tangled sheets with Nina staring up at the pale green ceiling, the white woodwork. She thought: How unreal to be here, in this bed in Omar's suite, in a place called Claridge's after

210

having dinner on a plane and a movie in mid-air and after a man called Chester had held the door of a car called a Daimler open for her. Nina had asked what kind of car it was and admired the sleek lines and Chester, in turn, had admired Mr Sarkis's newest American.

'How do you feel about dinner at a place called Odette's?'

Nina looked at his lean muscular body beside hers. 'I feel awfully awfully good about it,' she said in a not-half-bad English accent. Omar bent down to kiss her mouth again. That soft lush pouting mouth that looked as though it always needed to be kissed just once more, that mouth that seemed to swell under his touch.

Adele tried to sound light and unconcerned. 'Countess, it's been so nice to talk to you, again. Hmmmm. Oh, no! I was just curious, that's all. If you do hear from her tell her to call me. Thanks. Bye.'

Adele hung up the phone and felt prickles of panic. She sat down carefully on her black leather chair and leaned back, staring up at the floor-to-ceiling bookshelves of her white office. 'Damnit! Where are you?' she swore. 'Oh, Nina, please get my brain waves! I need you!' She grabbed her date book and began to furiously flip the pages. If she's with Omar and is having fun, she could be gone who knows how long! ' Adele slammed the book closed and thought. It could be too late.

'Oh, Countess! How could I not be having a wonderful time?' Nina lay on the bed with shopping bags around her. Their shiny labels attested to forays into Asprey's, Liberty, Laura Ashley, Fortnum & Mason, and Harrod's. 'What we do is have breakfast brought up to the room and we get dressed walking past each other from closet to closet from the bed to the bathroom and did I tell you? There's a living room!'

The Countess cooed trans-Atlantically. 'But, of course, darling!'

'And then Chester is down in front of the hotel in the Daimler and he drives us away into this amazing traffic situation with dozens of black taxis and little cars called minis and . . .' The Countess interrupted and Nina answered. 'We go out every night. We had pheasant last night at the Savoy Grill and we went to the theatre the night before that and to the ballet at Covent Garden the night before that and there's a restaurant called Odette's that has hundreds of different little mirrors on the walls, all framed, and arranged one on top of the other. Do you know it might be fun to do a bathroom like that . . . and oh, yes, I've been to the Tower and the Tate, and to the Victoria and Albert and Chester says I'm to call it the V & A . . .' Nina chattered on. 'You mean you don't mind if I stay?' Nina crossed her stockinged legs and pushed the pillow higher behind her head. The cream suit had certainly been a good idea to bring. Today she wore it with a taupe silk blouse and chunky earrings of topaz that Omar had bought from Carrington's after they'd admired them in the window. 'Just a few more day, but tell me if you need me!' Nina plunged in again. 'Promise me you'll tell me and I'll be on the next plane. Really!'

Nina listened as the Countess said nothing was happening except Dorothy had a touch of flu so hadn't come in for the past four days.

'Countess, do I hear violin music?' Nina toyed with the flowered silk scarf in her lap as she listened and then said, 'I should tell you, too, that we might have to go to Paris. Oh, how boring, I told Omar. *Have* to go to Paris he told me in a really gloomy way last night. Some meeting.' The two women made their goodbyes with Nina at last replacing the little cream-coloured receiver on the bedside table.

The Countess sighed loudly as she put the phone down in New York and pulled the scarlet negligee across one bare breast. Oh, I forgot to tell her Adele telephoned! Probably not urgent.

The well-muscled man, perhaps in his late forties, stood entirely naked at the foot of her canopied bed with sheets trailing in every direction; the brocaded bedspread was

212

beneath his bare size-eleven feet. He placed the violin under his chin and with eyes closed began to play again. 'Oh, dear,' murmured the Countess.

'Vut ees eet, my precious?'

'Well, Vladimir, I either tell Nina about you or else I go out and buy a stereo.'

Nina reached for the cup of tea on the silver tray and thought: How perfectly content I am in this glorious hotel reading *The Importance of Being Ernest* with the rain splashing down outside. Chester had driven her to the National Portrait Gallery and she'd seen Oscar Wilde's photograph: a young man with smooth dark hair looking languid in a sort of nineteenth-century smoking jacket. Buying the book at a corner bookshop had seemed an obvious thing to do. Besides, she was a little tired of the straight guidebooks. Omar had been rolling his eyes under her enthusiastic onslaught of information at dinner the evening before. Must say 'evening' and not 'night' unless I mean sleeping time, she reminded herself. The olive green velvet sofa was soft under her fingers as she plucked a crumb of bread from its surface. Cucumber sandwiches! Who would ever have dreamed I'd be in England eating cucumber sandwiches! She looked across the sitting room to the open double doors of the bedroom. And with Omar.

The phone began to ring and she reached for the extension on the little marble-topped table beside her. 'Hi!' She grabbed the gold pencil and the Claridge's notepad. 'No, I'll be here. I slogged around half the day and decided to be sensible and get dry after lunch. No, it was fine. Just a salad at some little place in Knightsbridge.' She listened with pencil poised. 'The desk in the bedroom or the top drawer out in the sitting room desk?' She groaned in fun. 'Yes, Omar! I can handle it! I'll probably be here for the rest of the day but at least' – she turned and looked out at the rain pelting the windows – 'until he arrives.' She listened. 'Okay. I'll make a reservation for tonight and surprise you. Bye.'

Nina stood and stockingfooted walked across the thick carpet into the bedroom. Prettier than any house I've ever been in, had gòne through her mind as her suitcases had been deposited by the porter . . . a week ago. Ten days ago? Nina opened the top drawer and pulled out the dark red folder. 'Oooooh,' she cried as page after page fell to the floor. On her knees she despaired of ever getting them in order again. They were telexes. Dozens and dozens. Something about oil drilling equipment. Getting it to Beirut. From Frankfurt. From Amsterdam. Telexes concerning bank accounts in Switzerland. Money transferred from Milan to Geneva. From Geneva to Milan. And oil drilling equipment being shipped from France to Asmara, Ethiopia.

Oil in Ethiopia? Nina tried to arrange the pages by dates but there were so many and after a few minutes she simply stacked them face-up inside the open file. The top one she read sitting on the celadon green rug as her tea got cold in the other room.

SARKEX OKAYS SHIPMENT MARCH 21 WITH DEPOSIT REGULAR ACCOUNT. TWO HUNDRED FIFTY THOUSAND POUNDS TO ARRIVE GENEVA NO LATER THAN MARCH 18. GOODS TOP CONDITION. END-USER CERTIFICATES. TELEX AGENT GENEVA IMMEDIATE DECISION REQUIRED. REGARDS. SARKEX LONDON.

Two hundred and fifty thousand pounds, thought Nina. Why, that was over five hundred thousand dollars! A half a million dollars! She reached for one telex after another and skimmed the contents. All deposits to 'regular account' in Geneva or in Zurich and several concerning a bank in a place called Guernsey.

The knock on the door startled her and she hastily, a little guiltily, rose to her feet.

'I'm Mr Sarkis's secretary,' said the young blond man in the dark blue suit.

His umbrella dripped on to the rug as Nina invited him in and then, thinking that she should, offered him a cup of tea.

'No, no thank you. I have to get back to the office.' He nodded as she handed him the folder and was gone.

214

Nina lounged in the enormous tub full of bubbles and tried to concentrate on Ernest and his problems with a house in the country, the nonexistent brother who was always in trouble and the best friend who was making life more complicated with every scene. After a few minutes she dropped the book over the side on to the thick white bathmat then sank up to her neck in the hot water. What is bothering me? she asked herself. She reached for the Floris soap and answered aloud, 'I don't know.'

That night at dinner she wore the pearl choker that Omar had given her. In the centre was one sapphire banded in tiny seed pearls. Nina reached up to touch it often, which pleased him.

'I love to give you presents, my little fox.' He reached for her hand and brought it to his lips. 'Do you know why?'

She shook her head. She'd pinned her hair up loosely and curling tendrils fell on her long pale neck. Nina was quiet; she hadn't been able to shake the mood of the afternoon which had fallen upon her like a cool mist.

'Because you always are as pleased as if it were the first present you've ever received in your life.'

Nina smiled. 'No man has ever given me presents before unless it's been at college with someone hiding a Hershey bar behind his back, or if you count a bottle of champagne . . .' Nina paused. 'I know my mother would say I should never accept gifts of jewellery from you but . . .' She shrugged in the royal blue bolero. 'And I never should have let you buy this either!' She touched the green and blue plaid taffeta dress beneath the short jacket.

'But it's fun for you, isn't it?' Omar winked.

Nina leaned forward. 'Omar, am I your mistress?'

He laughed at that. Really laughed out loud and then kissed her hand with fervour. 'Nina, don't you think it's a bit late to ask?'

'No,' she answered. 'I don't think it's too late. I want to know.'

Seeing her face, he tried to mirror her concern. 'Do you want to be? Does it appeal to you?' She was silent, watching him as he continued. 'Don't you think, the year is a little off

215

for that?' His eyes twinkled. When she didn't respond he kept on. 'I don't know what you want, little one.' A finger stroked one of her high cheekbones as she tried to ignore that sexual tension between them. 'I thought you were an independent woman of the twentieth century with your own job, learning something with the Countess, paying your own rent, and with lovely wide wings to fly as you please . . .' He brushed her shoulder and his hand made a 'shhh' noise as it rubbed against the taffeta puffed sleeve.

Nina reached for the glass of port and thought, how could we two be so far apart in our thinking and how could I only discover it now? Or did I know it and it just seems he had to spell it out? But how long can I follow the Countess's advice? How long can I stick to the standards of the peanut butter conferences? With great acting skill, she would congratulate herself later as she removed her eye make-up back at Claridge's, she smiled widely. A dazzling smile, really it was, she would report to the Countess.

'Oh, Omar, don't you realize what I really want from you?' He shook his head and she thought: Oh, Nina, don't say it! Be careful. Minefields ahead. Quicksand and trap doors. She fairly cooed, 'I want what I have. To be kept in my gilded cage at Claridge's wearing beautiful negligees and eating chocolates except when Chester drives me out for shopping or you take me . . .' Her eyes took in the crowd at Annabel's. The people were glossy and everyone seemed to be oh-so-happy. She finished her sentence. 'To places like this.'

Omar stared at her. His face was serious. His dark brows knitted together over the fathomless onyx eyes. 'You confuse me,' he said as he lit the Cuban cigar. A bright red glittering pulse of heat showed when he inhaled. He shook out the match and looked at her again. 'That's a big part of the attraction, you know.'

Nina sipped her port and breathed in the aroma of the tobacco. She congratulated herself yet again for not losing the game.

They flew to Paris the next day at noon. For Nina it was a Citroën Pallas with a new driver named Maurice, a new

216

hotel, but this time small and filled with antiques, and a new chance to be fey and lively and to make up for the conversation at Annabel's the night before. Why do I feel I must make up for it? she wondered as she hung the cream silk dress. The wardrobe door had a full-length mirror inside and its reflection showed a tall young woman with ivory skin and jet black hair wearing a lace teddy of green silk and a wisp of matching lace panties. What is bothering me? I am in Paris! With the man I love. The Countess won't need me for at least another week and . ... do I love him? Does he love me? Have my southern sensibilities caught up with me? He's married. How simple. That must be it. One word speaking volumes. Nina pulled the taffeta plaid dress from her suitcase and gave it a shake. The full skirt swirled widely in front of her. Married. And I cannot have him.

But do I want to marry him? Nina daydreamed of Omar smiling across the table from her in a candlelit restaurant and taking her hand. 'I'm happy with you. I love you. Will you marry me?' Then he would tell her that she had made him realize he had no marriage at all, that she had made him realize what he wanted and then he'd say, 'I want you. For ever.' Nina's daydreams had progressed to his bending over her as she lay in a pristine white hospital bed and with tears of happiness, kissing her and then their firstborn. But Omar wouldn't cry! thought Nina, sinking on to the little side chair of plum velvet. And I can't imagine crying in front of him either! And a crying baby? Nina sighed and with elbows on knees crushed the taffeta in her lap. He's never even said he loved me. Omar. Perfect in bed. Perfectly dressed. Every black hair in place Omar. The emotion might fluster him and Omar is never flustered. I'm the flustered one. The one who grabs forks for artichokes and stepped on Mayor Beame's foot in the Carlyle elevator and who had to go home to change clothes before the Addington dinner party. But I make love to him and I love to be with him and I love it that he has picked me when I see the way other women stare at him, watch us. The Countess would say I have more than enough. And Mother would say I have nothing.

Nina walked to the wardrobe and hung the dress beside

the dozen others. A little net-covered bag of sachet on a pink satin ribbon hung from the neck of each padded pink satin hanger. She turned away and began to pull shoe bags from the suitcases which sat open on the luggage rack. Nina dropped the black peau de soie heels on the floor and then the brown alligator pumps and then the black patents with the flat grosgrain bows. The Aubusson rug beneath them bloomed with pastel flowers. Maybe I should simply tell him what I want and stop the playing but . . . but it's the playing that he likes. Nina frowned as she remembered his face as he'd listened to her the night before. And if I stop playing too soon then I have no chance at all of his wanting me. 'But he does want you!' the Countess had said a couple of hundred times with raised goblet of skim milk. Nina could hear her mother's voice, and Ellen's too. 'But not the way he should want you!' is what they'd say.

Nina closed the wardrobe door, then turned and marched into the bathroom. In the doorway she spun around and surveyed the pretty room with its Empire furniture, its pale lavender walls, its silk swagged curtains printed with violets. Two more days in Paris, then we'll be on our way back to New York. Two more days of soaking this in while Omar has meetings. Two more lovely dinners, two more divine nights of making love with a man who may not love me. He won't say it anyway. Nina said, 'No' aloud and then stalked decisively in bare feet back to the wardrobe. She clasped its silver handle and pulled it open then began to yank all the dresses down. She turned to the yawning suitcases and began to crush them in.

The taxi slowed to a halt in the slush of 90th Street and Nina scrambled through the dirty snow to the wet sidewalk. She had left New York with one bag and now had two. The second contained new clothes, new shoes, three books on antiques, Floris soaps from Harrod's and *The Importance of Being Ernest*.

Nina paid the driver and then heroically made it up the steps and into the building without stopping to rest.

She struggled up the steep stairs, counting the flights as always, and then fumbled with the key, miraculously in the zipper part of her handbag where she had put it two countries ago. As the door swung open, the phone began to ring. Nina almost laughed with delight. My phone! My kitchen!

She was shocked to hear Adele's desperate voice, 'I'm coming right over! Thank God you're back!' and then the line went dead.

Within ten minutes Adele was coming in the kitchen door, stomping snow from her high boots and sweeping off the wide grey cape.

Nina embraced her. 'You're pale as a ghost! What is going on! What does that phone call mean? What . . . what are you doing in New York? How did you know I was back? Look . . .' she gestured towards her bags, still closed, festooned with airline tags.

Adele was thinking: She's here. Nina will know what to do. It's going to be all right.

'Do you want something hot or cold?' demanded Nina, as she yanked off her coat and pulled blue jeans from a bureau drawer in the other room. 'Come back into the kitchen, Adele, I think it's warmer.'

Adele stood in the living room, thinking of last summer. Snow was pouring past the windows like that fluff from dandelions when you blow on them.

Nina admitted, 'I'm afraid there is nothing, absolutely nothing, but hard liquor. I turned off the fridge.'

'Fine with me. Let's go all the way.'

Nina walked quickly past her and into the living room to the drinks cabinet. She pulled vodka out, and a bottle of scotch and then, with a shrug, grabbed the Grand Marnier. What the blazes was going on with Adele, anyway?

Across from each other at the kitchen table, both girls were in blue jeans, in knee socks, and either girl had a chair opposite her as a foot rest. Looking rather weary, they drank a toast.

'Here's to us!' Nina lifted her glass. 'Who's better? Damn few!' She grinned. 'Learned that in London from a

219

Scotsman we had dinner with.' I wonder what Omar will think, flashed through her mind.

Adele stared at the kitchen as though she'd never been here before. The plants hung from the mantel, and the old-fashioned stove in front of what had once been a fireplace looked warm, even though it wasn't. The black and white linoleum still startled her. The bathroom door was open and she could see the tub with its wide green racing stripe, like some magical vehicle from a children's story, about to take off for a better place, filled with giggling children and teddy bears. The Mexican paper flowers of yellow and fuschia and orange in the copper vase on the window sill were bright against the black and white back yard, silently filling with snow on the other side of the glass panes.

'Those paper flowers look more real than the sky and the snow,' she said. 'Might as well tell you my news and get it over with.'

Nina turned sharply to face her. It wasn't like Adele to murmur strange things about flowers and snow.

'I'm pregnant.' Adele lifted her glass of Grand Marnier in a mock toast to herself. She continued in an even, smooth voice. 'It's not Paul's. Those are the facts.' Nina stared at her. Adele suddenly looked helpless. Her face seemed to crumple as if it had taken all her energy to say the last two sentences. 'I . . . I . . . I kept thinking.' Her voice cracked. 'I thought that if you came back we could think of something to do . . . I thought if you were here . . .'

Nina pulled her chair closer and then leaned forward and took Adele's hands. If only she'd cry, Nina was thinking. Somehow this is worse than if she were weeping. There is some terrible courage inside her making her talk and talk instead of dissolving in tears.

'I came here a few days ago and checked into the Waldorf, and I've been staying in my room, thinking that any minute you'd answer your phone. The second time I called the Countess she didn't know where you were except "probably Paris". Your mother didn't know anything. I called the Ritz, the George V. I thought when you got back we could . . .'

Nina held her hands and listened. Obviously, Adele had

220

been talking to herself for days. Alone in a hotel room, how wretched she must feel. And I never think anyone is dependent upon me; I thought it didn't matter if I descended in a pumpkin next May, bearing presents and stories. I never thought anyone needed me.

'Okay, Adele, when did this happen? I mean, how late are you?'

Jesus, seven weeks pregnant. A one-night stand. He was nice enough, they had drunk too much, she had been curious to compare him with Paul. No, he didn't know. No, no one knew. Kim had flown to Hawaii because her father had had a heart attack and Adele had evidently taken the test, continuing to work and to telephone Nina's apartment all night long, night after night, and at last had caught a flight to New York.

'Paul always comes out,' Adele rambled on and, at first, Nina thought she meant to California. 'I forgot to mention that he had to come out.'

God, groaned Nina silently. Kid stuff and adult problems. How like Briarcliff it was. The godawful waiting for the twelfth day of lateness and then the test and then the next afternoon's results and then the celebration at dinner with lifted milk glasses and plates of chocolate chip cookies. In all the years at Briarcliff, only one friend had ever actually been pregnant, and she came back from Puerto Rico with a tan. Amazing, when you consider all the screwing we did and how screwed up we were. Nina could well remember the voices. 'Well, if I did go on the Pill, I might do it, and I'm not sure I want to, yet, so I won't go on the Pill.' 'The diaphragm seems so planned,' they'd all complained. 'Ugh, it's so unromantic.' 'Well, Freddy says he can't feel me if he wears anything. He says why should he wear a raincoat?'

'Adele, does Paul know anything?'

She shook her head, her blonde hair swinging, catching the light. 'He doesn't even know I'm here. I told Melinda at Grafton's that I'd be gone for a while. I insinuated that it was something to do with Kim in Hawaii and asked her to field any questions.'

'Okay.' Think. Think. Think, Nina was inwardly screaming. 'So Paul will call your apartment and he'll get your answering machine, and he'll call the office and he'll get a vague excuse.' Not good, she said to herself. 'Adele, look at me.' Adele's eyes were too bright and she seemed to have trouble focusing on Nina's face before her. 'When did you last eat?'

Adele shrugged and managed a tiny sad smile. 'You sound like me!' and then, with a ragged laugh, she began to cry.

Nina took the brandy away and handed her a box of Kleenex, then she went to her wardrobe and pulled on her tall knee-high black boots. God, they felt good! How she'd longed for them in London. She pulled gloves from a top shelf and her Isadora scarf. 'Come on! On with your coat! We have a lot of things to do!'

Adele blew her nose and looked confused, and then began to obey orders.

'Adele! You came without gloves? You should be shot! Here, take these.'

Out in the snow Nina hailed a cab and they leapt back as its tyres sprayed an arc of black water at them. Once inside, Nina told the driver to take them to the Waldorf.

'Got your key?' Adele nodded and they strode for the elevator. In five minutes all Adele's clothes were packed, the bathroom looked like a hotel bathroom again and they were in the elevator descending to the lobby. 'Want me to do it?' asked Nina. Adele nodded and let Nina use her credit card, only signing the voucher.

In forty minutes they were back in Nina's kitchen and Nina was making a grocery list. First, to be warm; second, to be fed; and then we think. She felt she'd been put in charge of a confused child. Adele was frail. She was exhausted with worry and the sharp edge of panic that must have got her on the plane to New York had dulled to an acceptance of the worst. She was paralysed in the situation, and all she could think of was to tell Nina and to stay out of sight.

'Okay, listen, Adele. I am going out to buy steaks for us and eggs and milk and all kinds of things. Brain food! Take any closet space you can get and unpack and watch the news.

222

See you in twenty minutes.' Then she ran back to call a warning in the kitchen door. 'Whatever you do, don't answer the phone!'

'What about the Countess or your mother?' wailed Adele.

'You're not here and I'm not here. Don't touch the answering machine; it'll look funny if it was off all the time I was away and now it's on. Just forget the phone. I'll be back soon.'

Nina strolled up and down the wide aisles of Gristede's, revelling in the clean floors and the bright packages wrapped in shiny cellophane. Hard to believe I had breakfast in London this morning, then lunch in Paris, Nina marvelled, as she tossed cookies and cans of baked beans and a chicken and potatoes, steaks, onions, and butter and milk and cereal into the metal cart. She staggered up the stairs with two bags of groceries, realizing she had never cooked for herself. This was going to be a new experience.

'What are we going to do?' she asked Adele as they finished dinner. The steaks had been a good idea. Adele has some colour in her face, thought Nina. 'What about telling Paul?' she persisted.

Adele looked alarmed. 'I can't. I can't. Oh, Nina! How could I tell him? "Oh, well, I'm pregnant. I went to bed with somebody. He didn't mean a thing," or, "Yes, I'm pregnant, I really adore him but not enough to marry . . ."'

'What do you think about an abortion? Tomorrow, or the next day. What do you think?'

Adele stared out at the falling show. 'I know it would solve a lot of problems, wouldn't it? But, even if I did have it, and I did cover my tracks, and Kim lied for me and said I'd been with her, even if Paul believed all that . . .' She gasped, as though about to cry again. 'I'd know. I'd always know.' Adele was thinking: I've made love to three men in my life. One, I never want to see again; one, I would love to have a child by but can't; and one is the man I am going to marry. If he'll still have me. She spoke: 'Nina, it isn't fair! I'm the one who was never late for class, I never jay walk, I never tell lies, I never do anything really *wroooong*! I grew up taught to do

223

the right thing! And now I can't get out of this!' She banged her fist on the table.

Good, thought Nina. The dinner has given her strength. 'You can get out of it. We just have to think how.' She hesitated. 'What if I call the Countess and ask her to come over here? Now, tonight. She's older and maybe she could help.'

Adele shook her head. 'I can't have an abortion, Nina. I could have done that in San Francisco. My doctor told me about a clinic.'

Nina sighed. Why did you come to me? she wanted to shout. I don't know how to help you. My best friend. I love you but I don't know how to help.

Her unspoken question was answered. 'I came to you because I want you to help me with Paul.'

'Look, he's wanted to get married for ages. Let him marry you if you insist upon having the baby, but you must tell him it isn't his.'

'He'll know it isn't his. We haven't made love since November and this happened in December.'

'Okay, he'll know. That takes some of the burden off you, because he'll be making a decision to stand by you. He is the only person who really has to accept what happened and has to accept the child, and he will be the only one to know it isn't his. I don't count.'

Adele smiled. It was a wan, grateful smile. 'I know you don't.'

'Now, let's see. If you tell him you are pregnant, what could be his reactions? They could run the gamut from rage to . . .'

'From rage to telling me he never wants to see me again.' Adele got up and opened the fridge. 'Chocolate chip ice cream? Did I see it before?'

'I was a little worried about you two hours ago, but now I know you're okay. Use the big dishes on the top shelf and Mother's silver dessert spoons. We might as well pig-out in style.'

'Milano Pepperidge Farm cookies!' shouted Adele with the joy of discovery.

224

Nina laughed. 'Just toss me the whole bag. Now, do you think he will tell you it's finished? Do you honestly think that?' Nina was thinking: Good riddance if he would be so judgemental towards someone he's professed to love for so long.

'I don't know.' Adele dug into the ice cream. 'There's a chance.'

'Do you want to marry him? Now?' questioned Nina.

'That's the best I can hope for at this stage, isn't it?'

Nina didn't answer. What was the best thing? 'If you have an abortion, and plenty of people do, every day, then that's one thing. If you decide to have the baby, then you can take care of it by yourself. You have money. You can quit your job, get a larger apartment in New York or out there. If you opt for here, I'll help you all I can. That goes without saying. Or you can have Paul at your side maybe as a friend. Maybe he won't want to marry you and claim paternity. Maybe he won't be self-righteous about it and throw you out into the snow, but maybe he'll say something like "Let's wait a while."'

'I hadn't thought of that,' admitted Adele, looking down and counting eleven chocolate chips.

'Or he might say "Let's get married. Let's have the baby. I will love it as my own and in two years we will begin the rest of our family."'

'That would be great of him, wouldn't it?' The blonde stared into space. She couldn't hear him saying that. Would he say that? Adele remembered overhearing Paul at Ivy Club comment on a friend's date: 'A slut. I don't know how he trusts her from one weekend to the next.' Maybe he'll never trust me again. 'Slut,' she said aloud.

'Oh, come on! You're hardly a slut!' retorted Nina. 'Do you think that Paul has never touched anyone but you? All these months in New York?'

Adele nodded.

'Well, I bet you're wrong!'

'Do you know something?' Adele asked, leaning forward in her chair.

'No! I only know that you've been sustaining this

"engagement" for – what is it, six months? – across the continent, and there are plenty of ski weekends that Paul goes to Vermont, and there are plenty of times when he must join friends from the bank for a drink, and there are plenty of parties where Paul must be a welcome male guest . . .'

Adele nodded. Nina's speech was not having the effect Nina hoped it would. Instead of doubting Paul's fidelity, she suddenly thought, I'm lucky to have him. There are hundreds, even thousands of single women in New York who could be after him. 'Maybe getting married to Paul is the best thing that could happen,' she said, sweeping her light hair back. Her voice had a hopeless quality to it.

'We'll talk in the morning.' Nina went to the wardrobe room and pulled out the fold-away cot. The two of them made it up with flowered sheets and a yellow quilt and wheeled it into the second bedroom. 'There are clean towels on the shelf above the mirror in the bathroom. Wake me if you're desperate for anything. It's not the Waldorf!'

Nina lay in bed, staring at the prints on the walls; her bedside green and white enamelled lamp cast warm shadows over the rocking chair and the desk that had been hers since she had been a child. Her mother had shipped it up as a surprise soon after she had moved into the apartment. Its brass drawer pulls gleamed in the light. Mother. I should call her. The Countess. I should call her, she thought sleepily. But tonight, I am not here. Adele is not here either. She rose up on her elbows. The kitchen light was still on. 'G'night, Adele! Sweet dreams!'

'G'night, Nina. Thanks. Thanks for everything,' echoed a tired voice.

For the first time since crossing the Atlantic, Nina thought of Omar. What will he do? she wondered drowsily and then with dismay realized she hadn't really left him for a point of honour, she'd left him with the hope he'd pursue her. Frustration gripped Nina. All the sure-fire attention-getters that worked so smoothly with other men didn't seem to faze the Lebanese. They never had. Am I losing my touch? Am I not so attractive any more? she worried fleetingly. But no, because when Omar was away she received plenty of invitations and plenty of notice at parties. Nina turned over restlessly and rearranged the blanket. Yes, plenty of notice, even adoration at times. But who really wanted it? I don't want Tad to think I'm out-of-this-world wonderful because, even if he is nice, he's dull as dishwater. And there's Peter Richardson and there's Stuart Morley and there's Sam and there's Sandy Decker and . . . oh, God! Nina pounded her fist into her pillow. This is like counting sheep! I'll just lapse into a coma from boredom. I want Omar and I don't know why I can't . . . He's different. I don't know where I stand so he makes me try so hard. I try to be spectacular with him and with anyone else at dinner I just play and they eat out of my hand like pigeons and it is so . . . so predictable. Nina thrashed over on to her back and stared into the darkness. And Omar is unpredictable. Will he fly back to New York and plead with me to marry him? She smiled, only half awake, thinking of travelling across Europe with him, planning which restaurant they'd have dinner in, meeting his friends, and charming all his business associates. Then maybe in a year when I get tired of that, perhaps we'll buy an apartment in New York and the Countess and I can do it up. She conveniently forgot that Omar already owned an apartment on Fifth Avenue in her excitement over a new one, one that was hers, as his wife. She conveniently forgot he had a wife. Nina's mind danced on; the need for sleep was dulling logic. And maybe we'll have something in Paris, too, and maybe . . . Nina closed her eyes and before she could decide on yet another city in which to take up residence, she was sound asleep.


James Lieberman folded his *Wall Street Journal*, tucked it under his arm, then leaned forward and spoke to the driver. 'Won't be going to the country today so you can have the weekend off beginning now unless Mrs Lieberman needs you for shopping.'

The long black Lincoln parked in front of Salomon Brothers, the door was opened, and the rather short stocky figure in the dark blue pinstriped suit stepped out. Almost March, the slush is turning to puddles, went through his mind as he passed the uniformed doorman, who touched his hat respectfully.

James Jeremy Lieberman would have been described by almost any Protestant as 'Jewish looking'. His hair was coal black and a bit wiry in texture, his straight black brows were full and rested above the darkest brown eyes. His beard was heavy, which meant he shaved very carefully in the morning and often a second time before a dinner party. It gave his strong jaw a slightly blue-black cast by three in the afternoon. Lieberman's gestures were those of a man used to giving orders – an aggressive walk, a tilt of his clefted chin, the direct gaze. All conveyed a faintly 'animal quality', a defeated tennis partner had once joked.

He liked to arrive early. It was half past seven, according to his Rolex, so he could telephone London and Zurich without being interrupted by local calls. Eileen appeared at eight and brought his morning coffee in, handing him a typed list of his appointments. When she left his office he reached for the fat round Roladex and separated the tightly pressed cards in the Ps until he found the listing. First, the room. This was something he never allowed Eileen to take care of for him. He enjoyed doing it himself.

'This is Mr Lieberman. I'd like my usual suite for the afternoon. I'll be arriving at two and checking out at six.' He waited on the line. 'Yes, I prefer 1011.' No sense in using phony names. There are hundreds of reasons why I might have business at the Plaza. It's a good place for a meeting. He smiled. 'Let me give you my American Express card number now.' All arranged. He replaced the receiver and thought how civilized credit cards were. It meant that afterwards he could walk through the lobby and out the revolving doors as though he'd just had a drink in the Oak Bar. Nothing to it. The notation on his AMEX bill didn't bother him. Eileen saw it, but she was a bright girl. Bright enough to realize it would behoove her to play dumb about certain things. He will have gone by now, decided James. He flipped open his brown calf address book and punched out

228

another number. 'Hello,' he purred when he had her on the line. 'Two thirty, same place.'

She answered, 'Fine', with no emotion in her voice at all. The maid a few yards away making her bed could have sworn that she was confirming a dentist appointment. 'Thank you for calling,' she said in her best prep school voice, which caused Lieberman to feel a tug in his groin. He put down the phone and clasped his hands behind his neck, leaning back in the chair thinking: Six more hours, then three with her, narrow it down to about two if you subtract shower and getting dressed time. God, it took her so long to get into her clothes again. And so little time to get out of them. So, two delicious hours with her and then there was the next Friday and the next and the next as long as there are Fridays.

'I'm having lunch with Paul,' announced Adele when Nina entered the kitchen, groggy and wondering what time it was. 'I've called him and told him I want to talk and he sounded happy that I'm here. Didn't ask me anything over the phone.' She paused. 'We're meeting at the Four Seasons at high noon.' Adele was trying hard to sound unconcerned.

Nina nodded, reaching for a Diet Pepsi and snapping it open. 'Oh, God! I can't watch!' Adele shook her head and turned away. 'Do you mind if I take a shower first? I want to wash my hair.'

'All yours.' Nina sat at the kitchen table and listened to the water running. 'The Four Seasons?' she exclaimed aloud. That's not the right restaurant for this kind of news. Nina made a face and swigged Diet Pepsi. Poor Adele. The appropriate setting. Some place where no one can hear a word you're saying. Definitely not the Four Seasons.

Thwak. Thwak. Thwak. Paul's legs pumped as he gracefully leapt from side to centre from back to front of the squash court. Thwak! he slammed the ball. Thwak. Sweat poured into his eyes until he thought he'd have to tear off the face mask. The muscles in his calves ached. His shoulder cried out in pain. Thwak. Thwak. He continued. Damn her, damn her. Thwak. Damn her. Thwak. All these years of waiting for her. Thwak. Pregnant. Thwak. Bitch. Silly bitch. Thwak. Can't hold her liquor. Thwak. Paul thought of her face at lunch. Ever beautiful but etched with strain.

'There's no right way to tell you this,' she had said and he had been sure she was breaking off the engagement. No, worse than that. Was it worse than that? A choice. She'd dared to say I have a choice? Thwak. Go to San Francisco. I don't mind. Thwak. Get a job and prove something to yourself. I understand. Thwak. I'll wait. Thwak. Whatever you want. Thwak. Don't do me any favours, Adele. Thwak. Must say I was calm. I was reasonable. Thwak. Damn her. Thwak. Damn her to Hell! He threw his raquet with all his strength against the court wall and watched it splinter in half. The sharp noise it made echoed in the suddenly silent chamber and the blond young man in white clenched his fists and whispered, 'Damn her!' one last time.

Tory Forrest Wickham walked down Madison Avenue peering in the gallery windows. She stared at a group of stone sculptures in one without seeing them and then looked nervously at her tiny Cartier watch. Don't want to be late. Don't want to be early. Don't want to cross the street again with all the melting snow. Tory could feel rising excitement suffusing her just-bathed, freshly scented with Chloe, body. Her shoes of pale grey suede would be ruined if she continued to walk but she would arrive too early if she took a cab. She glanced down at her long legs in their faintly patterned stockings, and then rearranged the royal blue cape. Her grey Gianni Versace suit felt good and she knew she looked well in it. What would he say? What would he do this time? She licked her lips nervously and resisted the urge to push a strand of hair in place under the grey fedora.

'May I help you? Mrs Wickham, isn't it?' A young man in a dark suit stood at her elbow. Tory was confused but smiled. 'Oh, I'm just looking.' She recovered as she realized he had sprung from the interior of the gallery and that she must have been standing there on the sidewalk for too long. 'I rather like the sculpture of the woman in the centre.'

'Lovely, isn't it? Would you like to come in and have a closer look?'

'Oh, no, I'm on my way to the Symphony. Nice to see you again.' Tory nodded and left him staring at her elegant figure as she walked purposefully towards 72nd Street. She felt almost light-headed. Tory couldn't seem to swallow anything but tea for her Friday breakfast and lunch was out of the question. She looked at her watch again as she decided whether to take a cab or not. One stopped for her, slowing respectfully yards away to avoid showering her with dirty water and she thought: Fate, and got in. The taxi curved through a brown and white speckled with melting snow Central Park as she powdered her much photographed face. Moments later, she handed the driver a five-dollar bill and allowed the doorman to open and close the taxi door behind her. The revolving doors of the Plaza spun around, embracing her in shining glass and brass. The thought occurred to her – one door after another, opening and closing behind me. All these Friday afternoons, all these doors. Tory stepped decisively across the flowered carpet to the bank of elevators and found herself all too quickly taking deep breaths outside the suite on the tenth floor. She raised her grey-gloved hand and knocked, feeling a rush of warmth almost like a blush as she did so.

'Door's open. Come on in, for Chrissake,' came the deep voice she knew so well. Tory squared her shoulders and turned the knob. She was suffused with exhilaration and the usual stomach-knotting ache of fear.

The green fern-printed wallpaper matched the heavy damask curtains, which were held back with tasselled dark green ropes. A sofa covered in pale lettuce-coloured silk was placed in front of the fireplace with a dark green wing chair on either side, and a French drop-front desk was next to the armoire. Tall windows looked over Central Park, fast emptying of snow as the sun blazed forth. Grey clouds like a herd of dirty sheep were being blown above the trees.

James Lieberman was led across the room by an appendage which, like a divining rod, pointed directly at a bottle of scotch on the table by the window. He was wearing a pale blue finely striped shirt, a Brooks Brothers tie of dark blue silk, a pair of black wing-tip shoes, and dark blue socks. His bare legs were covered in thick black coarse hair. He poured himself a glass of Johnny Walker and sipped it as Tory stood with head down in the centre of the enormous sitting room.

'Take off your clothes,' he commanded. Instantly, she obeyed, pulling at her wide silver bracelets and then at the silk bow at her throat. Within a minute she was wearing nothing but blue lace-trimmed bikini panties. Lieberman loved her like this. He stared at her slender body. Her small breasts were round and firm, with small pointed pink nipples, and her collarbones showed faintly under alabaster skin. Her perfectly manicured fingers curved towards her milk white thighs. Lieberman could plainly see the V of blonde hair beneath the thin strip of silk. My whore. The very paleness of her, the red marks his hands left upon her flesh, excited him. She was the penultimate WASP. The product of several generations of WASPs, beginning with those first arrivals on the *Mayflower*. And I, thought Lieberman, am a Jew, who went to Harvard, but was kept out of the fraternities, who graduated magna cum laude but whose father worked in a haberdashery in Brooklyn.

Tory felt the tension in her arms and legs. How long will he make me stand this way? I can feel his dark eyes, his almost black eyes, on my body. Don't dare move or he will shout again. I want a drink. Why does he always drink in front of me and never offer it to me? She could hear him breathing as he took four steps on the thick pale green carpet towards her.

'Make love to me,' she gasped, as he tweaked one of her nipples between his broad thumb and one sausage finger.

'Not yet,' he mocked her, 'not yet.'

At six Victoria Elizabeth Forrest Wickham was reading the

232

New York *Times* editorial page in her white living room. She was wearing cream flannel trousers and a pink angora sweater. A large ruby ring glittered on one finger and a gold chain encircled her long neck. The maid came in on tiptoe to water the ficus trees in the corner and Tory snapped, 'Can't you do that when I'm not here? I've been gone most of the day.'

'Yes, ma'am,' came the apologetic murmur as the girl retreated.

Tory didn't know her name, and would not have recognized her on a street corner. Her body still sang with what he had done to her. Lieberman always made her beg, made her cry out, made her plead for it until . . . Tory crossed her legs and crushed the paper on her lap, for once forgetting what the ink of the New York *Times* could do to anything white. She stared out the window and thought of the dark face above her. Red, he became, dark red, almost beet red with the exertion, with the waiting. She could hear herself, could hear her own moans as though she were another person. She remembered her voice, disembodied, though she was excruciatingly aware of her body. That voice did not belong to her. She could hear herself cry for him. She saw it all over again, the green wallpaper and the sheets twisted around his dark hairy body and her pale legs. When he'd tied her wrists with the silk scarf she had wept and tried to claw his face, but the panic of being helpless under his rather rough tongue, under his stocky torso, under his thick fingers, had only added to her excitement. Everything's worth it, Tory thought. What would all this be called? Lieberman. The electricity from him a year ago at that partners' dinner had been enough to cause her to flush quite pinkly when they had at last been introduced. The call on the following Thursday had been a great chance for him to take. She could have complained to Charles. She thought of it. But no, she hadn't, of course. She had gone to the Plaza as instructed. She had known that once she crossed the threshold of the suite with the green fern wallpaper, she could never complain; she was on her own with a strange man on an illicit journey. It excited her that he had known she would keep the appointment. It had been dozens of Fridays ago, that first time, dozens of nonexistent concerts ago. She sighed and picked up the paper and shook it. Her hands trembled and her face felt warm.

Tory suddenly rose from the sofa and walked quickly through the front hall. The black and white Beardsleys in their poses of mischievous sexuality seemed to snicker as she passed. She went through her white bedroom and into the bathroom where she locked the door and dropped all her clothes beside her dressing table. One bare foot brushed the pale blue-skirted stool as she turned to face the mirror. Lovingly, she touched the dark purple bruise on her shoulder then her fingers brushed the red welts on one hip. Pain hadn't mattered at the time for it had been such a small part of all that had been happening. The intensity of him and of his leading her farther and farther down a path away from the Tory she inhabited all the other hours of her life, all the hours not spent with him, all the non-Friday afternoon hours blotted out everything else. The fear and the pain and the passion are all mixed up, all becoming one, thought Tory as she rubbed her sore wrists.


Nina opened the kitchen door as Adele came running up the stairs. 'Quick! What happened?'

Adele was smiling, face flushed with the cold. 'Ran the last flight. Pretty good for someone pregnant.'

'Well, what'd he say? How did he take it?'

Adele threw her arms around Nina and whispered slyly, 'Will you be my maid of honour?'

'Oh! Fantastic!' Nina returned the hug. 'When's it happening?'

'Well, I have to tell Mother, of course.' Adele turned down the corners of her mouth. 'But Paul was the worst part, and that's over.' She looked very sombre. 'He was ice cold to me, Nina.'

'He has to get used to it. It's pretty surprising news, after all.' She walked into the kitchen. 'Come on in. We have to celebrate. You grab the wine glasses and I'll get the milk!'

*

234

Tory knew the head of Tiffany's, so the invitations could be ready in twelve days, then off in the mail after a working weekend with two elderly ladies addressing on card tables in the living room with pots of coffee and a tray of sandwiches nearby. Of course, that meant another two or three weeks. The earliest the wedding could possibly be and not attract undue attention was the last week of March. Adele would be three months plus, but that couldn't be helped. Speculation at the other end of the year would be dealt with when the time came. But, of course, hints could be dropped in a few months about early births running in the family. 'Why, Adele was born premature and on the way to the hospital,' she only had to say once to a dear friend at a cocktail party. Small and at home meant only Nina as maid of honour, which was wise. The reception would be large, but that posed no problem; help could be hired for the day.

Tory flipped back and forth in her address book, reaching for the phone. She was highly organized and always had been. This was far easier than planning a fund raiser for the Memorial Sloan-Kettering Cancer Center or a gala for the American Ballet Theatre. Flowers. Music. Champagne. Several cases of Dom Perignon. She wrote, 'consult Charles', for he had a well-stocked wine cellar. The dress for Adele should be bought immediately and there was the photograph for the New York *Times* to be lined up. Bachrach could do that. The list grew and grew, but so did the border of angled check marks on the left-hand margin as each notation was accomplished.

The list was the first thing that Lieutenant Farwell pulled from the Hermes black calf handbag. He noted the thick rounded prep-school letters in bold black ink and then dropped the paper into a manila envelope followed by the hairbrush, the Christian Dior lipstick, the tiny spray bottle of Chloe. The Gucci wallet was quickly unsnapped and examined. Four fifty-dollar bills, a twenty, a ten, and three ones. The credit cards from Saks, Bergdorf Goodman, Bendel's, Bloomingdale's, Bonwit Teller, gave the lieutenant all the information he needed.

He turned as the ambulance attendants pulled the black rubber bag over the naked woman. They exited, bearing the stretcher between them through the open doorway of the green and white room and down the hall to the elevator where they waited. Lieutenant Farwell put his hand on the phone and then, remembering the lecture he'd given his precinct only last week about public relations, removed it. 'Okay to use this? Just one call.'

'Of course. Dial nine for an outside line. I'll be downstairs in my office if you need me for anything else.'

The assistant manager, Lester Burroughs, wiped his long thin face with a white handkerchief and glancing around one last time as though assuring himself that all was in order, walked through the still open door. He carefully closed it behind him, wondering if he should go back and use the suite's bathroom. Lester's hands shook as he fumbled for the key among dozens of others on the chain and he hoped the ambulance attendants had not noticed. He pressed himself against the wall of the elevator as they entered with the stretcher and concentrated on inserting the small silver-coloured key on the brass plaque above the button marked PH.

'It won't stop between here and the lobby now.'

'Christ! No back elevator for stiffs!' muttered the stocky black man.

'Afraid not,' said Lester softly. He was conscious of heat under his arms and a strong churning sensation in his stomach. The body bag made a 'scrunch' noise as they adjusted it and the assistant manager winced.

'Goddamn, this is my first time at the Plaza and it's right through the fuckin' lobby.'

'I'll get out first and undo the revolving doors. They fold back flat . . .' explained Lester as he searched for another key and worried that he might be sick. Please, he silently prayed, don't let me throw up in the lobby in front of a hundred people. Please, dear God, give me five minutes to get to the men's room. He wiped his thin face once again and took a deep breath as the doors silently opened. The key was clutched between fingers wet with sweat.

Charles Wickham walked hurriedly from the dinner table to the living room. The trout almondine had been served and he'd had two glasses of white wine and still no Tory. It wasn't like her to be late and he was a little annoyed that she would keep him waiting. The maid handed him the phone and soundlessly disappeared down the hall and through the door to the pantry. She didn't hear him gasp for breath, she didn't see his face go white; she had no way of knowing that Charles Wickham would never be quite the same man again.

'Oh, bloody Christ!' swore the Countess aloud at the long dining room table. She put down the paper and carefully spread the square of wholewheat toast with strawberry jam. The New York *Post* headline fairly screamed the news. DEAD IN PLAZA LOVE NEST. Tory Forrest Wickham's face beamed below. The entire front page was devoted to her likeness, smiling as only she could smile, blonde hair fairly gleaming with sunlight, eyes sparkling as though she were being toasted with champagne. She turned the page.

'Tory Forrest Wickham, dubbed "The American Classic" by the fashion world, was found dead last night in a suite at the Plaza Hotel. The coroner's report was not yet available as to the exact cause of death but her nude body was removed at 7:25 p.m. last night and taken to the city morgue.'

Another column began with the headline: POLICE SEEK LOVER. 'The suite was registered under the name of James J. Lieberman who is a partner of Salomon Brothers, the investment banking firm, where Charles Lesley Wickham is Chairman.'

'Holy Christ,' whispered the Countess. She skimmed the *Post*, hurriedly reading a description of Tory's fame twenty-odd years ago and of her marriage to the entrepreneur, Charles Wickham. It listed her clubs, her favourite charities, her work with Sloan-Kettering, her interest in the ballet and the symphony. The *Post* dwelled on her fund-raising activities and on the benevolence of her wealthy husband. She turned the page and pushed it away.

The Countess sipped her coffee, staring at the painting across the room. It was crooked. At least I know that Dorothy cleans, went through her mind. Charles Wickham must be bleeding, she thought. She wiped her mouth with the white linen napkin and rose from the table. Poor man. Poor husband. Poor daughter.

Tears were coursing down Adele's face. She was so tired. So tired of wiping them away. She let them fall on the white lace.

'Darn it! Suck in! You've got to help me with this!' swore Nina who was behind her struggling with the zipper. 'Okay, that's better. Turn around.'

Adele's back heaved and Nina realized she was sobbing yet again.

'Hey, listen! You're getting married! Come on!' She threw her arms around her best friend. Adele gasped and then hiccuped. They both laughed. 'Great! Terrific!' Nina was sarcastic. 'You're going to remember this day for ever, and if you're not careful so will everyone else. I can see it now: "BRIDE HICCUPS 'I DO'."'

Adele laughed and hiccuped again. Nina thought, damn, why did I say that! The last thing we need to think about is the press. Their claws are dripping blood as it is. She called over her shoulder as she left the room, 'Brandy, Adele. Be back in a flash.'

Adele reached to untangle the white satin ribbons of the baby's-breath bouquet on the chaise. Mother ordered this. Hiccup. Mother helped me pick the dress. Mother sent the invitations. Hic. Mother told me to get this dress and not the one at Bendel's. Today is Saturday the twenty-third and Mother was buried on the fourth. Adele made no attempt to stop the tears.

Twenty minutes later she walked into the living room as

238

Peter Duchin played Mendelssohn on the piano. They'd toned everything down, deciding that simplicity was the only way to go, thought Nina. White roses were everywhere, almost engulfing the guests who sat in rows of Louis XVI armchairs.

She's so white, so absolutely white, went through Jack's mind. Her face looks like porcelain. Adele walked slowly, with great dignity, chin up, eyes downcast, on her father's arm. He looks ten years older than he did last summer. Maybe we all do, decided Jack. His mother stood beside him in a pale rose silk suit. She had debated over grey and then thought no, this is Adele's wedding day! We must give her that, after all that's happened! It's her day and not three weeks after a funeral. This day is hers. I wear pink and I wear a flowered hat and we all smile and we all drink champagne. She had told Charles that the night before in the living room. He seemed to be near the breaking point and grateful for her company. Their dinner together had been punctuated by long silences when she feared tears might roll down his face. They hadn't. And afterwards she had taken his arm as they walked into the big room for coffee and had been surprised that he had leaned quite heavily upon her.

Suddenly Adele lifted her eyes and focused on Jack standing before her on the front row. Her face showed such pain that the silent knot of people, only twenty in all, feared she might cry out. Jack felt a stab of sadness in his chest and longed to extend his arms and press her, the full white dress, the veil, against him. His eyes were wet but no one could ever have guessed the reason.

'It was awful!' cried Nina.

The Countess looked at the little clock on the mantel. Nine-thirty. A five o'clock wedding on Park Avenue on a Saturday afternoon.

'She . . . poor Adele . . .' Nina couldn't stop crying.

'Oh, darling! I know you're sad. It's been a strain on

everyone.' The Countess was very glad the wedding was over.

Nina still wore the yellow silk dress; the yards and yards of skirt flowed around her. 'You don't understand!'

'But I do! I know what the papers said. I know that your best friend's mother . . .'

'But listen! I just came from the hospital!' sobbed Nina. 'Adele lost the baby! The pains started during the reception and now . . . she's married Paul . . . and . . .' Nina ran from the room to the guest bathroom down the hall, leaving the Countess open-mouthed in surprise.


It was Sunday afternoon. Paul stared out the window at the skyscrapered horizon. No horizon at all, he thought. Grey masses of concrete. Adele slept behind him. As white as the pillowcase. A son. A little boy. Not mine, of course. Gone. Paul sat down on the ugly metal chair beside the bed.

Adele opened her eyes and saw him, shoulders slumped, head in his hands. The room was grey with that dull dusk colour peculiar to Manhattan in spring. I must have slept all day. Yesterday I got married and . . . her eyes focused on Paul's blond head again. He still had not seen her. He had not moved and had no idea he was the object of her attention. Adele thought: Great way to start a marriage, and with a dull ache of exhaustion closed her eyes again.

# 6

A large rectangular mirror framed in dark gold hung above the marble fireplace. Cherubs, with plump legs and round cheeks, hovered at each corner, covered in gesso. They look like babies, thought Nina, with pity for Adele. It was late on a spring afternoon and the two friends sat on the new peach-coloured sofa with a bottle of white wine before them. 'I like what you've done,' nodded Nina. 'It was far too . . .' She winced. 'Too decoratorish when you moved in.' She surveyed the pale terracotta walls and the dark Persian rug with approval.

'Not sure about the bedroom yet. What do you think of these swatches?'

'I like this one for curtains,' answered Nina, picking a blue cotton with a flamestitch pattern.

'Right. Done.' Adele leaned back and sipped from her wine glass. She was colourless and appeared frail.

'Oh, didn't tell you! A ticket for Boston!'

'Another invitation from Greg? Are you going?'

'I'll cancel Stuart for Saturday night and fish one or two things out of the cleaner's and get on the plane.' Nina put her empty glass on the shining lacquer coffee table. 'What have I got to lose?'

'Ever thought of Omar?' Nina was silent. 'What's going on with him, anyway? You haven't mentioned him since the last avalanche of white roses weeks ago.'

'I don't know what's going on.' Nina stared at the cherubs, thinking they reminded her of that lavender hotel room in Paris. 'I left Paris with the idea that it was over. I think that was the idea at the time. I suddenly felt like . . . don't laugh, please. I felt like a kept woman.' Adele didn't laugh, didn't smile. Poor Nina. 'I didn't like my place in his life which is . . . was . . .' She hesitated. 'A toy. A companion. For fun.'

241

'You don't think he loves you?'

Nina sighed and reached for her wine glass; Adele refilled it. 'Not enough to consider marrying me.' She rolled her eyes in exasperation. 'What is it in me, Adele, that can't be like the Countess? That can't be free and relaxed about this with Omar! That's what he wants. He wants me to be pretty and fun and free. No strings and no ties in return. And speaking of strings I feel more like a tightrope walker than anything else. I'm playing a role and he is the audience and I have to keep watching my step and not make a mistake.'

'What mistake do you mean?'

'Oh!' exclaimed Nina. 'The mistake would be to tell him how I really feel. That I am ill at ease, that I'm pretending and that what I think I want sometimes is to marry him.'

'You really want to marry him?' breathed Adele softly.

Nina frowned. 'When you put it that way' – she raised her black eyebrows – 'I don't know.'

'Nina!' Adele was exasperated. 'You're talking in circles.'

'Well, aren't I supposed to want to marry him?' questioned Nina. She went on, 'I make love to him and it's wonderful, it's good and I feel close and I can hear his heart beating and we hold each other afterwards as though we are the only two people in the world.' She stood up and plunged her hands into the pockets of her black linen trousers. Her thick hair fell over her face as she looked down at the shiny black patent flats.

Adele thought: Lucky Nina. I can hardly remember what that's like.

'But . . .' Nina stopped.

'But what?' insisted her friend.

'But sometimes, not in bed, he's far away. I'm not reaching him. I've thought about it and I can't put my finger on just what it is. I thought about it in London and on the plane coming back to New York. Omar does everything so well. I've heard stories about his polo playing, his backgammon, his tennis is unbelievable and even the way he makes love to me . . .'

'Is he mechanical about it? Cold?'

'No,' sighed Nina, sitting down on the peach sofa again. 'I

guess I want him to be madly in love with me and off balance about how I feel and he just isn't and maybe that makes all the presents he's given me and being with him in London and Paris seem . . .'

'Kept.' Adele's voice was flat.

'The problem is . . .' Nina looked confused. Oh! What is the problem? 'He doesn't mind if I see other people. I'm going to Boston to see Greg because Omar has been away for twenty-seven days.' Nina made a face. 'But who's counting?'

Adele absentmindedly twisted the gold wedding band on her finger.

'I miss him, but I don't know if I love him, Adele. And as for being in love, I wonder about that, too.'

'Don't ask me about being in love.' Adele's voice was so sad that Nina quickly turned to stare at her.

'Not so great these days, huh?'

Adele shook her head. 'Can't talk about it, Nina. Can't put anything into words.'

'Well, when you need to talk, you know where my kitchen table is. It simply thrives on disaster and heartbreak.'

Adele smiled wanly, remembering their kitchen conferences of a year ago. 'I want to hear about your weekend the minute you get back.'

'Call you on Monday,' Nina promised, yanking on her red jacket. She glanced at her watch and yelped. 'Have to run. Told the Countess I'd go to Clarence House and stop by to see you for fifteen minutes. I'm gone if she calls! I left ages ago! Bye!'

Adele watched her leave but remained on the couch staring at nothing. When Paul arrived from Wall Street he found her sitting like a statue in the dark apartment.


'Adele? Hi! It's me! Can't talk for long because the Countess and I have eighty-nine things to do before lunch . . .' Nina's sandal fell off on to the oriental carpet and she leaned under the little desk to retrieve it with one arched bare foot. The coral printed cotton dress rode up as she slithered down in the Empire armchair. 'Oh, don't ask how Boston was,' she sighed into the phone.

'I knew with you it would be fantastic or simply horrible. So? Horrible?'

'Nearly. I love Boston.'

'But not Greg?' Adele sipped coffee from a Meissen cup of her mother's.

'He's just pale after Omar.' Nina looked up as the Countess entered the room in a flowing robe of chartreuse green. The older woman smiled knowingly as she put her teacup down on the desk. 'But that's not why I'm calling. I'll tell you everything on my way home today but what I want to know is – will you come to Nantucket next weekend? We're all staying up till late, Monday, since it's a bank holiday.'

Adele's face was crestfallen. She couldn't go. Simply couldn't go. 'Nina, I – '

'Look, it's me, the Countess, Omar is coming Saturday night, Vladimir arrives some time, the Richardsons you've met, about six others. Millie Bancroft has two houses side by side in town and we'll all get bikes and . . .'

'Nina, I can't.'

This was predictable. 'Think about it. The city is making me ratty. Sun. Bloody marys every morning with lots of fun people. Sailing. You and Paul could have a great time and you wouldn't be alone with . . .' Nina caught herself but Adele knew exactly what she meant anyway. Alone with Paul. 'Have to hang up. But I'll stop by some time after five. Chill the white wine!' Nina replaced the receiver and cried out in exasperation, 'Oh! What can I do with her!'

The Countess held the letter-opener with the brass lion head on top and wordlessly began to open the morning's mail. The sun caught the reflection of the animal's topaz eyes and Nina thought immediately of the earrings Omar had bought for her in London. 'Do you think it'll be strange for us to be without male escorts, whatever, for part of this?'

'Poooh!' erupted the Countess as she dropped what looked like a bill from Greef into the blue leather wastebasket. 'How silly of you to even consider such a thing! I get ever so annoyed with hostesses who lose their minds scouting for that extra man for dinner parties. I mean, really, this is life in the seventies, not Noah's Ark.' Nina giggled. 'And unless we're all going to Nantucket to breed . . .'

'It's like a village of doll houses,' the Countess was saying. Her voice was lost in the clatter of the propellers as the plane took off from Hyannis. 'Millie said you and I can share a room on the first floor and when Vladimir comes he can go to a single little one nearby or else you can move into that one and move again when Omar . . .'

Nina wasn't sure she understood. Was the Countess at her age actually having a fling with a Hungarian violinist who'd just defected from the Houston Symphony because 'zat place eet ees plastic and full of svimming pools'?

'What did Adele decide to do?' the Countess asked.

Nina shook her head and cupped her hands around her mouth. 'Not coming.'

The little plane levelled out over a dark blue ocean that appeared to be a solid, hard-as-concrete, surface below. In what seemed a few minutes they began the descent over an island which curved itself into the wind. A ribbon of white beach was visible, a stretch of marshland, then immaculate streets lined with grey clapboard houses. Nina saw a cluster of children on bicycles and then the plane lightly tapped the tarmac as the Countess gushed, 'Arrived! At last!'

She flutters, she floats, went through Nina's mind as she watched the Countess in billowing yards of a loose flowered dress confer with a taxi driver over how to load the old woody station wagon. 'Never known you to be concerned about suitcases,' said Nina when they were settled in the back seat.

'Oh, it's the smoked salmon, darling! I called Dorothy from La Guardia and she told me she laid it in wax paper then put it in a Bergdorf's box from the hall closet and' – she threw up her hands which were beringed with turquoise and silver – 'put it – can you imagine! In with my lingerie!' Nina couldn't help but laugh. The Countess shook her head. 'Oh, that Dorothy! I'll simply strangle her if anything has leaked.'

245

She blinked heavily made-up eyes in agitation. 'Can you imagine me slipping into bed with Vladimir smelling like a smoked salmon?' Then she began to misquote. 'Oh, all the perfumes of Arabia . . .'

'Union Street!' announced Nina, surveying the houses along a narrow lane. Every dwelling sat practically upon the sidewalks; many doorways were festooned with red roses and one or two displayed large American flags at an angle over the front door. Millie, resplendent in white sharkskin trousers and pink flowered blouse, stood behind the screen door at number thirty-two, with arm raised in greeting. 'So glad you're here! Betty called me from Logan and she and Bill are taking the ferry because the fog's rolling in and all the planes are grounded.'

'Oh!' shrieked the Countess. 'We must have been the last to take off! How glad I am to miss anything at all to do with a sailing vessel. Why, the last time I was on water or even in water except for bubble baths of course was on Lake Tanganyika crocodile-shooting with the Earl of . . .' The driver was paid by Millie as two teenage boys materialized from the back garden to carry suitcases into the little house. 'My first crocodile,' the Countess continued as Millie and Nina exchanged glances and held the screen door for the Countess's flowing figure. 'My first shot hit the poor creature in the eye! Never forget that! It was a most . . .'

The shining wooden hallway led straight through the house from front door to back screened sun porch and rose-filled garden. 'I've never seen such roses in my life!' cried Nina in admiration at the enormous blooms.

'First floor, boys,' Millie directed, then turned to Nina. 'I love roses. My favourite way to spend an afternoon is to putter and fuss with them.' She called to the boys on the landing. 'The light blue bedroom is where all that goes!' Nina and the Countess followed her upstairs and down the hall past three other bedrooms. Those to the left had a view of blue water past grey and white houses and those to the right overlooked the bright garden behind with its white wicker chairs scattered among pink roses and large trees. 'Here we are!'

The Countess exclaimed, 'Charming, Millie! How utterly charming!' as she took in the navy blue mattress-ticking bedspreads, the matching headboards over the twin beds, the oval hooked rug of navy and white and turquoise.

'The bath is there and is all yours until Monday when the Stoddards arrive.' Millie nodded towards an open door. Its walls were covered in flowered blue wallpaper and its towels hanging over the old-fashioned tub were of the same shade.

'Who else is here?' asked Nina. 'Are we the first?'

'The Richardsons are next door, along with John Heiden and, Nina, have you met Ross Maynard who writes for the New York *Times*?'

'Reviews the theatre?'

'Yes, that's the one. He's not that scathing in person, though.'

'Actually, he's a little pussycat,' tittered the Countess. 'A marshmallow for a heart once you get him away from his typewriter.'

Millie laughed. 'I'm glad you get along because he's across the hall in the light green room. There are enough of us to avoid him at dinners but you will undoubtedly pass him on the stairs.' This last was said in a teasing tone meant to be overheard.

'Is my name being taken in vain?' boomed the voice behind her. Ross Maynard, tall, thin, tanned, stood in the doorway in a baggy pair of blue bathing trunks and a red T-shirt. His sunburned face made his thick white hair seem even whiter.

'Every hour, Ross! Have you met Nina McLean? The Countess, I know you know. Nina is the new assistant.'

'Assisting in what, may I ask?'

'No, you may not ask,' chirped the Countess quickly.

'Always up to no good,' grumbled the older man. 'Sit next to me at dinner tonight, Nina, and I'll give you the facts. You have to watch out for this Countess.'

'*Oooooh.*' The Countess hit a high operatic note. 'I think it's time to watch out for theatre critics.' She waved a blue chiffon scarf at him as if to shoo him out of the room and he laughed.

'I think it's time I changed out of this wet suit.' He laughed again at the Countess's dramatic flailing. 'See you later.'

Millie left with him and winked as she closed the door behind her.

Later was in two hours in the twilight holding a vodka with tonic in one hand and some of the Countess's smoked salmon on toast in the other. The air bore the delicious scents of the sea and the roses. The two boys Millie referred to as 'my butlers' were tending a fire in the barbecue as a maid in a white apron pressed hamburger meat into generous patties.

'I feel so good in a T-shirt and levis,' Nina said to the Countess. 'This is how I am best.' She wiggled her toes in the slip-on white sandals, feeling totally relaxed.

'Lucky you,' answered the Countess. 'You look so marvellous in anything. Why, I'd give all my millions to look the way you do in those white jeans.'

Nina felt it then as she had so many times before. Refusing to give in and glance around, she joked, '*All* your millions, Countess? *All* of them?'

'Well,' the Countess retreated, plucking at her aquamarine caftan, 'maybe save a few for just walking-around money.'

Nina laughed and then turned to see who was staring at her. Mickey Keeling was faintly smiling. Nina smiled back and then, praying he couldn't read lips, dared to say softly to the Countess, 'Why is someone, who shall remain nameless until he turns his head, always watching me?'

'Elementary, dearest Watson! Because you are ravishing to look at! Whoever he is is probably wondering if you had to writhe on the floor to zip those trousers!'

'Do you honestly think they're indecent?'

'I've already told you what I think! Almost, almost *all* my millions . . .'

Nina sipped the vodka and turned to watch as Ross came over to say hello and to slip his arm about the Countess's shoulders. The word 'distinguished' immediately springs to mind, thought Nina. He stood tall and straight in the white linen trousers and the oatmeal-coloured Shetland sweater.

The white collar of an oxford cloth shirt peeked out of the round neckline.

'Rumour has it, my dear . . .' He looked sternly down at the Countess's upturned face. She wore a come-on expression and her blue eyes twinkled. '. . . that you are deserting me for some Communist piano player. Is there any truth to that?'

The Countess fairly exploded with indignation. 'Communist! He's not a Communist! Why do you think he left?'

'I hear he just left Houston. One would think that anyone with . . .'

Nina tried not to laugh at the Countess's discomfiture. It was all an act. She loved the drama, and quite plainly adored being teased by Ross Maynard.

'And he's not a piano player anyway! How dare you!'

'Countess, how dare you?' said Ross quietly. 'You've known all these years the depth of my feelings for – '

'Your feelings! Why, a gila monster would be labelled hot-blooded and sentimental in comparison. You have no . . .'

Nina moved away laughing.

'They're at it again,' commented Betty Richardson. 'How are you, Nina?'

'I'm fine, thanks. How was the ferry?'

'I thought it was uneventful but don't ask Bill what he thought. He looked a little green those last few minutes. And driving here! Why, to hear him describe the crossing you'd think we were the survivors of something trans-Atlantic. Something that took days and nights!'

'You should hear the Countess on the subject if you want real drama!'

'I do want real drama! Will somebody here tell me something very exciting so that I don't have to drink too much and take off my clothes?' It was the Italian-accented voice of Anna Buccini who had materialized in a black and white striped sundress. It reminded Nina of her kitchen floor. As always she displayed 'one yard of cleavage', Nina would laugh with the Countess later.

'Are you threatening to take off your clothes again?' It was her manager, who trailed her everywhere. Nina couldn't decide if he were in love with her or not. 'As a man I'd love to see it happen but as your manager I must tell you the night air will surely chill your . . .' He cleared his throat loudly as they all laughed. 'Your lungs!' Anna squealed playfully.

Nina slipped the turquoise slave bracelet farther up on her arm. Banded in silver, it had been a present from the Countess for it had been too small for her to wear for years. The aquamarine jersey made Nina's eyes take on the same blue-green tint. She pushed her hair away from her face and retreated from the laughter only to walk straight into the drink of Mickey Keeling.

'Whoa!' he laughed, holding the dripping glass away from them both as the gin dripped on to the grass.

'Oh, I'm sorry! Really I am!' Nina was flustered by the accident, and by him.

He gave her one of his broadest grins – his eyes smiled, too – and consoled her, 'This is nothing! I've been swimming twice today already . . .' Mickey's face was very tanned, with fresh pink sunburn on top. Nina thought: This man literally catches me off balance. Except when I'm with Omar. Omar keeps him at a distance – or do I, when Omar is around? 'So what have you been up to?' he asked as he cheerfully wiped his muscular forearm with a cocktail napkin.

'I've been running amuck with the Countess.' She handed him her napkin and he took it and wiped his arm before wadding it up and putting it into the pocket of his white jeans. 'My first time on Nantucket,' she confessed.

'Well, then come with us tomorrow morning. Some of us are riding bikes on a grand tour.'

'It's such a tiny island from the air! How long will that take?'

'Oh.' He shrugged and looked as though he were making serious computations. 'If we all ride like the devil . . .' He paused. 'About two hours.' The two of them laughed. 'Where's the big bad Omar?'

'He's . . . ummm . . . he's . . .' Geneva? Paris? London?

250

What should I say? 'He's . . . I don't know exactly.' They laughed again.

'Tad?'

'I don't know.' Nina sipped her drink and then gazed up at him. 'Don't you think I can handle a little Nantucket houseparty on my own?' She was thinking of the Countess's comment about Noah's Ark but unfortunately the remark about breeding popped into her mind and she realized just how attracted she was to Mickey Keeling.

'You, Nina McLean, could probably handle a little hurricane on your own or a small war or . . .' He narrowed those gold-flecked eyes at her. 'Probably just about anything.'

'Don't know about a small war,' she said slowly. 'Never thought of handling one. How big a small war do you think I could handle? How big is a small war anyway?'

He fell into her light bantering. 'Well, what I had in mind was something civil. Perhaps in a banana republic.'

'Mmmm,' she agreed thoughtfully. 'That's quite a compliment, but I'll have to fake modesty and say I've had no experience with handling wars. Maybe I could start with something easier. What about a coup d'état?'

'He's very very nice,' she said sleepily to the Countess as she reached for the light switch between the two single beds.

'Who is very nice? Did I miss something?'

Nina realized she had thought of no one else all evening. 'Mickey Keeling.'

'Yes, he is. I saw the two of you together. Lila is sick, I suppose.'

'Lila? Lila Hutchins?'

'His wife. Oh, Nina, you knew . . .'

Nina was glad that the Countess could not see her expression. 'Well, no, I didn't know. Why is her last name Hutchins?' She was extremely uncomfortable with the news. Her throat felt tight as she swallowed and she was conscious of controlling her voice. Oh, boy! Did I ever flirt with him! And he . . . well, he hadn't exactly flirted back. No. Not really.

'She's the heiress to Hutchins Aerospace and people simply think of her as Lila Hutchins.'

'They're really married?' Nina burst out.

'Have been for years,' came the calm response in the dark.

'But . . .'

'I know. She looks decades older, poor thing. But he and she are the same age. I think he must be about thirty-nine or forty. That range.'

'But she's so . . .'

'She didn't used to be. She used to be a delight but in the last year she's changed. Mickey is very kind to her, very calm no matter what but I wouldn't want to spend too much time with her.'

Nina lay in the darkness staring up at the ceiling. Her hands were folded over the white sheet. I'll just have to avoid him tomorrow, she thought with disappointment. I was thinking how nice it would be to be alone with him. No, Nina. Don't finish the thought. But I am so attracted to him! Her mind raced along. Someone else's husband. And so is Omar! She turned over on her side and listened to the Countess's voice.

'She's changed so much. Arbitrary, contrary, exceptionally bad-tempered. And Mickey has changed, too! Imagine leaving the firm to become a poet. I wonder that between the two of them they have the common sense of a child!'

Nina couldn't imagine Mickey kissing Lila, making love to Lila. Why, she was positively old enough, in looks anyway, to be his . . . why, his aunt! 'Did he marry her for all that aerospace money?'

'Oh, no! I don't think so! She was a very pretty delicate blonde and if he started out with not a lot of money after Yale, he soon made it on Wall Street. Oh, no, it wasn't that.' There was a pause. 'Actually I've heard that Lila's brother made a mess at Hutchins and the stock hit rock bottom a few years ago. I think that Mickey probably has a lot more money than his wife does.'

Nina was amazed to realize that even that disappointed her. Why, he must be in love with her! Why does he pay so much attention to me then? Or did he? Yes, he did! But I was the flirt and I enjoyed it. Nina had perceived him as a challenge, and, thinking him single, a potential conquest. She had nurtured the idea of seeing him again, in between the times with Omar, of course. She felt thwarted and a little annoyed and yes, even foolish. Disappointed, too, for his sense of humour was so light and self-effacing and so . . . unlike Omar's.

'From what I've seen of him, and I've only known him a few years, he is simply tops,' the soft voice of the Countess continued. 'No one could be more considerate of Lila and, believe me, I've seen her in a very bad temper. But,' said the Countess sweetly, 'Mickey is always by her side.' She yawned and Nina heard the older woman turn over. 'Goodnight, darling.'

'Goodnight.' Nina lay there inhaling the cool, clear scent of the ocean. She thought of Omar's magic with her in bed and she thought of Mickey Keeling with those bright intelligent eyes and the delighted grin of someone about to blow out candles on a birthday cake. There is definitely something very attractive about him, decided Nina. But whatever it is, it's not for me.


The next morning six of them, in shorts, bright jerseys and espadrilles, took a vote on heading for the shore road or going through the town, and then compromised by doing both. The shops were all picture-perfect, thought Nina, often with tiny squares of well-tended bright green grass in front. Art galleries lined the area down by the wharves.

'This was all improved just a few years ago by a man named Walter Beineke Junior,' Mickey explained. 'It was a disgrace. He was the driving force behind rebuilding and renovating.'

A mile later, out of town, they abandoned their bikes and went on foot. Nina pulled down the rolled-up sleeves of the pink and white striped jersey as she shivered in the strong wind from the sea. All six bicycles lay in the sand behind her.

'Come on, Nina!' called Betty. 'You can still find shells here if you really look!' Millie raced after John Heiden who was a way down the beach picking up stones and casually skipping them on the surface of the rough water.

The waves curved towards the shore in lines of royal blue; the sky was almost white in comparison and the wind whipped her long black hair across her face and gave her goosebumps. Nina watched Bill Richardson hold his shirt tails towards his wife's latest acquisition in order to make a basket. The voice startled her.

'Lost in thought. As usual.'

'As usual?'

It was Mickey. 'I mean that I feel as if you are sometimes not quite all there. Not all here. Not in the same room with us. You watch.' Nina tilted her head and pulled a strand of hair from her mouth. 'You seem . . .' He hesitated and then turned up the collar of the dark green Lacoste shirt against the stiff breeze. His bare arms must be cold, thought Nina. 'You seem to belong to another dimension . . .'

'There are only three. Or so they tell me.' Nina didn't want to be alone with him. Didn't want to feel the way she had the evening before, before the conversation with the Countess.

'Do you believe that?' he teased.

Nina thought? I wish you didn't have such shining eyes. There were little white lines at the corners when his tanned face was not smiling. 'What about . . .' he began and then decided. 'What about dropping a collar stay and you know it's gone under the bureau and you get down on your hands and knees and it has simply disappeared. It has ceased to exist.'

Nina responded. 'That happens with the occasional earring. But that isn't another dimension. That's what scientists call a black hole.'

He laughed delightedly. 'That black hole business has never made me think of stars,' he smiled. 'I think of that rabbit in *Alice in Wonderland* disappearing or a crawfish darting into – '

'Crawfish!' interrupted Nina. 'How come you say "crawfish"?'

'That's what they are!'

'But not to somebody from . . .'

'I'm from Georgia.'

'How could you be?' demanded Nina. Mickey Keeling of Wall Street, Mickey Keeling without a trace of Southern accent. Smooth New York-y Mickey.

'Why, Nina! Surely you of all people know that once from Georgia doesn't mean always from Georgia.' He reached down for a stone and with one long easy underhanded throw skipped it across the surface of the bright blue sea.

'Three, four, five!' counted Nina. Then she returned to the idea of Mickey coming from the South, forgetting all resolutions to stay away from him. 'How did you get to New York?' she demanded.

'I believe there's Delta out of Atlanta.'

'Oh, come on, I know that! I've sat in that airport long enough to eat my weight in pralines, long enough to read *Gone With the Wind* thirty-seven times . . .'

'Love that airport. Especially when I'm on my way north.'

Nina remembered going back to Jackson for Daddy's funeral. She remembered all those trips home from Briarcliff, feeling different, and then on the way back to New York again wondering just how different she really had been over the vacation. Nina spoke after a moment of silence. 'Atlanta was always a point of no return for me. Just an hour away from Jackson. Leaving it or going back to it.'

'Gateway to the South.' He picked up another stone and Nina watched his strong tanned fingers stroke it absentmindedly.

'Escape.' Nina was surprised the moment the word was out, though Mickey's reaction was not of surprise.

'How true. Planes and trains, and if you think of the blacks – buses and feet.' A wave crashed loudly before them as the wind picked up. 'But,' he shrugged, 'it's really all in the head.'

'Escape?'

'Sure. There are lots of people who never get away but don't feel like being where they are.'

'Who do you mean exactly?'

'I don't mean anyone exactly. I guess I mean people who decide they're different, people who hate their marriages, people who hate their jobs.'

Nina rubbed her arms to get them warm. 'And the people who decide they don't belong where they're supposed to?' She thought: I feel like myself. I can say anything.

'Ah! Supposed to! Now that's a good phrase from a good little well-behaved Southern girl! You haven't really escaped, have you?'

Nina felt angry then. Who was Mickey Keeling to call her a 'good little well-behaved Southern girl'! 'Everybody has somebody or something telling them what they're supposed to be like, supposed to do,' she answered sullenly.

'I know what you mean,' he relented. 'Some people get out. The others make do. Hold fast. Give up. Turn to bourbon. Everybody knows people who didn't escape.' He stared at the faraway horizon. 'But some people are happy where they are. They fit. Or they tailor their lives to fit.'

Nina thought of smiling Sally Frances Stone being crowned 'Most Popular' in a high school gymnasium decorated with chicken wire stuffed with thousands of wads of pink Kleenex. 'So they stay.' Yes, Sally Frances had married the captain of the football team at Ole Miss after wearing his fraternity pin and before that his class ring, his football jacket, his clunky silver-plated ID bracelet and before that, his dog tag which had been the apex of status symbols in the sixth grade. The future: her ranch house, her station wagon, her charity work at the Baptist church, had been charted year after year in a path of metal trinkets, each more expensive than the last. Finally, the best trinket of all, the wedding band, had been slipped on her finger in front of four hundred and fifty pink perspiring witnesses one Saturday in June. She fitted. She'd filled out the baby blue gauzy prom dress with her full young bosom when Nina had still been a stick. She'd been photographed for every issue of the school paper 'with twenty-nine teeth showing' Nina had once told Adele. Yes, Sally Frances had been a success at age twelve. Why should she ever want to be anywhere else, be anyone else.

256

Mickey turned to her. 'But if you even think of getting away, that makes you different right there.' Nina didn't answer. 'I think most people don't even daydream about it.' He skipped another stone with precision on the back of a blue breaker as it peaked. 'That's my theory anyway.'

Nina began to speak quietly. 'I used to lie in bed at night and look out at my pine tree and hear the Panama Limited on its way to New Orleans. And I would wonder . . . so many things . . .' The wind had let up and the sun felt warm. 'Someone once told me that lots of people hear the whistle of the train but very few go down to the station and get on it.'

Mickey smiled. 'But you did. Figuratively.' He stared at her for a few long seconds and she thought what an open handsome face he had. 'And I did.' She smiled back at him when he continued, 'That makes us different. And that makes us strong.'

Nina accepted the statement happily. She liked him; she liked his thinking of her as strong. Perhaps, most of all, she liked his categorizing the two of them together. I care what he thinks of me.

It was during dessert after a long lunch in the garden that the Countess was summoned into the house for a telephone call; she reappeared after a few moments smiling absently. Ross stared as she, in her yellow flowered caftan, fairly floated into her chair again and seeing his face, she playfully wafted her white silk handkerchief and said, 'Now, Ross, I can't tell you everything, can I? I would lose all my mysterious appeal for you.' He snorted and poured her another glass of wine.

Plates and dishes were cleared and the group began to disappear one by one or in pairs either down to the beach or into the house for a quiet time with a book. The porch door opened and closed a half dozen times as this person or that went in to change into a bathing suit and as John Heiden loped back and forth searching for his tennis racket.

Nina was on the stairs when the Countess called from the landing above, 'Nina, I have to talk to you.' Their bedroom door was open and the breeze from the sea made the fresh white curtains dance in the shaded coolness of the blue room. The Countess closed the door behind them as Nina stood beside the chest of drawers littered with their talcum powder and perfumes and make-up, and several of the Countess's silk scarves. 'Omar called.'

'When's he coming?' burst out Nina excitedly. She'd planned to be bathed and perfect or else just out of the sea, quite wet and mermaid-y. One of the two. 'But why didn't he talk to m – '

The Countess was fluttering. 'Sit. Now listen to me and after that I'll get you a good strong something to drink.' Nina involuntarily clapped one hand over her mouth but otherwise remained like a statue standing beside the window. Dead. I know he's been in an accident. But no, she said he called. 'He's not coming. He's in Geneva. He said to tell you that.'

Relief rushed through Nina. 'Well, that's all right. After all,' she shrugged, 'it's not the first time he's cancelled.' Now she felt annoyed. Again let down by him.

'That's not all. He's in Geneva to be with his wife – '

'He told you that?' Nina's voice was angry now, and amazed.

'She's been in labour and . . .'

'In labour?' Memories like torn photographs flooded her mind: 'I don't find her physically attractive.' 'No, of course I don't sleep with her.' 'It's a marriage in name only. Only for our families – to please my father, really.' Had he said those things? Or did I want him to say them?

'Omar is now . . .' The Countess sighed dramatically. Might as well get it over with. '. . . the proud father of an eight-pound son.'

'I think I'm going to scream my head off,' Nina said slowly and distinctly.

The Countess ran from window to window pushing curtains aside and slamming them down closed. 'Don't you dare until I leave this room.' She held up one finger. 'If you're going to scream at least let me have time to get down the stairs to warn everyone that you're practising for your primal therapy class which meets once a week.'

'All right. I'm not.' Nina's voice was flat. Her heart was

pounding like a drum. A sick feeling poured through her as though she'd been held upside down by her heels and shaken.

'I'm sorry, darling.' The Countess put her arms around her. 'I put you two together; I encouraged it. He's not worth it. I wish I'd never introduced you.'

'I wanted him to love me!' Nina began to cry. With the first tears she thought of her mother's disapproval. Of Omar and of this making a scene.

'You picked someone you couldn't have,' the Countess said gently. She blamed herself for some of this pain. But didn't I tell Nina not to fall in love? At least six dozen times? 'It was up to you to decide what you wanted.'

Nina pulled away from her. 'Up to me?' She laughed mockingly. 'Nothing was up to me once Omar took me to bed. I was his little slave. I was determined to make him love me. I was sure I could make him fall in love with me.' Tears rolled down her face quickly now. Damn good manners anyhow! she swore to herself. 'Do you know that I'm the prize idiot! I'm the fool! Omar didn't do anything wrong!'

'What are you talking about? Of course he has treated you badly!' The Countess extended her handkerchief but Nina did not reach for it.

'Because I knew and I let it all happen. I went along with it. His game. Anything he wanted.' She gave a great gulp as tears filled her throat. 'I'll tell you something really horrible. Really awful.' She took the handkerchief then. 'I told him once I loved him. It was even after Paris. I broke all the sophisticated rules and confessed it once after we'd made love.' She looked with wet face, eyes streaming with tears, out the closed glass of the window. The room was stifling hot and still. 'I pleaded, "Omar, please tell me that you love me!" And when he didn't answer but left the room and came back with two glasses of champagne, I couldn't give it up! I insisted! Ha!' She began to sob silently then she surrendered to racking sobs that made her ribs jerk under the pink and white stripes. 'I said, "Oh, tell me what you think of me!"' She shook her head back and forth, hating the memory, as though she could nullify it. 'And he knelt,

259

naked, with one knee on the bed, and handed me the glass and smiled. And do you know what he said?'

The Countess whispered, 'No.'

'He said' – Nina's face was contorted with pain – '"I think you are a stroke of luck."'

The Countess left the room and closed the door behind her. Nina didn't see her go. Her shoulders were bowed and she leaned with elbows on the high-topped bureau, head down, hair in her face. 'I'm so stupid. So willing to please. To play games I hate. Making love a million times with someone who didn't love – ' She heard the footsteps behind her then and knew it was not the light tread of the Countess. Nina raised her tear-stained face and with horror, saw Mickey Keeling standing beside her bed. He seemed enormous in the little low-ceilinged bedroom. Larger than life, out of place, definitely not supposed to be there. With a deep blush of shame Nina realized he had heard everything. Her rage, her humiliation, her choked confessions to the Countess, everything.

Fury welled up in her like a wave. 'Get out of here!' she hissed at him and when he stepped towards her she put up her fists as though to go for his face. 'How dare you! How dare you!' she shouted. Mickey tried to step aside between the two narrow beds but Nina came at him like a tigress. 'I hate you!'

He easily grabbed her wrists and stared down at her. 'You hate yourself this afternoon.'

Mickey breathed inward sharply when he saw her face tighten with a new rush of anger. Instead of being crushed and sobbing and broken-spirited, the Nina whose hands he held was ready to fight. Her eyes flashed green, yes, almost a green, he would think later, many times, and her mouth looked swollen from crying.

'I hate you for listening. I'll – ' She jerked to get away but he held her tightly.

'No, you won't do anything. I'll let go of you when I feel like it so you might as well listen to me. You don't have a choice.'

Nina was aware of sweat soaking her; her face, arms, and

even her thighs under the white shorts were damp. Her hair combs had fallen to the floor. She looked up at him; yes, his hands hurt her wrists and yes, she did hate him.

His voice was quiet. 'You made a mistake. The Countess is right. You picked someone you couldn't have. Someone who probably will never belong to anyone.'

'I hate you for listening . . .' Nina whispered in a voice as cold as ice. Again she tried to pull her hands from his grip.

Mickey's face shone with sweat. Her struggling seemed to renew his resolve to hold her. 'Well, since I did, why don't you answer one question for me? Are you mad because Omar is with his wife or are you having this temper tantrum because, as you put it, you couldn't "make" him love you?'

Nina tried to wrench herself away with a vengeance but couldn't. She longed to slap his face. It would have given her keen pleasure to hear her palm strike his cheek.

'Have you always had any man you wanted?' he demanded.

'Yes!' She spat at him.

He pushed her backwards on to the bed then and she lay there with black hair fanned out on the blue and white spread; her eyes were bright with tears and with resentment, refusing to show anything but indignation. For a few seconds she thought he was going to kiss her but instead he roughly let go of her hands and walked to the door. He opened and closed it without looking back, leaving Nina staring up at the blue ceiling, despising all that had happened.


Saturday night's drinks and dinner came and went with Nina remaining close to the Countess and Ross Maynard. Like a child, thought the Countess, who needs to feel safe after an accident. Mickey Keeling did not exist for her as she laughed gaily at this quip or that little vignette, and he never came closer than four people to where she sat.

On Sunday, they all sprawled in various lawn chairs for most of the day with bloody marys on little side tables, passing the New York *Times* sections back and forth. The air smelled of freshly-mown grass.

261

Monday morning they lazed on the beach. Nina was feeling better. No one had asked where Omar was so either the Countess had told them he wasn't coming or they assumed he would arrive any minute, very late, but any minute. Vladimir had surrendered to food poisoning after consuming a mysterious fish on the West Side.

'The West Side!' the Countess had cried on the telephone. 'Why ever would you want to even *be* there, let alone *eat* something there?'

Nina stood and left the little encampment of bright umbrellas and beach chairs. The sun was warm and contrasted deliciously with the chill of the ankle-deep water. Tiny waves broke in front of her as she walked out to swim. How I love the ocean, she thought as she lazily did the breaststroke then the backstroke under the cloudless blue sky. Gulls squawked their lonely calls to one another, banking and turning against unseen aerial corners. Omar. Omar. Omar. A hollow empty feeling had been with her since the Countess had told her about the baby. We won't ever make love again. He won't ever call me his little fox again. She turned over and was surprised to see only deserted beach directly before her. Had they gone on without me? Is it that late? No, she saw them now. Yards and yards and yards behind her to the left. Nina was out much farther than she'd realized, and that realization was allied with a sharp little edge of panic. No, I'm not worried, she said to herself, treading water and then beginning her strong crawl. Soon she was tired and the surprising heaviness of her arms and legs made her a bit frightened. I am a good swimmer, she said to herself. I remember that summer at Watch Hill when everyone said so. She continued to do stroke after stroke directly for shore but then raised her head and realized she wasn't getting any closer.

'Nina!' The voice was behind her. It was Mickey Keeling.

'Please!' she hissed at him, as she began to tread water. She felt anger all over again. Adrenaline overwhelmed tiredness and apprehension. 'Just go away!'

'You idiot! You're in a rip current!' His face was coming

closer now, his dark hair was wetted straight back and his tan face was serious.

'I don't care what I'm in! Just leave me alone!'

He laughed. 'This is unbelievable!' He began to tread water beside her. 'You've been battling this for twenty-five minutes, someone has called for a lifeboat, everyone on the beach is watching and I . . .' He began to laugh again and got water in his mouth and began to cough.

'I can take care of myself,' Nina panted with dignity. Then she looked towards the sand and saw a cluster of perhaps forty people all standing, holding towels, wearing sunglasses. They were like dolls. Nina turned towards shore and with her strongest effort began yet again to flutter-kick towards land. After five minutes she was treading water and Mickey was beside her.

'Do I have to hit you over the head? Are you that proud?'

'Why were you in my room yesterday?' she shouted, oblivious to everything but her remembered humiliation.

'Millie told me to go up to your bathroom for a Band-Aid and right after I went in you and the Countess followed me and you – ' He took a deep breath. 'The door to the other bedroom was locked from the other side so I had no choice but to come out.' He sighed in exasperation. Nina with hair slicked back like a beautiful seal, eyes grey-blue with black long lashes wet with the sea, stared at him. 'I went to your bathroom for a Band-Aid. I didn't count on a Shakespearean tragedy.'

The water was cold and Nina's hands were going numb. She stared at Mickey's face. His mouth, serious; his eyes, promising the truth, shot through with the light of the sun; his black brows wet with shining crystal drops. Wordlessly, he held up one finger. It sported a tiny Band-Aid.

Nina began to cry and then she began to laugh and he stared at her in disbelief and then the lunacy of it swept over him, too. They laughed and laughed until they both had to float on their backs to keep from swallowing water and then Mickey, still gasping, said seriously, 'Look, those idiots are taking for ever with the boat. We've got to make it on our own. How are you?'

263

Nina nodded, wiping her mouth. She was crying but he couldn't tell. Thank God for that. I can say I swam in my tears.

'The trick with a rip current is not to fight it. You can't. We have to swim for about a quarter of a mile parallel to the beach and then we can head in. Are you okay?' Nina nodded again. 'You can hold on to me,' he offered. 'You're bound to be tired.' She shook her head. Never. I'm a strong swimmer, she said to herself once more.

So the two of them began. Nina found the idea of swimming beside the shore which often seemed so tantalizingly close and not directly towards it, was infuriating when her arms and legs ached so. Mickey's stroke knifed into the water cleanly; he moved with the grace of a powerful athlete. Nina rested with the breaststroke, feeling the cold water rush past her closed palms, then in a loveless caress the length of her body until her feet could kick those particular gallons away. Her shoulders were on fire and she told herself not to think of it; her ankles and calves were on fire and she told herself not to think of it. The wind picked up and little waves splashed in their faces as they swam. His presence was a comfort to her though only a splashing body nearby in the ocean. He could be a porpoise, she decided, and was glad that it was not necessary, indeed impossible, to talk.

'Tell me when you want to rest,' his voice came to her over the slapping water noise and she shouted, 'No', and tasted salt and then with a gulp of air put her head down again. It seemed hours later that he touched her shoulder, as Nina, like an automaton, ploughed onward. 'We can head in now.'

The crowd on the beach had grown; several people had been walking with them and now waved for them to come ashore. A white boat with oars was being pushed through the breakers. Its bow thrashed up and down as if it were fighting the idea of entering the blue-black water. Nina thought she recognized the tall thin figure of Ross Maynard in red trunks but couldn't be sure as she put her face into the water again.

At last Mickey was saying, 'Can you touch?' and she found her footing on the velvet sand. He grasped her wrist and pulled her towards him through the armpit-deep water which sucked at them as though attempting to drag them back towards the horizon. Nina felt the strength in Mickey Keeling. That same sense of power that took up space in living rooms, that aura of energy. They floated past the stretch of thrashing angry breakers then allowed themselves to be borne gently towards the land as if the sea had at last decided to relinquish them, to give them over from one element to another. Mickey's shoulders were out of the ocean first: smooth, bronzed, glistening with rivulets of water. Then Nina saw the deep ridge of his spine between the wide planes of his broad back. Yards later in the backwash of the waves she saw the tapered waist, the green trunks sticking to his flanks and then at last his tanned muscular thighs. Nina looked down at her own knees and saw them ringed in white bubbles and froth like lace garters. She wanted only to sleep for a long time.

'Oh, darling!' The Countess was near tears. She stood in the shallows; her lavender caftan was deep purple where it was soggy and trailed in the water. 'We were so worried!' She threw her arms around the dripping Nina.

'Good show, my boy.' Ross clapped Mickey on the back. 'Let's get some towels and get you two home.'

Nina's legs felt like jelly and she wobbled, almost falling.

'Darling, lean on me,' cooed the Countess. Brown rubbery-looking seaweed was caught in the chiffon folds and was being dragged along behind her, giving her the appearance of some wild queen of the deep, but all she could think of was her dearest beloved Nina. Safe.

That evening, back on 90th Street, her suitcase exploding with summer clothes on the floor beside her, Nina propped bare feet on the kitchen table and dialled Adele. 'Well,' she said slowly. 'Nantucket was a laugh a minute. And how was your weekend?'

*

Lieutenant Farwell had opened the file and was staring at a black and white glossy when Staff Sergeant Miller walked in. 'Are you hypnotized or what, Farwell? Been standing in the door for five minutes!'

Lieutenant Farwell tossed the photo across the desk. 'Take a look at that and tell me how to handle the Wickham broad's husband in fifteen minutes.'

Miller whistled, and his beefy face contorted with a scowl of disgust. 'S and M stuff? Looks like it, with those black and blue marks on the wrists. I hear Lieberman got picked up at JFK last night.'

'Think the DA'll go for manslaughter or murder or something in between?'

'It's a bitch of a case 'cause the press'll be breathing down our necks. Who knows what that bastard Sawyer'll do.'

A voice behind him announced that Charles Wickham had arrived. Miller clumsily stepped out of the path of the tall man. Good-looking, thought Farwell. Takes care of himself. Several hundred dollars' worth of suit. He knew from the files that there had been twenty years between him and this blonde ex-cover girl. The New York *Post* had described her as the personification of American aristocracy. And Charles Wickham had had enough something to marry her at the peak of her success. Maybe it was money. Maybe more. Farwell offered a chair with a sweep of one arm and Wickham sat down with an air of exhaustion. 'This isn't going to be any fun for either of us, I can assure you, but we have to go over a few things.'

'Lieutenant.' Charles leaned forward in the heavy wooden chair with the slatted back. He was unused to being the other man in an office with a desk. He usually sat behind the desk. 'Lieutenant,' he began again. 'I'm not even sure how my wife died. The last weeks have been spent in keeping away from reporters and dodging cameras when I arrive at my office. I don't know anything I couldn't have read in that damn rag, the *Daily News*. Or the New York *Post* or *People* magazine,' he finished with anger.

Lieutenant Farwell nodded. 'Okay. First, what we know.

She died of heart failure during sexual intercourse while inhaling a substance called amyl nitrate.'

'A drug?' Charles's face was full of shock. This couldn't be Tory!

'It's a capsule about the size of a Contac. When broken under the nose it speeds up pulse rate. The fumes are known to increase the intensity of an orgasm. It's not uncommon these days. They're called "poppers".' Lieutenant Farwell continued, 'We know that James Lieberman took the suite almost every Friday and had done so for the past year, except August. He did not register any Friday in August.' Charles was silent. He opened his mouth as if to speak but his voice didn't come. Tory was always at Watch Hill in August. 'Now, Mr Wickham, we don't know that your wife was with him every time he took the suite. This could have been . . . the first . . . the first time.'

Charles nodded mutely. Suddenly he blurted, 'Friday afternoon was Tory's day at the symphony. She always had lunch at home and then went to Lincoln Center. A subscription . . .' His voice trailed. How naïve he must think I am, he cursed himself.

Lieutenant Farwell nodded, his face carefully expressionless. 'Will you, or . . .' He found it difficult to say but did anyway. 'Someone, your staff, go through all her purses, all coat pockets, all drawers, all closets, and find any ticket stubs, any evidence of where she spent her time. Matchbooks, concert programmes, restaurant bills, anything would help.'

'But why?'

'The DA will try to link or not link. I don't know how Sawyer will work it, but he will want to understand just how involved Lieberman was with your wife.' He looked at the undisguised agony etched on the older man's face and added, 'Perhaps they were not involved at all. Or just this one time.'

'Do you mean there may have been other women, other people involved?'

The Lieutenant shrugged. 'We know so little. More of

this will be explained by Lieberman himself. He was picked up last night at Kennedy about to get on a flight to London.'

'Where has he been for Chrissake?' exploded Charles. Why had it taken New York's finest so long to snare him!

'He rented a car under an assumed name, paid cash, and drove to New Hampshire. He rented a small cottage and then changed his mind about staying there. Evidently, no one recognized him. No one was suspicious.' Farwell didn't add what he was thinking, and that was that he probably could have stayed safely tucked away for as long as his money had held out. And the cash he had had with him was considerable. 'Last night at Kennedy someone at the TWA ticket counter thought he looked familiar and tipped off airport security. He's now being held without bail. I get my shot at questioning him in exactly one hour. His lawyer's with him now.'

'The last anyone heard of Lieberman was the letter of resignation submitted to the board just after . . . after it happened. For personal reasons, it said!' Charles gave a snort of disgust. 'He called his secretary and dictated it over the phone.'

Lieutenant Farwell nodded. He'd spent two hours with that dippy dame, Miss Eileen Tribble. The police officer stood in a gesture of dismissal and Charles got to his feet and extended his hand. 'You'll be in New York for the next month or so, won't you? Sawyer will want to go over exactly what your relationship was to Lieberman and he'll want to know a great deal more about your wife.'

Charles concentrated on not flinching. 'Of course. Thank you for your time, Lieutenant.'

You'd think Tory was to blame because she died in a public place. No. Was murdered in the Plaza. Guess Farwell thinks I was not exciting enough for her and she turned to someone else. Lieberman! He felt like spitting when he heard the name, when he envisioned the big dark head set on broad shoulders, the beetle-browed face, the thick hands with the black wires of hair on top. Those hands folded on the boardroom table during a meeting, those hands snapping his briefcase closed, those hands on Tory. Suddenly Charles realized he was on the street and walking in exactly the opposite direction he wanted to go. He absentmindedly raised his arm towards a cab. As it slowed down, the young driver thought, funny, it looked like he was surrendering. All he needed was a white handkerchief. I'll have to put that in my novel.

James Lieberman lay naked on his cot. Two nights here. Maybe Cohen will swing bail today. What the hell is holding it up? I know why they call this place the Tombs, he thought. The cell was grey and the stiff sheets were grey in the sickly light from the bulb in the hallway. Even his skin looked grey when he bothered to look at his reflection in the steel plate soldered into the concrete wall above the stained sink. It stinks. Stinks of men and of me. He turned over on his side. The Tombs. A holding pen for all of us between life and death. Five in the morning. This had always been the worst hour for Lieberman. He had often woken in his penthouse on Fifth Avenue and 81st Street and allowed his mind to waver on the brink of despair. Lieberman thought of things that bothered him again and again, finding a masochistic satisfaction in his activity, like a tongue touching a sore tooth. Predictable pain. Controllable hurt. His wife bothered him, or she had. But now that she'd filed for divorce, he need never let her bother him again. She had come to tell him in person. Dressed to kill as usual. It had occurred to Lieberman as he looked at the diamond ring on her plump, stubby finger, the pearls around her fleshy neck, the gold earrings, the silk suit, the shoes at $250 a throw. I paid for all that. I paid for every inch of her. I paid for her food which has made her too fat, I paid for her exercise classes to remove that same fat, I paid for the clothes to cover that same fat. I paid for all the trinkets she thinks she needs. God, I am sick of the former Brenda Rosenberg, Jewish American Princess if ever one walked the earth. How many times had he lain beside her a few blocks from Tory, where Tory lay beside Charles Wickham, and thought: Tory Tory Tory. This is what I'll do to you in exactly three days and nine hours and twelve minutes. He felt a stirring of desire and almost smiled. I am not dead yet.

'What the hell are you trying to do?' shouted Matty Cohen.

'I'm trying to be comfortable until you throw me to the wolves in the courtroom,' shouted James Lieberman into the white bedside phone.

Cohen was standing beside his office desk. It was piled one foot high with papers, letters to be signed and open files. He ran his hand through the five grey hairs on his round pink head with a gesture of defeat and he sat down on the swivel chair with such force it threatened to shoot out from under his fat body in the shapeless black suit. 'I spring you on bail and you check into the Plaza! A suite! A goddamn suite for Chrissake! Does that make sense? Whaddya think the press'll do with this little bit of news?'

Lieberman held the phone away from his ear and looked unconcernedly at his watch. Almost noon. Time for a bloody mary. Downstairs in the Oak Room. I'll give Cohen three minutes of fire power and then I'll answer him. He switched the receiver to his right hand and watched the seconds slip by and sure enough after exactly three minutes Cohen's hoarse voice screamed, 'Well, answer me! Whaddya think you're doin' in the fuckin' Plaza!'

'I'm not fucking, that's for sure. Brenda's thrown me out and this situation hasn't exactly made me Bachelor of the Year.'

Cohen sighed and asked softly, 'Christ, Lieberman, there's plenty of hotels in town. Why the Plaza?'

'It's my favourite, Matty,' came an even softer reply.

'Don't you realize you want to appear contrite, in mourning for the woman you loved after her heartbreaking accident?'

'But I am! I wouldn't check in here if I had anything to hide, would I?'

Goddamn, realized Cohen. He is colder than a barracuda. A great white shark would come off as the Easter Bunny next to this guy. Case of my career, my ass! I may just toss it

270

to Racehorse who's been on the phone for three weeks begging to be a 'consultant'. But no, Cohen wouldn't do that. He smacked his fleshy lips over the big messy cases and manslaughter or murder, this was big. It had everything: a rich Jew, a loaded WASP, a beautiful society figure, two top Wall Street bankers, sex, kinky sex no less, the kind the *Daily News* devoted pages to, drugs, and the implication that lots was below the swampy surface about to spray more characters with shit.

'Look, don't talk to anyone. I'm sure your new address will be in the late editions, so don't move whatever you do. That'll be worse. Stay put even if the goddamn Plaza burns to the ground.' Cohen replaced the receiver with a bang and fumbled in his waistcoat pocket for his heart pills.

Lieberman laughed when he heard the dial tone. 'Cool it, Matty,' he said to no one, 'it's not the same suite.'


Burroughs wiped his face with the handkerchief for the third time since getting off the elevator and then opened the door of the suite. Jesus Jesus Jesus. And Peter's wife is having a baby so I, the assistant manager, get it on my plate again. Lieutenant Farwell walked into the room. Radio music was loudly playing. 'The maid didn't touch a thing. Just screamed her head off and then the housekeeper called me. When I . . . when I . . . well, I called you right away.'

A disc jockey's cheerful voice was chattering. 'So the last days of summer in the city, officially we've got till September 21st, for all you folks out there, on beaches, workin' on your tans, sippin' cool things, lookin' at hot things in those teeny weeny bikinis, gonna play some hits for you right now up to six p.m.'

'Turn that thing off,' barked Farwell and a policeman in a blue uniform hurriedly obeyed him. The room was silent now except for the hum of the air conditioner. Farwell passed the double bed where the quilted dark yellow and white bedspread was in place. He noted screws on the wall above the bureau where something had been hanging until recently. A white square also proclaimed its absence. A mirror? There was an expensive watch with an alligator strap on the night table nearest the bathroom and a man's clothes were draped over the armchair by the tall window. The sheer white undercurtain billowed out eerily from the breath of the air conditioner.

Farwell stepped to the open bathroom door where the brightness dazzled him. The shining white tiles reflected the naked body of Lieberman hundreds upon hundreds of times. The three-mirrored bathroom cabinet was open, there was a round shaving mirror on the edge of the tub, the mirror from the other room was propped against the radiator. All the surfaces endlessly duplicated the dark hairy body of James Lieberman hanging from the shower fixture. A blue and maroon striped necktie (label: Brooks Brothers) circled his purple neck. His brown eyes were closed and his hand held his penis as if in some last affectionate embrace.

'Okay, get the pictures,' growled Farwell, turning away. The photographer took his place on the threshold and began to snap-whirr snap-whirr snap-whirr.

Burroughs was as pale as a ghost. He said in a high-pitched voice, 'This has got to stop. Our hotel . . .'

Farwell put his arm around the man's trembling shoulders. 'Why don't you go downstairs and order a double something? I'll meet you in your office in twenty minutes. Let me just get him outta here.'

Farwell feared Burroughs was near the breaking point. His eyes were watering and his teeth were starting to chatter. Too young for World War II, too old for Vietnam, and he must've missed Korea for some reason. Must be the first time he's seen a corpse. No, the second. The second in six months. 'Go with him, Valensky. Go on downstairs with him.'

Valensky's young face crumpled. Seven months with Farwell and he got handed the babysitting jobs. Farwell nodded at the youth, who still sported a few adolescent pimples, and Valensky automatically responded, 'Yessir', and followed Burroughs through the door and down the hall.

In half an hour the men with the body bag had arrived and

272

gone bearing 190 pounds of what had been James Jeremy Lieberman. 'Incredible they don't have a freight elevator here, ain't it, Lieutenant?' commented Warren, who'd been present when Mrs Wickham's body was removed. 'Old man O'Neill told me when they found that dame Dorothy Parker dead in the Volney they had to take her down standing up 'cause the elevator was too small.'

Farwell, who was well read, remarked, 'Wonder what she would've said about that.'

'What?' asked Warren.

'I said yes, the Plaza is a great hotel to die in. All the amenities for the live or dead.'

Warren looked confused and then continued to drop wallet, keys, the watch, into a brown envelope. Fewster sat at the little desk by the window, opening and closing the drawers. 'No note, Lieutenant.'

Farwell shook his head. 'No, you won't find one because he didn't leave one.' Warren and Fewster turned to look at him. 'Lieberman didn't mean to die. This is just another accident at a suite in the Plaza.'


The press went crazy with it: SUICIDE AT PLAZA, MURDER SUSPECT TAKES LIFE IN PLAZA SUITE. One *Daily News* reporter had even measured the distance between the two 'death suites', as he called them, and decided that it had been fated to happen. The Plaza Hotel was not happy with the publicity.

Brenda Rosenberg Lieberman was interviewed on *Good Morning, America* and appeared to love every minute of it. 'She's very fat,' was the dry comment of Farwell in front of the station TV.

'No, no,' she almost whispered. 'I don't think he had a death wish. Of course, we have not been very close in the past few years . . .' her New York-accented voice went on.

'What is this new deal? Either you disassociate yourself or you hang in there as a loyal wife or you pull a Brenda Lieberman – half and half.' Miller was annoyed with the

273

whole scene. 'She'll probably get offers in six figures to tell what the *real* Lieberman was like.'

A reporter sipping coffee out of a styrofoam cup hooted, 'Yeah, kiss and sell!'


Adele opened her eyes and for a moment wondered where she was. She listened for the sound of water in the bathroom. Silence. The shades were pulled down to the window sill, reminding her to order the curtains today. Should have done it last week. Adele could hear nothing but the tick of the bedside clock. She reached for it and turned it to face her. 'Cripes!' she said, whipping the sheet off her. 'Ten fifteen!' Paul must have left hours ago. I didn't hear a thing. She stumbled into the bathroom and stared at herself in the mirror. I look terrible, went through her mind as she squeezed Crest on to her toothbrush. The phone was ringing.

Ann thought: Good. She's not at home, which means she's dressed and doing something. I'll let it ring just a few more times.

Adele didn't hear it for a moment and then she dashed into the bedroom to grab the receiver on what was to be its last ring.

'Adele! It's Ann! What about lunch today?'

Adele frowned. She really didn't feel like it. 'Ann . . . I . . . well,' she murmured.

'Come on. The sun's out and we can walk up Third Avenue to some place with tables on the sidewalk.' Silence.

'I just don't . . .'

'Do you have other plans?' Silence. 'Adele! Shall I stop by at twelve thirty?' Ann said with determined cheerfulness.

'All right,' Adele said. 'I'll be here.' She hung up the phone and closed her eyes. I don't want to go out. I don't want to see anyone. I don't want to leave the apartment. I guess I have to wash my hair, she thought vacantly as she stared at a dank strand between her fingers. I guess I'll have to. She stood up and slowly walked into the bathroom.

Ann arrived at half past twelve on the nose and followed

274

Adele into the living room. 'What about a glass of wine before we go?' asked Adele. 'Or did you make a reservation somewhere?'

'No, I didn't. Let's have a glass of something here.' Ann thought: She looks better than the last time I saw her. Clean hair. Clean beige linen slacks. White blouse. And at least the apartment is spic and span.

Adele handed her a glass of white wine and then carried her own to the opposite end of the peach sofa. 'Cheers!' she smiled.

'To new things!' said Ann. She began to talk about the last night at '21' and said that Charles had been in good spirits.

'I think he is beginning to come through all this,' said Ann, 'but I'm not sure about you.'

'My, my, nothing like being direct,' said Adele sarcastically. 'I told you that I'm fine. I don't know why you insist that I'm not.' Her face was disconsolate.

'I want you to be fine. I just don't think you're seeing friends or going out very much.'

'I talk to Nina a lot.'

'That's good. She's a great person. She's a good friend. Do you see her for lunch?'

'No, she usually comes here after leaving the Countess in the afternoon and we have wine together. Sometimes we have a quick talk on the phone after Paul has left for work.'

'How is he?'

'Okay.' Adele's lower lip trembled and she quickly brought the wine glass to her mouth. Ann waited. This silence feels tight, tense. I don't know what to say. I'll wait for her to speak.

A gasp came from Adele and Ann realized that hot tears were coursing down her face on to her white sweater. The voice was like an underwater gurgle. The words were nearly unintelligible. 'I want . . . I want . . . I want . . . Mother,' she sobbed. She dropped the wine glass on the floor where it rolled in a circle on the new carpet and then she put both hands over her face. Ann moved towards her with open arms. Adele clutched the sleeve of her brown wool blazer,

275

hanging on like a child. Suddenly she was still and Ann pulled away and then left the room to find a box of tissues.

When she returned Adele was staring into space. 'Sorry, sorry, really I'm sorry,' she said.

'Don't be sorry about it. You're so strong. Maybe too strong.'

'What do you mean?' sniffed Adele as she took the Kleenex.

'I mean that it's time you let everything out and said, "This isn't fair! This isn't the way it was supposed to be. I'm sad, and I feel terrible."'

Adele's face contorted with the beginning of new tears. She managed to nod and say, 'It wasn't supposed to be like this . . .' before the tears came in a flood all over again.

They never left the apartment. An hour later Ann went to the kitchen to make tea, but Adele didn't want it, so she filled glasses with ice cubes and they drank Perrier. At a few minutes past five Ann asked when Paul came in from the office.

'About six. Unless he plays squash at the Racquet Club.'

'Can you talk to him about some of this?'

Adele laughed mirthlessly. 'Ha! He doesn't want to know it ever happened! Mother never existed for him. And I let him down. He treats me as if I slept with every man in California . . .' She was suddenly angry.

'Did he say that?'

'No, of course he didn't. It's written all over his face when he looks at me. Usually, he doesn't look at me.'

'Adele, you might be imagining it. He might not be thinking that at all.'

Adele's lips were a thin line. She shook her head and her white blonde hair fell across her face. 'No, I'm not imagining it.' They sat in silence for a few minutes. Ann wondered if she should bring up the subject of a psychiatrist, of someone to talk to. Maybe only one or two visits would be enough. Adele broke the silence. 'Like mother like daughter!' She began to laugh uncontrollably.

Ann stood up and shouted, 'Stop it! Stop it! Whatever your mother did has nothing to do with you! We still don't know exactly what she did do! But whatever it was, it has nothing to do with you!'

Adele was stunned. She'd never heard her aunt raise her voice. Never seen her angry. Not in a dozen and a half summers of living in the same house at Watch Hill. Ann was a room-leaver.

'Adele! This is you we're talking about! You! You have just got married! You have just lost your mother in a terrible accident! You are the person who counts here!' Ann continued. 'Your father is going to be all right. I can feel it. But you need some help. You need to understand things.'

Adele said, 'Yes,' very quietly.

'How would you feel about talking things over with a psychiatrist? Going a few times?'

Adele shook her head. 'I don't want to.'

'Well, do you want to sit in this apartment, pretty as it is, for the next few years, dependent upon Nina's phone calls for fun? You're having a lousy time of it, I know. But things can be changed.' Adele stared at the cherubs on the mirror. Ann went on, 'You have to change them. I can only do so much. Nina can only do so much.'

Adele nodded almost imperceptibly. 'You're right,' she whispered.

Ann walked over to the mantel and smiled. 'Things are going to be better, Adele. I can promise you that!'

'Promises, promises,' Adele laughed and then suddenly she was in tears again. The two women walked to the front door together with arms entwined. Ann kissed her on the forehead and told her to wash her face. The girl nodded in an attempt to stem the tears. 'I haven't really cried since Mother died.' She gasped for breath. 'Except at the wedding. I simply couldn't. And now, I can't stop.'

Ann kissed her again and smoothed the hair off her forehead. 'Go and take a long, hot bath but first, take two of those steaks out of the freezer.'

'Thanks, Ann.' Adele's face was pink and splotched from tear stains.

Her aunt waved from the elevator. 'Call you tomorrow.'

*

277

Adele was up early. Paul was surprised to find himself alone in their big double bed. He stepped into the shower, realizing that she must have quietly managed a bath without waking him.

'Hi!' she smiled in the dining room. 'Do you want toast and scrambled eggs?'

Paul shook his head. He was mystified. He hadn't even been seeing her in the morning, and now suddenly she was up and dressed and offering breakfast. Paul's hair was wet from the shower and all the little comb lines showed. He wore a dark blue Brooks Brothers suit with a pale blue Oxford cloth shirt and a dark blue tie with wide bands of yellow across it. The table before him was set with straw mats and hand-painted china and lime green napkins. A tall glass of orange juice was beside his coffee cup.

'Come on, Paul!' she urged. 'Let me try to be the perfect wife for ten minutes at a time.'

'You look very pretty today,' he said quietly as he shook out the napkin. Adele smiled and waited. 'Okay, I'll risk it. Toast would be great.'

The only light in the small bedroom came from the window and shone on the two standing figures. Clothes were scattered on the bare wooden floor and the sheets of the double bed were rumpled and hung over the foot. 'Hey, hey,' she soothed. 'It's okay.' Her long dark shining hair fell against his smooth shoulder as she embraced him from behind. Her skin was very tan, with bikini marks in two narrow white stripes. Jack stood naked, as perfectly muscled as any statue of Adonis. He put his head down, palms flat against the window sill, and then frowned as he looked up and gazed out at the river without seeing it. The moon was hanging over Boston like a big white balloon. Someone was sculling over the black water of the Charles. Stroke stroke stroke, the shell glided towards a bridge and was lost from sight. Getting dark so early, thought Jack. 'Hey, Jack.' The girl kissed his shoulder blade. 'Come back to bed with me.'

He didn't reply. At last he turned and gathered her in his

arms. 'Sorry, Lisbeth. It's not you . . .' He stopped. 'It's not you.' No, it wasn't Lisbeth. It was the ghost of summers past. He swatted her on her white bottom and she shrieked. 'Let's get dressed and go to the Fellini film.'

She hid her disappointment. 'Sure, let's.'

In moments they had pulled on jeans and sweaters and the suede boots that composed their uniform. Lisbeth cursed the stickiness between her legs and went to the little green-tiled bathroom to yank off the boots and blue jeans and to wash. Damn! Getting worse, she complained to herself in frustration as she grabbed the green washcloth. I just can't reach him. I can't even seduce him any more, and that used to be the easy part. Her mind flashed back to that Saturday night of the previous January when they'd met at the Wursthaus in Harvard Square.

The place was always thick with smoke and the smell of beer and that night had been no different. People were laughing at nothing and Lisbeth suddenly felt the need for fresh air and quiet. She'd excused herself from the group at the long wooden tables and had threaded her way between the dozens of sheepskinned shoulders and ski-parkaed figures at the bar. Lisbeth pushed open the glass-panelled door and stepped with relief over the threshold and into the cold clear night. A fresh snow was falling and the tiny soft white flakes floated down between her and the lights of the crawling traffic on Massachusetts Avenue. Jack watched her for several seconds before she was aware of him beside her. When she fumbled in her pocket for matches, he extended cupped hands bearing an orange flame. Her dark eyes flashed to his face in surprise as she drew on the cigarette. 'Thanks,' she murmured.

'For aiding and abetting.'

'I know, I know.' She winced good-naturedly. 'I'm quitting tomorrow.'

'They all say that.' He put his hands in his pockets and stared straight ahead.

Lisbeth looked at his handsome profile. Stroke of the Harvard crew. How many times had she seen his photograph since her freshman year? How many times had she actually traced with her finger his perfect smile feebly duplicated on a piece of paper in black and white? Jack Forrest, the ultimate preppy from Main Line Philadelphia, top jock, Winthrop House. He probably had JFK's old room, she surmised cynically.

His voice startled her. 'Want to walk?'

She nodded in surprise and he took her arm as they approached the slippery sidewalk already powdered with fine white flakes.

'This is better than the Wursthaus by a long shot,' he smiled.

God, what a smile, thought Lisbeth. She could think of nothing, absolutely nothing to say. *I know all about him and he doesn't know I know. Shouldn't that give me an advantage?* She suffered as she paced her long blue-jeaned legs with his. *It's like suddenly being introduced to the Great Gatsby,* she worried. *What would I say? Oh, Jay, so nice to meet you, at last. He must think I'm a fool. He must be used to witty, effervescently witty, blonde girls who always know the perfect throw-away line and when to drop it, like a pearl, into the conversation. Oh, I hate myself.* Lisbeth almost ground her teeth.

'Let's cut behind Adams,' he said. Adams was one of twelve residences of Harvard; nine of them, called the river houses, were near the Charles, the other three nestled in the Quad in the northern part of Cambridge. Many had been christened for 'eminent worthies', was the joke among underclassmen.

Radcliffe students had now, in effect, become Harvard students and shared the houses. The girls' college had originally been founded to supplement the income of Harvard professors and to give women a higher education, but it had seemed ridiculous for one professor to give two identical lectures to two sexually segregated classes, and so the mixing had begun. Now, of course, it extended to everything and many girls accepted at Radcliffe as students would, when asked, say that they went to Harvard.

Lisbeth and Jack passed Kirkland and then Eliot and then Winthrop under the bare black branches of the trees which

280

bordered the sidewalks. 'This is where I misspent my youth,' he twinkled, pointing at two rather simple red-brick buildings. Lisbeth resisted the urge to say 'I know.' 'Have you been in?' he asked. She shook her head, wondering if he still had his key, wondering if he were inviting her. 'The dining room and the library are both halfway below ground which means that the dining room is rather depressing, but the library is my favourite of any on campus. The windows at the top of the room just pour in light. It's . . .'

'I know what you mean. I remember being there now. I had to do a paper on *Othello* and spent the afternoon there with a book I couldn't find anywhere else. It was last January and it was snowing like this and the light . . . the light was very special.' Her black eyes shone with the memory of that lovely room; even that clean smell, the smell of books came back to her. Her olive cheeks held a flush of dark pink from the cold and her heavy brown hair fell in waves over the turned-up collar of her pea jacket.

At last we began to talk, remembered Lisbeth. He, of course, was in Law School and she was an English major. He shared an apartment with a friend off campus and seldom went home. Wildwood, New Jersey, her home town, was light years away from the rarefied atmosphere of Chestnut Hill. Her father was a clerk in a hardware store and her mother was the kind of woman who would smooth her Penney's cotton print house dress and say, 'It's not what you do, it's how well you do it.' Jack had held her hand as they stood on Weeks Bridge over the Charles. They'd joked about ice skating to London; they'd laughed at the way the snowflakes clung to her long eyelashes.

Later, much later, early Sunday morning, they'd slowly walked past Lowell and back to Adams, where Lisbeth lived. At the front door before dawn she'd teasingly asked if he wanted a swim before breakfast. Jack followed her through the gloomy basement corridor to the indoor swimming pool.

'I knew this existed' – he shook his head – 'but I've never seen it before.' He pulled away his jacket, the green sweater, the shirt; the boots were janked off as he hopped on one foot and then the other.

'Come on! It's so warm!' Lisbeth's hair fanned around her shoulders like shining silk. Her nude body was a flash of tan in the blue water while Jack's was nearly white. Lisbeth lazily did the crawl to the far end of the pool. Half the lights were on in the tiled room and half were off, giving the sparkling water the eerie look of a lake at dusk. The room was a warm cocoon; they were alone in it as the snow fell softly, silently on the sleeping world outside.

Lisbeth clung to the edge and vaguely wondered what would happen next. She knew what had happened with Dave, with Mike, with Stephen, but she had known them. Known them much longer at least. So far, Jack hadn't even kissed her; not on the bridge, not crossing the campus under the trees, not at any of the spots she'd expected to be kissed, not at one landmark where she'd been kissed so many times before. What if he doesn't think I'm attractive, she panicked. Still, he didn't have to come in swimming.

'Aaaaah!' she squealed as he surfaced beside her. The length of his body had rubbed against hers. He laughed and kissed her quickly. Then a look of surprise had crossed his face and she had felt one large hand supporting her as though she were a child in the water as his other hand on the back of her neck pulled her face, her mouth, to his.

'Hey, Lis, you alive in there?' Jack called from the hallway. She hurriedly applied lip gloss and gave her face a searching look before she answered. 'We can't keep Fellini waiting,' he urged as she opened the bathroom door.

'Okay. Ready.' Lisbeth grabbed her trenchcoat and raced towards Jack, who tossed his key ring up in the air and caught it.

They hurried through the crackling fallen leaves beside the river, with Jack wishing they'd left five minutes sooner. Harvard Square is at least a ten-minute walk and we'll miss the beginning, he fretted. Fellini, the true romantic. That mad Italian! With humour, of course, but romance was the thing. Romance, sighed Jack to himself as he looked up at the star-spattered sky. Lisbeth tucked her arm in his, almost running to keep up with his long strides.

'Jack, do you remember when I met you on a Saturday night and we screwed our brains out till Tuesday?'

Bart wakened with a heavy feeling compounded by a headache. There was the meeting with the city planning commission at ten o'clock. He looked at his watch. Seven ten. Still time for a run. In five minutes he was tying the red and white Adidas shoelaces, and in seven minutes he was on the street. The air was still cool, for the October sun had not yet cut through the last patches of early morning fog. Bart inhaled and felt his head clear. A mile and a half later he allowed himself a short walk in the park. The leaves were pale green and the grass fairly sparkled with the glittering drops of dew. So clean.

He tried not to think of last night. No, it had been this morning. The night before always haunted him when he stopped running. He could no longer fool himself with the old 'boy, was I drunk last night'. It always came back to him when he gave himself a chance to think of something other than turning his ankle on the soft earth or wrenching a calf muscle as his foot landed awkwardly on an irregular edge of pavement. I'm not like them. I don't want to be like them. Why isn't anyone else ashamed? Why doesn't anyone else care if they're seen? I don't want to be like them. But it felt good once he started, once he got past the point of taking his clothes off. Bart still winced at the idea of kissing a man. The beard against beard he found unappetizing, but the hard body against his was exciting. The strong fingers, the muscles of a man . . .

He sighed and glanced at his watch, then turned out of the gates of the little park and began to run again. Cars were beginning to ease across the Golden Gate Bridge, and Bart imagined he could taste the acrid air of their exhaust. Seven o'clock is really too late to run. I'll get up earlier tomorrow, he promised himself. And I'll go to bed early tonight. His legs pumped harder up the hill towards his apartment building. And alone, he vowed.

283

# 7

The large, nearly square oak desk was covered with portfolios. A young man with blond hair bent over them, sun streaming in the window behind him, grey skyscrapers looming against a blue sky. That bright light of a clear December day illuminated the blue-carpeted pristine office. A steel sculpture on a pedestal was the only decoration.

Paul Rice was working in his shirt sleeves which he knew was frowned upon, but now that he had his own office he could risk it. He stared down at the figures on the page before him and carefully, in his meticulous way, began to mark the ones in the column that could be used for the stockholders' report. He didn't hear the door open and only looked up when the paper aeroplane glided literally under his nose and did a crash landing on the telephone.

'Hey, hey, don't let the boss catch you!' laughed Dexter from the open doorway. 'Half undressed and playing with toy planes! When are you gonna get something done around here?'

Paul smiled. 'I might ask you that question! Have you found your office yet? I've never seen you at your desk.'

'Ver-y funny. Très amuse-ant.' He closed the door. 'Hey, Paul-ie, how about squash tonight? Are you up for it? Let's make a night of it? Dinner afterward?'

'Sure.' Paul thought: Why not? Better than the bleakness I call home. He had hoped that a change of scene might lift Adele out of her apathy. She had remained more or less apathetic during the house-hunting – Paul had done most of that himself, and made the final choice of a house at Tarrytown in Westchester County more or less by himself – and Adele had just agreed to everything. But it hadn't made any real difference. A night out with Dexter would make a welcome break. Better than facing Adele looking miserable across the perfectly set dining room table. Better than an evening of sit-coms on the tube. Better than that awful moment of should I or shouldn't I make love to my wife.

Dexter retrieved his plane and stood in front of Paul's desk. He hesitated and then spoke. 'Hey, Paul. You don't have to have a game of squash and then dinner with me. You won't hurt my feelings if you say no. After all, you've got a wife waiting at home . . .'

Paul stared at him. 'I want to stay in town tonight. What's wrong?'

'You just don't look wild about the idea, that's all.'

Paul sighed. 'I don't think I'm wild about anything these days. I need a good game of squash.'

'Okay, you're on. See you about six, and we'll walk over and get suited up. I'll get a court for half past.' Dexter grinned and looked as though he were resisting the impulse to toss the plane again. He carried his two hundred and fifteen pounds very well and was surprisingly light on rather small feet. He spun, ballet-like, and closed the door with a flourish and a wave of the paper plane. Paul directed his attention to the pages before him once more.

Sherry always wore too much Charlie. People in the office smelled her before they saw her. She was a good girl, but her skirts were shorter than was the fashion and she did appreciate the men's open glances of appreciation. Paul was conscious of the heavy perfume but didn't raise his head until he heard her say, 'Mr Rice, do you think I could go early today?'

Paul wanted to say, 'Go where?' He found Sherry's English a little off, a little annoying. 'Leave early?' he asked her, knowing he was being a pain and not caring.

'Would you mind? Is it all right? I mean . . . if nothing happens. It's my birthday and the girls are taking me out. To P. J. Clarke's for dinner.'

'Fine. Good idea,' he assented absentmindedly. 'Have a good time.' He looked at her and realized what incredibly long legs she had. The black tights, the high heels, the red and black straight skirt; Paul absorbed it all with a funny feeling that he hadn't really seen her before. Dexter'd made plenty of lewd comments about Sherry but Paul hadn't paid

attention. Now, as he said, 'Happy Birthday', he realized
Dex was on the right track. Amazing, thought Paul, as he
watched her leave the room. Amazing. He picked up the
phone to call Adele to tell her he'd catch the last train and
not to wait up for him. 'Amazing,' he whispered to himself.

Dr Morton talked to Adele about having a child and she
agreed she'd like that. It might help things, she said aloud,
but he corrected her.

'No, don't become pregnant because things are not right,
only become pregnant because you want to add something
wonderful, a new dimension, to what you and Paul have.'
Adele wanted a child and she felt positive that once she was
pregnant with Paul's child, the marriage would really 'jell'.
He would feel important, he would feel protective, he would
concentrate on a future and not the past.

Adele guarded her feelings about Paul. She talked long
and hard about her mother, and eventually Dr Morton said
he thought she needn't return unless, of course, she wanted
to continue the appointments. She didn't want to. She'd
come through a much stronger person, and she felt that Ann
was to thank as much as the psychiatrist. 'Ann is more of a
mother than Mother ever was,' she once blurted to Nina.

Paul was happy when she told him she wanted to become
pregnant. Adele even thought that perhaps their lovemaking
might improve. She always knew when he planned to make
love to her because she could see his shadow on the open
bathroom door as he industriously cleaned his ears with
several Q-Tips. Why? She wanted to shriek. Why those
orifices? It seemed so calculated once she began to notice
the little ritual after he'd brushed his teeth, flossed them,
and gargled loudly. All she could do was lie under the sheet
and wait for him to pad towards her, with Listerine breath
and de-waxed ears, and turn out the light. That was at night.
The morning was different.

She would sense him waking and turning in bed. He
won't kiss me, she knew. Afraid of bad breath. Mine or his?
Adele didn't know. Then she would feel his hand pull her

nightgown up up up above her knees, and then he would fumble with his fingers for one, two, three, count four, then he would pull himself on top of her and in one, two, yes, he was inside. One, two, three thrusts, come on, Paul, see if you can last to four, but no, he never did. With a loud gasp of pleasure, he allowed himself to fall against her and then to roll off to her right. Stage left, thought Adele under him. She would turn and put her arms around his back and kiss his shoulders. Something about all the heavy breathing and the limpness of his flushed body afterwards awakened feelings of maternity towards him.

The alarm would begin its angry jangle and Paul would leap from the bed to silence it on the night table. He would sit on the edge of the mattress facing away from her and rub his eyes. A loud yawn, a shaking of the head the way a dog shook water from itself, and he was up and gone. She'd hear him turn on the tap water and then lift the toilet seat. Oh, God! I wouldn't mind hearing him pee! It'd be better than having him go to such lengths to not let me hear him!

Adele would rise from the bed. Annoyed and dissatisfied, she'd walk down the hall to the other bathroom and step into the shower. She thought of all those Friday and Saturday nights in the Princeton Inn. Don't let anyone tell you that marriage makes it better. Don't let anyone con you into believing that practice helps. Maybe with tennis but not with fucking. It made Adele feel good to think how the word 'fucking' would upset Paul. 'Fucking,' she whispered as the water splashed over her. She rubbed soap on her hands and, as she always did after these morning bouts with Paul, she thought of Jack.


Nina sat at the little French desk in her stocking feet and stared at the open chequebook. That was peculiar. According to the left-hand column of stubs not one cheque had been written since 3 August! And there were, let's see, Nina licked the tip of her pencil and then thought of all those lead-poisoned workers her mother had told her about. Something to do with the war. A clock factory. Luminous

287

numbers? She couldn't remember. The last deposit was $3,059.78 from Mrs Frank Watson and that left . . . exactly $110.14! Surely there must be another chequebook! There must be! Nina breathed an enormous sigh of relief. Yes, this was a Chase Manhattan account number and my salary cheques come from Citibank.

'Kachoo!' came from down the hall as Nina opened the Countess's desk drawer. A case of flu meant that Nina was running the show for a few days. She flipped the second chequebook open and saw that the last cheque, dated the previous Friday, was her salary. With two sets of sums on the phone pad Nina quickly deduced that the account held precisely $56.70. She felt horror sweep over her.

'The mail, Nina. It's been on the hall table all day.' Dorothy shuffled in and then shuffled out over the thick carpet.

Nina could hear her heart pound in her ears as she tore open one envelope after another. No wonder the Countess so jealously guarded all this! Every statement, from Greeff, from Sanderson, from Kroll, from Chelsea Antiques, from Clarence House, was stamped FINAL, URGENT, and least dramatically simply OVERDUE.

'Kachoo!' came from down the hall. Nina paper-clipped all the bills together and put them in her desk drawer. She replaced the chequebooks where she'd found them and then walked across the room to stare out the window. Every tree on every Park Avenue island as far as Nina could see was draped in white lights. Their glow cut through the damp Manhattan dusk like diamond bracelets lying on grey flannel. Well, I won't bring it up now, decided Nina. Not two days before Christmas when she's half dying with the flu. And I won't say a word about my salary until she tries to give it to me . . . and I won't . . . But, what *will* I do? Unless I can find another chequebook or the Countess keeps her money in a coffee can under her bed then her whole life is going belly-up!

\*

Bizarre Christmas, Nina was thinking as she poured champagne into the new flutes from Tiffany.

'They're lovely, Tad. So good of you to bring me something you knew I'd use!' The Countess reclined regally on the chaise of hot pink velvet with the folds of her emerald green silk caftan falling towards the floor. Her feet and head rested on numerous rose-coloured pillows trimmed in embroidered satin ribbons. She looked as though she might be preparing to issue a command to a retinue of minions or to sign a decree for an anxious head of state. 'Poor motherless children!' she suddenly sighed and both Tad and Nina looked at her with surprise, then laughed.

'Hardly!' grinned Nina. 'Mother is having the time of her life with Bart this year! I am so happy he thought of sending her the ticket.'

'Are you sorry you're not with them?' asked Tad.

Nina shook her head. 'Not really, but I guess I felt a pang.' She brightened. 'But we've talked on the phone and the Robertsons' Christmas Day party yesterday was pretty spectacular and I loved going to the matinee of *Blithe Spirit*.' She sipped at the champagne and thought: Last year Omar was in my life.

'A toast,' said Tad lifting his glass towards them from where he sat in front of the fire. 'To my parents in Nassau, to Nina's mother, Nina's brother . . . to absent friends.'

'Hear, hear,' cried the Countess huskily. How relieved she was to have broken it off with Vladimir!

'Don't you think you'd better go easy on the champagne?' asked Tad gently.

'Why ever on earth should I ever go easy on champagne?' The Countess was like an anxious peacock preparing to squawk. She nearly raised herself on her elbows but the effort was too much. With a sigh she sank into the pillows again. 'I mean I'm not going anywhere, am I? I'm not driving, for pity's sake! The prescription said not to operate heavy machinery . . .' Nina and Tad looked at each other and laughed; both conjured up an image of the Countess caftan-clad high atop a bucking tractor.

289

'Is there any heavy machinery in this apartment?' grinned Tad. 'A pencil sharpener? A corkscrew?'

'I shall valiantly fight the urge to curl my eyelashes . . .' The Countess sniffed as they laughed at her.

He's nice, thought Nina. I must never flirt with him. But why can't I be in love with him? Or someone like him?

He poured more champagne into her glass, almost losing his balance and tipping sideways towards the enormous Christmas tree to the left of the fireplace.

'Never drink champagne in front of a blazing fire,' ordered the Countess imperiously.

'Because you may fall into it?' queried Nina anxiously. She was beginning to feel light-headed herself. Never mind the Countess and all her flu pills.

'No! Because warmth tends to make one drink more quickly to cool off. It's very dangerous. Learned that in Malawi during the winter,' she said cryptically. Her audience waited but she was silent.

'Do they have winter in Malawi?' asked Nina. Wasn't it smack-dab on the equator? With a president named Pineapple? No. Banana?

'But, of course they do! Oh, darling, mind you it's ninety-seven degrees outside but it is winter and a fire would be lit and every afternoon one of the servants would ring a bell to gather us in the largest sitting room and in would be wheeled a trolley with cucumber sandwiches and little cakes on it. Steaming tea, a roaring fire, and all of us absolutely drenched in perspiration.' The Countess smiled at the memory. 'Best cucumber sandwiches I have ever eaten in all my life were in Malawi . . .'

As was often the case with the Countess's stories, Nina was hungry for every detail; she longed to drink the tea and to hear the voices. What were you wearing? Which husband were you with? Or were you between them? Or was it a lover? Or were you with a husband *and* a lover?

'I must go,' Tad was saying. 'I promised my aunt I'd stop by for a drink and if I don't hurry they'll be in the middle of dinner and ask me to stay and I don't really want to so I'll just . . .' He was bending down to kiss the Countess and she made a noble attempt to hold her breath and instead sneezed rather dramatically and he leapt away as though shot.

'So sorry, darling! I hope you are not infected! You may sue me if you catch this. I wouldn't blame you at all. Just call my darling lawyer Jason on the first business day and tell him you wish to claim damages . . .'

Tad saluted her and turned to Nina. She saw that familiar melancholy look in his eyes and as casually as she could, stepped forward and kissed his cheek. 'Merry Christmas, Tad. It was lots of fun, wasn't it?'

'It's Boxing Day! Happy Boxing Day!' corrected the Countess but Nina paid no attention and Tad didn't even hear her.

'I'll let myself out.' He waved from the doorway.

An hour later over big turkey sandwiches piled with watercress and cranberry sauce, the Countess suddenly asked, 'Are you all right, darling?'

Nina nodded. 'Absolutely. Especially all right eating this sandwich. I like the day after the holiday much better than the holiday. Cold turkey on rye with plenty of mayonnaise . . . mmmmm.'

'You seem distracted. Are you sure there's nothing wrong?'

Nina sipped champagne and carefully placed the glass on the coffee table, now sporting a white lace tablecloth and dinner plates rimmed in what looked like crushed rubies. Nina sat cross-legged in her black velvet slacks; her orange silk blouse was banded with a narrow gold belt. Black satin ballet slippers were beside the Countess's dark green brocade mules at the opposite end of the sofa. 'I want to say that . . .' Nina stopped and looked up at the Countess.

'Yes?'

'Look, if there are problems, I want you to know that I'll go on working without a salary. For as long as I can.'

'Why, darling! What a silly thing to say – '

'Countess,' said Nina firmly. 'I know. I saw the cheque-books. I thought I should at last pay some bills and . . .' The Countess always said she did the bill-paying. Obviously not.

The truth was out. The older woman's face seemed to sag. With a trembling hand she brought the glass to her lips. Several diamond rings and an emerald twinkled in the lights from the Christmas tree.

In the silent room Nina inhaled the clean smell of the spruce. 'Imported from the Northern Territory,' the Countess had explained to someone last week. 'You mean all the way from Canada?' the man had gasped. 'No, no, of course not! I mean Vermont!' To the Countess, anything past Harlem was en route to the North Pole and the Hudson marked the border of civilization. Points west were frontiers. Why anyone ever left Manhattan except for a beach place or another world capital was 'quite beyond me', she would laugh with a fluttering gesture of her pretty hands.

'Is it bad?' The Countess's voice was uncharacteristically soft, almost shy.

'You mean you don't know?'

The Countess shook her head and the gold coin earrings at her ears made a little tinkling noise.

Nina gulped champagne greedily, swallowed, then took a deep breath. 'Those two chequebooks – the Chase Manhattan and the Citibank – are they the only ones?'

'Well, of course, darling!'

'Then . . . then that's all there is? Just that money?'

The Countess nodded and Nina poured herself another glass of champagne.


Nina wondered if he had stayed at his aunt's for dinner, wondered if he'd be alone in his apartment with a pizza, wondered if he would have his answering machine on. He'd refused their offer of turkey sandwiches.

'Tad?' Nina's voice was tremulous. Good old Tad. I hate myself for calling him. Halfway hate myself, that is.

In fifteen minutes he seemed to understand everything. 'It's just that she's in the living room drinking champagne and I can't offer any suggestions. She refuses to believe that anyone living on Park Avenue could possibly starve to death.' Silence. 'Well, no, I didn't put it quite like that, but I – '

Silence. 'Tad, I don't know what to do. You're the only person who wouldn't embarrass her by knowing. 'You're . . .' He was on his way.

The Countess lay with eyes closed as the two of them spread bank statements, bills, and at last Nina's billings to the clients all over the Aubusson carpet. 'What I don't understand,' began Nina in a whisper but Tad stopped her with a roll of his eyes towards the 'sleeping' Contessa. Nina wrote on a pad and pushed it towards him. 'What has she been living on for all these months since the last deposit?'

Tad grimaced and then extended several bills from American Express; the last one was dated 15 December and was in the amount of $12,565.02. Tad sat with his coat off, his tie loosened and his Gucci loafers tossed in the direction of Nina's black flats. He examined every piece of paper thrust at him and then noted it, checked it off a list he had made and then put it in one of three piles he had organized to his left. Nina poured him another glass of champagne and whispered, 'What do you think?' He put up his hand and was silent for another twenty minutes. At last he put down his calculator and wrote figures on a clean sheet of paper and pushed it towards Nina, who leaned against the nearest pink wingchair. Tad had written in a clear hand, 'Countess owes' and the total was $72,480. The other column was 'Owed to the Countess' and totalled $149,670.

Nina felt better. Things weren't so desperate after all.

Tad's voice betrayed his disgust. 'These jokers don't pay their bills and if you look at the names they are people we know, people who come here and drink champagne and gobble smoked salmon! I'm making a list of the bills I think she should pay first,' he continued. 'There's Gristede's, and once she's on their bad list it'll be tough to get back in their good graces.' Nina winced at the idea of no more deliveries. Dorothy would have a stroke. 'And there's Clarence House. That's the biggest bill to a supplier. What do they supply?'

Nina pointed to the list of order numbers and metres. 'Fabric. Very expensive, very good fabric.'

'Then I think she should pay Charlton's. They're tacking on a penalty.' With Nina's help, Tad wrote down the most urgent debts and then sat back and shook his head. 'You know, Nina, we're doing this backwards. We should be going over the list of people who owe her money first.' And so they did. He was right. Nina recognized all the names; even the clients who hadn't paid for more than two years were often guests of the Countess.

'The nerve,' she hissed when Tad pointed to the Richardsons' bill of $17,000. The Countess had kept past billings aside. Nina had never been privy to the 'accounts due', but had begun billing with the first job she had helped with. It was as if the firm had been founded the day Nina began work.

'I think you should re-type all the bills and put a note at the bottom of each one informing them that as of now there will be a two per cent interest charge on all accounts overdue.'

'Two per cent?'

'Monthly,' Tad said firmly. 'Get tough with these people.'

The Countess suddenly sat up. 'You can't. I can't.' Her voice shook. '"These people" are my friends. "These people" invite me to their parties.'

'And you invite them to yours – ' began Tad.

'But to treat them as if I am Con Ed or the phone company! To dun them!' She shook with outrage. 'I will not allow it!'

'But will you allow them to not pay you! To drive you into bankruptcy!' Tad was as upset as the woman he faced. 'Because much as I hate to tell you this, that's what you're facing!' He held a page of figures in his hand. 'Either you – '

'Get out!' commanded the Countess coldly. 'Leave at once! I'm not a banker! And you plainly are and you – '

'Tad is only trying to help you! He has figured out that – ' Nina thought it was time to take his side.

'Yes! Figures! Numbers on a piece of paper!' Nina had never seen the older woman so angry. 'Now leave me! Please go!'

Tad was already pulling on his overcoat as Nina watched from her position on the floor beside the fireplace. The door slammed behind him. Nina kept her head down as she quietly gathered the receipts and closed the two chequebooks. A large sniff came from the Countess. Nina continued to straighten the papers but when she heard the second sniff she looked up.

The Countess's face was wet with tears. 'Pour me something,' she directed and Nina did so, anxiously watching the golden liquid rise to the top of the glass. The Countess never cried. Had never even told a story in which she confessed to shedding a tear and her stories were full of trauma and drama, of suicide and early death, of waving goodbye to lovers in train stations decades ago; foreign train stations, foreign lovers. 'I'll call Tad in an hour and apologize. I am ashamed for sending him away but there are some things . . . how could he know? . . . and I . . . there are some things I simply cannot have known . . .' she murmured and then held a white lace handkerchief under her swollen red nose. Nina sat at her feet like a handmaiden to a queen, staring into the fire. Wordlessly she began to open yet another bottle of champagne.

'Full of valuable trace elements,' nodded the Countess after the 'pop' had broken the silence. The fire crackled. 'Probably even essential trace elements.' The room was silent again. Nina added another log to the fire. She thought it must be midnight. 'I can't hound these people, Nina. Not after I've cultivated them. Not after I've been accepted by them.'

Nina looked away from the flames with amazement. 'After you have been accepted by them?' The Countess nodded. 'But you are a countess!' cried Nina. 'You are what you are and could have anyone as your friend. Everyone accepts you! You accept them, not the other way around!'

The older woman shook her head. 'No.' She took another sip from her glass. 'It has taken me a very long time to . . . to get here.' Nina waited. 'I wasn't always the Countess of Avondale . . .'

'Of course you weren't! You were born outside London – was it Surrey? – while your father was off in India seeing about his tea plantations . . . or was it his . . . his emerald mines in Burma . . .?' Nina finished lamely. Suddenly she felt a little confused.

The Countess pursed her lips and stared straight ahead, still lying majestically on the pink velvet chaise. 'I have been drinking, Nina, but I haven't been drinking enough to regret this conversation tomorrow. So listen to me.' She turned and extended her glass. Nina refilled it. 'I wasn't born in England and I haven't a drop of English blood in me.' Nina was dumbstruck. 'I decided at some point, probably after reading the Brontë sisters, that I simply would have some English blood, so I began with a long-lost grandfather and before I knew it I had a father from Surrey and a mother from Paris.' Nina didn't move a muscle to break the spell. She'd been sure that the Countess had told her that her mother was Russian. 'I grew up in a dreadful place and resolved to leave. I think I was six when I made that decision. Like you.' She turned the full force of her bright blue eyes on the figure at her feet. Nina's face glowed from the heat of the fire, from the effects of champagne. 'I won't bor~ you with stories of a cruel father and an alcoholic mother who lay in bed all day with a bottle.' Her face showed her distaste. 'Dickens is not my style. I prefer Noël Coward.' She pursed her magenta-painted lips. 'Imagine the most dreadful little town in Iowa and that's where I was born.' Her English accent, her tinkly voice, had died away and in its place came the nasal accent of a midwesterner. 'Once I had decided to disappear, nothing was difficult. No brothers. A sister who married a farmer and was so easily pleased that the idea of a movie in town on a Saturday night would cause her to change her gingham apron with great excitement. No, I wasn't like that. Couldn't ever be. And the lucky thing is to know it soon enough to escape.' Nina remembered the way the wind had blown on the beach at Nantucket as she listened to Mickey Keeling. All three of us. Escape artists.

'But . . . India? Kenya? The winter in Malawi with the cucumber sandwiches?' Nina felt panicked. Surely all this glamour, the adventures, were not to be swept away in one conversation the night after Christmas.

296

'Oh, yes!' trilled the Countess. She gestured towards the gallery of handsome men gazing at her from the forest of silver frames. 'Could I ever make up men as devastating as these?' Filled with relief, Nina poured them more champagne. 'But I didn't start out like Betty Lowell Richardson or Millie Bancroft and I cannot bear the idea . . .' Her voice quavered. Nina understood. 'And I cannot bear the idea that I was nobody and married up. I cannot bear the thought of anyone imagining that I was poor. Poor. Dirt poor. Too poor to go to the dentist.' Her face was filled with pain. 'That's not romantic. That's grey and sordid, and smells.' Nina realized that such words had never crossed the Countess's lips. Her descriptions were full of colours, were light as air, or else something was simply labelled 'horrid, dreadful'. The Countess's eyes were filled with tears. 'I know Tad is right. I know the two of you want to help.' One tear splashed down her face and left a dark track in her white rice powder. 'And I know I must get the money. I'm not totally in a dream world as you may think, but . . .' She put the white lace handkerchief under her nose again to ward off a sneeze. 'But you'll have to think of a way to not involve me.' The tears splashed down her face rapidly now. 'I cannot bear for any one of my friends – and whether they pay me or not, they are my friends – to think that I am desperate, to think that I am not one of them . . .'

Nina put down her glass and threw her arms around the Countess. The two women held each other. This proves, decided Nina, that if you have nerve and imagination you can be anyone you want, do anything you want to do. The Countess broke away suddenly and began to laugh. 'You know more about me than anyone, than even my husbands!' She laughed helplessly. 'I live in fear that some day someone from Iowa will see me on a New York sidewalk and call my name!'

'I don't even know your name!'

'No one does any more! It was the first thing I left behind! Horrid, common name and I was determined to never be common, usual, typical ever again.' She swallowed champagne as Nina pulled away and wiped her wet cheeks with

297

the back of her hand. The Countess began to titter. 'Imagine me in evening dress about to get into a limousine with the chauffeur holding open the door and a farmer in overalls rushing over and calling, "Why, if it isn't Minnie from Buffalo Center!"'


'Happy New Year, Paul!' Adele stood over his sleeping form with a silver tray. She had tied her hair back and was wearing a blue peignoir that she had changed into after her morning shower.

'What's this?' her husband groaned.

'Only freshly squeezed orange juice, French toast with honey, and bacon. Very crisp. The way you like it.' Her smile faded when Paul didn't answer.

He struggled to sit up and then struggled to look enthusiastic. I really tried, he'd tell himself later.

'I think it's awful that you had to work last night. New Year's Eve! It's unbelievable!'

Yes, it is, thought Paul. But you believed it. 'You didn't have to do this, Adele.'

'I wanted to! It's a new year and I . . . I just wanted to, that's all.' She sat on the edge of the big double bed with the tray on her lap. The bedroom had at last been finished with the same scheme she'd picked out for the apartment in New York. It suits us, thought Adele, why try to find something else I like as much? The walls were a pale blue with white moulding. The dark blue and pale coral flamestitch curtains and the dark blue fitted spread bound in white had been brought with them.

Adele sometimes went to the familiar curtains and looked out the window at the trees, and instead of feeling what she thought she should feel she felt disappointed. Weren't green trees and that long sloping hill towards the tennis club a better view than a skyline of concrete? Once she was pregnant she'd feel differently. Once there was a child involved things would change. Everything would change.

'This isn't just orange juice, my dear.' Adele tried to be light and sure of herself but she came across as merely trying too hard. 'It's laced with champagne and Cointreau. A mimosa recipe courtesy of Harry's Bar in Venice.'

Paul smiled upon hearing this. Last night he'd had enough champagne to float Harry's Bar clear across St Mark's Square. Or had it got really serious early this morning? Sherry'd borrowed a car and driven him home before dawn. It had been a triumph of sorts to get up the stairs, take off his clothes and fall into bed without waking Adele. He'd turned the bedside clock with the luminous digits around backwards, just in case she'd wakened and tried to see what time it was. But she hadn't stirred.

'Betsy and Jeff are coming at one and Lynn and Robert say they'll try but they'll be held up because of a babysitter problem. Thought I'd just put out a buffet in the dining room and let everyone wander back and forth from the library. I don't think Betsy or I will last through the Super Bowl. Lynn may.'

'She sticks to Robert like glue.'

'True. She knows more about football than he does, more about hockey than his sons. They're always together. Maybe she's determined not to be left this time.' Silence. She continued, 'Do you think people try harder at second marriages because they . . .'

Paul had the pillows propped up behind him and the tray on his knees. He was bare-chested, still a little tanned from Labor Day weekend at Oyster Bay. He concentrated on pouring honey on the French toast.

Adele didn't finish her sentence. He wasn't listening anyway, she realized. She always excused his inattention by: Poor Paul, he's tired. Poor Paul has so much on his mind. Poor Paul will miss his train. His knife and fork made that scratch noise on the china plate that set her teeth on edge and he murmured, 'Excuse me,' with his mouth full and Adele stood up and left the room.

Too much to ask that we ever talk at breakfast. Maybe it's too much to ask that we even talk, she thought as she descended the stairs. They were carpeted in dark blue and led into the rather grand front hallway with the blue and white wallpaper and the brass lantern lamp that hung a few steps in from the large panelled white front door. Nina told me I'd done a good job with this place. Ann loved the house. And yet Paul only notices when something *isn't* done, isn't finished. She walked into the kitchen and stared at her reflection in the microwave. I'm tired. Stayed up till one fantasizing that Paul would come home and we'd toast the New Year and that we'd make love and conceive the child he wants so badly. Instead she'd fallen asleep and wakened to find him snoring and the ice bucket on the floor beside her full of water and an unopened bottle of Dom Perignon. Adele walked to the refrigerator and began to take out the potato salad, the duck pâté, the cold pasta with shrimp and the platter of rare roast beef.


'All right, she won't be involved.' Tad lifted the gin to his lips.

The Stanhope bar is a perfect meeting place for all this talk of money and austerity measures, thought Nina, surveying the plaid carpets and matching upholstered chairs.

'I don't really understand why she . . .' Tad began.

'I can't tell you why. It's very personal and very upsetting to her.' Nina would never betray a secret knowingly. Her own, yes. Someone else's, never. She'd told Adele in freshman year that it was the only good thing in her character.

'Okay. I believe you. Now what'll we do next?'

'I don't know, but I was wondering what is done when a person simply cannot collect money owed to them.' Will we have to go to the Mafia? Nina imagined Mack Mason with a broken leg. And Bitsy Whitmore. And Mrs Lawrence Waters. And Tuttle Anderson. Why, *Town & Country* could do a big colour feature on everyone who was anyone suddenly having broken legs. Call it 'At Home' and have them all posed in casts wearing evening clothes in their splendidly decorated unpaid-for apartments.

'A law firm could become involved, but she won't allow that. Or a collection agency. Or an accounting firm.'

'That's it! An accounting firm!'

'But' – Tad was confused – 'if we aren't allowed to let anyone know that . . .'

'*We* are the accounting firm!' smiled Nina. 'Tad and Nina. The firm of . . . Thaddeus and Ninevsky!'

In three days the stationery had been printed and four days after that Nina had sent out the letters simply informing each client that, due to the increase in volume of the Countess of Avondale's business, henceforth all billing was to be done by the accounting firm of Tipton and McNamara. 'Remember John Beresford Tipton who used to give a million dollars away every week on television?' asked Nina excitedly. Tad laughed. He deeply resented ever being named Thaddeus and was delighted with dropping it from the masthead of anything, even something that didn't quite exist. They agreed that no address would incite suspicion, so used the downtown one of a loft that Tad kept meaning to fix up. The interest penalty was spelled out and one concise sentence directed any questions concerning the billing to Nina McLean at the Park Avenue office. 'The Countess hates anything to do with numbers so she'll put me on the line right away,' she said. 'I think we can get away with it.'

Adele stood in her kitchen for a full five minutes staring at nothing. The shining surfaces reflected each other. The microwave reflected the dishwasher and the dishwasher reflected the glass cabinets banded in oak, laden with the good china from Royal Doulton and the everyday china from Richard Ginori. Adele's platinum hair was reflected in the curved steel of the electric teapot, but it was the window pane above the stainless steel double sink that showed her sad face most clearly.

The Jensen clock said seven twenty-five. A Wednesday evening in January. Paul hadn't called. Again. Adele had given up cooking ahead of time, so now they ate later and later. She only began to put things in the oven when she got the call that he was at Tarrytown and did she want to pick him up or should he get a taxi. Usually she went, but she preferred his taking a taxi.

They embraced in the manner of all couples meeting at the station – the lean towards each other across the front seat, the peck on the cheek with the woman's left hand never leaving the steering wheel, then the anxious backwards glance, and the car, usually a station wagon, would move into reverse, then forward and out of the parking lot. Paul usually looked tired and said he was. Adele usually smiled and said, 'Hard day?' with as much enthusiasm as she could muster. Mustering was the word, she thought, as in summon troops, armies, in going into battle.

Paul resisted the urge to snap on the car light and to shake out the second and still largely unread section of *The New York Times*. Instead, he contented himself with staring at the trees, thinking of the landscape he left behind every day for ten hours of metal and asphalt and glass. There was never very much to say as Adele drove over the dark roads and up the long driveway, with him beside her and his big black calf briefcase from Gucci between them on the seat. Somehow, things went better at dinner if he walked in the door and then they said hello as she came out of the kitchen holding a dishtowel, or about to put a salad on the table.

Adele had begun to worry about what to say soon after they had moved to Tarrytown. The entire idea had been Paul's because, of course, she would be pregnant soon. She felt it was her fault and he felt it was his, and neither of them could speak of it to the other. Adele's period had come again. She touched the waistband of her wool skirt and frowned. She reminded herself to ask Paul if he would meet her at Dr Larson's office on Friday morning.


Morning after morning, Harry, the stout doorman at 799 Park on duty from six in the morning to noon, winced when he heard Nina McLean's boots approach the glass front door. She always lifted her palm as though to open it herself and always seemed pleased when he did it for her. Then it began. 'Has the mail come? Have you sorted it? Oh, is that all there . . .' – she would flip anxiously through the envelopes, still gloved, rosy-cheeked from the cold – '. . . is?'

She would appear agonized over the day's catch. Then as if to make up for her brusqueness she would thank him profusely and, clutching the letters as though she'd just as soon leave them behind, she would stalk to the elevator in high boots with that same determined stride. But on the eleventh morning her eyes widened and she dropped her purse, her canvas tote bag and all the envelopes save a pale blue one on the marble floor. Wrenching off brown suede gloves, she tore it open and shrieked. It was a cheque, Harry could see that, but had it been for ten dollars or ten thousand – or ten million for all the way Miss McLean acted – he simply hadn't been able to see.

Each morning after that was a call for euphoria for she behaved as though she'd won the lottery. Just as Tad predicted, she thought to herself as she said good morning to Harry, the cheques have begun to arrive.

'These people cannot stand the idea of losing money. They'll spend it but they don't like to feel it's being wasted. And the Countess has never pressed. Why, even Tiffany presses.'

'Well, speaking of pressing, before you start charging interest, before I get the urge to see Rio for Carnival . . .' Nina slid his cheque for five thousand dollars across the table to him. 'A few weeks ago' – she looked around the dimly lit Stanhope bar – 'when we met here, I was sure I'd have to deposit this.'

Tad tore it into small pieces and put it in the heavy glass ashtray. Then he grinned. 'When you're teetering on the edge of bankruptcy there's nothing like an old established accounting firm to set things right.'


The white blonde hair blew in the wind which swept arctically off Fifth Avenue, but the tall young woman in the mink coat ignored it. Nice to see broad streets and lots of taxis, and not shopping centres and highways and green trees and station wagons, she thought petulantly as she jay-walked with the aplomb of a born New Yorker.

Adele stopped in front of the Saks window and looked

critically at the bikinis and sandals and beach hats that were now labelled 'cruise wear'. Wonder if I will fit into a bikini this summer? Wonder if I will be –. she ticked off on her gloved fingers February, March, April, May, June – five months gone? She pulled up the coat sleeve and glanced at the tank watch. Well, I'll be ten minutes late if I don't get a cab immediately, she thought as she dashed towards Madison Avenue with one arm over her head. The bright yellow Chrysler swung over to the kerb and she got in gracefully.

'Daly's Dandelion,' she called through the little holes in the bulletproof barrier and the black driver answered, 'Right on, momma,' and pulled out into the traffic.

Nina had the feeling that she was going to cry out with joy when she saw Adele being led between the tables by the waiter. 'Missed you so much,' she gasped as they embraced and went through the 'should I check the mink or not' routine with the waiter, who plainly didn't want to be responsible for the expensive coat. They draped it over the chair between them and Nina put her two Bloomingdale's shopping bags on top.

'Wow! Adele! It's really something! Christmas from Paul?'

Adele nodded. She hadn't wanted the coat. She'd tried every way she knew to get him to consent to a few days in the Caribbean but the coat had been a pacifier, the 'isn't this wonderful? look what I bought for you' present instead of two tickets to Jamaica. Adele nodded when asked about a bloody mary and then stared across the table at Nina. 'So how is everything?'

'Great.' Nina pulled at the wide belt looped twice around her narrow waist. She wore a black sweater with white collar and cuffs showing and red and black plaid trousers.

Adele was silent. Nina was silent. Adele doesn't look very well, thought Nina. She doesn't look at all happy. Wonder if it's Paul. Wonder if I should ask. No, she'll tell me. If she's going to tell one living soul, it'll be me. 'Adele, isn't that my turquoise pullover?'

'I wore it for luck. I always do. And it goes with these fuchsia trousers, don't you think? You want it back?'

'No,' laughed Nina. 'So what do you need luck for, when you're having lunch with me?'

Adele's face was crossed with worry. 'Not for lunch with you. For my pre-lunch appointment with the famous and highly-esteemed-by-somebody Dr Larson.' She took a swallow of the bloody mary which had arrived in a goblet. 'I think I hate him, Nina.'

'What does he say?'

'He says to work on it.' She frowned. 'Ha! It is work.' She glanced around the restaurant at people arriving and departing. 'I wish I still smoked!'

Nina reached out and clasped the clenched fists on the red and white checked tablecloth. God, how much has gone on in the space of ten tables, maybe only five tables, since my life at Briarcliff.

Adele tried to smile. She succeeded only in looking insincerely glum. 'Nina, why don't I get pregnant? Why is it taking so long?'

'What does Larson say?'

Adele retorted angrily in a sing-song voice, 'He says there could be one or more of several causes, for as many as one in six couples in the United States have fertility problems which prevent conception. He says . . .'

'You sound like a scientist giving a speech. Now stop it! Tell me what he says to *you*.'

'Okay, sorry. I'm just mad. Larsen is so detached. Paul is so detached. The idea of a baby has become a business deal between men. I thought . . . you know . . . I was sure . . .' Her voice trailed off. 'Cheeseburger medium with bacon and another bloody mary without tabasco,' she said to the waiter.

'Same here,' echoed Nina.

'You know, I thought when we got married that the baby would be the answer. That baby was the problem but that the next baby would be the answer.' Her eyes filled with tears. They were pale blue like her mother Tory's beautiful clothes.

Mrs Wickham always used to dress in that colour, reminisced Nina. Nina remembered the wedding, the cry from Adele as she cut the cake, and then the clouds of white around her as she slumped to the floor of the Wickham living room. Ann Forrest had taken charge and directed Jack and Paul to carry her to the bedroom to wait for the ambulance. Nina remembered the bloodstains on the back of the dress and had strangely been reminded of some old movie, of the bloodstained sheets the bride was to hang out the window after her wedding night in a village in Sicily.

The two were silent. Adele was thinking of waking up in the hospital bed and seeing Paul's silhouette at the window at dusk. She had wanted to call for Jack and had stopped herself.

'Hey, Nina.' She pulled herself back to the crowded restaurant. 'I don't want to talk about this. It only depresses me. I wish you could help but this is one thing you can't do anything about!'

Nina nodded and slowly reached for the bloody mary before her.

'What are you thinking of?' asked Adele. She'd rarely known Nina to be so quiet. Even in the face of something ghastly, her father's dying, for instance, she was always fairly exploding with the drama of it. This gloom was unlike her.

'I may lose my apartment.' Nina held up her hand before Adele could speak. 'Correction. I am losing my apartment. They're tearing down all the buildings on that block to make room for high-rises.'

'My God!'

'Yes. I keep walking around saying that, too.'

'How long do you have to find another place? I know a really super realtor who found something for Laurie when she was – '

'I'm not going to look for another place.'

'What do you mean? You're taking up residence in Central Park?'

'I have another apartment is what I mean. In Rome.'

'You can't be serious!' Adele's face showed incredulity.

'I decided this morning when I woke up and have been thinking of it all day. Tonight, actually at one a.m., I'll call the owner of that hotel and see if his uncle still has the empty via dei Greci apartment.'

'But – to move to Italy just because – '

'No, it isn't just because of 90th Street.' Nina stared across the crowded tables. 'I want the change. Intensely.'

'Omar?' Adele's voice was soft. They hadn't mentioned his name to one another for months, nor had Nina mentioned him to the Countess. Not since the weekend in Nantucket. Hamburgers were placed before them. The ketchup was passed back and forth. 'I was an idiot.' Adele had no way of knowing what flashed through Nina's mind. It wasn't only the love affair with Omar; it was the searing humiliation of having Mickey Keeling's face above hers as she shouted 'Yes!' when he'd asked if she'd always got any man she'd ever wanted. 'Since Briarcliff, since really discovering boys . . . men . . .'

Adele corrected her. 'They discovered you.'

'Well, whatever. I have had this idea that I was invincible, could do anything I wanted. I flirt with Tad and he is speechless, so now I go out of my way not to smile too much around him. I flirt with Greg and he asks me to marry him. I'm in simply a good mood with someone who takes me to dinner and for some reason they think it has something to do with them and the evening becomes magic and before I know it . . .'

'They've asked you to marry them.'

Nina nodded. 'So I pick a big bad Lebanese who is married, who isn't particularly affected by my Southern belle wiles and I turn myself inside out trying to get him to . . .' She fell silent.

'What did you want from him?' Adele filled in.

'When I figure it out, you'll be the first to know,' frowned Nina. Adele waited. 'I feel foolish. Now. I didn't then. I think of all the parties with Omar and everyone knew I was his little – '

'Wait a minute! I've seen you with Omar at the Countess's and he always had his arm around you, the big brown eyes worshipping your every move, the protective air, the adoring manner. He appeared to drink you in. That is irresistible. It would be to me, anyway.' Adele thought: I've never had that experience. Maybe I never will.

307

'Yes, *it* was irresistible because something in me knew I wasn't irresistible. It was such a challenge. He didn't find me irresistible, did he? He commuted from a bed in New York to a bed in Geneva and . . .' She took a rather vicious bite of the big juicy hamburger. 'That doesn't matter really. Not now. What I really wonder is: Did I run after him because I secretly knew I couldn't have him? I know the games I played with him. What kind of game was I playing with myself?' The two friends sat for a moment, not speaking.

'It's always been so easy for you. I remember at Briarcliff when you would debate over four different dates for the weekend at four different colleges and you were bubbly and light about it. And what surprised me was . . .' Adele's voice faded to nothing in the noisy restaurant.

'What? Tell me.'

Adele looked at her plate. 'It was as if the boys you turned down . . . the ones you didn't see again after giving them a wonderful time at the football game or slow-dancing for seven hours at a party . . .'

'What about them?' insisted Nina.

'It was . . . I know this isn't true because you are such a kind person to me, to all your friends . . . but it was as if the boys you rejected didn't feel anything. You hurt them, Nina. And I don't think you ever thought about it.'

Nina flushed a deep red. Adele had never criticized her before. Oh, yes, she'd said, 'oh, don't wear that' or 'maybe you shouldn't have said that', but never anything like this. Nina nodded. 'I think I grew up in a strange household and . . . maybe I'll always trust women more. Maybe I'll always want them to think the best of me . . .'

Adele nodded, glad to create a bit of distance between what she'd just said and the present conversation. 'You are a best friend to women and they know that. I think it probably surprises them at first. I remember, again, back at Briarcliff, no matter how animated you were, or excited, or full of yourself, you would never go after anyone's date but your own.' She stopped. 'And at least one of his roommates and two of his fraternity brothers.'

Nina laughed. 'Oh, silly me!' she simpered, putting on a Southern drawl. 'Was I just unbelievably drippy?' She batted her eyelashes self-mockingly.

Adele nodded. 'But everybody loved it.'

'It takes a lot of energy, you know. To be on, like that. I have finally crashed into a steel wall. I feel . . . remember last year? I told you I felt used in Paris? Well, that's the word.'

'If Omar hadn't been married, you wouldn't use that word. If he had been free he probably would have wanted to marry you. I mean . . .' Adele put her fork down, 'every man does. Sooner or later with you.'

'Maybe I need a shrink. Maybe I went after him because I couldn't have him. And yet I used to daydream about marrying him, about having all the things he could give me . . .' Nina's face was troubled. She looked at Adele. 'What do you think?'

'I think,' said her always practical old friend of five years, 'that you had a very unhappy but rather typical affair with a married older man. Of course, it was more dramatic in ninety-nine ways because Omar is so attractive and whirls from continent to continent and seems to have . . .' Adele hesitated. Where did all his money come from, anyway? It had never been clear. 'Pots of money.' She looked very serious. 'Thank your lucky stars you didn't marry him.'

'Well,' mused Nina. 'He *was* divine in bed.'

'So what does all this have to do with Rome?' Adele had never seen Nina hurt in a love affair, could hardly fathom the idea that she had been so injured as to need to slink off to lick her wounds.

'I'm not running away. Please don't think that.'

Adele shook her head. 'It isn't like you.'

'I think Rome would be good for me. A total change. I want to throw myself into something brand new.'

'But your job with the Countess . . . it's what thousands of women anywhere in the world die for. Why, Mother told me once that the Countess has people who offer to pay *her* for the experience of working with her.'

'True. I've seen the letters. The latest one from a woman in Chicago who offered to move to New York. But . . .' Nina sipped from the goblet of tomato juice. 'The Countess has promised I can come back to her.'

'Well, that makes a great difference. Fantastic!' So Nina had told the Countess first. Adele felt a twinge.

Nina was pensive. Why am I going to Rome? she asked herself. 'Adele, to be honest with you . . . I have no idea why I'm going to Rome. It's not an intellectual decision. It's all emotional.'

'It is Omar, then?'

Nina shook her head. 'I really don't know any more. I feel at loose ends. I go to parties and never see anyone who attracts me the way he did. With that wanting deep in my stomach . . .' She laughed. 'Somewhere in the region of my liver.' Adele winced as Nina continued more soberly, 'I go out to dinner so often I don't have to read the menu at "21" or La Côte Basque. I can have the same flirty conversation, with minor changes of course, evening after evening, with . . .'

'With men who hang on your every syllable.' Whether you try or not, thought Adele, not without the tiniest pinprick of jealousy.

Nina didn't argue about it. It was true. 'I don't even wonder if I should make love or not, which used to be, pre-Omar, the $64,000 question. The biggest decision after working hours with the Countess is what to wear.'

'Do you still think of him?' Adele prayed she didn't. She was better off. He was too foreign. He was trouble. Adele had been convinced of it since he'd tickled her hand with his moustache in that oh-so-too-gallant to be true introduction months ago.

'Maybe that's it. I'm not moping but I am reminded of him all the time. Everywhere I turn. Every time I'm in the Countess's living room.' Her mind flashed to Mickey Keeling last Friday in the doorway, apologizing for the absence of Lila. 'She has her mother here from Grosse Pointe and I'm to meet them for dinner later. She wishes she could be in two places at once.' He had then turned to Nina who had tried to step out of sight behind John Heiden. The relief of a clean getaway was short-lived for she had bumped the Chinese vase of pink tiger lilies and it had tottered round and round in a maddening little circle on the hall table. Mickey and she had reached to steady it at precisely the same moment. His voice was roguish. 'Still breathing, I see. How is the unvanquished Nina McLean?' She'd answered 'fine' through clenched teeth. 'Where are your manners? Are you ever going to thank me for saving your life?' With eyes flashing she parroted, 'Merci beaucoup. Thanks ever so much. Etcetera.' He had laughed uproariously then. With that exuberance she'd once thought so attractive. Nina had moved away feeling hot and uncomfortable and above all, worst of all, ridiculous.

'But is Rome a plus?' Adele was insistent. 'Will living there make you happy?'

'Yes, I think it will. I'm going to learn Italian and get a job as a decorator. I know the names of some of the Countess's suppliers and I know a little about Italian antiques and why shouldn't I be able to talk someone into hiring me?' She grinned. 'I've always approached job interviews as just a minor variation of a blind date.'

'If anyone can crack the Roman job market, you can.'

'If I don't, for some weird unfathomable reason, then I do have money for a while. Mother's money. But . . .' Nina's face was lit by excitement. 'I just have a feeling about Rome. And' – she flipped hair behind her ears exposing the big black and gold chunky earrings – 'at the end of the summer I'll come back to New York. Bilingual and hopelessly sophisticated and wildly urbane and maybe even half as elegant as you.'

Adele laughed. 'I think you should go, when you put it that way. And don't worry about what you're leaving in New York or what makes you want to go. That job with the Countess is probably worth double all your men put together.' Adele looked at Nina and admired her. Would I ever have the courage to move to a foreign city and start over? Not having one friend, not knowing the language? 'You can spend all your free time in art galleries and museums non-stop. I think you should go. But, after all this, what if the apartment is not available?'

311

'I won't know until after midnight. I've made a deal with myself. If I call and it's rented then I stay here with an entirely different game plan. Working very hard. Maybe Italian class. At night of course. And more time with my antique books and less time with men who . . .' She sighed then brightened. 'But if it's free I'm off to Rome.'

Adele would miss Nina. Miss knowing she was forty minutes on a train away. 'When will you go?'

'Oh! Don't look like that!' Nina laughed. 'Not for a week at least. I actually have a blind date tonight.'

Adele leaned forward. 'Who is he?'

'Probably Manhattan's answer to Jack the Ripper. A client's son. Third time he's called. I practically have to go. I intend to keep my hand over my wine glass all evening long and if anything tastes the least bit peculiar I will leave the table and call the Poison Control Center.'

'Call *me* tomorrow! First thing!' Adele pleaded. 'No, better yet, come for the weekend. You haven't been out to the house for ages. Take the Croton Local on Friday night. Get the first train you can when you finish with the Countess.'

Nina nodded. 'I'd love it. I will.'

'Okay! All set!' Adele waved her credit card at a waiter who dashed over and bowed from the waist, hamming it up. God. Two good-looking women. Blew his theory of 'one beauty one dog'. All week long one beauty one dog. Nina slipped a ten-dollar bill under Adele's hand as she signed the credit card voucher.

'Never! You're on your own! I've got Paul to take care of this. That's Italy money,' Adele said definitely as she stood and gathered the mink coat. They made their way out to Third Avenue.

'I think it's Bloomingdale's money!' groaned Nina as she hugged Adele goodbye in a profusion of yellow shopping bags. 'The Countess gave me the morning off and it proved to be a very dangerous thing.'

'Speaking of danger,' Adele called over her shoulder as she opened the door of a taxi, 'keep your eyes open on the blind date!' Nina made a face at her. The door slammed closed and the taxi sped uptown as Nina turned to walk towards Park and to the Countess.

Sherry stared into the bathroom mirror as she applied the Helena Rubinstein mask. It was thick and pink and was made solely of herbs and natural ingredients according to the label. The once-white terrycloth bathrobe had orange make-up stains around the collar and dark grey cuffs. She kept forgetting to throw it in the laundry bag on Saturdays. Sherry read the instructions again: 'All over the face avoiding the eye area.' Okay. She put down the little jar and rinsed her hands. Sherry looked critically at her hair and decided that the roots could be retouched. Yeah. Saturdays. Always a lot to do.

She scuffed in her yellow terrycloth bedroom slippers into what served as living room and bedroom and dining room of her little studio apartment. It wasn't much but it was better than living with her mother and her mother's third husband, who was always giving her that look that saw right through her clothes. Disgusting. With his beer breath and his beer belly and his beer mentality. Sherry thought of Paul. He was different. Different from anyone she'd ever known. She flicked on the television but her attention was not on the screen. She thought of Paul's suits, the way he smelled in the morning, the way he went off to play squash at that club on Park Avenue. Park Avenue! That was it. The way he belonged on Park Avenue. Paul was a Park Avenue kind of person.

Sherry leaned towards the little low Formica table and started pushing magazines aside. Yeah, here it is. She flipped open last month's *Cosmo*, page eighty-seven: 'The Mistress who Gets her Man'. Sherry stood up and fumbled in the coffee mug by the phone for a ballpoint pen. She returned to the foam couch covered in tan Naugahyde, put her feet on the table, and began to read, underlining as she went.

*

313

Not bad for a little redneck from Mississippi, thought Bart as he pushed sapphire studs into his starched pleated shirt. Christmas present from Karen, he sighed. Jesus, Jesus, what am I going to do with her? Bart pulled the shirt on and, in his white undershorts, walked to the stereo to turn up the volume. The voice of Billie Holiday filled the bedroom. Just the thing before *Giselle*. He hummed to himself, 'Ain't nobody's business if I do . . .' And in two hours I'll be watching the 'willies' on stage in the dark with Susannah Stribling at my side. 'Ain't nobody's business if I do . . .' The last time he'd seen *Giselle* had been with Karen, but we're not an item, crossed his mind. And Susannah did ask me first.

Bart stared into the mirror above the bureau. One swipe with the brush and his black hair was perfectly smooth. One little touch of the bow tie and it was horizontal below his handsome tanned face. Bart squinted at the gold mirror frame which was jammed with white rectangular cards. He plucked one from the corner and thrust it into the pocket of his black dinner jacket. At least a dozen were left. 'Miss Diana Lane Landrum requests the honour of your presence at a Masked Ball', 'Miss Heather Louise Webster requests the pleasure of your company at a reception in honour of . . .' A few were handwritten. 'Bart! Please come up to the ranch for Daddy's birthday . . .' 'Dear Bart, hope you can come for drinks before the opening of the Noël Coward Revue then a theatre party after. We're meeting at my house in the garden at half past six Friday the 12th . . .'

The circuit, he'd nicknamed the round of dances, parties, benefits, dinners and weekends. The invitations which filled his mailbox and cluttered his mirror attested to Bart McLean's allure as a good-looking elegible bachelor. An escort. A well-suited or properly tuxedoed arm to be on. Bart winked at his reflection and then turned away. 'Ain't nobody's business if I do . . .'


Charles Wickham stood in his study by the window. The islands of Park Avenue were white with snow below him and

314

all around them swam gleaming taxis and cars with white headlights and red brakelights jockeying for position as they cruised north towards Harlem or south towards the gold façade of the Helmsley Building. He held the deed to Windswept in his hand. It had always been Tory's house, Tory's mother's house, the Watch Hill place he'd struggle to get to, the weekend place where he'd arrive too late for Friday dinner. The house with the obvious separate bedrooms. The house that smelled of that damned lemon furniture wax.

Adele now spent the summer weekends with Paul's parents at Oyster Bay. *Jack is in Washington. I haven't seen or spoken to Ann for months and months.* His mouth turned down at the corners. *I don't think any of us want to go back there.* Charles put his hands in his pockets and jingled his coins and then started to retract them guiltily. That was a habit Tory couldn't abide. He halfway expected her voice behind him, 'Charles, *must* you?' He turned to survey the room. It was dark blue lacquered like the hall. *I wanted dark bottle green! British racing green!* he thought angrily. Charles had always let Tory take over. It had suited him to devote himself to his work, to let his wife take care of him at home. Just the way his secretary took care of him at work. Tory had smoothed the edges just the way a capable secretary did. Rounded the corners. And she had been reimbursed for it. Credit cards and fur coats and enough jewellery to fill seven deposit boxes. Tory could have anything and everything money could buy. He'd given her a racehorse for her last birthday because he'd run out of ways to please her, because he simply couldn't think of anything else.

'Daddy?' Adele stood in the doorway bearing two coral geraniums in copper pots. 'Don't forget to tell Maria about these. Ann says they're just about un-killable, but still . . .'

Charles smiled. 'Nice of her.' Ann's pied-à-terre on Beekman Place was full of flowers. Tory had preferred silk ones . . . expensive, perfectly made, but nothing that had ever seen sunlight or felt a breeze, nothing that would need attention or die and make a mess. 'So, Del, are you for or against my selling Windswept?'

'I think everything you said at lunch makes sense. You can't keep it closed for ever.'

'Done. On the market on Monday morning.' He tossed the papers on his desk and followed his daughter into the living room.

'This was a good idea,' she said and Charles nodded. 'Yes. I feel like I'm playing hooky. Can't think when I last took a Friday afternoon off – ' He stopped and they both thought of Tory. 'It's hard to catch up with you now that you're in Westchester.'

Silence in the vast white room. Charles stared at the Italian antique desk in the corner by the window. Tory had kept her tickets to the symphony in that little top left-hand drawer and yet she had gone to see Lieberman instead. She planned it. Premeditated. All those Fridays.

Adele's voice was soft. 'I don't hate her any more.'

Charles jerked to look at his tall blonde daughter. She was calm. A study in white wool trousers and a pale blue cashmere sweater. It was belted in silver, just the way her mother would have worn it.

'I know we never used the word "hate" in our family. I remember once saying I "hated" cauliflower and Mother corrected me. So I started to "dislike" cauliflower.' Adele moistened her lips. For once she had her father's total attention. 'Same emotion, different, more acceptable word.' She twisted the wide silver bracelet around and around her wrist. 'Acceptable,' she repeated.

Dr Morton had encouraged her to talk to her father. 'Try,' he had insisted. 'Say anything you want but remember he is a fellow survivor of a tragedy. This is a family tragedy,' he had claimed.

'I don't hate her either.' Charles's voice was almost a whisper. 'I know that you know that . . . we . . . we weren't close these past few years.'

But, she never would have given me a divorce, he said to himself. She liked being Mrs Charles Wickham too much. It would have shaken her well-ordered life. She might have had to move her clothes to a different closet. It would have been disorienting for her and faintly embarrassing to explain to her friends at parties, and then there would have been mail to forward. No, Tory would never have consented to a divorce.

Adele folded her hands in her lap. 'I don't think we were close, ever.' She willed her father to not politely deny it, but was stung when he did not.

Charles thought of Tory that year after Adele's birth. He remembered that particular ermine-trimmed peignoir; he remembered the blue satin mules and the way she hissed at him like an elegant angry swan if he so much as put his arm around her shoulders in bed. She had been so angry. Angry during the pregnancy, angry at the hospital, angry afterwards whenever they were alone. A peck on the cheek became permissible only for the photographers at Adele's first birthday party. From then on this public kiss was the only affection between Mr and Mrs Charles Leslie Wickham. He had lain awake at night with a feeling that he was dying inside. It wasn't the sex, it was the thought that the woman lying beside him blamed him for something, loathed him, was repelled by him. Of course, the intensity of this anger dimmed over the months and years. Charles felt that Tory's anger became a distant antagonism below the surface of maintenance, the smooth surface of dinner parties and travel arrangements. He didn't threaten her any longer. No more sex. Separate beds. Separate bedrooms. Separate lives. Suppose marriages often become an armed truce, speculated Charles. And when all the feelings fade, when the colour has been bleached away like the past brightness of an old beach towel, then it is just two people with the same last name.

He realized that he had not responded to Adele's flat statement. Poor Adele. 'She loved you. You know that. As for being close . . .' He didn't know what to say. 'She did love you very much. Don't forget that.'

Adele felt tears. My aloof English father is actually trying to talk. 'Daddy . . .' she began. 'It was Ann's idea for me to see Dr Morton and he's been wonderful. He's made me consider so many things that I . . . maybe I wouldn't let myself even wonder certain things. Things about you and me and Mother.' She wondered where this was leading. Dr Morton would say keep talking, open a dialogue. Try to communicate. Reach out. 'I wish I understood more. Why she . . . why someone like Mother had to . . .' Adele heard her father sigh but continued, 'Why do you think she ever went to . . . to . . . to the Plaza?' she finished lamely.

Charles had prepared himself for this conversation. 'I think it was a domination thing. Obviously she was intrigued by something in . . . in him.' He couldn't bear to say his name.

Adele was quiet. Mother was always so dogmatic, such a perfectionist. Things had to be done her way when she wanted them done or there was hell to pay. Adele wondered how many dozens of maids they'd had over the years. 'So this man appealed to something in Mother that – that she couldn't control. Someone to control her.'

Charles stiffened then spoke. 'I must confess I've wondered when we would talk about this. Maybe it's best to get it all out in the open.' Adele's heart pounded uncomfortably. What more could there be? 'You know that your mother died by accident?'

'No. I thought that Lieb – '

Charles cut her off. 'I saw the police several times. The man in charge of all this was a Lieutenant Farwell who told me that the coroner's inquest ruled a heart attack.' He looked at his daughter. She was staring at him raptly. He uncrossed his legs and leaned forward with the palms of his hands together.

'Please,' said Adele. 'I want to know.' When he didn't speak again she insisted, 'Daddy, I'm grown up. A married woman. Please tell me.'

'The case was closed when . . . when Lieberman died. Lieutenant Farwell didn't think anyone could have got a murder or manslaughter conviction anyway. Your mother was . . . she was found with a drug in her bloodstream. That is just about the only thing the papers did get right.'

'Amyl nitrate?'

Charles was surprised. He nodded.

'Did Lieberman really kill himself?' Charles was even more surprised at this. 'I never thought so. I knew him – or at least I thought I knew him. It'd been years at Salomon Brothers – in meetings, over lunches, deal-making. We weren't great friends but we weren't enemies either. I know the way the man thought and the way the man handled things . . .'

'So what did happen to him?' interrupted Adele.

'He wasn't a man to backtrack, to say I'm sorry, to regret things – ' Adele leaned forward across the coffee table. Charles looked at her young face. 'Del, this is not a nice thing to tell you. He . . . he wasn't normal. He . . .' Adele was unblinking. 'Farwell showed me what he showed the press. His death certificate gave as the cause of death "asphyxiation" but the word . . .' Charles's lips were a tight line.

'I know that.' Adele remembered all the headlines.

'There is something called autoerotic asphyxiation . . .'

'What is that?' Adele wrinkled her forehead. 'I've never heard of it.'

'Neither had I. It's a practice by which a . . . a man puts something around his neck to . . .' Charles groped for words and thought he'd try to be as clinical as possible. What had he been told? Yes. 'To deplete the flow of oxygen to the brain. It heightens the senses. While they do that they are usually touching themselves and it seems that while hanging from the shower rod he lost his balance, blacked out, and strangled.'

'Oh.' Adele hadn't moved.

'He wasn't normal. He wasn't . . . It's deviant behaviour.' Charles's voice was almost inaudible.

Adele leaned back against the sofa cushions. 'I wanted to know. Now I can forget it. Does that make sense?'

He nodded. Adele stood and left the room quickly. Charles was staring out the window at the swirling snow when she returned with her coat on. The early darkness of winter dusk was settling in the still room.

'Daddy!'

He turned. She was crying then. He held out his arms and

she pressed her wet face against the sleeve of his dark blue pinstriped suit. Ann had comforted her at the funeral, he thought absurdly, and Nina. His daughter had not cried in his arms since . . . since she'd been a little girl stung by jellyfish. He stroked her hair as she gasped, 'Thanks for telling me. Oh, Daddy! Thank you thank you thank you for telling me.'

'Hey, Dex, can I talk to you for a second?' The two men walked into the small conference room and Paul closed the door. Dexter, tremendous in a light-coloured khaki suit, wondered what Paul wanted this time.

'Business or personal?' He tried to sound amiable as he pulled out one of the maroon wool upholstered chairs that lined the long oval oak table.

'Personal, my friend,' grinned Paul. 'You know I never discuss business with you in the office.'

'That's true.'

'Are you going to be around on Friday night?'

'The weekend this time! Hey, hey, hey, getting serious?'

Paul shrugged. 'I don't know about that. I know that she's great in the sack, really bangs like a bunny, and that . . . well, how about it? Just Friday night.'

'I'll be in Greenwich. Sure, it'll be all right.'

'I'm replacing the scotch, by the way. I realized we'd gone through almost the whole bottle.'

Dexter nodded. 'The place is yours for the weekend if you want. Just lock up when you leave and I usually keep one light on in the bedroom . . .'

'You're a pal. Thanks.'

Yeah, I'm a pal, Dexter thought as he stepped out into the hallway. Paul spends more time in my bed than I do and he sure spends more time with Sherry than he does with his wife. Dexter wasn't so sure that Paul was such a nice guy. Probably okay to do something like this once in a while but Sherry . . . Sherry wasn't a bad kid. Hell, she must be about twenty and this is her first job. And Paul's been married – what? A year? Two years at most. Dexter sighed as he walked into his office and closed the door behind him. He'd joked about Sherry's legs but that didn't mean he'd ever take a dive between them.

Paul knelt before the fireplace wadding up last week's New York *Times* and stuffing the pages under the logs with a poker. The flames were suddenly two feet high and he shielded his face from the heat and backed away. He stood up, brushing his brown corduroy trousers, and then put his hands on his hips. He wore a cream-coloured fisherman knit sweater and a pale blue oxford cloth shirt collar showed at the neck. Nina looked at him rather critically. Friday dinner he hadn't shown up, Saturday he'd been in a little bit of a bad mood over something no one had clued her in on, and today he'd been almost silent at lunch.

'So, Nina,' he said, 'how's life with the cuckoo Countess?'

Nina felt a wave of anger. 'It's wonderful.' Life with you should be so wonderful, she thought. She wondered if she sounded angry. Defensive? 'I adore her.' There, she thought. I didn't scream at him because he is married to Adele. That's the only reason, she told herself.

'Del!' he shouted up the stairs from the front hall. 'I'm going over to the club for a while. Don't know when I'll be back. I'll grab a hamburger probably.' He nodded at Nina with his sheepskin jacket in one hand. 'See you later.'

'Bye, Paul.' Nina pushed a pillow up behind her on the blue flowered sofa and extended one foot in a blue wool sock towards the fire as Adele walked in with *The New York Times Magazine*. She was wearing blue jeans like Nina with a red, white and blue pullover knitted in a pattern of stars and stripes. She kicked off the topsiders and tucked her feet in their bright red socks under her on the opposite sofa. Moments passed.

'Hey, what is it? I can feel the vibrations and they aren't good.'

Adele looked at Nina listlessly. 'No, they're not, are they?'

'Do you want to talk to me?'

Adele's expression didn't change in the slightest. She

321

shook her head. 'I'm not ready yet.' She put the tip of her index finger in her mouth, an old habit that Nina knew from Briarcliff. 'I wish I were like you. I wish I could just explode. I wish I could say I feel this and I feel that and I hate the way this is and . . .' She shook her head and her long straight blonde hair dipped forward off her shoulders. 'But I can't. Can't talk yet.'

'How are the classes? I didn't want to ask in front of Paul because I . . .'

'You're right. Boy, am I glad you didn't. He cannot stand the idea that his wife goes into the city several times a week. I'm not working. I don't get it. He'd have a fit if I wanted to have a job. But to study! You'd think he'd be glad for me. It's not as though I'm neglecting him or as if the house really needs me to sit in it all day. It's not as if he's home every night for dinner . . .'

'Why doesn't he like your going to Columbia?'

Adele shrugged and then fell into a heavy Southern accent. They'd seen *Cool Hand Luke* together years before. 'Whut we have heah is a fail-yuh to commun-ah-cate,' she drawled in her mimic of the cruel warden. Nina laughed and then Adele began to laugh, too. 'I'm going to fix cocoa! I want it and I need it! How about you?' Adele stood up.

'Good idea.' Nina got up from the couch. 'I'll follow you around in the kitchen. Tell me about your courses. Tell me all about what you're doing.'

Adele explained the graduate studies programme as she measured out the milk and tore open a plastic bag of marshmallows. 'I can have my master's next year at the rate I'm going.' She turned on a burner. 'I don't want it really! I want it but I don't want the classes to end, because Paul won't want me to get a job and I'll just be in this house again . . .' She looked exasperated. 'When I get it I won't be able to use it unless I commute to the city and even then I don't know what kind of job I could have.'

'What about an auction house? Won't the San Francisco experience help you with that?'

'Yes and no.' She popped a marshmallow in her mouth. 'The problem is I simply love the art, I love reading about it,

I love the lectures, I love the papers I have to do, but I can't visualize what to do with all this knowledge that's being poured into me. I know I don't want to teach, I have no technical skills so I won't ever be a painter or a restorer, and to make things worse, my favourite period and my favourite paintings are something nobody else seems to give a hoot about!'

'Now I'm interested. What possibly could Adele Forrest Wickham Rice be speaking of? Don't tell me! Let me guess! You are fascinated by infant Jesuses painted by Italians in the year 1543.'

'Close! Oh, you're really close!'

'Tell me, for pete's sake!'

Adele smiled as she poured the steaming chocolate milk into tremendous red mugs that said 'I love you' on their sides. God. These must have been bought years ago, thought Nina cynically.

'Come upstairs with me. No, go into the living room and I'll bring my books down. Won't be two seconds.'

'I couldn't be more surprised,' said Nina as she leaned back against the edge of the sofa. The two of them sat on the floor in front of the fire with all the art books opened around them. 'This stuff is so *unlike* you!'

Adele looked up from the book she held on her lap. 'What do you mean?' she asked almost shyly.

'It's just . . .' Nina thought: I shouldn't've said that. 'I thought you'd pick a French Impressionist because they are your colours and you speak French. Or even someone modern and sophisticated like Modrian, or even a fifteenth-century Italian like Fra Angelico . . .' Adele waited, her hand still on the plate she wanted to show Nina. 'These Indian paintings are so wild, so fresh, so earthy, so almost . . . well, there's something savage about them!'

Adele laughed. 'So, you've never seen my savage side!'

Nina thought: This is the closest we've come to talking about sex since that morning on 90th Street when we did the check list, deciding whether she should marry Paul or not. 'No, I guess it's not a word I associate with you.' She stared at the pale hair and the bright blue eyes, the nearly white

323

skin. 'I don't know anything savage about you. I guess the closest human adults come to being savage is violence or sex, and since I haven't been violent lately, I guess my savage side, if you define it as wild, or uncivilized, shows itself in bed. I was reading the other day that bed is the only place where adults are allowed to play.'

Adele thought of her wild side with Jack and she thought of making love with him. Her cheeks burned and she looked down at the book again. 'I really adore these colours, these strange animals, these strong dark faces, Nina. I really do.' Adele's voice was wistful.

'So become an expert in this period. And if there aren't hundreds of people as crazy about this as you are it simply means that you will have less competition.'

Adele considered this but didn't answer. 'I have some other books to show you.' She ran out of the room in her red sock feet and returned like a child showing her friend her favourite toys. 'Look.' She spread before them on the rug *A Viceroy's India*, *A Passage to India*, *The Raj Quartet*. She had twenty books – tattered paperbacks found in second-hand bookshops and brand new twenty-five-dollar coffee-table books of photographs. 'I've read them all,' she almost whispered.

Nina impulsively hugged her. 'You're great! Do you know that? You're really something great!'

Adele smiled back and responded very quietly. 'Sometimes I just want to be very, very good at something.'


The Countess stood at the open window, thinking what a warm day it was for February, thinking how much she would miss Nina. 'I just wonder,' she mused, almost talking to herself, 'is Italy – is Rome because of Omar?' The moment the words were out, the Countess regretted them. But perhaps it was time to talk, to clear the air. The Nina since Nantucket, as she'd begun to think of her, was not quite the Nina she'd met on Long Island the summer before. Now she seemed to move almost imperceptibly away from any member of the opposite sex, even as she sparkled with allure and flirted, even while fielding dinner invitations which numbered a dozen a week. Why, at this rate, Nina wouldn't have to go to Gristede's until the mid 1990s. However, the bruises of rejection were taking rather a long time to fade. She'd told Nina that it would not be her last unhappy love affair, that there was no inoculation against the very small-pox of it, but that it wasn't fatal by any means. She'd urged her to remember the attractive things about Omar, but feared she did. Suggested she remember the happy times, and again feared she did. Asked her to appreciate, too, all she'd learned from him. Paris and London had been hers and she played a mean game of backgammon and could make a martini like no one else on the Upper East Side. The jewellery was all good and the . . . at this point, Nina had excused herself and rushed down the hall to blow her nose loudly. They had never spoken of Omar again.

Nina shook her head and her long black hair moved on the shoulders of the red wool suit. No, she wasn't going because of Omar. She remembered the pain of losing him, but it was now in the abstract, like remembering a bad time at the dentist. The humiliation of his preferring someone else had even disappeared. After all, it was his wife and not just a run-of-the-mill other woman. That had to count for something on the scale of being squashed.

It was a Friday at four and the time that the Countess decreed herself 'in desperate need of red wine and company'. There was no company today for Tad was off skiing in Aspen and Ross Maynard, who had begun to stop by, was meeting with the producer of a newly opened Broadway show. Nina had been in the habit of having her dinner date meet her here but it had annoyed Tad no end, so she had stopped in deference to his feelings. Sometimes Adele arrived, with shopping bags, always a bit reserved, seeking Nina out like a safe port across the gulf of strangers. Sometimes Millie Bancroft or John Heiden or any of a dozen others put in an appearance. Both women thought of Omar suddenly and wondered if he ever thought of the garden in Purgatory on Friday afternoons.

'Well, then,' trilled the Countess, turning away from the

traffic noises of Park Avenue. 'That's settled! Let's have something sparkly to celebrate your new life!'

With the Countess's last two Baccarat champagne flutes they toasted 'Rome!' and 'Adventure!' 'Though you will discover,' said the Countess solemnly, 'that the two are synonymous.'

Nina stared at the older woman and then said softly, 'I hope some day . . .' She felt so shy about continuing. 'That I can be like you.'

The Countess tried not to let tears come. 'And I was thinking, just before you made that outrageous statement, that if I had a daughter I would wish her to be like you.' It was Nina's turn to feel teary. Both were slightly embarrassed, not to express their affection for the other, but to be the recipient. They would miss each other.

'I think it's the best thing.' Nina took a deep breath. She wanted to speak her mind. 'I confess. Omar debilitated me. All the hours of daydreaming, the planning. Planning everything from what I'd wear, to what I'd say, to what he'd answer, to what I'd say back.' Nina tried to smile, tried to pretend she wasn't serious, just in case the Countess laughed. The Countess did not. 'It's not that he's driving me out of town. Really it isn't.' She stood and walked over to the fireplace.

'Darling, stop me if I'm . . . interfering.' Nina looked at the concerned face, the bright orange hair, the falling folds of the poison green silk caftan.

'Never. Not possible.'

'I have often thought we are somewhat alike. Both of us love to flirt, love to play, love to bat the eyes and relish masculine attention.'

'Yes. I do love all that. Always have. I think I loved it when I was a little girl.'

'With your father?'

'Oh, no!' Nina recoiled. She had never said much about him but the Countess knew she couldn't stand him. 'With . . . it'll sound silly but here goes. With the fathers of my friends.'

'Mmmmm . . .' The Countess took a sip of champagne.

'At the risk of playing Freud, is it safe to say your father wasn't affectionate towards you?'

'He used to tell me he hated me once or twice a week. Does that count as affection?' Nina's voice dripped with sarcasm.

'How on earth could he have done such a thing! To his child! To any little girl! But to you, Nina!'

Nina shrugged, suddenly feeling hard and unsentimental. 'He was a rattlesnake and nothing I did ever pleased him.'

'Nothing?'

Nina shook her head with a blank look on her face. She could see him across the dining room table as though it were yesterday; as though, with some trickery, with mirrors, trapped in some nightmarish time warp, she were back in Mississippi. Helpless and small.

'You know, I kept falling in love with older men, time after time.' Oh no, thought Nina with surprise. The Countess is far too bright to give me the old 'father-figure' routine. 'Someone told me when I was in my late twenties to stop the pattern and I laughed and asked why. After all, it was so much fun! They had more money, they were where they were because of brains and ambition, and I felt sweet and adored.' Nina listened carefully. 'They had sexual experience, they were sophisticated, they taught me things and they took me to wonderful places.' Sounds just like Omar, agreed her audience. 'I didn't realize it then of course but the danger wasn't in being pampered, becoming spoiled but . . .' She sipped from her glass. 'The danger was inside me.'

'What do you mean?'

'Something in me was hungry for the approval that someone like that could bestow on me. I needed that respected older man to think I was worthwhile. I hadn't decided that I was bright, pretty, strong, capable.'

'Because your father had never made you believe you were?'

'Exactly. I'm not a Freudian and I've never been wildly New York-y and gone into analysis to lie on some couch talking about my dreams.' She threw up her hands and her bracelets jangled with disapproval. 'But some things go way back. I'm convinced of it. And . . .' She frowned. 'I think the kind of older man I chose said something about me in those days, too.'

'What kind of older man?'

'Usually I chose the biggest challenge I could find. Successful. Well-to-do. Handsome. That goes without saying. But the impossible task I set for myself was to make a basically unattainable man love me.' Nina winced, remembering her words when she'd heard that Omar was with his wife. 'I picked one man after another who loved himself best, who was usually ruthless in business and who, underneath all the fun and generosity and affection, was cold.'

'You're thinking of Omar, aren't you?' Nina's voice was thin and reedy, like a child's.

The Countess nodded. She didn't add, 'and I'm thinking of you, too, darling Nina.' 'There's absolutely nothing wrong with falling in love with an older man. Just make sure he loves you. Make sure you've picked someone who can love you.'

'You think I chose Omar, don't you?' The Countess nodded again. 'You give me credit for a lot of power, don't you?'

'Yes. I do. I've seen you take on three men at once in this very arena. I've seen them watching you, even wanting you, though not daring to make a move because you were Omar's property. And . . .' The Countess laughed a laugh like little bells. 'How many marriage proposals did you tell me you've had in New York?'

'Oh! I'm embarrassed about telling you that! Please forget it! Why, I was drunk when I told you!'

'Nina! Of course you chose Omar! Can't you see you have that in you?' she insisted. 'You have a glittering "catch me if you can" look and they fantasize about catching you. So whether you pull the vivacious "aren't you big, strong, and wonderful routine" or smile warmly and move away coolly – it works.'

'God! Am I that transparent?' moaned Nina. She sank to the floor in a faked swoon then recovered and crossed her

328

legs Indian style, pulling the full red skirt over her knees.

'I told you, darling. We do have our similarities.' The two of them laughed merrily.

'Oh, it's wonderful to talk this way. I've wanted to.' Nina gulped champagne. 'You might be the only person on earth who could understand. Omar . . . well, no one seemed as exciting as Omar. No one seemed as sexual. No one . . . well, don't you . . . well, I kept reminding myself that he seemed to have a faintly dangerous quality.' *Mickey Keeling has it, too*, she hated herself for thinking.

The Countess sipped a few drops and answered, 'It's up to you to decide if that faintly dangerous quality is truly dangerous or not. I suppose in a few years you'll be able to write a treatise on the *uomo Romano*.'

Nina rolled her eyes. She spoke simply not one word of Italian. 'A few years!' she erupted with surprise. 'Oh, I'll be back this summer!'

'If you are, you may certainly have your job again. I'll keep my promise and hire the next assistant making that crystal clear.' The Countess smiled. 'But if you are back in six months' – she looked amused, cynical – 'I'll give you this apartment, too!'

Nina's grey eyes were bright as she feigned innocence. 'What about all your millions?'

# 8

Rajiv Rajjin crossed the large dining room of Les Pléaides and allowed himself to be seated at his favourite table. The restaurant on Madison Avenue was a favourite with art dealers. He ordered a Coca-Cola and it was brought to him almost immediately by the same waiter who had served him yesterday. Rajjin never drank alcohol and the young man with a sympathetic nature seemed to want to make it up to him with lots of ice cubes and a slice of lemon, and several small white dishes of peanuts, crisps and pretzels.

The Indian was small – at least two inches under five feet, dark complexioned, with coal-black shining hair parted on the left side. His eyes were a deep brown and usually filled with interest and curiosity at all that was occurring around him. He wore Western suits tailored in London for the part of the year he spent travelling but always looked forward to his arrival in Bombay and his 'normal' wardrobe of cotton trousers and the loose tunic that he found so comfortable.

Adele Rice would be here in fifteen minutes if all went according to the telephone call. A dinner was all he needed to assess her character; he'd checked her birth date from her resumé and spoken to Collins, the professor who had recommended her so highly. She would be very suitable, he was positive. Tomorrow Rajjin would return to India and prepare the shipment of paintings for New York. Mrs Rice could handle this end of things and then he could arrive in time for the opening in mid-September.

Rajjin's large eyes, bordered by long lustrous black lashes, stared at nothing until he visualized the little chart he'd prepared in his mind. Adele Rice's life would change drastically in the next two years. The configuration of Venus and Saturn low in the winter sky was very interesting.

*

Like watermelon, speculated Nina. The air in spring has the sweet smell of watermelon. She turned on her left side in bed and gazed past the living room out through the terrace doors to the terracotta rooftops that populated her particular piece of Rome. The sun seemed golden. Nina easily understood why painters had come to Rome for centuries, for the light on her terrace changed with every hour and the black cool shadows of early morning were pale blue at dusk. Across via dei Greci were the six open windows of the art school with the blue-smocked students standing at their easels.

The music of Rome had to include the taxi noise, the *motorino* buzz, the shouting of 'Buon giorno!' from a window to a neighbour below. Nina often sat on her terrace and listened to the clear notes of a trumpet drifting down the narrow street from the Santa Cecilia Conservatory. Sometimes a soprano would practise her scales again and again at noon.

At a few minutes before one the metal grates across storefronts were brought down with deafening crashes as the shops were locked. At one, there was the cacophony of rush-hour traffic, for every Roman seemed to scramble home for lunch or, like some of the bachelors Nina knew, sit in Augusteo or Dal Bolognese for three hours of wine, conversation, and serious eating. How did they stay so narrow? she wondered. By half past one the *centro* was silent. No slamming doors, no one calling a reluctant dog, no children outside and hardly a yellow taxi moving. Nina was told that there was an ordinance against noise during the *mezzogiorno*, but since when, a friend had joked, did an Italian pay attention to a law? Still, the city was silent and it was true that one could be arrested for using a vacuum cleaner between the hours of one and three o'clock in the afternoon. At half past three it was as if the metropolitan yawning began, and by four o'clock, Rome had awakened and with it the noises of living.

I love it here, Nina decided dozens of times in the course of a day. I arrived knowing no one and now the shopkeepers call me by name and the man at the bar on via Babuino hands me my caviar sandwich and my Coke every morning as though I've been his customer for years.

And my first party was a success! Twenty-eight out of thirty people had come. A delightful thought had crossed Nina's mind as she set out the new wine-glasses – there is no one I should have invited, only people I want to see. A clean slate. She was Nina without a father; without Omar; she was Nina without a history. The friendships among the expatriates were sudden and often very close, very suddenly. It was all face, conversation, and 'will I see you again?' We are all in Rome without a past, decided Nina. Her friends ran the gamut from the romantic fly-by-nights to the corporates with a tour of duty. Fly-by-nights were in love with an Italian or, like Nina, in love with Rome. They arrived to study, to sightsee, and never went home again.

Rita had left England to work on a film in Greece in March and when extras had been sought for another film in Italy she had drifted there and at last, in the autumn, found herself in Rome not wanting to face the fog of London. She lived from day to day, apartment-sitting, dog-walking, baby-sitting, plant-watering. The apartment-sitting for absentee owners gave her a place to live, some privacy, and a refrigerator for white wine. Rita, with her copper-coloured hair and her crooked smile, was ensconced in the flat of a New Zealander who'd gone home to see his sick mother for at least a fortnight. 'God, I hope it's a lingering illness!' she exclaimed.

Lesley, tall, blonde, perpetually suntanned, had the look of an Australian who'd been born on a sunswept white beach. She had arrived in Italy as crew on a chartered sailboat. The owner, a fellow Australian, had asked her to marry him one halcyon day in the Mediterranean. She now lived with him in the old section of Rome called Trastevere and had recently discovered that he went through this every year, with every crew. Lesley knew it was only a matter of weeks before she moved on.

A few friends fell between fly-by-night and corporate and had reasons to be in Rome, i.e., an income. There was Solveig, the Swedish model across the hall who worked for

Giorgio Armani and the designing Fendi sisters, who chain-smoked, watered her wine, ate the occasional spring of finocchio, and talked incessantly about 'these Roman men they make me crazy'.

Two students from Harvard on fellowships had an apartment next door. Benjamin was studying the Church in Poland in the sixteenth century and practically living in the Vatican archives. 'The Church always, simply always, means the Catholic Church,' he teased Nina. Pauline worked all day in a lab measuring the length of mosquito legs. It is exotic medicine, thought Nina, who never really understood what Pauline was hoping to conclude. The pair were good fun, madly in love, and invited her to dinner more times than she could come. Many evenings Nina would lean against their refrigerator sipping wine as she watched them add spices to the vegetarian concoction simmering on the medieval-looking stove. Pauline seemed to be always saying 'Yes, Nina, if Stefano has asked you to Punta Rosa for the weekend he does expect you to sleep with him.' They talked about sex in the kitchen and discussed politics at the dinner table.

Kate Middleton, an aristocratic, petite brunette, with a faint English accent, was in Nina's exercise class. She and Bill had been transferred by Citibank from their last posting in London. They were East Coast and Ivy League. Nina was taken under their wing, for supper, for concerts, whenever they could catch her between her Roman rendezvous.

The via dei Greci apartment in the *centro historico* was a meeting place for all these wayward expatriates who might ring her doorbell at three in the afternoon or at ten o'clock at night. Nina would rush to the terrace and call down, then lower the front door key on a green ribbon. She always had wine and popcorn which was poured into a white basket about two feet in diameter. It was the only thing she ever cooked.

That first month sped by in a blur of getting dressed, going out, sleeping late, and getting dressed again. Italians she met at parties took her to dinners that lasted until they ordered dessert at one in the morning; they danced until four and later giggled in Nina's front doorway until the fat woman next door and one flight up threatened to pour buckets of water on them, '*come i gatti*, like cats', Nina would laugh until her evening's escort would stop her with his kisses.

Nina kissed a great deal and spent hours in the front seats of Lamborghinis and Alfa Romeos but she didn't make love. She couldn't get Omar completely out of her mind.


Adele gathered up the four heavy catalogues and her briefcase and then grabbed the car keys from the hall table. 'I'm taking the seven twenty today,' she called up the stairs. 'Okay if I drive the BMW to the train and leave the station wagon for you?' No answer. 'See you tonight.' She knew that Paul could hear her. How long could he not speak?

'You won't see me tonight,' she heard him mutter before slamming a bureau drawer.

Adele received the first really long letter at the gallery and shrieked. Nina in *adore* already! My God! She read the closely typed pages. Not quite love but heady stuff. A Venetian! A nightclub called La Bella Blu, a place for drinks in the afternoon called Il Baretto because it was 'miscroscopic, the tiniest bar in all of Rome'. Nina swore that it was ten feet by twelve and filled with women in sable coats. 'I am slumming it in my black velvet blazer,' she wrote, 'but Marco doesn't seem to mind, and Antonio doesn't care and Pietro says I am *bellissima* about six times an evening.' Adele laughed as she folded the pages quickly and put them in her bag to read on the train home.

The opening was to be on 30 September and Adele had agreed with Mr Rajjin on the phone that they should invite only the serious collectors to this first one. Perhaps the following January there could be a bigger opening when they had had more time to prepare and Adele had had this coming summer and the autumn to get her balance. India House was wonderful about supplying certain addresses and had even given Adele the name of a tiny woman who wore a little red straw hat with a dark blue rose on it to come and, in exquisite calligraphy, take care of all the invitations.

'Si, si, si,' she laughed and then hung up and raced to run the bath water. Luciano asking me if I will be home tonight so that he can call me back! Why do these Romans always call at seven and ask to call me back at eight? Nina pictured hordes of Roman men clutching *gettones* and address books lined up at pay phones all across the length and breadth of the Eternal Città. Infuriating but I'd better wash my hair, anyway.

At eight Marco called and said he had to call back in ten minutes. Nina sighed in exasperation. Now, if Luciano calls first and I'd rather go out with Marco, what'll I do? 'I am just not good at this!' she cried aloud.

Safety in numbers, Nina thought later in the ladies' room at Capello à Cilindro. She had arrived with Roberto and Franco. If I go out with so many and I don't sleep with any of them they all think I'm sleeping with the others, and they all seem to be fascinated with that idea!

She emptied the tiny gold evening bag on to the counter in front of the mirror and grabbed the little notes on folded index cards. '*Venire*,' she said to herself as she applied lipstick. *Venire* is 'to come' and *andare* is 'to go'! Why can't I ever get that straight! 'I literally don't know whether I'm coming or going!' she said aloud in irritation at her stupidity. She sprayed on more L'Heure Bleu as she recited aloud. '*Vengo, vieni, viene* . . .' She fluffed up her shining hair with two quick strokes of the brush and said, 'Okay, *andiamo*.' Cramming everything into the little purse, Nina returned to the blasting music of the nightclub.

Bart was conscious of Karen's perfume as the lights went out. The concert hall was filled and Leonard Bernstein walked on stage proudly, a bit arrogantly, thought Bart. He could detect a red handkerchief in the pocket of his tuxedo. The full head of grey hair bowed again and again to the applause and then he turned to the orchestra. They waited, anticipating his first move. Bart's muscles tensed unconsciously and then relaxed as the first notes wafted through the air. Then he felt Karen's hand in his lap and his muscles tensed again. My God! What did she think she was doing? The Mackelson box offered some privacy but not all that one would desire at a moment like this. Bart felt himself react to the gentle stroking in time to the Brahms.

At intermission they stood and Karen, smiling more broadly than usual, put her arm through his. Her auburn hair swung forward as she leaned down to reach for the silver evening bag. It was in the shape of a peanut with a topaz clasp.

'A drink?' Bart asked. She nodded and gave his arm a squeeze.

Bart told himself not to react. Only one intermission, he thought, then forty-five more minutes of Bernstein, then a late supper with six others and then home. He smoothed the finely pleated shirt and told himself to relax. In seconds the attractive couple was folded into the crowd in the lobby.

'To you,' she smiled and he nodded as she tilted the glass of gin and tonic towards his bourbon. Can't figure him out, Karen thought. Was sure that the emerald green raw silk dress from Magnin's would turn him on. Just a little bit, anyway. And Sandy told me last night to be more aggressive. I don't know how to be any more aggressive in the family box without holding him down between the chairs. Damn you, Bart! Notice me! I am a female, feminine person with certain instincts. He's just so caught up in his work. They say real estate gets in your blood. Especially California real estate. So much money to be made, so quickly. For the ones who run after it. And Bart McLean, as handsome as Warren Beatty, as steeped in Southern charm as Rhett Butler, well, he was running after it. He'd be loaded some day. I don't need to be loaded because I already am, she admitted, but I would like to be with Bart McLean wherever he is. In five years, or next year, or next week. 'Hey, Bart! Talk to me!'

'What do you think of Bernstein?' he smiled, sipping at his drink.

336

'He's a legend and he knows it.'

'I keep wondering about his brother, Elmer. How come we never see Elmer?'

Karen laughed delightedly. 'Bart! I can never predict what you'll say!'

'Well, I like Elmer and I want to know if he's got two heads and kept in a closet by the family back home in New York.'

It was easy to make Karen laugh, though he felt she always teetered on the brink of being terribly bored. Maybe that's why it's easy, he decided. She was good-looking instead of beautiful, with those wide strong cheekbones and the thick mane of hair. She looked well-bred and spirited. No one would dare describe her as delicate or pretty or sweet. Her face was familiar to anyone who skimmed the society pages, for old man Mackelson had made his mark in publishing and she, his granddaughter, along with her sister, would inherit it all.

A little banter, an introduction to one or two of her friends, the lights dimming and then that quick tipping of the bourbon so that the ice cubes hit you in the nose, the 'all right, Karen?' as she took your arm and you took her glass and soon you were sitting in the dark again with the music surrounding you. Simple, thought Bart. How many times has she invited me? When Sandy Richardson, her best friend, hadn't? Funny, these two women fighting over my company, he mused. Please don't put your hand in my lap, prayed Bart. Just another night out.

Like so many nights, he decided over the brandy after dinner. But suddenly, she turned the full force of her brown-eyed gaze upon him. The others were joking about the odds of a movie actor becoming President of the United States. 'He wasn't even a star!' cried Ginger. 'Ahhh, but perhaps he has star quality when you put him beside Ford! Always face-down Ford! On the tennis court or on the tarmac!' laughed Bob Austin. 'And what can we say about a peanut farmer from the wilds of Georgia . . .' asked someone rhetorically. Bart expected Karen to hold up her bag with a quick retort but she didn't. She was staring at him.

'Who is she?'

'What are you . . .' Bart was momentarily taken aback.

'Just tell me who she is. It's time we were honest with each other.' She bit her lip. 'Or rather it's time you were honest with me.'

'What do you want to know?' Bart asked, wondering if he should reach out to her, then thinking: No, that would be dishonest when she has just asked for honesty.

'Who is she?' Karen shrugged her tan shoulders in the strapless dress. She rode horseback every weekend and one could see the evidence of muscles in her forearms. 'Do I know her?' She looked down and stubbed out her cigarette. Karen's fingers trembled ever so slightly. Her smoking repulsed Bart, but he never thought it important enough to mention. He was silent. 'She must be awfully special.' Bart sipped the Courvoisier and listened to her. She was brittle, almost taunting. 'Or else she's married.' Karen looked pleased with herself. 'Ahhhh, Bart! So now I know! So that's it!'

Bart managed a weak smile. To his surprise she kissed him full on the lips and breathed, 'She's awfully lucky because you're awfully loyal. Tell her that for me.'


Nina was laughing. Mario had his arm around her and occasionally held a glass of champagne to her lips as Giorgio said, 'There, you see! That's why they must dub all the films, all the television shows! It's not just the language, it's the laughter. Americans they say, "ha, ha ha!" ' he mimicked her, 'and Italians laugh, "ho, ho, ho, ho!" '

The music was loud in the little club. A postage stamp of a shining dance floor was empty. The crowd filled black velvet banquettes and little gilt chairs which were sprinkled here and there. Nina wore the blue and green taffetta dress that Omar had given her. The bolero showed off her small waist and her slender arms as she reached for her emerald green evening purse. '*Scusi, la toletta,*' she explained to the men who stood politely to let her squeeze past their knees. Mario and Giorgio were her standbys. Best friends to each other, not to me, Nina realized as she made her way between the tiny black marble tables in the semi-darkness. Nina felt one of her rhinestone earrings drop; its cold metal touched her arm as it fell to the floor. She bent down with palms spread, hoping it hadn't bounced under the nearby bar, just as a tall man tried to walk past.

'Aaah!' he groaned as Nina stood and neatly hit him squarely in the stomach.

'Oh! I'm so sorry!' she cried pushing her hair back, grasping the little rhinestone star.

'*Futbol?*' he grinned.

'No, I . . .' Nina looked into his face. Mediterranean blue eyes – that colour you find near the Costa Smeralda, she would tell Adele – were set in a square-cut face with a high-bridged nose, black eyebrows, and a wide smile. Nina blushed in embarrassment as her entire Italian vocabulary vanished. Tongue-tied and silly is his impression of me, she suffered.

'Would you care to dance?' He extended his arm.

'Well, I . . .' she began as he took her hand and led her to the dance floor. The last record had been fast, so wouldn't you know it, thought Nina. Now Olivia Newton-John crooned something slow and melancholy as the stranger put his arms around Nina; she hurriedly clipped on her earring and clutched her bag over his right shoulder. He smells good, like lime, and he felt hard. Maybe he does play *futbol*, she surmised. Nina did a physical inventory as their feet stepped a few inches this way and then back again. Broad shoulders, big hands. He moved still closer and she stiffened and pulled away but he only laughed and pulled her to him with more force. Nina could feel her breasts pushing against his chest and the realization came to her: I like the way he feels, and with that in mind she allowed herself to relax and to float with him, for they were one graceful entity, gliding alone around the slick, polished floor. As he moved his head she felt his black hair, a little longer than the style and barely curling over his white shirt, brush her cheek. Soft, she thought dreamily. Wonder why he doesn't say anything, but maybe he doesn't speak English but then his invitation had been worded perfectly and his aura of total confidence was the first thing one noticed. No, second, after the eyes, no, third, after the mouth. Nina forgot about Giorgio whose love of the moment, Angela, was in Florence; Nina forgot about Mario who asked her out almost every night and whose invitations she accepted only every third or fourth time. The only thing Nina remembered was that she had not felt this way for a long long time. It must have been with Omar.

The music stopped and the staccato bang bang of an Italian rock group began. Nina and the stranger broke apart; his arm slid down her back as he looked long and hard at her. 'I'll probably be seeing you again,' he said as he led her down the two steps towards the clustered tables. 'Who are you with?' She nodded towards the two staring faces above their dark suits and they stood and shook hands with him. '*Come va?*' went all round and the nameless one nodded at her and walked away towards a stool at the bar. Nina sat down, ladies' room forgotten.

'We thought you'd slipped away to Jackie O's . . .' complained Mario. 'Until we saw you in this payssionate dance,' agonized Giorgio.

Oh, such a game, thought Nina. They don't mean it, but it's funny. She made a face. 'If you're not nicer to me, I *will* slip away.'

'Ohhhh, Nina,' they both cooed; Mario kissed her neck and Giorgio settled for kisses on her hands.

'Oh, oh, oh,' laughed Nina. These Latins. These games. The music pounded on.


On Sunday Mario persuaded Nina to go to the Polo Club and at noon he honked the horn of his little white Ferrari Sports Spider on the serene via dei Greci. She leaned over the terrace railing and waved at the figure in the open-necked shirt and blue silk ascot. These Italian men, she thought, would be well dressed anywhere. She noted his grey flannel trousers and dark blue blazer as she slid into the car. 'So tell me everything about the game,' exulted Nina as she arranged her black and white linen suit jacket on the red

340

leather seat. Mario shrugged; he was bored by so many things. 'It'll just be a couple of Romani on horses ploughing back and forth on a field.' The car roared past Piazza Venezia, dazzling white in the sun. 'Trying to hit a ball. The Argentines are the world's best. Today it's a team from France.'

Mario had never been athletic and the beginning of a pot belly could not be disguised by the best tailor in Rome. He gave up pasta one lunch a week and was convinced that it would make a difference eventually. 'I'd rather lose slowly,' he explained to a mocking Giorgio. Mario was a prince, and a prince with money, someone had explained to her. Nina had written to her mother who had excitedly written back, but Nina had neglected to describe him as 'a prince with a paunch', which did go through her mind once in a while. But he was rather more dependable than any of the first set of men she'd gone out with and he was fun and he no longer badgered her over sleeping with him. Giorgio was often with him as a sidekick and the three of them were relaxed together.

It was an April day of startling heat and the field looked less than golf-course green but the air fairly sparkled with sun. The little party of spectators in their white wooden chairs were dressed much as Mario and Nina. The Romans looked prosperous, well-bred, animated. There are only forty of us in all, Nina would count and be surprised. And only eight men on the field atop eight enormous highly-strung beasts and two referees in black and white striped shirts who rode past again and again and once in awhile put the ball back in bounds. The game had already begun when they found two places.

Nina grinned and pulled at Mario's coat sleeve. 'Oh, *bellissima*! It's so fast! And it looks so dangerous!' Mario leaned over and lightly kissed her lips. 'Oh, I love it!' she whispered back.

A programme was handed to her but she never found a second to glance at it, so riveted was her attention to the field. The noise alone was exciting. One man in the red and blue colours of the Polo Club di Roma, taller than all the rest, with a strong face under the helmet, with veins in his long tan arms clearly defined and muscles in his thighs quite visible above the gleaming polished black boots, fascinated her. He seemed to wheel his horse more sharply, seemed to ride faster than the rest, and ultimately – crack! would go his mallet connecting to the ball with an enormous circle swung over his head at full gallop – made more goals. Nina was mesmerized. Oh, if I were a man, she thought, I would play this. But I would want to play it the way he does. Roughly and not at all carefully, plunging into the thick of things like a cavalry officer in battle.

'Makes one think of *bushkazi*, doesn't it?' asked Mario.

'What is that?'

'It's the national sport of Afghanistan and it's much like polo except they use someone's head for a ball.'

Nina wrinkled her nose. 'Whose head? How do they decide whose head to use?'

Mario retorted, 'Afghanistan's Muslem, you know. Probably some adulterous wife's.'

'Uh-oh,' Nina winced. 'Machismo is alive and well in sunny Italy.'

Mario winked at her and at that moment they heard the lovely crack! of mallet connecting solidly with ball and looked up to see all eight horsemen galloping after it. 'Wow!' breathed Nina. The crowd applauded politely and someone shouted, 'Bravo! Bravissimo!'

'That's de Leone, again,' said Mario, studying the programme. He is lion-like, decided Nina as she watched him rein in his horse and quickly turn towards the opposite goal.

It was then that someone behind Nina bumped her chair and when she turned at the murmured '*Scusi*', the crowd moaned in unison. 'What happened?' demanded Nina, seeing a riderless horse and a man in white running across the field bearing a little white suitcase with a red cross.

'*Incidente* . . . not serious,' said Mario casually. The spectators strained in their seats to see through the cluster of horses and men, to see who had fallen, and to try to

342

ascertain the extent of his injuries. It was a Roman, that they could tell.

In front of the rows of chairs, just behind the fence, a greying blonde woman in a black and white silk dress paced back and forth in panic. Her black patent heels sank into the soft earth but she was unconcerned about them. She strained with flattened white-gloved palm held above her sunglasses to see the far end of the green field. Nina thought she must be early sixties, and thought, too, that she was very chic.

At last the man in white closed his case and two other men moved away and it was easy to see that the player was sitting on the grass and not unconscious, not lying down in agony. As de Leone stood, the crowd was hushed, and Nina saw the woman before her become motionless. Then the tallest polo player raised both his arms straight up and shouted, 'Mama! *Sto bene!*' and she waved back with one gloved hand and then, wreathed in smiles, returned to her chair as the crowd applauded its approval.

Rome won – six goals against the French club's two – but, 'Being adorably Italian,' Nina whispered, 'here they are giving a trophy to the losers!' The eight players astride their mounts were side by side in a line as below them a man in a black suit handed a silver loving cup to the French captain, evoking much cheering. Half an hour later in the little clubhouse surrounded by tall pines, a group milled around the bar in the corner as the barman handed out glass after glass of orange juice and champagne. The walls were wood-panelled and hung with photographs of the founding fathers of the 1930s. 'What are we waiting for?' asked Nina. There was an air of expectancy to the crowd. As if in answer to her question she saw the first of the players walk in from the path. Spattered with dirt on his white breeches, with a sheen of perspiration to his red face, he lifted his hand and called for a drink. Women clamoured to kiss his wet cheek, and men clapped him on the back and praised his performance. The heroes arrive, thought Nina and one after another, French and Italian polo players trooped in to be met with applause and handshakes and kisses.

343

'I love it,' she said to Mario. 'I know you think it's just normal and a so-so way to spend a Sunday but I don't.' She grinned. 'I think it's stupendous.' Mario took her empty glass from her hand and gave her another.

Then he was there. Nina would never forget the moment and even in the middle of it, she was sure of that, if nothing else. Not positive that the world was round, not sure if she had a middle name or not, not positive of her height if asked, but sure of this moment's unforgettability. Surrounded by women who tiptoed up to kiss him, greeted by men who bravo-ed him exuberantly, there he was. At six foot one inch tall, he was easily the tallest man within miles. But there were those sea-blue eyes and that grin that pulled you to him, made you fight not to smile back, and that sense of strength that Nina had felt on the dance floor when he had held her very close as she had made her rather half-hearted *de rigeur* protest.

Nina turned quickly to Mario and asked, 'Who is he?' and Mario said, 'You really don't know? You danced as if you knew.' Nina shook her head, pained at Mario's jealousy. Not now, she thought. Don't waste my time with this. 'What's his name?' she insisted.

'That's de Leone. You can see it on your programme.'

Mario was annoyed on the drive home even though the great de Leone hadn't approached her, not in his mud-spattered glory, his black boots dusty with bits of earth clinging to the spurs, nor later, showered and fresh, in his white shirt and cavalry twill trousers, from his place at one of the little tables at the club set up for lunch. It was warm and Nina had not worn the jacket, but had been bare-armed, with the square-necked black top dipping low. The long string of pearls the Countess had given her as a going-away present were wound around her neck three times and still fell inside the silk almost to her waist. De Leone had paid a ridiculous amount of attention to a blonde with short hair who seemed to laugh a great deal, enjoying her place at his side and wanting to be sure everyone else noticed what fun she was having next to the most attractive man in the room.

Back at via dei Greci Nina perfunctorily asked Mario up

for a drink and when he refused, she shrugged. He closed the car door on her side and stood behind her as she turned her key round and round in the front door's old lock.

'I had a wonderful time,' she said, thinking that sometimes she sounded exactly like a well-behaved little girl and sometimes she was sick of it.

'Yes, you did. I noticed,' said Mario sullenly.

'What does that mean?'

He laughed sardonically and shook his head. 'It's obvious. You were off in a dream world from the moment you saw him.'

'Who?' she demanded. Though she certainly knew.

Mario smiled then. 'Stay away from him, Nina.' He walked around to his side of the sports car. 'You're not ready for him.' He gunned the engine as she kicked open the ten-foot tall door, and with a snort of power the white car and Nina's prince disappeared.

A single perfect violet was plucked from the silver and white paper and tucked into the loose knot of hair she'd twisted on top of her head. Then another and another and another until half a dozen tiny flowers decorated Nina's crowning glory. It must be a terrible thing, she thought, to be so involved with what I wear and who rings my doorbell at nine o'clock every evening. She sighed. On Monday I will get a job. She clipped on Aunt Lilly's amethyst earrings. I will go to Rubelli first. After all, I pass them right near Piazza di Spagna six times a day. I'll simply talk them into hiring me. I know enough about fabric. Yes, it must be a terrible thing, she thought again. But it – she surveyed the lavender and black silk dress and the black patterned stockings with satisfaction – is so much fun!

'A job!' cried Lorenzo as they sped around Villa Borghese in the bumper-to-bumper traffic, all rushing to restaurants or to nightclubs, all in a hurry for the best table.

'Well, of course! Is that so bizarre?' Nina thought of Adele's euphoria over her gallery job on the telephone.

'Boh!' he shrugged, one thumb on the wheel, his hand

resting in his lap. The right hand punched at the tape deck in the dashboard.

'I don't even know what you do,' continued Nina. 'What do you do, when you're not with me? I mean, all day?'

Lorenzo turned his perfect profile towards her in the semi-darkness of the Alfa Romeo. 'I am very busy.' He smiled slowly, seductively.

'Oooooh, I know that! But what is your . . .' She hesitated. Sometimes speaking English here in Rome was not her own English, but had to be more precise. 'Your work?'

'Work!' he exclaimed as though she'd pinched him. 'Work is for peasants! I do not work!'

Ten minutes later, away from the lights of Rome, they were racing along the Appia Antica. She watched the large round stones of the road appear in the headlights and then disappear under the powerful sports car. They seemed soft as pillows, as though polished by water. Absurdly, the Bee Gees crooned on tape, as Nina thought of Roman soldiers and their horses marching proudly over the same stones. Lorenzo swerved sharply to the left between two stone columns and the car ground to a halt. A pair of uniformed attendants opened the doors and Lorenzo came to her and, taking her arm, led her across the driveway towards the villa. The music seemed to be absorbed by the branches of the tall trees just as the fresh air seemed to dissipate Nina's perfume. A shrill screech of tyres made them turn and the pinging of flying gravel caused Nina to flinch. *'La mia macchina!'* shouted Lorenzo, enraged, as he saw the little car being spun into a tight parking space between two Mercedes. Boys and their toys, thought Nina as she pulled him away from the scene and towards the party that awaited them.

It all began that evening, after she promised herself to find a job, after her resolution to pursue something she knew was important. The party overflowed into a back garden lit by torches that blazed every ten metres or so among the formal geometrically planted shrubs. It was all of darkest green, full of shadows, and smelled of the rich black earth and spring. A spot of colour would be seen and then lost again as a bright dress wandered down the path, its wearer shepherded along lazily by someone in a dinner jacket. She didn't know who he was at first, which worked to her advantage. '*Ciao*,' was all he said, as though of course she should recognize him.

'*Ciao*,' she answered, looking at a dark figure, tall, and faceless, for it was Nina who faced the light.

'You don't remember me?' he laughed as Lorenzo put out his hand. '*Ciao*, Claudio, *come va?*'

'*Bene. E tu?*' The stranger turned away from her then and the men talked about Lorenzo's father who had been ill. Lorenzo remembered his manners as he slipped one arm around Nina's waist. 'Are you friends?' he smiled. 'Or not?'

'I don't know yet!' Nina said in confusion. 'I can't see who this is!'

'Ah! Nina! This is a very good polo player. Claudio de Leone. Claudio, this is . . .'

'I know.'

'I saw you play once!'

'I know.' The voice held amusement. 'You should have come over afterwards and given me congratulations.'

So he had noticed me! 'With all the others?' she joked.

'*Certo!*'

'That's not the way I do things,' she countered.

'But it is my way!' he laughed.

A flirt, she thought. Too bad I cannot see his face. His face is heart-stopping. Lorenzo was communicating his unease with his hand pressed in the small of her back. As though aware of this, Claudio turned and called over his shoulder, '*Ci vediamo*,' and was gone. He was a tall figure walking slowly across the grass, holding a wine glass which became a reflected wink of light in the darkness.

The phone rang on Monday, late in the afternoon as she twisted the key, one, two, three, four, five, six, seven times in the lock. It rang again and again almost in time to the bolt turning. At last she was panting '*Pronto*' into the receiver.

Dinner. How simple. Picking me up at nine which is too early for dinner so he'll take me to Il Baretto for a drink first. How glad I am I didn't meet him a month ago for I would've known half as much as I know now! But he didn't take her to

347

Il Baretto, he took her to Harry's Bar where the barman in white linen knew his name and greeted him as though he saw him every evening. And he didn't take her to Dal Bolognese in the Piazza del Popolo or to any of the restaurants she knew but drove her out of Rome to a place with half a dozen tables in a garden. The conversation began as nothing special, she would tell Adele, but I found him irresistibly appealing. First, the tallness of him that had been so evident in the nightclub as he had held her; then the muscles in his thighs above the black boots, the muscles in his shoulders as he wheeled the horse back and forth across the polo field; the idea of his strength excited her. Though it was early in the summer, his face was bronzed, dominated by the bluest eyes. He often smiled at her as though he were halfway trying not to, trying not to give in to her, and she found it a challenge to amuse him.

'So where do you race this car of yours? I mean, when you're not terrorizing the populace of Rome?'

'I've almost stopped racing. There is Monza, of course, and the Grand Prix and the Mille Miglia, but one has to stay in form.'

'In form? I hear that all the time. In shape. A good figure. Maintain the line. In form.'

He smiled when she complimented his English. 'I spent six months in London for my English when I was eighteen.'

'Only six months?'

He nodded. 'I had an English nanny and I took it in school of course but it wasn't my best language. I know French much better and a bit of German. I think when one conquers the first foreign language, the second follows.' He noticed her dismay. 'Don't worry. The Italian will come to you. We spoke French at home at the dinner table all the years I was growing up.'

Claudio Massimiliano de Leone, it seemed, had gone to all the best schools: the Chateaubrian in Rome where only French was spoken, and then to Switzerland, then to London for a few perfunctory University of London courses and then, she was surprised to find, to Wesleyan in Connecticut.

348

'Briarcliff?' he echoed. 'Don't tell me I am having dinner with a "Cliffie"?'

Something stilted fell away from them then. He became another of Nina's would-be conquests and Nina blossomed as she relaxed in what she felt was familiar company.

'What year were you?' she questioned. 'What was your major? Did you join a fraternity?' If I can forget what he looks like, I can talk, she told herself. They ordered one course after the other, with no menu before them, only a short fat waiter who announced a litany of specialities like a proud schoolboy reciting a poem before his third-grade class. The wine was cold and bubbled like champagne. 'The best *pro-secco*,' Claudio told her. 'Pinot di Pinot.'

Nina tipped her glass towards his and her wide grey eyes stared into his face. He was the most attractive man she'd ever seen in her life. Perhaps the nose was slightly too large but it was a Roman nose, wasn't it? Generations of de Leones had had that nose since St Peter had been wandering along what was now the via Veneto. And his smile was ever so slightly asymmetrical, which gave him that look of detached amusement as though he would wait to choose to smile fully or not. The shirt was pale blue and seemed to have been laundered and pressed only minutes before, so perfect was the crease that ran down each sleeve. His trousers were fawn-coloured linen, and his shoes she'd noted at Harry's Bar as he'd rested them on the brass rail. They were slip-on, wine-coloured, with tassels. He put his hand on hers. It was large, with a coat of arms signet ring on the little finger. 'Tell me about this.' She touched it lightly with her free hand.

'My father's ring. He is Roman. My mother's family,' he began, 'is from Milano. She is what they call a Venetian blonde with light eyes. These are her eyes.' He looked up at her and away from the gold ring. Nina realized he knew the effect he was creating when he stared at her and she told herself to be cooler with him.

'And the de Leone part of you? Is that the part that makes you brave as a lion on the racetrack or the polo field or . . .' she smiled, 'or on the dance floor?'

'I wondered if you would ever remember that!'

So you did, she thought. Good. Point one for me. Except I was overcome and stupid and couldn't even speak a sentence of Italian. Maybe it was too bad he remembered after all. She shrugged as if it were nothing. The mannerisms of these Romans speak volumes, she had decided within days of her arrival. He laughed. 'You even shrug with an American accent!' he teased, and she made an outraged face at him.

'Oh! Unfair!' She pulled her hand away to take a swallow of the wine and he stopped her wrist in mid air and took the glass from her and then pulled her face towards his firmly. His mouth barely touched her lips when she had expected something hard from him, something aggressive in line with the mocking tone she had heard in his voice. His hand released her and she found herself looking into his face, lips faintly parted, as he moved away.

'Forgive me?' he said solemnly and she nodded, thinking: I feel as though I have been underwater and have risen to the surface too quickly; I feel the need to take a gulp of air. And yet, he seems unaffected by my touch. If I feel comfortable with the American part of him, that was the Italian part. American men don't kiss like that – like feathers.

'Forgiven,' she said in a clear voice and reached for her wine again. 'So tell me, Claudio, about the de Leones . . . were they stalking around Rome in togas with Caesar?'

He nodded. '*Certo*. What kind of Roman family wasn't?'

'Any popes?' she bantered. 'I adore the idea of your being descended from a promiscuous pope.'

Claudio's lips formed his half smile and then, with his blue eyes shining he put his hand on her cheek gently and shook his head. 'You, Nina, I like you.'

'Why are you shaking your head as if it weren't all right for you to like me?' With horror she thought: Now he'll tell me he's married. It's always the way, isn't it?

'Because . . .' He hesitated as though reluctant to say too much. 'Because my parents were so relieved when I

350

returned from Connecticut without an American wife and . . .' He smiled. 'And so . . . I like you.'

For a moment she was flattered into silence and then thought: It's all too pat, too fast, too Italian and I won't be lulled into this. He's done it before. They all have. She grinned at him as he took away his hand slowly. Her cheek could feel the coolness of his fingers as though they remained. 'American wives can be the best. It's the Roman husbands, however . . .'

'A volatile combination!' he put in.

'Poisonous,' she continued.

'Oil and water,' he agreed.

'Cats and dogs,' she inserted.

'But opposites attract,' he said seriously. It was the end of the teasing. He was looking at her across the table as though no one else existed. 'Do you have an understanding with Lorenzo?' he asked and when she didn't answer he continued, 'With Giorgio? With Mario? With someone I haven't seen you with?'

Nina lowered her big grey eyes to the grapes and cheese upon her plate. 'An understanding? How could I? I don't think I understand anything.' Her face with its lovely even features looked pale, the cheekbones were prominent and her beautiful mouth was pink and lush.

Claudio seemed relieved and took her hand in his. 'Then we will have dinner again.' He stated it and did not ask. 'Even opposites must eat.'

That is how it began with Nina and Claudio. The teasing about opposites, the trading of information about their families, the long dinners, the drives in the countryside. That first evening when he brought her back to via dei Greci he, with the impeccable manners the Italians of his class seemed to have, walked around to help her from the car and then took her key. He turned it in the lock and gave it back to her as she watched him in the yellow glow of the street light. When Nina positioned her face for the longed-for kiss he bent down quickly and kissed her forehead. She almost cried out, 'Why did you do that?' but of course she didn't.

Later in bed, she lay wide awake and thought: Thank

God, he didn't touch my mouth again. I might have invited him up and taken off my clothes and panted, 'Take me, I'm yours.' And he would have of course and then where would I be? She cursed herself for the attraction that made her 'weak-willed' and 'positively wanton', she wrote Adele. Her brain told her Claudio de Leone could have anyone and Lesley and Rita told her the same thing.

'You have to be different; you have to back away,' they insisted and she would sigh, 'I know. I know. But when you are about to lose consciousness from lack of oxygen who can back away? I keep thinking if I could just breathe normally – I could back away!'


'Oh, darling! Don't be discouraged by Rubelli!'

'Well, I am a little because it was pretty obvious I didn't understand a word of what Signor Ludovisi was . . .'

'But darling! If you're packing for a trip on the Count's yacht and he is feeding you I hardly think that Rubelli . . .'

'I did want a job! I did! Really!' insisted Nina, sighing into the telephone. She glanced around the one-room apartment as the Countess talked on. Three wooden steps curved up to what was a sleeping loft; the double bed was littered with coloured pillows she'd bought to cheer up that puke-green spread. More coral and yellow and lime pillows were randomly tossed on the same puke green of the sofa where she now sprawled. It helps, had been her melancholy response after she'd torn open the brown paper from her first shopping trip. Built-in closets lined the hallway into the bathroom which was noteworthy because it possessed a porcelain fixture that Nina first thought would be terrific for rinsing out stockings. There was also something called a hip bath which looked as though it would suit a dwarf. Nina always dangled her long legs over the side and laughed at the ridiculousness of it. But the tiles were pristine white and it was high-ceilinged, with plenty of storage cupboards. The apartment was basically L-shaped with one long hall where the refrigerator had sat humming until she unplugged it once and for all. For about a month there had been an egg sitting in solitary splendour on one wire shelf. 'I prefer terrace temperature,' she now claimed to guests as she bent over and plucked a bottle from behind a geranium. The kitchen consisted of two burners and a drawer that stuck open after it was opened and stuck stubbornly closed when it was finally closed again. Nina had shrugged when Adele had been mortified at the description. 'There is just one pot but you know how I adore popcorn.'

'Yes,' she was saying to the Countess. 'I love this apartment. The terrace is easily its best feature. Right now I have the glass doors open – that entire wall is glass – and can see hundreds of terracotta tile rooftops and, let's see, about five steeples. The sky is so blue you can't believe it's real.' She laughed. 'I know. When I found out he was a count I thought what a kick it all was! But it's his father who's really the count. It seems in Italy they call sons by the title they will inherit, on invitations and if they know them well, and really just if they feel like it. It's not proper, it's just Italian.' She listened. The Countess skipped back and forth from subject to subject. 'Maybe you're right. I'm not going to be too upset about it. I have left my résumé all over town. And embarrassed myself in a second language in five different shops.' Nina glanced at the bikinis piled on the nearest green upholstered chair; ten multicoloured piraeas were folded like giant handkerchiefs beside them. She'd been told they would live in the water or in the sun, so packing would be a snap. 'Claudio is wonderful. Really wonderful. I keep thinking he is the most fascinating mixture for me. You remember how I was intrigued with the very foreignness of Omar? Well, Claudio is exotic, but so American in some ways, so easy; he knows the East Coast, he knows New York. He's . . .' She laughed. 'Oh, Countess! I will be careful! Mother said the same thing last week. But there is such protectiveness towards me that I don't feel frightened of falling in love with him. I realize that part of it is the language and my dependence that goes with not knowing what's happening. Claudio is so sweet explaining a menu for instance and I . . . I feel so comfortable letting him take care of me.' She listened. 'No! He's never been married!'

The Countess chirped excitedly. 'Oh, maybe you will be the one! Then we can both be countesses!'

After they'd sent their love trans-Atlantically several times and at last hung up, Nina sat cross-legged on the sofa and smiled. Of course the Countess of all people wouldn't think it was awful of me to simply have a good time, wouldn't think it was awful to put off being practical. Just for the summer, anyway, decided Nina as she stood up and walked towards the bureau to decide what jewellery to take.

'*Ti amo*,' he whispered into one flat little ear. Claudio kissed her face then settled back upon the towels. Nina rearranged herself face down wearing her black bikini bottom and one silver chain around her neck and absolutely nothing else. What would Mother say? went through her mind when she felt Claudio's hand pat her fondly. They'd both been swimming all morning. Diving off the bow of the *Simba II* and then, after gambolling together – 'like porpoises', Patrizia called them – up the rope ladder for a peach or a wedge of watermelon which Claudio called '*pericoloso* to eat with Nina around. Yes, it was dangerous, for the two of them, like children, spat seeds at each other with terrifying accuracy and raced back and forth on the twenty-five-metre boat oblivious to the cries of their friends or the crew. Claudio had dripped all over today's *La Republica* and Nina had stepped on a sunbathing Antonio who had grabbed her by the ankle and brought her down amidst much giggling and a backgammon board. Thirty markers had rolled in thirty different directions.

Lunch was all eight of them or any number between that and just Nina and Claudio. There was a chef who was rowed to shore early in the morning for shopping and then out again by nine o'clock with bags and baskets of vegetables, fruits and fresh fish. When they didn't have lunch under the white umbrella on deck, they took the little rubber Zodiac and found a restaurant and drank wine and ate the specialities of the day. The ports of call were Capri, Ischia, Ponza, and Ventotene – all places of exile or holiday for

354

Roman emperors. Whitewashed houses overlooked narrow streets which led down to the harbour. After lunch, usually at around four, Claudio and Nina, hand-in-hand, and several of the others would stroll in and out of the shops buying the occasional postcard, trying on straw hats, replacing the last bottle of suntan lotion, and often bumping into friends from Rome doing much the same. Claudio festooned Nina with coral jewellery and seashells and she had 'ninety-nine piraeas' she claimed when he tried to buy her still another.

The afternoons on board were a quiet time of reading or naps below deck. 'Sleepy?' whispered Claudio as he unknotted the blue and aqua metre of fabric from Nina's waist. 'Mmmmm . . .' He licked her tan shoulder when she didn't answer. 'You look very tired,' she said as she reached for his bathing suit. 'Exhausted,' he sighed, feeling her fingers inside the narrow band of fabric. In seconds they were naked and entwined on the big bed of the master stateroom.

That first time of making love had been quick, passionate, crazy. Claudio had been so convinced by Nina of her 'differentness' he had hesitated to make a move. Nina, on the other hand, felt teased and fascinated by the respect he showed for her. She was more than ready to say 'Yes' when he pulled her down in the stall at the Polo Club before lunch one day in the spring.

Nina didn't think she had ever enjoyed looking at a man so much. Hadn't she read it was the male of the species, the human male, who could be so aroused by simply looking? But Claudio was glorious especially the Claudio of the summer. The Claudio who sailed *Simba II*. Nina loved his imperfection as others would love his beauty and always broke away to kiss his forearms with great tenderness. A fiery crash on the racetrack had left pink and white scars from the inside of his elbow to the tiny blue vein of each wrist. She pressed her lips to the different skin until he pulled her back into his embrace once more. His muscles were long and hard and his skin an olive colour from the sun and when he closed his eyes above her she saw the half moon of his lids and the black lashes like a child's curled on his ruddy cheeks. Straight black brows, thick and definite, framed the eyes which, when he opened them after a kiss, gazed into hers as clear as the sea, the colour of the Tyrrhenian they sailed upon. Nina felt the coldness of the big gold ring upon her skin as he stroked her and she admitted to herself that it, too, attracted her. That ring, that coat of arms, the idea that he was a count and that he, a count, was making love to her. Nina tried not to compare his lovemaking with Omar's, but she did invariably. But I love Claudio! she would insist to herself. That makes all the difference. So the few minutes he took with her and the few seconds he was inside her were explosively happy for Nina. He lay in her arms later totally satisfied, calmed somehow, with a sweetness to his mouth that made her love him all the more, after all the exertion.

Nina's first Italian summer was spent in pale blue–green water, in the sun, in bed, at tables laden with lovely food and bottles of wine. Her skin became one shade lighter than her adored Claudio's, she added four bikinis to her supply, gave up pasta, learned to love the bidet, and was sure she had never been so happy.

'God, I hope he didn't forget,' worried Adele in the taxi. She gave herself one last look in the compact mirror and smoothed the wide pale blue linen collar over her shoulders. Early September in New York was still hot, still summer humid, even at six o'clock in the evening, and Adele was still very tan, so she was bare-legged in the light blue and white slingbacks. Paul has been horrid for weeks. If only he can try tonight, just tonight; it's all I ask. She opened her compact again as the taxi jounced across a pothole on 72nd Street. Adele added rose-coloured lipstick with a frown and thought: I'm okay, I'm okay. No one would ever think I've never been this happy and this miserable in all my life. It should make me come out even. But, she smiled, I look better than normal. Suddenly she thought of Jack and all her self-confidence rushed away like wine spilling from a glass.

Her heart pounded as the driver stopped in front of the awning and Herbie came rushing out to open the door.

'Mrs Rice, very nice to see you.' He tipped his hat. 'Your father told me abut the gallery. How's it going over there on Madison?' They stepped into the elevator, the doors clanked close, and they began the ascent.

'Just fine, thanks. I'm having a nervous breakdown,' she laughed. 'But the gallery is fine.' He laughed with her and opened the door into the Wickham hall.

That's good, thought Adele. Don't think about him. I should have asked if Mr Rice had arrived. I should have asked Herbie. I could have waited downstairs – no, that would have looked . . .

'Adele!' It was Ann, looking radiant in a cream silk dress. The women embraced.

'My daughter, at last!' said Charles with his arms out. Adele felt a rush of affection. The last time I saw him, she thought, I cried all over his blue suit.

Jack stood by a long window in the living room with the light behind him. He held a glass of scotch in one hand and with the other he nervously pushed back his hair, which was almost white after a summer of sailing off Nantucket. His mouth went very dry when he saw her in the hallway and he felt his heartbeat quicken. Ass, he said to himself. Get over it. She's been married for years, can't stand the sight of you because of what we did and you still, you ass, you still can't think of anyone else. He remembered the wedding right here in the living room and the look that had crossed her features as she stepped towards Paul. Had it been directed at him or had he only imagined it?

'Adele!' cried Melanie. 'It's been ages!' Short, with brown hair cut very short; childbearing had added ten pounds to her figure. She, however, seemed satisfied with home and hearth and more at ease than Adele had ever seen her. 'You remember Henry, don't you?' Melanie's sharp voice never failed to get on Jack's nerves. 'There are five of us now,' she gushed. 'Little Henry, and Beth, and little Ann who's just starting to crawl.' She added with a laugh, 'And to get into trouble!'

Jack was alone in the living room but he could see the knot of family through the archway. Adele's hair shone like pale yellow silk; he could squint and see it blowing in the wind as she pulled down a spinnaker. He could see strands across her face as her eyes closed and she whispered his name.

'Jack!'

He jumped. 'Oh, Uncle Charlie, I was . . .'

'Don't tell me! Dreaming of corporate mergers?' His uncle put a hand on his shoulder. 'It's almost eight and I've got a table at "21" for half past. We'll give Paul another fifteen minutes and then do you think you could call his office and just ask . . .'

'Sure. Be glad to.'

'Adele's very embarrassed about it.' The older man walked towards a maid in uniform to instruct her about the champagne. 'Can't wait for Paul! I'm certainly not going to make this announcement in a restaurant!'

Jack heard Adele's light laugh. 'Rome! Fourteen dollars! Can you stand it? Nina sent them!' She was holding on to Ann's arm and kicking out one foot as they looked at her sandals.

'I think we should all go over there once a year just to buy shoes,' Ann was laughing.

'At that price,' agreed Melanie, 'it's ridiculous not to!'

Ann still had Adele's arm and guided her into the living room. 'Don't think you two cousins have seen each other for a while,' she smiled.

Adele hadn't noticed him standing there. She'd refused to look past Ann, Melanie, Henry, her father. There he was. Strong and straight and tall with the blue eyes that mirrored her own. She nodded, not trusting herself to speak.

'Adele,' he said with a nod and then left the room, excusing himself. 'Uncle Charlie's asked me to take care of something.'

Ann was mystified. Jack usually had better manners. How could these two have had a fight? They haven't been in the same room for years. 'Tell me about Nina. What do you hear?' she asked brightly.

358

Charles came in, followed by Agatha bearing a silver tray and tulip-shaped Baccarat glasses. 'Everyone sit down, please! Except for Ann!' he amended.

Melanie and Henry entered from the hallway; Ann looked near blushing as she took Charles's outstretched hand in the centre of the big white living room. The son and daughters were silent. Brent poured champagne and hurriedly served everyone.

'I think they've guessed!' laughed Ann as Charles put his arm around her and proposed a toast with lifted glass.

'To Ann, who has consented to be my wife!'

Jack made the best toast, thought Adele later on the train. And Daddy's in heaven and Ann looked very beautiful, whereas a year ago I would have only described her as attractive or pretty. He called her 'darling' and I've never heard him call anyone that, ever. Adele began to cry. For no reason! She reproached herself as she stared at the dark glass of the window, watching the pin-pricks of light sweep by. Miles later she thought of the black woods outside and saw only herself reflected and the interior of the train like a gloomy oil painting and thought: Why am I on this damn train? Going back to that house – a pile of bricks and wood and stone. I'm going there because of Paul. Paul, who didn't even show up tonight. Because I'm doing the right thing and I'm his wife and I have to fix his breakfast tomorrow. That's what it's boiling down to. No more dinners, no conversations, no kiss goodnight for weeks. Not that I miss that! Adele blew her nose and then felt anger. Damn it, she thought as the train clattered into the little station at Tarrytown. I'm sick of this train!

'Adele, it's Rajjin.'

She was surprised. He wasn't due to arrive until the day after tomorrow. 'Are you here? Are you in New York?' She tried to decide if he sounded long distance or not.

'I'm at Kennedy. I'm staying at the Carlyle. Can you meet me there later?'

'Of course.'

'I won't be able to get into town until about six with all this traffic and my bag hasn't shown up yet. Is six all right? Six fifteen?'

'Perfect.' Adele put down the phone and wondered if she should call Paul. No, he never called and he wandered in at midnight and later. It didn't matter any more.

Adele stared out at 80th Street and suddenly wondered if she loved him. What if . . . what if she had simply stopped loving him in the habits that had become their lives? What if in between making orange juice and feeling the bed move in the dark long after she'd found sleep, what if all those hours in between he had stopped being a part of her life? The only part of her life that concerned Paul was where she was when he wanted her to be at home. It had become a game of appeasement. I'll make a very special dinner because I know you don't like my going into the gallery every day. That had stopped after two weeks because he did not bother to show up for these very special dinners. He was always working late. Paul was a success, no doubt about that. S.U.C.C.E.S.S.

'It sucks!' she complained aloud.

'What sucks?' laughed Jack, standing before her.

Adele looked up, astonished. She blushed above the red suit and was so surprised to see him that she forgot to be her cool self, the persona she assumed like a cloak when he appeared.

Jack grinned. 'How about closing early?' Christ, I'm pushing my luck, he worried, but couldn't stop himself. 'Let's go somewhere and have a drink.'

Adele became wary. Don't play with me. Just because there is no Lisbeth of the moment. She hesitated and then said, 'No, thanks,' as casually as she could manage.

Jack flinched. He felt like grabbing her and shaking her.

Adele, suddenly awkward, shy, wondered: What is he doing here?

'Are you happy about those parents of ours?' He tried to be nonchalant but she had stung him again.

She nodded. Adele sat at the desk and stared at the calender in front of her. The numbers swam before her

360

eyes. She could feel him breathing beside her but couldn't look up at him. Then she heard the door close and saw him stride quickly across Madison Avenue, his trenchcoat over one shoulder held by one finger, his blond hair blowing back in the wind.

Adele felt like crying.


Bart was grinning in the lobby of his apartment building. He put down his briefcase and studied the postcard. The fountains in front of St Peter's were spraying forth on one side and Nina's bold turquoise ink covered the other: 'Come to Rome. I miss you. A zillion things are happening every second. Just get on a plane and come! I am drinking champagne non-stop and there are flowers on every window sill. love Nina.


Rajiv Rajjin stood on the east side of Madison Avenue and stared across at the black sign with large gold letters. THE RAJJIN GALLERY. They're not too brassy, he thought. Rather classical. Not too big, not too showy. Adele has very good instincts about things. She'd done quite well. He looked at his watch and then at the 'Don't Walk' sign and waited on the corner to cross. Beginning to get dark and people would be arriving in an hour. Adele was home changing her clothes. Rajjin could see into the lighted gallery. The bartender was in place, the waiters were adjusting bow ties, but most important of all, on the walls hung the tapestries of oranges and pinks and greens and blues and lavenders and yellows, radiating a life all their own. Rajjin was happy with the New York gallery. It was the newest star in the constellation he dreamed of.


'Adele Rice. I don't think we've been introduced yet.'

'Oh, so you're the energy behind this gathering! I'm Alistair McKendrick.' The plump man with red hair nodded. 'A great success! I marvel at the selection!'

361

'I can't take credit for that. That's all to do with Mr Rajjin.' She nodded across the room at the dapper little Indian in the dark blue suit and the highly polished black shoes.

'So nice to meet you, Mrs Rice,' gushed a woman in turquoise with a tremendous full-brimmed hat.

'I just wanted to say . . .' plucked another woman at her arm.

Jack stared at the animated face from where he stood at the front door until someone wanted to pass and then he backed out on to the sidewalk and told himself to walk away. The track lighting played havoc with the other women's make-up but Adele looked beautiful, radiant, in control. Her sheaf of blonde hair had been cut a few inches and dipped to chin-length when she laughed or turned her head. He could see only the shoulders of the persimmon-coloured silk dress and the diamond clip earrings when they caught the light. Jack felt the familiar ache inside and almost said aloud 'I want you,' before turning to walk up Madison Avenue and home to his apartment on Park.

'Nina! It's Adele! How's the *dolce vita?*'

'My God!'

'I miss you! Tell me all about everything!'

'Adele! This call will cost a fortune! I was going to write you tomorrow!'

'Oh, I don't care what it costs! It's the day before Thanksgiving and the gallery is closed and I had to hear your voice. I'm standing in the kitchen; there's snow outside. The very first snow . . .'

Nina could hear it. That strong brave resolve to not say something. 'What is it, Adele? I know you didn't call for no reason.' There was silence from Tarrytown except for the slight echo of Nina's last word which meant the phone connection was via satellite.

Adele laughed. Not really a laugh, thought Nina.

'Okay, I wish you were here. Something happened last

362

night and I don't know what to do about it. I wonder . . .'

'What happened?'

'Paul had to work late. He always has to work late. Sometimes he calls, sometimes he doesn't even bother doing that. I never know when I'll see him. Usually I don't. He gets into bed beside me but I don't even wake up any more. I don't know what time he gets home.'

'Adele . . .'

'Last night at six he called and said he was working late. Then at seven I got a call from a woman who said I really should stop thinking that my loving husband spent so much time in the office. She sounded like a normal person, not a crank. I don't think she was even disguising her voice . . .'

'What did you do?'

'I asked her who she was and she said that didn't matter but why didn't I try to call my husband and see where he really was? So I called the main switchboard, forgetting, of course, that it's turned off at six and then I remembered the extension in Paul's office for after hours. I dialled it a dozen times and, of course, he wasn't there.'

'Maybe he was out getting a sandwich or in the men's room or maybe the phone line . . .'

'Nina!' Adele was nearly shouting. 'I've been trying to ignore all this but I can't any more. We don't have any feelings for each other.'

The teary quality of her voice belied that, thought Nina, or was she crying over having to face something she didn't want to face?

'What are you going to do?'

'I . . . I don't know . . . You know that Ann and Daddy are getting married soon and I wonder if I should disrupt things by . . .'

'Forget about everybody but you for a second. Do you want to confront Paul? Do you want to patch it up?'

'I don't know what I want.' Adele sounded near tears. 'I . . . we don't even like each other. It's as if he's punishing me for loving the gallery so much. It wasn't this bad when he was so angry over my going to Columbia. He is furious that I am not at home all day! He says he works hard to give me

363

everything I want and look at this big house, etcetera and that he has to have a supportive wife, an understanding wife, a wife who will devote all her time to him and to his needs after a day doing battle at the bank!' Adele took a deep breath and realized how angry she was. 'He says he doesn't want a partner in marriage, he wants a wife waiting at home to care for him and soothe him.'

Nina thought he sounded like a spoiled brat – peevish and self-centred – but then she'd always thought this about Paul Rice, which made her doubly hesitant over voicing an opinion.

'Paul says he doesn't want "his wife" to work. It's as though I am his toy, his possession and he doesn't want a wife of *his* to work. It doesn't have a thing to do with me or what makes me happy.'

'Do you really think that your working or your degree is at the bottom of this?'

'No, I don't,' Adele said quickly. 'I think he's been angry at me ever since I told him I was pregnant.'

'You might be right.'

'What'll I do, Nina?'

Nina exploded with her stream-of-consciousness questions one after the other. 'Do you want to go on this way?' 'Do you think anything can be changed?' 'What is the best thing that could happen?' 'Do you want to give up the gallery to bake apple pies for him?'

'No, I don't, because he wouldn't be on the train if I were sitting there in the station wagon waiting for the Croton local to roll in every evening at seven twelve.'

'Do you want to divorce him?'

The word was out now. Like a black cloud hanging somewhere in mid-Atlantic between Nina's voice in Rome and Adele's ear in Westchester County.

'Yes, I think that's what I want,' came whirring back over the wire.

Nina was surprised. 'You know, Adele, you can try a separation, you can talk to him about changing things, you don't have to leap . . .'

'I am not leaping. I think I will pay more attention to these

364

late nights at the office and then after Christmas tell him and then Daddy what I think.'

'That's a month away. Can you speak to him, behave normally all this time?'

'Nina, we don't speak, anyway! I serve him his breakfast in silence. We don't make love – haven't for months. There is the occasional weekend brunch or dinner party but it's easy with other people. We should hire people to live with us.' Nina laughed and Adele saw the humour in it, too.

Nina had to ask. Had to make sure. 'Adele, you said you haven't made love for months but still . . . you're absolutely sure you're not . . . I mean, there's no chance you're pregnant, is there?'

'No!' Adele was triumphant. 'I confess. I've been on the pill for the last four months. A baby won't help my marriage and I know it.' Nina was amazed. 'Paul used to make love to me only about once every three weeks, anyway, but I couldn't keep taking the chance. I have been on the verge of getting out for longer than I let myself realize. And I got into it because I let myself be pushed by a baby I didn't really want into marriage I didn't really want.' She paused. 'I'd feel worse if Paul had consented to all those tests. You know, the ones where his sperm have swimming races?' Nina yelped with laughter as Adele continued. 'He's such a macho monster that he wouldn't consider that the "problem" could possibly be his. But I couldn't take the chance of a baby changing my life again.'

'Very smart, Adele. Keep eating the pill. And listen, you finally have something in your life you love to do. The gallery. Don't give it up. You need it more than ever now.'

'True. It's my only contact with the world outside my kitchen. It's people taking my advice, it's organizing and planning, and it's Mr Rajjin making me feel I am competent.'

'I'm so glad that you have it! Hang on and call me in the middle of the night if you need to talk.'

'What about you? How's Claudio, the lion? I devour your postcards but more juicy details, please!'

'He's wonderful!'

'Write me all about him! I must hang up, but Nina . . . thanks!'

'Come and visit me!'

'Maybe I will surprise you. Have a good Thanksgiving!'

'We don't have it here, silly! The Romans were being frightfully urbane at the time those rustic pilgrims were eating corn . . .'

Adele laughed. 'Much love!'

Nina called '*ciao*' into the phone and hung up.

Six hours' difference between Rome and New York. Eleven o'clock in the morning there and here it is dusk. Nina stared through the wall of glass at the students at their easels across the street. Church bells began to ring and a faraway flock of swallows like a handful of pepper swooped back and forth across the white November sky.


Sherry clung to the metal loop above her head and thought how much she hated the subway during rush hour. It was loud, dirty, and hardly economical at fifty-five cents a ride, and she sometimes wondered why she didn't give up this ridiculous Manhattan dream and get a job in Brooklyn the way most of her friends had. Especially tempting after the events of the last week. That bastard, Paul Rice! He had actually had her spend the week interviewing her replacement and then told her that she would be transferred, same salary, of course, to another department. He'd evidently picked up the phone, called personnel and told them there was a personality problem! After all this time of being his slave in the office and then being his lover after hours!

What does that prove? Sherry asked herself. Only that Paul Rice is a creature of habit, from the way he lays his shirt carefully over the chair in that apartment to the way he touches my left breast first and then my right one. Sherry wondered if she could scream and not be heard above the deafening racket of this damn train. It would feel so good.

Screaming alone wouldn't do it, though, she realized as the train ground to an ear-splitting screech of a stop, tossing everyone first forward, then backwards. Angie's idea had taken some getting used to but was not such a bad one now that they'd put it in action. After all, her best friend had rationalized only the week before as she sat cross-legged on the sofa and drank Tab from the pink can, 'He's bound to be screwing someone else now, and doesn't his wife have a right to know?'

The car emptied of people and the pretty blonde in the raincoat, wearing Charlie, found a seat. Yes, she said to herself, Angie is right.


It happened on Lesley's birthday. She'd wanted Nina and Rita to take her to some place 'absolutely Roman', some place she'd 'never been before' and some place she'd 'always remember', even if she were to become an old maid in the outback. This was doubtful since her streaky blonde hair attracted more masculine attention than she cared for. The three of them, all long-legged, still tanned, and smiling, were treated like a trio of *principessas*. A waiter at the Café de Paris on the via Veneto waved them to a prized back corner table. 'I love it!' said Lesley. 'How come we never meet here for lunch?'

'Don't answer her, Rita! It'll spoil her birthday!' put in Nina.

The maitre d' gave them menus and took a deep breath, preparing himself to address them in English. Lesley looked at the prices and gasped. 'That's right. Exactly right,' murmured Nina.

The third carafe of wine had been taken away empty but they were still sober enough to discuss the possibility of another when Nina saw him.

'What is it?' asked Rita seeing the colour drain from her face. 'Are you all right?' she persisted in her English accent.

'No. I'm not.' Nina's voice was dull. She felt hypnotized as she watched Claudio only metres away kiss a woman wearing a red dress. They sat, holding hands across a round table, both leaning forward, faces and mouths pressed together in what seemed the longest kiss on record. Nina's eyes filled with tears. Maybe it wasn't Claudio, after all, she

367

wanted to believe. But then she saw the couple separate and saw Claudio, with that gesture she'd seen every day for months, lift his hand casually for the bill. Rita had met him and instantly assessed the situation.

'Quick. Put this on!' She plopped her big-brimmed hat on Nina's head, who sat as if in a bad dream staring down into her wine glass. She imagined she could smell him, that lime aftershave, as he and the stylish brunette walked past their table.

'He didn't see you,' decided Lesley as she turned in her chair to watch the couple disappear in the crowd crossing the street in front of the Excelsior.

'His sister,' said Rita.

'He's an only child,' Nina murmured.

'His cousin,' said Lesley.

'His great old friend from school,' put in Rita.

'I don't know who she was but that *was* Claudio,' said Nina definitely.

'That *was* a shit,' said Rita just as definitely.

But it was Lesley who had the last word. 'What do you expect? That *was* an Italian.'


Adele felt the arms embrace her, the lips against hers, searing her with their warmth, and the strong muscles of his body pressed down the length of hers. She held onto his shoulders and said, 'I love you. I love you.' Suddenly she was snapped into wakefuless. She reached out and found that the bed was empty, then she heard the bathroom door open and sank back and lay very still, watching Paul through slitted eyes in the semi-darkness. He tiptoed past the foot of the bed and began to fumble with his belt buckle and then she heard the zip noise of his trousers. He sat in the wing chair and pulled off his shoes and socks, then he stood again and pulled the trousers off, holding them by the cuffs upside down. Adele watched him and thought: I feel like Margaret Mead. I haven't seen my husband undress in months.

Paul pulled at his shirt buttons and in seconds the Brooks Brothers shirt was on the floor where she found it every morning. He walked slowly to his side of the bed and Adele felt the cold air on her legs as he lifted the covers and slid in. Only when she heard his regular breathing and was sure that he was asleep did Adele turn over to look at the little clock. Half past two. Always darkest before the dawn, went through her mind. Confusing the time change, she thought of Nina, probably entering a restaurant at this hour, perfumed, wearing something drop-dead beautiful in black with noise and music and an attentive Claudio toasting her with flowery compliments. Never mind, she deserves it, thought Adele. Nina deserves everything good.

The dream. That was good. She almost turned and reached out for Paul beside her. Warm and naked and her husband no matter where he'd been. But she didn't, for as she stared at the outline of the windows facing on to the back yard filled with snow, she thought something about that dream was . . . off . . . not clear. What was it? Adele lay with the duvet pulled up under her chin for a long while, eyes open, willing herself to remember what had been awry. Then it came to her. The man making love to her, the man she had said 'I love you' to . . . the man was Jack.


'*Ti amo.*' He kissed her nose and Nina believed him. The music reminded her of that first time they'd danced, not knowing each other's names, each other's place in the world. They had been male and female only. Tonight they were in the Hostaria dell'Orso listening to the piano player pick out this song and that, in English, in French, in Italian. The club chairs were covered in dark brown velvet, the walls were coral and the dark brown beams of the ceiling gave the large room a solid warm feeling as though it would be safe from enemy troops, battering rams, stampeding horses. This room was one of three floors of a palazzo occupying a corner facing the via dell'Orso or 'Street of the Bear' and the Tiber. The first floor was a dining room of marble and mirrors; candles were reflected hundreds and hundreds of times. The second floor was a disco that literally pulsated with the beat of the music. Stone stairs led from one entirely different ambience to another. Nina and Claudio preferred the relative quiet of the ground floor with its music which made talking possible and its new arrivals who were often old friends.

Nina held Claudio's hand and loved him. The scene on the via Veneto had taken on the unimportance of a very blurred photograph. It was something to look at once and then throw away. For Claudio was beside her, wasn't he? At lunch, at dinner, in bed all afternoon during the *mezzogiorno* – with his intensity, with his warmth, his clear blue eyes, his firm grasp of her hand, and now this evening, the pressure of his thigh against hers on the little velvet-covered banquette. 'A one-shot deal,' Nina told herself. The woman in the red dress meant nothing. Nothing to Claudio, the extremely attractive Roman, and if I'm smart, nothing to me, the American, either. She resolved to forget it once and for all.

The autumn had passed in a whirl of what she thought of as 'being available'. Her finances were amazingly healthy since she spent nothing on food, her rent was nearly exactly the rent of 90th Street, and taxis in Rome were cheaper than Manhattan by far. Nina calculated that with her living expenses so minimal it was practically like working for the Countess!

Nina's lire went towards looking as prosperous as possible, for the Roman women made an art of looking well-tended. From their chic haircuts down to their waxed legs and pedicured toes peeking out of open-toed stiletto-heeled pumps, they fairly gleamed with moneyed good looks. Damn it! thought Nina when she tied and re-tied a silk scarf. Do little Roman girl babies get born knowing how to handle this kind of thing? A lapel pin of lapis lazuli, a big brass ring of cornelian, diamond earrings set in a triangle of onyx. Nina looked, told herself not to gawk, was envious of the flair and then began to try harder. But it seemed to take money to keep up with this league. The women's suit jackets were lined in heavy silk, the hems of their skirts hung as a designer planned. Crepe blouses had fine pleats across a bodice or a cuff with a covered button that Nina had never noticed looking like that in New York. The women wore patterned stockings of all colours to match their dresses: emerald green, cherry red, royal blue, and lots of black. Shoes were glove-leather soft, of many colours and always – Nina ground her teeth – looked brand new. Nina's dressing and undressing and her hairwashing and the changing the neckline of a suit with a scarf and the shopping for slingbacks that were perfect and under $50 were a big part of her life now.

Nina loved Rome, loved her little apartment, but most of all she loved being with Claudio. Now she often spent the afternoon watching him on the polo field; she was the one to kiss his sweaty beaming face afterwards. She was the one he escorted to the French Embassy dinner at Palazzo Farnese in honour of the Italian president. She was the one he held in his arms at the end of the evening, the one he called in the morning about plans for lunch or the afternoon. I am the one he loves, she thought. I am sure of it. For, she echoed the Countess all those months ago, during the Omar days, how could he have time or energy for anyone else?

The piano notes died away and Claudio squeezed her hand. 'Are you there? Are you with me?' and she nodded. 'Daydreaming.' 'I'd like you to meet Sandra Martinelli and Carlo di Persio.' Nina stood and had her hand kissed. The very pretty young woman nodded and smiled at her. 'Still together. What a fool,' said Claudio in a low voice as the couple walked towards two empty chairs across the room.

'Who's a fool?' asked Nina.

'She is. He's married.'

'Thought that was pretty normal for Rome.'

'Mmmm,' grunted Claudio. 'She gives herself so easily.'

Nina was shocked. 'But,' she began, 'do you think it's all right for him, for his wife . . .'

'Oh, Nina!' He shrugged his massive shoulders and sipped the champagne. 'What he does is his business. His wife won't know. He's careful. But for Sandra! She gets nothing. She gives everything. She has cheapened herself.'

Nina was silent. She was thinking of herself and Omar. Living for the phone calls, the dinners, the few days here and there, and knowing all along. Sustained on a diet of daydreams. How much more painful to have the wife in the same town, to know, to be sure that he lived with her! But in the end, maybe more painful to be lied to and to discover it so . . .

Claudio was speaking again. 'I have only contempt, no sympathy, for a woman who gives herself that way. She knows what she is doing.'

'Claudio,' said Nina, thinking of love, thinking she needed another glass of something, 'you can be very hard sometimes.'

'I haven't written in so long,' began the familiar voice on the phone.

'Adele!' cried Nina in delight, putting down her hairbrush. 'It's only half past nine here. What are you doing up at three-thirty in the morning?'

'Can't sleep! Tonight was the big dinner for Daddy and Ann and I've just got home. The wedding's at noon to-morrow.'

In minutes Adele had poured out all her news. She had filed for divorce and become Adele Forrest Wickham again. Her voice was calm as she told Nina that Paul had 'been screwing this secretary and that one for ages. I was very slow to catch on.'

She told Nina that she saw Paul so differently. He had kept all his feelings buried inside. His anger about the baby had come out only after she'd actually told him she'd seen a lawyer. 'I'm getting my balance again.' She stared down at the pale mark on her left hand where her wedding ring had been. 'I really lived alone for so long. Paul was just someone coming and going in that big house – someone to make sure there were flowers on the hall table for, someone's laundry to worry about. Someone to buy bacon for. There was so little conversation, and no affection, I might as well have charged him rent as a boarder.'

'Oh, Adele!' Nina was horrified.

'True. So now it's easy to live within ten blocks of the gallery, to have my own time. And it's far better to be a little lonely on my own than to be very lonely in the same room with someone I was married to.'

'Do you ever see Jack?'

'Oh, we're thrown together once in a while. He seems to go through periods of every night at "21", when he's not at the Sign of the Dove with these rather gorgeous society types, like Phoebe Haffenraffer and then, according to Ann, he turns around one hundred and eighty degrees and plays squash during his lunch hour and works every night till ten.' Adele no longer felt the need to confide in Nina. *I came so close to it all those years ago at Briarcliff, before the evening with Charlie Brewster, before drinks at the Palm Court. How glad I am I didn't. I'm grown up now. I can keep away from Jack. It's in our own best interests to leave each other alone.*

When asked about Claudio, Nina stated she was very much in love with him. Adele couldn't understand why Nina hadn't met his family, or why he, in his mid thirties, still lived at home. Nina was hard pressed to explain that most Italians lived with their parents until they married and that meeting parents was simply not done until they were practically married. Home she described as a stone monster festooned with ivy – a palazzo in the centre of Rome. Claudio had pointed it out as they'd driven by and told her that his family occupied the *piano nobile* which was the floor with the best frescoes and highest ceilings. The rest of the structure had been divided into enormous apartments and rented. She described Claudio's life as pretty glamorous: a life filled with racing, his polo-playing and summers on the *Simba II*.

'But does he work?' Adele's belief in the Protestant work ethic was evident in her voice.

Nina talked about the chain of magazines his father owned and the half-dozen newspapers. Claudio did go to an office, did work at the financial part of things, did go to Switzerland on business. This pacified her old roommate who, at last, agreed that the young Conte de Leone didn't sound half bad. Nina laughed. 'The wedding is in eight hours! I must stop talking!'

There was silence between the phones for neither one of them wanted to hang up. 'Nina, you know you're invited any time. You could have a bedroom to yourself at the apartment with Daddy and Ann, or stay here with me slumming it on the couch. I'd love to see you. Been too long.'

'I know it has. I miss you.'

Suddenly Nina felt very far away. 'Bye!' 'Goodbye!' they called like two people on trains moving out of the station in different directions. 'Bye!'

The tinkling notes of Domenico Scarlatti filled the little chapel of St James Episcopal Church on Madison Avenue. Below its vaulted blue and gold ceiling stood the fifteen guests: a few of Charles's associates, a few from Ann's circle of Chestnut Hill.

Ann Louise Beaufort Forrest soon-to-be-Wickham made her way slowly, regally, down the red-carpeted aisle. All faces turned to see hers and there were several sharp intakes of breath as members of the congregation appreciated her gentle loveliness. The groom turned, too, and stared as the slender figure in pale silk approached him. He remembered her in his arms only the other night. With Ann, at last, he had overcome all the reticence that years of sleeping alone had inspired in him. With Ann he was the man he'd always wanted to be – a man of passion and tenderness.

Adele was near tears as she watched her father put the ring on her aunt's finger. She thought of her own wedding, of her own promises, of Paul, of what was supposed to have been. She was giving up and she knew it. But it was time to give up and to be alone.

Jack was staring at his cousin from where he stood beside his uncle as best man. He was thinking of the *My Fair Lady* monologue that is delivered in irritation by Professor Henry Higgins as the minister intoned the vows between his mother and his uncle: 'Words! Words! Words! I'm so sick of words!' They don't work with Adele. I can't reach her! Was it that ridiculous pact we made all those years ago not ever to be alone again? Is it that she hates me or does she hate herself? Why does she become the original ice queen when I try to get near her? When I, of all people, know that she is anything but icy? Perhaps that's it. She hates how well I know her.

Their eyes locked for a few very long-seeming seconds. Adele was frightened that Melanie could hear her breathing; Jack was afraid he would reach out to her. The electricity was still there, whatever else neither of them knew.

Two hours later in the crush that was the reception in the apartment on Park Avenue Jack squeezed his way through the celebrating crowd.

'Hey, your hair's the colour of Dom Perignon!' he laughed, handing her a full glass of champagne and expertly putting her half-empty one on the nearby secretary. There was loud laughter behind them. 'Anyone tell you that before?'

'No, that sounds like something only you would say, Jack.' She hated saying his name because she loved it so much, because she remembered crying it out, the one syllable that made sense when he had pinned her like a butterfly to the dock, to the boathouse floor, to the ground.

'Well, how come yours is getting lighter and mine's getting darker? We're supposed to be the same.'

'Because this is your winter hair and because mine has gone quite pale from stress.'

'Oh, I see. That explains it.' He smiled slowly in that lazy irresistible way he had.

Adele looked down into the gold-coloured liquid in the tulip flute. The twin sapphires at her ears were no brighter than her eyes.

'How is it, Adele? Are you all right?'

She nodded with a lump in her throat. His voice held such concern that she thought: Maybe I'm not all right, after all. Anyone else who's asked me that has got a dazzling smile, but with Jack I know he is really asking and I know that I could really tell him. He stirs all the same old feelings in me. 'Better get back to the living room,' she said politely. 'Daddy's . . .'

'Wait.' He put his hand on her bare arm. The warmth coursed through them both but he didn't release her. 'Could I . . . could I talk to you some time, Del?'

'About what?' she asked, trying to sound casual, unconcerned, refusing to look at him.

His voice was deep. 'About you. About me.'

She shook her head and tried to move away again. His hand slipped easily to her narrow wrist. He could feel the fine bones. Jack held her until she looked up at him and said, 'Let go. Let go of me.' There was such pain in her face that he knew she meant it and released his grasp instantly. Adele turned and disappeared through the laughing, talking people.

Jack stared at her bell of blonde hair as she bobbed between shoulders and faces and thought: Oh, Del, I don't want to let go.


They were late; the dressing room was nearly empty as they struggled out of their clothes. 'I cannot believe it!' cried Kate as she pulled on the red tights.

'How do you think I feel?' answered Nina, brushing her long hair back into a pony tail. 'I thought I was going to have to be put into intensive care.'

'In Rome, forget it,' said Sarah dogmatically. She made it a habit of chiming into conversations whether she had heard the pertinent bits or not. 'The hospitals here . . .'

'*Ragazze! Ragazze! Andiamo!*' In seconds all fifteen women had taken their places at the barre and were anxiously surveying their figures in the wall of mirrors. '*Va bene!* Today we will work on the tummy area . . .' With great thuds they positioned themselves on the floor and stared up at the jewel box ceiling, waiting for the torture to begin.

Fifty minutes later in the dressing room Kate picked up where Nina had left off. 'Okay, intensive care. What did you say to him?'

'What could I say?' grimaced Nina as she yanked off the

black ballet slippers. 'Why aren't you taking me to Cortina for Christmas? Who are you taking? How dare you? Don't you love me? Aren't you ever going to' – her voice dropped – 'ask me to marry you?'

Kate struggled to keep her balance as she pulled on first one leg of her pantyhose then the other. 'I think you're too up front, too honest, for this man. I think . . .'

'Don't ever be honest with Italian men.' It was Sarah again. 'They'll leave tread marks on your trusting face.'

Nina had to laugh. 'Kate, I think' – she paused dramatically – 'we should go somewhere and have a coffee.'


'When I have a plan,' said Nina, 'I'm all right.

Kate pushed the sugar bowl away. 'Okay. A plan. First, Claudio loves you, doesn't he?'

Nina sighed. 'I think so. He says so.'

Kate resisted making one of her anti-Roman-male comments. How happy she was, how grateful she was to have an American husband like Bill! 'And you do love Claudio?'

Nina nodded. 'I went out for a long time, had an affair with – whatever you want to say – a married man. And I thought I was in love with him, but now I see that I wasn't. I am in love with Claudio.'

'I think all this is very simple. Claudio adores you, has fun with you, but he is too sure of you.'

'Well, how can I make him unsure about me when I see him every day?'

'You aren't going to see him every day, remember?' Nina's face fell. Her grey eyes were sad above the rosy cheeks; her hair was tied back with a dark blue velvet ribbon which seemed suddenly wilted. 'You have, or had, so many admirers, so many dinner dates, when I first met you. Dig up one of those princes and bat your eyes. Become fascinated with someone you simply liked six months ago.'

'Wish I could, Kate, but the worthwhile ones, the ones in Claudio's league, are all friends of his. And any other one wouldn't pose much competition.'

377

'Good point.' Kate was thoughtful. 'What about a different nationality? Someone he doesn't know? That's it! If he doesn't know him, he'll be twice as interested in what you're up to with him.'

'Oh, Kate! I just told you I'm in love with him! I don't want to do anything with anyone but Claudio.'

Kate waved at the waiter and ordered another round of espresso. 'It's still before noon. We have time to burn off the caffeine high.'

Nina laughed. 'Rita had a friend from London who just loves coffee. One day she had seven espressos and they had to take her to hospital. Went into shock. Right on the via Condotti. In front of Gucci.'

Kate stared. 'Should I cancel the order?'

'No. I haven't had a good caffeine buzz in weeks. It'll cheer me up.'

'So don't you know anyone, any attractive male, who'd be willing to feign love for you over Christmas?'

Nina suddenly thought of Tad. 'No. It's mean!'

'Oh, I'm thinking of someone who knows the score. Maybe someone who loathes Claudio . . .'

'It's too scary. This has to be foolproof and you know what they say about crimes . . .'

'No, I don't. But Nina, you know scads of men in this town. Can't you dream up just one who'll – '

'That's it!' Nina downed the nearly black liquid in one neat tip of the tiny cup. 'I'll dream him up! What could be safer? What could be more effective?'

'But . . .' stammered Kate, 'how can you be seen with him in all the right places if he . . . doesn't exist?'

'I . . .' thought Nina aloud. 'Either I'll leave Rome to be with him or we'll spend an awful lot of time in my apartment. Maybe he'll take on the characteristics of someone I knew in New York . . .'

'Have him from New York! Have him a love-crazed novelist who has never stopped lusting after you since your last tryst in the Bahamas – '

'Kate!'

'Do it up right. Give him a house on Long Island, an

378

apartment on Park Avenue and a passionate, romantic nature. He's flown over here to surprise you for Christmas!'

Nina was aghast at the breadth of Kate Middleton's imagination. She of the practical, common-sense nature, mother of a one-year-old, wife of a corporate banker, was all for inventing a wild, reckless love affair. And she knew the details that would swing it, too. They ordered fat cornettos gooshing with creme, 'to soak up the ink,' insisted Nina. 'Brain sugar,' nodded Kate as she wiped her mouth with a handful of napkins.

In twenty minutes, Nina had plans for Christmas. Richard Hanes Lattimer III, a Harvard graduate, independently wealthy, outstandingly good-looking, an excellent tennis player, maybe even Davis Cup, and an all-American skier, was to arrive at Fiumicino on 21 December.

'Nina?'

'Mother, Merry Christmas! I got your present yesterday and opened it an hour ago. It's beautiful!'

'I bought it at a little country store out here and thought it would be fun to wear over a sweater . . .'

'I love it! I can use the chain for other things and the silver bird is adorable. Thank you!'

'And I just opened the white cardigan and it is perfect!'

'I wish I were there!'

'So do I! It's funny having this Christmas without either you or Bart, but my life has changed so much in the last year that I guess we just have to think things like "onward and upward!" '

Nina laughed at the expression. 'Oh, Mother! Are you still doing that volunteer work? How is the clinic?'

Virginia's voice was full of life. 'Every day I am there something happens.'

'Is Ellen still involved?'

'Oh, yes. At least two or three hours a day. Then she goes out to a Mrs Morton to clean her house three times a week, and there's the Ross house, and there's an office building she cleans early in the morning at around seven before the secretaries arrive. I don't know how she does it all.'

'Well, Mother, now tell me what your plans are.' Nina was hoping that her mother wouldn't be alone. She felt guilty that she wasn't there.

'Weeeeeell!' said Virginia with teasing in her voice. 'First I am going to the clinic to serve Christmas lunch. The place should be mobbed since we put up posters downtown in the bus station and all up and down Farish Street. I've got fifteen turkeys donated by the Jitney Jungle and fresh vegetables by the Farmers' Market and cornbread made by the Broadmoor Methodist Ladies Club . . .' Nina smiled and thought: Mother sounds different somehow. These last months she's changed so much since she feels needed. Virginia continued, 'And then at three o'clock I'll drive back here to change into good clothes. Then I'm going to . . . I don't know if I've mentioned him to you . . . Dr Thorpe is having a Christmas party for all of us who work at the clinic.'

'Mother? Who is this man?' Nina was very curious. Her mother had never mentioned any man at all since Duncan died.

'Why, he's a general practitioner who comes to the clinic to see people almost every morning. He really started the clinic. We work together.'

Nina stifled her impulse to ask more about him. Wouldn't do to act too interested. She knew she'd have to wait for her mother to tell her if there was anything to tell.

'Thanks again, Mother, for the necklace. Kate gave me an address book – for all Roman names, she said. I was there for Christmas Eve last night. Lesley and Rita are coming here for wine in two hours. The Countess sent the new Graham Greene novel and Adele sent something too big for my mailbox and the *portiere* had flu so it's being held hostage at the post office.'

Virginia laughed. 'Wonderful! Much love to you. I'd better hang up.'

'Bye, Mother.' How good of her not to mention Claudio. I wonder if she wonders why I didn't. Oh, Claudio! Nina punched the yellow pillow in her lap as hard as she could. 'You monster!'

# 9

3 January. Almost time for Richard to leave, decided Nina as she pulled on the jogging suit and the heavy socks. The day was bright with sun, the air cold and clear as she ran past the little shops shuttered for the *mezzogiorno*. Maybe all this was good for me, she thought as she reached the pavement which ran beside the Tiber. I've read three novels, caught up on letter-writing and decided not to depend on Claudio. I have a busy day tomorrow. Back to Rubelli with my newly typed résumé which I will insist they keep on file. Adding the Countess of Avondale as a personal, along with professional, reference can't hurt. And her idea to have them call her collect is pretty bold. Then the new place that just opened on via della Scrofa. Even if it does seem to only sell furniture maybe they would have some use for me. Maybe it would lead to something.

She passed the Palazzo di Giustizia which was draped in the green veils that signified that it was being renovated or cleaned and/or that things were in danger of falling on Roman heads below. '*Bella!*' called a man on a bicycle. Then a car slowed down and someone called, '*Stupenda!*' and she ignored it but sensed that she and the driver were travelling at exactly the same speed. How irritating!

'Come on, Nina! You're only going twelve kilometres an hour!' It was Claudio. She stopped and walked slowly to the kerb. Smiling, she bent down for him to kiss her. He was tanned; his eyes were bright. '*Che cosa?*' he grinned.

'Didn't you know I run? I have to work off all these midnight dinners!' She wanted to ask, 'When did you get back, did you have a good time and *who* did you have it with?'

'How was your holiday?' he asked, and Nina tried not to smile too widely.

'Very good,' she nodded.

'What did you do?'

'Oh, ummm, a friend came from New York.' Wonderful that English has no gender for friend.

'A friend? Adele?' Claudio turned off the ignition and ignored the cars who had to go around him.

'No. Not Adele. I did talk to her, though. She's fine.'

'A friend.' Claudio turned the corners of his mouth down. 'Boh.' He made a gesture with his hand as it rested on the leather-covered steering wheel. Nina had become so convinced, through her long rehearsals with Kate, of Richard Hanes Lattimer III's existence, she was almost disappointed not to trot out any of his attributes. Exercise coolness. Drive him crazy with curiosity. That was Kate's advice. 'And you won't tell me anything more about this friend?' Claudio's eyebrows were raised.

'Of course I will! What do you want to know about him?' Go ahead and lie, Lesley had urged. He's lied to you. Count on it.

'Aaaaah!' Claudio actually shook his finger at her when he heard the 'him'. She laughed. So Italian. Her face was flushed and her black hair swept back in a red ribbon. A white terrycloth sweatband gave her the look of a very pretty American Indian.

'Well, Claudio,' she said casually. 'He insisted on coming and I . . . He's a great friend. A little wild – '

'Where did he stay?' Claudio interrupted.

'He took a suite at the Hassler.' Nina knew that Claudio had had a fight with the manager over something years ago. He'd never check. 'Claudio, you look so serious. What's the matter?'

'He flew all the way to Rome to see you?'

'Sure. Why not?'

'Is he in love with you?' he demanded.

Nina shrugged, thinking how proud the Countess would have been of her performance. 'I don't know. He says he is.' I could get mileage out of Richard for ages, thought Nina with glee.

Claudio was silent. Nina felt her control of the situation ebbing away. Had she gone too far? What was he thinking?

382

'Are you free for dinner tonight?'

(Nina would howl on the telephone to Kate, 'I don't know what came over me!') 'No, Claudio, I'm not. I'm seeing – '

'All right.' Claudio's voice was cold, full of dignity.

Nina bent down to kiss him on the cheek and then waved as she jogged away, heart pounding. She castigated herself mercilessly for two bridges. I can't play these games! I've ruined everything!

'Kate! I'll never hear from him again!' moaned Nina into the phone. She clutched a lime green pillow to her chest like a life preserver.

'Don't be ridiculous!' Kate, in her kitchen outside Rome, leaned forward to extend a spoon of baby food towards little Alice's heart-shaped mouth. 'You've whetted his appetite, that's all.'

'How could I have turned him down for dinner? How could I?'

'It was the perfect touch. You've given old Claudio something to think about. It's one thing to go away and not see you but it's another thing to ask to see you and not be able to. Your stock has risen to the stratosphere.'

'Oh! Do you really think that?' Nina frowned. She didn't think that. I used to be so good at all this but then there was never a Claudio involved. 'The Roman men are masters of flirtatious intrigue. It's a sport.'

'But you're covered. It's the perfect crime. We didn't overlook a thing.'

Nina ticked off what could give her away. 'Well, no one actually saw me with anyone over Christmas so I always could have been somewhere else. And if the phone was busy I do have the duplex system I share with the Mancinis on the second floor so they could have been on the phone. I didn't go to restaurants with you or Rita or Lesley or Solveig. Or with anyone at all, which means I was always possibly with this mysterious American.'

'Relax, Nina. You're in great form. You just don't realize it.'

383

An hour later Nina was staring into the mirror saying to herself: Sure, I'm in great form. I'm in love with someone unattainable again. But this time a confirmed bachelor, and last summer, last fall, three weeks ago even, I thought he was in love with me! And now – she sighed, turning away from her pouting reflection – I'll never hear from him again. He took someone glamorous to Cortina, probably a fabulous skier, someone frightfully sophisticated, and now he's back in Rome and I said no, I can't have dinner with you. Oh, how could I? 'But he's a bastard!' she said aloud. How could he make love to me and then go off with someone else? I wouldn't do something like that! And I'm so good. I didn't even scream about it; I didn't even say who is she? Which would be normal, but then I'm trying not to be normal. I'm trying to be Italian or . . . what *am* I trying to be?

Nina went outside on to the cold dark terrace and stared at the lights before her. No stars. Only golden lights of a terracotta Rome. Oh, Claudio, Claudio, Claudio, I miss you! She thought of his blue eyes and his mouth and the way he . . . oh, stop! she told herself as the lights blurred and she wiped her cheeks impatiently. I wonder if I have picked someone who won't, who can't, like the Countess said, love me. Nina stood unseeing until she realized she was shivering, then turned slowly and walked back into the apartment to a hot bath, to bed, to dreams of Claudio.

Nina ran to release energy; she ran so she wouldn't stare at the phone. She rang because it always made her feel good. Two afternoons later the purr of the Giuletta engine was beside her again. Claudio demanded out the window, 'How long has he been here?'

'He came on the twenty-first,' she panted, thankful for all the rehearsals with Kate.

'When's he leaving?'

'He has a board of directors meeting in New York day after tomorrow.' Nina's feet pounded on as the car, like a giant pilot fish, cruised two metres away. So he's leaving

tomorrow was the implication. There were only morning
flights from Rome to New York.

'Nina! Stop this ridiculous running!' burst out Claudio
and Nina turned with a look of innocence on her pink face.

'What is it?' she asked calmly. Can't believe how easy this
is.

'Can you come to lunch tomorrow? At the palazzo?' Nina
fought to suppress a tap dance of victory in her red Adidas.
'I want you to meet my parents.'

'Oh, yes. I can come.'

Claudio smiled. It was the first smile since Richard had
become known. 'I'll pick you up at one o'clock. *Va bene?*'

'Va bene.' Nina stood ankle-deep in brown leaves on the
pavement, a slim figure in a scarlet sweatsuit.

Claudio thought how very beautiful she was. '*Ciao, tesora,*'
he waved as the car moved forward and was swept into the
Roman traffic of the Lungotevere.


'Have you grown since I've seen you last?' teased Nina as
Claudio leaned over in the front seat to kiss her. His grey
suit was elegant. The blue silk tie matched his eyes and his
skin was almost olive above the white shirt.

'What do you mean?' he laughed, pushing his black hair
back with one hand.

'You seem bigger than life today. Skiing must agree with
you.'

Claudio smiled one of his half smiles. 'Whatever you did
over Christmas agreed with you, too.' He leaned over to kiss
her yet again, not caring about the lipstick she'd so carefully
applied with the tiny brush only ten minutes ago, just before
the doorbell sounded. '*Bellissima,*' he breathed. '*Bellissima.*'
Claudio and Nina were locked in an embrace that made
their hearts pound when the horns started. Via dei Greci
was one car wide and it was lunch time. Claudio finished the
kiss and then opened the door and leaned out. With palms
outspread he shouted to the irate drivers behind him, 'I am
kissing! *Va bene?*' and the honking stopped. Someone called
'Bravo!' He pecked a blushing Nina on the cheek once more

385

and then moved the car forward towards the via del Corso, past Piazza Venezia, up corso Vittorio and then down a little side street towards the massive archway that led to the courtyard of Palazzo de Leone.

The *portiere* waved the shining dark blue car through the tunnel-vaulted entrance which marked the centre of the palazzo's façade. He glanced up from *Il Messaggero* only long enough to nod recognition. Gravel scrunched under the wheels as Claudio swung into a parking place. Nina smoothed the red and black plaid skirt and wondered if she looked all right. It was lunch after all, Lesley and Rita and Kate had emphasized. The red cashmere sweater, her best, looked just fine with a string of pearls and her low-heeled shoes. Her black velvet blazer she'd debated over then decided it had always been right so grabbed it at the last minute instead of her good black wool coat with all the military buttons. 'Always cars here now,' he was saying in a tone of acceptance. 'The Paraguayan Embassy' – he gestured towards a flag hanging from a balcony – 'and the Bolivian Consulate to the Holy See.'

The palazzo was four storeys tall with the largest windows on the first floor. Pilasters decorated the wall between each arched fenestration. Nina looked up as Claudio pointed to the first floor. 'This is where we live. My apartment is' – he swung around – 'in this corner.'

'Your apartment?'

He nodded. 'Well, my rooms. I call it an apartment. I have two bedrooms and a dressing room and a bathroom of course. It is normal.' He made a face. 'My escape from the family.' Nina quickly repaired her lipstick as he watched. 'I only want to mess you up again.'

She snapped the compact closed. 'Anything you want to warn me about?'

He knew what she meant and hesitated. 'Mama loves me a lot. All mothers go too far in Italy. They spoil their sons.' He stared at his hands on the steering wheel. 'You know that.'

'And your father?'

'He will love you.' Claudio opened his door and went around to Nina's side and helped her out.

'My Italian isn't perfect. I – '

'Oh, don't worry!' He squeezed her hand. 'My parents speak English at the dinner table. French, when I was growing up. Now it's English for the last couple of years. You'll think you're in London.'

Relief suffused her. Nina turned to gaze up at the fountain framed by dark evergreens in one corner of the courtyard. Water poured from one chalice-like bowl to the other in tiers, splashing bright in the sunlight.

'It's been called the most beautiful in all of Rome,' remarked Claudio. 'I'll tell you the history of everything after lunch if you want. But you should ask my father to tell you. It will please him.' Nina took his hand and was led to the left towards a vaulted ceiling under a colonnade. An elderly man in livery nodded, 'Conte, Signorina,' and pulled open the double doors.

'His silver buttons are engraved with the de Leone coat of arms. You are looking at five hundred-year-old buttons,' grinned Claudio as their heels tapped over the stone floor.

'Don't make fun of me, you bad thing! I'm only a little American, after all!' They marched up a wide, curving, white marble staircase where another footman materialized and took Claudio's briefcase and, with a bit of reluctance, Nina allowed him to remove her jacket. The temperature in the grand reception room was identical to the January day outdoors.

'*Caro! Carissimo!*' trilled a tall woman coming towards Claudio. She was elegant beyond description. Blonde hair going grey was coiled in a fat chignon, crowning a fine-featured face with Claudio's blue eyes. Nina recognized her from the polo game. Her dress was of blue paisley silk, her stockings a shade of light blue and her shoes the finest high-heeled dark blue leather. One narrow band of gold embedded with dark sapphires circled her long neck and the matching earrings caught the light at each tiny ear. She even has his ears, thought Nina. 'And you must be Nina!' She was

387

dignified, she was reserved, but there was sincere warmth. Wasn't there? Nina wondered. The Contessa had quite an English accent.

She waved them to a seating arrangement at one end of the enormous high-ceilinged room. The interior was decorated in Renaissance style, grandiose and sumptuous. The door frames were elaborately carved and pedimented. There were heavy cornices and niches along the walls, each bearing a life-size marble statue. The walls themselves were frescoed in rich shades of blue and yellow and red and green. Giant figures loomed twelve and eighteen feet above Nina and above them were latticed windows. The french windows, letting in light, led off to the loggia which, Nina realized, was directly over the archway entrance. 'They've been sealed closed to protect the frescoes,' explained Claudio. The furniture, decided Nina, was early seventeenth century. It was brocaded in rose and pale green and looked spindly and insubstantial below all the opulent busyness of the room itself. The coffered ceiling was twenty-four feet above, in white and gold. The marble floor was geometrically patterned in rose and green and white marble.

'Would you care to take something before lunch?' the Contessa was asking. A maid in a black dress with a white apron and a little fluted white cap stood by.

'No, *grazie*.' Nina shook her head. I want to keep my wits.

'We never take anything before lunch but, however, you are American so . . .' She fluttered her hands.

'Mamma!'

'Oh, *Caro!* I want Nina to feel at home here! To be relaxed!'

Nina was thinking: Please stop. I feel like a little schoolgirl in these clothes; a little girl dropped off at the dentist's.

'Claudio!' It was his father, thank God, went through Nina's mind. He kissed his son and then turned to her and dipped towards her extended hand, his lips not touching her. He was an extremely handsome man in his early sixties, quick to smile – and he smiles with his brown eyes, too, noted Nina. She felt relieved to have him on the scene though in the dining room she couldn't think why. Nothing helped. The atmosphere fairly ticked with tension. It was like a wire being turned tighter and tighter between two invisible points. Maids served one person at a time as all the others watched the silver spoons dip into the pasta, the sauce, the broccoli; the fork jabbed the guinea hens, the knife flashed in the light as the cheese was sliced. Wine – first white, then red – was poured into goblets over Nina's shoulder until she resolved to never take another sip, so terrified was she of doing something disgraceful. It seemed that Claudio's parents spoke of everything in the world but of her. No questions, no 'how do you like Rome?', nothing she could warm to, nothing she could seize upon to show her enthusiasm, her wit. To make it worse, Claudio's grandfather was seated at her right and he simply chewed breadsticks loudly for long periods of time and then would fairly explode with some comment about 'the war'. My God! Which one? panicked Nina. She heard him put his fork down and thought: There he goes again. 'Did you know that Mussolini was expelled from school as a boy for stabbing someone?' the old man demanded.

'No, no.' Nina shook her head. 'I didn't know that. How terrible.'

'Happened more than once.' The white head turned away from her, back to breadsticks.

And he's not the only strange person here, thought Nina. There's that woman across from Claudio who hasn't said a word. Not one word, not since we were introduced. A cousin of Claudio's. Big as a house, with a vacant look. I don't think she's quite with us, Nina decided.

'Usually, Nina, we have ten or twelve for dinner, what with family and so forth, but lunches are very casual. Anyone who is in town, anyone who wanders in.' The Contessa smiled at Claudio on her right.

Nina turned to the Count. How terribly good-looking he was! Claudio may have inherited his mother's features but the look of an athlete came from his father's side. 'When was the palazzo built? It is so beautiful.' Nina's eyes shone as her glance took in the jewel box ceiling with the gold rosettes.

The floor seemed to gleam of malachite, but then it must have been green marble, mixed with the black and white and topaz-coloured.

'Oh, do you like history?' His tanned face showed pleasure.

'I do. My major in college – in university,' she corrected herself. 'But of course it was American history so . . .' She shrugged. 'There was less of it!' He was delighted at that.

'Yes, it's a young country.' He reached for a piece of gorgonzola and put it on a slice of bright yellow apple.

'So tell me all about the palazzo,' she urged.

'First it was a fortress; probably goes back to the early 1300s. They say the hill we're on is composed of ancient buildings that collapsed. Seemed any promontory was good for defence so they picked this as the place. Became a centre of fighting for several generations. The de Leone family owned land – controlled it rather – from here across the Tiber. We even owned Castel Sant'Angelo.' He shook his head at the loss. 'For a while.' Nina thought: I must read about this. I'm too stupid to comment. But the Count didn't seem to notice her silence. 'In 1482 the fortress was overrun and some of it was burned, but that marked a rebuilding and it was transformed into a palace.'

Finally some dates popped into her head. 'The Renaissance palace it is now?'

He nodded, pleased. 'Get Claudio to walk you through the *pinacoteca*,' he urged. 'Many of the paintings were sold, unfortunately, about fifty years ago, but we have some worth seeing.'

The Contessa interjected, 'The ones you see now were hidden from the Nazis in the catacombs.'

Claudio spoke from his end of the dining table beside his mother. 'Nina knows a lot about furniture and architecture. She was an interior decorator in New York.'

'Oh, really!' was the response from the Contessa. Nina wondered if Claudio had told them anything at all about her. 'Then the fifteenth-century frescoes and the tapestries in the yellow room might interest you.'

'I'd love to see them.'

At last everyone had put down knives and forks; white linen napkins had all, save Nina's, been pushed through their monogrammed silver rings, and five pairs of eyes were on the Contessa. With a faint smile as though assessing the situation she nodded and Claudio immediately rose to help with her chair. The Count pulled Nina's away from her, and she was grateful, for it was large and solid and weighed an absolute ton. They all adjourned to the reception room once more. The grandfather was busy lighting a pipe and dropping matches on the floor which a footman picked up in one quick motion after another, bowing at the waist again and again like a big mechanical toy soldier. Claudio lit a cigar and his mother complained. He smiled and said, 'Nina loves the smell,' and Nina made a face that caused him to laugh. The Count said he would take a spot of whisky, that 'It was a bit of an occasion,' and Nina saw the Contessa give him a withering look. And there staring out of the window, as big as a Volkswagen, Nina thought, was this strange woman: elegantly dressed – obviously her clothes were made for her – and with manicured fingernails and lovely shoes, but with a face as blank as someone in a mental hospital. Claudio leaned back on the rose-coloured brocade sofa and blew smoke rings into the air. The grandfather began to cackle and then to squeal like a child and, dropping the pipe, tried to put his arm through this one or that one as they floated upward and disappeared. The same footman materialized at Nina's feet to stomp out the live coals on the marble and to neatly scoop up the mess of ashes with a brush and a silver silent butler.

'Oh, Claudio! Stop it! You're exciting him!' commanded his mother.

'I have to go back to the office,' announced the Count as though he'd had enough of it all. He tossed back the whisky, neat, and stood. His clothes, thought Nina, are like Claudio's. Something so expensive, so perfect about the tailoring. The cuffs that obviously had openable buttonholes, the lapels that . . . 'Nina, it has been a great pleasure,' he was saying and then kissing her once on each cheek.

Suddenly there was the clicking of little claws on the

391

marble floor and the jingle of leashes being dragged as lickety-split two brown dachshunds with ears flying raced down the long room towards the group of humans. La Contessa was beside herself. 'I will not have these creatures in this part of the palazzo!' she cried as they, as if to mock her, circled her chair.

The butler pursued them and then two maids, each shouting in Italian, '*Vieni qua! Vieni qua!* Keats, come here! Shelley! Stop!' The grandfather began to clap his hands with joy and Nina started to laugh. Claudio thought it was a great joke, too.

'My Anglophile sister left them to me in her will,' explained the Count to Nina. 'They are little maniacs!' he grinned as the dogs raced down the length of the reception room on their short legs. '*Vieni qua!*' echoed in the long marble hallway as everyone, but the Contessa, laughed.

By four o'clock it was over. Nina stood in front of number six via dei Greci and thanked Claudio. The *portiere*, Signora Cadlolo, clicked her knitting needles and pretended not to notice anything from the gloom of the *terreno*. She sat in a little room behind a glass door at a wooden table, surrounded by her art collection. Her taste was eclectic and the walls were covered by reproductions of George Romneys, Van Goghs, Rembrandts and Modiglianis. '*Buona sera,*' called Nina and she answered with a smile and a clicking of her needles. With a grandchild due in the summer she had no time to waste.

'My father may be going back to work, but I'm not.' Nina smiled and they ascended in the swaying little open cage of an elevator. Nina's apartment was for lovemaking, as far as Claudio was concerned. They never had a drink there, other than sipping wine from one glass on the headboard shelf; they never sat on the terrace, never sat in the living room and talked. They locked the door and undressed and went to bed. Nina walked up the three little steps wearing a white lace teddy and stared at this big strong tanned body waiting for her among the white sheets. She slid into his arms with a sigh of pleasure. Those broad shoulders, that warmth, the lime smell of him. He held her face in his hands and stared at her. Then he began to kiss her softly all around her waiting mouth. Those little kisses that made her hold her breath with anticipation, those mere brushes of his lips against hers, that teasing that made her want him pressed as hard as possible against her. The kisses are the best there are, she thought later in his arms. Nina curled closer to the firmness of his shoulder, in the curve of one perfectly sculptured arm and thought: I love this man.

'No! That wasn't it at all!' Claudio laughed and sipped red wine. 'Well, okay, I confess. It was part of it.' He lifted an eyebrow and gestured with his glass. 'But only part of it.'

'I don't believe you.' Nina tried to look serious.

'Maybe I was giving you a chance to look them over.'

'Hmmm. Maybe.' Nina didn't look too convinced.

'You little cynic!' He pulled her face to his and kissed her mouth. It was dark outside the terrace doors, but they could still see each other's face. 'Look, I thought it was going to be just you and me and my mother and my father. I didn't know that Nonno would be there, or Elena. Usually they . . .'

Nina had not seen Claudio embarrassed before. He had never had anything to be embarrassed over for as long as she had known him. He dressed perfectly, his manners were impeccable and no situation had ever arisen in which he seemed less than positive about how to comport himself. Nina felt a rush of love for him. 'Oh, Claudio, I was glad to meet them. You don't have to keep things from me. I want to know all about you.'

He seemed surprised at this and took her hand in his and studied it for a moment. 'I don't invite my friends home with me.'

'I'm complimented that you asked me.'

They lay on their sides with the sheets around them. The dark green quilt had been pushed to the foot of the bed. Claudio touched her face very gently with his forefinger, the way an artist or a sculptor would outline a cheekbone or the fine curve of a jaw before trying to copy it. '*Ti amo*,' he whispered.

'I know,' was all she answered.

Claudio had told her to wear boots and dress warmly. He'd refused to give her any hints at all about his plans. It was ten o'clock.

'Where are you taking me?' she laughed.

The car buzzed along the highway at 140 kilometres an hour. They were leaving Rome. 'Wait and see,' murmured Claudio. Lights flashed by them, the music from the radio filled the car. The speed excited Nina – in this she was like Claudio – and with him, she felt total confidence. His hands on the wheel were firm, his eyes on the stretch of road ahead unblinking, his reflexes instant.

'The Polo Club! Fantastic!' Her voice became full of concern. 'Hey, is one of your ponies sick?'

'No!' The car slowed as they entered the gate and Nina rolled down her window. It was a warm night for February and the air was scented with the clean smell of horses and hay and sweet grass. The grounds were dark, deserted. 'We're having a picnic.'

'Here?'

Claudio nodded and opened the trunk. The basket made a clink noise as he lifted it out from under the pillows. He tossed the plaid blanket at her. 'Can you manage that?' he grinned.

'"Can I manage?" he asks? Can I manage? I can manage you, so I can manage a little blanket!'

'Okay, you shrew! Let's march. I thought . . .' He squinted out at the dark field. 'That corner over there by the goal.'

Nina was exhilarated. 'I love you!' she suddenly said.

Claudio turned in the starlight and put everything – basket with clanking bottles, pillows, the lap rug of his mother's he'd borrowed without her noticing – plop! on the wet grass and took Nina in his arms. His mouth was warm, soft, yearning. 'I love you, too, Nina McLean.'

She could feel his heart beating under the thick dark blue sweater. I love you, I love you, hummed in her ears like a song. It was something she saw behind her grey eyes, a landscape of great serenity; it was something she tasted in her mouth like honey.

Somehow the two of them managed to make it to the desired patch of emerald grass, cold and damp with dew, and settled themselves like pashas in a foreign northern clime, among velvet pillows and the mink throw. Pop! went the champagne cork and 'ooh!' went Nina when she saw the silver dish of truffles. There were silver forks and white linen napkins and the wine glasses Nina recognized from lunch two weeks ago. 'Your mother will have a fit!' she said, and Claudio erupted with laughter. 'My mother doesn't count tonight.'

He leaned forward and demanded, 'Open,' and she did and he placed a truffle on her tongue. 'They've been scraped, washed and soaked in cognac. I like them raw like this with a little salt.'

'Bliss! Ecstasy!' she enthused, lifting her arms up towards the sky. 'Shooting star! I get to make a wish! Oh, Claudio! Did you see it? Did you make a wish?'

'I did on both counts.'

They devoured the midnight supper, talking, teasing, both thinking what a perfect night it was. Claudio was suddenly serious. 'Nina, you've never mentioned lunch again . . . I mean, my family . . . we've never really talked.' Nina didn't speak. 'I want to talk. My mother is difficult to any woman she perceives as competition. She . . . I'm her only child. I heard from my aunt when I was a little boy how she almost died having me . . .' Claudio was staring up at the sky. Nina curled herself in the crook of his arm and rested her head on his chest the way she always did after lovemaking. 'So . . .' he sighed. 'She is sometimes a problem.'

'She is a very elegant, very intelligent woman,' Nina said carefully. 'And I don't blame her for loving you.'

Claudio closed his eyes for a moment as though grateful for something. 'And my father . . . well, we don't get on.'

'Oh, I like him. He's all right,' said Nina.

'He likes you, too.' Neither spoke for a few minutes then

Claudio broke the silence. Nina was warm against him. 'My cousin was kidnapped two years ago and that's why she is the way she is. It was nice of you not to ask about her.'

'My God! How terrible for her! For you all!' Nina sat bolt upright, full of sympathy.

'It was,' he nodded and then pulled her to him again. 'The police froze the bank accounts so we couldn't pay the ransom but then friends chipped in, we got her back, the bank accounts were unfrozen and we paid everybody.' He sighed. Life in Italy was sometimes difficult but problems were solved with a bit of imagination.

'I feel so close to you knowing these things,' Nina said softly. 'I am finally getting to know you.'

Claudio turned his face to hers and smiled that half smile. 'Do you like what you know?' he said in a very uncharacteristic, shy way.

Nina's first reaction was to punch him playfully, but something stopped her from the elbow jab, from the quick retort. Claudio was more tame since Christmas, since the introduction to his parents. He had allowed her into his space at last. His clubs, the *Simba II*, the dinners, the nightclubs, the parties with friends, the receptions, even the lovemaking, were all preliminaries to letting her touch him now. Under the widest black sky she'd ever seen. Under more stars than she'd thought existed. 'I love what I know. I want to know more. I don't think I can ever know enough about you.'

They were Nina's words, the excess of feeling, the sentiment that overflowed, the heat from her generous spirit that Claudio loved. 'Will you marry me?' he asked just as they both saw the shooting star flash like the diamond he'd forgotten to take out of his pocket, just as they both wished to be with each other for ever.


Bart took his sister's arm and joked, 'Even though you're married in the eyes of Italy, these steps give you time to reconsider!' Nina winced as she looked upward at the nearly vertical stairs of stone. At the top was the simple Roman church of old bricks. Three shields affixed to it were in sight. The arms of the reigning pope were painted on the left one, the middle one she couldn't decipher, and on the right shield were the letters 'SPQR' signifying that the church belonged to the people of Rome. So steep was the grade that the door below these could not yet be seen. The church. This was it. The civil ceremony yesterday had been . . . well, perhaps civil was the word. 'I don't feel married!' Claudio and Nina had chorused afterwards. A ceremony in Rome's city hall made it legal; church was optional. Church was this dress and everyone watching. Church was the last step; Nina smiled at this figure of speech.

'Remember, Bart! You're not giving me away! I refuse to be handed over from one man to another like a chattel, like a pig.'

Bart laughed. 'You don't know what's going to happen to you at the altar, do you, my little pork chop? How good is your Italian anyway?'

'Stop it!' insisted the Countess from the landing above them. 'Don't frighten her! I'm nervous enough for a dozen brides as it is!' Virginia laughed. Both women had started the ascent ahead of the others and held their little veiled hats in place with white-gloved hands. Their pastel flowered dresses blew in the slight breeze. 'Well, Virginia! Onward and upward!' They giggled together.

'Have they got into the champagne back at the Hassler?' Nina asked Adele, who panted beside her.

'Not that I know of! But' – she rolled her eyes – 'anything's possible!'

'The Countess,' Bart said in a low voice as they lock-stepped upward, 'would be a bad influence on anybody!'

'I wouldn't say that. Look what she did for me!'

Bart grinned. 'I'll let that pass, baby sister! Wouldn't touch that line with a ten-foot pole!'

Adele grabbed Nina's arm suddenly and the trip stopped. 'You were with me when I got married – and here I am with you. I . . .' Her blue eyes filled with tears. 'I . . . oh, Nina! I wish you all the luck in the world!' Bart yanked his handkerchief out of his pocket and handed it across. They continued up the stairs. 'He adores you,' sighed Adele. 'Why, every time you're in the same room he is hypnotized with love for you.' She sniffed loudly and Bart laughed.

'Adele! You're supposed to wait until we're in the church!'

'Oh, shush, Bart!' frowned Nina. 'I feel like crying, too!' But somewhere between the first and the one hundred and twenty-sixth step, Nina stopped feeling anything. She became detached from the experience of getting married. She would later recall the excitement of her mother's arrival in Rome, then Adele's voice on the phone saying, 'I'm two minutes' walk away! Hurry!' and Bart ringing her doorbell shouting for her to let him in. There had been so many lunches, so many dinners; the introducing of Claudio and his parents to the four people in the world who were Nina's family. She did miss Ellen, and had always imagined that she would be at her wedding, but her mother had promised to bring back pictures of everything. There was lunch at Romolo's with Kate and Bill and Lesley and Rita and Benjamin and Pauline, and the surprise that it was warm enough to sit in the garden after all.

The little via dei Greci apartment became their head-quarters though Bart, Adele, the Countess and Virginia took rooms at the Hassler, just at the top of the Spanish Steps. Virginia had pronounced herself 'Breathless!' at every view, and at every course at every meal. The Countess spoke French to all the waiters for some reason no one understood, least of all the waiters, but she couldn't seem to stop.

Nina had chosen a less formal dress than Virginia thought she should have but it was lovely on her. The only way she could describe it to Adele over the telephone was 'a garden party dress'. It was entirely of white lace, full-skirted, floor-length, with the tightest bodice possible, a square neckline and puffed sleeves ending at the elbow. Virginia altered it as the Countess and Adele sipped white wine and talked. The train Nina fought against, but the Contessa wanted her to wear it for it had been in her family for a long time and the Countess and her mother both said she had to accept the offer. 'I feel like a peacock dragging my tail along behind me,' she complained. Instead of a picture-book hat such as

398

the one Adele was wearing, the florist had designed a crown of tiny white roses to sit atop Nina's dark curls. Virginia had brought Aunt Lilly's diamond and pearl earrings for her to wear, and the Countess had brought Nina a small diamond pin that she placed in one corner of the neckline. Adele gave her a blue garter trimmed in seed pearls and the most delicate white nightgown and peignoir of matching lace the women said they'd ever seen.

The via dei Greci apartment fairly exploded with merriment for four days. Nina plugged the refrigerator in and they had bottle after bottle of wine as Nina and Adele packed boxes of books and clothes. Nina would later remember that very few opinions were offered about Claudio. The Countess said, 'You really love him, darling. It's wonderful,' and Adele said, 'I think he's divine and I think being a Countess is just the way you should end up.' The words sounded peculiar to Nina. Is this the end? she wondered. But no, of course not. She turned as her mother pinned the bodice a little tighter under the left arm. I've found Claudio and marriage is simply the beginning. Bart said, 'He's okay. He's all right. It's his mother who's the shark.' All the women screamed and Nina threw a green pillow at him where he sat on the terrace outside the open doors. 'Nina! Be still!' her mother sighed in exasperation. Nina dropped her arm and said gloomily, 'Bart's right.'

'You'll win her over. Give yourself a week,' spoke Adele from the floor as she taped a cardboard box closed.

'She has been extremely sweet to me,' put in Virginia, 'so I think you should give her the benefit of the doubt.'

'Well said,' toasted the Countess with a glass of wine.

Nina sighed. 'Mother, you haven't said a word about Claudio. What is bothering you? Don't you like him?'

'Oh! He's wonderful! He just . . .' she began. 'Well, he is wonderful.'

'Come on, Mother! Out with it!' called Bart from the terrace.

'Why I . . .'

'Mother!' insisted Nina. 'Is it because he's Italian?'

'Well, Nina . . . he's . . . he's Catholic!'

The Countess began to titter and Nina spoke. 'I did sign a paper about the children and I promised to take classes but the Count says as far as he's concerned I can remain a Protestant. He has enough pull for the wedding to go through with me as I am. It's just the children.'

'Nina!' Virginia was shocked at how lightly her daughter was taking such a step. Her grandchildren were to be raised as Catholics!

The Countess made another noise and Nina demanded, 'What is so funny?'

'Oh,' laughed the Countess, dabbing at her eyes with a handkerchief trimmed in lace. 'He's not really Catholic! He's Roman!' Everyone was mystified. 'The Romans abhor the Vatican. Why, they're still furious at things that happened fifteen popes ago. Romans beat up priests on the street here!'

This news amazed them all and pleased Virginia particularly. Bart came inside and opened a new bottle of champagne. 'Now,' he said solemnly, 'if anyone present knows any just cause why my little sister and Claudio Massimiliano de Leone should not be joined in holy matrimony, speak now or forever hold your peace!'

Nina looked from face to face. A taxi honked in the street below. Then they all lifted their glasses and toasted, 'The bride!'

Five steps to the top. Nina and Bart and Adele could at last see the open door of the church and the Countess and Virginia being greeted by the Count de Leone and the Contessa. Nina was happy at how much everyone seemed to like one another. Her mother, if a bit shy at first, was so charming and looked so lovely that her very awe at her surroundings was attractive. And of all the surprises, Nonno, Claudio's grandfather, got along like a house afire with the Countess. She seemed to know an awful lot about Mussolini and the two of them had been at one end of the dining room discussing Clara Petrarci as though the dictator's mistress had just excused herself to powder her nose. Bart and Claudio had gone to the Polo Club together and the two of them had ridden in the Villa Borghese early one morning. They had posed with much clowning at the fountain on via del Babuino as Nina fumbled with her Nikon and implored them to be serious. Adele had been seated next to the Count at lunch one day and pronounced him 'so charming you can't believe he hasn't stepped out of a movie. Who writes his lines for him, anyway?'

Moment of truth, thought Nina, squaring her shoulders, licking her lips. 'Wait! Let me straighten the train for you!' Adele scampered down a few steps and pulled the white tulle into a wide swath.

'Did you say "tail"?' Bart looked innocent and Nina resisted the impulse to punch him. Nina took a deep breath; Bart squeezed her hand and winked at her and together the brother and sister climbed the last five steps.

The Count kissed her on both cheeks, then the Contessa did the same. Bart, too, was kissed by both parents as Nina asked for Claudio. 'He's inside, waiting for you at the altar,' the Count told her. Nina tried to smile back. Her heart was pounding. Nonno took the Countess's arm and they entered the church, then a nephew from Milano took the Contessa's arm and the Count guided Virginia through the door. Nina could see nothing but darkness past the portals. 'Ready?' Bart nodded then he gave her a kiss on the cheek and said, 'Here's thinking of you, kid.' Nina remembered crying on a sailboat with him, remembered hundreds of afternoons in the kitchen or on the front steps leaning against the fat white columns as he told her stories; she remembered the wild ride down the country road racing the train. She looked at this handsome man and thought: My brother. 'Ready,' was all she said.

Why am I doing this? Why am I here? he asked himself with every step upward. He'd arrived in Rome that morning and taken a room at the Hassler for a nap, a shower and a shave. Now he was the last person to enter the church. His first impression was of perhaps a hundred chandeliers hung from the ceiling. Small chapels of Rome's oldest families lined either side of the enormous church. They sat with their secrets behind wrought-iron grilles. Statues, crypts and frescoes were barely discernible in the cool semi-darkness. But the apse and the sanctuary were brighter than the spring day outside its walls. In the centre of it all was a slender woman in a white dress; yards of the lace train lay on the cherry red carpet. The same carpet that led to where he stood one hundred and fifty yards behind her, unseen by anyone. His hands were cold and his mouth was dry as the bride turned slightly and allowed the groom to put the ring on her finger. 'Okay,' he said softly. Now I know. He turned and silently, without one backward look, left the church. The expanse of Rome from the top step was lovely, even for the most jaded of Romans, but he did not notice the view. He kept his eyes down, watching his feet in brown leather shoes, descending. With each step he was walking away from the woman he had loved. It's over, he thought. The taxi driver helped him into the yellow Fiat. 'Fiumicino, please.' He leaned back in the seat but could see nothing but an unreasonable expanse of white stairs which appeared to lead nowhere. The taxi whirled past Piazza Venezia in the afternoon traffic. By the time it had passed the Colosseum the passenger had lit a cigar and said, 'It's over,' one last time.

An hour later the round pink-faced priest perspiring heavily under his vestments had finished his murmuring. The register had been signed by Nina and Claudio and then by Adele and the Count as witnesses. The bride was on the arm of the groom standing again at the top of the steps with the Campidoglio, Rome's city hall, below to the left. The monument dedicated to the unification of Italy and to the first king was to the right and directly in front of them stretched the peach-coloured rooftops of Rome. Steeples, and terraces, and laundry formed a mosaic so alive it almost sang. Two photographers snapped away, jockeying for

402

position in front of the couple like dancers, each trailing long black cords.

'*Carina* Nina, Nina *carina*,' Claudio said softly. She turned to him. His face was bronzed from riding every day and his eyes were shining. 'Happy we did it?' Nina kissed him on the mouth, oblivious to the crowd who 'oh-ed' their approval and pelted them with rice. Claudio led her down the stairs then as people closed in from all sides to embrace them, wish them well, to simply see them close-up, for they shone with a radiance unlike ordinary mortals. '*Auguri!*' many cried. 'Best wishes!' 'The most beautiful bride I've seen in all my life,' said one Roman banker to the Count and then added, 'And I've married four daughters, you know!'

Dante stood behind the white Rolls-Royce on the street and helped them in. It was so strange, Bart thought, to have an English car drive the newlyweds to the reception. The parade began with a joyful honking procession around Piazza Venezia and then they sped through the city. People waved at Nina and Claudio and they waved back; passengers in other cars at traffic lights sounded their horns and shook handkerchiefs out the windows and children on sidewalks jumped up and down, shouting '*Auguri! Auguri!*' Once out of Rome the convoy raced along at 120 kilometres an hour towards Grotta Ferratta.

The country house was rarely used, Claudio had explained to Nina. His parents preferred to spend time at Porto Santo Stefano by the sea and he preferred to be with his own friends on *Simba II*. It was an estate, a compound, Nina now saw, of several tremendous houses that had been built several generations ago for this de Leone brother, for that cousin, for that daughter and all their respective spouses and children. The lawns were bright green and peacocks, with their tails dragging, sauntered majestically across the grounds. They appeared and disappeared among the white and fuchsia and pink flowers that bordered the paths. 'We've just opened one house for this,' Claudio was saying. 'The others we never use. If you and I proceed to have eleven children the old place will come in handy.' Nina exploded with laughter as the Rolls purred to a stop. 'God! I feel like starting now!' sighed Claudio as he pulled her face to his for a long kiss. Dante, compact, white-haired, stood patiently holding the door for them. He smiled with delight when he caught Nina's eye and she laughed back, a little embarrassed.

How wonderful that Claudio's mother had volunteered to plan the wedding and the reception. I wouldn't have known where to start, Nina thought as she surveyed the thirty or forty round tables set up in the distance on the other side of the turquoise swimming pool. It was fed by fountains of ferocious, roaring marble lions. Three hundred guests wandered among the palm trees clutching glasses of champagne, pursued by waiters bearing enormous silver trays of hors d'œuvres.

'What is it?' Adele asked as she took a square of bread with tomato on top.

'*Bruschetta!*' Kate answered. 'And no one will dance with you after you eat it.' The typically Roman dish was bread fried in garlic.

'I will!' declared Bart. He took a second one as the waiter began to move away. Nina turned back to Claudio who was introducing her to some old friends of his, but she was thinking of her brother. Bart was so attractive, Adele was so beautiful, and they liked each other and yes, even flirted. But both of them kept their distance. Neither was the least bit interested in the other. Nina couldn't understand it.

Dinner was served to them by twenty-five waiters in white coats, black trousers and white gloves who, in perfect formation, came into view from the opposite end of the garden. Each bore a silver-domed platter at shoulder height and each walked with determination towards a table of ten guests. Course after course came: asparagus mousse, two kinds of pasta, trout, zucchini, lamb, potatoes, two kinds of salad, and at last a fruit torte. Three types of wine were served and seven waiters did nothing but circle the tables with bottles of champagne. Lanterns had been strung through the trees on the slight hillside; white candles in the pool were lit spelling out 'Nina e Claudio' among floating white blossoms. 'It's like fairyland,' said Virginia to the Count.

The tiered wedding cake was pushed up the incline on a trolley covered by a white cloth. It was very tall and with the blowing skirt of satin beneath it the Countess had a sudden eerie image of a woman in a wedding dress being propelled across the dark landscape. 'Fellini-esque,' she murmured aloud without meaning to and when the handsome lawyer from Florence on her left said in perfect English, 'I beg your pardon?' she smiled and said, 'More champagne, please. After all, this is a celebration!' But the vision had chilled her; there was such sadness suggested. It took several glasses for her to feel warm and bright once more.

'I don't want this night to ever end,' sighed Nina as Claudio led her in the first dance. Guests still nibbled at wedding cake, and drank, and smoked, with pushed-back chairs. Many wandered from table to table and visited. 'Let's stay up all night and not let it end,' whispered Claudio as they waltzed as one, as he pressed his lips to a fragrant white rose tangled in her dark hair.

Most of the guests drove back to Rome at two in the morning but Nina's family had all been assigned rooms in the house and would stay. Nina and Claudio kissed everyone goodnight at half past three and went up to their enormous antique-filled bedroom on the third floor. The double bed had carved lions of oak as a headboard above the white square pillows. One lamp with a silver base glowed on a large chest. Nina put on the white nightgown peignoir Adele had given her and went out on to the balcony to inhale the scent of the countryside in spring. The last week had been unseasonably warm for March. She wondered how many lire the Count had given the orchestra to keep playing. Every hour he had conferred with the leader who had made a show of putting his baton away and then taking it out again to the 'bravos' of the guests. 'It's so Italian!' the Countess had tittered. 'Such a performance!'

Nina looked down at the few occupied tables and could make out Adele and the Countess and Bart still drinking, still talking. Claudio came up behind her then, naked, and put his arms around her waist. 'Sleepy?' He kissed her neck. 'No.' She smiled dreamily. Darkness stretched in all directions away from the little islands of tables in the candlelight. A Strauss waltz drifted up in the night air. Nina took one last look at the scene below and then faced Claudio, her husband. The young Conte de Leone led the new Contessa through the doorway, into the bedroom and at last to his bed.

Married eight days, she thought happily. France by helicopter had been Claudio's idea. Clattering over Paris in the transparent stomach of some fairytale insect toasting the spires with champagne in the spring sunlight, alighting at different chateaux for dinner, hovering over green hillsides, bobbing over vineyards – all was like a dream for Nina. They'd had a *bouillabaisse* lunch in Marseille, dinner at Paul Bocuse's restaurant in Lyon and evening after evening of wine and music and lovemaking. We've made love on via dei Greci, at Grotta Ferratta, at the Ritz in Paris, and now in his bed, the bed he's slept in since he was a little boy. Nina turned towards Claudio and embraced him.

'What's this?' he teased, feeling the narrow strap of the green silk nightgown. She sat up and pulled it over her head and then tossed it away from the warm dark world that was now their bed. Claudio wrapped her in his arms again and it seemed a second homecoming, as heady as brandy: that span of seconds of separation, that rush of cool air on skin and then to be next to his muscles and warmth once more. They weren't sleepy, just drowsy from wine at dinner, sated from afternoon lovemaking. They each wanted the same kind of snuggling, of touching. 'Glad you asked me to marry you?' Nina whispered coyly.

'Mmmmm,' smiled Claudio, kissing her silky shoulder. She played with the soft curls at the back of his neck. He needed a haircut but just because his mother had said so at lunch he would wait another week.

'I used to wonder . . .' she began.

'Wonder what?' he said, pressing his cheek against her.

'Wonder if you asked me because of . . . Richard.' Might as well play it out. Claudio stiffened and did not answer. She found his mouth with her fingers and kissed him long and gently. When they broke away he looked at her and answered, 'I couldn't stand the idea of another man . . . having you. Did you sleep with him?'

'No, I never did. Not once.'

Claudio kissed her very tenderly this time. 'Nina, I've never wanted anyone but you.' Longer than a night, is what he means, she thought. 'I've always had what I wanted,' he continued.

'Always?' asked Nina, still close in his arms. He nodded.

'I can't think of any time I didn't.' He lay back and Nina rested her head on his chest as he played with her hair. 'You are the first thing I've ever wanted that my father or mother couldn't give me. That I couldn't buy. I picked you myself, and fell in love with you . . .'

'And I fell in love with you!' she insisted.

'And I couldn't bear the thought of your being with anyone else, couldn't bear the idea of losing you. During summer, on the boat, I wondered how I could keep you without marrying you . . .' He couldn't see Nina blinking with surprise in the dark. Everyone else always used to want to marry me. Except Omar. Always make an exception with Omar. 'But even then I knew you were too good for that, too special.' Nina turned her face to his chest and kissed it. 'I knew you were too good for an affair, for a fling; that you valued yourself too much to be a toy.' A toy. Sounds like something I once called myself. In a conversation with Adele, thought Nina. Claudio kissed her forehead. 'So now you are my wife. I do feel you belong to me.'

Nina was uncomfortable with the phrasing. Usually his English was so precise. She pulled away. 'We belong together. We belong to each other.' Claudio nodded and she nestled close to him once more. 'Claudio?'

'Mmmmm.'

'What if I – I didn't – but what if I had slept with Richard?'

He was instantly alert. 'I would hate knowing it and I would never want to meet him and I would try never to think of it again.' His muscles relaxed when he finished speaking.

They lay in each other's arms for a long time, curled as closely as possible like two forest creatures. The last thing

Nina saw before closing her eyes was the canopy above them like the sail of some mysterious boat. She imagined herself and Claudio adrift on the Mediterranean in the big four-poster bed. Nina pressed herself even closer to him and, lulled by a sense of wellbeing and the merry splash of the fountain in the courtyard, was soon asleep.


Claudio's friends numbered about a dozen between the ages of twenty-five and forty-five; they were mostly married, but there were a few bachelors and some *separato*, which was a common state in Rome since divorce entailed seven years of separation. These men were the constants. The women at their sides seemed interchangeable to Nina. Many appeared one evening with their wife and the next dinner with a *fidanzata* which translated to fiancée, but meant nothing of the sort. Nina wished so much that Kate and Bill could be a part of this crowd but knew it was impossible. Even if Kate could get a babysitter to stay with Alice until four or five in the morning, how could Bill get up at seven and hope to function at the bank? These Romans did not work, for there simply weren't enough hours in the day for it. Inherited money meant they did not ever expect to work though a few experimented with playing at it. Giuliana talked of hand-painting silk scarves and selling them to a friend who ran a boutique on via Frattina but no one ever saw one of these scarves. Antonio had the idea of building greenhouses on his four hundred acres outside Rome and selling flowers to the hotels in town, but the plan was forgotten in the confusion of getting his boat delivered from Riva. It was soon apparent to Nina that Claudio's appearance at Fabia Srl. was a joke.

Many of them had gone to school together or known each other since childhood. They all spoke impeccable French as well as excellent English but Paris and London and New York were usually discussed in terms of nightclubs, restaurants and dress designers. They were, to a person, quite good-looking with strong features, athletic bodies, and that well-tended look. The exception was Principe Vittorio from Florence, who had miraculously survived a motorcycle accident in his teens. Some plastic surgery had been performed but the skin grafts on his face did not hide the angry red scars. The men were titled or would be but used their living father's prefix. Three sons of a living Barone were all called Barone and no one batted an eye. They preferred it, as did their friends, as did their servants. Nina was the young Contessa de Leone though Claudio was not technically yet a count.

Talk was of each other, the last trip, the next trip, a new place for dinner, for drinks. Talk of politics became their favourite game of vying for who knew the name of the prime minister's latest mistress, then who had met her, then where they had been seen together, what she had been wearing, and finally where she shopped. They were casual with money and laughed at Principe Mario for losing one hundred million lire one night playing cards at Il Circolo. Money meant champagne and polo ponies and clothes and jewellery and new cars. They were casual with love, too, for love meant 'a flirt'.

Nina was popular among Claudio's male friends but she soon realized she was not very well liked among the women. This disturbed her so she began to down-play the flirtatious-ness that was second nature to her. She told herself it was for Claudio's sake; she told herself it was for the other women's sakes, but she knew differently. Self-preservation, she wrote Adele. For how long have I ever been able to exist without female confidantes, female allies? She badly wanted these Romans to like her.

For the most part these evenings were full of fun, full of humour. There was little rowdiness for they all understood the importance of *la bella figura*, which not only meant to create a good impression but to keep up appearances. They seldom drank too much, with the exception of Principe Romolo who was described as a colossal alcoholic. Nina opened a bathroom door at Stefano's villa in Tuscany and found the descendant of Julius Caesar passed out and snoring on the white tiles beside a pan of kitty litter.

The high spirits of these young Roman aristocrats were

409

tempered by the sirens of Rome, for the capital was gripped in fear. Nearly every day someone else disappeared and usually the victim was known by at least one of Claudio's friends. Their parents warned them incessantly about being conspicuous with their wealth. They spurned the bodyguards their fathers hired but did drive bulletproof cars and Claudio did sell his Alfa Romeo Sports Spider convertible. A few even bought Cinquecentos which were the cheap little cars of the middle class. They did carry guns. Claudio preferred to tuck his pistol into his waistband, which horrified Nina, but he disliked the way the shoulder holster stretched the fine cloth of his suit jackets. 'It's madness!' cried Nina when she hugged him and felt the cold steel against her for the first time. 'It's life in Rome, Nina.' Claudio shrugged then his eyes twinkled. 'No one's going to take me alive!'

'They may not get all of you is what worries me!'

To an American, the most famous kidnapping was that of Paul Getty Jr the year before. His ear had been cut off as a grisly warning that those responsible were ready to kill. Sirens wailed 'wah wah! wah wah! wah wah!' night and day as dark blue vans hurled through intersections and sped past pedestrians who feigned disinterest. Piazza di Spagna was cordoned off every week or so and Nina would be asked to open her shopping bags and show her passport as two dozen guards wearing flak jackets stood nearby with machine guns. There were traffic jams all over town as the *polizia* flagged down cars and inspected identity papers. Many buildings had twenty-four-hour guards; among them, of course, was the Parliament and the several political party headquarters. Midnight-blue cars of the Carabiniere raced along the Lungotevere, packed with men in business suits as the passenger in the front seat held out a red signal like a giant lollipop. They would be protected by a phalanx of motor-cycle police roaring ahead, on either side, and behind the speeding sedan.

'But who is doing all this?' Nina asked one night at La Tartarughino when they had been told that someone's aunt had been abducted the evening before.

'It's the Mafia from the south,' sighed Sergio. 'It's quite a good business for them.'

Claudio disagreed. 'A lot of these kidnappings are engineered by the Sards. They had nothing until the Aga Khan developed the Costa Smeralda and most of them still have nothing.'

Mario nodded. 'And so many of the Sards in Rome take care of racehorses. They have a network. They know who has money, who doesn't. They work together and ftttt!' He made a particularly Italian noise and waved his hand. 'The person disappears into the wilds of Sardinia. The family back home feeds them and gets paid to make sure they don't walk away.'

'For months . . .' nodded Claudio.

'But how does a person ever get over it, when they come back again? I mean, when they are free . . .'

Claudio looked at her. 'Most of them are all right. But you live with Elena.'

'They go to clinics, they go to psychiatrists . . .' said Massimo.

'My mother's best friend is still terrified of the dark,' spoke up Laura. 'And she was released eight or nine months ago. She couldn't stop crying for weeks, but now she is better.'

'Enough!' interrupted Stefano. 'Champagne *per tutti?*' They changed the subject as one and turned with smiles to the person beside them.

'You're not serious!' cried Francesco after a moment.

'I'm always serious,' insisted Nina with demurely downcast eyes. The piano music in the background began the song 'New York New York' and she thought: How far away I am.

There was general laughter all around the table and Claudio took her hand. 'Cara, you don't need a pet. I am your pet!'

Nina smiled at him. 'But I want a useful pet. When is the last time you found a truffle?' Claudio gave her his darkest frown as they all laughed again. 'I am not asking for the moon. Just a little truffle pig to keep in the palazzo. We'll put

411

him in your dressing room. He'll have a good time in there. I'll put a pink ribbon on him and we'll drive north for the weekends – can't you just see him leaning his little pig head out of the window with his ears flying back in the wind – and he can run through the woods finding truffles for us.' She took another breath as they laughed at her. Claudio was trying to look out of sorts. 'It's an economy measure. You know I can eat my weight in truffles in one sitting. Zillions of lire per kilo! That's four hundred and fifty dollars a pound!'

'What about my mother?' said Claudio, pretending to be serious.

'Oh, can she find truffles?' popped out of Nina before she could think. The table rocked with laughter then. Even Claudio couldn't stop.



'Lesley!' called Nina at the tall figure in front of the fountain in Piazza de Spagna.

The blonde Australian threw her arms out. 'Wow! Didn't recognize you! Is that sable?' It was a very chilly day for April after the surprising warmth of March, but now Nina wished she hadn't worn the new coat. The Contessa had told her not to, but for a different reason.

Nina nodded. 'I've missed you, you loony tune! How is everything?'

Lesley rolled her eyes. 'Okay. I'm still dating Renato who is still driving me crazy. You knew I'd moved out of Trastevere, didn't you?'

'No. When?' That meant she'd left the seafaring philandering Australian at last.

'Months ago. Must have been before your wedding but of course there was too much going on to call you and say, "Oh, by the way" . . .' They laughed.

'Oh, Lesley! It's good to see you. Why don't you come home with me and we'll sit and have a real talk. It's been so long. I'm going to grab a taxi and – '

'Oh, I can't. I'm meeting Renato in twenty minutes at his office . . .'

'Oh, okay.' Nina sighed. 'Another time. Call me. You can, you know! I'm usually there!'

'Yes, well . . . sure. I will.' Lesley kissed her on both cheeks and then her lean figure in blue jeans and parka disappeared in the crowd on via Frattina. Nina frowned at her reflection in a shop window. It's the coat. It's the palazzo. It's my life.


'Oh, Kate! I'm so happy to see you!'

'Wow! You look gorgeous,' enthused her friend.

'Window table? Or in the back where we can get good and drunk?' Nina said wickedly. Kate laughed as she told the maitre d', '*In fondo*.' They followed him past a dozen tables with white linen cloths. 'I am starved for your company!' growled Nina, putting the menu aside and ordering a bottle of white wine. Kate was allergic to red.

'Tell me everything! I am still staggered by the wedding, staggered that you have almost become a full-blown contessa but, by the way, you're thinner. Full-blown isn't the word to use.'

Nina shrugged. 'Stress, I guess. Tough life.'

Kate put her hand on Nina's. The nails were long now and polished a bright coral which exactly matched her sweater and the ropes of cornelian and coral beads around her neck. 'Are you all right?' she asked.

Nina bit her lip. 'Why do I feel I'm going to burst into tears all the time?'

The waiter hovered and then like a trained parrot sing-songed the specialities. '*Penna alla vodka per me, e dopo la trota*' ordered Nina and Kate nodded, '*Per me anche*'. He retreated after a scratch on his pad and a soft, '*Grazie.*'

'Alone at last,' giggled Nina as she gulped the wine.

'I've never seen you like this,' said Kate. 'You are so mercurial. Talk to me.'

At that moment Kate was very like Adele and Nina felt something akin to homesickness sweep over her. 'I'm very glad to see you,' Nina said again with great emotion.

'Is it Claudio?' Stunning he might be, adorable he might

413

be, but trustworthy, Kate didn't know. Kind, Kate didn't know. A good husband, Kate feared not.

Nina shook her head vehemently, her eyes filling with tears. 'No! Claudio is wonderful! Really wonderful!' She grabbed the heavy damask napkin and held it to her nose and blinked rapidly. Then she took an enormous swallow of wine and coughed, then laughed.

'Nina! Calm down!'

'I am. I am perfectly calm.' Nina flipped her black shining hair over one shoulder and took a deep breath.

'Now slowly, tell me what's happening.'

'Nothing's happening. It's just . . . I'm just living, that's all.'

'Is the Contessa giving you problems?'

'Not really. I know she was devastated that I was not of their social status but now, what can she do but be nice to me? So, she's all right. There's an edge to her voice and she calls me *tesora all* the time, never Nina. We've gone shopping together. Suppose she doesn't want me to disgrace the family by appearing under-dressed.'

'You look fabulous, Nina. You always did, but there's a little difference . . .'

'It must be the manicures twice a week and the facials on Thursdays and the haircut that costs more than I used to pay for a pair of shoes . . .'

'Well, how sorry I am for you!' The words were out before Kate could stop them. Nina's head snapped back as though she'd been struck. 'I didn't mean it,' Kate apologized. 'I really didn't. I'm sorry, Nina. I know you're having a hard time.'

It was as though a cold wind had swept the noisy restaurant. Nina twirled her wine glass then looked up and said, 'I'm not, really. I'm okay. Now, tell me everything. How's Bill? Have you found a new exercise class? I nearly died when I heard Monica had disbanded us. I feel abandoned, as do my stomach muscles.'

You're such an actress when you want to be, thought Kate. 'There's a place way out in EUR but it's just too much of a production to actually get there. I'll . . .'

414

The pasta came and they both sprinkled it with parmesan and began to eat. 'Kate.' Nina's voice was pleading. 'It's not that I feel sorry for myself. Really. I don't.'

'I know you don't. I didn't mean to say you did. I am sorry.'

'No,' Nina continued. 'You make me think. You are my voice of reason. Always have been, here in Rome.'

Kate smiled. 'I am reasonable. Even my husband says so. But I'm so . . . I'm such a grey little guinea hen beside you.'

Nina erupted with laughter. 'My God! Is that how you see yourself? And I see someone my own age with this calm rather aristocratic coolness that I'll never have in a million years!' They both laughed then.

'Nina, are you all right?' Kate asked quietly.

'It's not Claudio. It's not marriage per se.' She rolled her eyes and thought. 'I don't know what it is. Do you remember when you came over a month ago and I showed you Claudio's apartment?' Kate nodded. How could I forget? Twenty-four-foot vaulted ceilings covered with flying cupids and floating clouds and horses stampeding over robed bodies as gold angels hovered in the corners ignoring the carnage. The walls were covered in dark portraits of long-dead de Leones glowering from their rococo frames. There was a bust of a cardinal beside the bed that Nina waved at, laughingly. 'He loves watching us do it.' The furniture was the same style as the other rooms: delicate, ornate, gilded. Claudio evidently sprawled with ease all over everything but Nina sat with her spine straight terrified of hearing a 'crack' noise, particularly after a heavy dinner. 'Well, the canopied bed is wonderful. I think I've always fantasized about a bed like that . . . with satin curtains, and when I wake up and see that pale green . . .' She stopped. 'But the heavy mirrors and the draperies shutting out the sun and the formality of it all just seem to wear down my spirit.' She shrugged. 'Ridiculous, isn't it? That must be it. Don't you think that's why I'm a little spacey?'

'Look, you've leapt from total independence into life with a strange family. I know you married Claudio but you're living with his family and it takes a bit of adjusting. You're used to being on your own and this is a jolt.'

'You're right. And the side of me that longs to have three tiny rooms painted white with just Claudio and me and lots of flowers and simple watercolours on the wall instead of these masterpieces . . .' She digressed. 'Do you know that in the palazzo they have a papal canopy where, just in case a pope pops in, he can be received?' Kate was unblinking. 'Only one of five Roman families is so equipped, said my mother-in-law.' She began again. 'Well, anyway, so I don't get to live exactly the way I'd like: in blue jeans, playing with Keats and Shelley. The flip side is I don't worry about housework, have to shop for a piece of veal at the butcher's or cook it or' – she lifted her eyebrows – 'or do laundry or . . .'

'Or cope with a Roman plumber! I waited four afternoons for him to deign to come and he spent two hours tinkering away, singing opera the entire time. Something from *Tosca*. I was getting very curious about the state of the leak when he walked into the kitchen and asked me for a cork! All I had was something fancy to keep the fizz in champagne . . .'

Nina laughed. 'The palazzo plumber is no better because he cannot ever come. I heard Maria talking about him. She's the maid who takes care of my clothes. Isn't it unbelievable?' Nina rolled her eyes. 'This plumber works for the Vatican – evidently a lot of these old churches have things dripping on ancient frescoes – and for the president of Italy and for the de Leones. Three clients. But the catch is Cesare is never in Rome! Caesar! A plumber named Caesar! But he's never to be found. He shoots grouse in Scotland, quail in Spain and goes off to Austria for the pheasant shooting. Has the little bearers, the whole thing!'

Kate laughed. 'Makes me wonder why Bill insists upon being a banker!'

'Oh, Kate! I am glad to see you!'

'Why do you keep saying that? I'm sure you're making friends.'

'I think I am, but honestly I don't know. The women are nice to me when I'm with Claudio but they won't accept my invitations. They won't ever have lunch with me or go to a movie in the afternoon or go to a museum or . . .' She

416

sighed. 'I even asked Patrizia to go running when she said she admired me for doing it.'

'Keep trying. I wish I had Italian women friends. There are two that I talk to when I bump into them in the park with Alice, but they never come up for coffee afterwards or ask me to come to their house either.'

'Well,' shrugged Nina. 'It's a foreign country, after all.'

'How is the key figure in all this?'

Nina smiled. 'I am happy just being in the same room with him. I still cannot take my eyes off him. Can't quite believe we're married. He is moody. He does have these amazing fights with his father. He does throw things when he's mad. Though not at me!' she hastened to add. 'He's had some real rows with the Count and broke a really ugly vase one night after dinner. A million pieces!' Nina chortled. 'I just loved it. The butler, that nice Franco, came in to sweep it up and I sent him out for some brandy and he arrived a few minutes later with a brand new bottle and two glasses on a silver tray. And a smile on his wrinkled old face.'

'What happened then?'

'I locked us in the apartment and we got rip-roaring drunk and turned on the Stones so loud that the Contessa herself pounded on the door and told us to stop it and I was almost cowering under the bed like a little kid and Claudio told her to leave him alone and thank God refused to open the door. I mean, we were both naked . . .'

Kate laughingly reached for the wine. The waiter materialized with their trout and placed it before them. 'Maybe that's it. It's like being a child, a little girl in that place. I'm trying to be well behaved and I feel tight all the time.'

'Sounds like it's a lot more fun to misbehave.' She could hardly imagine the regal Contessa raising her voice, let alone making a fist and pounding on the twelve-foot-tall panelled door.

'Ha! It is!'

'Well, if you and Claudio love each other then you can liven up the palazzo. You can overlook his mother and the gloom of those rooms . . .'

417

Nina burst out laughing. 'Oh, Kate! Mick Jagger was howling "Let's Spend the Night Together" and Claudio was dancing with his polo mallet and I was wearing his boots and helmet . . .' She began to laugh and couldn't stop.


The bathroom still took Nina's breath away. Every single inch of it, save the gold dolphin fixtures, was of a marble called *gialla antica*. The shades ranged from amber to honey to topaz swirled with white. The tub was an alabaster sarcophagus brought from Egypt by Claudio's eccentric archaeologist great-grandfather. Sometimes the newlyweds filled it with bubbles and climbed in after dinner. They placed Amaretto in little glasses on its ledge and sipped and talked; Claudio often puffed on a cigar. Later they washed each other and dried each other and then made their way to bed and to lovemaking.

There they go again, she thought, as she heard her mother-in-law scream at her father-in-law. It's nice they fight in Italian so I don't have to be embarrassed at the next meal. She turned the water on full force to shut out the angry voices which echoed down the long hall. It must be Thursday, decided Nina as she pulled off the stockings and the lacy suspender belt. Franco's day off. They don't seem to fight as much when he's around. Claudio had told her that every servant – Franco, the maid Maria who was his wife, the chef, the two maids who served at the table and cleaned, and even the chauffeur, Dante – had been with the family for at least twenty years. Franco and the chef were second-generation servants for the de Leone household.

Nina stretched out full length in the warm water. Cannot believe that the Contessa de Leone just called the Count de Leone a pig. A crash of broken china made her jump. Heavens! but these marble halls do echo. People wouldn't believe it, she thought as she reached for the nail brush. Another crash! then the Count's voice saying that he was going out and then an anguished scream of rage from the Contessa. Nina leaned back and closed her eyes. Oh, these Italians.

*

418

'*Cara mia, mia Nina!*' sang Claudio as he opened the door. Nina was in the second bedroom which had become her dressing room with its make-up table, its wardrobe, its long mirror. The carved oak day bed between the windows, covered in pink and white brocade, was the only reason to call the room a bedroom.

'I'm in here, darling!' He threw his arms around her, white towel and wet hair and all, and kissed her upturned face.

'Missed you today.'

'I missed you, too. Your mother was not in a great mood when you called to cancel and then your aunts didn't arrive till after the table had been cleared and . . .'

'Never mind about that.' He pulled a little box from his suit pocket. 'A present. Forgive me for missing lunch.'

Nina smiled. 'I don't forgive you for missing what we do after lunch.'

He grinned. 'I married a shameless sex-starved wanton.'

She took the box. Bulgari. 'Oh, Claudio!' The emerald ring sat upon a little throne of black velvet. She threw her arms around him and as she did the towel fell away. 'Oh, I love you! You crazy Romano! I love you!' She squealed as his cold belt buckle dug into her flesh and then he kissed her as she writhed like a fish against him.

'Come on, Americana,' he ordered. 'Follow me around while I shave and change for dinner. I want to keep you in my line of vision for as long as I can. And try the ring.'

She let him slip it on her ring finger. 'Perfect.' She extended her slender hand and admired the square stone set in platinum. Claudio looked at her long lean body, the firm breasts, and echoed her, 'Yes, perfect. You know, Nina, I don't have to get ready for dinner just yet.' She leaned forward and kissed him for a long breathless moment and then, breaking away, she led him to their bedroom and to the big bed under the green satin canopy.

Nina smiled across the dinner table at Claudio then she said softly, 'First, a diamond as big as the Ritz and now this!' He

419

winked back at her as the salad was served to the bishop from Florence at her left. 'What's the biggest hotel in Rome?'

Claudio shrugged. 'Don't have any idea, Nina.'

'Well, couldn't this be an emerald as big as the Hassler?' He erupted with laughter and coughed as wine went down the wrong way. Everyone turned their attention to the young couple.

One of the Contessa's twin sisters asked, 'Is the younger generation telling secrets? Plotting against us?'

'You do quite enough of your own plotting,' said Claudio smoothly. His aunts doted on him though he made no secret of his dislike of them. It was hard to say which one he disliked more. And it scarcely matters, thought Nina, for they are identical.

'Claudio!' His mother's voice was sharp. He looked at her but did not respond. Nonno's crunching of the breadsticks became louder and louder. The Count's father, in his late eighties, gazed into space, no doubt seeing Mussolini's troops advancing from the far end of the dining room. His white head seemed to bob on a thin filament, nearly too heavy for the scrawny neck with the pink wrinkled skin that gathered above his buttoned shirt collar. He had shrunk inside the expensive suit as though it had been meticulously tailored for quite another person. He turned his head suddenly and the extra skin at his throat flapped like a turkey's wattle. 'That Abyssinia business!' he shouted. 'Now that's a big mistake!'

'Yes, I agree with you,' said the Count quietly, then he turned to his niece and asked if she wouldn't like another glass of wine. Elena was the only child of his sister who had died of a heart attack during the time her daughter had been held hostage. She nodded, unsmiling. Her two hundred and fifty pounds were encased in several yards of light blue satin. The stitching seemed to have pulled loose under one arm as the flesh fought to get out of its sausage casing.

'I'll do the via Condotti tomorrow,' Aunt Livia was saying. 'Silvia, are you coming with me?'

'I have an appointment at lunchtime but yes, I'd like to come all morning.'

'Go to Maximilian's across from the Hassler to see the shoes. It caters to movie people so it's a bit avant-garde but just stop and look. It opens at ten and then . . . Shall I plan lunch for you here?' the Contessa was asking.

Oh, thought Nina, why don't you go *out* to lunch with your sisters? You never go anywhere.

The bishop was talking about the Vatican and the Christian Democrats and telling the Count that two of his magazines could lean a bit more towards the Christian Democrat party. The Count was enjoying the discussion. 'If I lean any more in that direction, I'll fall on my face!' The bishop didn't seem to understand that Count de Leone couldn't make all editorial decisions. 'We have a board for this,' he joked with the older man. 'I'm not the pope, you know!'

Nonno was murmuring something about Somalia. His plate was taken away untouched as he reached for another breadstick.

The talk droned on. Nina leaned back in her chair and thought: Even if I die of boredom I'm well dressed, well fed. The new Valentino of lime green silk felt rich under her fingertips. She inhaled and thought of that third fitting. Killingly boring and now it fits perfectly and I sit in it being bored. At last the cheese plates and the bowls of fruit had been cleared away. The identical twins, blonde, blue-eyed, chattered on. They resembled their older sister very much: all three were tall, small-boned and elegant. Their dresses were in three different shades of blue. Silvia and Livia prattled as though they never saw one another though in fact they lived not a mile apart in Milano and had never been separated for longer than their honeymoons. Both husbands worked in the twins' late father's publishing empire, as did La Contessa's husband. All three women had married well. They had never needed money but they had no name; with marriage they gained social acceptance many rungs up from their bourgeois backgrounds.

Count de Leone had married a wife and a fortune and a career. He had taken all his father-in-law had offered and of the three sons-in-law had been the most ambitious and the brightest. Now seven of the ten magazines were his. He could wallpaper a hotel with all the pages of print he produced each week. The plants, the presses, distribution and labour problems were all his. His share of the stock was seventy per cent, with his two brothers-in-law splitting the rest.

Claudio was to follow in his footsteps but so far seemed to be walking away. This enraged the Count. His only son, with the best education money could pour into him, was a spoiled young man whose idea of a productive day was to score at polo. Work meant a morning on the phone arranging the evening's schedule and gossiping with friends as he skimmed *La Republica*. Then there was the three-hour lunch and the odds were against his returning to his desk afterwards. The Count gave him money because 'If I didn't,' he often shouted at La Contessa, 'you would!' And it would have been more money, too. But he felt it was undeserved and that his son threw it away. His son, on the other hand, felt it was a pittance and chafed at the leash he said he was on. Claudio often declared that he wanted independence but he was the first to admit that that didn't mean an apartment of his own for he was quite comfortable in the palazzo. Neither was getting a job a consideration that crossed his mind. A job would take time away from his other activities. No. Claudio's definition of independence was his inheritance in advance. At fifteen when he'd wanted a very expensive sports car, and his parents had both said 'no', he had proposed they subtract it 'from what I'll get when you die'. His father had never forgotten his son's face at the dinner table that evening as he calmly presented the idea. Good-looking, yes, with a face women will always stare at. His mother will adore him no matter what he does and didn't he usually charm his English nanny out of a spanking? Used to getting his own way but worse than that, he holds the self-truth that he deserves his own way. He will age with a petulant sulk on those handsome features and no matter how strong I am with him, his mother will undo it.

The Count liked Nina but he saw her marriage to his son as doomed. If Claudio had married a Roman girl of his own

422

class there might have been a chance. But Nina was too strong-willed, indeed too American, too idealistic, to overlook his indiscretions, to put up with his selfishness which was sure to surface *fortissimo* before too long. Some of this must be my fault, thought the Count. But he thought it infrequently. He had emotionally pulled away from the ongoing fracas years ago. He still fought and argued but it was more of a habit than a vocation. He no longer cared very much what Claudio did, or what the Contessa did, for that matter. The palazzo was there for him; it had stood for six hundred years give or take a few decades. The Count came to change his clothes, for the occasional meal, and went away again in the bulletproof Fiat 130 with his bodyguards Ugo and Enzo. They each carried 9-mm Barettas and he felt so safe with them he often forgot their existence. My life is somewhere else, he thought as he turned once more to the bishop. The Count tried to glance at his wristwatch without being caught at it. For fourteen years, Simona had been on his mind and in his heart every time he wondered what time it was. He would try to be early, he might be late, or he might have to call and say he couldn't come at all. But every time he rang the doorbell on the narrow street in Trastevere she let him in. And the Count, with great happiness, knew he was welcome in her arms and that he was loved.

Finally all eyes turned to the Contessa and she gave the nearly imperceptible nod which signalled that they could leave the table. Nina and Claudio walked hand in hand to the salon where they sat next to each other on the little brocade love seat. Seeing poor Elena, Nina asked in a low voice, 'Couldn't I ask her to have lunch with me in town tomorrow? Do you think she would come with me?' Claudio looked at the broad back of his cousin as she stared out of the window. 'You could try. She hasn't been out of the palazzo for . . . since . . . since we brought her back.'

Nina got up and went to her side. She's only a few years older than I am. She must be bored out of her mind staying inside all day, week after week, month after month. 'Elena,' she said and waited for a response. Elena looked at her but didn't speak. 'I wondered if you'd like to . . .' The living room was full of chatter and laughter behind her. The bishop was telling an amusing story about the Vatican Secretary of State and an African ambassador. The twins were off in their own world discussing leather suits: the care and maintenance of and the pros and cons of having them made here in Rome as opposed to the tailor they trusted in Milano. Nina tried again. 'I want you to have lunch with me tomorrow. It would be fun. We could have Dante drive us in and . . .' Something was registering on Elena's usually blank face. Nina thought: 'I've got through. Maybe she will speak. We see each other every day after all. Wouldn't it be wonderful if . . . She was pointing out the window. Nina nodded and smiled. 'That's right. Outside.' And with that realization, Elena began to scream in long piercing shrieks of fear. One after the other they came from her as she stood beside the window with her arm pointing towards the courtyard.

Franco ran down the stairs and out of the building to summon Dottore Martini. In half an hour Elena had been sedated and had been carried – it took five men – to her bedroom. Nina was trembling when it was all over and they had taken their chairs again in the salon. Her mother-in-law was the first to speak as the coffee was at last served. 'Tesora, why on earth did you decide to frighten her?'


'Oh Claudio! Again?' Nina's face was reflected over his shoulder in the mirror of the open wardrobe door. The shelves were stacked with shirts from Caleffi at one hundred thousand lire apiece in neat rows. They were all the palest shades of the rainbow and two dozen white ones for good measure.

'Well, yes. Again. You know I don't do it for fun. Zurich is not exactly my favourite city . . .' He pulled a pale yellow shirt from the top row, put it on and began to button it. 'Those Swiss. I wonder if they ever make love.'

Nina wasn't really listening. She was thinking: Every week now, and it used to be every third week and it means that I have dinner alone with the Contessa again since the Count never seems to be here in the evenings. She looked down at the twinkling emerald and thought: Yes, this is because he knows I don't want him to go. How original. He makes things up to me before he does them. So Zurich is why we're having breakfast together for a change.

'Don't let my mother get you down. She's not happy these days.' Nina almost winced, remembering the humiliation in front of Zia Silvia and Zia Livia.

'Claudio, she must know I didn't do anything on purpose. She must know after all this time that I am not a mean person.'

Claudio sighed as he tucked a white handkerchief in his suit pocket. 'She knows. Forgive her.' He gave himself a quick look then turned and kissed Nina on the forehead.

'I will if you want me to. I'll . . .' Nina hesitated. 'I'll send flowers to her and to Elena, too, while I'm at it. Do you think that would be a good idea?'

'*Stupenda!* They'll both love it.'

'Has that ever happened before? I mean, screaming like that?'

'No. She has been totally silent for years. We have hired psychiatrists but obviously if she won't speak then they cannot help her.'

'What about hypnosis?'

'She resists it.' He was packing his briefcase. Nina applied bright red lipstick and surveyed herself in the looking glass. The red linen trousers and the white sleeveless blouse were the simplest things she owned for she hated to be more dressed up than Kate. She looped a leather cowboy belt with big incised designs around her waist and pulled on high-heeled brown sandals. There! She removed the gold lion-head earrings Claudio had given her for fun and replaced them with simple gold hoops. Grabbing her red and green striped Gucci bag she announced, '*Pronta!* Come on, de Leone! Get your act together!' He snapped his briefcase closed, snatched the overnight bag from the bed in the other room and then swatted her soundly on the rear. With a squeal, Nina opened the door and they tap-tap-tapped down the marble hall together for breakfast.

*

425

Nina's mind wasn't really on picking out the flowers. She stood in the shop doorway and felt ever so drowsy after the wine at lunch. Kate was a trustworthy confidante and had urged her to make it up with her mother-in-law. 'Especially if the two of you will be practically alone at dinner for the next three evenings.' Alone unless you count Elena who doesn't know what day of the week it is and Nonno who doesn't know what year it is. The dinner table seemed to gather all the unhappiness, all the tension, and the mental illness of the household in one place each evening. Nina's chest always felt tight and she could hear herself chewing. My God! she'd thought the week before with a flash of recognition. It's just like being back home in Mississippi.

Nina turned away from the slow clerk and the indecisive customer and walked to an outdoor stall near via dei Gamberi. Those bright yellows, she pointed. They looked gay. Not my favourites, but cheerful. The little boy hesitated and she said, '*Per favore*,' again and he began to wrap them in the white tissue paper. Something more sophisticated for the Countess. Yes, white roses, she nodded. A dozen. He shook his head and added a thirteenth. 'Oh, no, no!' cried Nina. She then plucked a few more from the bunch standing upright in the pail of water. He looked at her and said, 'Signora?' with a frown and then with an air of resignation apparent on his nine-year-old face wrapped them, too, in white paper. '*Molte molte grazie*,' she smiled, and paid. It never would have happened if his mother hadn't been drinking a coffee in the bar across the street. She was horrified when he told her. 'Ahhh, foreigners!' She threw up her red raw hands in exasperation and shaking her head sat down on the overturned barrel she used as a stool. Massive legs apart under the black canvas apron, dusty lace-up shoes planted firmly on the cobblestones, grey hair under a babushka, she shook her head again. 'They're all crazy!'

Nina felt refreshed by the air, by the knowledge that she was taking a definite step in healing the wounds of the previous evening. Nothing was my fault, she told herself, and even though Claudio was close to his mother, he had agreed. So it shows that I am thoroughly well-meaning to arrive with flowers. And her sisters are gone so maybe this will thaw the Contessa and she will be able to show it without losing face or considering a power play. She went first to Elena's bedroom. Nina knocked on the half-opened door then peered in. Elena was sitting in a large chair reading the Bible. There's too much furniture in here, Nina thought. The shutters were closed and the lamps on, giving the room the appearance of night, and the windows were closed, making it airless. 'These are for you,' she motioned as she put the chrysanthemums in the silver vase on the table beside the bed. Elena stared at her and then at the flowers and began to weep silently. 'Oh! I'm trying to say I'm sorry! Can't you see that!' Nina stood helplessly in the middle of the large room. When the woman didn't stop crying, Nina thought: I'd better leave; I have a bad effect on her, and she hurried towards the door.

'Can you bring a vase for these?' she asked Maria who had materialized in the front hall. Nina held the white roses under her nose and inhaled. Tiny white buds. Each one perfectly formed. The blue and white ginger jar and the Contessa arrived at the same moment. 'I wanted to apologize for . . .' For what? thought Nina. She should apologize. 'For last evening.' The Contessa smiled, actually smiled as she watched the maid arrange them. Then at precisely the same second the two Italian women noted the number.

'How could you?' spat her mother-in-law. Nina was mystified. The flowers were so beautiful. The Contessa and Maria then heard loud sobs. Elena was running down the hall when they met her. The chrysanthemums were upside down, dripping water, clutched in one chubby hand. 'You did this?' The Contessa turned to Nina accusingly.

'I brought her flowers! I brought you white roses!' What had gone wrong!

Elena at last flung the wet yellow blooms on the floor and then still sobbing padded barefoot back to her room. 'You don't know anything, do you?' shouted the Contessa. Nina was amazed. She'd never heard her shout at anyone but the Count that way. Nina thought of the months of snide remarks, the cold looks, and now at last the woman was actually screaming at her. 'What did you mean doing something like this?' Nina didn't hear the words. She saw Maria in her black uniform rush down the hall, she saw Franco out of the corner of her eye and then he, too, disappeared, and still that voice shouted on. The Contessa's blue eyes were wide, her mouth was red with lipstick and her very teeth showed in anger.

Nina felt feverish as the adrenaline pumped through her. She shouted as loudly as she could, drowning out the crying down the hall, drowning out the wrath of her Milanese mother-in-law. 'You're right! I don't know anything!' She shook her fists in the older woman's face. 'I don't know anything except you make everything harder for me! You love making it harder!' Her voice echoed down the marble hallway. All the maids heard her where they huddled with questioning faces in the reception room; the chef stood in the dining room with a spoon in his hand, his white hat on his head, and Franco hid behind the piano in the galleria. Nina's face was white with rage. 'I don't know anything! Except I'm' – she almost choked on the words – 'except I'm doing the best I can!' The amazed Contessa watched Nina walk away. She marched down the hall, past the pop-eyed faces of the staff, and then down the opposite hall and with a slam that could be heard from one end of the palazzo to the other she sequestered herself in Claudio's apartment.

Claudio returned while Nina was at an Italian class and when she walked into their bedroom he greeted her with laughter. Gales of it. He couldn't stop. Nina ran into his arms, then pulled away and demanded that he tell her what was so funny. 'You are! My silly Americana!' and with that he began to laugh again, unable to speak. At last he explained. 'You brought chrysanthemums to Elena. In Italy we only put them on graves. She thought you were wishing her dead. And then' – he wiped the tears from his eyes – 'and then you brought white roses to Mama . . .' Nina stared at him as though he were drunk and to be humoured.

'Seventeen of them. It's terrible luck.' It was also terribly funny and when Nina's initial thought of 'what a stupid country this is' had passed, she too began to laugh. 'You never bring seventeen of anything to anyone. We even worry about Friday the seventeenth.'

It was decided to go out early on *Simba II* this year. Nina was delighted. Paperbacks galore from one of the two English bookshops in town, her Italian grammar, bathing suits and piraeas, ten glittery dresses for evenings on Capri, and not much else were heaped into suitcases. Nina was dressed or undressed as the other women were: she was topless all day, with an endless wardrobe of bikinis and lots of gold jewellery, for Claudio was generous. She had gold and silver high-heeled sandals, two dozen pairs of slip-ons and quite a collection of straw hats. Nina lay in the sun and thought of the last summer, the Claudio of a year ago, the Nina of a year ago. He was very much the same person. For that, I'm grateful. And me? she wondered. I am doing the best I can. She could now joke with the others in Italian, she read the newspapers and kept up with the political gossip as much as anyone could. It seemed a morass of contradictions and with the government always rocked or about to be rocked or simply falling; why, it was hard for an Italian to follow. The days passed in a haze of swimming, backgammon tournaments, lazy talking, the lunches on the various islands, taking the Zodiac to a favourite deserted beach. Claudio made love to her less often but that was probably normal, Nina decided. They still cuddled together on deck watching the moon rise over the sea, still held hands as they walked around the little ports, still nuzzled one another in the water like two playful animals. One afternoon in June they talked about having a baby and, every night of the summer, after a day in the sun, they fell asleep holding hands, thinking with the same thrill of their secret. Maybe the next time, maybe it was this afternoon, maybe it will be soon.

*

429

'Oh, the idle rich!' Kate embraced Nina and they both laughed with happiness to see each other.

'It's been for ever!' Nina sat down on the banquette in Ranieri's red dining room and said, 'My treat. Just thought we needed to try something new.' Kate gazed up at the sconces, the rich red brocade wall covering, the old mirrors. 'It was founded in 1843, says the sign outside. Ranieri was born in Naples, somehow became chef to Queen Victoria, then to Emperor Maximilian in Mexico, and finally took over here and spent the rest of his life in Rome.' They ordered white wine and both began to speak at once. 'The boat? The boat was fabulous. I was so disappointed you couldn't meet us for that week.'

'Well, Bill had a really tough time this summer. He fired someone and you evidently can't do that in Italy and the awful woman has come back and threatened to sue the bank and then for all four weeks of August . . .' Kate shook her head. 'You, you lucky thing, have never had to have Ferragosto with all the working stiffs in the Eternal Città. I swear you count the days till September and wonder where you are going to buy food. Everything, but everything closes. The newsstands take turns staying open. Anyway . . . the air conditioning at the bank went on the blink for the entire month and there was no one in this entire city – this is a capital city, Bill kept saying – to fix it.'

Nina laughed. Bill was usually so calm. 'What did they all do? Just go to work naked and hire Nubians to fan them?'

Kate shook her head. 'They arranged for men selling ice cream to come through the offices four times a day.'

Nina giggled. 'It's so Roman I can't stand it!'

'That isn't the worst of it . . . Bill gained six pounds!'

'Tell him to sue the bank.' Nina flipped open the menu. 'How's Claudio?'

'Adorable. He's simply adorable.' Nina couldn't keep the secret a minute longer. She didn't feel close enough to any of the Italian women friends she knew for they never confided in her, and she feared that they would tell their lovers or husbands anything she conveyed anyway. 'I'm trying to get pregnant.'

'Oh! I'm so happy for you!' Kate had watched Nina progress from starry-eyed 'he is so handsome and he is a count' to near despondency when he gave her a hard time that Christmas, to marriage with all the odds against its working out. 'Why do you say that?' Bill had demanded at dinner one night. 'Because.' Kate passed him the roast beef. 'Because he is Italian and she is an independent American. From another world. How long will it take them to crash headlong into the face of their differentness?' 'Oh, Kate!' Bill had moaned. 'Don't you have any American friends married to Italians who are happy?' Kate ticked off seven friends and said, 'Before I answer that, tell me what you think of Giorgio and his wife from Chicago.' Bill groaned. 'So to answer your question,' concluded Kate, 'no. Not one.'

'I have felt from the beginning,' Nina continued, 'that the Contessa would be happy, that the Count would be happy, that it would somehow solidify things with me. Claudio told me I'm the only foreigner a de Leone has married since seventeen something. She was French and dazzling and produced nine children and everyone loved her. And here I am. So far, only the servants like me.'

Kate was philosophical. 'That's crucial. The Contessa can't use poison.'

'Well, if looks could kill, I'd have just had my ninety-ninth funeral.'

'Claudio still going to Switzerland?'

'Yep. And don't ask what he does there. It's plainly not my place to ask.'

'You can't ask?'

'Oh, I can ask all I want. Ever heard that Southern expression of "askin' ain't gittin'"?'

Kate laughed at the exaggerated redneck drawl. When they'd met in the exercise class she had all the polish of a New Yorker, and now she had a glow that marriage had given her. A polish that came with being a countess, or simply a sheen of self-confidence. Her Italian was progressing, though much more slowly than she wished, and her clothes were the most elegant Rome could offer. They were culled from the best shops with Nina's sense of colour, and worn with Nina's flair on Nina's spectacular body. If anyone deserved to arrive in Rome and marry a count, it was Nina McLean.

The two women chattered on. The *vitello tonnato* came and was devoured. Big salads of *rughetta* were eaten and the bottle of white wine was nearly empty. At last the pastry cart was wheeled over amid their soft moans of, 'Oh, I shouldn't,' 'Oh, don't let me but look at that mountain of whipped cream!' As Nina was lifting a bite of almond cake she suddenly said, 'If I don't get pregnant in the next two months I think I'll go insane.'

'*Pazienza*,' Kate advised and then seeing her friend's face realized she was nearly serious. 'Almost everyone has to wait. I waited three years. Bill and I were discussing adoption when it finally happened.'

Nina remembered Adele's waiting. 'I feel that so much hinges on it.'

Kate nodded. 'You don't have enough to do, do you?'

'No. I get up, do exercises while Claudio sleeps fifteen minutes longer and then I take a bath while he shaves and we talk and it's fun, I guess. We both get dressed and I kiss him goodbye and then I have breakfast with the Contessa. We're polite. We talk about clothes mostly. She keeps notebooks of what she wears. Then it's lunch with you or with myself or with a friend from Italian class. Italian class is four times a week. I would go every day but I wouldn't have time to soak it in. Then I go to antique shops on my long walks, or read, or go to a museum, then I jog. Then I take a bath and try to look beautiful for Claudio and for dinner.' She shrugged and took another sip of wine. Her face was solemn. 'That's it. I feel like a plant sometimes. Taking up space on the earth.' She grinned suddenly. 'But then I'm not quite that since I can't even manage to pollinate.' Kate smiled. 'Propagate? Procreate?'

'How does La Contessa spend her day?'

'She seems to be biding her time, waiting for something. She has no friends that I can tell, other than the people she sees at these oh-so-social functions. She does do some kind of charity work but it's not even every week. I dropped enormous hints about wanting to do something like that at dinner one night but she plainly would rather exclude me.' Nina frowned. 'The bulk of her time is spent in maintenance. She must have her hair done nearly every day and her nails are always perfect. A woman comes to the house a hundred times a week. And there are facials, massages, etcetera. She didn't understand why I wouldn't have a private tutor come to the palazzo for my Italian.' Nina was silent for a minute. 'Kate, I'd love a job. If it takes a while to get pregnant, why couldn't I do something while I'm waiting?'

'I'll keep my ears open. Sometimes I think it would be wonderful to get dressed for the day, leave home for an office, and do something and be paid for it. Then I think the job market will still be there in two years. Alice will be in nursery school before I know it.'

'You have plenty to do. I don't. Please tell me if you hear of anything. I have half a mind to go back to Rubelli and give them my new phone number.'

'While you're at it, give them your new name.'

'What do you mean?'

'Well, Bill and I were at a dinner party the other night and the conversation was all about how Romans are concerned with who you know, not what you know.'

'How awful! You mean that they might hire me now and I wasn't good enough for them a year ago?'

'Maybe they'd hire you now just because they have an opening but . . .'

Nina's sense of democratic fair play was offended. 'I don't like that.'

Kate was not so sure. 'I admire your sentiments but Rome isn't New York. You may have got jobs on your merits before but you're here and you may as well play the game the way the Romans do.'

Nina was adamant as she placed a one-hundred-thousand-lire note on the silver salver with the bill. 'No. I like being a countess and I like being married to Claudio but if someone wants to hire me, they're going to get Nina McLean.'

*

433

Nina decided in the taxi that she missed having friends. Thank God for loyal Kate! Rita and Lesley had come to see her only twice since the wedding and the Contessa had sat with them a while. They'd been in awe of her and of the tapestries, and of the paintings and of the servants and of the very air – so rarefied was it all. The Palazzo de Leone is not for the faint-hearted, thought Nina, lifting her hand in a friendly wave to the *portiere*, who smiled back. She walked beneath the long colonnade towards the door where little Massimo, belying his name, waited in his de Leone livery. 'Contessa,' he smiled. '*Buona sera.*'

'Contessa Contessa Contessa' echoed in her ears. She thought of Minnie from Buffalo Center, then she thought of Mickey Keeling saying 'crawfish'. The heels of her hand-made pumps of brown alligator went click click click up the marble staircase to the *piano nobile* where still another foot-man awaited her in beige and mustard livery. But what if, thought Nina as she nodded '*Buona sera*' to him, what if you escape to the wrong place?

October and November came, the *tempo d'oro*, the time of gold. Rome pulsed with life as the dog days of summer were replaced by bright clear days of autumn. Nina ran by the river in the crackling leaves every afternoon. She thought she could measure the passing of the seasons by the purchase of new clothes, by the fittings, and by the boxes delivered and then unpacked by Maria. Every morning the hall table was piled with large envelopes addressed to both counts and both countesses for this ball, this dinner, this party. Nina was instructed to buy six new evening dresses and she dutifully did. Her mother-in-law allowed herself the pleasure of knowing that Nina would choose well. When she and the Count were at the same party or reception she noted the impression her young daughter-in-law made. She was charming, she looked happy, she gazed at Claudio with undisguised adoration, and she was undeniably quite beautiful. All this odd running, wondered the Contessa. Could that have anything to do with it? But no, she decided, many Americans run and as a group they dress atrociously and do lack any savoire faire whatsoever. Nina on the other hand had immediately comprehended the concept of *la bella figura*. The Contessa thought of the wedding. Her mother was a lovely, delicate, well-bred person. Yes, mothers have so much to do with how people turn out. Nina was also quite popular with Claudio's crowd, among the men anyway. Her mistakes with her stumbling Italian were often amusing and she had a way of telling a story that made everyone at a dinner table listen to her every word, so worried were they of missing something. At the American Embassy dinner in honour of the visiting Secretary of State, Nina had been surrounded by Americans wanting to know about her. And she had, the Contessa had to admit, delighted them with her bright-eyed recital. She was a bit of an actress; she did perform when the spotlight was on her.

Nina knew her mother-in-law watched her and knew, too, that she could not remain oblivious to the compliments she received. But so far there was no thaw in sight. The Conte was sweet to her when she saw him, but she never passed him in a corridor, nor did she see him in the morning. It was at a formal gathering or at the occasional dinner. Claudio was attentive when he was in Rome but that was only half the days of the month now. Nina was still not pregnant.

'Maria, I think I'll wear the raspberry-coloured dress and maybe that dark green sash that came with the other. Yes, that one. Let me try it on quickly and then I'll give it to you to press.' Nina removed high-heeled dark blue leather pumps and the dark blue Chanel suit and walked across the room in her lacy underwear. The maid slipped the dress over her head and together they wrapped the green length of silk around her tiny waist like an obi. 'It's not Scarlett O'Hara's seventeen-inch one but it'll do.' Maria nodded in admiration. The young contessa had told her the story of Scarlett O'Hara in halting Italian one long afternoon as they'd sorted summer clothes from autumn clothes and decided which could not be worn again, for the Contessa had a strict 'visibility rule' and once an outfit was photographed it was retired. She kept lists of dresses, jewellery and accessories, and a photograph meant an X in the far left-hand column. The phone rang and Nina looked at it impatiently. She knew she wasn't allowed to pick it up; that Franco would answer '*Pronto*' in his perfect accent and then knock on her door if the call were for her. This time the knock came. 'Contessa, *il telefono è per Lei*.' '*Grazie*,' she called happily.

It was Kate. 'How would you like to be on the radio?' Nina listened as Maria fussed with a hook and eye at the back of the strapless ball gown. 'It doesn't pay much, maybe nothing at first. What do you think?'

'I think,' grinned Nina, 'I'll be there tomorrow at eight o'clock.'

It isn't easy, thought Nina as she practically ran through Piazza Barberini with its big round planters filled with marigolds. The Triton fountain gurgled in the sunlight. No, and I have to lie, too. Nina now woke up and hurriedly dressed, grabbed her bright red canvas sausage bag, drank a glass of milk at the table with her mother-in-law. Then with talk of an early exercise class she sprinted out of the house. She hailed a taxi when she saw one but usually leapt on to a bus, and then just past Piazza San Silvestro would decide the traffic was so terrible she'd make better time on her own two feet. In minutes she was in the building, past the *portiere* and up the stairs and in the *toletta*. She pulled off the beautifully-tailored wool trousers and folded them carefully and then with a sigh of pleasure would slip into her oldest, most faded pair of jeans. With a simple sweater and her necklaces tucked inside, she told herself she looked 'reasonable'.

The station was owned by Americans, run by an Irishman, and staffed with English and Australians. The technicians were Italian. Everyone was young, good-natured, casual, and had to be. The station squeaked by on such a little bit of advertising revenue that often no one was paid for weeks at a time. 'It's all highly unprofessional,' Nina confided to Kate, 'and more like a club for expatriates than anything else. No wonder they hired me! It doesn't matter when I arrive. The news goes on any half hour I want to show up!' Nina liked the easy-going atmosphere and the dozen people she worked with. Best of all, none of them ever connected Nina with the Conte de Leone, the publishing magnate, or with his polo-playing son.

'Okay, Nina. Ready?'

'Whenever you say.'

'No, not whenever I say! Whenever I drop my arm! Then you're on.'

Nina adjusted her headphones and took a deep breath. She sat in a glass box of a room facing Steve, the morning disc jockey, in his adjoining glass studio. He also wore headphones and spoke into a microphone. Record covers surrounded him in colourful profusion, a poster of the Stones and one of John Lennon were taped to one wall, a tomato sandwich lay on Kleenex next to the telephone and she could see his clothes for the gym stuffed into the Rinascente shopping bag on the floor beside his size-twelve feet in their white Adidas.

I wonder if Clayton is in his office listening? No, it's too early for him to be here. He could be listening as he shaves or on the car radio as he sits in traffic, though. Clayton Reilly had told Nina to lose her Southern accent, so for the last two days she had been walking around the Italian capital murmuring, 'The rain in Spain falls mainly on the plain.' Steve had made fun of her and said, 'Nina, with you, the rain in Spain is simply more so. Accept it.' Nina had retorted, 'I can, but Clayton can't! I've talked this way my whole life. Steve! You have to help me!' So Steve had put a rather long tape on the air and Nina had sat on the floor awaiting his instruction. Almost immediately the classical music disc jockey had arrived with his English accent and joined them, his little grey goatee wagging as he crouched like a frog at Nina's level and helped her to enunciate.

Now Nina sighed and straightened the Associated Press clippings in front of her. Thirty seconds. Fifteen seconds. She stared at Steve as Dolly Parton sang the last notes of

'Here You Come Again', and then heard the music that signalled the newscast. Steve's arm came down and Nina began in a clear voice, 'This is Nina McLean with the 8:30 news for WROM.' One-two, she counted silently. 'Early this morning in Beirut, five people were injured as a . . .'

One of Claudio's friends must have told him, thought Nina. She stood in the dressing room and he stood over her. She'd never seen him this angry. 'So you've taken a job! A ridiculous job! Why do you think you must work? Why, with all this?' He waved his hand at the open wardrobes fairly exploding with clothes. Rather absurdly, Nina thought, he's gesturing at his own things. His suits cost a thousand dollars each.

'Because I want to work.' Nina tried to keep her voice from trembling. She loved her job, though they had only paid her once, but they were so nice about it and the disc jockeys laughed and said they'd get by. It was normal for Rome. Normal people had talks with their landlords and their grocers and everyone shrugged and life went on. But money wasn't the problem.

'Because you want to work!' Claudio's sneer was ugly as he mimicked her voice. 'You are my wife! You are the young Contessa de Leone! You don't work! You don't get out and get a job! You are no longer Nina McLean!'

'I am Nina McLean!' she shouted back, enraged at his idea that she had become his property at some point during the wedding ceremony.

'No, you're not! There is a ring on your finger. Look at it!' His face was a dull red colour. 'Actually there are several rings on your fingers. Given to you by me, your husband, in case you have forgotten!' Then he began to fight in Italian and Nina joined in. She called him a crocodile which was the only animal she knew which didn't appear on a menu. She was sure of pig but that was what the other Contessa called the other Count. Claudio continued his shouting as she slammed the bathroom door and began to fill the sarcophagus. They had a dinner in one hour at the

438

Argentine Embassy. The visiting polo players and all their wives would be there in full force. Crash! Claudio must have broken the urn on the desk – the one with the rose petals in it. Nina brushed her teeth and thought: A miracle there are any antiques left in Italy at all!

Nina had always thought that one good thing about the Italians was that they exploded with all their anger and then it was dissipated. No one went to psychiatrists because they let every emotion show so freely. She'd heard as a little girl that Latin men actually cried at funerals and had fewer heart attacks than Anglo-Saxons. Now, in her marriage to Claudio de Leone, she wasn't so sure of these maxims. There were more trips to Switzerland, more days of not seeing him and more nights without him in bed.

Claudio was still angry with her at Christmas time and the holiday was marred by his sulky silences. No more picnics on polo fields, Nina thought as the family gathered around the decorated tree in the chilly marble-floored salon. 'It's a pagan northern custom,' the Count was saying. 'Still unusual to have a tree in Rome.' They opened presents and drank champagne. Nina called the Countess in New York and cried when they had to hang up. Then she called her mother and cried when they had to hang up. Adele called and they both cried when they had to hang up.

Christmas night Nina turned to Claudio in bed and put her arms around him. He had his back to her and feigned sleep. 'Do you realize if I get pregnant tonight we could have a baby in the fall?' She kissed the nape of his neck but he didn't speak, didn't move. 'A tiny Claudio,' she teased. She stroked his back and kissed his shoulder blades. His skin was warm and smooth; he still smelled of the sun, and Nina did love him. In silence she touched him gently until he turned over and took her in his arms. Instead of kissing her he put his face against her cheek and then with a minimum of fuss, a few movements, he was inside her and it was over. Nina felt tears stream down her face when he rolled away from her and though she was sure he knew she was crying he made no move to comfort her. Soon she heard his deep measured breathing in the dark room. Was the job so important? Was it so terrible that I lied to him and to his mother? What has changed everything? This man I once thought such an exciting mix of cultures – both American and Italian – is now one thousand per cent Latin. But I'm going to make this marriage work. If I can get pregnant, if I can please his mother, then he'll want me the way he used to. We will be happy again. Nina breathed aloud, in a whispered prayer, 'We will be happy again. Oh, please.' She listened to the chalice fountain for a long time and, at last, slept.


'How are you getting a tan in the office?' she asked as they dressed to go to the dinner at Principe Vittorio's. Claudio didn't answer. He fumbled with the bow tie, glancing at Nina's bright reflection in the white satin dress behind him. 'Well, you are tanned,' she insisted.

'From the sun.'

A simple thing really but then the next day on via del Babuino she'd been grabbed from behind by Mario and had shrieked in surprise and then delight. They'd kissed each other and then he'd demanded, 'Nina! Where have you been?'

'Right here in Roma!' she laughed. 'Trying not to get arrested as a Red Brigade.' When the Carabinieri sirens had screamed past them and circled the block, Mario pointed down the street. 'A judge lives there. He has twelve guards to get him in and out of his apartment. Every morning and every evening. He must be going home for lunch. By the way, what are you doing now? Come with me.'

First, they stopped in an antique shop to see a seventeenth-century silver chalice Mario was thinking of buying, then they sauntered, window-shopping and talking, to Dal Bolognese at Piazza del Popolo. How much fun he is. How much fun it is to flirt again, to joke again, thought Nina, as she let him order for her, as he filled her glass with wine. They were joined by two of his friends who made much of her and teased her about Claudio's handicap at polo. 'It's ten,' she said proudly. 'In the stratosphere.' Ten was the best. Claudio was one of only five left-handed players in the world. After 1973 it had been deemed too dangerous, and no other left-handed players had been allowed.

'That de Leone is tough. But the way he plays! Don't you worry, Nina, about his getting hurt?'

'No,' she shrugged. 'He's so good. I feel sorry for his ponies. Six weeks on a boat from Argentina. Then they get to crash around on that field twice a week with my husband on top of them.' She blushed the minute the words were out. The men laughed but they were gentlemen and it was all good fun.

Mario gazed at her fondly. 'Why don't you re-schedule your Italian class so that your lunch hours are always free?'

Nina was confused. Surely he didn't mean, after all this time, that he wanted to begin something? And asking in front of his friends? Claudio's friends? 'What do you mean?'

'We miss you at Grotta Ferratta,' said Giorgio.

'Yes, we go almost every day to take the sun and Claudio says . . .' Mario stopped.

Nina looked at the three faces and thought: No hysterics, please. *La bella figura*. 'I would love a coffee, after all. Do you have time?' she asked sweetly.

'*Certo*,' said Giorgio, stepping into the breach. 'It's only half past three and this is Rome. You know what they say? "Milano works, and Rome eats."'

Nina managed a bright smile. 'None of us would last very long in Milano, would we?'


Nina held Claudio's arm as they strolled down the Corso. The marble majesty of Piazza Venezia with its wedding cake temple, its typewriter shrine to Italy's unknown soldier, gleamed very white below the full moon. 'Italy's answer to the Taj,' Nina quipped and Claudio laughed. It was such a glorious night she had persuaded him to walk home from the party. Nina's copper-coloured evening slippers felt paper-thin on the pavement. She pulled the rust velvet cloak about her shoulders more closely. 'Claudio, I must talk to you.' She hesitated then plunged forward. 'You seem to merely tolerate me except when there are people around. Will you tell me – '

'What do you want me to tell you?' He stopped and put his hands out in a gesture of helplessness. A few cars passed the figures in evening clothes.

'Don't you even like me any more?'

'*Certo.*'

Nina examined his face in the half light of the moon. His mouth was set in a frown, his eyes were staring past her, not seeing her. 'Why is it that you are different when you – '

'What do you mean "different"?' he snapped.

'I mean aloof. Even hostile. You look as though you don't want to see me, have me in the same room with you, and certainly you're not happy to have me in the same bed.'

'Boh.' He shrugged.

'What is it? What's happened? What have I done?' Oh, I sound like my mother now. It rains on the family vacation and it is the mother, the wife, who apologizes for the weather. Nina took a deep breath. 'What happens in Switzerland?' she demanded.

His voice was cold. 'I work. Your emerald ring is Switzerland. Your topaz necklace is Switzerland. My new Jaguar is Switzerland. It's money my father won't give me.'

'But why have you changed so much since the trip before Christmas?'

'You've been listening to my parents!' said Claudio defiantly.

Nina walked in step with her husband. This husband who was prickly and defensive again. Isn't there anything I can ask, anything personal we can discuss without retreats into silence, after the anger and the shouting have died away? Franco had moved all breakable bric-a-brac from their rooms. Even the little sixteenth-century snuff boxes Nina loved so much had disappeared. 'I try not to listen to your parents,' she responded. 'I know you fight with your father about money, though that seems to have stopped; I know that your mother fights with your father about why he isn't home more. That's all I know.' She felt such frustration at not being able to get at the truth of the matter with Claudio. What *did* happen in Switzerland? 'I'm talking about us. About how you are with me.'

Claudio gave a bark of a laugh. Nina refused to remove her arm tucked in his. Maybe this is our only contact, she considered. We don't make love more than once a week. There is dancing, arm-taking at receptions, his removing my coat upon arrival at a party or restaurant. A civilized brush of skin.

'You really don't listen to my parents, do you?' It wasn't a question. It was an expression of surprise and yet Claudio was very angry. 'My father . . . my father! You don't know about his . . . you really don't know what's going on, do you?' Claudio stopped and wheeled to face her. The pavement was empty. It was two o'clock in the morning. When she didn't reply he continued, 'He has a mistress. Has had since I was old enough to know the word and . . . he knows my mother knows. And now I know – don't ask how I know – that the mistress is pregnant. And that means that . . .' Claudio looked up at the dark sky and cursed in a stream of Italian. 'That means that I share my inheritance. It's the law now. That my mother's money managed by my father will go to this little bastard.' Nina was amazed. She had tried not to hear, tried not to understand, and because it was in Italian she had managed to avoid comprehension of the words. 'All the servants know. Christ! I can't believe you didn't figure this out!'

Nina decided to ignore the obvious slur on her intelligence. 'What do you mean, your mother's money?'

Claudio sounded as though he were explaining a multiplication table for the twelfth time to a very dim-witted child. 'My father's father lost all the de Leone money in the 1930s. At about the same time, my mother's father, who started with nothing, was making a fortune. My father was a conte with no money, but he was landed gentry, with a palazzo and one thousand acres outside Rome. My mother was beautiful, with lots of money and did not mind being a contessa. Simple. Money marries name. It's normal.'

'How did your grandfather lose all his money?' Nina thought: I will milk him for information until I do understand. I rarely see him unless he's changing clothes these days or part of a crowd.

'In a card game! Sounds so romantic, doesn't it? Like some Mississippi riverboat gambler. He got involved with a group in Napoli and they cleaned him out over the course of three days . . .' He spread his palms and raised his arms heavenward. '*Magnifico!*' he said sarcastically.

'What happens now?'

'Nothing happens, really. We all wait for the child to be born and then my mother and I pretend it doesn't exist the way we've always pretended the mother didn't exist.'

Nina decided to forget about asking about Grotta Ferratta, forget about asking him about another woman. Forget about asking him why he so seldom makes love to me. It could wait. Maybe tonight he will let me be close to him. 'Let's go home, darling. Let's go home and have a brandy and go to bed.' Claudio took her extended hand and together they walked through the silent streets. When they entered via dell'Orologio the moon greeted them low in the sky above the clock tower. It washed the cobblestones in its pale light as they ventured towards it. Then the ivy-covered archway came into view; they nodded at the groggy *portiere* and entered the courtyard where the fountain splashed in the dark. Like children who had stayed out past suppertime they tiptoed under the colonnade, through the front door then up the marble staircase, and down the hall to bed.


Dinner alone with Claudio! Nina dried herself in the marble bathroom with the enormous white towel. Maybe tonight we will be able to talk, really talk, thought Nina as she patted cream around her eyes. The facial this afternoon had left her face very pink and the run had added to her feeling of wellbeing. Well, certainly not pregnant yet. She stared at her flat stomach in the mirror and sighed. She massaged in skin lotion from her pedicured feet up to her broad shoulders. Then she sprayed L'Heure Bleu, the perfume she'd worn that year they'd met, up and down her legs and inside her elbows, between her breasts and on her throat. For luck. Then she hurriedly fastened the cream lace suspender belt and pulled on the silk stockings, a new find at the strangest little shop near Campo dei Fiori, then yanked on cream lace bikini underwear. Maybe, just maybe he will maul me in the taxi later. The Giuletta is sick and the Jaguar attracts too much attention, he had told her that morning, so could she meet him at his club at Largo Fontanella Borghese? At last Nina pulled the peach silk dress off the hanger and slipped it over her head. The neckline was low and square and she hesitated to add jewellery, then thought of the way the Roman women festooned themselves and added rope after rope of the coral beads Claudio had given her that first summer. She twisted the last length of palest coral, pink really, in with the Countess's pearls and was quite satisfied with the result. She'd written Adele that everyone wore twice as much jewellery as any New Yorker would dream was in good taste. And it looks striking. Nina's black hair hung a few inches below her shoulders and shone with health. Maybe it's the olive oil, she surmised. Her face glowed with anticipation. She snapped on the coral and pearl earrings and then applied a lipstick just the colour of the lightest coral. I do love him, she said to herself as she applied mascara to her black lashes. I'll tell him that we should start again. I'll tell him that we should get a place of our own, that I want to fix it up in a simple way, that I want to cook for him, that I want to wear blue jeans and that I don't care if it's one big room or three tiny ones. She sat down on the little brocaded stool and asked aloud, 'Or do I?' She crossed her legs and the feel of the silk stockings gave her pleasure. But didn't suntanned skin and a black bikini give her just as much? 'I don't know,' she said aloud. But I know I love him and I want to be a part of his life. I don't want to be shut out. Out of his lunches with friends twenty miles from Rome or shut out of his thoughts when we lie in bed and don't touch. I will tell him how much I love him. Tonight!

*

445

'*Ciao!*' Claudio opened the taxi door for her and helped her out. '*Bella! Molto bella!!*' he enthused as he led her through the courtyard and into the narrow, one-person-wide elevator. Torpedo-shaped, Nina had called it the first time. Its doors opened one floor above the Embassy of Spain on to the *piano nobile* where a large brass plaque informed them that this was *Il Circolo della Caccia, Foresteria. Foresteria* meant guests were allowed in this part. Claudio opened the door and they entered the hallway with its several dozen black and white photographs on the right-hand wall; Prince Charles and the King of Sweden stared down at them. All the monarchs of Europe are automatically made members, Claudio had explained. The reception room with its eighteen-metre high ceiling was massive. Four storeys, fifty-eight feet high. Liveried waiters in beige with red and white striped waistcoats took drink orders and later served at table.

'This is exciting,' she teased after Claudio had asked for champagne. 'Dinner with my own husband in this super, elite, Ritz of all time, big-deal club!' He smiled. She was happy he was in a good mood for a change. 'And don't do anything outrageous.' She tried to sound stern. Raising her eyebrows, she said, 'I'm known here.' Claudio laughed. He'd been a member since he was eighteen and Nina knew very well she would not be allowed one inch inside the door without him as an escort. 'How did they let you in anyway?' She sipped from the glass and smiled.

Claudio gave a half smile. Nina was terribly attractive tonight. She sparkled. This was a good idea. Conversation was so limited at dinner at home with 'a cast of thousands', as Nina said. 'I was put up and seconded by two members and then voted on just like everyone else.' He took a swallow of champagne. 'It all takes place on a Saturday afternoon with stamps at a table. You must have five white balls for every black one.'

'I am impressed, you know.' Nina tilted her head backwards and tried to take in the enormous space, covered in frescoes and gilt.

'You should be, my little Americana. We blackballed John Paul Getty.'

Dinner was at one of eight tables in Pauline Bonaparte Borghese's bedroom. Napoleon sister had lived life to the hilt and the outline of the hidden door for her lovers could be seen in the frescoed room if one looked carefully. Anyone watching the young couple would have noticed affectionate glances – particularly from the woman to the man – heard lots of laughter, and as the last plates were cleared away, observed the woman's hand on the man's. She stroked his thumb suggestively, a slight smile on her full lips, until he moved it away. 'Is there someone else?' she asked suddenly.

'Not really,' he answered, and took a last sip of the wine. He nodded to the waiter that they were leaving. No bill was ever brought. Nothing was ever signed. Charges would appear on next month's statement.

Nina felt that the blood had drained out of her at that 'Not really!' 'What does "not really" mean?' Claudio gave her a terribly Italian shrug. It said everything and nothing. 'Do you still love me?'

'*Certo.*'

'Claudio, could we go somewhere and talk? I need to talk to you about how I feel.' Nina's voice was tinged with tears. She heard it and hated herself for letting down her guard so soon. This was to be a seductive dinner, a night of fun, a night of playing in bed, a night of making things up, and maybe a night of conceiving the baby.

He was standing then in his perfectly-tailored beautiful grey flannel suit with a pale blue shirt that matched those eyes and a silk tie from Gucci that cost a fortune. They were '*buona sera*-ed' out into the March night. Nina was wrapped in sable but Claudio wore only his wool scarf with the stripes of maroon and navy.

'We're invited to a party. *A dopo cena,*' he told her as he held the taxi door open. He'd made up his mind when Nina had pleaded yet again 'to talk'. I'm not an American husband, he thought. I don't sit around and analyse endlessly nor do I have to explain myself! Not to Nina. Not to anyone. It was another side of Claudio's nature to call '*Aspetta*' to the driver, bidding him to wait. He sprinted in a few quick steps to the flower seller at one corner. Nina watched him fumble in his pocket and hand the old woman a few thousand-lire notes. He returned to the taxi, smiling like a pleased little boy, with the bouquet behind his back and only after he'd slammed the door and told the driver to drop them at via Borgo Pio did he present them to Nina. She held the coral roses to the sable coat and thought: I do love him, but the words 'not really' flashed into her mind the way one wakes in the morning from a nightmare and remembers only the splinters of fear.

The 'after dinner' party was at an apartment not far from the de Leone palazzo, just across the river. They heard the music as they alighted from the elevator and when the front door was opened Patrizia gave a squeal of delight and threw herself into Claudio's arms. He kissed her on the mouth as Nina felt her flesh crawl. Isn't it funny, she thought as Patrizia proceeded to kiss her coolly on both cheeks, that I grew up hearing about the right thing and now I am trapped by something called the *bella figura*. She took Claudio's arm and looked around the room. It was all the women who had been on the boat with them over the past two summers. She recognized many of the faces. Most were dressed in short black dresses with lots of jewellery, but several were in bright orange and bright red with the big rhinestone earrings that were the most recent fad. Or, Nina thought, knowing their husbands, maybe they were the real thing.

The excited Italian flowed around her quickly, the rock music was loud, insistent; a tall woman she'd met only once pulled Claudio from her and proceeded to dance in the middle of the living room. Nina was given a drink by Francesco and turned her back to the others. '*Come va?*' she began bravely and then had a conversation about his skiing trip to Cortina which didn't keep her from thinking about Claudio dancing behind her with Laura. Laura of the big breasts, most of which were showing in the clingy red dress, Laura of the blonde mop of hair à la Farrah, Laura of the deep throaty laugh. Gianna joined them and Nina complimented her new haircut. It was shaggy and layered around her pretty face, making her eyes seem bigger than ever. 'I've known Claudio a long time,' she said in Italian. 'He's a wonderful man.' She smiled broadly and walked away. Nina turned and saw that Claudio was now dancing with Paola, clutching her to him and moving very slowly. It was the kind of dance she remembered from that first night he had held her to him in the dark nightclub. Susanna stepped forward to the applause of the other women and Paola kissed Claudio on the lips long and hard before relinquishing her place.

'They don't like you.' It was Mario's voice. 'Nina, don't . . .' He saw the tears in her eyes and grabbed her wrist very very hard and squeezed. 'Drink this,' he ordered and she swallowed the salty tears gathering in her throat and then the drink. 'You're not one of them and they're out to show you that. They don't understand you and it frightens them so it's easy to hate you. You might steal one of their men.'

Nina wasn't listening. I have to leave or I have to stay. I have to not let anyone know I'm hurt. 'But this was planned!' she breathed. The light was dim, her vision was blurred. She really couldn't see his face.

'He's let everyone know he has problems with you.' Anna came up behind Claudio, who was still the sole man dancing; she removed his jacket and rubbed herself against him. He raised his eyebrows and grinned and the crowd applauded. Nina kept her back to them all. Mario was speaking softly. 'You can get through this. I know you.'

'I feel as if you're talking to an accident victim waiting for the ambulance to come.'

'Maybe I am.' Mario tossed down his wine and poured cognac into Nina's glass. 'But look, I know you and I know what you're made of as those Americans say – the right stuff.' Nina managed to laugh. It was a hoarse laugh, like a cough because she was choking on tears, but a laugh nonetheless. 'I've known you longer than Claudio has known you and tonight is going to be over and no one is going to see you break. Don't give them the satisfaction.'

Someone had put on 'The Stripper' and Claudio was laughing as Anna did bumps and grinds a foot away from him. 'I am going home.' Nina put the glass down on the table and with a last look at her husband turned to walk past the group on the sofa, the people standing behind it. Amazing, she thought. There are about four women here for every man. It was planned. The room was big and white, with the rugs rolled up against the doors leading out to a terrace. Built-in modern shelves held art books and records. Nina entered the bedroom and found her coat with its monogram inside lying on the double bed with the two dozen other furs. A tall brunette materialized beside her. Her perfume was heavy. She smiled and said, 'So you're Nina. I've heard all about you.' Nina could not return the smile. There was something wrong about the tone. Then the woman in the black velvet dress said very slowly, 'Claudio. Mmmmmm . . .' The pursed lips, the suggestive deep murmur of appreciation as though she were rating a dessert – it was too much.

Nina's hand connected with the perfectly made-up face in a fraction of a second. The noise seemed explosive in the bedroom, but no louder than Nina's heart as she walked quickly through the living room where Claudio was still dancing, past Mario who tried to grab her arm, and out the front door and down the stone stairs.

I'm dying, went through Nina's mind. I'm dying. I loved him. I did. He was my husband. The sable coat dragged on the paving stones behind her as she mindlessly rushed towards the river, towards the bridge, in the direction of the palazzo. Her breath came in gasps as though there were no oxygen in the spring night. Her heels seemed to land at angles on the cobblestones and she felt off balance, unsteady. It's the wine, it's the cognac, she told herself. I will go home and I will . . . but she didn't know what she would do. She was halfway across the Bridge of the Angels when he called her name. 'Nina! Nina! Wait!'

Nina turned then and saw him, coatless, without his scarf, running towards her and she shouted, 'I hate you! I hate you!' His black hair was blown back by the wind, his face was lit by the street light. *'Ti odio! Ti odio!'* she sobbed in Italian so that there would be no mistake, so that he would not come closer, so that he would not touch her. She pulled at the wedding ring on her finger as he watched.

'Nina!' he shouted. 'No!'

She threw the gold band over the railing with all her strength, using the strong overhand Bart had taught her. It gave off one last gleam of light and then fell silently into the dark water thirty feet below. It left as much of a mark upon the old river as a pebble and then disappeared.

Nina waited until the serving maids had left the dining room and then said clearly, 'Contessa, I want a divorce.' The older woman dropped her usual three teaspoons of sugar into the little coffee cup and stirred. 'I want it as soon as possible. I know that you will know how to take care of it. I don't have a lawyer but I'm sure the family does. Please give me his number and I will call him.'

Nonno said, 'Mussolini is secretly using poison gas against rebels in Libya,' and the two contessas and the cousin ignored him. They they heard Claudio's footfalls in the hall and his 'Ciao!' as he opened and closed the front door. Nina had not seen him since the night before on the bridge. She had slept in her dressing room on the ornate little daybed, without brushing her teeth or washing her face, with no sheets, using her sable coat as a cover. She had locked the door and opened all the windows as though fresh air would help.

'Claudio is the one you should talk to.'

'I have.'

'The Count is away for a few days. You must wait to speak with him about this matter.'

'No. I can't wait.' Nina felt very tired, very near tears. Nonna was talking about Abyssinia. Cousin Elena was humming.

'Divorce in Italy takes seven years,' her mother-in-law said with a calm Nina found maddening. 'I hardly think a few days will make a difference.'

Nina bolted from the table, calling 'Scusi' before she made it out of the dining room, and down the hall and arrived in her bedroom in time to be very very sick. She spent the day making lists of what to do, what to pack. First, she would speak to the Count and then to the lawyer. Surely there would be no problem. Not even Claudio – no, no one – would want to be married to someone who didn't want to be married to them. He plainly doesn't want me anyway. The tears came and again she went into the bathroom and washed her face.. She skipped lunch and forgot to tell Franco or Maria. Maria knocked at her door at two o'clock and asked if she wanted anything. She tried to smile and thanked her and said she wasn't at all hungry. Maria gave her a very sympathetic look under the little white cap and Nina, for one second, wanted to be embraced by the plump grey-haired woman. 'I'm fine,' she kept saying under her breath as she moved about the room. I've come out of this marriage with a lot of clothes, haven't I, she noted as she looked at the two large bureaux filled with underclothes and sweaters. The two tall wardrobes held all her evening clothes and sports clothes. Everyday suits and silk blouses were in a wardrobe in Claudio's dressing room. So, a few days, thought Nina. I can get Maria to bring me sheets and make up this bed properly and I'll be . . . just fine. She blew her nose. And when the paperwork is done I'll be on a plane for New York. Maybe the Countess will be between assistants. Maybe . . . Nina went to the little ivory-coloured phone and dialled New York. In the few seconds before Adele's phone rang she heard the click! of an extension being picked up. She pushed the button down and replaced the receiver. Kate. I'm having lunch with Kate tomorrow. My voice of reason, Kate!

It was a warm day and Nina wakened hearing birds singing. Everything is going to be fine, she said to herself. She looked at the Sèvres porcelain clock and thought: Only seven; Claudio won't even be awake yet. She tiptoed past his sleeping form into the bathroom and locked the door behind her. In fifteen minutes she'd taken a quick bath and applied make-up and was back in what she now thought of as her room. She pulled on the green wool suit and draped three strands of silver beads around her neck, then snapped on the matching earrings. Franco greeted her in the front hall with a look of surprise.

'*Buon giorno*,' she nodded as he held the door open for her. 'Would you please tell the Contessa that I won't be home all day? *Grazie.*'

'Dinner?' She shook her head. Getting a divorce from Claudio meant no more dinners with his mother. This was certainly going to be fun.

Ranieri's was crowded when Kate arrived and found Nina reading the *Herald Tribune* at a table in the back of the red dining room. They kissed and ordered white wine immediately. Kate was wearing a dark blue suit which could have been the twin of Nina's and big blue enamel earrings. Her straight dark chin-length hair had been pushed behind her ears by a navy velvet hairband. 'Getting dressed up and having lunch like this is such a treat.' She shook out the big white damask napkin. 'I was wearing blue jeans with apricot baby food stains on them until an hour ago!'

'Kate, I'm getting a divorce.' Nina's voice was calm. After all, she'd spent all yesterday being weepy and now it was over. It was a time of plans. Plans made calmly, with logic. No more screaming on bridges. No more broken antiques. She told Kate of the party. 'Do you know how a lot of Roman women look so striking, so dark – so really lustful, I guess? Well, the other night they took on a new quality. It was sensual, sensuous – damn, I get those words mixed up – but something else, too. They looked almost whore-like. They were seductresses and they all wanted me to know it.'

'What did Claudio say after you threw your ring into the river?'

'Oh.' Nina shrugged. 'He was sorry.'

'Sorry about the ring? Sorry about the party?'

'I don't know.' Nina sipped the wine.

'I don't think he wants to end the marriage,' Kate said quietly. Nina began to speak but Kate silenced her. 'Listen to me. Get inside his head. He did set it up, I agree with you. But he didn't plan on your calling it quits. He is Italian. His father has had a mistress for years and even though he feels sorry for his mother, he is a male. I think he wanted to put you in your place.'

'My place?' Nina was disgusted and confused.

'Yes. He was telling his independent American wife that he could do as he pleased and that she'd better accept it.' Nina listened. 'In his mind he gives you clothes, food, shelter, and a full social life at his side as the Contessa de Leone. You will bear his children. Now, why isn't this good enough for you?'

'Because I am – I was in love with him. Because I expected him to be faithful.'

Kate looked into the sad face across the white linen tablecloth. She put her hand on Nina's. 'I know you did. But Claudio didn't know it.'

They ordered *bucatini* with cream and Nina pushed her plate away. She tried to eat the calves' liver, thinking: I forgot to eat last night, actually all of yesterday, but it was difficult to swallow. 'Try,' urged Kate. Nina was quite pale. After they had discussed finding a lawyer if the Count would not help her, after Kate had offered to let her stay with her and Bill, Nina suddenly excused herself and left the table. Ten minutes later the maitre d' stood over Kate and said quietly with a worried face, 'La Contessa. She has fainted. Come with me, please, Signora. We have called a doctor.'

Nina opened her eyes and saw the green canopy above her. Lettuce green. How pretty, she thought vaguely. Then she sat bolt upright, realizing she was in Claudio's big bed. Had it all been a dream? The party, the scene on the bridge, the . . .

'Now, Nina, darling,' soothed her mother-in-law. 'Lie down. You need rest.' Nina's expression was of undisguised horror. The Contessa actually patted her hand. Franco's face was worried and so was Maria's.

'Kate!' she cried and her friend came over and sat on the edge of the bed. 'Kate!'

'You're going to be okay. You certainly livened up Ranieri's today!' She tried to be light about it. Tried to smile.

The Contessa was regarding her daughter-in-law with

454

something akin to affection. She patted her hand again and said, 'I'll leave you now. Dottore Martini has given you a sedative so you'll probably feel very sleepy for several more hours.'

They all left except Kate, who remained motionless staring at Nina's face, at the dark hair spread on the big pillow. White linen sheets, she thought. Wonder who has to iron them. The room was oppressive, filled to bursting with velvet and brocade, and paintings. It made Kate remember the time she'd toured the Royal Palace in Madrid. She looked up. A chandelier the diameter of the table in her kitchen hung over the scene.

Nina grinned then and mimicked her mother-in-law's English accent. ' "Martini has given you a sedative." Ha! I wish old Martini had given me a martini!' She stopped when Kate didn't laugh. 'What happened to me? I was on my way to the bathroom and then – then nothing.' She looked at Kate's face. Something was very wrong. 'This is a big fuss to make. That's all I can say. A little bout of stomach flu. Too much wine.'

Kate remembered the gleam in the Contessa's blue eyes when she had been told. Such triumph. Her face was split with the first sincere smile Kate had ever seen registered there. She was an unhappy woman, anyone could tell, but she did take care of herself and had looked slim, immaculate, perfectly groomed in the light grey silk dress with the grey pearls. Yes, she had looked cold but elegant right down to her hand-made grey suede pumps as she watched the men carry Nina through the palazzo on the stretcher.

'Nina,' Kate began, and then her eyes filled with tears. She couldn't stop them.

Nina leaned up on one elbow rather weakly and demanded, 'Tell me! Kate, what is it?'

Everyone else knows, why shouldn't you? thought her friend. But it isn't fair. It isn't fair. 'Nina,' she said softly. 'You're pregnant.'


Nina cried herself to sleep. Maria came in at dusk and

closed the shutters against the cool night air, then she smoothed the cream satin quilt over the young Contessa. '*Un bambino! Buona notizia!* What happy news!' she whispered to herself.

Hours later Nina opened her eyes and realized that the little lamp by the door was on. It cast a yellow glow in the shadowy big room. Claudio was standing at the foot of the bed staring at her. He'd been on the polo field and hadn't yet changed out of his sweaty clothes. His mother had been angry at the mud he'd tracked in but Franco had shrugged as if to say, what next? It doesn't matter. Claudio's face was very tanned from the sun. 'A baby. Nina – '

'I can't have it,' she said.

'This changes everything.'

'No.' She looked at his handsome face and saw something else. She saw how spoiled he was. There was that sullenness around the mouth. There was the I-get-anything-I-want attitude she had been attracted to, mistaking it for strength of purpose. 'It changes nothing. I want a divorce from you as soon as possible.'

'There will be no divorce.'

'And there will be no baby.'

At that moment he lifted the riding crop and said grimly, 'I'd like to beat you with this until you understood.'

'Go ahead,' she said. 'You've done worse than beat me.'

He turned away then. A giant in the gloomy over-furnished room, shoulders damp with sweat. He went to the bookcase and pushed a button. To Nina's surprise, the shelf swung out exposing a little bar. Claudio took the bottle of Rémy Martin and poured into a glass. He turned back to her. 'There will be no divorce, Nina. You are carrying my son.'

Oh, how like him to expect a son! 'Not for long, I'm not.'

'For nine months.' His jaw tightened. His hair lay in wet ringlets on his flushed forehead. He tossed the brandy down his throat and then looked at her long and hard. She was sitting up in bed now, a thin figure with the masses of black hair about her shoulders, her white lace nightgown exposed above the sheet. Her eyes were almost green with anger.

He'd seen that before. 'I know what you're thinking,' he said. 'But you can't. This is Italy . . .'

'No one can make me have a baby!'

He laughed at her then. 'As I was saying, this is Italy, my dear American wife.' He fairly spat the words at her. 'And it's too late. I can make you have a baby and you can't stop me. This *is* Italy and you need my signature for an abortion.' He poured another few ounces of the dark liquid into the glass and then drank it quickly. The room was so silent the clock's ticking could be heard from the mantelpiece metres away.

Nina watched him move about quietly as though it were a sickroom. He sat on a chair and pulled his tall black boots off, then he pulled his jersey over his head and she looked at the strong muscles in his back and thought: Once I loved touching you. Once I loved you. Now all she felt for this enormous male animal was hatred for what he had done to her, to her life, and hatred for the power he wielded over her future.

The household became solicitous in the extreme and Nina was fussed over until she felt like slamming doors. The next week Kate came for lunch and Nina pleaded tiredness and Franco arranged for it to be served in what Nina now called her room. It was a sunny day and Nina felt almost happy. 'Don't telephone me, Kate,' she said quietly. 'I always hear someone pick up an extension when I dial out. I assume it's the same if I get a call.'

Kate nodded. 'Look, I did my homework. Rather Bill did and it isn't good news.'

'Haven't I had all the bad news possible?'

'There has to be a way to work this out,' said Kate, trying to be cheerful. 'I keep thinking that with a little imagination . . .'

'Tell me what Bill says.'

'Evidently it's true. The father has to sign a permission paper when there is an abortion. It isn't hard to arrange an abortion if you're in the de Leone class but if Claudio won't sign . . . forget it.'

'I've already said how much I want to see Mother, how much I miss her at a time like this.' Kate nodded. The Italians were positively gaga over mothers, babies and motherhood in general. 'And the Contessa knew immediately what I was up to and said she'd send her a ticket to come here. Such was her joy at becoming a grandmother, etcetera, that it would be her treat, etcetera.'

'They're afraid you'll get an abortion or that you just won't come back.'

'They're right, too.' Nina sipped her wine. The little intarsia table was set with bright yellow plates. There was cold pasta as she'd requested and *insalata caprese* and *prosciutto* and cheeses and olives. An ice bucket was on the bureau nearby. Nina had been amazed at having all her wishes granted.

'So it looks like I'm having a baby.'

'You haven't heard the rest.' Nina shrugged as if nothing else could matter. 'If you insist upon a divorce the de Leones can easily declare you an unfit mother and take custody. Even if they don't do that they can prevent you from seeing the child, visiting it or ever taking it out of Italy.'

'What!' Nina's face was horrified.

'That's the worst. It won't happen. I shouldn't've told you.'

'But do you know what that means?' cried Nina.

'It means you're having a baby.' Kate stabbed a piece of *mozzarella* with her fork.

'It means I'm producing an heir for this demented family just like one of Claudio's polo ponies!'

Maybe that isn't exactly the case, thought Nina. Her mother-in-law had been so nice to her, so gentle, since she'd found out about the pregnancy. 'Sit here, *tesora*.' The Contessa patted the dove grey brocaded love seat and Nina obeyed. She had never been invited to the Contessa's rooms before and there was so much to look at, to take in. There were four rooms, each quite large, giving her more space than Nina and Claudio shared. The Count's apartment was across the hall. All was decorated in the same style as the rest of the palazzo with profusions of floating gessoed cupids holding bouquets of flowers, trailing ribbons across the vaulted ceiling. The room they now sat in on this sunny May afternoon had walls covered in the palest watered green silk. A green Murano chandelier hung above them. Still another group of long-dead de Leones on canvas gazed down at the two women.

'I have something for you,' she smiled. ('She really smiles at me now,' Nina had told Kate in wonder.) 'It was given to me by Claudio's grandmother when I was pregnant with him.' She walked to the bureau and opened a box painted with gold leaf; lifting a ring out she handed it to Nina.

'Oh! It's so beautiful!'

'It's a star sapphire. One of the best.' She turned back to the bureau and to the jewel case. 'This is from Claudio's great-grandmother. A dinner ring which I think would be lovely with your pink evening dress.' She handed the oxblood ruby banded in diamonds to Nina who held it up to the light and blinked in wonder. There were more. It seemed that the afternoon passed with the Contessa turning from Nina to one jewel box after another and back again. There were twelve rings: diamonds, emeralds, rubies, sapphires; there were seven brooches including a very fine cameo. Many many pairs of delicate earrings were given to Nina, some with a single stone dangling from the gold wire, others ornately clustered with gems. The five necklaces took Nina's breath away. One was a choker of diamonds and rubies, another was composed of one hundred and twenty diamonds, all pear-shaped and designed to lie flat like a magnificent collar. 'This,' the Contessa explained, 'was designed by Jeanne Toussaint in Paris who did so many pieces for the Duchess of Windsor.'

'But that can't have been in the family very long,' remarked Nina.

'It was given to me by the Count but I would like you to have it.'

Nina took the diamond lion pin with topaz eyes almost

459

reluctantly. She looked up at her mother-in-law. 'Thank you for this as much as for all the others put together.'


Life changed for the Nina who was having a baby. An Italian tutor was hired to come three afternoons a week and the young woman and Nina sat in one of the smaller reception rooms by an open window and conversed. She told Kate that she first felt it was to prevent her from leaving the palazzo and resented it, but perhaps no, for no one objected to her penchant for long morning walks. She prowled the antique shops of via del Babuino, the art galleries of via Margutta, found a marble works on a side street and knew dozens of print shops and their owners by name.

Claudio and she shared the big bed again but they never touched, not even in sleep. He was polite to her and when others were present would take her arm or help her with her chair and even bend to kiss her on the forehead in a respectful manner. It was plain that he had a life without her. In the hour before dinner he was usually with his mother behind the closed panelled doors of her apartment. Nina had no idea what they talked about. She did remember all that time ago, at that first polo game, the woman in black and white silk waiting anxiously for her son to stand and shout, 'Mama! *Sto bene!*'

The Count was rarely home but when he was he gently questioned her with interest as if to make up for the non-conversation between himself and his wife, the bad blood between himself and his son. For him, thought Nina, I am happy to have the grandchild.

As the baby grew inside her, Nina was beset with confusion. She had always wanted a child – no, she had wanted children – but she wanted a good father for them. Adele was euphoric at the news; the Countess sent a tiny pale yellow sweater from an elegant boutique on Madison Avenue; her mother was thrilled. Nina had only written that she had fainted in a restaurant, was pregnant and what a nice surprise. The initial urge to write Adele or the Countess to find out about her legal rights had been dispelled by Kate's help and Bill's research. Nina knew that her freedom to come and go in the household depended on her being too far along for an abortion. As her stomach swelled she would be barred from getting on a plane without a doctor's letter stating her month of pregnancy. She had lain in bed every night of the first month and considered creeping out with a raincoat over her nightgown and getting into a taxi for Fiumicino. A credit card could do wonders. But then she thought of the de Leones giving up their grandchild and she thought of living in New York, worried about the baby being kidnapped or, at best, the legal wrangling. The family had clout. Her father-in-law was very well known, and not only in Italy, she had discovered. The world of publishing was the world. Then she thought of the alternative: to have the child born into a household that would adore it, spoil it terribly, but treasure its very existence.

What happens to the mother? Nina vaguely wondered. When she thought of divorce after the birth and of going back to New York, of leaving a child behind, tears were hot behind her lids. Leaving her baby to be raised by a mother-in-law who had proved herself cold and vindictive and jealous for so long was something she hated imagining. But now, Nina was greeted by kisses on each cheek at breakfast and cordial welcomes at the dinner table and sketches for the dressmaker as her figure changed. Nina was trying very hard to like her, trying to feel comfortable and, sad as it was, the two women had so much in common. Our marriages are the same, decided the daughter-in-law.

Life was happier for Nina though Claudio was really no longer a part of it. That knowledge was an ever-present sadness for the young wife. 'It's a pain somewhere in the region of my breastbone,' she once told Kate. On the afternoons without her tutor she read in the reception room, curled on a pink velvet chaise, feeling at last that the palazzo was no longer a hotel. Nonno didn't annoy her any more. The old man was pleased that he would be a great-grandfather soon though he confided to her solemnly that he hoped the war would be over before the birth. Even Cousin

Elena sometimes came and sat in the same room with her in a peaceful, companionable silence. It was usually at about five when Franco would approach her. He was proud of his English. The kind butler would walk quietly across the long room towards her with a silver tray bearing a goblet of milk and three or four of the *biscotti* he knew were her favourites. She would look up from her book and smile and then he would ask politely, 'Contessa, would you like a little snap?'


'Oh, do you speak Italian?' asked the woman holding a marble carving before her in the shop.

'Yes, I do. Do you want me to find out about this for you?' It's nice to hear an American accent, thought Nina. Kate had been away for an entire month. Nina played broker for the sale and the woman in the dark blue sun dress and the big hat was grateful. Brenda was the wife of someone in the film business and would be in Rome for eight months. She had American friends she was meeting for lunch. 'Come with me!' she urged as Nina hesitated.

In five minutes they were at Toto's, a little restaurant on a corner of via delle Carozze.

'This is Nina, everyone! She used to be an interior decorator in New York and now she's married to an Italian and having a baby!' There were gushes of greeting as three faces turned to her. 'And this is Cynthia from St Louis.' A short streaked blonde with an open face and freckles nodded. She looked as if she might be very athletic or perhaps was merely a sunbather who dieted religiously. 'And this is Lorna from Connecticut who is a fabulous painter!' Lorna was pretty, with light hazel eyes and light brown hair, but her smile was nervous. She seemed strained, tense. 'Linda is from San Francisco and has five children sprinkled all over the United States and two grandchildren and you'd never know it, would you?' Linda laughed. She had touches of grey at the temples and perhaps had had a face lift. 'Aerobics every day of my life!' They were all well dressed, well jewelled, ranging in age from thirty to perhaps early fifties. All three were married to Italians, all having had

462

another marriage or even two in their past back home. All full of jokes about how they coped with Rome and the Romans.

'I swear I would sleep with my plumber if it would help him fix my hot water heater.'

'Try mine. He is not mechanical but he has a wonderful voice. I'm learning so much about opera.'

Nina thought of Kate's experience with the cork. '*Tosca*, by any chance?' she asked and they all laughed. 'I know that man.'

'Listen,' said Cynthia in a mid-western accent. 'Does anyone have any pull with the phone company? I have been incommunicado for seven weeks!'

'Plumbing problems? Broken telephones?' laughed Brenda. 'How can you complain! This is a country of artists. Painters, lovers . . .' They all booed her.

'SIP! It must stand for "such impossible phones"!' They each told a story more maddening than the last. 'I asked Giovanni about your phone problems and he said, "Everyone knows SIP is a bad animal." And then,' she laughed, 'he shrugged!'

'The shrug!' cried Lorna. 'Is anyone writing a book called *The Shrug*?'

A waiter in a white jacket stood over them and smiled. Silence fell on the table as they listened respectfully to his recital of the specialities. '*Per favore, senza sale,*' pleaded Brenda. '*Senza olio, per favore,*' begged Linda. He nodded, smiled, and disappeared. 'He knows us,' explained Brenda, 'and we love this restaurant because we never hear anyone else speaking English.'

'Lorna, have you decided?' asked Linda.

'May I shrug?' They all laughed. She sipped wine and said, 'It's certainly been on my mind since our last lunch.'

'I have thought and thought and I think it will save your marriage.'

'So do I. It's the only way to play with these men.'

'What? Play with other men?'

Nina watched the animated faces. What fun to be out of the palazzo. Franco had promised to tell the Contessa she'd

463

met a friend at the centro. Let her think it was Kate.

'He's American. He won't tell on you. I think it's a perfect solution.'

'Otherwise you are going to get more and more strung out and you're liable to leave Giuseppe, and do you want that?' insisted Brenda.

Nina asked in a quiet aside, 'Have you known Lorna a long time?'

'I met her last week but I understand the situation.' Brenda turned her attention back to Lorna.

'No, I don't want to leave Giuseppe. He treats me very well but he just won't . . .'

'Make love to you!' they chorused, oblivious to the others in the trattoria.

'The Sicilian cleaning woman told me he has someone else. She said she can always tell,' Lorna said mournfully.

'So you get someone else!' Cynthia was adamant.

'Does every Italian male have a mistress?' asked Nina. All eyes were on her.

'How long have you been married?'

'A year and a few months.'

'What do you think?'

'I think my father-in-law probably does,' Nina said carefully. 'But is it common? I mean, do your husbands?' There. It was out. The question she'd been dying to ask Alessia, her tutor, for weeks.

'I think mine does,' nodded Cynthia.

'Lorna's cleaning lady thinks Lorna's does,' said Brenda. She went on, 'I'm married to good ol' Steinberg and he knows if he so much as had an erotic dream I'd – ' They all laughed. Beverly Hills tough, thought Linda.

It was like a club – a very small club. These women called each other on the phone, when their phones were *funzione*, every day to chat, to bolster spirits, to hear the smallest bit of news. They had long ago and quite separately vetoed the American Club of Rome as for fuddy-duddys involved in tours of gardens and little lectures. No white gloves for them. Lunch was a long affair with talk a-mile-a-minute, confessions poured forth, complaints commiserated over, and all of it washed down with a nice house white. Their waiter, Pietro, would periodically materialize at their corner table in the back dining room and plop another carafe down, knowing they liked to pour it themselves, knowing which one added water, knowing they were so involved that they didn't want to pause and say '*Grazie*'. Lorna was still talking. 'I can't just get on the train to Florence for heaven's sake and call him from the station and say, "Will you make love to me?" '

'Why not?' cried Brenda. 'He will, of course.'

Lorna was unconvinced. 'I only met him once, for heaven's sake.'

'Look,' began Linda. 'You are attracted to him and if Giuseppe hasn't touched you for two months, don't you think that . . .'

'I think I'm losing my mind.'

'Of course you are. You wouldn't be sane if you weren't,' someone said positively.

Brenda poured too much wine in her glass and it overflowed. Immediately four fingers were dipped on the tablecloth spot and then touched behind ears.

Nina was an observer. She dreaded the moment when they were likely to turn to her and ask questions about her life, her husband. But it seemed Brenda's introduction had been sufficient. There were so many other things to talk about, she decided with relief.

Speaking English gave them the airy freedom of talking in code. They had each revealed the truth about themselves – as they saw it, of course – and analysed each other later on the phone to others. They had, over the course of the last year or two, revealed the most intimate details of their first marriages, first sexual encounters, first loves. They practically voted on why a great love had gone wrong, why a marriage had soured, why divorce had been the obvious solution. The stories were repeated, sometimes altered but the women were remarkably patient while listening to a saga for perhaps the third time. They knew each other's faraway families – not only their children, but their parents and ex-husbands as well, and in Linda's case, the personalities of her grandchildren. They shopped for birthday presents together, a trio of chattering Americans cruising in and out of the chic shops. They shopped for Christmas presents together, fur-coated and gloved against the damp Roman December. Then, laden with glossy shopping bags and boxes tied with ribbon, they would vote on having wine at the Hassler or kir at Harry's Bar.

They lived vicariously through one another. If Lorna gave a dinner party the others called the next morning for a detailed account of each woman's dress, the conversation and who was who. 'His wife or *amante*?' they would each demand over the wire separately. Their husbands weren't friends, nor did they think they would be if introduced; indeed most of them never so much as caught a glimpse of another's husband though they each knew how he felt about his mother, how much money he made and if he were a good lover. Dottore Luca Perrini, married to Cynthia, would not have been happy to know that five American women had spent twenty minutes discussing the probable reasons he made love wearing socks.

The closeness was born of a loneliness, even a desperation. They recognized their great need for familiarity, for empathy, and realized that they were part of a smaller world than any they had known in their respective cities.

'Cooking?' Lorna was saying. 'It's the most creative thing in my life since I haven't been able to interest a gallery in my paintings. I gourmet this man to death. He is Cordon Bleu-ed senseless everynight at nine o'clock.' Laughter.

'How did you all meet?' Nina asked when there was a break in the conversation.

'I was buying the *Herald Tribune* in my atrocious Italian,' said Linda, 'and Cynthia laughed at me.'

'I couldn't help it! You were just so funny! You were trying to give him enough money to buy his whole newsstand and he didn't want to take it!'

'Do you have Italian friends?' Nina asked.

'Of course! Friends of my husband, and their wives, but – '

'I don't consider myself close to any Italian women I've met,' put in Lorna.

'I have Gianna but I rarely see her. It's evidently not the thing for Italian women to meet for lunch and at night they are with their husbands or with their man of the moment. They still cancel something with a woman if a man comes along and invites them afterwards,' said Cynthia.

'I think,' began Linda, 'that women's lib is such a new thing here that there is an enormous difference in the way we American women think . . .'

'It really seems to be gaining inspiration from the American movement, though.'

'I agree completely with that,' nodded Cynthia. 'But I was talking to Gianna who is a lawyer here, believe it or not, and she said one of the things that is affecting it is this rush of southern Italians taking over a lot of the jobs. This migration from the south to the north – to Rome, to Milano – is incredible.'

'And we all know, economics is the name of the game when it comes to liberation.'

'That, and education,' said Brenda.

'Yes,' put in Linda. 'You have to be educated before you enter the job market.'

'Well, I think women here are miles behind American women in their thinking,' insisted Lorna. 'There is no spirit of sisterhood and that is because it is so important that they have a male to take care of them.'

'Yes.' Brenda poured more wine. 'I saw an amazing fight between two women at a party over the weekend. The flirting can get nasty.'

'But they're on the Pill, the birth rate is going down and there is divorce. It's all changing and changing fast,' said Lorna.

'But sisterhood – what a word!' said Linda, who'd had quite a bit of wine. 'What if all the women in Italy decided to stop spoiling their sons so that their daughters could have nice men to marry so that – '

'It does start with these mothers. I couldn't believe my mother-in-law was for real. She used to call Giorgio at his office six times a day. When we moved into an apartment of our own she'd call in the morning and ask me to make sure he was dressed warmly and did he have his raincoat because the sky looked grey . . .'

'My husband didn't like his mother and when she died he was right there at the hospital bed along with his sister and his father and she ignored everyone but him.' She rolled her eyes heavenward. 'The only precious son. He nearly had a nervous breakdown that year. Guilt.'

'They spend their entire lives taking care of their husbands and sons and when the son gets married, woe to the daughter-in-law.'

Nina realized she wasn't alone in a morass of problems. They were general problems. Maybe I can put it all into perspective, she thought. 'I don't know what my mother-in-law does all day,' she murmured.

'Mine takes hours shopping. You know how you go to the butcher for meat and you stand and gossip and then to the wine store and you stand and wait and chatter and then to the bakery and then to the store for pasta . . . ooooooh!'

'I'd give my life for a station wagon and a good old A&P!' cried Cynthia in her mid-western twang.

'Well, in New York I never had a car so that isn't it with me. It's just the time everything takes. Have you been to the bank lately?' She groaned. 'Four men have to go over five pieces of paper to cash a cheque. You wait in one line for a receipt and then you wait in the cashier's line for the money. I was in the Banco di Santo Spirito for an hour and a half yesterday.' Someone laughed. 'Where but in Italy would you find a bank named after the Holy Ghost?'

Nina couldn't imagine the Contessa shopping or in a bank. Dante must do the banking unless of course she'd arranged for someone to come to the house! 'I don't think my mother-in-law has any friends,' Nina said, thinking aloud.

'I don't think Italian women are friends the way we are. I really don't.'

'Oh, come on. Maybe that isn't fair. We don't know for sure.'

'I think it's the competition for male attention that is still so rampant,' insisted Brenda.

'Well, speaking of male attention, I, for one thank the militant feminists for what they've done about it.'

'What do you mean?'

'I mean that I haven't been pinched for ages and that is all because of the women's movement in this country.'

Brenda laughed. 'Is it true what I heard?'

'What did you hear? That bands of young women are roaming the streets pinching men and grabbing them by the you-know-what?' The table rocked with laughter. 'That's exactly what I heard!'

Each woman tossed a few thousand lire into the pile beside the last empty carafe and Pietro pocketed it with a big smile. Then he rushed from one to the other helping with chairs and shopping bags. Out on the street they scribbled phone numbers on scraps of paper and thrust them at Nina. Cynthia took Nina's arm. 'Oh, you are so young. I hope we didn't horrify you. We're all such jaded old birds. We'll be at Toto's next Wednesday as usual.'

Linda was laughing at Lorna who had four enormous shopping bags. Two from Gucci, one from Fendi and one from Giorgio Armani. 'The weight is cutting off the circulation in her wrists!'

'This is why I stay married, Nina!' grinned Lorna. 'I'm paid well. I spent three million lire today and I wasn't even trying!'

Brenda laughed. 'Oh, you must make him happy! Since he doesn't pay taxes . . .' They all laughed, standing in a circle in the cobblestoned street. It was empty for it was not yet four and the mezzogiorno was still upon the city. 'Only person I know who launders money on the via Condotti!' teased Brenda. Nina left them there, all shouting '*Ciao!*' pledging to call tomorrow, Cynthia promising a new plumber to Linda, and Brenda exhorting Lorna to go to Florence 'and do it!' Five minutes later they had disbanded, for a last errand 'if the shop opens at four', to pick up *Time* magazine at the newsstand, and then to Piazza di Spagna for a taxi home to an Italian husband.

*

469

Nina didn't go to Toto's the following Wednesday. She tucked all the phone numbers in her jewellery box and wondered if she were glad that she hadn't given out her own. The Contessa had swatches for her to choose from for summer dresses, and the two of them spent a few hours going through magazines and drinking lemonade together.

'I like this one,' said her mother-in-law, holding up a photograph of an Empire dress from the Italian *Vogue*. 'You'll get bigger of course but you could hide the bambino for quite a while!' They decided on eight dresses and then the Contessa asked, 'Has Claudio talked to you about where you're going?'

'No. He hasn't said a word.' For weeks, is what she didn't add.

'You are welcome to come with me and the Count to Porto Santo Stefano, of course. The villa is pretty and high up and overlooks the sea. But' – she pursed her lips – 'you might get awfully bored having no young people around.'

'Couldn't I just stay here?'

'Oh no! Why, no one stays in Rome! It's hot and deserted. All the shops will close. It's out of the question. Why, even Franco and Maria will come with us to the villa.' She wrote something down in her notebook on her lap. 'I think perhaps you should go with Claudio on the boat. It will be lazy days of sunning and swimming and you liked that before, didn't you?' Nina didn't answer. 'It'll relax you both.' She closed the Papiro notebook and breathed, 'There. That's decided. And perfectly all right on the boat to wear a bikini these days and to live in a piraea the way you did before. I think it's a splendid idea.'

Well, what are my alternatives? Nina asked herself that evening before dinner. I can't even mention the idea of going to the States, for the goose about to lay the golden egg might fly the coop. Can't stay in Rome and, no, I don't imagine it'll be fun to be at Porto Santo Stefano with my parents-in-law. The boat. She began to slowly wash her feet in the bubble bath. I get it! She's trying to get us together again! Nina squeezed out the soapy sponge. I don't love him any more. We co-exist. Share the same cell. We don't fight because we don't care enough. And the baby in me is all that links us. And it will link us for ever, thought Nina. Claudio de Leone will be my child's father for ever. As she dressed she wondered: Should I seize the chance? Should I let the Contessa help me? Maybe it's all been leading up to this, all those conferences in her room. Maybe I'm the last to know that this is the best thing. I don't love him any more but there is the marriage. She smiled bleakly at her image in the mirror. How Italian I sound. She put on lipstick and sprayed on perfume then walked with a sense of purpose towards the salon for a glass of wine before dinner.

They were all there that evening. Nonno in one of his too-big but very expensive-looking suits, cousin Elena in a yellow silk dress with a flounce around the hem. Nina hated herself for being reminded of a circus elephant wearing a frill. La Contessa wore a pale blue linen dress with a low neckline and a sapphire and diamond necklace. Nina was experimenting with wearing such jewellery and had decided on the simplest diamond earrings with a pink and white printed silk dress. The Contessa had advised her to attract attention away from her fuller figure towards her face with low necklines and pretty earrings and she thought the advice was good, and followed it. Claudio rushed in as they were sitting down at the table, with apologies, with a kiss for his mother's cheek and a peck on the forehead for Nina.

Two business associates then arrived with the Count and discussed politics in an animated fashion until Nonno joined in, furious at what Mussolini was doing to Italy's international reputation. The Count smoothed things over but he was tense and distracted. As fruit was being brought in, the telephone rang down the hall and he looked up anxiously; he seemed to be counting the seconds until Franco picked up the receiver. The Count assumed the posture of someone waiting to be summoned and when Franco appeared in the doorway of the dining room he was already halfway out of his chair and making his regrets. 'Dante is waiting, sir,' nodded the butler.

Whisky was served after dinner but the two men did not stay long, then Nonna and Elena went off to their rooms. Nina sipped Amaretto until she, too, felt sleepy. When she arrived in her bedroom she heard the pinging of the phone which meant someone was dialling. Thinking suddenly that tonight was the perfect chance to spend time with Claudio and how good it would be to have his mother present – who was certainly on her side – she quickly returned to the hall. She heard Claudio's voice asking about the condition of a Signorina something and then heard his voice say, '*Il bambino? Morto?*' There was silence and then '*Grazie*' and the phone was put down.

Oh, God! A baby has died, thought Nina. The Count was summoned to the hospital. She hesitated outside the double doors of the salon. Perhaps Claudio and his mother want to be alone. Then she heard the laughter, and the clinking of two glasses. 'Here's to the de Leone family!' It was the Contessa's voice. 'The legitimate one!' laughed Claudio.

Nina felt her knees tremble as she realized what had happened. The Count's baby. She put her hands over her face in horror and thought: What kind of people are they? What kind of man did I marry? Did his mother make him the way he is?

Weeks passed. It's an armed truce between two pairs of counts and countesses, thought Nina. A pack of lunatics living in the Sistine Chapel.

The emerald green linen blazer needs something. Nina critically surveyed herself in the wardrobe looking glass. Beginning to show but this hides a multitude of sins, she decided. The earrings are fine and the sun dress beneath it but . . . Nina pulled open Claudio's top drawer. A handkerchief tucked into the pocket, a touch of white, will liven this up. She looked at the stack of freshly laundered squares and wondered why any man would need several dozen all identical. She took the top one and had started to close the drawer when she glimpsed a scrap of paper underneath the pile.

472

As Nina unfolded it she was swept by an eerie sense of recognition. The thick black curves of the handwriting were strangely familiar. Nina read: 'Sarkex agrees to pay C de L one per cent of all monies transferred in his name.' There were two scrawly signatures Nina could not read and then the one that took her breath away and made her hand shake. 'O. Sarkis.' Oh! God! Claudio and Omar! Know each other! Are business partners! Or were . . . there was no date. But has Omar told Claudio he knows me? Or knew me? Nina leaned against the bureau, heart pounding. So there was probably no other woman in Switzerland. It was Omar all along. Omar told him or let him guess. Nina remembered that night in bed soon after they were married. 'I knew you were too good for an affair, for a fling, that you valued yourself too much to be a toy.' Nina's heart was beating very fast as she folded the note and tucked it back under the pile of handkerchiefs. I used to tuck notes into my father's handkerchiefs, she thought absurdly. It isn't fair! she wanted to scream. Omar was so long ago! But Claudio is so proud. He couldn't have borne the truth. No wonder I couldn't smooth things over. I didn't have a chance. He hated the sight of me after that certain trip to Switzerland. It was after the brawl about the radio, but before Christmas. That's why he couldn't seem to get over that fight. 'It is so Italian!' she shouted aloud, slamming the drawer shut. She walked back into her room and sat down heavily on the little daybed. It isn't fair! But it doesn't matter, she decided looking down at the curve of her belly. It's too late. It doesn't change a thing.


The boat was a mistake. Nina felt all the muscles in her body tense as she lay in the sun. Relax, she told herself, everyone knows. It's not as if Patrizia and Enrico and Carla and Gianni are talking about me. They know. They know Claudio and I aren't getting along. It's obvious I'm pregnant and it's obvious we don't speak unless it's to say 'scusi' when we pass. And of course I would look like a hippopotamus and I would have some sort of rash on my hands which is so outstandingly attractive. Relax, she told herself again. The sun is warm and the boat is so soothing rocking back and forth, back and forth, back and forth. Nina bolted up from the towel and raced to the railing where she was sick quite noisily. Patrizia raised her eyebrows; Claudio looked disgusted. Nina went below, considering a slow breaststroke to Sicily.

Capri was Nina's favourite island; land of geraniums she called it, for the narrow winding streets were bedecked with them. Window sills were filled and even the elegant shops often had a few pots of the flowers on either side of their doorways. Long a haunt of intellectuals and the movie crowd, it was crowded with everyone in the summer. Elsa Martinelli, the actress, shared their table sometimes at the disco Number Two; Gianni Agnelli, the head of Fiat, often ate at La Capannina; Valentino had his favourite place in the Piazzetta; Gianni Versace had greeted Claudio in front of the clock tower. It was a village of Italians who knew each other, of Caprese who endured the annual invasion good-naturedly and of foreigners who arrived and saw only the sun and the sea and the surface of the life.

This afternoon was spent browsing up and down the hill from the Hotel Quisisana to the Piazzetta. The little piazza had been aptly nicknamed Capri's living room and was filled with tables and chairs and people watching people while being watched. Young waiters in white shirts wriggled through the crowds with trays held overhead to deliver this coffee, that *spremuta* to that postage stamp of a table. The round ones had their blowing tablecloths held in place by giant embroidery hoops. The women were dressed as Nina and Patrizia and Carla were. They wore bikinis with piraeas slung low over narrow hips with masses of gold jewellery around necks and around wrists and hung from ears. Faces behind giant sunglasses were adorned with only eye make-up and a touch of pale lipstick. Nina's wide-brimmed hat of hot pink straw matched her nail polish and the pink and white piraea she'd knotted high under her arms. A delicate silver chain necklace matched her silver love-knot earrings.

She felt much better today and joked with Enrico about an outrageous gold lamé bikini in a shop window and challenged Carla to a backgammon game with dinner as the stake. Claudio, gloomily handsome, silently stared across the piazza as new people came up from the *funiculare*, the cable car linking the port a hundred metres down the cliff. Suntanned bodies were arriving from the beach by bus and in the taxis which were old American convertibles – brightly coloured, highly polished, in mint condition. Nina thought they looked as though they'd been driven off the set of a Rita Hayworth film. Claudio's face was impassive behind the designer sunglasses. He wore a white shirt of thin Egyptian cotton open nearly to the waist of his white linen trousers. Espadrilles of faded blue were on his feet. The gold signet ring caught the sun and shone on his darkly tanned hand.

At six they returned to the boat to shower and change for dinner. Nina pulled on a silver strapless dress which showed off her full breasts. 'I'm getting well endowed if nothing else out of this,' she remarked to Claudio, who grunted. It didn't bother her tonight for some reason. Maybe it was Capri, maybe it was that she felt hungry after two days of losing everything she ate, maybe it was something about the baby growing inside her. That morning she had lain beside a sleeping Claudio and felt the baby move. She had laughed delightedly and put her palm against her rounded stomach and with tears of joy in her eyes decided: It's going to be worth it. You're going to have a good life. 'I promise,' she whispered in the still cabin.

Dinner at La Palma had taken hours but Nina had relaxed in her chair and gazed up at the darkening sky and felt happy. She often thought of what Kate had said sarcastically so long ago at lunch: 'Well, I feel sorry for you!' I don't feel sorry for me, Nina had decided. When the baby is born I will be a good mother and then when I feel ready I will try again to get a job as a decorator. The Contessa wants me to be happy and if she gave me all that jewellery she doesn't expect me to vanish into the sunset, or more likely, get on a plane for the States the minute the hospital lets me out of bed. She'll bring Claudio around. Nina glanced at his face.

But then, perhaps he no longer cares what I do. How convenient. The Italian chatter continued. Nina ordered chocolate soufflé and she and Enrico split his vanilla one and hers with great groans of delight.

Afterwards, they decided to see what Pentothal was like and walked down the hill to the disco. Music pounded as the door was opened. Nina took Claudio's arm and smiled at him. He tried to smile back and succeeded in looking uncomfortable, even surly. I don't care, thought Nina. I love my dress, I love my diamond earrings, I love my silver shoes with heels as high as they can be. She thought of Myra so long ago at Briarcliff. She would have called them 'fuck-me' shoes. I feel sexy and I love the music and Gianni will dance with me even if Claudio looks as if he's coming down with a headache every time I look at him. Her husband excused himself the moment they had seated themselves at two adjoining tables and Nina watched him disappear into the dark. She said to herself: Bad-tempered, spoiled brat, and resisted the very strong urge to stick out her tongue. The strobe lights blinked and the dancers moved jerkily like figures in old movies. Everything white became blue-white and everything shiny shone like stars. Nina listened to the others talking about a group of Romans they knew who had come in after them and it was then that she saw Claudio. He was across the room on the other side of the dance floor in the arms of a woman with waist-length blonde hair. It was tawny and tumbled down her bare back. Claudio was kissing her and the kiss didn't stop as Nina watched. A mirrored ceiling globe turned slowly, spattering the crowd with thousands of little lights like sequins on a bullfighter's suit. The music pulsed on and still Claudio kissed her.

Nina rose and, clutching the silver heart evening bag, walked carefully up the steps, past one tier of tables after another, past giggling girls, past laughing men, past everyone. I need oxygen. I need to take a deep breath was all she could think as she pushed her way past couples in the narrow hallway towards the front door. Claudio had seen her silver dress give off a last shimmer as she turned into the corridor and now he ran interference through the patrons to reach her. She sprinted the last few steps, someone opened the door for her and in seconds she was out on the street gulping the clear night air. The tears of rage were blinding. When she felt his hand on her arm she cried out and recoiled. She wrenched away from his grasp thinking: Don't touch me, don't keep me, let me go. The spindly heel of one elegant silver pump caught between the paving stones and with a cry of surprise Nina fell face downward. At the moment of impact her life was for ever changed.

It might have been the smell of disinfectant that wakened her or the feeling that her fingers were frozen, had been dipped in ice water. She opened her eyes and realized she was in a white room in a white bed and that Claudio was standing over her. Without the riding crop this time, she thought sourly. His face was sunburned, handsome, tired. He still wore the white linen blazer but there was a dark smear of grease on the left sleeve, perhaps from helping with the stretcher. His blue eyes glistened with moisture. 'You got your wish.'

'No,' said Nina softly. She realized there was a smear of scarlet lipstick on his mouth. 'I don't have the strength for any wishes any more.'

# 10

'My ears kept ringing with the words, "it's over it's over it's over".' Nina sounded very tired on the telephone.

'But what about a hospital. Is there a decent one on that little island?' Adele's voice held an edge of hysteria.

'An Arab that we'd had dinner with a couple of times had his boat there and it just so happened to be equipped with his own personal helicopter. Monogrammed no less . . .'

'But – '

'I remember this tiny ambulance. It was literally a yard wide so that it could manœuvre the streets of Capri. Part of that time I was awake and I could see Claudio's face . . .' Tears rolled down her cheeks unheeded now. 'So I went from a doll's ambulance to a little motor boat out to the Arab's yacht then into the helicopter and then Naples and an ambulance to a hospital. I think I slept after that. I woke up in bed and Claudio was there. He cried on my feet. We barely spoke and then he cried. He had his face and hands bent down over my ankles. I had such a mean thought then. It's too late to kiss my feet, went through my mind. I've done everything I can to make you want me, to make you keep loving me and it's over . . .'

Adele thought: Oh, poor Nina! And it ended with Omar, too, with a baby. 'Nina, is it really over?' Adele remembered the Claudio and the Nina of their wedding day.

'I haven't told you a lot of things, Adele. Just because . . .' Nina sighed and swung her stockinged feet under her on the couch. 'Because I didn't know how to write them. And maybe because I thought I could work them out and that if you knew all that had happened and I did sort it out then you wouldn't have been able to ever like Claudio again.' Silence. 'I didn't want to give up.' Or I wasn't allowed to. Some day I'll tell Adele everything.

'Nina!' Adele's voice was pleading. 'What has Claudio done?'

Nina thought: Loyal faithful Adele. She reacted exactly as I thought she would. 'Maybe he hasn't really "done" a thing except behave the way he was programmed to behave with a mother and a father like the ones he has. I mean, the Count plays around and . . .'

'How do you know that?' Adele thought: It's a terribly emotional time to make big decisions. Right after losing a baby is not the time to decide things.

'Because his mistress got pregnant and the baby was born dead and I overheard Claudio and his mother celebrating.' Nina was as matter of fact as someone reading a grocery list.

'My God!' Adele breathed. 'So Claudio was unfaithful to you?' she asked at last.

'*Certo.*'

'But it's not fair!' shouted Adele from her apartment in New York. 'You loved him and I know you – you were good to him! And you are beautiful and you are interesting and you were going to have his baby! Why did – '

'I didn't want the baby, Adele.' She heard the gasp from four thousand miles away. 'I wanted a divorce and then I was told I was pregnant, and I wanted an abortion. Claudio said it was impossible. He would never sign the papers for the abortion.' Adele was thinking: All this is so new. All this time I thought of Nina as happy and looking forward to the child. Nina swallowed. 'But I changed. I began to want the baby. The morning that . . . the morning of the . . . the accident' – she took a deep breath – 'I felt the baby move inside me and I wanted it.' She began to cry. 'I made promises to it. I promised it would have a good life. I promised . . .' She couldn't go on. Adele was without words. Too much was swirling over the telephone line. 'It changed me. Maybe for the first time I was willing to – no, had to is more like it – take care of something, someone not as strong as I am. Maybe that was the only really unselfish moment I've ever experienced.'

'That's not true!' Adele was adamant. 'You of all people to say that! You love so unselfishly when you do love . . .'

She thought of Omar, she thought of Claudio, she thought of the way Nina was with her.

'The Countess said something to me before I came to Rome, before I ever met Claudio. It was in relation to Omar but awful as it is, maybe it could be applied to my Roman husband, too.' Nina stretched her legs out on the coffee table. 'She said that a person might pick someone to love them as a challenge because something inside that person was missing.'

'I don't understand.'

'I liked the idea that someone as handsome as Claudio, as worldly, as well educated, would pick me to love.'

'Normal. Obvious,' pronounced common-sense Adele.

'But I didn't see that he is not a person who would love me. Who would be loyal to me. I can see this now. It was apparent. I knew when we were going out there were other women, even when we were sleeping together.' She thought of the Cafe de Paris that autumn afternoon.

'But – '

'But all the rest of Claudio was too wonderful, made me feel too wonderful to see beyond this façade of great dinners, and the polo games and being on his arm at parties.'

'I still don't understand.'

'I picked someone to make me feel like someone! To make me feel wonderful! And I thought being well dressed and fun and loving him would be enough. I neglected to notice that he really isn't capable of love! Oh, he loved me, in his way, but there wasn't enough love to keep him from turning to other women, not enough love to trust me with his business secrets, not enough love to come to me and talk, to confide his feelings.'

Adele was confused. 'You are saying that being with Claudio, being his wife, was something you subconsciously wanted or needed to make you feel good about yourself?'

'Maybe, Adele. I don't know. I do know that when I was with him I was someone. And with the wedding ring I was the young Contessa with a place in a palazzo. I automatically belonged somewhere. It was so easy in a way. Like buttoning a warm coat. I didn't marry Claudio to be a contessa and I

know I certainly didn't marry him for his money but . . .'
Nina reached for the glass of white wine. The clock Adele
had given her so long ago said half past three. The night was
black outside the terrace glass doors.

'Look, Claudio is a terribly attractive man, and he did love
you and he wanted you as his wife. You loved him and
married him. No matter what psychology the Countess fed
you, I think some of the problems were simple differences in
expectations between an American woman and a Latin
male.'

'You sound so much like Kate. Or she sounds like you.
She says different expectations can finish off a marriage as
quickly as infidelity. It just doesn't sound so dramatic.'

'I think Kate's right. But what did you mean a minute ago
when you said Claudio didn't love you enough to trust you?'

'Oh, Adele! So much has happened!' She despaired of
telling it all. 'I found out that Claudio and Omar are
business partners and that – '

'Omar!' Adele thought she'd heard the last of the Leb.

'Yes! I found something in a drawer. Claudio was putting
money in bank accounts for Sarkex, Omar's company . . .'

'Laundering money?'

'Maybe that was it. I didn't understand. But that makes as
much sense as anything. Claudio and his father used to have
incredible screaming matches over money and then they
stopped. Claudio spent more and more time in Switzerland
and then I found this paper in his bureau.'

'But how did they even know each other? Isn't this the
most insane coincidence in the world?'

'I realize they went to the same schools in Switzerland.
And they both play polo. That's a sort of international club.
You know they are remarkably alike. Lots of schools, lots of
money, and both expected the wife to sit at home and
produce their heirs . . . but it's more than that.'

'How could it be more than that?'

'I think Omar told Claudio about me or allowed him to
guess or maybe I misjudged him and he tried not to let
Claudio know. It doesn't matter now.' She twirled the wine
glass stem between her fingers and watched the little waves

481

of liquid almost splash over the top. Oscar Wilde always used to call white wine 'yellow'. An image of Claridge's, of Omar's suite, flashed into her mind. 'I don't think Claudio could stand the idea that I'd had an affair with Omar. I think he was too proud to accept it.'

'But that was so long ago!' insisted Adele.

'But Claudio wouldn't think seventy-five years was long enough ago. He told me once that he'd got everything he'd ever wanted and I was something he wanted.' There was a pause. 'I had the uncomfortable feeling that I fell under the category of "possession".'

'Did you ever talk about Omar?'

'No. I didn't find the note, the memo, until the beginning of this summer. It was too late. I honestly don't know if it would have changed things between us to talk. Even if we'd been able to scream and break a few priceless antiques and then make up . . .' Nina shook her head. 'No. You see, Claudio thought of me as his. He wouldn't have been able to consider that I might have fallen in love with someone else, might have even been hurt. He was angry. And seeing Omar every other week, having to be reminded, didn't help either.'

'It's back to "you are my possession" time,' said Adele coldly. 'Paul made me feel that. And speaking of time, how I spent my days somehow reflected on him. He didn't want me to study. He wanted me to sit in that barn in Tarrytown. He wanted to control me and what I did. And what better way than to exile a city person to the suburbs?'

Nina laughed and thought: When did I last laugh? 'I was thinking of Elba but I guess anyone can be exiled anywhere. My mother-in-law has exiled herself in the palazzo. No interests. No friends. Two sisters in Milano who came to Rome without their husbands – to play around, according to Maria, the maid. She would tell me little titbits when the Contessa and I were on really strained terms, but when I got pregnant and things became better, she turned off all info. Afraid I'd repeat it, I suppose.'

'Nina! It's almost four in the morning there! Aren't you afraid someone will hear you on the telephone?'

'No. I have complete privacy at last. I'm at via dei Greci.'

Adele was speechless. 'The Count and I talked yesterday in the car on the way back from Naples and the annulment shouldn't take more than three months.'

'It's really over, then?'

Nina nodded, looking at the still-unpacked suitcases in the hallway. '*Finito*. It never happened.' Though a settlement would be worked out and Nina had been given a generous cheque already. Annulled. Null and void, like sending in your cornflakes box top past the deadline. 'You know, Adele, I never did become a Catholic.'

'How did you escape that?'

'Your Episcopalian upbringing is showing!'

'Don't tell me those priests just forgot about the new Countess of the Lion!'

'No. I told Claudio I wasn't keen on it and he said to talk to his father. I told the Count the same thing. The children – ' Her voice cracked. God. There'd been so much blood. She'd left pools of it on the black rubber floor of the helicopter. And the stretcher . . . mustn't remember. Nina cleared her throat. 'I told the Count I didn't object to the children being brought up as Catholics. Italy is a Catholic country, their schools would be, their friends would be, and if they're twelve and scream they've had enough . . .' She shrugged. 'I liked the Count. He must've . . . taken care of it.'

'Oh, Italy!' laughed Adele. 'But why don't you come back to New York? Why don't you?'

'Because I want to sort things out. I don't want people to ask what happened and I don't want anyone to feel sorry for me . . .' Nina realized she was crying again. I feel sorry enough for myself, she thought. Sorry enough for forty-five sympathetic people.

'Nina, are you sure you want to stay over there? I know how different everything is when you're suddenly on your own again after being married. I know that New York City is a familiar place and that that made it all so much easier . . .'

Nina held her breath until she could speak. Tears were clogging her throat. She nodded as though getting ready to recite her lines. 'Yes. I'm going to stay for a while. I'm going to try to get my old job back. I have to pull myself together for an interview.' She put her hand quickly over the receiver so that Adele could not hear her gasps.

Adele thought: One more time. 'Are you sure you want to stay in Rome? If you don't, I can have five realtors on the phone within minutes. I can ask the Countess . . . I saw her last week and she told me that Tad had got married.'

Nina had a sad feeling then. A feeling of being left. 'I hope she's wonderful to him.'

'Evidently she's from Virginia, with dark hair and looks a little bit like you!' Adele went on, 'The Countess had drinks with him and he told her the strangest thing . . .'

'What?'

'He told her that he got on a plane the night before your wedding and flew to Rome and stood in the back of the church. He said it was the only way he could get you out of his mind once and for all.'

'Oh, how awful! I didn't see him . . .'

'No! That was just it. No one did. He just – ' Adele stopped. 'But are you sure you don't want to come back to New York?'

'I'm sure. If if if I get the radio job back then I can start a new life here.'

'Your Italian is so good now. Why aren't you trying to get a decorating job?'

Nina wiped her nose. 'It's not that good, Adele. I don't feel quite up to selling myself. So much of that job is pleasant conversation and convincing people and I feel a little shaky. The radio would give me a place to go every day and some money and I did like it before. It's temporary, I know that. Decorating is my real love.'

'Will you call me right away if you change your mind about coming back here?'

'You'll be the first to know.'

There was silence between Park Avenue and via dei Greci. 'Nina, I have to tell you something.' Adele wondered if she should. 'You've been my best friend ever since I met you and I . . . I am ashamed . . . but sometimes I've been jealous of you.' Nina laughed and then held her nose with a

Kleenex pinched over it. 'Men adore you. And you radiate something that *everyone* wants to be near . . .'

'Stop!' Nina took a great gulp of air. She had to speak. 'I've always been jealous of *you*. Always. If not flat-out, green-eyed jealous then I have envied – what a terrible word! – what you have, what you are.'

Adele was dumbfounded. 'What! What I am?'

'You belong somewhere on this earth and right now, more than ever maybe, I'm not sure I belong anywhere. But you have always known it. Why, you'd be the little girl who twirled round and round in circles with your arms out and when everyone stopped and was dizzy, you'd be the only one not to fall down in the grass.'

'But don't you see?' cried Adele. 'Because you are not sure of this, you have always had to be braver. And it makes you stronger.' Mickey Keeling came into Nina's mind, unbidden. 'It's your bravery that makes you what you are. It must be that in you that attracts people. It must be that as much as anything that makes me jealous.'

'Oh, Adele!' Nina wept. 'I don't feel very brave sometimes!'

'But you are!' her friend insisted. 'You know you are. I know you are.'

At last, at quarter past four, each woman hung up her telephone. Then the two of them, best friends since the day they'd met, stared at their respective pieces of the night sky. Adele thought: It must be nearly dawn in Italy. Doesn't Nina understand that her courage means she belongs anywhere she chooses!

Nina looked out at the stars hanging over the silent city. I must not ever allow myself to think that Omar broke up my marriage. That's not true. It's too simple. That's being too easy on myself. She thought of Claudio in the big bed with the green canopy, she thought of the palazzo full of shadows at this hour, and then she crossed her arms over her stomach and thought of her baby who would not be born. A fingernail moon low in the early morning sky would soon be melted by the heat of the August sun. Nina contemplated the stars, making no sense of anything, until her tears

485

doubled and trebled every point of light, until the vista became a cracked kaleidoscope.


A man with a cigar paced back and forth in front of the long expanse of glass which overlooked the East River. It's a grey day, a grey river, and it matches my mood, he thought. He reached for the phone on his desk. 'Sally, would you get Gaston on the line for me. Yes, try the Nice number first. Then the Paris office.' He replaced the receiver and waited, striking a match from a book that said, le Cygne, and relighting the Cuban cigar carefully.

'Yes, Gaston. Funny connection. Can you hear me? Listen, I want you to do some leg work.' Pause. 'Sooner the better.' He puffed on the cigar and listened. 'She's American, about twenty-five years old and she's in Rome. Can you find her for me?' As he listened he blew a smoke ring over his head. 'Oh, yes, her name's Nina McLean.'

Two days later Gaston called back. 'It wasn't difficult. She's registered with the police for some sort of residency permit and they have her address.' He switched the phone from one ear to another.

'What is she doing there? Do you know anything about her life?' came the questions from New York.

'She evidently married a Roman count but the marriage is being annulled. She has a small apartment in a very chic area near Piazza di Spagna. It has a terrace, is my guess from the street.'

'Where are you now?'

'I'm back in Paris.'

'Don't you think it'd be nice if she had a job?'

'What are you up to?' asked Gaston. One minute, gold, then buying all that silver, then the tin mines that were turning out so well. Awfully well. Gaston raised his eyebrows and waited.

'Do you remember when you tried to get me interested in a vineyard deal and I said no, too slow?'

'I remember it well.'

'What do you know about vineyards in Tuscany?'

486

Gaston laughed delightedly, for it was this kind of project that excited him. 'In a week I can find out everything!'

'Okay, call me back as soon as you've found one for me to buy. I want some kind of a house on it. A house to live in. Doesn't matter how run down it is. Just as long as it's no more than three hours' drive from Rome and has possibilities.'

Gaston said something in French to himself and then repeated, 'Aaaaah, possibilities! I like that! Where will you be one week from today?'

The man in the grey suit glanced down at his open appointment book. 'I'll be in Geneva. The Ortega people are letting me use an office of theirs for a few days. You have that number.' He pencilled in 'Gaston re: Tuscany' and then concluded the call.


Pauline and Benjamin, Nina's neighbours, had returned to Harvard just after Nina's wedding. A taciturn German woman with an eyepatch and a poodle lived in their flat now. Solveig was modelling in Milano. Her apartment was empty but the little Swedish flag was still taped to her door. For Lesley and Rita it was no place to live; it was no money and the sudden realization that they weren't even slightly in love with the men who took them to dinner. Lesley had gone to India on a charter flight that left Fiumicino in the middle of the night. She planned to spend six months with a yogi in a tiny village outside Calcutta studying yoga, and then to make her way home to Australia to give classes in Eastern philosophy. Rita had left a few weeks later, deciding that it was time to stop playing, as she put it, and to go back to London and 'real life'.

But the person Nina missed most, indeed needed most, was Kate. Her postcard hurriedly scrawled then mailed from Fiumicino had read: 'Mother had a stroke two days ago. Off to New Canaan for as long as I'm needed. Hope your summer is wonderful. much love, K.' Nina had held it in her hand for several minutes after Franco had given it to her, after Dante had deposited her bags inside the apartment.

The letter from Nina's own mother was exuberant about 'my little Italian grandbaby'. Nina would not call her, not yet, and she knew Virginia would not try to reach her at the palazzo either. A call from Mississippi to Italy connoted an emergency.

I'll get on with life, thought Nina. Life in small letters. I'll pretend I'm someone else, she said to herself as she stood surrounded by open suitcases, and I'll imagine what someone else would do. She reached for a blue striped silk scarf and refolded it carefully. A beginning. I won't consider life in capitals yet; I'll concentrate on the business of maintenance until I'm stronger.

Nina took morning walks and afternoon naps as the doctor had advised. At five she strolled to Piazza di Spagna to see if the *Herald Tribune* had arrived. One morning she very deliberately sorted her clothes. The next morning it was her jewellery and her cosmetics. One evening she put on blue jeans, rubber gloves, and the radio, and scrubbed every inch of the apartment.

It's not easy, she thought in the Villa Borghese. An ocean of schoolchildren was meandering home for lunch in dark blue smocks and white knee socks, chattering like birds, holding hands. Nina stared at their shining hair, their faces, the way they wore their little book bags like parachutes. She swallowed hard. Nina often turned away from a newborn in a coffee bar or at the *giornalaio*, as often as not in the arms of a proud moustached father. Customers in a shop would ooh and aah over the pink face and the tiny perfect fingers showing at the edge of a snow-white crotcheted blanket. Nina told herself not to think too much when she tasted tears in her throat. There will be another baby for me. Some day.

The Contessa telephoned to ask how she was and they had talked, in a very friendly normal way, Nina thought later, about Nina's health and then about her plans.

'Yes, I'm staying in Rome,' Nina said. 'After all, I do love Italy.' And I did love Rome before I loved your son, was what she didn't say. The Contessa was surprised that she wasn't going back to the States but had been very gracious in inviting her to call if she needed anything, 'anything at all'. Nina replaced the receiver with a smile. She is human. But how funny that she didn't mention the Count or the annulment. Suppose she thinks that is being taken care of and, in a way, is between her husband and me.

Exactly a week after the Contessa's call, as Nina was considering whether to call back and ask that Maria pack the rest of her things, the flowers began to arrive. Pink roses in white tissue paper were left with Signora Cadlolo on a Tuesday, then white roses in green tissue paper on Thursday, and then violets wrapped in silver foil beside her apartment door the following Monday. A heavy white card was tucked in each bouquet. '*Ti amo ancora*' was scrawled in Claudio's dark blue ink.

Nina filled the smallest wine carafe in the kitchen sink and, to her surprise, wept. She almost tenderly tucked the pale green stems in the narrow-necked bottle as tears raced down her face. 'I love you still,' she said aloud cynically. Adele would tell me not to be surprised, that no one would want to let me get away because I'm so wonderful. That's what Adele would say. And Kate would say – Nina blew her nose on a paper towel – Kate would say, I didn't think it would work and you tried and now it's over. Nina took the flowers into the living room and put them on the coffee table. The phone rang and she picked it up, quickly computing the time change between Rome and New York, anxious to talk to either Adele or Kate.

'Nina? Nina? Are you there?' The deep voice was a jolt. She didn't answer. 'Nina! I want to talk to you. *Per favore.* Are you there?'

She could only manage one pleading syllable before hanging up.

'No.'

'But don't you understand? Nina! You have power! You're not pregnant and you're not in the palazzo. You have the power, at last, to say "no" and mean it!' Kate was adamant. She stood in her parents' bright yellow kitchen in Connecticut and sighed into the receiver of the wall phone. The flowers, the notes written by Claudio who supposedly never so much as wrote down a telephone number. *'Ti amo ancora'* every day of the week now. Nina is being worn down and I can't help her. If only Bill had been able to have dinner with her his last night in Rome! But no, the fates had given him one final meeting to clear up affairs before the transfer took effect. Back to good old New York. The Middletons had had a love/hate relationship with the Eternal Città for two years and then Mrs Chase's stroke and a week later word of Bill's new position. While Nina lay in a Neapolitan hospital bed. When she needed me most. Kate listened to the faraway voice, trying to reason things out.

'What if, just what if, Kate, all this is a turning point and the person I married is still there, does exist, and the Claudio I wanted wants me enough to change?'

'Nina,' Kate said slowly. 'It's almost Christmas and you haven't been able to get a job. I think you should think about coming home.'

Home? Where is that? thought Nina. Ninetieth Street is no more and Mississippi is certainly not home . . .

'Look, except for the new exercise class, you're alone all the time.'

That's true, agreed Nina. She did sometimes have a coffee after class with two English girls but she never allowed them to become confidantes. They accepted her simple 'I was married to an Italian but it's over.' There were no invitations or telephone calls from any of the Italian women in Claudio's circle and she rejected invitations extended by Italian males for they usually knew Claudio, and sometimes the story of her marriage to him, too. And as for her story, if questioned she never said anything other than 'It was very disappointing. I don't discuss it.' Nina spent one evening with Mario but it became a hand-holding session at an upstairs corner table of Da Luigi's and the waiters had hovered, looking concerned and wondering if they should offer handkerchiefs.

Kate hesitated but couldn't stop herself. 'I don't think you should go back to him.'

'I didn't say I was.' Nina's voice was clear. 'I said I was thinking of seeing him.'

Kate remembered how tall Claudio was, how striking were his good looks, how attractive his laugh. Damn it. Nina doesn't have a chance.

'He is my husband, after all. Or he was. Or he almost was. Bad grammar.'

'The kind of husband you want?' Kate frowned and twisted the curly yellow cord in her fingers. 'Nina, I'm sorry. I just can't tell you what you want to hear. I hope we'll always be friends but I – '

'Don't worry.' Nina's voice was light, playful. 'I'm still hanging up on him!'

'Oh, Nina! Please think about coming back – '

'I will think about it. Right now all my options are open.'

This did not console her friend one bit. 'Call me any time and let me know what's happening. I'm at home in Greenwich every day except Thursday and Friday. Then I try to be here with . . . oh, I have to go now.' Her voice dropped. 'It's changing of the guard time for the nurses and Mother doesn't like this one so I want to be upstairs with her . . .'

They said goodbye then, with uneasiness in the Connecticut kitchen and dissatisfaction in the Roman living room. Nina felt Kate was totally unsympathetic towards Claudio and no help at all, and Kate thought that Nina was beyond help if she returned to her Italian husband.


Rome is full of surprises, thought Nina.

What could happen to me in Caffe Greco at half past four on a Wednesday afternoon? Nothing but good things, she decided as she pulled on a violet silk blouse and black leather trousers and scuffed her feet into black flats. The last time she'd met anyone there had been before Claudio. B.C. They had been two Moroccans who'd wanted to give her a ten per cent share in a Rafaello they were selling, which came to ten per cent of a million dollars. The catch was they wanted her to take it to New York for them and it was a national treasure and the whole set-up was wildly illegal. In her haste to leave, frightened of being seen plotting with them, Nina had spilled wine all over one Moroccan's elegantly French-tailored trouser leg. Wow! construed Nina. I hope those characters are not trying to pull me in using this Gaston! I'm going to be terribly careful, she promised her reflection in the mirror as she secured her hair with a pair of black enamel combs.

Gaston was unprepared for her to be so beautiful. American and about twenty-five hardly describes this creature of bright fire crossing the crowded room, thought Gaston. He rose and took her hand, a small bow, the merest brush of his lips, not really touching her hand at all and then, 'Mademoiselle,' as he helped her with a carved oak chair upholstered in red velvet.

She flipped a black leather jacket trimmed in grey suede on to the banquette and smiled, 'Who are you, really?'

Gaston returned her direct gaze. 'I am Gaston Pibault, as I told you on the telephone.'

Nina brushed back her hair and Gaston thought how shining it was. Her eyes seemed to have a violet cast. 'Do you have anything to do with Claudio de Leone or with those lunatic Moroccans who wanted me to smuggle that painting out of Italy?'

'Mon Dieu!' whispered Gaston. He was thoroughly used to saying 'My God!' except when he thought being more French was a plus. 'Absolutely not!'

Nina was amused at his dismay. A waiter approached them with all the solemnity of an orchestra conductor and Nina asked in perfect Italian, 'May I have hot chocolate with masses of whipped cream?'

'Perchè no?' responded the waiter.

'And for me,' said Gaston, 'a glass of red wine.'

'Where are you from? Paris?' asked Nina. 'Do you like Rome? How long have you lived here? And please, who is the friend?'

'I am supposed to be finding out things about you!' he murmured. Typical American. Forthright, to say the least. 'Yes, I like Rome, but I live in Paris and sometimes in Nice.'

He stopped. 'Will you listen to me first, Mademoiselle?'

She nodded. He seems nice enough. He has kind eyes, and those microscopic hips I associate with Frenchmen. His raincoat is Burberry, she noted from the red and black plaid exposed on the red velvet banquette. His gold signet ring looks old enough to have been another generation or maybe he has simply scratched it in fistfights. Oh, panicked Nina. I wonder how good I am at assessing people. Gaston's features were fine. Almost delicate, with a longish thin nose above narrow lips and very white teeth. His blue eyes seemed without guile. Brown hair, cut short, nothing special; I might not recognize him again in a crowd, she decided. 'My phone number. I am not listed.'

He paused. 'I told you, a friend. Please don't be so alarmed.'

She stirred the chocolate. 'You know, when I first came here my Italian was so bad that I kept ordering hot chocolate with bread, because *pane* and *panna* are so similar. And I'd order beans for dessert instead of strawberries and I'd order bread with my beans instead of strawberries and cream!' She shook her head. 'I am still doing the silliest things, but the Italians are so kind I'm sure half the time I don't even realize it!'

Gaston liked her. She has a great generosity to her, he would tell his boss. 'I represent a man who wants to buy a house and a vineyard in Tuscany. The house will need to be renovated and furnished. This is where you come in.'

Nina stared at the Frenchman. 'You must explain who told you to find me.'

Gaston tightened his lips. She was fighting herself, he could tell. Her nature was exuberant and trusting. What was the English expression? 'A nature that leapt first and looked later.' And now she was trying to be careful. 'A friend. This friend has recommended you to my client, who shall remain nameless for the present.'

'Oh,' said Nina softly.

'Now, the house will be purchased within a fortnight and then, if you agree, we can drive to look it over and make plans.' He stopped. 'You will be paid, of course.'

'Of course,' she said rather hollowly. He didn't look like a white slaver but then, they never do, do they? She resisted the impulse to demand to see his shoes. You could tell so much by a man's shoes. 'I may have a job with a radio station here in Rome,' she confided. 'A newscaster is leaving and they've promised to call me. How often would I need to dash away to Tuscany?'

Gaston shrugged. He had been told to convince her, to make her trust him, to use his own judgement about making her agree. 'I don't think more than once every week because . . .'

Nina looked perplexed. 'Do you mean you will want me to supervise the workers? Because if you want that I'll have to practically live there . . .'

'No, just help me with the drawings and give me ideas of how it should be furnished. I will fly to Paris and Milan for the ordering and see that the workmen are following your instructions.'

'You only want ideas?' Nina frowned. 'It sounds so simple.'

'Ahh, it's not so simple. The man I represent wants someone who speaks Italian, someone with young ideas, someone who lives near Tuscany, and you have had interior design experience.'

It doesn't sound strange when he explains it that way. There's the Countess, of course. How many of my friends in New York knew about her and her reputation? All of them, she considered. There are a lot of people who might have given someone my name.

Gaston swallowed the last of his wine then looked at the bill and wondered if she would say 'yes' or 'no'. He considered whether to mention money again. Funny, the money didn't seem to hold any allure at all and yet, she must need a bit of money. Everyone seemed to these days. No, if she turns me down now, it's all right. I will come back to her. But if I sound too eager at this first meeting I might spoil things, make her suspicious.

'Yes,' said Nina clearly. 'Yes, I'm game.' She extended her hand and shook his small one.

'It will be very nice to work with you, Miss McLean.'

'Will you go back to Paris soon?'

'I am driving north to see some property tomorrow and then I'll fly to Paris the day after.'

'Well, thank you for the cocoa.' She stood and held her jacket in front of her, draped over one arm. 'You know how to find me. Just call. Any time.' She smiled and was gone.

He watched her thread her way between the tables, head high, black hair long and shining halfway down her back. She vanished between the shoulders of customers waiting to be seated. Gaston imagined her striding up the via Condotti looking in the shop windows and then turning left on to via Babuino for the walk home.

'*Senta!*' he called to a waiter, with the ten thousand lire note in his hand. Gaston couldn't wait to telephone Geneva. He'd place the call as soon as he reached the hotel.

'Thanks, Rob, I really appreciate this,' said Bart in a hoarse voice. He accepted his mail from the older man's outstretched hand and put the mailbox key in his bedside table drawer.

'Are you warm enough?' Rob looked down at the figure under two blankets and a duvet. The bed was obviously a sickbed, with books at the foot and a tray on the floor beside the phone. A half-drunk glass of orange juice was on the bedside table along with a box of Kleenex and a thermometer in a white case like a ballpoint pen.

Bart nodded. 'Don't know what's happening. I've never had a case of flu I couldn't shake in two days. This goes on and on . . .'

Rob picked up the three magazines on the floor and placed them on the bureau. He was in his early fifties, with brown hair flecked with grey, youthful in appearance. He was a man who appeared to be and was an excellent tennis player. Never married, always living alone, he had spent his considerable inheritance on a life filled with travel, the theatre, the symphony, the opera, and art. He wore elegant but conservative clothes and frequented the best restaurants.

This life had also been filled with loneliness, the occasional one-night stand when he could no longer deny his sexuality, and the inevitable morning after of guilt and the intense desire to forget the purely physical assignation. Things were different now.

Rob took off his Harris tweed jacket and draped it over the leather and chrome chair. He shook his head and said jokingly, 'You, who are so immaculate. Look at this! I go away for a week and you fall apart.' He began to toss clothes in the hamper, put shoes in the closet, and to crush old newspapers in the wastebasket, then he approached the bed with clean sheets and pillowcases.

'Oh, you don't have to do that,' protested Bart weakly. He was embarrassed but very grateful all the same. Rob helped him to pull on a tan robe when the bath was ready and they walked together into the bathroom. Then Rob returned to change the sheets.

Bart lowered himself into the warm water and felt the steam clear his sinuses. He almost groaned with the feeling of pleasure it gave him to breathe again through his nose. The sound of the bed being moved came to him from the adjoining room.

Rob! What would my life be without him? thought Bart for the hundredth time since their meeting at the symphony. It had started with a chance conversation during the intermission as they waited to buy champagne for the women they had escorted to the gala. Then Rob had called him at the office and asked him if he were free for lunch to talk about an investment. Bart had accepted and had arrived at Ernie's with a briefcase full of brochures and a planned speech about California real estate opportunities and tax shelters. After bullshots, Bart realized that he was with someone very like himself. An attractive man, pursued by the wrong sex; not daring to make his sexual preferences known to anyone with whom he did business or to his family or to even his closest friends. He is like me, mused Bart. He has somehow fallen between bureau drawers like a missing sock. Rob was interested in all the things Bart loved: sailing, music – why, they had probably been at half a dozen of the

496

same art gallery openings in the past year. They even had Karen Mackelson in common, for she had pursued both of them relentlessly with invitations to this ball, to that fund-raiser.

The weekend after that lunch Rob had invited Bart to his house in Carmel. A Chinese manservant prepared their meals and brought their drinks as they lounged in bathing suits on a cedar deck high over the beach. Bart had not expected to be the only guest, but within an hour was flattered and at ease. They talked, they read, they took long walks on the sand and, Bart realized, Rob was as lonely as he.

'Men without wives,' Rob said on Sunday morning.

'Yes.' Bart picked up the thought ruefully. 'Wives are confidantes, and helpmates – though I wince at that word – and allies, and accomplices.'

Rob had nodded and put down the latest John Irving hardback. 'I will always miss being married or miss what I would have liked my marriage to be.'

'Tell me,' urged Bart from his deck chair. The early morning sun was very warm on their skin, the little glass-topped table between them held two mimosas in goblets; the remains of scones, butter and strawberry jam littered two plates.

'I mean that I would have liked a wonderful marriage to someone who loved me, someone I loved very much.' He stared out at the blue sparkling sea. Gulls as white as paper soared over the wall of surf rising and falling with a roar. 'I would like children, too. But . . .' He shrugged. 'That will not be. That is not in the cards.'

Bart thought of all the women in San Francisco who would jump at the chance to be Mrs Robert Auden Cabell, who would like to be listed on every opera and symphony programme as a patron, who would like to be at his side in receiving lines.

They stared at the ocean in a companionable silence. The making love had come after the friendship, after the being in love; it had come in tandem with the respect and the trust. Neither man had ever been so happy.

*

Nina strode across the lobby of the Hassler looking to the right and to the left, past the gold velvet chairs, past the doorway that led through another large reception room and out to the terrace. At last she saw him walking towards her. 'Bart! Can't believe you're here!' She threw her arms around the tall, thin figure.

He grinned as he crushed her to him. 'I can't either! Nothing like a phone call and a credit card . . .'

Nina's eyes were shining, full of sudden emotion. 'Christmas! I don't know if I could have got through it without you . . . without this visit . . .'

'Hey!' Bart put one arm on her shoulder and steered her towards the elevator. 'You always get through everything!' Nina stepped inside the lift and nodded wordlessly. He gave her a kiss on the forehead and seeing her near tears asked gently, 'It's been a bad time, hasn't it?'

His sister nodded again and then, flipping her black hair off the shoulders of the dark green velvet suit, forced herself to smile. 'But it's getting better by the minute.'

The elevator doors slid open and they stepped out into the hotel's rooftop restaurant. The lights of Piazza di Spagna and of the arteries of via Condotti, via della Croce and via Frattina competed with the candles on each table. The skyline beyond the glass was pale, with church domes, spires and steeples laid over it as if they had been cut from black paper. 'Glorious,' decreed Bart after telling the maitre d' they'd be having a drink before dinner. 'I understand why you stay,' he said as they seated themselves at the bar.

'Glad you do. No one else does.' Nina thought of her last phone call with Kate. The last talk with Adele. The most recent one with her mother. She nodded when Bart ordered champagne and then finished, 'I don't even understand why I stay.' Bart opened his mouth to speak but Nina continued, 'Yes, I do. I think it's because of the villa in Tuscany.' She told her brother of Gaston, of the project, of the excitement she felt when she first realized she would be in charge, not under the tutelage of the Countess in New York. 'All my ideas!' she smiled. 'All the colours I want. All the flowers for the grounds are to be picked by me and all the – '

'But who is this client of yours?' interrupted Bart.

'I'm dying to know. Maybe when I see the house in January Gaston will tell me. Maybe it's a hijacker's hideaway.' She sipped the champagne. 'With his moll, Yasmin.' Bart laughed. 'When I last spoke with Gaston on the phone he told me he was not a movie star but he would not deny that he was an Arab. Maybe I'm getting close. After all, Gaston is French and it could add up. He could be a Lebanese ducking out of Beirut, or a Saudi, or a Kuwaiti – that certainly explains the money. Gaston told me there was no budget when I remembered to ask.' Nina had listed her questions beside the phone and the Frenchman had answered them all save, of course, the identity of the villa's owner.

'What do you mean? No budget?'

'I mean,' said a wide-eyed Nina, putting down the glass. 'That the sky's the limit. I can spend anything I want.'

Bart whistled softly. 'Sounds very exciting and possibly illegal. When you find out who he is, ask him if he'll cut you in.'

Nina frowned. The note in Claudio's handkerchief came into her mind. She remembered sitting on the celadon green rug of Omar's suite that rainy afternoon and reading telex after telex. Two hundred and fifty thousand pounds, again and again, being moved from this place to that, to Geneva, to be deposited to a bank in Zurich. One per cent of that was only two thousand five hundred pounds but with enough transactions . . .

'Nina, our table's ready unless you want more champagne.'

'I always want more champagne,' she responded quickly. 'But I want dinner too.' She took the last sip and then got to her feet and followed the maitre d' to their table by the window.

'The de Leone emeralds?' Bart asked as he eyed the flat collar of green stones above the scoop-necked cream silk blouse.

'My mother-in-law told me to keep them while I was

thinking about the annulment.' Nina grinned ruefully, remembering the Count as he relayed the message. Even he had been amused.

'Ha!' Bart chortled. 'She doesn't even feign altruism.'

'She's pretty straight, actually. I'm grateful for that. But a benevolent soul, no.' Then Nina remembered the lion pin and felt remorse for the snap remark. Then she remembered the toast with her son when the Count's baby had been born dead. She shuddered.

'Nina!' Bart's voice cut into her thoughts. 'Are you okay?' She nodded and opened the menu. Too much for anyone to understand. He put his hand on her arm. 'I'll listen to you. Anything you want to tell me. I know it can't have been easy – '

'I want to know what you were doing in London last night and why you have to go back tomorrow.'

Bart flashed a quick smile. 'What do they say about gift horses?'

'Oh, come on! Tell me!'

'It was a spur of the moment thing. I'm meeting a friend there tomorrow. But last night when I heard your voice and realized it was just two hours to Rome . . .'

Bart was never secretive, thought Nina. 'It's Karen, isn't it? Wasn't that her name? Is she still in your life?'

He shook his head. 'Just a friend, Nina.'

The wine steward appeared. 'Shall we keep on with champagne? Or why not the Beaujolais nouveau? This may be the last time this year we can drink it.' The French wine of the autumn harvest had to be consumed before the New Year.

'Both!' enthused his sister. 'I think it's perfectly all right to get drunk with a brother!' They ordered more champagne, a pasta with salmon and cream sauce to be followed by wild boar and the red wine.

'Bart, you've lost weight.'

'I had a touch of the flu last month. It's not that many pounds actually, but I just haven't gained any of it back. I need a tailor, I guess.' He winked at Nina as the pasta was placed before them. 'Or a week in Rome.'

They ate in silence. Nina thought how thin her brother was. Bart thought how subdued his sister was. 'How are you really?' His voice broke the silence between them.

She put down her fork and reached for the champagne flute, sipped and swallowed before answering. 'Really?' she said brightly, then her face became serious. 'Really I don't know how I am.' She told him then of her walks in the Villa Borghese, of her Italian class, of the exercise class, of the antique and print shops. 'I don't know where I belong sometimes.'

'Do you think you belong with your husband?'

'My husband . . .' she said softly. 'No one has called him that in so long.'

'What do you call him?'

Nina didn't answer but opened her green satin bag, and brought out a pink ribbon knotted at one end. A simple gold ring hung from it and glittered in the candlelight. 'This came yesterday. Tucked in with a bouquet of violets. To replace the wedding ring I threw in the Tiber.'

Bart sighed. 'Have you tried it on?' She shook her head. 'What are you doing to do?'

'I guess I'm going to keep putting the damn flowers in water!' Nina's hand holding the ribbon became a fist.

'You love him, don't you?' Nina moistened her lips. She looked stricken, anguished. She did not answer. 'Then go back and try again.'

'But you don't know – '

'No, I don't know. I don't know what happened. You are the only person who knows that. Mother doesn't know. Adele doesn't know.' He paused and tasted the red wine, then nodded as the waiter filled their glasses. 'I know I was there when you married him. I know you, too. And you still love him.' Nina was beset with confusion. Bart was talking sense but he didn't know that it didn't apply to Claudio, to her. It was so sensible for other people, other marriages. 'Could so much have changed in a few years?'

The boar came. Nina wanted to tell Bart everything, to have him weigh the evidence. She longed to have him say 'do this'; to have him put an end to the doubts that nagged at her every waking moment. She wanted to feel anger right down to her bone marrow or unmitigated delight at the flowers that came several times a week. She hated the Nina who sniffled while trimming the stems of pink roses and she hated the Nina who, in a rage, had pulled all the tiny heads off the violets and thrown each purple flower off the terrace into via dei Greci one midnight. 'Bart, I'm serious when I say I don't know where I belong.'

He took a swallow of the red wine. 'I know the feeling, my dear.' His voice was bitter.

'Remember when Daddy used to tell me I was stupid? Over and over again when I was little. And I don't think I ever thought I wasn't.'

'Well, you're not.'

'I don't think I ever really believed him but even if I didn't it's been with me somehow. Like a hangnail that stings when you get into the bathtub. Through school when I struggled with French or algebra. It was like a curse. I hear his voice sometimes when I can't understand something in Italian and I think: Maybe he was right. After all, he knew me from the moment I was born and – '

'So did I. I knew you when you were one day old.'

Nina went on, 'And maybe he could have seen the truth.'

'Nina – '

'No, listen to me for a second.'

Nina felt she was figuring things out. Answers were floating past written on clouds and if she could just say it aloud to Bart, could make Bart understand, then maybe she could understand it, too. 'In New York I was . . . with someone for a while . . . older, sophisticated . . . and I remember being with him and it was just like being with Claudio. It wasn't really me. I never told either man how I grew up, how frightened I was of not understanding a conversation, how terrified I was of being dressed the wrong way. They knew a part of me that was attractive enough, lively enough, flirtatious enough to make them feel masculine and in control and I . . .' She swallowed. 'I was dependent on them because they pulled me along in their wake into a world I didn't know. And so I used enormous amounts of

502

energy pretending to belong. Trying to predict the mistakes that I might make. Being well behaved. *La bella figura.* I craved their approval the way I need air. I wanted to be perfect for them.' She remembered the Countess and her conversation about approval. 'I wanted to be perfect so they'd keep loving me and that would mean I wasn't stupid. That I deserved to belong with them.'

Sins of the fathers, thought Bart with rage. Beautiful Nina at last realizing she's brainy and worthwhile. If it takes being alone and spending all day walking through Rome, then that's what it takes. But no, maybe this was bound to evolve anyway.

'I used to think that if I were entertaining enough men would like me enough to not discover the truth. And the truth was I never felt I belonged anywhere. But if I persuaded Omar or Claudio that I belonged with them then I did. I was like an actress in a play. It was a game. I loved them, but it was still a game. I guess I played it with myself. All by myself.' Nina held the white napkin in her fist.

A terrifying game, thought Bart. Where the ground must give way under your feet all the time. Like the game I used to play before finding Rob.

'Bart? Are you listening?'

'Yes.' Bart felt near tears himself. 'I'm listening to every word.'

'Bart . . . I think I've stopped playing the game.'

It was after *crème brulée*, after Amaretto, and long after two o'clock when the brother walked his sister home.

People still strolled through Piazza di Spagna, but the scene was quiet enough to hear the gurgle and splash of the Bernini fountain. Nina thought of the fountain in the courtyard of the Palazzo de Leone and of Bart's advice. Do whatever you want but do it your way. Do it on your own terms. He loves you, he wants you back. Go back a new person and with new ways of looking at him, at his family. Bart had shushed her objections, had not wanted details, and at last she had listened to him.

'Yes, he has hurt you. And you are too bright and shining to be hurt,' he had said, looking into her troubled face across the candlelit table. 'But being hurt, hurting him, may have changed the way you are together. Maybe you should think about a second chance.' Bart had smiled then. 'I'm only saying this because I feel you still love him. How will you feel when it's too late to go back and you realize you let something slip through your fingers that might have been wonderful?'

They were on the silent via dei Greci when the coughing began. Bart's face contorted with the effort of it as Nina watched helplessly. Deep racking coughs caused him to bend over with one palm spread across his chest; with the other hand he leaned against a building.

When he was quiet, Nina touched his arm. 'How long have you had that?'

He shook his head, wiping tears from his eyes. 'Since the flu. It's just not going away. I have a little breather thing, but I forgot it tonight. Remember what Daddy used to carry around for his asthma?' He tried to smile. 'Mine's just like that.' Seeing her worried face he consoled her. 'I'll be fine, really. This wild flu swept San Francisco last fall. Everybody who's anybody came down with it. Hong Kong, Siamese, I don't know what it was.' He held his arm out to see his watch. 'I'd better get some sleep. I have to be at Fiumicino in seven hours.'

'Merry Christmas, Bart. Thanks for the best Christmas Eve I can remember.' She kissed him on each cheek then held him close to her for a few seconds, feeling how thin he was yet again.

'Merry Christmas to you. And remember – you can do anything you want.' His voice was strong, sure. The handsome face looked down at her in the glow of the street light.

'I really love you for saying that,' Nina breathed. 'I needed you tonight.'

Bart grinned, then lowered his voice in a Bogart imitation. 'Always thinking of you, kid.' He winked, then turned and in seconds his tall figure had turned the corner onto via del Babuino and was lost from sight.

*

The connection from Rome to Hong Kong was very clear. Gaston lit a Gauloise and inhaled deeply. It was nearly eight according to the little gold clock on the mantel and his reservation at Charly's Sauciere was for nine. Gaston felt famished for French food.

'Does she like the house?'

'She went through it like a whirlwind and then came back to the front door with a notebook and progressed slowly from room to room. She's bright. She can handle it.'

Hong Kong harbour twinkled with the lights of early morning activity, for it was nearly dawn. The man on the phone had obviously been wakened by the call for the only light in the room was the bedside lamp. It lit a double bed with covers thrown aside and a naked well-muscled man. He stood beside the bedside table and ruffled his fingers through his hair tiredly. 'Listen! Gaston! No clues. Nothing to give me away. It's very important that she not have any idea . . .'

'She's full of curiosity. Full of life. Insists I call her Nina instead of Miss McLean. And she's full of questions.'

'Yes, she will be, but put her off. Do you think this Nina business is a good idea? It's a dropping of formalities . . .'

Gaston shrugged. 'If you knew the way she is you'd . . .' What can I tell him? he wondered. 'She is so open, so totally at ease with things. She . . . she has the chauffeur giving her Italian lessons.' Laughter. 'And she has decided that you are an Arab!' More laughter.

'Gaston, just don't give her any answers. I must be protected until . . .' The Frenchman wanted some answers himself, but all the subterfuge seemed harmless, so he could wait. There was an audible sigh all the way from the Hotel Mandarin. 'Until I am ready.' The voice took on its usual crispness. 'The meeting with Duarte is for Friday. Can you meet me in Geneva then?'

'Absolutely.'

'I'll get Swissair day after tomorrow. Until I fly out you can reach me here.'

They rang off. The man in Hong Kong sat on the edge of his bed for a few minutes, then reached for a cigar. He looked at his watch where it lay on the table and decided it was too late. Or was it too early? He sat one minute more and thought of Gaston spending the afternoon with her. Then he turned off the ormolu lamp and swung his legs into bed and tried to find sleep.


January second. I made it, thought Nina. Never thought I'd get through the holidays. The telephone had rung and rung – Adele, Kate, the Countess, her mother, a goodbye call from Bart before he left London to return to San Francisco on New Year's Day. Nina's eyes swept the little apartment. She'd thrown out the last of the Christmas roses and placed the last note under her favourite paperweight. The green china frog sat on a pile of white cards two inches tall. The pink ribbon curled beside him, the ring still on it.

There were no flowers the next day, nor the next.


Gaston called Nina and told her that the property had been purchased and that he was anxious to begin the renovations. Was she free the next afternoon? Nina held a green sofa cushion on her lap and nodded, 'Yes, yes, I'm excited.' Noon? 'Okay.' She smiled. *'Perfetto.'*

Lisa rang the doorbell as she hung up and then Peggy arrived from a job interview. 'Don't be so silly and don't be so cynical,' Nina defended herself with great dignity as her friends from exercise class howled with laughter.

'You're just driving off to Tuscany with a Frenchman who bought you a cup of cocoa in the Caffe Greco!' Lisa struggled with a cork.

'Who is the friend?' insisted Peggy. Nina shrugged. 'Well, go, but be careful and wait . . . one minute . . . I . . .' Peggy fumbled in her tan jacket and then brought out a long evil-looking metal object.

'What the devil is that?' cried Lisa, pouring the wine. Nina stared in horror.

'I have been all over the world with this!' proclaimed Peggy in her English accent. 'It's a knitting needle, you idiots. Haven't been very domesticated, have you?' she continued, unconcerned by the looks on her audience's faces. 'Looks worse than it is; just stick it up your sleeve and if the chauffeur or this frog tries anything strange with you . . .' She fumbled desperately inside her blazer as they laughed. 'You simply . . . you just . . . there!' Peggy cried triumphantly, fishing it out with all the flourish of a Musketeer. 'My mum gave me this before I left Dorset.'

The afternoon conversation turned as always to money, to work, to survival. 'The only things for us here are au pair jobs and teaching English, and I am not excited about continuing with those English lessons,' sighed Lisa. 'I spent two hours with Signor Amadio today and he has the worst breath.'

'Garlic for one hundred generations will do that.' Peggy looked glum as she reached for the wine bottle. 'I answered that ad in the little English-language paper for the proofreader job and they told me there were over four hundred applications!'

'You're joking!'

'Wish I were, and the pay is not even a pound an hour. That's slavery!'

'And we, the poor little "my Italian isn't so great" foreigners, are begging to be slaves!'

'It's the blue skies and the wine,' sighed Nina as she reached for her glass. 'And the *spaghetti con vongole* and the shoes and the . . .'

'And the men!' chorused her friends, lifting glasses in a toast.


'Made it! I was afraid you'd leave without me!' Nina settled herself in the back of the Bentley and gave a deep sigh. She pulled off the yellow jacket and placed her notebooks and sketchpads on the seat.

'Nev-air!' cooed Gaston as Giorgio carefully steered the car past the silversmith, the framer's, the Santa Cecilia Academy of Music and out into the bedlam that was the via del Corso.

'Gaston! *Come va?* I am happy to see you!'

The little Frenchman nodded and smiled. 'I am very well and yes, happy to see you, also!'

Nina looked with appreciation at his expensive-looking dark brown leather shoes, his khaki-coloured wool trousers, the tweed jacket and the brown silk tie. Those shoes, considered Nina. I know he's all right. She unwrapped the black and yellow plaid scarf from around her neck and snatched off the black leather gloves. 'I have some drawings here to show you, and a lot of ideas about putting up beams in several of the rooms. I was going through some books an architect friend has . . .' Nina opened an enormous spiral-ringed pad on the seat between them. 'What would your friend think?'

Gaston looked at the finely drawn pencilled sketches. He was impressed. 'My friend is not worried about the money.'

'Yes, you said that,' answered Nina, 'but what about the ideas?' Gaston liked the beams and was about to speak but Nina spoke first. 'You know, if you could describe him to me, tell me what he's like, it would be such a help. I don't know what colours he prefers. I don't know anything other than it will be for a couple who will arrive and want to be comfortable.' She threw up her hands. 'Gaston! Really! Couldn't you just tell me his nationality?'

Don't be drawn in. Don't be drawn in. He had been warned on the phone. Still, considered Gaston, she is not being at all unreasonable.

Nina continued. 'You know a house has to feel like the person to make them at ease there. It sounds easy but it isn't easy to make surroundings comfortable. Does he like Italian antiques? Does he like formality?' She sighed in exasperation at the silence.

'I weesh I could help you! I want to . . .'

'But it is imperative that his identity be kept a secret!' she finished in a faint French accent.

Gaston laughed and then pulled the sketchbook on to his lap and examined it. 'This is good. Use the beams. I can get the timber and have the workmen plaster them in place . . .'

'Okay. What about our timetable?'

He shrugged. 'There is no hurry.'

'Six months? Six years?'

'Something in between.'

Nina clapped her hand to her face. 'Gaston! You must urge this man to allow you to tell me . . .'

Gaston nodded. 'I weel try again with heem. Perhaps we weel talk tonight.'

The silver Bentley hummed along the Highway of the Sun, heading northward. The greenness of the fields startled Nina as it had on the first trip to see the house. She knew only Rome with its busy streets, terracotta buildings, its churches, and the Tiber as her part of Italy. This landscape has a soft serenity to it, she decided as she leaned back in the plush upholstery. The occasional farmhouse perched on a hilltop near the horizon made her imagine the interior and sent her mind into a daydream of what the Tuscan villa would be like upon completion. When it was clean and freshly painted and filled with flowers and copper and brass and pictures and four-poster beds . . .

'The setting is sensational,' she had said the first time she had seen it. Now she thought it all over again. Giorgio read *Il Messaggero* in the car with the door open and Gaston had gone inside to look for the fountain pen he'd left behind. Nina stood on the hill behind the house and stared down at the sea. The Frenchman had purchased all the property between her and it, preferring this house without a vineyard to the two he'd seen with vines. The back garden would be planted with lemon trees and magnolias soon, but the flowers could wait to be chosen until the early spring. A stone path would need to be laid first and even then it would be a fifteen-minute walk down the hill to the ocean. Nina turned back to the house.

It was a four-storeyed structure of stone built in the early eighteenth century for a wealthy landowner. Gaston explained that he had been a Roman, hence the nearly square design which mimicked the shape of a sixteenth-century palazzo. The rooms were high-ceilinged, marble-floored, and nearly every one had a fireplace. In the 1920s the house had left the hands of the original family and the new owner had installed quite lavish bathrooms. Mullioned windows in front looked out over a grove of peach trees which hid the driveway from view, and windows in the back looked down the sloping hill to the water. At the top of the third-floor staircase was a red door. Through it a much narrower set of marble steps led to what Nina called the tower. This fourth storey was much smaller than the others and sat atop the building with terraces on four sides, giving the house from a distance the look of a birthday cake. Its walls were almost totally mullioned windows, with two sets of double doors opening outside. The floor was of a rose-coloured marble and the white plaster ceiling had once been brightly painted with pink and yellow flowers intertwined with green tendrils. The effect, thought Nina when she first saw it, was of a child's room – a place to play. The only sound was the wind and the birds' chatter. To the north the south, the east was spread the spectacular Tuscan countryside, and to the west glittered the bright blue Mediterranean.

On the way back to Rome Nina couldn't stop imagining possibilities for the villa. 'I worked for a woman who could have gone through it once and in half an hour given you a total plan for renovations. She would have known where every lamp would be placed six months from now. I am sorry I am not that gifted' – she made a face – 'but this second time has made me see it pretty clearly and I do have distinct ideas about what will be good and what won't work at all.' Gaston listened. 'If this man is going to use it in the winter months I think the natural white plaster walls will be too cold in feeling. A pale terracotta colour, almost peach, would make it more inviting. The only real structural changes in the downstairs will be putting in the beams.' Gaston looked at his notes and nodded. 'And making sure all the stones are steady around the fireplaces and the chimneys. The marble hearths should be cleaned. And all the floors! But that's last. The kitchen and all the bathrooms need work. I'm glad they are almost as large as the six bedrooms, with dressing areas and built-in closets. That makes them so luxurious. I can pick up tile samples and . . .'

'I will bring you the plumbing brochures for the kitchen, kitchen cabinets, dishwasher and the washing machine, and equipment for the laundry room. That way I can order them and take care of the shipping.'

'Good.' Nina crossed out a line of handwriting on the pad in her lap. 'There's the central heating. Better let me talk to – '

'Let me do that. This way I will show you what's available and you can say "yes" or "no" and which one, and then I will have it delivered, probably from Milano.'

'Okay, sounds fine.' Nina made another note. 'What about the sauna? What about the swimming pool?'

'I will ask about the pool and I will bring booklets on the sauna fixtures. Where will you put it?'

'I think it should be on the *terreno* behind so that if someone has gone for a swim, or is about to, they won't have to go through the house, but, of course, there should be a staircase from the master bedroom directly to it. Maybe one other entrance from the hall.' She stopped. 'And don't forget shower fixtures for the sauna area.' She suddenly decided, 'The potting shed is very large and in the right place for showers, sauna, a small kitchen and changing rooms for the pool. It's exactly where the pool house should be.'

Gaston wrote something down as she spoke. 'Then I think we should have a small potting shed built for the gardeners, for equipment. Another potting shed. Perhaps behind the stables which will be . . .' He hesitated.

'The garage.'

'Oh, Nina, you said six bedrooms, but there will only be five because there must be a study, a sort of office – a working place for the woman.'

This surprised Nina but she merely noted it on her pad. She wrote 'five' and circled it. She had pictured this Arab arriving with several wives, dozens of suitcases, and a staff. A woman who needed a desk and privacy for work jarred all her preconceptions.

'My favourite part of the entire house, Gaston, is the tower,' remarked Nina. 'It's a bit awkward to deal with since it's all windows with no centre, no fireplace. It's really a tower – it belongs to the countryside more than to the house.'

'I see it as a special place. Wouldn't it be nice to have a drink there and watch the sun set?'

'Yes! Exactly! Not a bedroom, certainly, and not a work room, but a place to go and think or talk or read or simply admire the view.' Nina decided to have Franco touch up the ceiling where the flowers had faded. This room alone would be left white, for the pink marble floor and the ceiling give it enough colour. 'Maybe several big comfortable chairs with a long chaise off to one side. And a telescope!'

'I can get an antique one from Paris,' said Gaston. 'It's on a wooden tripod and dates from the eighteenth century.' He'd long admired it in the window of the Left Bank shop.

'Perfect! And a really elegant backgammon board! I think with the doors open to the terrace it should be an outdoor place. The gardener can put lots of pink and white geraniums in clay pots on all sides. We should have chairs for sitting outside and a table, of course. I think wicker, with pink cushions. Bright geranium pink, Gaston? Or sort of dusty rose like the marble floor?'

'Dusty rose!' said the Frenchman definitely. He visualized the effect and sighed, '*Très jolie! Très, très jolie!*'

'I know the furnishings come last but what about Italian antiques? Nothing fussy or too, too delicate, but country antiques. I know more about French provincial but I can certainly learn about the Italian equivalent.'

'*Très bien.*'

Nina was thinking of the winding via dei Coronari for the desks and tables and chairs. Old mirrors could be found on a street just behind the Campo dei Fiori market. Nina often passed the very fat man with the long scar on his face as he set up his mirrors in their gold frames right on the narrow street. The passers-by could examine them without making the commitment to enter his dark little shop. At last, an excuse to enter!

'A double bed or twin beds?'

Gaston's head jerked almost imperceptibly. 'Pardon?'

'Well, what do you think? Is this a happy marriage with separate bedrooms or a happy marriage with separate beds or what?' She began to laugh at Gaston's discomfiture. 'The Countess in New York always told me that you find out absolutely everything about a person when you decorate their house. I am at a great disadvantage since there are no traces of him there now, but' – she smiled – 'I will know a lot about this couple before I ever meet them!'

Gaston looked uncertain. I don't want to give this game away too soon and, of course, there will be no one to blame but me, Gaston! 'Nina, listen to me. It is better that you stop trying to find out who this man is.'

'Is he a criminal?' suddenly occurred to Nina.

'Oh, no.' Gaston shook his head.

'Is he a movie star?' Gaston shook his head again. 'He *is* an Arab, isn't he, with a liberated wife or wives, or . . .'

Gaston threw up his hands in exasperation. 'You mustn't do this to me. I do want to help you. I do want to tell you what I know,' Gaston said, 'but I made a promise to a friend.'

Nina smiled rather sympathetically this time. 'I'm sorry for making you upset. All I need to know, I guess, is that he has enough money to pay me.'

'He does. He has made several millions of dollars in the last three weeks alone and before that a fortune in the span of only months.'

'My God!'

They drove in silence – Nina not daring to risk another question, Gaston hoping she would not ask anything else, and Giorgio, poor Giorgio, with a very bad headache. He had closed the partition for the entire trip back and forth.

'And you?' asked Nina. 'What are you to this man?' Gaston didn't answer. A friend. His partner. His tax adviser His counsellor for the various stock exchanges in Europe. A contact. 'Can you tell me even that?'

The car was pulling up via Babuino. Gaston grinned. 'I am . . . a . . . troubleshooter!' He looked inordinately pleased with this and with himself.

Nina laughed and, getting out of the car, called, '*Ciao!*

Troubleshooter!' The silver Bentley moved slowly and with great dignity down the little cobblestoned street.

No more flowers, thought Nina as she nodded to Signora Cadlolo. And just when I've made up my mind what to say when I hear his voice again, no more telephone calls. Nina stepped into the little swaying elevator, slid the iron grating closed. He's given up and I'm on my own again. At last not waiting for his next move, she thought as the cage moved upward. She clanged the iron gate shut behind her and turned.

Claudio Massimiliano de Leone leaned with arms crossed against her door. Taller than she remembered, with broader shoulders than she remembered, with bluer eyes. Nina clutched the sketchpad across the front of her canary yellow jacket and simply stared.

'I want to talk to you.' He wasn't smiling. He hadn't moved.

'Fine.'

'May I come in?'

Nina hesitated then shook her head. 'No. Let's go downstairs. A walk. A coffee.'

'No. I don't want to talk to you like that. May I come inside?'

'No.' Nina thought: Neutral territory, that's what I want. Some place without memories. Some place where we're not alone.

He uncrossed his arms and stepped towards her in the hallway. 'Will you have dinner with me?' Nina's eyes took in the sunburned face – probably from skiing, she thought – then the brown leather jacket and the checked wool scarf knotted loosely over the tan sweater. Any absence from Claudio had always made his reappearance larger than life. She was acutely aware of his closeness to her. He still hadn't smiled. 'I said, will you have dinner with me?'

'Yes.'

He stepped out of her way then; his shoes made a soft noise on the stone stairway. Five steps down he called to her. 'Tonight. *Alle nove.*' Nina's fingers trembled as she turned the key in the lock. She did not watch him go. Nine o'clock. It had not been a question.


'Why can't I have everything?' Nina asked herself in the bathroom mirror. She held the ruby earrings up against the pale pink silk dress then made a face and thought: No, I won't wear any de Leone jewellery tonight. She clipped on pearl earrings and then pulled the Countess's pearls over her hair and looped them around and around her neck, at last dropping the last foot of beads nearly to her waist. The dress was off the shoulder with small puffed sleeves and a fitted bodice that made her look very narrow and yet pushed her breasts upwards. Nina continued her monologue as she patted on charcoal-grey eye shadow. 'I'm young, energetic, educated, American, independent, have a fabulous project as a decorator . . .' She stopped and snapped the little compact closed. 'Why can't I be married to an Italian count and still be myself? Why should I let it all drop away as though I'm stepping out of one dress and into another?' She took a plump sable brush and applied rose-coloured powder to her cheekbones.

The downstairs doorbell rang as she tucked pink lipstick into the red sequinned bag. Nina raced out on to the terrace and peered down over the railing at the black Lamborghini. Claudio waved one hand as she called, 'Be right there!'

She locked the glass doors then sprayed on perfume one last time, wondering if she were wearing too much. Then she grabbed the bag and her sable coat and suddenly was reminded of the first time Claudio had taken her to dinner so long ago. The delicious tickling tension, the last spritz of perfume, the shining car in the street below, the shout from the terrace, the excitement of possibility. One long look in the mirror and she shook her head, more than slightly nervous. 'This is where I came in.'


'*Bella*,' Claudio said seriously as he helped her into the car.

Nina looked at the white scarf hanging over his dinner jacket and retorted, '*Bello*, yourself.'

They both smiled slightly then, not looking at each other, but straight ahead as Claudio started the engine.

'I don't want . . .'

'*Si? Che cosa?*'

Nina had nearly forgotten his inflection of the musical Italian words. 'I don't want to go anywhere we used to go.'

'We won't, then.'

They drove in silence along the river and then made the turn into Trastevere. In minutes a man in a tuxedo was taking Nina's coat and another was waving her to follow him across the candlelit dining room. '*Ho prenotato per due*,' Claudio was saying as the maitre d' nodded. '*Certo, Conte. Qui.*'

Wonder how many times he's been here without me and with whom, thought Nina, and then told herself to stop it as she took her place at the corner table. Champagne came and they lifted their glasses in silence, Nina not looking into his blue eyes. The waiter refilled the flutes as Nina thought of Bart's words. What if you let something go, something that could have been wonderful?

Claudio at last spoke. 'Why don't we just get drunk?'

Nina laughed at that, her face dipping towards him, her eyes bright. She looked down at his large hand on the white tablecloth. No matter what, she knew she was still attracted to him physically.

'Contessa, Conte?' A waiter was placing menus on the table. Nina realized it had been a long time since anyone had called her that. Here we are: the young Count and Countess de Leone, easily recognizable from newspaper photographs. Claudio nodded him away, imperiously, then allowed a second waiter to again refill their glasses.

I was going to tell him about the villa, thought Nina. I was going to talk to him about having a life of my own. I have to tell him about wanting to feel like myself again. I want to be totally honest, absolutely straight, and I want him to be the same. No more secrets, no more quiet nursing of wounds solitarily. And I must tell him about Omar. It has to be

516

understood. And he has to tell me about the other women. I have to know. We have to trust each other. She took a swallow of the champagne and heard him then. A gasp. He put the glass down to cover his eyes with his hands. His face was wet with tears. Nina was reminded of him in the sea, surfacing, streaming with water.

The Claudio she'd never seen cry, the Claudio she'd never heard apologize, was weeping, was saying he was sorry. 'It was my baby, too,' he whispered as he fumbled with a white handkerchief. His broad shoulders shook slightly as Nina put her hands on his cheeks and helped him mop away the tears. At last, overcome with her own emotion, she pulled his head towards her and felt his tears upon her bare shoulders and he inhaled her sweetly perfumed ivory skin. That was the moment everything changed, Nina was to realize later. He raised his head. 'I want you back,' he stated. His strong face was full of sorrow, his lips parted as he raggedly inhaled. 'I want you back.'

Nina forced herself to look away from his eyes. They fairly burned her with his pain. She had forgotten how blue they were. Claudio leaned back on the banquette as though very very tired. Nina thought: He's suffered, too. Bart was right. We have hurt each other and then I left so we could each suffer alone. Tonight I expected compliments, promises, and even a plan of change presented to me with all the finesse of a New York lawyer. I expected a sophisticated discourse on how marriage is different in Italy. She picked up the champagne with trembling fingers. Claudio immediately put his hand on hers and she felt the familiar heat.

'I won't send any more flowers. I won't call you again or try to see you after tonight if that's what you want.' Nina was shocked. 'I won't disturb your life.'

Oh, thought Nina. This vulnerable man I've never seen before is giving up. On me, on us. On a future together. But I had so many things to tell him. I had to make him a promise that I could have certain freedoms, that he would be faithful, that we would be honest . . . His voice was gentle. 'I may be very unhappy, I may be filled with many regrets, but . . .' Nina stared at him and thought: Yes, it was our baby. It was our marriage. This is the man I wanted. He removed his hand from hers and with the gesture she suddenly smelled the lime scent of him and her mind was awash with memories. His voice was very soft. 'We'll have dinner and I'll take you home.' He put aside the menu as the waiter approached them. 'What about a steak? You used to like that, my little Americana.' She nodded as he ordered two of them *al sangue*, rare.

'Claudio.' It was the first time she had spoken his name. 'I want to talk about so many things.' She pushed the hair away from her forehead. 'I want to talk about Omar Sarkis.'

'I know about him. I don't want to know more.'

'But can you understand how long . . .'

Claudio shook his head. His voice was firm. 'I don't want to know anything else about him. I won't ever mention him again if you won't.' Nina opened her mouth to speak. 'It's finished. Isn't it?'

She nodded. Nina had expected his voice to change, his temper to flare, but now all she could do was believe him. Finished. Red wine was poured, tasted and their glasses were filled. 'There were other women, weren't there?' I have to know. He has to tell me. Her voice was meant to be flat but it betrayed her anguish.

'Yes.' They stared at each other. Man and woman. Husband and wife. 'Things were not good between us but I always loved you.'

What do I expect him to say? Nina screamed at herself. Do I want their names, do I want apologies for every one, for every time? Do I want promises that it'll never happen again? What do I want? Now I'm in the quicksand between the Roman reality and the American idealism and my shoes are covered with mud.

'Tell me what you've been doing,' he said when she didn't speak.

Nina sipped the wine. 'There is a villa in Tuscany,' she began. And as she told him about Gaston and the mysterious owner and about the land leading down to the sea the villa itself became a symbol. It was Nina's first independent job as a decorator, her first in Italy. It was someone believing that she was professional, someone who was willing to trust her implicitly, someone willing to pay her well. 'It means a great deal to me,' she finished.

Claudio lifted his wine glass to her and smiled. 'To the villa.' She returned the smile, unsure, then pleased. The steaks were put before them and they began to eat. So much was on Nina's mind. How could every issue have been waved away so easily? How could every single doubt have evaporated? She had asked all the questions and Claudio had looked her in the eye and answered them. She believed him. He had had a bad time. They had been apart. He had thought about all that had happened and decided that their marriage was important. Yes, it was. In Italy, marriages always were. But Claudio had decided that a good marriage was important. There was one more thing.

'I can't . . .' He put down his fork and gave her his attention. 'I can't have a baby soon. I want to wait. I want to be . . .'

Claudio leaned towards her. 'I understand. You want to be happy first. You want to be sure.' Nina nodded. A man in a white dinner jacket began to play the piano. 'I want you to be happy. Do you believe that?'

Suddenly she could not speak. She remembered the Claudio standing over her with the riding crop. The Claudio kissing the blonde in the nightclub on Capri. His face was close to hers and though her arm nearly brushed his jacket he made no move to touch her. Nina's cheeks were flushed with the wine, her grey eyes were alight, her bare shoulders creamy above the pink dress. 'I want you back,' he said.

Their plates were taken away and Claudio ordered more champagne. Why can't I have everything? she asked herself yet again as she stared at his aristocratic profile. Why can't I have a villa to renovate, a palazzo to live in, a baby, Claudio, whatever I want? Am I pushing happiness away with both hands? Nina realized she wanted him to touch her, to stroke her arm, to put his index finger to her cheekbone and slowly outline it the way he used to. He was tantalizingly near, surprisingly gentle, as attractive as ever. The piano player sang all the songs of their past. 'Am I being set up?' Nina

519

asked Claudio cynically and he actually laughed and made a gesture as if to take her hand, but then drew away again.

They stayed for hours, sitting on the black velvet banquette side by side, inches apart, listening and thinking. Nina could hear Bart's logic; then she could see Kate's face; then she could imagine Adele's reaction which would be right in the middle of the other two. A yes, a no, a definite maybe. Her favourite song. The notes of the music brought tears to her eyes. Nina's Italian had not been good enough to understand the lyrics for a long time but now she heard the chorus clearly. '*Aaaaan-cora, aaaan-cora, ancora* . . .' sang the young man as Nina visualized the entry in her dictionary: '*Ancora* – still, yet, again, once more.'


'I feel very good about everything,' said Nina as Claudio poured the Amaretto. The others had gone to bed after an animated dinner of welcome for her; Franco and Maria had long since closed the shutters of the reception room against the January night and then retired to their quarters. 'Everyone seems to be happy to see me.'

'*Certo*,' smiled Claudio, pulling at the knot of his tie.

The day had begun with Dante arriving for her bags, then Claudio bounding up the stairs to take her to lunch with friends at Dal Bolognese. That afternoon they'd spent at the Polo Club to oversee Claudio's newest pony being put through its paces by Lorenzo, the groom, then at six Nina had taken a bath in the sarcophagus and prepared herself to see the family for the first time since the previous summer. They last saw me when I was pregnant, unhappy, about to go on a boat trip with a man I thought I no longer loved. And now, she mused, I am me again. With a husband who has come around to my way of thinking. The triumph and the liqueur were both sweet.

Their silence was companionable; of a man and a woman who'd shared a day in a beautiful city, in and out of a fast car, with fresh air and good food, excellent wines, and people who seemed happy to see them together.

'Sleepy?'

'Mmmm,' nodded Nina. Claudio took her glass and placed it beside his on the ornate intarsia table. They rose from their chairs and made their way side by side down the hallway to Claudio's apartment. He still has not touched me, not today, not the other night, not so much as held my hand, thought Nina.

She went into the dressing room and changed into her nightgown. As she pulled the silver-backed brush through her long hair he was behind her in the mirror, slowly unbuttoning the white shirt. 'I'm waiting for you,' he said, staring at her reflection, his eyes over her shoulder.

Nina turned, as always aware of his proximity. 'But I . . . Claudio.' She shook her head. 'I told you when we talked . . . the other night . . . I thought you understood. I'll sleep here.'

His voice was firm. Each word cut through the silence of the room definitively. 'No. You will sleep with me.'

She shook her head again. 'I told you I can't have a baby yet. I can't even think of it.'

His eyes narrowed and he gave her a sardonic half smile. 'I'm not talking about babies. No baby doesn't mean no love.' Nina could hear the Sèvres clock ticking on the mantel. She had wanted to hold him at arm's length, quite literally, until she felt that the marriage would be a success, until she knew he accepted her terms, until she had a firm footing in the palazzo. But seeing him this way, half undressed, feeling his stare through her black silk night-gown, she knew she had been wrong. It would only anger him and drive him to some other woman's bed. Besides – her heart pounded quickly and her skin felt warm – I want him.

'Do what ninety per cent of the good Catholic women of Italy do.' He grinned. 'I won't tell the Pope on you.'

Nina smiled faintly, thinking: What power he has over me. How sure he is.

Claudio pulled at the cuffs and then took off the shirt. Nina had not moved. Her right hand still held the hairbrush but her arm was limp at her side. He stepped towards her and cupped her chin in his hand. A spark seemed to leap between them. She saw the familiar pattern of black hair on his tan chest before he forced her to raise his eyes to his. 'I've told you I want you back. All of you.' Nina wanted him to kiss her. The longing overrode any words he could be saying. She felt irresistibly drawn to him, the planes of his face, the prominent cheekbones, the straight black brows, that wide mouth. 'You are my wife.'

Nina dropped the hairbrush as he gathered her in his arms and carried her into the bedroom and placed her in the big bed with the green canopy. There he made love to her as he never had before. With his fingers, his mouth, his body, and his heart. Nina dug her nails into his hard shoulders and cried out again and again, '*Ti amo, ti amo, ti amo!*'

'April is the cruellest month,' said Rob. Bart nodded from the hospital bed. The room was filled with roses, carnations, potted plants. A vase of tiger lilies had been delivered yesterday. They took place of honour on the small white and chrome bedside table. The card simply read, 'Love love love from Nina.'

'Just be glad I don't have hay fever,' quipped the thin figure beneath the sheets.

Rob managed to smile though he didn't feel like it. He was so worried that he could barely eat, never slept, and thought ceaselessly of Bart. The doctor had told him that the latest test results might at last throw light on Bart's illness. He had lost about a third of the one hundred and eighty pounds he carried on his six-foot frame and his face was gaunt; fever gave his grey eyes a supernatural brightness. His hair seemed blacker than ever above the paper-white complexion.

The door swung open admitting first a nurse with a thermometer and then Dr Parker, short, compact as a fire plug, with red hair.

'Nurse, not now.' He waved one hand with a pen and she cruised silently away on rubber soles. The physician sat on the chair at one side of Bart's bed and motioned Rob to be seated, also.

'Look, I want to be straight with you.' He sighed as the two men stared at him unblinkingly, holding their breaths, preparing for bad news. They braced themselves as he looked down at the clipboard which seemed to be covered with numbers and initials.

'I have just received the lab reports and I'm afraid that it doesn't look good.' He continued. 'Bart, you have a virus which is attacking the, uh – let's call them the T-cells. These T-cells coordinate your system of immunity.'

Rob had pulled the green plastic chair close enough to Bart's bed to hold his hand with its clearly outlined veins. Bart was too weak to return the squeeze which bade him to be brave.

'These T-cells defend your body, your system from disease and these T-cells are being destroyed by this virus.' He had purposely gone around in a small circle, almost insulting their intelligence, for he dreaded the inevitable desperate questions.

Rob spoke in a calm voice. 'What can be done?'

Dr Parker felt a very clear pain as he shook his head. 'Not very much, I'm afraid.' How many times had he had to say these words in his thirty years as a doctor? 'I am supposed to heal,' he had wept once as an intern upon realizing that he could only watch as one of his patients waited to die.

'We'll have to watch you very carefully' – he hated using the word 'watch' but it slipped out, anyway – 'because without these cells giving you immunity, even the most minor infection could be very serious.'

Bart thought of Eskimos catching cold and dying after their first exposure to the germ. Rob thought of pneumonia. Dr Parker thought: What do I tell them now?

'What will you treat him with? Is there a medicine he can begin taking?'

'I'll up the dose of penicillin. That is what I and two of my colleagues have decided would be best.' He stared at Bart and wondered if his fever had risen since that morning when he'd checked the chart. 'I've been consulting with Dr Brad Waterston and Dr Richard Markley. If you want to talk to either of them I can tell them to stop by.'

Parker was standing now. 'Bart, I'll be in in the morning and look you over again.' He nodded at Bart and left the room. Rob followed him into the hall and touched his white-coated sleeve.

'Dr Parker, is this a rare disease? How did he get it? What is the prognosis?' His voice was tinged with fear.

'All we know is that the majority of patients are either intravenous drug users or homosexual males.' Dr Parker was careful not to look into Rob's face. He knew the name

Robert Auden Cabell well and he also knew that the two men had been inseparable since Bart's admittance to the hospital twelve days ago. 'It can be spread by sexual intercourse, by secretions from the male into the bloodstream. The disease has been virtually unknown, or at least unidentified, until the last year. Research is still in the primary stages.' He sighed and held the clipboard to his chest.

Rob noticed the three ballpoint pens in his breast pocket and thought: Only a few marks on a page confirm that Bart is pale and thin and suffering. 'What next? What happens now?' he demanded with furrowed brow.

'So far, there are few things we can do. There has been experimentation with bone marrow transplants but it has failed to influence the course of the illness.'

'What are you saying?'

Dr Parker gazed into Rob's face and, without a word, communicated what Rob was most frightened of knowing. He put his hand out then and touched the broad shoulder in the tweed sports coat. 'Try to get some rest, Mr Cabell.'

Nina was happy with the way the house was coming along and surprised at how conscientious the workers were in following her absentee directions. There was a gardener who had two helpers from the town of Capalbio and an electrician and a plumber and their assistants, several tile layers, and the painters. The slender man resetting roof tiles was also a part-time chimney sweep.

'Spectacular!' breathed Nina as the Bentley pulled up the long hill towards the house that April day. The front walk exists to walk upon, she thought excitedly. The front door she had bought for almost nothing in Rome had been sanded and varnished and the brass lion knocker shone like gold. 'Never guess that the door is four hundred years old!' laughed Nina as she petted the leonine nose.

'Bellissima!' exclaimed Giorgio as he squeezed past her carrying the fabric samples and the catalogues from the trunk.

'Gaston!' she called excitedly from the front hall. 'Look at this!' She pointed towards the kitchen.

'You like it?' he grinned.

'Oh, they've done a magnificent job!' she cried as she ran into the large open area. She'd decided to leave the kitchen fireplace as it was and to make it into a place for grilling steaks. From waist-level to ceiling were the green and white tiles she'd found in the village between Capalbio and Rome. Nina had been almost asleep in the back seat of the Bentley when the car had slowed, then swerved to pass a horse-drawn cart carrying stacks of the bright glazed ceramic. She'd begged Giorgio to stop and ask where she could buy some and the old man had been delighted to guide them to his brother's kiln. The Bentley had eased along behind the black horse and the little cart through the village as the children, just let out of school, called, '*Inglese! Inglese!*' at the silver car.

Kitchen equipment would be sent from Milan, the shutters had been ordered from the carpenter of Capalbio and would be finished within a week, the new bathroom tiles were being laid, and the beams in the living room were already in place.

Nina was delighted with the progress. She made more notes. Gaston had the idea to make floor-to-ceiling windows in the master bedroom to take advantage of the view of the water. Then Nina decided to make the windows begin at seventeen inches from the floor so that deep window seats could be built. She pictured rich velvet cushions and pillows piled up at each corner. Drawers could be disguised underneath for storage. Gaston nodded. He was beginning to like the house.

Nina put her arm through his as they took one last look at the sea before getting into the car. The air was full of hammering and the buzz-saws were wailing.

'One question, Gaston,' she said, looking at him sternly.

'Ah, ah.' He waved his finger at her. 'The Directeur . . .'

'Is you!' she finished triumphantly amid his gales of laughter.

*

526

'Don't!' There was the crash of breaking glass as the little silver box hit the seventeenth-century venetian mirror dead centre. Nina closed her eyes, put her arms over her head and shouted, 'Look what you've done! You spoiled brat!' Her dark blue linen dress and her bare arms gleamed as though coated with Christmas glitter.

'What are you then?'

Nina resisted the urge to go at his impassive face with her fists. Whenever Claudio became angry enough to throw something, then after the noise he became horribly aloof and taunting. Nina didn't throw things but felt positively feverish with rage and later her arms and shoulders and the back of her neck ached as though the tightening of muscles needed to resist destruction had somehow stayed with her.

'I know what I am!' she fairly screamed. 'I am what you call "independent".' Her voice dropped. 'The most disgusting thing a Roman male can call his American wife.'

'For once we agree.' Claudio turned on his heel and walked out of the dressing room. He stood before his own bureau casually knotting the dark green silk tie as though he had nothing more on his mind than a leisurely breakfast and a glance at the morning paper.

Nina was behind him then. She told herself to calm down. To meet him on his own icy level. There was the tinkle of falling glass from the next room as the last shards fell. 'You know what, Claudio?' He didn't answer her or respond with even a flicker of his eyelids. She watched him adjust the knot. 'I think you're jealous. You're jealous of the villa, of the time I – '

Claudio scowled. 'Of that little frog?'

Nina was enraged. Oh, how like him! To not understand anything but sexual jealousy. To have any other kind simply too incomprehensible. Okay. On your own terms then. 'But you met Gaston and you liked him! And he charmed your mother and I thought you liked him!' Nina had invited him to dinner way back in February when things had been so perfect. When he and Nina had been inseparable, when the servants, when friends had joked about how adoring they were and when they couldn't seem to stop touching each other, stealing kisses behind people's backs, at parties, in hallways. The dinner with Gaston had been a marvellous idea. It had only been marred by Nonno's insistence that Gaston must be a collaborator to have not had trouble crossing the border. There had been confusion about that until finally the Count had told his father in rapid-fire Italian that Gaston was not really French at all but affected the accent for the war effort. Gaston had praised the Tuscan wine in blissful ignorance and dinner had proceeded.

Claudio turned away from his reflection and strode past her, plucking his suit jacket from the blue brocaded chair. 'Tell me exactly why you're so mad at me!' implored Nina. Her face was pink, her fists were clenched at her sides. She took no notice of the glass covering every bare inch of skin. Some sparkled in her hair. 'What am I doing wrong?' she shouted at his back.

He turned then as he shrugged the shoulders of his jacket into place. His voice was so soft she had to strain to hear. 'You're doing what you want to do, Nina. Isn't that why you came back to me? Isn't that what *you* decided?' Nina was confused. 'So go ahead. Go to the villa three times a week. Go eight days a week. It's what you want.'

Claudio's jaw tightened. Nina saw the little muscle under his cheekbone move. 'And I will let you do anything you want.'

'Let me!' she shouted as he walked from the room. 'You'll let me! *Molte grazie!*' she shrieked as the panelled door closed behind him.


The two men in Burberry raincoats were laughing.

'I am so nervous I will say your name, that I now refer to you as the Directeur,' explained Gaston as the London taxi crawled through the traffic. The grey sky was spitting rain and the cars moved inches, then braked again.

'Directeur! I like it,' laughed the other man. He snapped closed the latches on the Mark Cross briefcase and turned to face the little Frenchman beside him. 'Tell me how she is.'

What was going on? wondered Gaston. Why did he ask how she was and not how the house was? 'Nina is . . .' He gave a Gallic shrug then broke into a smile. 'She is glorious.' The Directeur laughed as the Frenchman continued, 'We get along very well, you know.'

'Yes, yes, I'm sure,' said the Directeur a trifle impatiently, 'but what about her life? Does she say anything – '

'She is back with her husband but I know nothing more.'

The Directeur was frustrated. Were there no details? The car pulled to the kerb and the driver pushed back the glass which separated the passengers from him. 'Here y'are, guv'nor. Turnbull and Asser.'

'The sun is beautiful on those waves as they curl towards the beach.' Rob nodded in assent as he stared out of the sliding glass doors. He had his hands in the pockets of his tan linen trousers. The green Lacoste shirt and the espadrilles suited his athletic build. He turned back to the pale, emaciated stranger who lay under the tan duvet in the chrome four-poster bed. His beloved Bart. 'I know what you're thinking,' he teased and then his face became serious. 'And the answer is "yes".' Rob sat on the edge of the bed and took the thin hands in his.

'I keep thinking what a waste of energy so many things have been,' said Bart.

'What specifically, for instance?' Rob stared down at the perfect little half-moons of the other man's fingernails.

'Subterfuge. Why should anyone have cared that we . . . that we . . .' He stopped and his grey eyes glistened with tears. Rob looked at his face and thought: Your poor face. Your poor, handsome face. Bart moistened his lips and continued in a whisper, 'That we love each other.'

Rob nodded, feeling his own control ebbing away.

Bart wanted to talk about everything. He'd been that way for the two days since leaving the hospital. 'I wonder if I'm this textbook case. If you are the first man to love me, when my father should have been; if all these years, with all those women, with all the Karens of the world, I've been looking for you – for someone I loved to love me and that that person had to be a masculine person . . .'

'Don't know.' Bart had teased him the summer before about being the least introspective person he'd ever known. 'You and my sister, Nina,' he'd joked.

'I think this is going to be all right with Mother. I have never doubted that she loved me. And Nina! The tigress of the family!'

'They will always love you, but are you sure . . .'

Bart nodded and then his eyes turned to look at the rows of bottles on the glass and chrome bedside table. Rob surveyed them mockingly. Nothing in them would do any good. Parker had just about put it in those words.

'Don't you remember your father at all?' asked Bart suddenly.

'No, I was at boarding school in England when they told me he'd had a heart attack. I must have been . . . it was my first year so I was eight. He had always been away. Long trips.' Rob paused. 'Building an empire.'

'The Cabell Empire,' interjected Bart as he remembered having someone explain that Cabell Inc. owned Cabell Oil, known as Caboil, twenty-three daily newspapers, four magazines, forty-seven radio stations, several dozen television stations, and a swath of California coastline that could qualify for statehood.

'And me, the heir apparent, without parents, without wife, without heirs.' He shook his head. 'My father came from nothing and sweated blood to gather all the poker chips together and' – he smiled sardonically – 'here we sit looking at the ocean.'

Bart knew what he was leaving unsaid. 'If my father could see me now. I blew it. I was supposed to get married and have children. I was supposed to do the right thing.' He was reminded of the way Nina said that phrase, with sort of a taunting twang in her voice. The right thing.

The two men sat together for hours that afternoon – Rob, looking much younger than his fifty-two years, tan, muscular in the casual clothes of someone who knows who he is, where he belongs, and Bart, in light blue pyjamas with that

530

hair the colour of ink above the big grey eyes that dominated his drawn face more than ever.

As the sun set over the water Rob's hand tightened ever so slightly over Bart's. He turned and said very softly, 'You known I'll never leave you.'

In Carmel the next few days elapsed without hours; they were punctuated only by the elegant meals that Ching prepared, the occasional steak that Rob grilled on the terrace, or the bloody mary he made for Bart who was exceedingly pleased to be treated 'as a real person', as he put it. The hospital had been a very depressing experience for both of them and loomed as a threat if Bart's condition, or rather when Bart's condition, worsened. Neither could summon the humour to joke about the food, the stout nurse who used the royal 'we', as in 'how are we feeling today?' or the drabness of the view which was a parking lot for the ambulances.

Bart stopped taking the medication one morning, simply asking, 'What's the use?' as Rob handed him his orange juice and counted out the dozen capsules from various bottles. Rob didn't answer.

Bart could still walk leaning on Rob's shoulder and asked to be helped on to the wooden deck. It was a warm day for April, the flowers were bright in the cedar buckets, and they sunbathed as they had so many fine days of the summer before. A pitcher of water was between them on the little table, Ching came out once in a while to ask if they wanted anything, and the sun was high in the sky making them feel warm and giving them a sense of wellbeing.

One afternoon, after a lunch of eggs benedict, Dr Parker telephoned and said he'd like to drive out in the next day or so. Rob told him they were getting along just fine and that Bart was eating quite well, with a good appetite and yes, of course he was taking the medication. No, the long drive really wasn't necessary, he said firmly as Bart watched him talk on the terrace phone. He hung up and walked sombrely back to the chaise longue.

531

'Rob, I have to tell you something,' Bart said almost childishly, as though he had left his bike at a neighbour's house or torn his best school jacket.

Rob looked up. 'What is it?'

'I weighed myself and if those scales are right then I've lost eight pounds since the hospital.'

Rob shrugged. 'They're . . . they're always screwed up. Don't worry about it. Ching probably moved them when he was cleaning the bathroom.'

He sprawled on the deck bed parallel to Bart. They were both thinking the same thought. Finally Bart broke the silence.

'Is he coming tomorrow?'

'The day after.'

Bart turned to look at Rob and Rob opened his eyes and squinted at him in the glaring sunlight. They had decided.

The next day was a Thursday, bright white and clear, with the Pacific spread before them like liquid lapis lazuli. They awakened at the same instant and felt for each other's hand. Bart turned and smiled into Rob's face.

'Funny, but I feel so good today.'

'I know,' sighed Rob, 'almost as though it's Christmas or my birthday.'

'A new day,' said Bart. 'All kinds of possibilities. Are you . . .'

Rob laughed and put his hand on Bart's face. 'Stop playing devil's advocate! You know I will do what you do!' His voice became soft. 'I told you I'd never leave you and I meant it and I mean it for ever.' Bart's big grey eyes in the sunken face filled with tears. 'Hey, hey,' teased Rob, 'real men don't cry.'

Bart started to laugh so suddenly that the tears fell on to the white sheet. 'No, you've got it wrong!'

'Don't say another word,' called Rob, slipping out of bed. 'I'm getting the champagne. Ching has the next couple of days off.' He returned in a knee-length red terrycloth bathrobe, carrying a silver tray with two glasses and a bottle of Dom Perignon.

'As I was saying' – Bart sipped leaning on one elbow – 'I was saying that real men don't eat quiche.'

'No,' argued Rob, grinning. 'It was macho Mailer who started this garbage. It's real men who don't dance.'

'Well, real men don't get AIDS, either.' They laughed until they cried. Bart spilled champagne on his pillow and then said, 'Not one minute more in bed.' Rob helped him through the sliding glass doors and on to the chaise in the sunlight. The morning passed with showers and sunbathing and banter and omelettes and bacon and champagne. Bart called his mother at the clinic and talked for nearly an hour, telling her that he felt better than he had for several months and that, please, she was not to worry about him.

Rob wrote a cheque for eight hundred thousand dollars to Ching and put it on the dining room table. The bank could handle it easily. His will was in the hands of his lawyer. All had been squared away – tightly, legally – in that one recent appointment. It had been the only time in the past four weeks that he had left Bart's side for more than five minutes.

The bright morning became one of those afternoons of almost fearful beauty. The sky was a robin's egg blue above the sweep of dark water. The sand shone like acres of diamonds in the sun. Rob felt good and drunk.

'Hey, listen, I don't want to do it out here on the deck.'

'I think that would be good,' slurred Bart. 'I want to be warm, and it's a good view. A spectacular, magnificent . . .'

'No, no,' Rob insisted, shaking his head. 'Can't do it out here where the sun'll get to us. S'lutely no.' He poured more champagne and then replaced the green bottle in the silver ice bucket.

'Why the hell not?' demanded Bart.

'Well, remember all the photographs of Jonestown?'

Bart exploded with laughter, spraying champagne all over his bare stomach with its prominent ribcage. 'It might be an improvement on the way I look now.'

Rob started to laugh. 'No, I refuse,' he sputtered when he could speak again. 'I don't do one hundred sit-ups every morning of my life to be found looking like some fat middle-aged . . .' He couldn't finish. The thought seemed hilarious to both of them.

'Puff adder,' finished Bart, and they began to rock with laughter again.

At sunset, as the vivid orange and lavender fingers of light blazed over the ocean, Bart lay on the lounger and thought: I've never been so happy, laughed so much. Loved anyone so deeply. He called to Rob who was carefully lining up the eleven empty champagne bottles against the ledge of the deck.

'Hey, Rob, I must be a Christian because I'm not afraid.'

Rob walked over to him in his yellow bathing suit and the open sports shirt. 'Me, too, unless champers makes you brave. I'm sure there isn't nothing.' Bad grammar, he thought disjointedly.

'Hey, wanna call Billy Graham and ask him anything?'

'Christ, Bart! You are drunk!' He sat on the edge of the chaise. 'I think he'd tell us we're Christians. He might think we were blotto but he'd tell us we were Christians.'

Bart reached for Rob's hand. 'Let's go inside and light a fire. What about sitting in front of a fire? I'm so cold since losing all this weight. Heat, would that be so bad? Another Jonestown syndrome?'

Rob helped him to his feet. He weighed little more than a child, it seemed to the older man. They made their way slowly into the house. After showers, they changed into sweaters and slacks, joking about what they should wear and about final appearances creating a lasting impression. The carpet felt so soft under their feet, the modern art on the walls seemed so bright to their eyes, Beethoven's *Pastorale* sounded so gentle to their ears, the air smelled so clean and sweet from the open bedroom window.

It was dark outside when they took the pills, passing the one glass of champagne back and forth. Rob kept filling it as one after the other they would drain it with a handful of the capsules.

'I feel like a little boy, as if you're my best friend,' said Rob.

'I know. I was thinking the same thing. As if we are doing

534

something secret in the woods and we're a little bit afraid of getting caught at it.'

'As if we've made thousands of promises to each other.' He stared at Bart's face.

'We have,' said Bart quietly.

A few minutes later, as they lay beside each other on the zebra-skin rug with the black silk cushions under their heads, Rob turned to Bart and said, 'I'm afraid of one thing.' His fingers closed on his friend's shoulder.

Bart stroked his face and shook his head. 'Nothing to be afraid of now.'

'I'm afraid of going first but I'm more afraid of going second. I'm terrified of your leaving me for even one minute.'

'I won't. I promise I won't.'

They stared into each other's faces, feeling drowsy and warm, talking softly. The fire lit the two figures on the floor in hues of pink and coral. They finished that last bottle of champagne and both heard the settling of the ice in the silver bucket and both felt the same wave of sleep, alluring and then insistent and at last irresistible, and both succumbed to its spell at the same moment. Bart kept his promise.

'Adele?'

'Yes, this is she. Hello?'

'Adele, it's me. Nina.'

'Nina!' Adele unsnapped the big gold earring and dropped it on the open auction catalogue on the desk. She put the phone closer to her ear. 'I didn't recognize your voice! How is Rome?'

'I'm not in Rome. I'm in San Francisco. I really . . . I couldn't seem to call. I wanted to days ago but . . . I just couldn't . . .' Her voice broke.

'Nina?' Adele stood up as though she could reach out in a standing position and be closer. 'Nina what's happened? Why are you in San Francisco?'

'Bart died. The funeral was yesterday.'

'He what? Bart? But why? But, I mean, how?' She

535

fumbled with the collar of her pink blouse and told herself not to cry out. 'Please, Nina. Are you all right?' What a stupid question, colossally stupid, she thought immediately after uttering it. How could she be? Her adored brother had just died. 'Nina, can I come there? Can you come here? Can I do anything?'

'No, no, I have to get back to Rome. I've been here with Mother since Saturday. It was the fastest I could get here and now, I have to hurry back . . .' Her voice was vague.

'Nina, are you sure I can't do anything? You know that . . .'

'I have to tell you that . . . he killed himself.' The last phrase was spoken almost as a question, with surprise in her voice.

Adele sat down heavily in the desk chair. 'But why? Why would he do that?'

'He was very sick and he didn't think he was ever going to get better and he just . . .' Her voice faded to almost a whisper. 'Did it.'

Adele grabbed a Kleenex out of the top desk drawer and held it firmly under her nose. Her tears were sliding rapidly down her face. The gallery was so quiet and the Madison Avenue traffic so strangely muted that Adele could hear the plop plop sound the liquid made as it fell on the colour reproduction of the Cézanne up for sale at the next Sotheby's auction.

'Adele, I have to go now. I'll try to call you again before my plane tonight. I wish I could stop in New York but I'm trying to go over the pole so it'll be a shorter trip. Are you all right? How is everything there? The gallery? Is it wonderful?'

Nina was so brave, Adele thought later. She had given an almost superhuman performance in that last moment on the phone.


Nina clutched the Fendi carry-on bag and waved one last time before going through gate twenty-three. Virginia blew her a kiss and nodded as if to say, yes, I'll be fine, to the unasked question. Dr Thurston Thorpe, the founder of the clinic where she did her voluntary work, stood beside her, one arm around her shoulders protectively. Thank God she has found someone. A widower. Handsome in a rough outdoorsy way. Thank God there is someone special, someone kind for Mother, thought Nina as she handed her boarding pass to a uniformed attendant.

On the plane she took her window seat and put a pillow between her head and the glass. Poor Bart was going through her mind, poor Bart, and then she thought: No. Poor Mother, and then, poor me. We never get to see him again. Nina dozed fitfully, lulled by the hum of the plane.

She dreamed of Bart. He had his hands on her shoulders, introducing her as his little sister. Nina wakened suddenly. I'm not his little sister any more, she thought, and won't ever be again. Years will go by and some day I'll be older than Bart. That realization was more painful than anything else that had occurred to her in the past five days. She pulled a blanket over her stocking feet and stretched out on the three seats across, resolving to think of nothing until Dante at Fiumicino. Claudio was 'in Switzerland' which means, Nina frowned, he is unreachable. All it really means is that we had a fight eight days ago and no one knows where he is. Tears of anger and self-pity began to roll down her cheeks. Nina blew her nose then rearranged her pillow and wished she could sleep. Mother's Thurston had been wonderful. He'd sat them down and gently explained that this acquired immune deficiency syndrome had only recently been identified in the United States and that it was incurable. There could be a remission but no one has ever been cured. Dr Parker, Bart's doctor, had come to the hotel and they'd all talked quietly in a corner of the restaurant over endless glasses of iced tea which was not nearly as good as the tea that Virginia made at home. He told them that Bart had lost so much weight, his blood count had been so radically altered, with no white blood cells at all, that his resistance to even a sore throat was nonexistent. While a patient at the hospital, Bart had requested that he be allowed to read all medical reports of the research that had been done. He had asked endless questions and then he had begged to be discharged, promising to take care of himself. It was Parker's opinion that Bart knew he was going to die and could not face months, or perhaps only weeks, in a hospital environment.

Thurston said acquired immune deficiency syndrome wasn't hereditary and Parker had said there was the idea of it being spread by transfusions but, the doctors agreed, there were still few clues as to its origin.


Curiously, neither sister nor mother seemed to have the faintest idea that Bart may have been homosexual. The mention of a suicide pact of sorts had shocked both the McLean women, but then they had seem relieved to know that his best friend, this Robert Cabell, had been with him when he died. Before learning this, on the way in from San Francisco airport, Nina had said how sad it was to have your very last moment on earth, breathing and seeing and thinking, in such sadness. Such sadness, she said, she couldn't imagine. Thurston had turned to look at her and a new expression had come into her eyes then and he realized that, yes, she had remembered something, and he knew she could imagine those depths of misery.

Those eyes as beautiful as her mother's, those slender lovely hands with the same gestures, that same way of pushing the shining black hair away from the same oval face. Bart looked like Mother, too, she'd said as she caught him staring at her. Lucky anybody to look like Virginia, he'd responded, and Virginia had smiled. Virginia McLean was still a very beautiful woman.


The de Leones were emotional and solicitous. The Contessa greeted Nina in the front hallway and wept. '*Tesora!* I am so sorry . . . so sorry. Your mother! How is your mother? Her only son!' Franco took her suitcase and Maria followed him with the carry-on bag and her pocketbook. Claudio's apartment had been filled with flowers, but Nina's heart sank with disappointment as she realized that Claudio had not come back. The maid kissed her on both cheeks and then smoothed her hair maternally. Franco told her in his self-conscious English to call him for anything she might need at any time. Nina smiled and thought: I feel pregnant again, but was touched by all the little kindnesses of these Italians who, as the Count told her, 'think of you as part of our family, with your family very close to us, too'.

Claudio's absence was not alluded to, but his empty chair at dinner that evening might as well have been painted bright red.


The dreams began that night. The dreams that she was helping Bart to pack, that he wasn't dead at all, but only going away. He wanted Nina to help him fool everyone and thought it would be easier for Mother if she thought he had died. Bart was in his room at the Old Canton Road house, laying out shirts and socks on his bed as Nina watched from a chair much too big for her. Her feet dangled, not touching the floor. She tried to make him stay, but she was only his little sister, after all.

Nina wakened with pounding heart and frantically grabbed for the light switch beside the bed. She sat up, hair matted against her face, which was wet with sweat. Sleep came to her again, fitfully, filled with half dreams. There was a smiling photograph of Bart on the floor and she could not pick it up. There were suitcases in the back of a car and she was a little girl waiting in the driveway at home for Bart to come. There was a letter from Bart. He was asking her to do something for him but the writing was blurred.

The days edged by in a haze of feeling sad and being tired after nights of not sleeping well. The newly returned Claudio was kind to her but no more than that. He held her in his arms after her nightmares but Nina detected no passion in him. More than once she had signalled her desire to make love but he moved away. Nina suspected there was someone he met in the afternoon, that there was someone he spent his evenings with when she had dinner at home with his mother, his cousin and his grandfather. Sometimes she wanted Claudio back and sometimes she hated him. His capacity for coldness frightened her. He could sleep in the same bed as she lay awake; he could walk into her dressing room as she chose jewellery to wear to a party and not speak; he could sit across a dinner table and not appear to notice her presence. Nina almost wished for the return of the shouting husband who threw things – anything would have been easier to bear than the silent tensions of two obviously sexual animals in close proximity. It is sexual, decided Nina. She had caught him staring at her fingers wrapped around the stem of a wine glass with such longing. Impetuously she had put her other hand quickly up to his cheek. To her acute embarrassment he had turned away and joined the conversation between Luciano and Marco who had seen everything. Nina had been welcomed back to the lunches around town, the meetings for drinks at Harry's Bar, the dinners, the parties, for it was very common to be *separato* and then together again. They like me enough, thought Nina, but Claudio is one of them. They've known him all their lives.

She realized her own friends had all left Rome and she had not troubled to replace them. Peggy and Lisa were sharing a flat in London. The Middletons were ensconced and content in Connecticut and the occasional letter told of gardening and dinner parties and suburban life. It was the life that Adele had left behind. She wrote of gallery openings, of auctions and of Mr Rajjin's plans for a gallery in Paris. Once, she forwarded a letter from Myra, addressed to both of them at the Park Avenue apartment since 'Nina has vanished'. Myra was pregnant with her third child, happily married to an investment banker in Chicago, and running a boutique. Adele had written in the margin, 'Sounds as if she has it all.'

Nina wondered what it 'all' was.

Dear Kate, when told of Nina's decision to return to the palazzo, had said to give it her best, to love Claudio and to be happy. She had claimed to be glad for her but at the end of the phone call had offered, 'I'm always here. Call me collect if you need me.' Adele had never fully absorbed the idea that Claudio had been unfaithful, for Nina, in her eyes,

540

was the most attractive, most vivacious of all women. She
had thought it only a matter of a cooling-off period before
the separation ended. Virginia in Mississippi was delighted.
Her daughter was 'safe' again; living with her husband
where she belonged.

But Nina thought of the villa as the centre of her life these
days. She spent her afternoons prowling the antique shops
for this or that table, for that perfect print to be framed in
blue and silver, for that lamp that would probably need to be
cleaned and rewired and fitted with the cream silk shade.
She lingered over dark blue velvet, touching it lovingly, and
spent a rainy hour picking out antique drawer pulls on her
knees in a dusty storeroom. She walked home in the
amethyst dusk of that Roman spring and felt the excitement
of creation. The villa would be alive with her colours, her
ideas, with the Persian rugs she'd bid on at Christie's, with
the lion doorknocker, with the hand-painted plates, with the
silver pitcher to be filled with flowers.

Decorating the villa was a focus for her energy, for her
originality, but Nina longed for affection from her husband.
She missed Adele, the Countess, Kate. She missed Bart and
wished she could have stopped him. The only consolation
was Thurston's telling her about all the empty champagne
bottles.

Time. Time measured by I'll never see you again. Time
measured by a baby growing inside you. She thought of the
Claudio of the midnight picnic on the polo field. So long
ago. So much between then and now. Time measured by
nights of not making love.


'No, I won't!' Claudio was saying. 'I will not take her!' He
spoke in his precise English as his mother answered him in
Italian, telling him he was being very silly and making
matters worse. Nina hesitated at the open bedroom door and
then walked quietly down the hall to the reception room.
The Contessa never came to their quarters. Take me where?
she wondered.

In minutes Franco and Dante had manœuvred past her

with the luggage. The dark blue canvas bags Claudio packed for the boat. Maria clutched a basket of bright royal blue and white striped towels, and another maid carried a stack of the freshly ironed white silk shirts Claudio enjoyed wearing on summer evenings. Dante had gone to bring the car around as Claudio and his mother appeared in the front hallway.

'*Cara*,' said the Contessa, with real affection evident, 'I thought you'd gone out.'

'No, I decided it's too close to one o'clock. I'll go out after the *mezzogiorno*.'

Claudio didn't look at her. The Contessa stared at her son as he pointed a finger at each of the eleven bags and counted, '*sei, sette, otto* . . .' She seemed to be willing him to speak to Nina. The trio stood beside the open front door as Franco and Maria rushed back and forth. Nina's hands were moist with perspiration and she wondered if the great tension she felt was evident under the immaculate white piqué dress. She glanced down at her bare toes in the white sandals, manicured and polished bright coral, and thought they seemed ridiculously vulnerable. All the bags had been removed, everything was in the car awaiting the drive to Civitavecchia and the unpacking aboard *Simba II*.

Claudio moved to kiss his mother goodbye but she stepped back, displeased. Only then did he meet Nina's unwavering gaze. 'I'm going away, as you can see.' Nina didn't say anything. She stood very still, very straight, her eyes never leaving her husband's face. Claudio stood framed in the doorway facing the two most important women in his life. There was no way to please his mother and himself; no way to please himself and Nina. So he gave her a half smile which appeared as a wincing expression and said, 'Switzerland', and turned and was gone. The two contessas listened to his topsiders pad down the marble steps, heard his voice ask Dante, '*Pronto?*' and finally heard the engine of the blue Mercedes come to life.

Nina thought that her expression must show her pain but the Contessa silently noted her cool reserve, admired her dignity. She closed the door and turned to her daughter-in-law. 'Switzerland,' said Nina softly. The lie wounded more than angered her. It made a mockery of every trip he'd ever taken, of every explanation of every absence.

The Contessa put a soft hand on Nina's shoulder. '*Carissima*.' It was the first time she had lengthened the 'dear' to 'dearest'. 'My son is a fool.' Nina blinked in surprise as she continued, 'I am very glad you are back.' The two women, both without husbands, walked slowly into the dining room, where the serving maids stood at attention, and took their places for lunch.

'We'll never really know, but yes, I'll level with you. The odds are that he was.'

'And Robert Cabell?'

'Looks that way.'

Virginia bit her lip and then reached up to smooth the hair from her face. Turning her back to Thurston she walked quietly to the edge of the porch and listened to the 'shhhhhhhh' noise of the drops falling on the tall grass, and the gurgle of the gutterspout. The Mississippi drought was at last over. Virginia's voice faltered. 'I don't believe Nina could stand to know. I hope she never . . .'

Thurston stood up and reached for his wallet. It was years old and curved almost into a C after tens of thousands of hours in his back pocket.

'This came in June. From Nina. I don't think she'd mind your reading it now.'

'From Nina? Nina wrote to you?' Virginia was mystified. She took the page covered in Nina's slanted hurried handwriting; she studied the curves of peacock blue ink.

Dear Thurston,

You were with me and with Mother at perhaps the hardest time of our lives and I thank you for all your kindnesses to us.

Because you were there, I think you know how much we ache inside and I know that you will help Mother as much as you can. I have been reading about the sickness that Bart had and putting things together and it's all right. I loved Bart. He will always be the brother I love, the brother I miss. Whatever he did or was or was not, he was always Bart, a person I love. I hope that Mother never has to know, or that if she does find out you will help her to absorb it as just something that Bart had in his life. I am so sorry that he felt he had to hide it from us because we loved him so. Sometimes I wish I could have known Robert, the man who died with him. If Bart loved him then I am sure he was worthy of it, and I miss knowing him. Robert Cabell must have been spectacular for Bart to have loved him enough to let him be with him in the last moments, and he must have loved Bart enough to never want to be without him. That must be more love than I have in me.

Please take care of Mother. I am so far away.

Thank you for being so good to us both.

with love, NINA

Virginia handed the page to Thurston and looked up at him. The pain had left her eyes and her face was relaxed and smooth. 'Some daughter I have,' she said softly as he folded the note and placed it back in his wallet.

Thurston took her in his arms then and she reached up to embrace his broad shoulders. He murmured, 'Some mother she has,' and kissed her wide forehead, then her closed eyelids and, at last, her mouth.

The Directeur was laughing. He stood at his desk in his London office and smiled at the sheets of paper before him. He'd bought low and sold when it was high. The market had done just what he thought it would. He looked out the window at the expanse of river before him and thought: Love this address. Lower Thames Street, Sugar Quay. And I love sugar! He laughed again and picked up the phone.

'Helen! Will you track down Gaston Pibault for me? Yes, try his suite at the hotel in Geneva first, then the Paris office, and then . . . God, wonder if he's still in Rome. That's always the Hassler. I want to catch him this morning. Thanks.'

Gaston lay dreaming of Catherine. Mmmmmmm, he murmured as his mind's eye watched her approach him in the bikini that was barely a G-string. Mmmmmm, the sun felt good on his body. 'Mmmmmmm, Catherine,' Gaston moaned. Suddenly there was a fire engine on the beach at St Tropez! Mon Dieu! How terrible! The noise!

Gaston sat bolt upright and stared stupidly at the phone and then grabbed it. '*Bonjour!*' he shouted, his hair standing straight up, his eyes wide.

'Gaston! Why are you asleep at this hour?'

'*Quelle heure . . .*' he whispered like a man caught with his fly down. 'It's only five o'clock in the morning!' he shouted as he plucked his watch from the bedside table.

'Are you in New York?' The Directeur apologized. 'New secretary. I told her to find you but I never thought she'd wake you up. I'll call back in a few hours.'

'*Non, non, non.* I am awake now. I got in yesterday from Rome.'

'How is she?'

'She is fine.' There is only one 'she' in his life, thought Gaston. 'I wish you'd let me in on this. How you say in English? I am the "fall guy"?' – Laughter.

'You're not a fall guy. I'm just glad you don't mind playing front-man and interior decorator for a while.'

'I'm not really doing the work. It's someone I hired in Milano. You'll get the bill later.' The little Frenchman pulled the sheet up over his bare chest. He looked very small in the big double bed. The Pierre suite was dark, with only slivers of light showing between the floral curtains where dawn was edging through.

'Nina is all right, then?'

'I couldn't reach her for a while, you know. She went back to the States . . .'

'To see her mother?'

'No. Her brother died. She told me he killed himself. San Francisco.'

'My God!' came the strangled oath. He pulled at his silk

tie and stared out the window. Pale sunlight shone on the Thames.

'She didn't tell me anything else,' continued Gaston. 'Went to the funeral and then flew back and got right to work again. She's strong, you know.'

'Anything I can do?'

'No, not unless you want to tell her and me what you're up to.'

'All in good time. Speaking of which, I called about the Callison deal. Did we get the stocks?'

'Tell me again. How many?'

'We decided to put in for 175,000 pounds' sterling worth . . .'

'Yes, yes, we have them. I was notified yesterday in Rome. The telex went to Paris. You should receive a confirmation from there this afternoon at the latest.'

'Wow! You know what! We have just made ourselves a bucket of money!' Gaston laughed. The Directeur was like a little boy with his games. 'With the stagging next week we'll do awfully well.'

'Can I go back to sleep now?'

'Sweet dreams.'


Adele walked into her apartment and sighed, dropping her keys on the bureau. London in August. No one could predict the weather there. Ever. She opened the Gucci suitcase on her bed and stood staring at the lining. Last night had been so ridiculous. Me, a grown woman, grappling with that investment banker who collects stamps and who just assumed I was dying to go to bed with him. She shook her blonde hair as if to forget it. New York's not so easy when it comes to men.

She walked to the closet and slid open the doors. Silk dresses, perfectly simple for every day, and then good jewellery for the dinner with Rajjiv and the clients. She took out the white silk, and then the pale blue silk print. She picked the peach flowered silk dress and the high-heeled cream-coloured sandals. Silver sandals were thrust into the shoe bag alongside them. The black silk suit with the white piqué camisole, two evening bags, a deep blue evening jacket which looked well with everything, in case it was chilly and damp. The little collapsible umbrella was thrown in. Adele plucked half a dozen pairs of bikini panties from her bureau drawer, tossed in several unopened packages of pantyhose and thought: That's it. Only four days in London. Two for meetings and two for me. She stripped off her cream linen dress and, naked, marched towards the bathroom for a quick shower.

Two hours and twenty minutes later Adele sat composedly reading a magazine in the VIP departure lounge. The British Airways flight was due to depart on time, her bags were checked, and her seat assignment sticker was on her boarding pass.

The man hurried down the long hallway to gate twenty-three. There was two minutes before boarding and, according to the manager of British Airways, the seat next to her would be empty. He pulled at his tie. His hair was still damp from the shower and he wondered if he were wearing shoes of the same colour, for he'd practically dressed in the speeding taxi once he'd found out where she was going and had made the decision to go, too. In great strides he was soon at the gate and saw her all in white – a white linen suit, her blonde hair a perfect cap of shining silk. She carried a small canvas bag in one hand with several auction catalogues peeking out of the top. He waited until the line snaked its way past the smiling attendant. She, in her dark blue uniform and white blouse, gave every single person the same automatic smile as they passed. Like a magnetic eye on a door, he decided. No fuss, please, no fuss. I'll wait till we're airborne and then I'll sit down beside her. No, I'll wait till one minute before take-off. No, he decided. I can't wait that long. I've waited long enough as it is.

Jack was the last person to board the plane. He saw her immediately, sitting in first class, the second row by the window. He took the aisle seat and handed his carry-on bag to the flight attendant. His pulse quickened when she opened her pocketbook to pull out a notepad but she began to write without glancing at him. At exactly seven-fifteen, when the plane began to move down the runway, Adele leaned back and closed her eyes. Oh, no, you're not, said Jack to himself. You're not going to sleep. You're going to listen to me. For five hours if that's what it takes.

'You can't avoid me any longer.'

'I beg your pardon?' Adele opened her eyes. 'Jack!' Adele, known for years as the Ice Queen, was flustered.

He smiled slowly. 'Amazing what a small world it is, etcetera, etcetera, etcetera.'

Adele felt her face go crimson, much to her dismay. What was he doing here? 'Are you going to London?'

'Gee,' he grinned. 'I hope so. I thought this flight was non-stop.' Adele laughed. Jack motioned for the flight attendant to bring them champagne. 'We're beginning to celebrate,' he said cryptically.

'Celebrate what?'

Too soon. Too soon. Watch out. 'Going to London, of course.' It only took one bottle of Dom Perignon – half a bottle for Jack, half a bottle for Adele. Jack reached over and, grasping her hand, said, 'I've missed you.'

'I've always been there. We live seven blocks apart.' Adele was confused, had skipped lunch, and the alcohol was certainly not helping her to straighten things out.

'I mean I've missed you for years.' Jack thought of the recent parade of Phoebe Haffenraffers, and of the nights alone when I dreamt of holding Adele; the theatre parties, the dinner dances, and I was always with the wrong girl.

'I've missed you, too.' Adele thought of Paul. 'But you didn't miss me!' she recovered enough to protest.

'Well, yes, I did!' retorted Jack fervently.

'What about Sandra, and Lis, and Phoebe, and . . .'

He put his finger to her lips. 'Funny you remember those names, because I don't.'

His touch was electric. Adele found herself leaning closer and closer to his handsome face. He was tan, with a blush of

548

pink beneath it; his teeth were very white; his hair that sun-bleached colour of her own.

Jack was ready to kiss her and then drew back. Let her wait. Let her decide. He poured the new bottle of champagne into their empty glasses and waved the dinner trays away. 'To us,' he dared toast.

Adele nodded. She felt a little giddy and quite bold. 'I've missed you, too, you know,' she said seriously. Her blue eyes were troubled as she searched for words. 'Paul wasn't you,' she sighed dramatically. 'He had blonde hair, of course, and he played squash and he was' – she fell into a mocking Long Island lockjaw accent – 'strictly top drawer.'

Jack grinned. 'I wanted to warn you. But how could I?'

Adele thought of how lousy Paul was in bed. 'How could you have known?'

'Known what exactly?'

Adele blushed and made Jack laugh uproariously. He took her hand and put it to his cheek. She felt the soft just-shaved skin and longed to put her face against his.

'Lousy, huh?'

Adele swallowed the champagne the wrong way and began to cough, then giggle. 'The worst.' She coughed again and started to say, 'Sometimes I pretended he was you,' but held herself in check.

'Adele, Adele.' Jack wanted to say, 'I love you, I love you,' but contented himself with saying her name. 'There were all kinds of things you never could have known.'

'Like what?' Adele was fascinated.

'Like Paul is the kind of guy who'll try to cheat at squash.' Adele gasped. This shocked her. It simply wasn't done.

'Thank God it's over. My marriage, I mean. All those years of being by myself with him.' Was she making any sense, she wondered? She could hear her voice; she was being awfully open, awfully free; was it all right to talk this way? Of course it was. This was Jack. He's known me longer than anyone.

He stroked her hand, with his thumb moving back and forth. She didn't object, so he continued. 'Not sorry about anything?'

'I think I'm sorry about everything. I'm sorry I got pregnant, I'm sorry I lost the baby, I'm sorry I got married. I'm sorry we moved to that tomb in Westchester, and I'm even sorry the marriage was a flop.'

Jack suddenly felt a wave of sympathy for her. Nothing had worked for her, had it? He'd been in limbo emotionally all these years, wanting her, but she had been trying to make something go – a marriage, a life. Adele had been expending emotion on a man who didn't deserve her, but he, Jack, had been saving his emotions, using his energy to hold them back.

'Adele,' he said softly, continuing to stroke her hand. Those tiny bones, that delicate wrist. How well he remembered leading her to the boathouse and . . . no, not now. You've relived it tens of thousands of times. Not now. 'Adele, could you ever want me again?'

She sipped her champagne. Her blonde hair dipped forward towards her mouth and his hand came up naturally to flip it away. His fingers touched her cheek as he did so. Could I ever want you, Jack? she repeated to herself. God, he doesn't know. He really doesn't know. I can pretend to be more drunk than I am and say anything and then pretend I didn't say it when the plane lands, or I can try to sit up straight and say, 'Whatever do you mean?' which is the Adele I have been trying to be with him. Or I can tell him the truth.

'I've never stopped wanting you.' Her words were clear and precise. Let the consequences be damned, she thought.

They sat in silence for a few minutes. His thumb stroked that soft delicate mound of her thumb as they listened to the jet's engines and considered what would or might not happen next. Adele took another sip of champagne.

Jack turned to her, blue eyes alight. 'I love you. I've always loved you. Always. Hasn't changed. Except you're a woman and I'm a man. We're not little kids playing tag on the porch and we're not teenagers out in a sailboat pretending not to notice how our hearts pound when we brush against each other. I love you. I want you. I don't want to take you off to the Dorchester for one night or for one week. I want you for always.' Adele thought she'd never seen his eyes so bright. 'I want you to marry me.'

Adele moistened her lips and unblinkingly stared at his face. This face she loved. This face she often visualized in the last seconds before falling asleep at night. She had daydreamed of marrying Jack once. After all, didn't Egyptian pharaohs marry their brothers and sisters over and over again? But this is New York and hadn't he ever seen pictures of the distorted head of the Egyptian king, Akhnaton? Had't he seen, she thought a bit drunkenly, the movie *Deliverance*, with all those inbred Southern hillbillies drooling into their harmonicas and playing banjos from dawn to dusk?

'Jack, we can't.'

'You don't want to?' His flesh went cold. Disappointment was a wave of pain. 'You don't . . . Do you love me?' he demanded.

'Yes, I love you.' I've said it, at last. It feels so good to hear the words, to tell him.

'Then for Christ's sake, marry me!'

'But we can't . . .' Adele thought: Hasn't he considered . . .

Suddenly Jack realized why she wouldn't say yes. 'Adele,' he insisted impatiently, 'we *can*. I'm a lawyer, remember? A hot shot, hot shit Wall Street lawyer, and we *can*. It's legal in nineteen states and the other thirty-one I don't care about!'

Her sapphire blue eyes showed astonishment. 'Are you sure? Do you really think so? Are you sure?'

'I looked it up years ago! Now will you just say "yes"?'

Adele smiled slowly at first and then her face became so radiant, so luminous, it seemed lit by candlelight.

'Yes.'


'This never happens!' exclaimed Nina. 'Absolutely never!' She stood in the middle of the beamed living room and surveyed the progress. Gaston smiled beside her, a dapper figure in a summer suit, holding an expensive-looking briefcase. 'Nothing is ever done on time, on schedule, when you think it will be done, in decorating a house!'

The little Frenchman laughed. 'Giorgio, what do you think? Do you like it?' he asked in Italian. The Sicilian driver answered in the affirmative, peppering his response with '*bellissimas*'.

The fireplaces were clean and the stones had been replaced where necessary. Giorgio brought the andirons and the copper buckets for firewood from the trunk of the Bentley. Nina made notes to buy towels when next in Rome. She thought she'd carry through the same colour scheme and have white ones, rust, or pale coral in every bathroom. The oriental carpets she'd bought at the Christie's auction at Piazza Navona lay tied with twine in one corner of the room. She instructed two of the workers to spread them out and they all admired the soft shades of blue and fawn and copper on the marble floor.

'I think we'll roll them up again until the very last,' she decided, and Gaston nodded.

'Nina, there is a surprise for you upstairs!'

'What! What! What!' She clapped her hands in delight, following Gaston up the stairway. The ceiling had been painted in the upstairs hall and even the bedrooms were finished.

'Look!' motioned Gaston in the doorway of the master suite.

'Oh, it's here!' The four-poster bed had arrived. It dated from the seventeenth century, according to the man in Rome who had sold it to Nina. The oak gleamed with the soft patina of age and the loving attention of a refinisher.

'And the mattress, too!' Nina bounced up and down. Her face was alight. Gaston was charmed by her, as always.

'Get out your notebook, Miss McLean. I have some more things the Directeur wants you to find for him.'

She raised her eyebrows and said, 'I've stopped being curious, really, honestly I have, Gaston. You won't get any more questions from me, so you can just relax and' – she hesitated and said with a straight face – 'and tell me who he is!'

Gaston grinned. 'No dice. Is that how you Americans put it? No dice?'

'No dice is right. I don't get anywhere with you.' She folded back a few pages of the spiral tablet she carried and commanded, 'Begin.'

'He wants you to stock the bathroom for a woman.' Nina looked up. 'Well, for a woman who arrives with no luggage. The things . . .'

Nina burst out laughing. 'I think you are involved with a very strange man, Gaston!'

'I am French, Nina. I am used to these things. Try to be a little sophisticated, please.' This speech was so unlike Gaston that Nina continued to laugh. At the look on his face – sheer embarrassment – she abruptly stopped. 'Soaps, bathrobe, nightgowns, a toothbrush, everything a woman would need to spend the weekend here.'

'Okay.' Nina was thinking: I'll go to that really chic place at the top of the Spanish Steps on the via Francesco Crispi and then to the via Condotti for the lingerie. 'Size?'

'Hmmmm, I have it somewhere. She is rather tall,' he began.

'Oh, this is so like a man.' Nina groaned inwardly. Next he will describe her measurements with his hands outstretched.

'Size eight American.'

'Right.' Nina wrote it down, wondering if the woman were, in fact, American. Probably not. Probably Gaston is trying to throw me off the scent. 'Gaston, you said things for a weekend. Do you mean I should buy slacks and sweaters and bathing suits, too?'

'The house will not be ready until the autumn but it will be warm, so all of that. I think one bathing suit, one . . .' He faltered. 'You know, whatever you would bring if you were to be invited here for a few days as the guest of the Directeur.'

'Price range?'

'No limit.'

'Wow!' yelped Nina. 'This'll be fun.'

Gaston was glad that was over. The Directeur had been insistent. The house must be ready for a woman to arrive and be at home. The wine cellar was fully stocked already

553

and a new lock had been made for the door so that no workmen were tempted. The champagne had been delivered only this past week. All of the kitchen utensils were still in the boxes from Milan, waiting for the two local housekeepers to unpack and to put away.

'So, Gaston,' said Nina from the upstairs sitting room off the master bedroom. 'I need to buy towels and bathroom things, like paper and . . .'

'No, the toilet tissue has arrived. Hundreds of rolls wholesale, along with the paper towels and things for the kitchen.'

'Okay.' Nina marked through one line on her list. 'The big things to come are the mirrors for the downstairs hallway, for the bedrooms, and all the prints and etchings I've had framed. I wonder if I should hire a truck to get them driven up here from Rome?'

'Give me the address of the framers and I'll do it.'

Nina handed him the small engraved card. 'Ready after Wednesday. I think there should be eight mirrors and forty-five pictures. He's honest, his name is Pietro, and he'll have it itemized.' She continued. 'Living room furniture will come from Milan. The leather sofa from D'Alessandro, the velvet settees from the Roman upholsterer, and the antique bedside tables are coming from this little place on the outskirts of Rome. There are eight of them – four pairs – no, three pairs and two which are good together. Three wardrobes are from there, too. I think it's fine to have guest room wardrobes, don't you, Gaston?' He nodded, head down, writing. 'They're so beautiful and the guests won't need masses of closet space the way the master bedroom will have.' 'Coathangers,' she wrote. The silky padded kind – pale blue for some bedrooms, pale green for others. 'Did the Piranesi linen arrive for the beds?'

'*Oui*, the housekeeper will take care of it.'

'Dining room table? Living room table for in front of the fireplace? Dining room chairs?'

'*Oui, oui, oui*, they are in the garage. The next time you come the floors will have been cleaned and polished and we can put them in place.'

'Gaston, I am going to buy some copper and brass vases for the flowers. And silver, too. Does the Directeur like flowers?'

'*Oui*.' Gaston was worrying: I'll need another day in Rome to organize this. 'The gardener is a sorcerer and when we go out the back you can see that the lemon trees and the magnolias are in full bloom.'

'Can he do something for the front door? Something maybe in white? And for along the path to the sea, too.' If we're going to have a full-blown gardener, might as well put him to work, thought Nina.

'Right.'

Nina was thinking: I'm going to buy things like candlesticks and paperweights and little carved boxes and things for the tables. A silver bowl for the hall table to put keys in. A silver tray for the mail. A handsome letter opener. Good soaps for all the bathrooms.

The ride back to Rome was quiet. Nina stared out at the green hills of Tuscany and felt comforted by the land. She glanced over at Gaston and saw that he had dozed off and was curled in one corner of the back seat. Dusk was full of smoky grey and pinky streaks above the fields. The air smelled of the rich scent of growing things, of fertile earth. Nina closed her eyes and let the wind from the open windows blow her hair as she leaned back on the soft upholstery. Oh, this Directeur, I hope he loves the house half as much as I do. She smiled and slept until Giorgio gently touched her arm. '*Il palazzo*, contessa. *Siamo arrivati!*'

Nina rather liked the deserted palazzo. It was just Francesca to take care of her, and Vittorio who did any heavy work and watered the trees and flowers in the courtyard. The Count and Contessa, Nonno and Elena had gone to Porto Santo Stefano taking Maria and Franco with them. Dante, the cooks and the other maids had the month off. Nina thought she might go to the family villa for the last half of August when the entire city was closed. She no longer felt uncomfortable with her mother-in-law and realized that the older woman liked her company.

Nina strode quickly under the archway. Vittorio appeared,

and dropping a length of green rubber hose raced to open the ground-floor door for her. She smiled a '*grazie*' and rearranged the heavy wallpaper book across her chest. Ascending the stairs, she was pleased at the thought of a supper of whatever she wanted, an evening reading or watching Italian television, wearing shorts and a T-shirt. Wish Kate were here, or Adele, or just someone to enjoy it with me! A long supper, a long talk, and someone to listen to all my news about the renovating. She pushed open the door, surprised it wasn't locked, then frightened that something was amiss. 'Oh!' she exclaimed when she saw him. 'I thought you were on the boat!'

'No. I'm not on the boat.' Claudio's voice was angry. His skin was nearly mahogany from the sun; he wore white linen trousers and a red and white striped jersey. 'I'm here. Watching you arrive in that damned silver Bentley with your little frog escort! Your pimp!'

'What are you talking about?' Nina told herself not to show panic. What had happened? She walked to the hall table and put the notebook down. The pink linen dress was damp where it had pressed against her. This heat, suffocating, she thought vaguely as she pushed her hair away from her temples.

'Why do you think you can do anything you like? How much do I have to put up with?'

'What are you talking about?' she asked again. Nina tried to keep her voice soft, calm. He's been drinking, she decided. There was a very real menace in his manner.

'Flaunt yourself in front of my friends! Be driven away for the afternoon and then come back here – so happy. So well taken care of!'

'Claudio! Please stop and – ' The man before her was sinister, not a person she knew.

'Luciano was in town last week. He saw you with Gaston on the via Veneto . . .'

'He took me to pick up some fabric and then we drove to the country.'

'Do you think I believe – '

'I don't know what you believe but I don't think you

should believe your friends. I think you should believe me.'
Nina turned to walk into the reception room, thinking that
the shutters should be opened now that it was evening. The
long room was full of cool shadows. She was unprepared for
Claudio's rough grasp. He jerked her by the arm, causing
her sandal to slide precariously on the slick marble floor.
Some terrible fragment of memory – of the last time he had
grabbed her, of that street in Capri, of that fall – came into
her mind. 'Let go!' she cried out, upset, no longer able to
feign unconcern.

'Listen to me!' He shook her then, hurting her, not
caring. 'You leave me and you move to via dei Greci, you
stay in Rome, you show everyone how independent you are,
how free you are! You drive out of the city with a man every
week and at the end of the afternoon – '

'Claudio! Stop it!' Nina gasped. 'You're hurting me!' She
tried to pry his fingers from her forearm.

'Then you come back to me and I want to make it all right
and you insist on your project, your work. No baby. *Va bene*.
Whatever you want. *Va bene*. My mother insisted you were
worth it.' Nina's eyes were wide. 'Whatever Nina wants!'
Claudio's mouth was sneering. 'And months later still you
go to meet him – whenever you please! My friends have seen
you! All Rome sees you!'

'Him? Go to meet him?' repeated Nina. Surely Claudio
didn't think –

'You humiliate me!' He spat the words at her.

Nina was confused. What was he accusing her of? 'I
haven't done anything to humiliate you,' she replied calmly
though his fingers were digging painfully into her flesh.
Where was Francesca? Vittorio? Then Claudio's hand
swung back and struck her across the face. Again and again
until Nina tasted blood. Until she felt it pouring out of her
nose. Still he held her and shook her like a rag doll as she
tried to put one arm up to fend off the blows.

'Stop!' she screamed. 'Stop hitting me!'

This Claudio she didn't know shouted back at her, 'This
is Italy! I can kill you if I want!'

Nina tried to cry out, liquid bubbling in her throat. 'Who

is he?' demanded Claudio. 'You don't make love to me! Who is he?'

'There isn't anyone!' Nina shouted. She could see blood spattering the front of her dress. 'No one!'

Claudio hit her one last time, which knocked her off her feet. She fell backwards over the low end table where Nonno kept his humidor. Francesca came running into the room, crying, then stood and stared at the Count as though she were awaiting directions. Claudio looked down at Nina where she lay motionless then without another word he left the palazzo, slamming the front door behind him.

Nothing is broken, thought Nina as she stared into the bathroom mirror.

Little Francesca ran the bath water in the sarcophagus and wept loudly. '*Sto bene. Sto bene. Calma,*' Nina said. Don't cry or I'll start again and won't be able to stop. Suddenly he was there in the doorway and both women jumped in surprise.

'Don't come near me again. Not ever again,' whispered Nina. Her face was still bleeding. There were five little crescent cuts where the de Leone coat of arms in twenty-two-carat gold had left its mark. The pink linen dress was halfway off her shoulders, stained with dark red. Claudio was calm now. That icy calm that had taken them through the months of the previous spring. He walked into the bedroom, opened a bureau drawer and selected a dress shirt and a wide black cummerbund. Then he was gone.

Gaston called Nina the next week and they had a talk about all that was left to do. 'I've bought lots of things to make it look as though someone lives there.' Nina put a finger to her still swollen mouth, grateful that he could not see her. 'They're here in the bottom of my closet.'

'I think they must wait, for the Directeur and I have several meetings together and we will be flying between

Hong Kong and Geneva the last two weeks of August. Do you mind holding on to everything?'

'No, of course not. So this means I shouldn't plan on going there until September?' Nina was both disappointed and relieved for her face was still a horrible sight. As a matter of fact, the black eye seemed to be worse. Why do they even call them 'black'? she wondered. Her eye and then her cheek had become several sickly shades of lavender, yellow and grey.

'I think it will be the first week of the month. You and I can put things in order that last time.'

'Oh, the last time,' she repeated. 'That makes me so sad. I love the villa.'

Gaston agreed. 'So do I. It's a place with feelings now.' He hesitated. 'I have a thought. Do you have the clothes ready?'

'Yes. Boxes and boxes.' Behind big sunglasses and pancake make-up, she'd had no choice but to get the shopping done before Ferragosto. I look too awful for a fall downstairs she'd said to Francesca, so they'd decided on a car accident; but in shop after shop clerks seemed to go out of their way not to stare and certainly no one had asked the young Contessa de Leone anything about her poor face. It had been so much fun to take Gaston at his word and buy just what she would have wanted to have for a weekend at the villa in the Tuscan hills that Nina had soon forgotten what she looked like. She bought a black and white print bikini, a wide-brimmed straw hat, a fluffy white terrycloth cover-up, a hot pink and white striped jellaba, gold sandals, three negligees with matching peignoirs in black lace, in white lace and in a goldey cream colour. There were white raw silk trousers, black raw silk trousers and hand-knitted sweaters of lime green and pale coral embroidered with tiny seed pearls. She couldn't resist the powder blue linen shift with the silver belt, the silver sandals and the pale blue cashmere sweater. Nina's practical side had tracked down Fiorucci jeans and Gianni Versace T-shirts in six primary colours and a western-style belt studded with turquoise. Several pairs of espadrilles would be put in the closet along with the gold and silver sandals and the white leather thongs to wear around the pool. September could be any kind of weather, thought Nina, so she'd also bought lightweight cream wool trousers, a silk blouse from Armani, and a cream cardigan trimmed in ivory ribbons. A dozen pairs of the laciest underwear would fill the sachet-scented drawers.

At the *profumeria* on Franceso Crispi Nina had told the man behind the counter what she was doing and he had become as enthusiastic as she. He brought out eye pencils in various colours, wands of mascara and palettes of eye shadow in little triangles; there were handfuls of brushes for make-up, several shades of blusher, a neutral foundation for any skin tone, corn silk no-colour powder, and all the cleansing creams and moisturizers and sun blocks one could imagine. Nina had gasped at the bill and paid it in cash that Gaston had given her. Signor Peroni had then added eight tiny bottles of perfume and had gift wrapped every single item. '*Sconto! Discount!*' he cried when she paid him, handing her back some of her ten-thousand-lire notes. '*Grazie, grazie,*' she had smiled, practically staggering under the weight of the shopping bags as he held open the door for her.

Gaston continued, 'Giorgio can pick everything up tomorrow and drive it to Tuscany. Then the last time we go will really be the last. It will just be a time of hanging pictures and putting things in place.'

'The pictures can be hung without me, Gaston. I made a diagram of the entire house and numbered each mirror and each print. All the workmen have to do is put the nails in the walls where I marked with white chalk.'

'*Mon Dieu!* You are organized!' exclaimed the Frenchman.

'Let Antonio handle it. I think he was the one I explained it to.'

'Fine. *Va bene*. Then the pictures can be hung and Giorgio will pick up all you have tomorrow. Is the afternoon all right?'

They agreed on two o'clock. Nina did not want Giorgio to see her face, so Francesca could help her prepare the boxes ahead of time and then be there to make sure all was taken away.

'Gaston, good luck with all your meetings in August.'

She is so sweet. Such a sweet girl, thought Gaston. '*Merci!* I will tell the Directeur.'

She laughed then. 'I just know he is an Arab, Gaston! I've figured everything out!'

'You will know in good time. I will call you in September.'

'*Ciao*, Gaston.'


'There's only one person in the world happier than I am.'

'That's me,' said Jack.

'Okay. I accept that.' Adele smiled. She could hardly believe that she was here in a suite at the Dorchester with her cousin. 'Happier than we are. That's my father.' He had been elated on the telephone and had promised to organize a great celebration upon their return. Adele thought of how different he was now, married to Ann. How outgoing, how affectionate, how open about his feelings.

'I think he's tied with my mother on that score,' put in Jack. 'Cripes, those two are happy together! Do you think something runs in the family?'

'Good genes?' Jack moaned as Adele continued, 'And Rajjin! I think he may be as excited as I am!' She clipped on the sapphire earrings.

Jack came up behind her and with strong hands circled her small waist then kissed her bare shoulders. 'I don't know if that bodes well. I don't know if the boss of the bride should be as excited as the bride.' He nibbled the back of her neck.

'Now for the good news.'

'Mmmmm, I'm busy,' he sighed, thinking that she smelled faintly, very faintly, of vanilla.

'Rajjin told me to stay an extra week if I want. He said the gallery in New York can wait. Everyone's still away, anyway. They won't be dragging back from the Hamptons for at least another week.'

Jack abruptly disentangled himself and walked quickly to the telephone where he dialled New York. Adele couldn't help but hear. 'Right,' he was saying. 'No, I think I'd prefer

561

to be unreachable. Let Larry handle it and I'll call in every few days. Okay. See you next week.'

'May I use the phone now?' She smiled as she sat down on his lap. The white bath towel fell away from her breasts. Adele held the receiver in one hand and with the other stroked Jack's sunburned neck. It was all she could do to get out the words. 'Yes, suite 620. Yes, yes. Dom Perignon. Yes.'

Jack took the phone away from her and spoke into the receiver. Totally American was he to the room service operator. 'You'd better hurry!'


Ferragosto literally translates as the 'pit of August'. The holiday was 15 August on the calendar, but shops were closed from the Saturday afternoon before or the Wednesday before or perhaps from the eleventh to the thirty-first, or even the entire month of August and through until mid September. It was the Roman way to express individuality in all things. The only people who wandered through Piazza San Pietro or Piazza di Spagna were tourists, with glazed eyes, clutching guidebooks, taking photographs. From the first blush of dawn, the city seemed to labour under a dome of stifling heat. The daytime sky was a deeper blue than the sky of the spring, the river didn't move, the trees seeming to be waiting for a breath of air, and everyone walked around licking ice cream cones, talking about the weather.

Still showing bruises, Nina was relieved to have no obligations, no reason to go out of the palazzo. When the Contessa telephoned on the twelfth about sending a car to pick her up, she told her. I am a tattletale went through her mind. The Contessa was shocked, then angry, then very sympathetic, and at last, embarrassed at her son's behaviour. She spoke of boat races and of her sisters' friends from Milano, of the glorious sea, as if she were bound to make it up to her American daughter-in-law, as if she could make it better. Like the lollipop the doctor gives you after the polio shot.

'Carissima!' she exclaimed at last. 'I know you are a strong girl but – '

'I'm fine.' Nina felt near tears at the sudden show of sympathy. 'I think I want to be alone for a while.' She tried to laugh. 'Besides – I don't want to frighten the houseguests!' Nina hung up the phone quickly before giving in to tears yet again.

I didn't want to know it, but I did. Have known it for months. Nina paced up and down the enormous reception room in shorts, a blue T-shirt and bare feet. The marble was pleasantly cool. 'Infidelity,' she said aloud. '*Fede* means faith, trust, fidelity.' She spoke as though practising her Italian. My husband hasn't made love to me since April or was it March? And yet he is on the boat and no one expects him to sleep alone. 'Lovely double standard we have here,' she addressed a red-robed floating figure above her. 'Forget fidelity. Let's talk humiliation,' she said rhetorically to an angel who smiled down at her from above a frieze. 'Hey, you! You with the fifteen-foot wingspread! Humiliation . . . one of the big sins. I left him, the Roman husband in question, but I must have humiliated him by staying in Rome and playing sane. If I'd been anywhere else he could have told everyone he'd thrown me out. "My bonkers American wife. My mistake thinking she could adapt to the Italian way of doing things. Couldn't handle it." But no, I stayed.' She waved her arms up at the fresco of spectators. 'And then we have a Bentley and a Frenchman and a mysterious villa owner . . .' Nina stopped. Suddenly she realized what Claudio had been 'letting' her do! She opened her mouth in shock and clapped one hand over it. He'd actually decided that I was having an affair and it had been all right until . . . Nina could scarcely believe it. As he'd been hitting me he'd shouted that I'd humiliated him! That all of Rome, that all his friends had seen me!

Nina marvelled at the gulf of misunderstanding. The marriage is over. I am the fool. Claudio can't change. She tilted her head backwards and willed the tears to defy gravity and roll back into her eyes. The ceiling so far above her was rich with colour. Italy. A country I love. And I love little Francesca even though she is prone to hysteria, and Franco with his little 'snaps' and Maria and Vittorio and Dante . . . Nina took a swipe at her runny nose and winced. It still hurt. She remembered Claudio's chilling words: 'This is Italy. I can kill you if I want.' Mad country for men and women. For marriages. She thought of the Contessa whom she now regarded as a wealthy woman who lived with servants. She has one child, her Claudio. No wonder she clings to him so, suffered so over me, his wife, in the beginning.

'So,' she said aloud. 'Send your sons to England and to Ivy League schools but don't count on their ever being Anglo-Saxon.' She walked to the other end of the room feeling the silky marble beneath her feet. 'It's over,' she whispered. I was so stupid to think Claudio could be different. 'I don't love him any more,' she said aloud. And with that sad declaration she felt a wave of grief. Loss. Letting go of dreams. Nina crossed her arms around her ribcage as though she could stop the deep sobs. Let go, she told herself. I must let go of this marriage which isn't a marriage anyway. Let go of a Claudio I don't know. I must, she nodded, face wet with tears, head down, start over. First I finish the villa. The villa will be the last thing in Italy for me. 'Then' – she raised her head to a golden-haired angel carrying flowers across the vaulted ceiling – 'then I start again.'


Thomas Y. Butler was in his office overlooking the Bay of San Francisco. 'I'll put you through to Mrs McLean,' chirped his secretary.

Thurston would tell her later that he'd counted five 'Oh my Lords' and this from a woman who never swore. At last he took the telephone from her and sat down on the kitchen stool with a pencil and introduced himself. Mr Butler then repeated the information, which hummed over the long-distance wires like some mad music and upon reception into

Thurston's ear, and comprehension by Thurston's brain, elicited one very clear, very loud, '*Oh my God!*'

Adele opened her eyes and smiled slowly. The pale light of dawn showed between the folds of the not quite drawn blue curtains. Love this room, she decided. The baby blue ceiling was twelve feet above her with its white panelled trim. Love this bed, she decided. The blue and white flowered print of the armchairs also covered the cushioned headboard behind her. And I love this man. She curled herself around the golden-skinned sleeping form beside her.

When she awakened again Jack had ordered breakfast and was sitting beside her, a tray on his knees, carefully buttering a flaky croissant and reading *The Times*.

'What have I missed?' She rose to a sitting position and kissed his cheek.

He grinned. 'You've missed watching me yawn twelve times.' She laughed. 'You know, Adele, I think we should get out more. I don't think we should limit ourselves to just one restaurant per night, one theatre per night, only one discotheque, only one nightclub. I think it's silly to come all the way to London to hang around the room . . .' She laughed helplessly and then reached for the telephone. 'What are you doing? More theatre tickets?' he moaned.

She shook her head. 'How do I dial Rome?' she asked the operator. 'I have to tell Nina. I have to tell her!' she said, pushing the button down. 'Do you mind? Is there anyone you want to tell first?'

Jack looked serious. 'You mean . . . you mean, you will? You mean, you'll really marry me?'

Adele giggled and allowed him to kiss her nose as she dialled the numbers. He was kissing her neck as she listened to the phone ring and ring at the de Leone palazzo in Rome.

Nina seldom read *Time* magazine any more. Or anything American for that matter. She'd only picked up this issue at the newsstand at Piazza di Spagna because the cover story was about Italian fashion, Italian cuisine, the new American interest in anything Italian. Now she lay barefooted on the daybed enjoying the silence of the *mezzogiorno*. The sun was hot outside the closed shutters but the thick stone walls meant the apartment interior was cool.

Nina thumbed to the People section as she always did first. The photograph leapt out at her, then the name. For a few seconds they didn't register. He was smiling that 'I can do anything with one hand tied behind my back' smile of his, the tiny black moustache perfectly trimmed, the teeth white as pearls, the nearly black eyes shining with excitement. Of course he would be in white tie, of course he would look unbelievably handsome. The background was blurred but there were other people behind him, in evening dress.

> This Manhattan society figure will hold court in court soon. Omar Sarkis, the Lebanese-born banker and entrepreneur, has been arrested in New York City as part of investigations into suspected arms deals linked to Middle East terrorism. The patron of the Metropolitan Museum, the Metropolitan Opera, generous contributor to many American charitable organizations, polo player and bon vivant has retained legal eagle, Roy Kohen. Sarkex, the multimillionaire's privately owned corporation, has offices in twelve cities including London, New York, Paris, Beirut, Cairo, and Geneva.

Nina stared at the picture for a long time. She remembered putting her face against that white piqué shirt front, remembered touching the onyx studs teasingly with her fingers as she leaned towards him, nearly knocking over a pair of silver candlesticks. She thought of guns, of gun-running. She thought of all the newspaper stories which usually began: 'Last night in Beirut seventeen people were injured as . . .' And Claudio laundering money. Isn't that what Adele had said? That must be it. If Omar couldn't move the funds around himself, if something weren't legal. Maybe Claudio had been using the Fabi Srl. accounts . . . Had or was? Anything that Claudio did in Switzerland was

566

synonymous with 'it doesn't concern you!' How Nina hated 'Switzerland' – a country she'd never set foot in.

She stood up and padded across the cool marble floor to the bookcase then reached behind the novels of Moravia and grasped the neck of the bottle. White wine would be nicer, nice and cold, she decided, but I don't really want to call for an ice bucket and have Francesca know that I am drinking alone. The ruby-coloured Chianti splashed into the silver mug Claudio kept his fountain pens in.

Nina pushed open the heavy shutters and stood there for a long time. She watched the light change; thought of dusk falling on the city outside the palazzo. Darkness was falling on Porto Santo Stefano, on Capri, on the *Simba II*. It was nearly time for dinner. Nina lifted her wine to the first evening star above the dark roof of the palazzo across the courtyard. 'Here's to you, Omar,' and 'Here's to you, Claudio.' She sipped then raised the mug once more. The wine looked blood red in the rich rosy light of the August sky. 'And here's to me. Here's to not being at your side.'

## 12

'Still no answer, Mr Butler.'

'Her mother seemed to think that any time after one p.m. local time we'd be likely to reach her . . .'

'It's early evening there now.'

'Afraid we'll have to wake her up, then. Make a note to try again just before five this afternoon.'

Margo smiled as she scrawled in capitals on her desk pad: CALL ROME.

'Prime time,' she sighed, 'but I don't care. She punched the numbers once again and once again listened to the ringing phone in Rome. 'Where is Nina?' she said aloud in exasperation. She snapped on the pearl earring and resolved to think of something else for one whole hour.

Adele was tearing brown paper off a newly framed tapestry when the phone rang. She walked quickly past the paintings on the floor to take the call standing beside her desk.

'Hi, caught up on your sleep yet?'

She laughed that tinkling little laugh her mother had had and made a face at no one. 'Don't think I ever will with you around.'

'Aaaah, let us now discuss insatiable appetites.'

'Jaaaaaack!' She blushed. 'It's exactly ten-o-four in the morning. Are you at your desk?'

'You guessed it.'

'Well, you're on Wall Street so start being staid. This minute.'

'Staid?' he mocked her accent. 'Is that a synonym for stiff? I could start be –'

'Jaaaaaack! Please! I've been in the gallery exactly

fourteen minutes and it's far too early for an obscene call . . .'

Someone cleared their throat behind her and Adele whirled so quickly she nearly upset the tiny brass horses on the corner of the desk.

'Oh, good morning. Yes, I'll be with you right away.' She hung up on Jack's laughter and, smiling demurely, turned to the elderly woman who stood before her. Complete with cane and chauffeur, she would groan to Jack at dinner that evening.

The Directeur was excited. 'Gaston!' he fairly shouted into the telephone. He could wait no longer. 'Why not tomorrow? Nina at the villa. Why not?'

'*Mon Dieu!*' Gaston always lapsed into French when surprised or losing his temper. This boiling Persian Gulf. The Frenchman wiped his face with a monogrammed white handkerchief.

'Can you be there? At Fiumicino? Can Giorgio be there?'

Gaston was drawing cubes-within-cubes doodles frantically on the cream-coloured paper beside his phone. The air conditioner was going full blast and he still felt as though he were suffocating in a closet. His alligator suitcase was opened on the luggage rack.

'*Oui! Oui! Oui!* I weel get a plane out of here immediately!'

'Now, listen. Don't answer any questions! I want to tell her everything!'

'You? You weel be there?'

'At the house. Just get her to the house as usual and let me take over . . .' His voice was euphoric.

'But . . . what . . . but . . .'

'The house is ready, isn't it?'

'*Oui!* I put the last touches myself!'

'The pictures are hung, the clothes are in the closet?'

'*Oui!*'

'And now, while I've got you on the line, how're the Arabs treating us?'

'They're not happy about the dip in oil prices. Not happy

569

at all . . .' He hesitated. 'And I must try to not look too happy when I am with them.'

The Directeur grinned. The silver market had made them both millionaires many times over. He and Gaston seemed to have turned tin into gold, and oil into gold, and coffee into gold, and . . . those little pieces of paper they'd been playing with on Wall Street . . . 'Well, try not to look too much like the cat who swallowed the canary and maybe something long-range can be hammered out that will make us all happy.'

Gaston hated these confusing English sayings and sputtered, suddenly assuming a very strong French accent, 'Whut ees zees canary zing?'

'Don't worry about the canary!' came the amused response. 'I will see you at about six, old friend!'

The connection was broken. Gaston looked down at the page on his desk. Boxes within boxes. All he'd managed to write in his exhilaration was 'Nina'.

Gaston changed his last meeting to that evening and checked out of the Intercontinental early the next morning. At the airport he was told that his flight would depart on time and given a boarding pass denoting his first-class status. The Frenchman roamed the air conditioned airport aimlessly. Why am I, how does he say, 'wound up'? I am just flying to meet Nina. Just a normal day in the first week of September to meet Nina. This was planned months ago. All very normal, he repeated. He wandered into the duty-free shop and stared at the glass counters displaying perfume. Then, restless and strangely excited, he ambled out into the main lobby again.


'Everything to your satisfaction, sir?' John Dawkins, the young English steward, inquired solicitously.

'Fine, thanks,' nodded the sole passenger on the executive jet. The craft seated ten very comfortably and sported a spacious galley, two baths and two good-sized bedrooms. The Directeur's was decorated almost totally in light tan suede, with a large double bed, a writing desk, a television

570

and stereo system set into the wall, a bar hidden within a Bombay chest of mahogany and brass; the adjoining bath was complete with king-size tub.

He leaned back in the tan suede-covered armchair and flipped the safety belt closed. The steward took his suit jacket and put it on a hanger in the rear closet, then returned to ask if he'd be wanting something to drink before take-off.

'When is take-off?'

'The captain told me twenty minutes. Evidently, we're in the middle of mid-morning traffic.'

'Well, flying west, we'll gain time. Do you know how many hours from Hong Kong to Rome?'

John smiled ingenuously. 'Not any idea. This is my first time in either city.' He recovered his professional manner and promised to find out.

'I think I will have a bloody mary, after all.'

The twenty minutes seemed much longer as he puffed on the cigar and stared out the porthole-sized window at the little yellow trucks scooting like toys across the tarmac. He owed his muscular leanness to squash and tennis and swimming no matter what the country or the season. There was usually an hour in his day for it, and always a hotel with facilities or a colleague's club ready to welcome him. The grey suit with the faint pinstripes had come from London, the blue and white striped shirt with the white collar along with thirty-nine others had been custom-made for him at Turnbull and Asser. The shoes were Italian, of soft burnished leather. He had pairs the colour of chocolate and pairs as black as ebony. The silk ties were Hermes on some days, other times he wore Sulka. Even the Mark Cross briefcase on the drop table before him was new. He glanced at the watch and shook his head, smiling to himself. Gaston had given it to him as a present since he claimed he would never buy anything that expensive for himself. It had cost over eight thousand dollars. Trappings. But I am the same man who has thought of her for a long time, he mused. The earlier euphoria had been replaced by a tense anticipation so, though usually a man of steely discipline, he signalled John for another bloody mary.

\*

The young couple at the corner table of Lutece talked non-stop, noted the maitre d' with pleasure, and they had also ordered the best white wine the cellar offered. Jack Forrest. Second time this week for lunch. I will have to remember him. Impeccable taste. He watched the blonde lift a heavy crystal wine glass, and smile. She wore a simple pale pink silk suit with no blouse beneath its jacket. The neckline was filled with pearls as white as her skin. Tory's ruby earrings glittered in the soft light when she tilted her head back in laughter. The maitre d' did a pirouette and fluttered towards the door to greet Henry and Nancy Kissinger, but his eyes lit once more on Adele. He said to himself: Yes, impeccable taste.

'Still can't reach her. No one answering the phone in a big household like that!' Adele lifted a spoonful of raspberry sherbet to her lips. 'Remind me to try very very late tonight and then again very early tomorrow morning.'

'It'll be difficult to get to a phone,' Jack said seriously. With a rather wicked grin he explained, 'Those are the hours you and I are busiest.'

The telegram was addressed to Nina McLean de Leone. 'Please contact me immediately. My firm is the executor of the estate of the late Robert Auden Cabell. Sincerely, Thomas Y. Butler of Spencer, Butler and Kennington, San Francisco, California. Telephone 415-722-2200.'

It gave Margo a thrill to send it all the way to Rome to a countess in a palace! She pulled the file labelled 'R. A. Cabell', then opened it on her desk and reread the first page.

Three million dollars tax free! 'To be left to Nina, the sister of my beloved, Bart McLean, and the same amount to his mother, Virginia.' Incredible, she sighed, then slipped the telegram copy on top and closed the brown folder.

The private jet was due to land at Fiumicino airport in forty-five minutes. Its passenger was staring at a financial report detailing the rise of diamond prices due to the uncertain political climate of South Africa. He was thinking, however, not of diamonds, not of Mr Botha, but of Nina's silky skin, white as a magnolia in winter and tan as an Indian's in summer. He remembered her mouth and her flirtatious grin, that gamin quality when she looked up behind the long black eyelashes . . .

'More coffee, sir?'

The Directeur raked his hands through his hair. 'Aah, John! You startled me!' He sighed and answered, 'Yes, a black coffee should bring me back to reality.' John nodded and poured.

Reality, theorized the Directeur to himself. What power it is to make your own!

Giorgio's brother, Gianni, proved a most skilled driver, and the Ferrari he'd borrowed for the day fairly flew through the Tuscan countryside. Gianni was movie-star handsome with a glossy black moustache that, noted the Directeur, was perhaps shampooed and combed hourly. He often flexed his biceps over the wheel as though even while driving his mind was never far from the consideration of muscle tone. This was shown to great advantage in the short-sleeved skin-tight red jersey. He wore a black chauffeur's hat as a sign of his new station but other than that, the Directeur would laugh to Gaston, 'I wasn't sure whether I might be in a stolen car with the thief.' He did drive well, but at breakneck speed, as though the *polizia* might be screaming over the highway giving chase to the sleek black sports car.

Gianni spoke no English other than 'okay' accompanied by a dazzling smile, but he did feel it necessary to be cordial to his back-seat passenger. This resulted in loud one-sided conversation as the Directeur nodded in polite confusion. '*Tempo d'oro*,' Gianni called over his shoulder. '*Il tempo più bello in Italia.*'

The Directeur smiled. At last he understood something. French helped a little. The time of gold. Perhaps a golden time. Yes, it was that. The fields were lush, the sky the bluest of all blues, and the feeling in his heart made him know that, yes, it was a golden time.

Nina stared out at the green fields. *Tempo d'oro*, she thought. That magic time in September is upon us. The Indian summer of Italy. I keep barely surviving Ferragosto, she thought. The de Leones and servants will be back next week. I will speak to the Count and start the annulment all over again. She sighed at the thought.

Gaston tugged at his maroon silk tie and smiled. 'It wasn't easy to reach you . . .'

'I was so surprised to get the message. The palazzo telephones haven't worked for two weeks!'

'Our office in Milan managed to contact someone in Rome but . . . it was quite involved!'

Nina laughed. 'I am so happy to see you, Gaston! Now tell me what the pool is like. I don't even know what shape you and the Directeur decided on. I can hardly wait to see it! Are there palms around it the way we planned?'

'It's almost square, but a very, very large square so that the Directeur can do laps. The palms are just the way we planned. But the big surprise is the colour. Emerald green!'

'I love it already,' exclaimed Nina. 'But now . . . now is the time to tell me about the Directeur. Tell me, Gaston! Tell me now!' cajoled Nina. 'Please! We have twenty whole minutes to drive!' she pleaded.

She leaned over the front seat and spoke to Giorgio in Italian who laughed and answered her in his own rapid-fire Sicilian-accented Italian. 'See? Even Giorgio says twenty minutes is nothing! Can't hurt to tell me now!'

Gaston teased. 'If twenty minutes is nothing then you can wait twenty minutes!'

'The Directeur . . . Can't you give me any hints?'

He waved a finger at her. '*Non, non, non!*'

Giorgio turned around and said, '*Pazienza, signorina!*'

'Boh!' she mimicked the Italians. '*Pazienza*' – she folded her arms and sat back in a gesture of defeat – 'is not one of my strong suits.'

*

574

The well-upholstered and very gregarious Signora Grazzini had made him feel at home but the house itself, he thought, welcomed me. It is Nina. It is her spirit. The cypresses which lined the long curving driveway, the brass lion knocker on the front door, every shining stone, every candlestick, every etching, bespoke Nina. Signor Grazzini who was caretaker, and his wife who was renowned for her Tuscan cooking, had been on hand to greet him, to lift his bags from the Ferrari, to take Gianni into the kitchen for coffee. Moments later Signora Berbotto, the housekeeper, had introduced herself rather shyly with large brown downcast eyes. She had giggled when the Directeur had mispronounced her name and smiled, '*Lori*,' behind one hand.

The Directeur stood beside the fireplace in the living room and surveyed the long leather sofa with the cinnamon-coloured cashmere lap robe folded over one arm, the antique side tables with brass drawer pulls, the porcelain lamps, the rug of soft rust and coral and tan. A nineteenth-century tea caddy of tortoiseshell with ivory fittings was centred on the glass *étagère* to the left of the mantel. Nina had left most of the bookshelves bare since Gaston had refused to divulge the native tongue of the Directeur, but she had collected a tiny menagerie of brass and glass and carved wooden animals who paraded across a shelf at eye level. A malachite bowl of potpourri assailed the senses and the Directeur inhaled deeply. He glanced at his watch and sighed. Almost seven o'clock. She should be here any minute. Had Gaston . . . ? No, he had been so careful all along. What if . . . no, no, stop it, he castigated himself. He took off the grey suit jacket and then put it on again.

Signora Grazzini was drying her hands on her bright blue apron in the doorway. She made a clucking noise and said firmly, '*Pazienza*.'

The Directeur nodded, trying to look composed, relaxed, indifferent, but at that moment he heard the Bentley's tyres on the gravel outside and all confidence vanished.

'Oh Gaston!' cried Nina as she saw the house through the trees. 'It is my first glimpse of it in a long time, and my last

575

glimpse from this direction for ever. The last time! I am very sad.' Impetuously she grabbed the little Frenchman's hand as the Bentley drew up.

The sun still shone brightly behind the house but the driveway was in grey shadow. Gaston smiled. '*Entrez*, Nina. I think your questions are about to be answered at last.'

Where did he disappear to, wondered Nina as she stood in the hallway. The chandelier had been a good choice, she decided, and someone had filled the tall silver vase with white irises. Thinking she was quite alone, she walked through the marble archway into the living room and gasped when she saw a man standing beside the fireplace. She did not recognize him at first; it was not possible for her mind to connect, the surprise was too great. He smiled then, that slow, slow smile of his and Nina breathed, 'Mickey Keeling!'

'The one and only.' He drank her in: the dark hair, the long-legged figure, so familiar and yet so foreign. The sleeveless lavender dress, the silver earrings.

'You can't . . . you can't just be here . . . like this! In this house in the middle of Tuscany . . . you're not supposed to be here . . .' she stammered.

Mickey stood very still with his hands in the pockets of his suit, his jacket open, and regarded her silently.

'How can you . . . you shouldn't . . . why . . .' Her heart pounded in her throat and she felt her face flush.

'Aren't you happy to see me?' he asked gently, teasingly. 'The least bit pleased?'

At that moment Nina didn't know. She remembered the last time she'd seen him. In the Countess's living room in New York. She'd been embarrassed; she'd been ridiculous; she'd been another person. Now staring at Mickey before her in this room, in Italy, she felt a mixture of panic and shock as though the world had been turned upside down, as though she were a snowflake in a tiny paperweight and someone had casually shaken it for a moment. Soon, she thought, they will put it back on the desk, and all the snowflakes, and I, will settle.

'What about a drink?' God, she was beautiful. More lovely than ever. The slenderness that invited protection, the litheness that made you imagine her knifing into a pool, running across a field, under you in bed. And the face of an angel. Now a very confused angel, with enormous grey eyes seeking, asking questions, mystified.

'Have you had a glass of champagne lately?' he joked.

Nina's stare never wavered. 'Three years?'

'Longer,' was the quick reply.

She stood still on the spot where she'd first seen him, toes on the oriental rug, heels on the marble floor. She had not taken a step or moved, as though she feared he might vanish before her. He looks just the same but better, she decided. His face is very tan, his eyes are very bright.

Dust danced in the pale golden bars of sunlight which crossed the room. The windows were open towards the sea.

'I hated to turn the lamps on so soon,' Mickey was saying. Maybe if she would sit, if she would relax, if she would stop staring. 'I haven't been upstairs, yet, I wanted to wait for you. I wanted you to show me everything.' He continued to talk. 'Especially the tower.'

An Italian woman in a black dress and a white apron put a brass tray on the coffee table. Nina sat on the soft leather sofa she'd picked out of a catalogue so many months ago. It felt cool under her bare thighs where the dress rode up. She folded her hands in her lap and stretched her suntanned legs straight out, looking at her feet in the slingback sandals. It was the first instant she had taken her eyes from Mickey.

'You are so terrifyingly beautiful,' he whispered, nearly to himself.

With parted lips and mind awhirl with things to say, Nina looked back at the figure before her. She fought all her instincts and was silent. She remembered being in the ocean with him. Sounding blasé, she inquired, 'Well, Mickey Keeling, what are you doing here? Are you friends with Gaston?'

He nodded, then wondered where to begin. All these machinations to get her here and I have no opening speech.

'I think the Directeur is coming. Do you know him?'

Mickey threw back his head with laughter and Nina stared at him as though he'd gone mad.

577

'Nina! I *am* the Directeur!'

'But you can't be . . . you . . .'

He laughed again. 'I know. I know. I'm Mickey Keeling, too,' he teased.

'But why aren't you in New York? Where you are supposed to . . .' Nina's face showed such confusion that he felt sorry for her. The game had gone on long enough.

Mickey took a glass from the tray and lifted it in a silent toast as she watched. 'I planned this. All this.'

Nina waited for him to explain. Mickey was the Directeur?

'Gaston found you in Rome and you know the rest.'

'But what about New York? How can you be here . . .'

'I don't live there any more.' He moistened his lips. They sat in silence and watched the light in the room change from a soft gold colour to the rosy hues of the sun as it set on the line between sky and sea. 'Do you remember a long time ago . . . all the things we talked about?'

Nina nodded.

'So many things have happened to me since I met you.'

'To me, too,' Nina said quietly as she reached for the glass of champagne.

'I go in and out of New York but it isn't the same for me. I . . .' He really didn't know how to tell her everything. 'When I met you, Lila, my wife, was very ill. She refused to tell anyone. She was very proud, wanting no sympathy, wanting no curiosity. When she was told she had cancer we had a long talk and I decided that if there were five years left or only one year, I wanted to be with her for as many minutes as there were in that time.'

Nina was amazed and horrified, too. All those people commenting on how old she looked. Why, even I thought it, and the Countess, too. We didn't know!

'I was with a firm on Wall Street and simply told my partners that I wanted to do something else. That I was going back to writing poetry.' He smiled wistfully. 'Everyone laughed at me. I'd had three – let's call them slim – volumes published a year after Wharton. Anyway, I pulled out of finance but the rest of my life continued with the parties and the dinners that Lila loved.' He took another sip of the champagne. 'But she changed. She wanted me to leave her, claiming that she was a burden, that she was unattractive, that I really could not love her as she watched herself get thinner, more frail. But, you see, I did love her and I know . . .' His voice cracked. 'That she knew I did. It was almost as if she had to behave horribly in order to prove to herself that I did love her, that she really couldn't drive me away.' He stared out at the sea, afraid that Nina would see his eyes fill with tears. 'So, we kept up with our friends and our life in New York as long as we could and still she refused to reach out, to let anyone know that she was sick. And she made me promise – nearly every day we had the discussion – that I would never betray her secret.' He sighed.

What a terrible time he's had, thought Nina. Such pain.

'Not long after the last time I saw you it was apparent that she would have to be hospitalized so, still keeping up appearances, Lila picked a private clinic in the Bahamas and we flew there and . . .' He downed the liquid in his glass in one impatient toss. 'About a month later she died.' He put the glass down and sat back in the celadon green velvet wing chair.

The Tuscan countryside around them seemed to muffle all sound, the silence was such that the very light in the room seemed to breathe with the two of them. Nina was positive that her thoughts were ringing in her ears.

Mickey suddenly rose and walked to the fireplace. Bending forward, he lit the paper beneath the carefully laid logs. The scratch of the match was loud. In a few graceful movements his suit jacket was off and he was back in the chair, hands clasped behind his head. Nina stared at the blue-striped shirt, the white collar, and his raised arms. 'I decided to leave my life. Most of it, rather.'

'Tell me what you mean.'

'My old life. My New York life. I decided not to go back to Wall Street.' Mickey refilled his glass as Nina watched unblinking. He thought of the apartment in Paris on the Ile St Louis and the two-storey flat being renovated on Eaton Square. 'I met Gaston who was representing a French firm investing heavily in Eurobonds. We had lunch, we spent the afternoon together, and by midnight, after a long dinner, we had decided to join forces.'

Nina interjected, 'He's the best.'

Mickey nodded. 'I know.' He gazed into the fire. 'We separated for a month and he outlined all the European companies, all the commodities that might be lucrative investments, that would show us a profit within a year.' Nina was rapt. 'I did the same for North America and South America. We agreed during our first meeting that our objective would be to make as much money as quickly as possible and exactly a year later we would decide what should be ploughed in again, what should be taken out, and what should be moved.'

'Sounds like a game.'

'It began as a game . . . to forget. Or to stop me from thinking. Gaston and I made some lucky guesses the first few months and did build up some capital. But what happened with the silver market staggered us. We went in on the backs of the Hunt brothers. They were hoarding and buying on margin and got caught short but Gaston and I sold just before silver peaked.' Mickey hesitated. 'The Hunts lost over a billion dollars but we made money.' Understatement of the decade, he thought. He and Gaston had gone over the figures several times during that early morning phone call from New York to Paris, each man convinced there were far too many zeros to their net worth. The gold market had been immediately affected but Mickey had pulled their money out in time. A game.

Nina noted the expensive-looking watch, the Italian shoes. Mickey continued, 'Gaston investigated companies that were on the edge of change, of takeovers, of mergers. We'd study the earnings, meet with people, and then decide about investing, about buying.' He thought of those sessions and of Gaston's face alight as he described this or that which was bound to follow if such-and-such happened. 'Once, in Paris, after a really superb dinner, we ran out of paper and Gaston and I did all our figures, due dates and projections on the next thing available.' He laughed. 'We had to buy the tablecloth!'

580

All this talk. All this explaining. Her eyes have never left my face but what is she thinking? 'Nina.' His voice changed. 'You've had a bad time of it, haven't you?'

She nodded. 'It's okay, now.' He didn't press her to tell him anything but she sensed that he would be able to understand it all.

'You can tell me if you want.'

She nodded again and they sat in the silent room. The fire crackled and two yellow sparks were spat out upon the marble hearth and then extinguished themselves like dying fireflies. 'This morning at the palazzo I tore every page of an old *Time* magazine in half and scrunched them up and, from twenty feet, aimed at the wastebasket.' It had been just over a year ago that she'd lost the baby. Now she had finished her marriage and was starting over.

'Were you by yourself or with an audience?' he asked very quietly.

'Alone. And with every throw I always say, "I'm going to live for ever".' Nina thought of all the years she'd been saying it and watching paper, all kinds of paper – history notes, bright wrapping paper from presents, Kleenexes, math homework – teeter on the rim of wastebaskets in two countries.

'And?' Mickey raised his eyebrows expectantly.

'I may live for ever.'

'You just may.' How do I proceed from here? he asked himself. 'You made me think about things . . .' His voice drifted off into nothing.

'What things?' she asked.

'Too many things . . .' Then he recovered a bit and answered, 'I thought about you. The chameleon holding her own at parties.'

Nina blushed. 'Was I so easy to read?'

'No. I just felt . . .' He stopped. How much can I tell her? 'You made me think of a villa in Tuscany, too.'

Nina's eyes sparkled. I am happy to see you, Mickey Keeling, went through her mind. Nina sipped champagne and then placed the stemmed glass on the tray. Her heart pounded like a drum as she felt his eyes upon her. She folded her trembling hands tightly in her lap and felt the texture of the lavender raw silk, the little nubs, beneath fingers that seemed unreasonably, inexplicably sensitive. She brushed her hair back with one hand suddenly.

Mickey's voice broke the silence. 'Nina . . .' He waited for her to look at him. 'I suppose I have stalked you. I have watched you and waited for today. I wanted everything in order. I waited for the right time.' Nina swallowed. 'Maybe it was selfish of me to watch you offstage, to choose my moment, but I wanted to confront you as an equal, not to fear that I had taken advantage of situations.'

He shook his head and stood up, pushing hands in pockets and then staring into the fire, then restlessly, distractedly, patting one elbow on the mantel. 'Am I making sense?'

She did not answer him.

'Nina . . .' He turned again towards her and she stared at his muscular frame, his broad shoulders, his deeply tanned face. His eyes were flecked with gold as she remembered. 'I want you to do anything you want. Live in Rome, live here, just . . .' His voice was almost choked with emotion. 'Just be with me. If you want. When you want. If . . .' Mickey waved one hand out at the sea, out at the path she'd had the gardener line with white flowers. 'The house is your house, or our house, whenever you want to be here . . .' He stumbled over the words.

Nina stood then, tall and straight, her grey eyes shining. 'Mickey, what are you saying?'

The fire crackled as a log fell and orange sparks danced up the chimney. It was dusk outside the villa but the room was bright with the fire's glow. 'I'm saying . . .' His voice betrayed his susceptibility, his longing for her. 'That when two escapees from other places . . .'

'Other lives,' she said softly.

'Find themselves in Tuscany . . .' He began to smile.

'Drinking champagne . . .' Nina smiled slowly back at him.

Mickey put his hand out and Nina took five steps towards him, extending her own. His words were almost inaudible. 'They should never have to escape again.'

# FAME AND FORTUNE

## Kate Coscarelli

In glamorous Beverly Hills, casual sex is taken for granted, driving ambition is commonplace – and true love is the rarest commodity of all.

In search of that elusive emotion are four women, close friends, and all facing major upheavals in their lives:

PEACH – blonde, beautiful, wealthy and newly widowed – shocks her set by taking her pleasure with a younger man – Hollywood's hottest glamour boy.

Within the walls of her exclusive beauty salon, GRACE shares the whispered secrets of the super-rich. Few suspect that Grace's glossy veneer hides a brutal past and dark secret of her own.

For years, MAGGIE has played second fiddle to her high-powered husband Kirk. Now she's the most sought-after designer in Beverly Hills. But is Kirk man enough to take his wife's success?

LAURA – perfect wife, perfect mother, perfect hostess. Surely that's enough to keep any man? So why is her handsome doctor husband seen around with sex-symbol Ghilly Jordan?

In the bestselling tradition of LACE and SCRUPLES, FAME AND FORTUNE has it all – exciting sex, horrifying violence, passionate struggles for power, security, survival – played against a glittering background of wealth, glamour and luxurious sensuality.

FUTURA PUBLICATIONS
FICTION

ISBN 0 7088 2611 3

# MANDALAY

## Alexandra Jones

Burma, late nineteenth century – land of vast wealth, sumptuous beauty and unthinking savagery. In fabled Mandalay the king lies dying, and his ruthless queen is determined to set her own puppet on the Dragon Throne.

Against this richly exotic backcloth, three unforgettable characters act out a drama of passion and betrayal:

Captain Nathaniel de Veres-Vorne – American remittance man, handsome, reckless and deadly enemy of the vengeful queen.

Minthami – his young and utterly enchanting Burmese mistress, loves him with a touching dignity and strives to bridge the cultural gap that forever divides them.

Angela Featherstone – a rare free spirit in a corsetted world endeavours to earn his respect. And, for the sake of Minthami, tries to hold at bay her passionate love for him, which alone could bring her fulfilment.

As Burma seethes around them, these three, locked in a triangle as old as time, struggle with fate and each other to work out their destinies, separate but tragically entwined.

MANDALAY – an epic saga of passion and sacrifice, romance and lust, and history and imperial ambition, a compelling drama told on the grandest scale.

FUTURA PUBLICATIONS
FICTION

ISBN 0 7088 3680 1

# SUMMER HARVEST

## Madge Swindells

'a spellbinding read' Sarah Harrison

Set between 1938 and 1968 in a land where gruelling poverty rubs shoulders with remarkable opulence, and moving from the Cape to London and the West Coast of America, SUMMER HARVEST is a family saga in the finest tradition.

At the heart of the story is Anna, a woman as strong and passionate as she is ambitious, who fights her way up from near destitution to become one of the Cape's most prominent and powerful businesswomen. Only love eludes her. For Simon — a poor farmer when they marry — has too much masculine pride to stand on the sidelines while Anna plunders her way to a success that threatens tragedy and loss.

'Anna van Achtenburgh mirrors the strengths and the weaknesses of her beautiful, harsh country: the toughness, the dazzling material success, the moral dilemmas, the tragedy. I was gripped from start to finish.'
Kate Alexander, author of *Fields of Battle*.

FUTURA PUBLICATIONS
FICTION

ISBN 0 7088 2528 1

All Futura Books are available at your bookshop or newsagent, or can be ordered from the following address: Futura Books, Cash Sales Department, P.O. Box 11, Falmouth, Cornwall TR10 9EN.

Please send cheque or postal order (no currency), and allow 60p for postage and packing for the first book plus 25p for the second book and 15p for each additional book ordered up to a maximum charge of £1.90 in U.K.

B.F.P.O. customers please allow 60p for the first book, 25p for the second book plus 15p per copy for the next 7 books, thereafter 9p per book.

Overseas customers including Eire please allow £1.25 for postage and packing for the first book, 75p for the second book and 28p for each subsequent title ordered.